ALISON WEIR is the top-selling female historian (and the fifth-bestselling historian overall) in the United Kingdom, and has sold over 2.7 million books worldwide. She has published eighteen history books, including her most recent non-fiction book, *Queens of the Conquest*, the first in her England's Medieval Queens quartet. Alison has also published several historical novels, including *Innocent Traitor* and *The Lady Elizabeth*.

Anna of Kleve: Queen of Secrets is Alison Weir's ninth published novel and the fourth in the Six Tudor Queens series about the wives of Henry VIII, which was launched in 2016 to great critical acclaim. The first three books in the series – *Katherine of Aragon: The True Queen*, *Anne Boleyn: A King's Obsession* and *Jane Seymour: The Haunted Queen* were all *Sunday Times* bestsellers.

Alison is a fellow of the Royal Society of Arts and an honorary life patron of Historic Royal Palaces.

Also by Alison Weir

The Six Tudor Queens series
Katherine of Aragon: The True Queen
Anne Boleyn: A King's Obsession
Jane Seymour: The Haunted Queen

Six Tudor Queens Digital Shorts
Writing a New Story
Arthur: Prince of the Roses
The Blackened Heart
The Tower is Full of Ghosts Today
The Chateau of Briis: A Lesson in Love
The Grandmother's Tale
The Unhappiest Lady in Christendom
The Curse of the Hungerfords

Fiction
Innocent Traitor
The Lady Elizabeth
The Captive Queen
A Dangerous Inheritance
The Marriage Game

Quick Reads
Traitors of the Tower

Non-fiction
Britain's Royal Families: The Complete Genealogy
The Six Wives of Henry VIII
The Princes in the Tower
Lancaster and York: The Wars of the Roses
Children of England: The Heirs of King Henry VIII 1547–1558
Elizabeth the Queen
Eleanor of Aquitaine
Henry VIII: King and Court
Mary Queen of Scots and the Murder of Lord Darnley
Isabella: She-Wolf of France, Queen of England
Katherine Swynford: The Story of John of Gaunt and His Scandalous Duchess
The Lady in the Tower: The Fall of Anne Boleyn
Mary Boleyn: 'The Great and Infamous Whore'
Elizabeth of York: The First Tudor Queen
The Lost Tudor Princess
Queens of the Conquest

As co-author
The Ring and the Crown: A History of Royal Weddings, 1066–2011
A Tudor Christmas

ALISON WEIR

SIX TUDOR QUEENS

ANNA OF KLEVE
QUEEN OF SECRETS

REVIEW

First published in Great Britain in 2019
by HEADLINE REVIEW
An imprint of HEADLINE PUBLISHING GROUP

1

Cataloguing in Publication Data is available from the British Library

ISBN 978 1 4722 2772 0 (Hardback)
ISBN 978 1 4722 2773 7 (Trade paperback)

Typeset in Garamond MT by Avon DataSet Ltd, Bidford-on-Avon, Warwickshire

Printed and bound in Great Britain by Clays Ltd, Elcograf S.p.A.

HEADLINE PUBLISHING GROUP
An Hachette UK Company
Carmelite House
50 Victoria Embankment
London EC4Y 0DZ

www.headline.co.uk
www.hachette.co.uk

SIX TUDOR QUEENS

ANNA OF KLEVE

QUEEN OF SECRETS

ENGLAND
HOUSE OF TUDOR

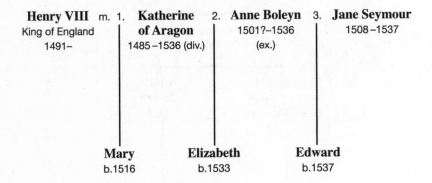

Henry VIII	m. 1.	**Katherine**	2.	**Anne Boleyn**	3.	**Jane Seymour**
King of England		**of Aragon**		1501?–1536		1508–1537
1491–		1485–1536 (div.)		(ex.)		

Mary
b.1516

Elizabeth
b.1533

Edward
b.1537

KLEVE
HOUSE OF LA MARCK

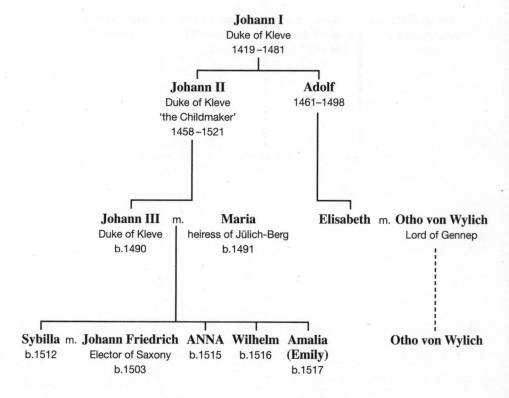

Johann I
Duke of Kleve
1419–1481

Johann II
Duke of Kleve
'the Childmaker'
1458–1521

Adolf
1461–1498

Johann III m. **Maria**
Duke of Kleve   heiress of Jülich-Berg
b.1490   b.1491

Elisabeth m. **Otho von Wylich**
Lord of Gennep

Sybilla m. **Johann Friedrich** **ANNA** **Wilhelm** **Amalia**
b.1512   Elector of Saxony   b.1515   b.1516   **(Emily)**
         b.1503   b.1517

Otho von Wylich

To John and Jo, with all my love.

And to Beth, with thanks for your generous help.

Part One

Princess of Kleve

Chapter 1

1530

Anna peered through the window of the gatehouse, watching the chariot trundling through below, enjoying the rich sensuousness of the new silk gown she was wearing, and conscious of her parents' expectations of her. At fourteen, she should have learned all the domestic graces, and to impress their guests with her virtues.

Every summer, Vater – or Duke Johann III, as his subjects knew him – brought his wife and children here to the Schwanenburg, the great palace that towered on a steep rocky hill, dominating the mighty River Rhine and the fair city of Kleve. Joining them today for a short visit, were Onkel Otho von Wylich, the genial Lord of Gennep, and Tante Elisabeth, who never let anyone forget that she was the granddaughter of Duke Johann I. With them would be Otho, Onkel's bastard son. For all the reputation of the court of Kleve for moral probity, bastards were not unwelcome there. Anna's paternal grandfather, Duke Johann II, had had sixty-three of them; not for nothing had he been nicknamed 'the Childmaker'. He had died when Anna was six, so her memories of him were vague, yet the living testimony to his prodigious fertility was all around her at court and in the great houses of Kleve. It seemed she was related to nearly everyone in the united duchies and counties of Kleve, Mark, Jülich, Berg, Ravensberg, Zutphen and Ravenstein, over which her father ruled.

Duke Johann was lavishly dressed as usual, welcoming his guests as their chariot drew up at the gatehouse – dark hair sleekly cut, fringe and beard neatly trimmed, portly figure swathed in scarlet damask. Anna looked at him affectionately; he did love to make a show of his magnificence. At his command, his wife and children were attired in

3

rich silks and adorned with gold chains. Anna stood in a row with her younger siblings Wilhelm and Amalia, who was fondly known as Emily in the family. Vater and Mutter had no need to remind their children to make their obeisances, for courtesy had been drummed into them since they had been in their cradles. Nor were they allowed to forget that they were royally descended from the kings of France and England, and were cousins to the mighty Holy Roman Emperor Charles V, Vater's overlord. Their awareness of that must be reflected in everything they did.

As young Otho von Wylich stepped down, Anna's heart almost stopped. To her, this cousin by marriage, two years older than she, seemed like a gift from God as he alighted on the cobbles. Oh, he was fair to look at, with his wavy, unruly chestnut locks and his high cheekbones, strong jaw, full lips and merry eyes, and he was charming too as he greeted everyone, displaying the proper deference to his host and hostess, with little of the gaucheness often seen in boys of his age. When he rose from his bow to Anna, his smile was devastating.

She was already betrothed, as good as wed, and had been since the age of eleven. When people addressed her formally, they called her Madame la Marquise, for her future husband was Francis, Marquis of Pont-à-Mousson, eldest son of Antoine, Duke of Lorraine. They had never met – she had not even seen a portrait of him – and although she was always being reminded of her great destiny, the prospect of marriage still seemed unreal. Some of her dowry had already been paid, and she had long expected her wedding to take place as soon as Francis reached marriageable age at fourteen, this very year.

She had been too young for a betrothal ceremony: her consent had been implicit in the contract her father had signed. She had accepted without question the husband chosen for her, having been schooled in her duty from infancy; but now, having seen Otho von Wylich, she wished for the first time that she was not spoken for. She could not drag her eyes away from Otho's engaging smile.

As she struggled to hide the fact that her world had just shifted seismically, Vater led the guests through the majestic Knight's Hall, his serious, craggy features becoming animated as he pointed out the decorative sculptures to Otho.

'This hall is said to have been built by Julius Caesar,' he said proudly.

'I well remember the great ceremonies that took place here,' Tante Elisabeth said.

Slowly, they processed through the state rooms. Anna was aware only of Otho, standing just inches away, and of his eyes on her.

'We had these apartments built on the model of the great French chateaux on the Loire,' Vater boasted, waving a beringed hand at the fine furniture and tapestries. Anna saw her uncle and aunt exchange envious glances. Mutter seemed serenely unaware. All this splendour was no more than her due, for she had been a great heiress, and had brought Vater rich territories and titles. She graced the court of Kleve in a manner that was regal yet humble, as deferential as a woman should be. Both she and Vater were strict in maintaining the elaborate code of etiquette laid down by the dukes in the manner of their Burgundian ancestors; in matters of courtesy and style, the court of Burgundy had led fashionable Christendom for nearly a hundred years now. Mutter and Vater also welcomed new ideas from the magnificent court of France, not far to the west of Kleve, and from Italy, which permeated north by means of visitors travelling up the Rhine. Anna sometimes sensed that Vater's court was too sophisticated and free-thinking for Mutter's taste; it seemed much more liberal than the court of Jülich had been. But Mutter would never criticise what went on in Kleve.

When they reached the private apartments, wine was served, the sparkling Elbling that Vater regularly had brought upriver from the vineyards on the Mosel. Onkel Otho and Tante Elisabeth accepted their goblets with alacrity. It was as well that it was not evening, for the rules at court were strict, and all wine, even the Duke's, was locked away at nine o'clock by his Hofmeister, who took his duties very seriously.

As they sipped from their goblets of finest Venetian glass, the adults talked, stiffly at first, then gradually relaxing, while their children sat silently listening, Anna intensely aware of Otho, who was sitting beside her.

'Your father has a wondrous palace,' he said.

'I hope you will be able to see more of it,' she replied. She felt sorry for him, for he had no hope of inheriting any great houses, even though it was no fault of his that he was a bastard. 'But I am sure you live well in Gennep.'

'Not as well as you do here, Anna,' he told her, with another of those devastating smiles, and she thrilled to hear her name on his tongue. 'But I am fortunate. My father and stepmother treat me like their lawful son. They have no other children, you see.'

'But you have friends?'

'Yes, and I have my studies, and an amiable tutor. One day, I will have to make my own way in the world, probably in the Church.'

'Oh, no!' she exclaimed, before she could stop herself. 'I mean, you could surely have a happier life doing something else.'

He grinned. 'You are thinking of the pleasures I would have to give up,' he said, making her blush. 'Believe me, I think of them too. But I have no inheritance, Anna. It will all go to a cousin when my father dies. What else can I do?'

'Vater will find you a post here, or Dr Olisleger, his chancellor, I am sure!'

'How kind you are, Anna,' he murmured. Their eyes met, and she read in his gaze all she could have hoped for. 'I can think of nothing I would like more than being at the court of Kleve. It would mean I could see you more often.'

His words took her breath away. 'Then I will ask for you,' she promised.

She noticed her mother watching them, a slight frown on her face. Vater was warming to his favourite topic. She knew for a certainty that she would hear the name Erasmus before too long. The great humanist scholar was Vater's hero, the man he admired above all others, and whose advice he sought on religious matters.

'Erasmus says the Church is not the Pope, the bishops and the clergy,' he declared. 'It is the whole Christian people.'

Tante Elisabeth looked dubious, while Mutter's expression remained inscrutable. Anna knew Mutter did not agree with Vater on religious matters. Devout as a nun, she was probably wincing inwardly to hear the Holy Father in Rome dismissed as if he were of no importance.

'Erasmus preaches universal peace and tolerance,' Vater went on, oblivious. 'There can be no higher ideal than that. It inspires the way I live my life, the way I govern my duchy and my court, and the way I nurture my children.'

'It is a high ideal,' Onkel Otho observed, 'but a dangerous one. Even if he does not intend to, Erasmus encourages those who attack the Church. It's a short step from that to the heresies of Martin Luther.'

'Luther speaks sense in many ways,' Vater countered. 'There *are* abuses in the Church, and they need to be rectified.'

'My lord has banned Luther's works,' Mutter said quickly.

'I have indeed, twice,' Vater confirmed. 'But some of his protests against the Church are justified. No one should have to pay priests to forgive their sins and save them from Purgatory, and it's wrong that the princes of the Church live in luxury when our Lord was a simple carpenter. But to deny five of the sacraments is plain heresy.'

'Your son-in-law would not agree with you,' Onkel Otho replied.

'The Elector of Saxony has extreme views,' Vater said, looking pained, 'and I fear Sybilla has become infected with them, for a wife is bound to follow her husband. The Elector wants me to join his Schmalkaldic League of German Lutheran princes, but I will never do that.'

'Yet you allied yourself to him by marriage,' Onkel Otho persisted. 'You are linked to the League whether you like it or not.' Now it was Mutter's turn to look pained. It must have gone against all her beliefs to see her daughter given to a Protestant.

It seemed an argument was stirring, but just then, the bell at the top of the Johannisturm in the inner courtyard chimed four o'clock, and Mutter seized her opportunity. Anna guessed she did not want her offspring hearing any more talk against the Church and the true faith in which she had nurtured them.

'Children,' she said brightly, 'why don't you show your cousin Otho around the rest of the castle?'

The young people all jumped to their feet, Anna secretly rejoicing.

'It will be our pleasure,' thirteen-year-old Wilhelm said earnestly. Anna knew Otho would soon be receiving a lecture on the architecture of the Schwanenburg and the glorious history of Kleve – and she was right. As they returned through the state apartments, Wilhelm, who had all the virtues save a sense of humour, humility and empathy with others, started waxing forth on how he had been born here in the Schwanenburg and how rich and prosperous the duchy was.

'Our father is called Johann the Peaceful, because he rules so wisely,' he boasted. 'When he married our mother, she brought him Jülich and Berg, and lands stretching for four thousand miles. When I am duke of Kleve, I will inherit all that, and I will be as wise as my father.'

Anna saw Otho smothering a smile.

'Otho did not come to hear all this, Bruder,' she said. 'It's a beautiful day, and you've been excused lessons for the afternoon.' She turned to Otho, and felt herself grow hot. 'Would you like to go up the Schwanenturm? The views are wonderful, and I can tell you all about the legend of Lohengrin.'

'It's too warm to climb all those stairs,' Emily protested, her rosebud lips pursed in a pout.

'Emily, you are such a lazybones,' Anna sighed.

'But I should love to see the views,' Otho said, his twinkling eyes still on Anna, 'and the exercise will be good for us.'

'I think Otho would prefer to see the Spiegelturm,' Wilhelm said, as if Otho had not spoken. 'The ducal archives are most interesting.'

'Oh, Wilhelm, it's always what *you* want!' Emily cried.

'You can take Otho there afterwards,' Anna said firmly. 'But first, he wants to see the Schwanenturm.'

'Then you take him,' Wilhelm ordered. 'I will go and look out some things I want to show him.'

'I'm coming with you,' Emily said. 'I can help find them.'

'You're just too lazy to climb the stairs,' Wilhelm scoffed, looking none too pleased at the prospect of his twelve-year-old sister's company.

'Come,' Anna said to Otho. 'Let's leave them to their squabbles.' She led him away before Wilhelm could stop her. She had never known such luck. Her life was hemmed around with rules, ritual, sewing and her mother's endless vigilance, and the chance of a short time alone with this most handsome youth was beyond her wildest imaginings; it was incredible that it had been afforded her so easily, without any effort on her part. It was an escapade of which Mutter might well have disapproved, for she had always enjoined that a young lady should never be alone with a man, lest her reputation be compromised. She had never explained exactly how that might happen, though it was clearly a dreadful thing. But Otho did not count, surely? He was family, and he was not much older than Anna.

The mighty Schwanenturm loomed above them, its square shadow falling on the cobbled courtyard. Anna was headily aware of Otho walking just a pace behind her. She was glad she had donned her new red silk gown with its gold bodice embroidered with loops of pearls. She felt beautiful wearing such a dress, with her fair hair loose down her back. Sybilla, whose portrait showed off the slanting eyes and long golden tresses that had captivated the Elector, was the beauty of the family, everyone was agreed on that; but Anna revelled in the thought that she too could look pleasing.

The guards on duty at the door stood to attention as they approached.

'My ancestor, Duke Adolf, built this tower,' Anna said, pushing open the heavy door.

'Allow me,' Otho said, taking its weight. Anna went ahead, lifting up her gorgeous skirt to ascend the stairs.

'The old tower fell down about a hundred years ago,' she went on, trying to conceal her nervousness behind a barrage of facts. 'Duke Adolf rebuilt it much bigger than before.'

'It's certainly high!' Otho said. 'These steps go on for ever. Shall we rest for a moment?'

Anna turned on the stairs to see him looking up admiringly at her.

'You are very pretty,' he said, 'and that gown becomes you so well.' His eyes travelled up appreciatively from her slender waist to the swell of her breasts beneath the velvet bodice.

Thrilled by his praise, she smiled down at him. She could not help herself. She knew she should not be allowing him to say such familiar things to her, or herself to acknowledge them. Yet she was bursting with such joy that she had no will to walk away, or to spoil the moment.

They were slightly breathless by the time they ascended the final flight of stairs leading to the turret at the top of the tower and entered a narrow, sparsely furnished room with windows at each end. The Turkey carpet must have cost a fortune in its day, but it was now threadbare. Anna crossed to the window overlooking the river. Below, the town of Kleve lay spread out before her, a patchwork of red roofs and spires.

Otho stood right behind her.

'It is a fair sight,' he said, looking over her shoulder. She could feel his breath on her ear. 'So tell me about Lohengrin.' His voice was like a caress.

Anna tried to focus on the legend she had promised to recount, but her mind was too overwhelmed by this strange, heady feeling. Was this love? She had seen how deeply her parents loved each other, and had learned, from listening to the ladies and maids gossiping, that love could also be a kind of madness that made people act like fools, as if they were out of their senses. It could make you ecstatically happy or desperately sad. And now, standing in this dusty little room, alone with a young man for the first time, she understood what it was to be powerfully attracted to someone. It was a glorious feeling, and frightening too, as if she were being impelled towards something momentous and dangerous, and had not the mastery to stop herself.

But she must! She would soon be a married woman, and had been schooled in absolute loyalty to her husband-to-be.

'Do you know why this is called the Swan Tower?' she asked Otho, forcing herself to collect her thoughts and speak. 'I don't suppose you hear much about the legends of Kleve in Limburg.'

'My mother used to tell me stories when I was little,' he answered, 'but I have forgotten them mostly.'

'Above us, on top of the turret, there is a golden weathervane,' Anna said, a touch breathlessly. 'It bears the swan that the old counts of Kleve blazoned on their coats of arms, in honour of the Knight of the Swan, the mysterious Lohengrin. See here.' She turned and drew from her bodice an enamelled pendant. 'This is my personal device. The two white swans stand for innocence and purity.' Otho cradled her hand in his as he bent to look in her palm. Suddenly, he kissed her lightly on the wrist. It gave her the most pleasurable jolt.

She was not quite mad – not yet. She had been taught that no virtuous woman would let a man kiss her until he made her his affianced bride. She withdrew her hand, and Otho straightened up.

Her voice shook a little as she continued her story. 'Lohengrin's boat was guided by two white swans when he sailed along the Rhine long ago to visit a countess of Kleve named Elsa. She was in deep distress because her husband had died and a tyrant was trying to usurp his place by forcing her to wed him. Lohengrin came to her aid. He overthrew the tyrant and married her.'

Otho's eyes were shining into hers. 'If she was as beauteous as another princess of Kleve I could mention – then I take my cap off to Lohengrin.' His voice sounded a little hoarse.

Anna's cheeks suddenly felt very hot. She had no idea how to respond to such a compliment.

'He was a renowned hero,' she said, struggling to act normally. 'But on the day after their wedding, he made Elsa promise never to ask his name or his ancestry. Unknown to her, and to all, he was a knight of the Holy Grail and was often sent on secret missions. She agreed, and they lived very happily together, and had three fine sons. They were my ancestors.'

'You are going to tell me that it all went wrong,' Otho said.

'It did. Elsa was desperate to know if her sons would have a great inheritance from their father. She could not contain herself, and asked him the question she had sworn never to ask. When she did, Lohengrin fell into anguish. He tore himself from her arms and left the castle – this very castle. And there, on the river, waiting for him, were the two swans with the boat that had brought him to Kleve. He sailed away in it, and was never seen again.'

Otho was shaking his head, his eyes holding hers. 'And what happened to Elsa?'

'She was so overcome with grief for her loss that she died. She had loved Lohengrin so much.'

For the first time, it was dawning on Anna how terrible Elsa's loss had been. That sad realisation must have been plain on her face, for, without preamble, Otho stepped forward and folded his arms around

11

her, drawing her close to him. Before she could stop him, he had pressed his lips to hers and touched her tongue with his. It was the strangest thing, at once wonderful and repulsive. She had never dreamed that kissing could be like that, but she knew it was wrong to be doing it. What would her parents think of her?

'No,' she said, pulling back.

He held her fast in his embrace. 'Yes!' he breathed. 'Please don't deny us this pleasure! It can do no harm. You need not fear it.'

'I might have a baby,' she protested, and was surprised when he laughed. 'I might,' she warned. 'Mother Lowe told me kissing leads to babies.'

'And who is Mother Lowe?' he asked, nuzzling her nose with his as she struggled half-heartedly to free herself.

'She is my nurse.'

'Little she knows! You can't get a baby from kissing. It's harmless. And you were enjoying it, I could tell.' He was still holding her tight, grinning at her so engagingly that she felt her knees melt. It was thrilling, talking about such things with a man.

He kissed her again, gently, tenderly this time, and then he was drawing her down on to the carpet, kissing her eyes and stroking her cheeks. His hands strayed elsewhere, and the glorious sensations he was awakening in her drowned out the alarums ringing in her head. He had said there was nothing to fear, and she believed him. He was a guest in her father's house – a well-brought-up young man who, she could count on it, knew how to behave. And there was a rising, breathless excitement in him that she found infectious.

'Oh, Anna!' he murmured, his eyes on hers as he twined her hair around his fingers, his breathing becoming more rapid and tremulous. 'Let me love you! I will not hurt you.' His lips closed on hers again, with greater fervour, and then he reached down, pulled her beautiful silk skirts and chemise aside and – to her astonishment – began gently touching her private parts. She did not resist him: she was too far immersed in feelings and sensations she had never dreamed of.

'As you have lips here,' he whispered, caressing her mouth with his tongue, 'so you have them here, for the same purpose.' His fingertips moved rhythmically, exploring more boldly, and Anna felt the most exquisite pleasure mounting within her. There was no shock, just surprise at how little she had understood her own body – and no shame. Here it was, the madness of which the women had spoken! Had she lived until now?

What followed was utterly glorious, and she gave herself up to it without further thought, being incapable of reason. A little pain – and then she was ascending to Heaven. As the pleasure mounted, she felt Otho's body spasm. He cried out, and then, as he slowly relaxed on top of her, and inside her, holding her tightly and murmuring incoherent words of love, she was overcome by a wave of unstoppable ecstasy, building and building until she thought she would pass out.

She lay there stunned as he turned his head to face her, and smiled.

'Did you enjoy our kissing, Anna?'

She nodded, thinking how beautiful his eyes were.

'Oh, sweet Anna,' Otho murmured, his lips on hers, 'you loved it, didn't you? I could tell.'

'Yes,' she breathed. 'I never dreamed there could be pleasure like that.' She lay there in his arms, feeling blissful, wanting to prolong the moment for as long as possible.

'This is what God intended for men and women!' he smiled.

'It wasn't wrong, was it?' Her sense of fitness was returning, and with it the awareness that she had been a party to something forbidden.

'Of course not.' He released her and sat up, lacing his hose. 'But let's keep it as our secret. Our parents wouldn't understand. They think such pleasures should be kept for marriage, but I see no harm in enjoying them before.'

Anna began to feel guilty. Carried away on a tide of madness, she had betrayed the precepts drummed into her by her mother. But it had been so beautiful! Why, then, did she feel a creeping sense of dread? It was the fear of being found out, she realised; that was all. How could she regret something that had brought her such joy?

'Can we be married, Anna?' Otho asked, gazing at her longingly.

'Oh, I do wish that!' she cried. 'But I am promised to the Duke of Lorraine's son.' Her voice caught in her throat.

He stared at her. 'I did not know.'

She shook her head. 'It is not what I want, but my father is set on an alliance with Lorraine.' Belatedly, she realised that what she had done with Otho was meant to be saved for marriage; they had stolen what rightfully belonged to Francis.

'Betrothals can be broken,' Otho said.

Anna shook her head. 'I doubt it.' She felt tears welling, and knew her misery must be written plain on her face.

She stood up, tidied herself and moved towards the door.

'Where are you going, *Liebling*?' Otho asked, looking bewildered.

'We should go back. We have been here too long,' she said.

He pulled her into his arms and kissed her again, long and yearningly, leaving her in no doubt as to his feelings. They belonged to each other now, and nothing could change that: it was what his lips were saying to her. She was drowning in emotion. She wanted the moment to go on for ever, but made herself break away. She dared not stay alone with him here any longer.

'I love you, Anna,' she heard him whisper.

Ignoring the soreness between her legs, she hastened down the stairs, bereft, and desperate to cry out her sorrow in her chamber, where there would be clean water, soap and towels to remove all trace of her sinfulness, and she could take off the gown of which she had been so proud, but which now bore the stains of her fall from grace. Otho was right. What had passed between them *must* remain a secret; besides, Anna did not have the words to describe what had happened. If her parents found out, *she* would be blamed. She should not have been alone with Otho in the first place, let alone allowed him to kiss her and lie with her. They would say he had dishonoured her, a princess of Kleve, when he was a guest in her father's house. Yet it had not been like that! She had lain with him willingly – and she had been in ecstasy. Otho had said he loved her and had spoken of marriage – yet they could never belong to each other. Tears welled again in her eyes as she emerged from the tower. She prayed the guards would not notice her distress.

'Anna?' Otho cried, behind her. 'Are you all right?'

'The Spiegelturm is over there,' she called back, her voice catching.

'They'll be waiting for you. Tell them . . . tell them my head is aching and that I've gone to lie down.'

Leaving him standing there, she hastened away to her chamber. Mercifully, it was deserted. Mother Lowe was enjoying her usual afternoon nap.

Crying, Anna unlaced her bodice and sleeves and let her gown fall to the floor, then poured some water from the ewer into the bowl beside it. It was while she was scrubbing herself that she noticed blood on her lawn chemise. Was this the monthly visitation Mutter had warned her about? When Anna had asked why women had to bleed, Mutter had simply said that it was God's will, and that Anna would learn more about it when she was about to be married. Anna wondered if it had anything to do with what she had done this day.

She changed her chemise and put the soiled one to soak in the bowl of water. What to do about the dress? There was blood on the lining of that too, so she took the damp cloth she had used to wash herself and rubbed it away. Soon, the stain was nearly gone; if you were not looking for it, you would not see it. She laid the damp dress away in the chest, and put on another, of creamy silk banded with crimson. Then she stared at herself in the mirror, checking that no one could see she had been crying. Her eyes looked a bit red, but she could put that down to the headache. And it was true, her head *was* aching, from the burden of love, guilt and desperation she now carried.

When the bell in the tower summoned everyone to supper, she sped down the stairs and arrived in the dining chamber on time. Vater never could abide unpunctuality.

Otho was there already, with Onkel Otho and Tante Elisabeth. She wanted to fly into his arms, but made herself avoid his eyes, aware that he was avidly seeking hers. No one must guess the secret that lay between them.

'Is your head better, my dear?' Tante Elisabeth asked her.

'I am much better, thank you,' Anna told her.

'You've changed your dress, child,' Mutter observed.

'I was too hot in the other one.' She was praying Otho would not give them away, by some chance word or glance. Mutter could be sharply observant.

The meal was an ordeal, and she struggled to behave normally, and to eat the choice carp and roasted pork served to her. She dared not think of what had happened earlier, lest her face flame and betray her. It wasn't easy, with Otho sitting so dangerously near to her, looking so handsome, and her stomach churning with love and desire. It took all her inner resources to behave as usual. She did not think anyone noticed anything amiss.

After supper, the Duke's consort of musicians arrived with their trumpets, lutes and harps. Mutter would always have harp music if she could; it was her favourite, and she bestowed one of her rare smiles on the players when the last note had been struck.

'I wish we could dance,' Emily said wistfully, 'or sing.'

Mutter frowned. 'My dear child, you know it is immodest for a woman to dance or sing in public.'

'I know,' muttered Emily gloomily, 'but I do so love music and dancing.'

Tante Elisabeth regarded her with disapproval.

'She inherited her love of music from me,' Mutter said. Elisabeth gave a thin smile.

The men were talking of politics.

'The Emperor has ambitions. He wants the duchy of Guelders for himself,' Vater was saying. 'But it will go to Anna's betrothed.' Anna saw Otho's expression darken, but Vater continued, unheeding. 'Duke Charles is childless, and Francis, as his great-nephew, will inherit. I myself have a claim to Guelders, but I relinquished it as part of the terms of the betrothal contract; I am content that my daughter will be duchess of Guelders.'

Anna struggled to maintain her composure. She most certainly was not content at the prospect. Her imaginary image of Francis had metamorphosed from a courteous, smiling boy into a disapproving, suspicious man.

'The Emperor also has a claim to Guelders, does he not?' Onkel Otho asked.

'Yes, through his mother,' Vater told him. 'But if he presses it, we will be ready for him. Kleve may be part of the Holy Roman Empire, but it is also one of the leading principalities of Germany. We will not let the Emperor dictate to us. We protect our independence. We have our own courts and our own army, and I keep control of our foreign policy.' Wilhelm was listening avidly.

'But Charles is very powerful. You would have a fight on your hands,' Onkel Otho said.

'Ah, but he might well be going to war with England, if King Henry continues in his attempt to divorce his Imperial Majesty's Aunt Katherine to marry a courtesan. I count on Charles being too pre-occupied with that, and with the Turks encroaching on his eastern borders, to concern himself with Guelders. I have the means to raise a mighty army.' The Duke paused as a servant refilled his goblet. 'I met King Henry of England once, you know. Eight years ago, I visited his kingdom in the train of the Emperor.'

'What was he like, Vater?' Wilhelm asked.

'Handsome. Bombastic. Full of his new title. The Pope had just named him Defender of the Faith for writing a book against Martin Luther.'

The conversation dragged on interminably. There had been no chance of any conversation with Otho, as Wilhelm and Emily were sitting between him and Anna, and now, at precisely nine o'clock, the Hofmeister was arriving to remove the wine, signalling that it was time to retire. It was forbidden to the courtiers to sit up any later, playing cards, drinking or even just chatting, and Vater liked to set a good example.

Everyone bade each other a good night. As Anna was leaving the room, she felt a hand close on hers from behind, pressing something into her palm. She swung round, to see Otho giving her a longing look. Fortunately, no one seemed to have noticed, and she walked on, out of the dining chamber, to receive her parents' blessings and hasten up to her room.

Only then did she open her hand. She was holding a tiny package wrapped in a scrap of damask; inside was a ring enamelled in red. There was a note, too. 'Sweet Anna, please accept this token of my esteem. My family's coat of arms has a red ring, so it is special to me. I hope you will wear it and think kindly of your servant.'

He had given her his special ring! If only it could have been her betrothal ring! And yet, even though it was not, it still symbolised eternal love.

She dared not keep the note; though it broke her heart to do it, she tore it into tiny pieces and threw them out of the window. But the ring she hid under the loose floorboard in the corner of her bed-chamber.

When the von Wyliches left, two days later, Anna was torn between misery at having to bid farewell to Otho and relief at not having to fend off his earnest, covert attempts to speak with her. Once he had gone, taking with him the fear of exposure, she was able to relax, telling herself she must not think of him, for the sake of her sanity; nor did she dare ask her father for a place for him, lest her evident interest in his affairs led to awkward questions. Yet it was unbearably hard to resume the endless routine of her days, which she and Emily spent largely in their mother's apartments, among the women. Rarely, except at night, in their shared bedchamber, were they alone.

Wilhelm was luckier. From the age of seven, he had received a fine education under Vater's scholarly councillor, Herr Heresbach, who had been recommended by Erasmus himself. Wilhelm never stopped boasting that Erasmus had dedicated a book to him when he was only five. He was now fluent in Latin and French, whereas Anna and Emily could speak only German. Mutter did not believe in educating women beyond teaching them to read and write.

'It is immodest for great ladies to be learned,' she said, often. 'It is not necessary for you girls to speak any other tongue.'

Anna could not imagine her mother ever succumbing to the kind of passion she herself had experienced. Mutter, whose resemblance to Anna was marked, physically, but not (Anna felt sadly) in many other ways, was too dignified, too serene, too devout. She supervised her daughters almost constantly. Even when Anna and Emily took some recreation in the fresh air, there she was, following at a distance with her ladies.

'We are never far from her elbow!' Emily grumbled as Mutter watched them perambulating the garden, and Anna found herself chafing even more now against such vigilance.

'The Duchess is a wise lady,' Mother Lowe chided when, back indoors, the sisters complained about Mutter's rules. 'It is rare to see a mother who looks after her children so strictly.' Mother Lowe was also a lady of great dignity, for all her plumpness, her apple cheeks, and her plaits tight-coiled around each ear. Anna and Emily knew beyond doubt that she loved them, but she colluded with Mutter in constraining them to be modest, chaste and humble. Everything they learned from mother and nurse was intended to mould them into the virtuous future wives of princes; and if they strayed from the narrow path mapped out for them, or fell to daydreaming, well then, Mutter and Mother Lowe would be sure to keep them busy and distracted with religious devotions and needlework. Heaven forbid, Anna prayed, that they ever learned how far she had fallen short of their exhortations!

'You must be like nuns,' Mutter enjoined yet again. She was prone to giving little homilies as they sat plying their needles. It was now a week since their guests had left, and Anna wondered, in some alarm, if her mother had noticed her reaction to Otho. 'You must learn custody of the eyes. Never let them stray where they should not go. Be discreet in your gestures and your expressions.'

Even if she had noticed, Mutter could not know the whole of it, Anna reassured herself, suppressing the guilt that nagged at her constantly. It still surprised her that she had been so heedless of Mutter's training. Custody of the eyes? She had kept custody of nothing! I am not worthy to be married, she told herself miserably. I am not worthy of my family's love. If they knew what I really am, they would spurn me, as I deserve.

She said nothing of her unhappiness. She must keep her secret, bearing her joy, her sorrow and her guilt in silence – these were her punishments.

She yearned now for more distractions. Her days were a repetitive round of prayers, needlework, weaving, cooking and instruction on how to run a great household. At least there was always music to listen to; however, playing and singing were condemned as indecorous. Emily cleverly circumvented that rule. She had a lute hidden amidst the jumble of possessions crammed under her bed, which she would play softly at night or in snatched moments, and she was forever scribbling down the words to songs she had made up. But Anna lacked her temerity and boldness; besides, she could not play any instrument, and certainly she could not sing.

It seemed that her world was forever to be limited to the boundaries of castle and chapel, though occasionally, she and Emily were allowed to entertain guests at dinner with the Duke and Duchess, for in Kleve, parents brought up their daughters to be good hostesses. The guests – who were chosen for them – were invariably humanist scholars, churchmen, or councillors Vater wished to favour. They praised Anna's charm and graciousness, as Mutter looked on approvingly. She thought she had done well in so virtuously bringing up her daughters.

For all Mutter's strictness, Anna loved her. She was the rock on which their world was built, their lodestar when things went wrong. The sight of her composed face, the sound of her calm voice, represented all that was good and safe. And her faith was an inspiration.

Like Vater, Mutter was a friend to humanist scholars, but those who were welcomed into her circle, and at her table, were of one mind in opposing the teachings of Martin Luther. Mutter relied for spiritual consolation on her confessor, Father Gerecht, prior of the Charterhouse at Cantave, near her native Jülich. He was a monk of the very strict Carthusian Order, yet, although he had embraced the ascetic, secluded life of his cloister, he had a tender pity and love for those souls still living in the world, and visited court weekly. He had written two tracts against Luther, but there was no hatred in him. Anna loved to hear him preach, because all he spoke of was love.

'Never lose sight of God's love for man,' he enjoined, smiling benevolently at her and Emily as they sat at table with Mutter. 'You are Christian princesses, and must keep the Sacred Heart of God before you as the subject of special veneration and imitation.' Anna tried to do as he counselled, but she was finding as she grew older that the world offered too many distractions – most of which were forbidden to her.

Mutter, of course, was above worldly distractions. Her mission was to make good Catholics of her children. 'I am always reminding them of the family motto: *Candida nostra fides* – "Our faith is pure",' she said, sipping her wine delicately. 'And so it must be. My husband's court is a school of this New Learning. It is true that we can learn much from these lately rediscovered texts of ancient Greece and Rome, yet I fear they inspire men to question the teachings of the Church.'

'A new study of the works of antiquity seemed a marvellous thing a few years back,' Father Gerecht declared, as fruit was served, 'but your Grace is right, it has proved dangerous too, for it has indeed led men to question matters of faith and doctrine.' He looked distressed. 'Some think the Scriptures should be available for all to read.' He did not mention the name of Erasmus; he did not need to, for they all knew that Erasmus advocated the translation of the Scriptures into the vernacular, and had translated some himself. And it was well known that Vater agreed with him.

Mutter would never criticise Vater, or openly disagree with him. And because Vater loved Erasmus, she would not criticise him either. She just sat there daintily cutting up her food, looking pensive.

Father Gerecht shook his head. 'If laymen are permitted to read the Scriptures, they may boast that they understand them better than the clergy, who are trained to interpret them and invested at ordination with the spiritual power to do so.'

Wilhelm, listening with interest to the conversation, suddenly spoke. 'Forgive me, Father, but I have heard it said that not all priests have the learning to interpret Scripture properly for their flock, and that some interpret it selectively for their own ends.'

'Wilhelm!' Mutter exclaimed, shocked.

The old monk smiled. 'Your Grace, it is natural at the boy's age to question, and if he has heard this, then he needs to hear that it is very rarely the case. There are venal souls in all walks of life, even in the priesthood, regrettably. But most are devout and conscientious in their calling. Does that satisfy you, my young lord?'

'Yes, Father.' Wilhelm did not look convinced.

'I should hope so,' Mutter said, severe.

Wilhelm bowed his head.

It would not be long now until Anna's fifteenth birthday. Her birthday was in September, Emily's in October, and they always had a joint celebration, usually a staid little supper with their parents and a few choice guests, who would come with felicitations and gifts. At least it was a chance to dress up.

Anna was standing in her chemise in the middle of her chamber, studying the fine garments spread out on her bed. Emily fidgeted impatiently, already dressed in a gown of moss green with a wide black velvet belt and elaborate slashing on the tight sleeves.

'The black velvet is too sombre, Anna,' she said.

'Yes, but it's my most costly dress.' Anna bent over a rich pool of crimson velvet. 'I'll wear this one. And perhaps my new headdress, with my plaits showing.' She lifted up the beaded *Stickelchen*; it was beautifully embroidered, with a decorative forecloth of gold.

'Very fitting, Madame la Marquise,' Mother Lowe commented, as she bustled into the room with a pile of clean linen for the chest at the bottom of the bed. 'Now that you are almost a grand old lady of fifteen, you must look the part! But that crimson clashes with your headdress. Why not wear your red silk?'

Anna hesitated. She had not worn the gown since June, and did not want to do so now. It bore an indelible reminder of what had passed between her and Otho, if anyone looked closely enough.

'No, I think I will wear the black,' she said quickly. 'That gold belt with the big buckle will go well with it.'

Mother Lowe laced her into the gown. 'I do declare, my lady, that you have put on weight,' she said. 'I was lacing it tighter last time.'

'That's because she likes her *Kuchen* too much,' Emily scoffed. Anna did not laugh. She had enjoyed no more cakes than normal, yet she was aware that her bust had developed rather rapidly in the past weeks, and her stomach was rounder. It was all part of becoming a woman, she knew, but she did not want to become fat.

She put on the belt. It was true. Her waistline had thickened. 'I shall have to look to my diet,' she said.

''Tis common for young ladies of your age to get plump,' Mother Lowe consoled her. 'If you eat less, it will all fall off, mark my words.'

But it didn't. A month later, as the wind was whistling around the towers, the cobbles were slippery with damp russet leaves, and the household were preparing to move to Düsseldorf, as they did every winter, Anna had to face the fact that her belly and breasts were definitely swollen. Could she be ill when she felt very well? And what disease would manifest itself like this?

An awful possibility occurred to her. When the married ladies of her mother's court were *enceinte*, their stomachs swelled up. They would disappear to their estates for some months, then reappear at court, slim as reeds and full of gossip about their new babes. But she could not be *enceinte*. She was not married, for a start, and Otho had assured her that kissing, even the more intimate kind, was harmless. Mother Lowe had just said it wasn't to put her charges off kissing any young man they fancied.

But what if Otho had been wrong? What if kissing was not as harmless as he'd said?

Chapter 2

1530–1531

November came in with mists, and the packing was nearly completed. They would leave Schwanenburg tomorrow.

That night, Anna lay wakeful, her hands on her belly. There was a definite thickening there. And she had to keep hurrying to the close stool.

She got up and knelt down by the bed. Prising up the floorboard, she retrieved Otho's ring. It must go with her; she could not bear to leave it behind. It was all she had of him.

When she got back into bed, sleep still eluded her. Dare she risk consulting one of her father's physicians? Doctors swore an oath not to reveal anything about their patients, but would Dr Schultz account loyalty to his Duke more pressing, morally speaking? And how would Anna ever find the words to tell him what she had done with Otho?

But she had to know what ailed her, otherwise she might die – or, Heaven forbid, have a baby, which was almost worse. She could not keep her symptoms a secret for much longer. Already she was fastening her belts as tight as she dared, and making sure she was clad in her warmest, most voluminous chemises before Mother Lowe arrived each morning to help her dress. Soon, surely, her nurse would notice that something was wrong.

She could not fool Mother Lowe. The very next morning, that redoubtable lady sailed into the room before Anna had had time to get out of bed.

'Hurry up, Madame la Marquise!' she said. 'We have a journey of a hundred miles ahead of us, and your lord father wants to be on the road as soon as possible, to make the most of the daylight. I'll just pour you some hot water and put your chemise to warm in front of the stove.'

Anna slithered out of bed. Not so long ago, it would not have bothered her to strip and wash in front of her nurse. Turning her back, she lowered her night-rail to her waist, took a clean cloth and began to soap her face and arms, praying that Mother Lowe would not notice the changes in her body.

'Anna, face me!' Mother Lowe's use of her Christian name, as if she were a child again, and the sharpness of her command, left Anna in no doubt that her secret was rumbled. Clutching the damp night-rail to her breasts, she turned. Mother Lowe's face bore such a look of horror that it chilled her.

'Is there something you need to tell me, child?' she stuttered. '*Mein Gott*, I had my suspicions, but I told myself, no, not my Anna, it is not possible. She is a good girl, and innocent of such matters. Anna would not do such a thing. Tell me you have not shamed us all!'

Anna burst into tears. 'I don't know!' she wailed. 'He said it would not be harmful.'

Mother Lowe's hand flew to her mouth. 'He? You had best tell me everything!' She was visibly struggling to regain mastery of herself, but her shock was plain.

Anna hung her head, bracing herself to face the consequences of her wickedness, knowing that this was one thing her nurse could not make better. All the same, as her sorry tale came tumbling out, in fits and starts and clumsy euphemisms, she felt relief at unburdening herself.

While she talked, Mother Lowe dressed her with trembling hands. This would reflect badly on her nurse, Anna realised. Mutter would say she had not properly looked to her charge, or instilled in her a sufficient sense of propriety. And that would not be fair, for Mutter herself had suggested that Anna, Emily and Wilhelm show Otho around the castle. She had not told them to find Mother Lowe, because she had known that Mother Lowe would be napping. And, for all that Mutter herself had drummed into Anna the need to be virtuous, she had failed in her duty too, because she had not told Anna what she must guard against.

'He was definitely inside you?' Mother Lowe barked, her cheeks pink.

'Yes,' Anna whispered. 'He told me it was kissing, and harmless.'

'Harmless my foot! It is what a man and woman do to get a baby. And it looks like you have got one, poor lamb.' The nurse sighed deeply. 'What's to be done, I cannot think. Your lady mother will have to be told.'

'No!' Anna cried, suddenly furious with Otho for misleading her – had he done it deliberately? – and devastated at the prospect of Mutter's shock, her disappointment in her daughter, and the anger that must surely follow.

'I have no choice,' Mother Lowe stated firmly. 'She has to know, so she can decide what to do. But you must leave it to me to tell her, in my own way, to make her understand that, while you acted foolishly and with impropriety, you were taken advantage of by a young scoundrel who should have known better!'

Anna was trembling. She wanted to protest that no, it had not been like that! But she dared not. She needed Mother Lowe on her side.

'What do you think she will say?' she whispered.

'What any mother hearing such news would say!' the nurse snapped. 'And you must allow her her righteous fury. But I think I know her well enough to say that, when she has calmed down, she will be just.'

'Are you going to tell her now?' Anna faltered.

'No, child.' Mother Lowe lifted Anna's cloak from its peg. 'We have to be on our way. It's best to wait until we get to Düsseldorf.'

'But we won't be there for three days!' Anna cried.

'And there'll be little privacy on the way. No, it must keep until we arrive, for I need time to think how I'm going to approach your lady mother.'

Never had a journey seemed so long. It was an eternity before the walls, spires and onion domes of the ducal capital appeared in the distance, wreathed in fog.

Anna had been born here, in the palace overlooking the River Rhine, and it was from here that Sybilla had departed to marry the Elector of

Saxony. But today, Anna could not take her usual pleasure in what was normally a happy homecoming. She was too full of dread. As she alighted from the chariot in the outer courtyard, all she could think of was that tonight she would know her fate. She could not imagine what it would be. Would her betrothal be broken? Could they consign her to a nunnery, to live out her days in shame? Worst of all, would her parents disown her? Or – and she began to cherish a golden beacon of hope – would Otho be made to wed her? Maybe things would turn out well after all.

Vater was dismounting, looking up in satisfaction at the two towers flanking the open end of the great courtyard, each surmounted by a cupola. Mutter was directing her maids to see to her personal luggage.

'You girls, go up to your rooms,' she told her daughters. 'And, Anna, do try to look more cheerful. It will be Christmas soon.'

'Yes, my lady,' Anna said, forcing a smile, then turning away quickly so that Mutter should not see the tears brimming. By Christmas, she might have been cast out from her family.

She made for the stairs, Emily following, and they ascended to their chambers on the second floor. The sumptuousness of the private apartments, which always struck Anna anew each time she came here, made no impression on her today. She closed the door of her chamber behind her and sank down on a carved settle, choking back her sobs. Her maid came knocking, asking if she should unpack, but Anna sent her away.

She was too restless to read or embroider. She found herself staring out of the window at the grey-tiled roofs of the gallery and loggia below her, which fronted the quayside. In the rooms beneath hers, Mutter would be settling in, unaware that her world was about to be shattered. At the thought of that, Anna wept again.

Supper, as usual, was served to the ducal children in their own chambers. Anna took one look at the *Sauerbraten* and fried spinach before her, and sent it away, feeling nauseous.

'I am not hungry,' she told her maid.

She was in a fever of anxiety to discover whether Mother Lowe had spoken to Mutter yet. It was not until the bell sounded seven o'clock that the nurse came to her chamber, her face grave.

'Your lady mother wants to see you,' she said.

Anna rose shakily, unable to speak. Her throat felt as if it was closing up. She went ahead of Mother Lowe, down the stairs and through the public rooms to the door leading to Mutter's chamber, her legs feeling as if they might give way. The guards stood to attention, raising their crossed pikes. An usher sprang forward and pushed open the door.

'Madame la Marquise de Pont-à-Mousson!' he announced.

Anna walked past him, her eyes searching out her mother's face as she curtseyed.

The Duchess was alone, seated in her usual chair. At her nod, the doors closed behind Anna and Mother Lowe. Anna was utterly shocked to see that Mutter had been crying. Mutter never cried. She offered up her troubles to God, certain that He would succour her. But evidently this trial Anna had inflicted on her was beyond divine help.

'Sit down, Anna,' Mutter said, indicating a stool. Her voice shook. 'You know what this is about. It is too painful for me to reiterate what Mother Lowe has told me, so we will not dwell on that. You must go to confession, do penance and make your peace with God. What concerns *me* is what happens now. Mother Lowe reckons that you are about five months . . .' She gave an involuntary shudder.

'Yes, my lady,' Anna whispered. 'I am so sorry.'

'I am sure you are.' Mutter's voice was tart. 'When I think of all the times I exhorted you to virtue, I could weep. If you had heeded me properly, we would not be having this conversation today. But what's done cannot be undone, however much it grieves us. And Mother Lowe has told me how deeply it has grieved *you*, having to live with the consequences of your sin. I bear in mind your tender years and your innocence. I like to think that you were more sinned against than sinning, as appears to have been the case.'

Anna bowed her head. Such understanding was more than she deserved. She would be eternally grateful to Mother Lowe for giving such a sympathetic account of her transgression.

28

Now was the moment to plead for her future. 'My lady,' she ventured, 'we were wrong to do what we did, but we love each other. Otho wants to marry me!'

Mutter stared at her. 'Are you out of your mind, girl? Do you really think that your lord father would marry you off to a bastard?' Anna had never heard her mother speak so vehemently.

'But it would avoid disgrace, my lady,' she whispered.

'There are other ways of doing that!' The Duchess shook her head, as if despairing. 'Anna, heed me. On no account must anyone ever find out that you are with child. Have you told anyone?'

'No, Madam. But shouldn't Otho be informed?'

Mutter's eyes widened in astonishment. 'Absolutely not! He should be horsewhipped for what he did to you, but it is better that he remains in ignorance of what has come of it. And your father must never know either. It would break his heart . . . as it has broken mine.' Her voice trembled again. Anna was overcome with remorse – and resentment. She had hurt Mutter badly, yet Mutter was being very unreasonable.

'So,' her mother's voice was brisk again, 'we will say you are ill, with a humour of the stomach. Mother Lowe tells me your appetite has been poor lately, so maybe others have noticed too. You will go to stay at Schloss Burg, where the air is healthy, and there, in the spring, you will make a full recovery, God willing. Mother Lowe will accompany you, and she will arrange for a midwife to attend you in due course. When . . . when all is over, you can return to court, as if nothing had happened, and no one will be any the wiser.'

'Yes, Mutter,' Anna replied dully. Her punishment could have been a lot more severe, and she might even have forfeited her mother's love, but couldn't Mutter have been a bit more understanding and exercised her considerable influence to persuade Vater to let Anna marry Otho? How happy she would have been! But now . . .

'What of the child?' she asked, playing her last card. 'It needs a father.'

Mutter's lips tightened. 'You should have thought of that! It will be put out to nurse and fostered. None shall know who its parents were. Mother Lowe, you will arrange that while you are at Solingen.'

'Yes, Madam,' the nurse nodded.

The Duchess turned to Anna. 'You may not believe it now, but this is all for the best. All I ask of you is your cooperation and your discretion.'

'Yes, Madam,' Anna whispered, unable to contain the tears any longer. 'Shall I have to confess to Father Gerecht?' She felt sick at the prospect – and suddenly frightened at the thought of facing what lay ahead without Mutter's reassuring presence.

'No. Mother Lowe will arrange for a priest to visit you at Schloss Burg,' her mother said. 'Someone who does not know you.'

Despite her resentment, Anna knew she had been very lucky. 'Madam, I cannot thank you sufficiently for your goodness to me, which I know I do not deserve,' she said tearfully. 'I am very sorry to have grieved you so; and I will miss you.' She sank to her knees, crying hard now, her shoulders heaving, her face in her hands.

A gentle hand rested on her shoulder. She raised her wet face to see Mutter bending over her. 'I will miss you too, my Anna,' she said, her voice softer. It came to Anna that her mother's reserve did not arise so much from disapproval as from sadness. She was holding on to her emotions, as she always did. Anna had not yet mastered that art. She flung her arms about her mother's waist.

'Do not forsake me utterly!' she cried. 'Please do not cast me out. I would rather die than lose your love.'

Mutter prised her hands away and held them. 'No one is casting you out, Anna. I am doing what is best for you *because* I love you. Now, go to your chamber, take to your bed and pretend to be ill. And when you are away, we will write to each other and you can let me know how matters are progressing. Go with my blessing, and God keep you.'

Schloss Burg had always been one of Anna's favourite places; she had spent much of her childhood there. Isolated on its rocky plateau high above the River Wupper, and surrounded by dense forests, the magnificent palace, formerly the chief stronghold of the Duchess Maria's ancestors, the counts of Berg, was also a favourite abode of the Duke, on account of the good hunting to be had thereabouts, and because it was perfect for hosting the courtly festivities he loved. In its distant days as a fortress, it had commanded a sound defensive position. Now, it was a cluster of pepperpot towers and pretty black-and-white timbered buildings surrounding a massive donjon. Vater appreciated it for its splendour, the security it afforded his family, and because it was a much healthier place for his children than the city air of Düsseldorf.

Leaning on the arm of Mother Lowe, accompanied only by the maid her nurse had chosen, who had been waiting inside the great arched Zwingertor to greet them, Anna walked slowly across the courtyard, aware of the two knights of her escort watching her with sympathy. Clearly she'd made a convincing show of being ill, and no doubt they thought she had come here in the forlorn hope of prolonging her life. Fortunately, it was now winter and her heavy furred cloak concealed her burgeoning stomach.

She ascended the grand processional stair one slow, careful step at a time, until they reached the public apartments on the first floor and entered the Rittersaal. This vast aisled Knight's Hall had long been used for the great ceremonies of state hosted by the dukes of Kleve, and before them, the counts of Berg. Mutter and Vater had been married in this hall twenty years ago, and Sybilla had been betrothed to the Elector here. Today, fires had been lit in the two elegant French-style fireplaces against their coming, but the room remained chilly, as if it needed warming by the presence of a great throng of people. The candles were unlit, giving the hall a gloomy aspect, and as Anna walked past the stone pillars that supported the lofty beamed ceiling, she shivered from both the cold and a sense of loneliness.

Beyond the Rittersaal were the spacious private suites used by the ducal family. Anna had spent many a day in Mutter's ladies' chamber, the Kemenate, where the women of the family lived when Vater was away. All the windows afforded beautiful views of the spectacular scenery outside. Beyond the Kemenate was the chapel, where, when she was in residence, the Duchess daily observed the liturgy of the Hours, herself reciting the Divine Office, with her children kneeling behind her.

The servants had prepared Anna's bedchamber. The green-tiled stove in the corner had been lit, the feather bed was airing, and floral tapestries had been hung on the walls. Mother Lowe had the little maid, Gerda, hastening to unpack Anna's chests, and soon the room seemed like home again – except that nearly everyone who made Schloss Burg home was missing.

As winter set in, and the child grew and kicked within her, Anna kept mostly to her chamber, looked after by Mother Lowe and Gerda, who had been told her mistress was suffering from a severe dropsy. Whether she suspected the truth, Anna never knew. For all that the girl was an unlettered farmer's daughter, she had a vivid imagination, but she was willing, and very kind to Anna. Hopefully, she did not think to question her betters.

Feeling her baby move for the first time had brought home forcefully to Anna the reality of the child growing inside her. She wept to think it would never know the love of its mother – or its father. She tried not to think of Otho; if she did, she knew she would go mad with longing and misery. He should be here, at her side. It was wrong to keep him in ignorance. It was cruel to make the babe an orphan.

Mother Lowe made discreet enquiries locally, and found an experienced midwife, who was spun a tale about one of the Duchess's married ladies being in an unfortunate predicament, and told that, having obtained permission to seek refuge in the castle, this lady required assistance and absolute discretion, and that the midwife would be paid well for both. Pleased with her good fortune, the midwife had undertaken to find a reputable wet nurse when the time approached. Her own sister was with child and might be able to help; she had had plenty of milk with her last babe. Mother Lowe had visited the midwife's house, and that of her sister, and reported that both were spotlessly clean. Better still, the midwife knew of a family who had lost six infants at birth, one year after the other, and were desperate for a child. The husband, Meister Schmidt, was a prosperous and respected swordsmith, a craftsman with a fine house of timber and stone, and his wife was very devout. The nuns in the cloister of Gräfrath in the town would take care of the fostering. It was all arranged.

Anna knew she had no choice in the matter. It was for the best, Mutter had said firmly. Anna would never believe it.

Time dragged. The days were spent sewing a layette for the child to take with it to its foster home, or taking gentle exercise, or in prayer. Every week, Anna wrote to her mother, but there was not much to report, except that she was in good health and eating well. The fresh air of Schloss Burg had seen to that. Each day, she walked around the castle precincts, through a postern gate and into the gardens on the steep hillside beyond. They ended in a sheer drop, with the River Wupper far below.

In this hilly fastness, surrounded by forests, it was easy to believe in all the tales she had heard of witches and fairies and ghosts. Gerda held that the castle was haunted, but Mother Lowe was brisk to tell the girl to hush up and forget such nonsense. Expectant mothers, she murmured in Anne's ear, must not be affrighted!

But Anna, desperately in need of some diversion, found herself wanting to know more. Had Gerda seen or heard anything herself?

'No, Madam,' the girl had to admit. 'But my cousin is a groom here, and he once saw a tall black-hooded figure standing by the window in the Rittersaal.'

It could have been me, Anna reflected. Me, in my dark cloak. I am sad enough to haunt this place – a ghost from the present. 'I have never experienced anything odd here,' she said, 'but I do love ghost stories.'

Gerda had a fund of them, to while away the dragging hours. Thrown together as they were, notwithstanding the difference in their rank and station in life, they had become friends. Mother Lowe, normally a stickler for etiquette, did not discourage it. She knew how lonely Anna was, how homesick for her family, and how greatly she needed company. And here was Gerda, about her age, flaxen-haired, cheerful and garrulous. As soon as she had finished her duties, there she was, in Anna's chamber, chattering away. The final weeks of Anna's pregnancy were enlivened by many dark and magical tales.

As the child grew heavier inside her, so the evenings lengthened and the first buds of spring began to unfold. And one morning, in the middle of March, she felt the first pangs of travail.

The midwife, installed with her birthing chair in the castle two weeks earlier, had told her what to expect. Afterwards, she said it had been an easy birth. But nothing had prepared Anna for the force of the contractions, or the pain. It went on for hours and hours. Yet she was young and strong, and bore it well. Only at the last did she feel she could not endure any more – but then, urged to make one final, supreme effort, she felt her child slide into the world, and her ordeal was over.

Mother Lowe laid the tiny infant in her arms, just for a few moments, so that he could receive his mother's blessing before being parted from her for ever. Anna's heart turned over when she saw him; he was perfect, so adorable – and she could see Otho in him. She had never wished for anything as fiercely as she yearned to keep him, but she knew it was out of the question. It was a terrible moment, the worst one of her life, when Mother Lowe came back to take him away. Bravely, Anna swallowed her tears, kissed his sweet head and handed him over.

'His name is Johann,' she whispered, 'after my lord father.'

Left alone, she lay there sobbing, feeling as if half her heart had been torn away.

Mother Lowe came back and found her thus.

'Have it out, my lamb!' she cried. 'There, there. It was for the best, believe me. I have arranged for word of him to be sent to me from time to time, so that you will know he is happy and well. But now, you must look to the future. You have your destiny as a princess to fulfil, and I know you will do so with pride. You have had an easy travail, and your trouble is all behind you. You have been lucky.'

'Lucky?' Anna wept bitterly. 'Not when my arms are aching for my little baby, my *Liebling*! Not when I am missing him so dreadfully. If this is being lucky, what does bad luck feel like?'

As her body healed and her milk dried up, her empty arms continued to ache for the child she had lost. She returned to Düsseldorf fully restored to health, but with her heart bleeding for what might have been. It felt impossible to resume life as she had known it, for she would never be the same again. And yet, as the months passed, and her secret grief turned to numbness, she began to see the wisdom of Mother Lowe's words. As far as avoiding scandal went, she had indeed been lucky. But she still felt like weeping every time she thought of how different her life could have been had she been allowed to share it with the man she loved and their child.

Chapter 3

1538–1539

Vater was dying. There was no hope. For the past four years, he had suffered a slow but steady mental decline. Where men had once called him 'the Peaceful', they now nicknamed him 'the Simple'.

Anna did not know what ailed him, and neither, it seemed, did the doctors. It had begun three years after she had returned from Schloss Burg, with Vater forgetting little things, making remarks out of character or addressing people by the wrong names. Sometimes Mutter wondered if there was anything wrong with him at all, but then he would do or say something odd, and they would all fall to worrying again.

In October, he had suffered another illness, a mere ague, which had given his physician, Dr Cepher, an opportunity to examine him closely. 'His confusion is in his head,' he had told Mutter, who had been waiting anxiously outside the bedchamber with her children, 'but his bodily reflexes are also deranged. This is a new development, and I do not understand it. I have never seen it before.'

'Could it be serious?' Mutter had asked, anxiously.

'Alas, I do not know, Madam. We shall have to see how he progresses.'

'I will pray for him,' she had said, and had led her daughters to the chapel, where they spent the next few hours begging God to make Vater well.

They had known something was really amiss in November, when, without warning, Vater had fallen headlong on the floor. He had not tripped or stumbled; he had just lost control of his limbs. The doctors had stood around helplessly, frowning and looking grave.

His disease had followed an inexorable course until it reached the stage where he did not always recognise Mutter. Sometimes he called her Mathilde, his own mother's name. By Christmas, he was bedridden, and had trouble speaking. On one of the rare days when he had known who Mutter was, Anna had watched as he tried to take her hand in his, gazing at her with eyes full of love. 'You must . . . be . . . going through . . . the tortures . . . of the damned,' he murmured, finally getting the words out over long, painful minutes. That had been the last coherent thing Anna had heard him say.

It was now January, and his condition had worsened. The doctors kept shaking their heads and saying there was nothing they could do.

Mutter went about wraith-like, trying to convince herself that this was God's will.

'He has gone from me, the man I loved, and it is too painful to be with the shell of him that is left,' she said.

Anna's heart bled for her parents as she stood by her father's bed and looked down on him. He was sleeping fitfully, a trickle of drool running down his grizzly chin. Was this wasted husk really the debonair chevalier who had dazzled his subjects in his flamboyant satins and velvets and feathered bonnets?

'It will not be long now,' Dr Cepher murmured to Mutter. She crossed herself and sent for Wilhelm.

For months now, Wilhelm had been duke in all but name. At twenty-two, he had grown to be of middle height, with good looks, a muscular build, and a bushy dark brown beard that matched his hair, which he wore cropped to the ear. He was as serious and humourless as ever, but winning praise for his courtesy and his virtue. Wilhelm would never be caught in a tavern or in the arms of a whore, but Anna was sometimes irritated by his sanctimonious manner and unshakeable belief that he was right.

And yet, watching him now, as he sat by Vater's bed, his angular features taut, his fine eyes clouded by tears, she had to concede that he had the makings of a great ruler. He was impressively learned, with a reputation among the princes of Germany for being the most fluent in French, and the most accomplished in Italian manners.

And he was determined to make Kleve respected throughout Christendom.

It would all be his soon – Kleve, with its duchies and territories. Anna had long been wary of him. If he discovered her secret, she would suffer for it. Once – she had never forgotten it – hearing that the sister of one of the ducal councillors had abandoned her husband, Wilhelm had exploded in rage and said that, if it had been his sister, he would have killed her. Anna prayed he would never find out about the existence of his unknown nephew, who – she heard from Mother Lowe, all too infrequently – was thriving in Solingen and desired to be a swordsmith like his adoptive father. A swordsmith – and he the grandson of the Duke of Kleve! Missing him was a dull ache she lived with daily.

His face pained, Wilhelm gazed down at his dying father. 'What a tragedy. He was the most peaceable ruler of his day.'

As they left the stuffy bedchamber and opened the windows in the gallery beyond, letting in the clean, cold air, Anna kept her voice lowered. 'Mutter thinks Vater's illness is a punishment from God because he rejected the authority of the Pope and the Church of Rome. She said it was never the will of God for the Church in Kleve to be placed under the control of the state.' Goaded by grief, their mother had been unusually outspoken.

'Mutter would think that,' Wilhelm observed. 'She is a devout daughter of the Church of Rome. But Vater believed he was doing what was right. And, unlike the King of England, who broke with the Pope just because he wanted a new wife, Vater acted on a principle, and took care to maintain as friendly relations as were possible with the Vatican. I shall not change things, whatever Mutter says.' He looked down his long nose at Anna.

She raised her eyebrows. It was no secret that Wilhelm was a reformist, like Vater, and a friend and protector to his Lutheran subjects, even inviting one to preach at court; but he was a Catholic at heart, and orthodox, and many expected him to heed his mother's urging and return in obedience to Rome. He often said himself that he took no decision without consulting Mutter, and Anna anticipated that he would do so in regard to religion. Whatever he decided, Mutter would not challenge him; as it had been with her husband, so it was with her son.

Since Wilhelm had assumed sovereign power, Anna had felt the constraints tightening. He was zealously protective of his womenfolk, and far more severe in his views on female decorum than Vater had been. Mutter was strict, but Wilhelm was stricter. It had already been made clear that, until they married, Anna and Emily would stay secluded with their mother in the private apartments, except on state occasions. Yet, since her betrothal had been broken four years ago, there seemed no prospect of Anna marrying. She was twenty-three now, and no other prince had asked for her hand. Even if they did, Wilhelm would probably turn them down. His treasury was depleted; how could he afford a dowry?

Sitting in Mutter's chamber, sorting through embroidery silks with Emily, Anna wondered what her life would have been like if she had married Francis of Lorraine. She had not felt sad when Vater told her that the precontract had been annulled, a thing easily done as neither she nor Francis had been of the age of consent when it was made. No, all she had felt was relief. Once upon a time, she would eagerly have begun hoping anew that she would be allowed to marry Otho, but that was years in the past. She still kept his ring locked away in the little casket that contained her few personal treasures; even after she had heard he was married, she had not been able to bring herself to get rid of it. She had not seen him since that fateful visit, and sometimes wondered what he was like now, and if he ever thought of her. When she thought of him, it was as a poignant memory, and with gratitude that she had at least known the wonder of physical love – especially since she might now never know it again.

Maybe the breaking of her betrothal had been part of God's plan to ensure that she was here in Kleve when her mother needed her. Maybe He had saved her from becoming embroiled in a war. For, much to the impotent rage of the Duke of Lorraine, the childless Duke of Guelders had been persuaded that his duchy would preserve its independence more effectively in the hands of Wilhelm than in those of Francis, and had designated Wilhelm his heir. This was why there had no longer been any reason for Anna to wed Francis. And when Duke Charles had died last year, Wilhelm had become duke of Guelders, further expanding the territories controlled by Kleve.

But the Emperor had been furious. Guelders, he had announced, was rightly his. People were saying he would have it whatever it cost him.

'Of course he is angry,' Wilhelm had said, his eyes gleaming. 'He knows that possession of Guelders gives me great strategic advantages. He now has to cross my dominions to get to his duchy of Burgundy. Hitherto, Kleve was landlocked, but now we have access to the Zuyder Zee and the North Sea, which increases our military potential.'

There might yet be a war. Even if Anna had married Francis, and they had taken possession of Guelders last year, the Emperor might still have objected, and she could have been caught up in the conflict.

She wished she had some marriage in view. She could not help envisaging what it would be like, sharing physical pleasure with a husband she could love. Many times, she had been tempted to commit what the Church taught was a mortal sin, which could consign her to damnation if she did not confess and repent. But she shrank from mentioning such a thing to Father Gerecht, or to any other priest, for how could they understand, being vowed to celibacy? They would surely be shocked at a woman admitting to such base desires. Moreover, repentance meant resolving never to commit the sin again, a commitment she feared she might not sustain. St Paul had said that it was better to marry than to burn, and she understood exactly what he meant; but with no prospect of marriage in sight, all she could do was burn.

Anna was alone when Wilhelm came to the ladies' chamber at Düsseldorf in the last week of January. Mutter was in the chapel, and it was Emily's turn to sit with Vater.

Anna poured some wine. Wilhelm accepted it with a nod and sat down.

'I have some news that concerns you,' he announced. 'Sybilla has written to say that envoys from the King of England have arrived at the court of Saxony and approached the Elector's Vice Chancellor touching the possibility of an alliance with Kleve. Vater's health is known to be failing, and they know the Elector to be my firm ally. In this matter, he can be trusted to do right by me, because he wants to draw Kleve into the Schmalkaldic League. You will remember his Vice Chancellor, Franz Burchard, from his visit two years ago. He has been in England, and knows the people. He's a good man, sound and reliable. We can count on him to handle the matter properly, and discreetly.'

'How does this concern me?' Anna asked, sipping her wine.

Wilhelm straightened in his chair. There was a rare air of suppressed excitement about him. 'It seems that King Henry's Principal Secretary, Lord Cromwell, has recommended you as a bride for the King, and that the King has intimated his interest in proceeding with an alliance. Anna, you could be queen of England!'

For a moment, Anna was speechless, then she found herself trembling. No. No! Henry of England's matrimonial career had fuelled the gossip of Christendom for years. He had had three wives, and all had died miserably, the first, rumour had it, poisoned, the second put to the sword, and the third in childbed, only the year before last. By all accounts, he was a tyrant, both in the bedchamber and out of it.

'You don't seem very pleased,' Wilhelm observed, looking a little deflated.

'Do you wonder?' she asked. 'What price a crown, if the man is a monster?'

'Some would say he has been unlucky. His first two queens failed to give him an heir; the third died doing so.'

'But he had the second beheaded! Would you have me risk such a fate?'

'She was a strumpet who betrayed him with other men. You, Anna, are cut from different cloth. No breath of scandal would ever attach itself to you.'

Anna felt her cheeks grow hot with guilt. 'I should hope not,' she said, inwardly in turmoil. What if the terrifying Henry of England discovered she was no virgin?

'I do not want to marry this King,' she declared.

'But, Anna, an alliance with England will be of great benefit to Kleve,' Wilhelm protested, severe. 'It is your duty to aid your country by making a good marriage.' It was clear that he was already set on it. With a sinking heart, Anna realised she had little choice in the matter.

'But why does England want to ally itself with Kleve?' she asked.

'Let us take a walk, and I will explain.'

They fetched cloaks and gloves, and Wilhelm led Anna down to the gallery and loggia that fronted the quayside, where they stood watching the boats sailing along the Rhine or offloading their goods on to the wharves.

'The Pope has recently excommunicated King Henry,' Wilhelm revealed. 'Consequently, those two devout sons of the Church, the Emperor and the King of France, have allied themselves to each other, leaving him isolated. England is not as powerful as the Empire or France, but until recently, by allying itself to one or the other, it has maintained the balance of power in Christendom. Henry has long been in negotiations for a marriage with the Duchess of Milan, the Emperor's niece, but this new pact between Charles and King François has wrecked them. The King is most put out; he is preparing for war and seeking other friends, and another bride. He needs an ally who will support him against his enemies; an ally bound by the ties of kinship.'

Reluctantly, Anna found herself understanding why King Henry was attracted to Kleve, which was one of the foremost principalities of Germany, and able to command a great army.

'An alliance between England, Kleve and our friends, the Protestant German princes, would tip the balance of power in Europe in England's favour once more,' Wilhelm said, indicating that they should move on, as the wind was chilly. Anna followed him through a door in the wall that led to his garden. 'As you know, the Protestant states of Germany are thorns in the Emperor's side, resisting his attempts to enforce the Catholic faith throughout the Empire; an alliance between them and England would divert Charles from any thought of joining with France to make war on Henry. You can see why the King is keen to ally with us and marry you. Lord Cromwell, his Majesty's chief adviser, is pushing for the match. He is a reformist, like Vater and myself.'

Anna paused by a sundial, tracing its pattern with her finger. It sounded as if the King too was resolved on the matter. What good would it do her, a mere woman, to protest?

'You are thoughtful, Schwester,' Wilhelm said, coming to stand beside her. 'It is a great match. You would be a queen.'

'I would be in danger.'

He sighed. 'Not while I am here to protect you.'

'The Emperor, for all his might, did little to protect his aunt, Queen Katherine, when King Henry set her aside!'

'I am not the Emperor. And, to be fair, King Henry's fear of Charles invading England made him stay his hand against Katherine. Anna, I always knew that your virtue and your sweet looks would get you a good husband. The King will love you, never fear. Besides, he needs my friendship; thus you can be assured that he will never mistreat you. Above all, *we* need this alliance. We too are threatened by this new pact between France and the Empire. If François were to back Charles's claim to Guelders, we would have a war to fight. With English aid, we can win it!'

Against Wilhelm's zeal, the will of King Henry and the threat to her country, Anna knew herself powerless. She made a final attempt to save herself from the fate that was being thrust upon her.

'Could not the King marry Emily?' As soon as the words were out, she hated herself for uttering them. How base she was, wishing upon her sister a marriage she herself found repellent!

'You are the obvious choice, Anna. As the elder of my sisters, you will inherit Kleve if both I and Sybilla die childless. Sybilla has her three boys, of course, but the King, of all people, has good reason to know that young children can die of any number of unhappy mischances.'

Anna crossed herself. 'Heaven forbid!'

'Amen!' Wilhelm said fervently, taking her arm and steering her back towards the door. 'While King Henry thinks he has a chance of gaining Kleve through you, you will always be his first choice.'

Anna turned to him. 'What would Vater do in this matter?'

'The same as I am doing,' Wilhelm said firmly. 'He would be for the alliance.'

Anna was watching over Vater, praying he would wake up and be himself again, if only for a few moments. If he knew that the peace he had brought to Kleve was under threat, he would be appalled; but would he give his daughter to a tyrant as a remedy? She believed he would not, despite what Wilhelm had said.

But Vater did not wake. He was oblivious to the world around him, almost with the angels.

Sadly, Anna stood up, straightened the counterpane, and poured some cordial that would, most likely, never be drunk. Then she went to find Mutter.

Mutter knew all about the discussions that were going on in Saxony.

'I admit, I am torn,' she said, as they settled to embroidering the opposite ends of an altar cloth. 'It would be a great alliance for Kleve. But I shrink from giving my daughter to an excommunicate whom all true Catholics must revile, for his apostasy and his morals. When the Duchess of Milan turned him down, she said that, if she had two heads, one would be at his Grace's service! How I applaud her!'

Hope began to flower in Anna. 'Have you said this to Wilhelm?' she asked. Wilhelm always heeded what Mutter said.

'I told him that *he* must decide. Even though I approve of the alliance, I will not be a party to your marrying that man.'

There was no hope, then.

The Elector had written to Wilhelm. King Henry wanted to know if both dukes of Kleve, father and son, still bore any allegiance to the Bishop of Rome, as he was pleased to call the Pope; were they of the old Popish fashion, and, if so, would they be inclinable to altering their opinions?

'I think we can safely satisfy the King on that score.' Wilhelm smiled at Anna. 'And on another too, for his ambassador was asking discreetly about your beauty and personal qualities. He wanted to know all about your shape, stature and complexion, your learning, what activities you enjoy, and how you conduct yourself.'

Anna felt herself growing hot. 'My shape? Isn't that rather indelicate? Bruder, I do hope you will not answer to that!'

Wilhelm shrugged. 'Anna, when princes cannot meet their prospective brides in person, they must rely on the descriptions sent by ambassadors, and on portraits. The King has asked for one to be sent to him.'

Anna was fuming. 'So this vitally important alliance hangs on his liking my face, my figure and my behaviour! Of course, it doesn't matter what *I* want, or if I have preferences in regard to the kind of man I shall wed; I have to marry for the good of my country, never mind that the King is a vile man!' She was shaking with indignation.

'Calm yourself, Schwester,' Wilhelm said, getting up from behind the table and pulling out a stool for her. 'Nothing is decided yet. In fact, I think I am going to stall for a pace.'

She was astonished. 'Why?'

'I dislike the attitude of the English. Their ambassador is fencing with us. The Elector complains that Henry will not ask outright for you; rather, it seems, they mean to prod *us* into offering you to him, which my pride forbids, for it is the man's part to play the suitor. His envoys act as if your marrying their King is the noblest and highest honour that could come to the House of Kleve. He must be seen to be conferring a great favour on us.'

'Then you are right to stall,' Anna seethed. 'I have never felt so insulted!'

Vater's death in the first week of February was a merciful release, but despite having long been expected, it brought great grief in its wake. Mutter donned deepest black, and a lawn *Stickelchen* like a nun's wimple, and withdrew to the chapel to pray for Vater's soul. Anna and Emily knelt behind her, bereft and weeping copiously.

Leaving them to mourn in private, the new Duke Wilhelm V, stricken-faced and burning up with a fever, followed his father's coffin to its burial in Kleve. When he returned, he took to his bed, seriously ill, and for some weeks it seemed he would be following Duke Johann to the grave.

If Wilhelm died, which God forfend, Sybilla would be sovereign duchess of Kleve. Would she pursue the alliance with England? Almost certainly, because her husband the Elector was all for it. Between brother and sister, there was no way out for Anna.

Slowly, to everyone's relief, Wilhelm improved. By the third week of March, thin and pale, he was able to sit in a chair and receive visitors. From her window, Anna saw a messenger wearing the Elector's livery galloping into the courtyard. An hour later, Wilhelm summoned her to his bedchamber and told her, with a hint of gleefulness, that the English deputation were frustrated at having made such little progress, and that King Henry was dispatching ambassadors to Kleve itself to treat of the alliance. The envoys had asked the Elector to exhort Wilhelm to weigh the matter seriously, as it concerned the King's own person.

And what of my person? Anna fumed inwardly.

'The English grow anxious!' Wilhelm said. 'The Elector writes that they keep reminding him that the Protestant cause would be greatly advanced by the influence of a Lutheran queen of England, this King being so uxorious that the best way of managing him is through his wives.'

'But I am no Lutheran!' Anna protested. 'How dare they assume that!'

'They are but cozening favour with the Elector, Anna. Already he has promised to do his best to advance this alliance. He exhorts me to consent to the marriage, and has promised to send your portrait to England.'

'He should have consulted you first,' Anna said. 'He had no right to act on Kleve's behalf.'

'Schwester,' Wilhelm said, patiently, 'he *is* acting on my behalf; he has had to, as I have been ill. But the picture will not be sent – not yet, anyway. To give me time to weigh the matter, he has told the envoys that his painter, Meister Cranach, is sick.'

One must be grateful for small delays.

'I suppose no one has suggested that I might like to see a portrait of the King,' Anna said. 'Is he as handsome as reputed? Does it not occur to anyone that that might matter to me?'

Wilhelm regarded her severely. 'It ought not to. There are higher matters at play in this betrothal. It will be your duty to love your husband, and you must endeavour to do so, and study him well, so that you can please him.'

'Of course I hope to love my husband!' she retorted. 'But there is a world of difference between the dutiful love of which you speak, and the true love that was between Mutter and Vater, and which Sybilla has clearly found with the Elector. *That* is what I hope for from marriage.'

'Then I will pray you will have it, Anna. Yet there is more to a princely marriage. King Henry has already been told of your beauty and your virtue. Sybilla and the Elector have been praising your fairness, your honesty and your gravity.'

'I hope they don't make me sound too much like a paragon of loveliness and womanly perfection, for I am but human! I hope the King will not be misled.'

'Speaking as a man, Anna, I think most men would find you pleasing.' It was a rare compliment from Wilhelm, who deplored the sin of vanity. Touched, Anna kissed him on the cheek.

'So you will be conformable?' he asked, one eyebrow raised.

'Yes,' she conceded, sighing. 'I will look forward with good grace to the coming of the English ambassadors.'

As she returned to her chamber, she took comfort in the knowledge that all was as yet tentative, that marriage negotiations could drag on for a long time – and that betrothals could be broken. Picking up her mirror, she gazed into the burnished silver and appraised her image. Yes, it was pleasing, but beautiful? No. She had a rosy complexion, and a heart-shaped face with a pretty mouth and finely arched brows, but her eyes were too heavy-lidded, her chin too pointed, and her nose too long, too broad at the tip. Yet she was tall and graceful, with a good, slender figure and delicate hands. Was it enough to please a man like King Henry, who had probably been pursued by beautiful women all his life? Or was the King, like her brother, one to appreciate the more sober qualities in ladies, such as modesty, humility and piety? She prayed it was the latter.

* * *

In early spring, amidst much speculation at court, Dr Heinrich Olisleger, the Vice Chancellor, and other high officers of Kleve, arrived back from Cologne and hastened to report to the Duke. Wilhelm had bidden Anna, Mutter and Emily be present at the audience, and they were sitting discreetly in the corner of his presence chamber.

Dr Olisleger was a sturdy man in his late thirties, with a spade beard and a bushy moustache. Wealthy, of bourgeois origins, and utterly loyal, he was a dedicated humanist, and had been one of Vater's most trusted councillors.

'Your Grace,' he said, 'we have met the English envoys and had preliminary talks with them. Dr Wotton is their spokesman; he is a lawyer; Herr Carne is a scholar and diplomat, Herr Berde a member of the King's Privy Chamber. Herr Barnes you know of, as the King's chief emissary to the Protestant princes. They have sent him in the hope that he will find favour with you. All of them speak good German.'

Wilhelm nodded. 'Have they told you anything of their instructions?'

Dr Olisleger permitted himself a wry smile. 'Certainly they were keen to learn about the Lady Anna's appearance and character.' He bowed to Anna. 'I think they were happy with what we told them, for they immediately said they were empowered to offer King Henry's friendship to your Grace. They crave an audience. I suspect they wish to ensure that you are genuinely interested in an alliance. If so, they would like to have sight of the Princess, and her portrait to send to the King. If he likes her, he will be glad to honour your Grace's house and family with an alliance.'

Anna could barely contain her indignation. It was outrageous that King Henry should make this crucial alliance dependent on her personal appeal! But gradually it dawned on her that perhaps, like her, he wished for a marriage in which love could flourish. And who could blame him for not taking any chances this fourth time? This might not be the marriage she had once dreamed of, but maybe, with a willingness on both sides to make it work, it might just be a success. That was in everyone's interests.

Wilhelm was thoughtful. 'I do not wish to appear to be rushing into the English King's open arms, exulting at my sister's good fortune.

Keeping his Majesty in hopeful anticipation may enable us to obtain greater advantages. More importantly, I mean to ensure that the Lady Anna will be well treated in England, and accorded the status she deserves. His Majesty should be made aware that she has been raised virtuously in our lady mother's household. I am concerned about how she will fare as queen in a court known for its licentiousness. In view of what has happened to the King's other wives, I must ensure my sister's happiness.'

Anna felt a warm rush of gratitude to Wilhelm, but Dr Olisleger looked dubious. 'Your Grace, the King may not be disposed to wait. He might be offended by any delay on our part, and then we shall lose any advantage we have, for the match will be off. In my humble opinion, the negotiations should be concluded as soon as possible.'

'Very well,' Wilhelm said. 'Tell the envoys to present themselves in Kleve in two days' time, and I will receive them.'

Two days had passed, and Wilhelm was still tarrying in Düsseldorf. Only in the evening did he depart for Kleve.

'It seems rude of him to keep the envoys waiting,' Anna observed to Emily, as they sat up late, wrapped in their nightgowns, on Anna's bed. 'He needs this alliance, as does King Henry. I wish they would stop playing games and get things settled.'

'You are growing to like the idea of marrying the King,' Emily said, plaiting her long tresses.

'I'm not sure,' Anna confessed. 'I was horrified at first, but I do see the advantages of an alliance, and I want to do what is right for Kleve.'

'The noble maiden sacrificing herself for her people!' Emily hooted, tossing the plait over her shoulder.

Anna smiled. 'Something like that.'

'I will miss you,' Emily said, and Anna saw she was near to tears.

'I haven't gone yet, and there is no certainty that I will,' she replied, feeling a constriction in her throat at the thought of leaving Kleve, her sister, and all those whom she loved – perhaps for ever. She had been brought up knowing it might happen one day, had seen Sybilla depart for Saxony at just fourteen, and knew that she herself had been lucky to remain at home for so long; but the prospect of saying goodbye to her family and her country was heartbreaking. She was certain she would suffer the most dreadful homesickness. 'We will write to each other, and maybe you can visit me in England,' she said, with as much brightness as she could muster.

'I would love to go to England and be queen,' Emily sighed.

'And marry a man who has buried three unhappy wives?'

'Maybe they made *him* unhappy.'

Anna was dubious. 'I suppose it's possible.'

'Think on it,' Emily said, throwing herself back on the pillows and stretching out like a cat. 'He needed a son, so he tried to divorce his first wife because she couldn't give him one. She was stubborn and refused to agree; you can see why he got angry with her. And then the second wife, Anne Boleyn, she couldn't give him a son *and* she was unfaithful to him. That's treason. She got what she deserved. He was happy with his third wife, but it wasn't his fault she died in childbed, was it?'

'No,' Anna had to agree. 'It's just that he is so much older than me – more than twice my age. I fear I will not please him – and, if I don't, that something awful will befall me.'

'Nonsense, Anna! Any man would be lucky to have you. He will fall in love with you instantly, as soon as he sees you.'

'I hope you are right. If I find the kind of love our parents shared, I will be content.'

She lay wakeful after Emily had gone to bed. Clearly the King was well disposed towards her, and looking for marital happiness. If she pleased him and took care never to offend him, and conducted herself in such a way that none could reproach her or accuse her of anything, and King Henry did not notice anything amiss on their wedding night, then nothing ill could befall her. She might even find happiness herself. Oh, but there were too many ifs!

Wilhelm returned from Kleve. Anna was discouraged to hear from Mutter that he had not seen the envoys, even after keeping them waiting an unconscionably long time. In his wake came Dr Olisleger, who *had* spoken with them. When Wilhelm summoned Anna to his cabinet to hear about their meeting, Olisleger was there waiting for her.

'My Lady Anna,' he said, 'I have spoken at length with the English-men, in company with Chancellor Hograve and other officers of the Duke.'

'You did not speak to them yourself?' Anna challenged Wilhelm.

'Vice Chancellor Olisleger excused my absence, as I had directed.' Wilhelm smiled faintly. 'It does not do to appear too eager.'

Anna threw him an exasperated look. His stalling might well cost Kleve the alliance.

Olisleger spoke. 'I assured the English envoys there was no deliberate delay on our part. But, Sir, they still behave as if the King is doing us a great favour, and express astonishment that you are not falling over yourself to accept the Lady Anna's good fortune. They believe you are procrastinating to wring the most advantageous terms from their master.'

'They are right,' Wilhelm said. 'I'm not sure I can afford to provide the Lady Anna with an appropriate dowry. And I want to know more about the terms King Henry is offering, and what dower he will settle on her for her maintenance. Then I will determine what answer I will give the King.'

'So I told them, Sir. I also informed them, as you commanded, that they will have portraits of both ladies within fourteen days.'

'*Both* ladies?' Anna echoed, surprised.

'Yes, Madam. That is what the King has asked for.'

Anna looked sharply at Wilhelm. 'But I thought that I, as the elder sister, was the one under consideration?'

'So I was given to believe,' her brother said, 'but his Majesty wishes to make a choice.'

Anna did not quite know how she felt. On the one hand, she was relieved that she might not have to leave Kleve after all; on the other, her pride was a little wounded. What if the King decided he fancied Emily best? How humiliating that would be for Anna, for her younger sister to be chosen over her and married first! Always she would be remembered as the rejected bride.

Wilhelm was speaking to Olisleger, oblivious to her discomposure. 'They can have the portraits that were painted six months ago.'

'No, not mine, please!' Anna protested. She had been painted in profile, wearing a ghastly hat chosen by Mutter. She looked lumpen and fat, and too heavy in the chin – and she did not want King Henry, or anyone else, seeing her like that. Emily's likeness was much closer to life, and very winning. There was no doubt who the King would choose.

Wilhelm frowned.

'If I may offer an opinion, Sir,' Olisleger intervened, 'that portrait of the Lady Anna does her no justice.' Anna smiled at him gratefully.

'Then we will have to arrange for another to be painted,' the Duke said, 'and find a better artist.'

'I will see to that, Sir,' Olisleger promised.

The envoys had been wasting time in Kleve for five weeks now. Even the Elector of Saxony was losing patience with Wilhelm, and had sent Vice Chancellor Burchard to urge him to ensure that negotiations moved forward. Wilhelm insisted that Anna and Emily be present when he received this most respected and influential statesman, and ensured that the English envoys were there too. Anna was bracing herself to make a good impression, but then Wilhelm mentioned that the envoys were not to be presented to either her or Emily.

'You will not mingle with the throng. You will stand behind my chair, and you will both dress as our mother decrees. I have asked her to ensure that you are modestly and discreetly attired.'

That meant being swathed in voluminous black gowns from neck to feet, and wearing floppy feathered hats that overshadowed their faces. Really, Anna thought, they could not have appeared more unbecoming!

'We look like frights!' Emily complained, as they walked sedately to the presence chamber.

'They will think Wilhelm is hiding us from view because we are deformed or ugly,' Anna protested.

'Your brother has his reasons,' Mutter said firmly, and would not be drawn further.

* * *

Vice Chancellor Burchard, in his sober black gown, bowed before Wilhelm. He had a world-weary face, shrewd eyes and heavy jowls. Discreetly, Anna swivelled her eyes to the English envoys, who were standing some distance away. Their spokesman, Dr Wotton, had a gaunt, kind face. They were all staring at her and Emily with undisguised interest.

The audience consisted of mere pleasantries. Only in the afternoon, when Burchard retired with Wilhelm and Olisleger to the private cabinet, did the real business of the day begin. Anna, seated with Emily and Mutter at the table, watched Wilhelm resist Burchard's attempts to get him to approve the alliance.

'The English are weary of delays and excuses,' Burchard argued. 'They say that you, Vice Chancellor Olisleger, know that well enough.'

Olisleger mopped his brow. 'I do indeed.' He glanced despairingly at the glowering Wilhelm. 'What troubles them most is that they have not seen the young ladies here – or not properly. They complained at dinner about the apparel their Graces were wearing this morning. They called it monstrous – saving your presence, my ladies – and said they could see no sight of their faces or their persons. I'm afraid I got rather testy and asked if they wanted to see them naked!'

'Really!' Mutter exclaimed. Anna squirmed with embarrassment. Emily giggled.

'My apologies to your Graces.' Olisleger looked abashed. 'They said they just wanted to see the ladies. I said I would arrange that presently.'

'Please, my lord Duke,' Burchard intervened, 'will you not send ambassadors to the King to offer the Lady Anna? At least, then, you will know where you stand, and what terms the King offers.'

Olisleger nodded his approval.

'I cannot spare anyone now,' Wilhelm said irritably. 'I need my diplomats for a meeting in Guelders.'

The chancellor sighed. 'My lord, this is getting us nowhere. Maybe you should unburden yourself of the real reason why you are worried about proceeding with the marriage – which I have had to divulge in confidence to the English envoys.'

Anna stared at her brother. Wilhelm looked nonplussed for a moment, then recovered himself. 'Anna, I am concerned that your betrothal to Francis of Lorraine is still valid, and that you are not free to marry.'

She was stunned. 'But Vater said the precontract had no force because the promises were made only between the fathers, as Francis and I were too young to give our consents. Vater told me we were at liberty to marry where we would.'

'He said as much to me too,' Mutter declared firmly.

'And that is the truth of the matter, as I have assured his Grace here several times,' Olisleger said, 'and the envoys.'

'Then, my son, what is there to worry about?' Mutter asked.

Wilhelm sighed. 'Madam, I know my father considered the precontract void, but it was never formally annulled.'

'It did not need to be,' Burchard chimed in. 'Evidently the Duke of Lorraine agrees, because he is negotiating for his son to marry the French King's daughter.'

Olisleger turned to Wilhelm. 'I assure your Grace you need not worry any more about this. For the love of God, let us proceed to negotiations!'

There was a long pause.

'Very well,' Wilhelm said. 'I will send my ambassadors to England.'

Anna tensed. It looked as if she might become queen of England after all.

Chapter 4

1539

It was hot in Schwanenburg that July, and Anna found it hard to concentrate on reading or embroidering. It was not just the stifling heat that plagued her. Mutter had just come to her chamber and revealed that King Henry himself had expressed concern about her being free of her precontract.

'His envoys want written proof that the betrothal was formally annulled,' she said. 'The King is very keen to have the matter resolved, for he has heard of your virtue and wisdom, and other things to your praise. If you are not free, he will ask for Emily, but he would prefer you, since you are the elder. All he is concerned about is that there is no impediment to your marrying him.' She smiled. 'I think Dr Olisleger can satisfy him on that score.'

'I am sure there is no need for concern,' Anna said.

Mutter reached across and laid her hand on Anna's. 'I trust you are happy with this marriage, child?'

'Yes, my lady. I admit, I did not want it at first, but I know my duty, and will do my very best to make the King a good wife, and to make you and Kleve proud of me.' She was reconciled, she realised. She was even a little excited about her great destiny.

'The envoys want to meet you, and I think it is high time, since you are to be their Queen.'

'Of course. I shall be happy to receive them.'

'Good. I will arrange for them to meet us in the garden this afternoon. Tell your maids to dress you in the crimson velvet gown. It becomes you well, and you want to look your best.'

Anna agreed. The crimson gown was the richest she had. She had outgrown the red silk with its telltale stains. How dearly she had paid for her pleasure . . . and might pay more yet. It had begun to prey on her mind, now that her marriage to the King seemed likely. Could a man know if his wife was no virgin? Worse still, would he be able to tell if she had borne a child?

Resolutely, she thrust away her fears, and went to her chamber to change for the envoys.

She knew she looked every inch the princess as she waited in the garden, seated to one side of Mutter on a stone bench, with Emily on the other. The round skirt of her gown, banded with gold, fell in soft folds about her feet; its long sleeves, gathered above the elbows with matching ornamented bands, trailed almost to the ground. Draped across her bejewelled bodice were heavy chains and a crucifix studded with gems; and on her head she wore an elaborate *Stickelchen* of silk damask atop a sheer winged cap of lawn and a gold embroidered forecloth. Her fingers were laden with rings.

When the envoys approached and bowed low before her, she nodded graciously at them. Dr Wotton, acting as their spokesman, was most courteous, clearly practised in the art of diplomacy.

'I was told that your Grace's beauty excelled that of the Duchess of Milan, as the golden sun excels the silver moon,' he said, 'and now I can see for myself that it is the truth. His Majesty is a most fortunate man. It is said that you have many gentle qualities.'

'The Lady Anna has been well schooled in all the virtues, and in the accomplishments that befit a wife,' Mutter said. 'She can read and write, and cook, and is most proficient with the needle.'

'Admirable, admirable!' Dr Wotton exclaimed. 'And are you musical, my lady?'

'I do not sing or play, Sir, but I enjoy music,' Anna told him. Was she mistaken, or did she see a momentary chink in his bonhomie?

'What languages do you speak?' he asked.

'Just German, Sir,' she told him, feeling at a disadvantage. Surely he had not expected her to know English? 'But I am sure I could learn English quickly.'

'Very good, very good.' Wotton turned to Mutter. 'Your Grace, has any progress been made in obtaining the portraits his Majesty requested?'

'Alas, no,' Mutter admitted. 'We hoped to have them painted by Meister Wertinger, but he is otherwise committed. We have sent to Meister Cranach in Saxony, but have not yet received a reply.'

'No matter, Madam. His Majesty will send his own painter, Master Holbein, if that is acceptable.'

'Of course,' Mutter smiled. 'I am sure the Duke will give his permission. We have all heard of the fame of Hans Holbein.'

'I am also instructed to tell you, Madam, and the Duke, that if there is any difficulty about the dowry, my master prefers virtue and friendship to money.'

Henry *must* be eager, Anna thought. All kings wanted money.

'That is extremely generous of him,' Mutter said, her eyes widening in surprise.

Early in August, the court moved to Schloss Düren, Wilhelm's hunting lodge in the high lands of the duchy of Jülich. Here, the Duke spent much time closeted with Dr Wotton and the envoys. At length, he appointed Dr Olisleger and Werner von Hochsteden, Grand Master of the court of Kleve, as ambassadors to England.

'They shall have the power to treat and conclude everything,' he told Anna, as the family sat together over supper that evening. 'And we *will* be offering a decent sum as dowry, despite the King's hint that he would waive it.'

'Thank you, Bruder,' Anna said gratefully. She did not want to go to England without a dowry; she would feel like someone of little worth.

Mutter finished eating and turned to her. 'It looks, my dear child, as if you will be leaving for England soon.'

'If the King likes my picture,' Anna said, feeling a great lump rise in her throat at the thought of parting from her family.

'He might prefer mine,' Emily piped up.

'Then I will be happy for you,' Anna said. In truth, she still did not know whether she would be jealous or relieved.

'I think he will ask for Anna,' Wilhelm said.

'I will be loath to suffer either of you to depart.' Mutter looked sad. 'But I know my duty, as I know you know yours. It is for this that you have been carefully reared.'

'Dr Wotton asked me a strange question, Anna,' Wilhelm said. 'He asked if you are inclined to the good cheer of this country.'

'What did he mean, I am a drunkard?' Anna was aghast. Emily spluttered into her drink.

'Such impertinence!' Mutter exclaimed. 'Especially as you, my son, are well known for abstaining. These English are impossible.'

'But it's a fair question,' Wilhelm observed, 'especially as we Germans are known for our love of beer and wine – and regrettably, for our carousing. Even Luther calls us boozing devils, and no doubt our reputation is known in England.'

'Perchance the King fears he will be marrying a wine barrel!' Emily giggled. Anna laughed.

'I should hope not!' Mutter retorted, but even she had to suppress a smile.

They were at Düren when Hans Holbein arrived early in August.

'The painter is here!' Emily cried, leaning out of the ornate bay window of the Duchess's Tower, built by Vater for his womenfolk. Anna joined her, but caught only a glimpse of Holbein's back as he disappeared through the door below. They watched as his easel and other equipment were unloaded from a cart in the courtyard. 'Maybe we should call our maids and start looking out our finery.'

'I am going to wear the crimson velvet,' Anna said. 'It made a good impression on Dr Wotton, so I hope it will please the King.' Her eyes followed the stocky figure of Holbein as he emerged again, following an usher towards his lodging in the red-brick guest range opposite the tower.

'He looks rather grumpy, doesn't he?' Emily observed.

He did. As Anna discovered at her first sitting, he was a taciturn man with lion-like features in a square face, a spade beard and a severely cut fringe. He took his work very seriously, and did not encourage chatter.

At least he was able to converse with her in German when he felt inclined, though mostly he did not.

'Please keep still,' he told her. He had done a few preliminary sketches, and was now painting a little disc of vellum he had cut out.

'Is it to be a miniature?' she asked. 'It will be easier to send a miniature to England than a large portrait.'

'Yes, your Grace. I will make a large portrait later. Now, please, no talking.'

'Can I watch you drawing?' Emily asked, sitting at the side of the room, fidgeting with boredom.

'No, Princess.' He looked up at Anna. 'Keep still, my lady, and stay facing me. Rest your right hand over your left.'

As the morning wore on, and the sun rose in the sky, Anna began to swelter in her rich gown. She longed to remove her headdress. Beneath it, her hair was clinging to her head, wet with sweat. She raised a hand to mop her brow.

'Keep still!' Holbein barked. The minutes dragged by. The silence, like the heat, was oppressive. Emily was yawning.

At last, Holbein laid down his brush. 'That is enough for today.'

'May I see?' Anna asked.

'Not today. When it is finished, hopefully tomorrow. Good day, your Graces.' He began tidying away his brushes.

Anna realised that she and Emily had been dismissed. Thank goodness the painting would be finished soon. She prayed it would be a good likeness, and appealing. Thankfully, Holbein had a good reputation.

She was not disappointed. When, the next day, he announced he was finished, and let her see the portrait, she was thrilled to see herself so delicately delineated, smiling demurely. Her complexion was clear, her gaze steady, her face pleasing.

Dr Wotton, summoned to see the miniature, was delighted with it. 'Master Holbein, you have made it very lifelike,' he declared.

Now it was Emily's turn to be painted. To Holbein's obvious annoyance, Dr Wotton stood at his shoulder as he made the first sketch and barked for Emily to keep still.

'That's marvellous!' Wotton pronounced, grabbing the finished drawing. 'To the life! No need to paint a miniature. This will do perfectly.'

Holbein looked furious. 'My commission is to paint two miniatures,' he snapped. 'The King himself commanded me.'

'The King wants to see the portraits as soon as possible,' Wotton replied. 'Yesterday, preferably! Let me send this, and the miniature, today. I assure you, his Majesty will be delighted. I will answer for it.'

Holbein rolled his eyes. 'Very well, Dr Wotton.' He did not sound happy.

Anna looked at Emily's portrait. Her sister looked unusually grave-faced. What the drawing did not show was her fine attire, but doubtless King Henry would be more interested in her features. Would he prefer her to Anna? She did not think so, for this sketch did not do Emily justice. It did not capture her sunny personality or her quick wit. Had that been deliberate, to ensure that Anna was chosen? Or would Emily have looked different if Holbein had had a chance to paint her miniature?

Anyway, it was too late now; their likenesses would be dispatched to King Henry today, and soon they would hear which of them was to wear the crown of England.

Wilhelm seemed unconcerned as to which of his sisters the King would choose – so long as he chose one of them. In the wider scheme of things, Anna realised, it did not matter which princess's name was on the treaty; it was the alliance itself that was the crucial achievement.

'His Majesty was enchanted by the Lady Anna's portrait,' Dr Wotton said, beaming, 'and declared at once that it was she whom he wished to marry.' He bowed to her, as if she were already his Queen.

They were in Wilhelm's cabinet, gathered in haste at Dr Wotton's request.

Gratified at having been chosen, but not quite sure how she felt now that her marriage was a virtual certainty, Anna smiled at the ambassador.

'The King does me a supreme honour,' she said, glancing at Emily, who must be feeling some mortification at not being chosen, but was hiding it well.

'His Majesty is impatient for your Grace's arrival in England,' Dr Wotton told her. 'It is already September.' He turned to Wilhelm. 'Are you ready to proceed to the alliance, Sir?'

'Indeed I am, Dr Wotton.' Wilhelm looked jubilant.

Anna watched from the dais as her brother signed the marriage treaty, scrawling his name with a flourish before the entire court. Then, at his nod, she stood up, aware of the expectant faces eagerly looking her way. She had been dreading this moment, never having spoken in public before, but knew she must accustom herself to it, for the Queen of England would have many public duties. She took a deep breath.

'I should like to express my hearty thanks to his Grace, my brother, and to the people of Kleve, for having preferred me to such a marriage that I could wish for no better.' There – it was done, as Wilhelm had bidden, and her voice had not faltered once. She curtseyed and sat down, as Mutter looked on approvingly.

Wilhelm, seated in the great chair next to her, beckoned forward his envoys. They would negotiate the many matters to be discussed, such as the dowry Anna would take with her, the dower King Henry would settle on her, her household, and how she would travel to England.

Dr Olisleger was to act as ambassador, and Wilhelm handed him his commission. 'Tell his Majesty I desire him to treat with you as if I myself were present. God speed you all.'

That evening, Anna asked Mother Lowe to attend her in her chamber.

'Something is troubling me deeply,' she confessed, standing by the window and gazing out into the night. 'Soon, I will be leaving for England. When I am there, how will I learn how young Johann is faring in Solingen?'

'The same way you do now,' the nurse assured her, 'although it will take a little longer for news to reach us. Your lady mother has already told me that I will be going with you. Frau Schmidt will keep me informed on Johann's progress, as she has always done.'

Anna sagged in relief, yet still her mind was not quietened. 'We must be careful. The risks will be far greater now. The King thinks I am a maiden. What would he do to me if he found out? It has been preying on my mind.'

Mother Lowe laid a reassuring hand on her shoulder. 'No one has found out these eight years, *Liebling*. We've been careful, and discreet, and will continue to be so. If anyone asks, I will say I have a nephew on whom I dote in Kleve, and like to hear of his progress. What could be more natural? There is nothing to connect you with him.'

'No, of course. I am worrying unnecessarily.' Anna paused. 'Mother Lowe, I am leaving Kleve soon, probably for good. I had always hoped that, one day, when he is older, I might see my son, but that now seems a vain hope. Is there any possibility that I could see him now?'

To her dismay, Mother Lowe shook her head, looking perturbed. 'No, Anna. It is not possible. The agreement was that you would never see him again. As far as Johann is concerned, the Schmidts are his natural parents. They think his mother is a friend of mine who went to the nuns for help when she found herself in trouble. *Liebling*, you cannot meet the boy, lest it arouse suspicion. Your name is famous throughout Christendom now, and a visit from the future Queen of England to a humble swordsmith of Solingen would draw comment!'

'Yes, of course. I understand that. But could I not just see him from afar? I long to know what he is like, before I have to go away. I might never get the chance again.' Tears welled in Anna's eyes. Always there was this unsatisfied yearning for her child. 'Please!'

Mother Lowe was turning down the bed, frowning. 'In truth, I do not know how it can be managed. You cannot travel thirty miles from here to Schloss Burg without good reason. How would you explain it?'

'Could they not come here, to Düsseldorf?'

'But what reason would they have to do that?'

'You could tell them I wish to purchase a fine sword as a gift for the King, and ask Meister Schmidt to bring a selection for me to see. You could say you had praised his craftsmanship to me.'

Mother Lowe still looked doubtful. 'And why would he bring his family all the way here on business?'

'I have it!' Anna cried. 'You could suggest that, if Johann is to be apprenticed to him, which he must surely be soon, the boy might enjoy a visit to court.'

The nurse shook her head. 'The matter is fraught with risk. It seems such a strange thing to suggest. Meister Schmidt might smell a rat. He cannot but have wondered all these years who Johann's mother is. He'd know it was natural for her to want to see him.'

Anna took off her necklace and laid it in her jewel chest. 'Now *you* are worrying unnecessarily.'

'No, Anna. I will not do it. Your lady mother has relied on me to maintain discretion, and I've never failed her. She would be horrified if she knew what you are suggesting, especially with your marriage to King Henry going forward. *Liebling*, I know it is hard, but it is impossible.'

Anna knew herself defeated. As Mother Lowe helped her prepare for bed, she fought back the wave of emotion that threatened to engulf her; but when the door had closed and she had blown out the candle, she gave way to a storm of weeping – and not for the first time.

At supper one evening in October, Wilhelm announced that he had received a letter from Dr Olisleger. 'They had a good journey, and when they arrived in London, Lord Cromwell himself invited them to dinner and showed himself sympathetic to our situation here. He said that it was dishonourable of the Emperor to scheme to steal Guelders from me. Truly, I think this treaty will prove advantageous for us.'

Anna felt proud to be doing her country such a service. 'Have the envoys seen the King yet?'

'Yes, they rode to his castle at Windsor, then travelled in his train to the palace of Hampton Court. He showed them every honour, and entertained them with hunting and feasting. They say he is in a joyous mood, in very good health, and eager to see the negotiations brought to a conclusion.'

'Will that take long?' Anna asked, passing a platter of meats to her mother.

'There is much to be decided and arranged on both sides,' Mutter said. 'We need to provide you with a fitting escort that reflects the magnificence of Kleve. We have to choose the lords and ladies who will accompany you, and determine which of them will stay with you in England, at least until you acclimatise yourself to the customs there. Remember, Anna, that while you are a princess of Kleve and should do everything in your power to benefit your homeland, once you wed, you will be an Englishwoman, and must behave as such. The King will expect it.'

Anna drained her goblet of good Rhenish wine. 'It is a slightly daunting prospect, I admit. I will do my best to learn English ways, and hope the King will be patient with me. But it will be a comfort to have some Germans about me. I am so grateful to you for allowing me to take Mother Lowe.'

Mutter smiled. 'She has been a second mother to you from your infancy, and I trust her like no other. She will be your confidential attendant and have the rule of your maids. I hope the King will agree to her staying on permanently to run your household.'

'I shall have to work hard at learning English!' Anna said. 'How else can I communicate with the King?'

'I have been thinking about this,' Wilhelm replied. 'It may be too late in the day to find you a tutor here. I will ask Dr Wotton for his advice.'

'When do you think my wedding will be?' Anna ventured.

'Before Christmas, I hope,' her brother answered.

'It is so soon.' It was hard to believe that in a few short weeks, her place at this table would be empty, and she would be celebrating Christmas in a strange land. It was devastating, knowing she would be saying farewell for good to her family, and that she might never again look upon the beloved face of her mother. Her hands were clenched in her lap, the knuckles white with tension.

'It will be upon us before we know it,' Mutter said briskly. 'There is *so* much to do.'

News reached Kleve at irregular intervals. There was much discussion about Anna's dowry, but King Henry proved most accommodating. Although a sum of a hundred thousand gold florins had been agreed, he generously insisted that Wilhelm did not actually need to pay it. And he agreed to Wilhelm's request that Anna be granted the same dower as her predecessors, which amounted to twenty thousand gold florins.

'And if, after the King's death, you are left a childless widow,' Wilhelm explained, 'you shall have a pension of fifteen thousand florins for life, even if you wish to return to Kleve. And if you do so wish, you can bring with you all your clothes, jewels and plate.' He gave her a rare grin. 'Anna, if all goes as planned, you will live in luxury and never want for anything again.'

'And Kleve will be the safer for it,' she replied, warming a little more to King Henry. Maybe he *had* been more sinned against than sinning. For both their sakes, she wanted to believe the best of him.

Wilhelm was scanning Dr Olisleger's latest, highly detailed, report. 'It has been agreed that you will travel to Calais at my expense. Calais is an English city, and King Henry will meet all the costs of conveying you thence to him in England.'

He turned the page. 'Provision has also been made for you in the event of my dying childless. Sybilla would, of course, inherit Kleve, and you and Emily would jointly receive one hundred and sixty thousand florins and several castles, with five thousand florins a year for life.'

'So everything is settled then?'

'Almost. There has been much debate about how you will travel to England. As it will soon be winter, I told Dr Olisleger I thought it better for you to travel to Calais by land, for if you were transported by sea – and you've never been in a ship, Anna, so you don't know what it's like – the rough weather might make you sick or mar your complexion, and you'll want to be looking your best when you meet the King.'

'Then I shall travel overland,' Anna told him.

'Even that's not as straightforward as it might seem,' Wilhelm sighed. Rummaging in a drawer, he drew out a map. 'You can see here that the route to Calais lies through the Netherlands, which are the territory of the Emperor, and governed by his sister, the Queen Regent. There is no guarantee that the Emperor will grant you a safe-conduct to pass through his dominions. The only way to circumvent that is to go by sea. But even were you to risk the voyage, there might be danger from the ships of the Emperor's subjects. What if you fell into their hands without a safe-conduct?'

'Does the King have a view on this matter?' she asked.

'The King is the founder of England's navy, Anna. They say the sea is in his blood, and he sees no reason why his fine ships should not carry you to his kingdom. He wants you to sail from Hardewijk on the coast of Guelders. But then you would have to navigate the Zuyder Zee, and it is hazardous for ships to manoeuvre through its dykes and dams, even in good weather. The King is aware of this. He sent two experienced shipmasters to Guelders to draw up a pilot's chart, but they warned him that no ship could come near the coast, lest it founder on sandbanks.'

Anna was perplexed. 'So how shall I get to England? Envoys seem to go to and fro without hindrance, but it appears that I encounter only difficulties.'

'*You* are precious cargo,' Wilhelm smiled, rolling up the map. 'Dr Olisleger has asked the King personally to request a safe-conduct from the Queen Regent in Brussels, permitting you to travel overland through Brabant.'

'And are you hopeful of the Queen Regent granting it?'

'Reasonably hopeful. If she does, you will travel by land along the northern coast to Calais. It's about two hundred and fifty miles away. The King is arranging for the Earl of Southampton, his Lord High Admiral, to receive you there with a fitting escort, and accompany you across the sea to England. Dr Olisleger writes that Lord Cromwell is already ordering the fitting-out of the ships that will take you, and determining where you shall land, who shall be there to meet you and where his Majesty will receive you.'

'I would rather not be the cause of such a fuss!'

'Anna,' Wilhelm said, stern, 'you are to be the wife of the King of England. Everything that touches you must reflect his own magnificence. From now on, you will be the cause of a lot of fuss and ado, so you had best accustom yourself to it. I too am determined that you shall go honourably to Calais, and I will provide gold and jewels and all things

66

suitable, as befits the intended bride of so great a king.'

Anna wished Wilhelm did not sound so pompous. 'And what if the Queen Regent refuses a safe-conduct?'

'Then we will have to find a way for you to go by sea with a suitable convoy of ships. But let us hope it does not come to that. I have promised to keep the King informed by letter of my plans for your journey, so that he may time his preparations for your reception.'

He leaned forward in his chair and took Anna's hands. 'Schwester, this will be a good marriage for you. The King has shown nothing but solicitude for your comfort and honourable reception. Dr Olisleger has enclosed a letter from him, thanking me for the goodwill I have shown in negotiating the alliance. He urges speed in concluding the treaty, as winter is approaching. Anna, he wants to be married as soon as possible. You have an eager bridegroom!'

Mutter, busy with preparations and endless lists of things to do, was delighted to hear that Lord Cromwell was equally busy ordering the refurbishment of the Queen's apartments at the King's principal palace of Whitehall, and improvements to St James's Palace, where Henry and Anna would spend their honeymoon.

'I hear that the initials H and A are being carved on all the royal fireplaces and ceilings, embroidered on hangings and linen, and chiselled on stonework,' she said, as they sat in Anna's chamber surrounded by piles of body linen and towels, all to be embroidered with Anna's new royal monogram, A.R., for *Anna Regina*. 'I'm told that St James's lies secluded in a park.'

Anna, busy with her needle, suddenly felt chilled. The honeymoon. Her wedding night loomed ahead, and with it the fear of exposure – and what might follow.

She could not contain herself. 'Mutter, I am frightened,' she blurted out. 'Is there any way the King could guess that I am not . . . that I have borne . . .'

Mutter came to her rescue. 'No, my daughter, I do not think so. And I am sure you know that, when you do your duty, as he requires you, you must act as if it is all new to you.'

For all Mutter's wise advice, Anna realised that she did not really know the answer to the question. And there was another that Anna could not ask her. Was a virtuous woman supposed to feel pleasure in the marriage act? She could not imagine experiencing with the King the kind of ecstasy to which Otho had awakened her, yet she had so hoped to know again that glorious completion, and find it in the nuptial bed. Henry must be a seasoned lover, having had three wives and – it was said – many mistresses in his time, but he was nearing fifty now, and the fires of youth would long have been dampened. Truly, she had no idea at all of what she could expect from him, yet one thing was certain: he would want her to bear him sons, for the future of his dynasty was vested in one small boy, just two years old. God send that she herself prove fruitful!

'I hear that the principal English lords have bought much cloth of gold and silk against your coming.' Mutter's voice interrupted Anna's reverie. 'You are going to have a splendid welcome!' She gave her daughter a searching glance. 'Do not look so worried, child. There is nothing to fear in the marriage bed.'

Chapter 5

1539

King Henry had signed the treaty! The English court, Dr Wotton reported, had been plunged into a flurry of excitement and lavish preparation.

Anna was henceforth to be addressed, and deferred to, as queen of England. Immediately, she felt set apart, even from Mutter, who, like Wilhelm, she now outranked, and who must now curtsey to her. Everyone had to address her as 'your Majesty' or 'your Grace', and observe greater ceremony in her presence; at table, she sat at the high chair. Had she thought her previous life constrained? Already, she was missing it. At least she had enjoyed some informality.

And then young Mrs Susanna Gilman arrived from England. Presenting her to Anna, Wilhelm explained that she was the daughter of the renowned Flemish painter, Gerard Horenbout, and was herself a painter and illuminator of great competence in the employ of the King; more importantly, she could speak German.

'I will leave you to get acquainted,' Wilhelm said, and closed the door of Anna's chamber behind him.

'I am delighted to receive you, Mrs Gilman,' Anna said.

'His Majesty has sent me to wait upon your Grace,' replied her visitor. 'He understands that you know little of England, and thought I could tell you about the ways and customs of the English court.'

'You are come as a godsend,' Anna said, beaming. She had taken instantly to Mrs Gilman's broad, wholesome face and pleasant manner.

'I very much hope so,' Mrs Gilman smiled. 'I know the court well, as I work there. I served the late Queen Jane as a gentlewoman of the privy chamber. My father is one of the King's painters; he taught me my craft.'

Anna was impressed. 'I did not know that women could be painters. I never heard of such a thing.'

Susanna smiled. 'Your Grace, at the English court, they make no distinction, so a woman has the ability. And there too you will find women who are scholars, writers of songs, poets and musicians.'

'It sounds so different from Kleve,' Anna said, a touch dismayed. 'Here, it is frowned upon for women to do such things. I fear that, in England, I may be at a disadvantage, for I have none of those skills.'

'Not to worry, your Grace, for there are also many women who have the kind of virtues and skills for which you yourself are especially renowned, and which the King much admires.'

'So I am spoken of at the English court?'

'Madam,' Mrs Gilman declared, 'you may be sure that every word that is reported from here is repeated around the court within five minutes!'

'Oh dear,' Anna said, and they both laughed.

'Your father must know Meister Holbein,' she went on.

'Certainly he does,' Susanna told her. 'Meister Holbein was his pupil. A most difficult man!'

'Indeed.' Their eyes met in amused agreement, and a friendship was born.

'I am so grateful to you for coming all this way, Mrs Gilman,' Anna said.

'It is my pleasure, Madam. The King was generous with my travel expenses, and he paid for my husband to accompany me. We were married only recently.'

'How long have you lived in England?'

'Nearly eighteen years, Madam. I am quite settled there. I hope your Grace will be happy there too. The King is longing to see you. It is the talk of the court.'

'Then I trust I will live up to expectations!' Anna smiled. 'I want you to tell me all I need to know, and how I can please the King.'

'Oh, I think you will do that very well,' Mrs Gilman said. 'And his Majesty has asked me to teach you some English, so that you will be able to observe the courtesies when you arrive.'

Anna was relieved to hear that. Mutter arranged for her and Mrs Gilman to have their lessons in the ladies' chamber, the finest room in her apartments, while she and her attendants retired to a smaller room. The lessons went fairly well, although, willing to learn as she was, Anna found English difficult. In some ways it was akin to German, but it didn't seem to follow consistent rules. She made slow progress.

Mutter agreed that Anna might invite Mrs Gilman's husband to supper with his wife one evening. The couple were most appreciative of the honour of dining at the ducal table, and Anna found herself liking the merry Mr Gilman, a successful vintner who was clearly in love with his bride.

'We met when I was delivering wine to Whitehall Palace,' he told her. 'She was about to trip over a barrel, and I saved her.' His eyes twinkled.

'It was not the most elegant start to a courtship,' his wife observed. Anna felt wistful, seeing them together. They were so obviously happy, so in harmony with each other. How wonderful it would be if she herself could find that kind of easy contentment with King Henry.

Susanna – for so Anna was soon calling her – was full of the splendours of the royal palaces of England, the celebrations that were being planned for the wedding, and the great household Anna would have.

'The highest ladies in the land will serve your Grace,' she said, 'and you will have your own council and officers.'

'I will not know where to begin!' Anna cried.

'There is no need to worry. You have been well schooled in all the requisite courtesies, and there will be many to guide you.'

'Including yourself, I hope!' Anna said fervently.

'Indeed. His Majesty assured me of a place as gentlewoman to your Grace before I left England.'

'That makes me feel much happier,' Anna smiled. 'You will be the foremost of my gentlewomen.'

'You honour me more than you realise, Madam,' Susanna told her, 'for there is great competition for places in your household. I assure you that, for every post, there are at least a dozen applicants, some ready to offer inducements. Of course, many places will go to those who served the last two queens and are experienced in their duties.'

'I do hope I will be allowed to keep some of my German servants,' Anna said.

'That will be a matter for the King,' Susanna told her. Anna hoped she was not being evasive.

Anna was sitting at the table in her mother's chamber. She was supposed to be embroidering the chemises she would take with her to England, but she kept slacking, fascinated to watch Susanna painting exquisite little miniatures of biblical scenes.

'They are for a book of hours,' Susanna explained.

'I don't know how you can paint such detail in such a small space,' Anna marvelled.

They had become friends, for all that they had known each other for only a few days, and presently, as it grew dark outside and the maids withdrew after adding more wood to the stove, Anna ventured to ask the question she had been aching to pose for a long time, a question she could never ask any ambassador. 'Susanna, what is the King like?'

'Does your Grace mean as a person?'

'Yes. Please tell me the truth.'

Susanna laid down her paintbrush. 'I have always found him most charming. One never forgets he is the King, of course, but he has perfect manners and is always most friendly and pleasant to the ladies. He has what people in England call the common touch: he can be familiar and royal at the same time, if you understand what I mean. And he has always been kind and generous to me.'

'He has been kind and generous towards me too,' Anna said. 'And yet I have heard he can be cruel and ruthless.'

'So people say,' Susanna replied, 'but I have never seen that side of him.'

'But what of Queen Anne? He had her beheaded. His own wife!'

Susanna shook her head. 'She was a whore. She paid a musician for his favours. She even slept with her own brother. And she would have murdered the King if she had not been stopped by Lord Cromwell. It was he who discovered what she was plotting.'

'Truly?' Anna was dubious. 'Most people I've spoken to here think Lord Cromwell made an occasion to get rid of her because she couldn't give the King a son.'

'Oh, Madam, it was not like that at all,' Susanna hastened to reassure her. 'The King had forgiven her for her last miscarriage; he was hopeful she would soon be *enceinte* again. But then her crimes were un-covered . . .' She paused. 'Madam, her name is not spoken at court. You would do well to avoid mentioning her to his Majesty. Her betrayal was so insulting to him, as a man, and as a king.'

'You may be sure I will never mention her,' Anna promised.

'She deserved to die,' Susanna said, with some vehemence. 'It was she who made the King treat Queen Katherine cruelly. Queen Jane said that his Grace was a good man at heart, but that he had been led astray by Anne.'

'She was in a position to know,' Anna said, feeling much heartened. 'Tell me, did he love Queen Jane greatly?'

'Yes, he was devoted to her, and mourned her deeply. He was in seclusion for weeks.' That too, sad as it was, was encouraging. It proved the King could be a good and loving husband. No wonder he was hoping to find a similar kind of happiness in their coming marriage.

'And what was Queen Jane like?' Anna ventured.

'Gentle, and quite shy, although she strove to overcome that. She was much upon her dignity as queen. But she was a kind mistress, and open-handed too. It was tragic she did not live to see her son grow up.'

'He is so young,' Anna said. 'He needs a mother.'

'Madam, he has a lady mistress who dotes on him, and a huge household of servants. Never was child so cosseted and fussed over.'

'Nevertheless, I will do my best to be a mother to him,' Anna resolved. 'And to the King's daughters, although the Lady Mary is about as old as I am!'

'It is the Lady Elizabeth who needs mothering,' Susanna said. 'She lost her mother when she was tiny, and her lady mistress to Prince Edward.'

'It must be awful growing up in the knowledge that your mother was beheaded,' Anna reflected. 'I cannot imagine how it is for her. I will make it my business to befriend her, poor little girl.' If she could not care for her own child, then she would lavish her frustrated maternal affections on Henry's.

Wilhelm asked Anna to join him in his library, his favourite sanctum where he kept the precious books Erasmus had sent him, his maps, and portraits of his ancestors. Anna was moved to see the one of Vater, looking so healthy and lifelike, kneeling in adoration before the Blessed Virgin and Child.

They sat on a bench scattered with cushions bearing the arms of Kleve.

'Anna, you should know that the King's decision to marry a German princess has led to much speculation and rejoicing among the Lutherans. The Elector is not alone in hoping that this marriage will lead the King further down the path of religious reform. Some even anticipate that you will persuade his Majesty to convert to the Protestant faith.'

'But I am a Catholic. Why would I do that?'

'Indeed, Schwester, but that is not widely known. Many make the mistake of thinking that, because Kleve has broken with Rome and is sympathetic to reform, we must be Lutherans. Dr Olisleger writes that the English reformers are hoping their new Queen might be another Anne Boleyn, who was a friend to Protestants, and that they will soon have a friend and champion on the throne.'

'Then I am sorry for them,' Anna said. 'These are vain hopes.'

'And dangerous too. While the King may have been sympathetic to reformists when he was under Queen Anne's influence, he has withdrawn from that position, and is now much more conservative in his opinions. Earlier this year, he forced the English Parliament to pass an Act signalling a return to the old doctrines. It is now dangerous to champion reform or show Lutheran sympathies. I know we have not always held the same views on religion, but now I think it as well that you are an orthodox Catholic.'

'And always will be,' Anna told him. 'I fear the Protestants are destined to be disappointed in me.'

'Have nothing to do with them,' Wilhelm counselled her. 'In England, they burn heretics.'

Mutter was much occupied with equipping Anna with an entire new wardrobe fit for the queen she soon was to be. Her apartment was littered with bolts of rich fabrics delivered for her inspection by the mercers of Düsseldorf.

'Everything must be in the German fashion,' she said. Anna did not like to gainsay her mother, but she was aware of Susanna frowning.

'Surely an English queen should wear English dress?' she ventured.

'No!' Mutter said. 'I have heard it is immodest. You must be seen in decent German gowns and headdresses.'

Behind her, Susanna was shaking her head. But it was not her place to comment.

Mutter was most put out when King Henry sent a tailor called William Wilkinson to Kleve.

'Does not the King deem me capable of choosing my own daughter's wedding clothes?' she asked. 'This Meister Wilkinson wants to make you gowns in the English style. I have told him no!'

'Surely,' Anna said, 'it will be a compliment to my new country to wear its fashions?'

Mutter shook her head. 'No, child. Modesty aside, you go to England as the representative of Kleve, the living embodiment of the alliance. You must wear the best that Kleve can provide, and in our customary fashion, as a reminder of your standing in the world. Your father would have wished it.'

Against the views of her late, much-lamented father, Anna knew she could not prevail. But Meister Wilkinson was of sterner clay. The gowns he made would be in the English style. The King had commanded it. And so, for the weeks he was working at court, Anna had to endure her mother's complaints. The English gowns were not as becoming; they were indecorous, and that neckline was positively indecent . . . When Mutter had gone, Anna held up one of the gowns to show Emily, and both collapsed in giggles.

'Wilhelm would die!' Emily spluttered.

By contrast, the garments made by the German tailors and seamstresses, under Mutter's direction, were cut high to the neck; their skirts were round, without trains, which made the English tailor shake his head. Anna spent ages trying them on, feeling the rich pile of the velvets, the silky contours of the damasks. The gowns were designed to be belted above the waist, and had long hanging sleeves, often edged with fur or banded with velvet or gold embroidery; many were heavily adorned with goldsmiths' work. There was a selection of belts, most with decorative buckles. Mutter had ordered kirtles of damask and silk, to be displayed beneath a gown open at the front. There were, too, new *Stickelchen*, heavily beaded and bejewelled, with a few of white linen, as well as forecloths and lawn caps. Anna's jewel chest – a thing of beauty in itself, for it was made of chased silver bound with ivory – was filling up with heavy gold collars and chains, jewelled necklaces and pendants, and a large assortment of rings.

Her new wardrobe increased daily, for Mutter kept everyone busy. There was no time to lose, as winter would soon be setting in. Before then, Anna and her whole train had to be fitted out for going to England.

She could not help fearing that Mutter's efforts would be wasted, and that the King would not permit the wearing of German dress when he had provided Anna with a new English wardrobe. Secretly, she thought the English gowns were very becoming . . .

In the third week of October, Wilhelm's ambassadors returned to Düsseldorf. Anna was present when he received them and Dr Wotton in his cabinet.

'Your Grace, King Henry wants the Lady Anna to come to England as soon as possible,' Dr Olisleger said. 'We are here to conduct her to Calais.'

'Sirs, we still await word from the Queen Regent about a safe-conduct,' Wilhelm told them. 'The King himself has pressed the Emperor for one. Without it, the Lady Anna cannot depart.'

'His Majesty is confident it will be obtained soon,' said Werner von Hochsteden, a personable, congenial man, devoted to the ducal family.

'Lord Cromwell sent you this, my lady,' Olisleger said, handing Anna a sealed letter. 'He wishes to congratulate you on your betrothal.'

Normally, Anna reflected, it was the lucky bridegroom who was to be congratulated, having won his chosen lady.

Dr Olisleger read the letter aloud, translating it into German. It was courteously phrased in just the right tone of deference.

Anna smiled. 'I am most grateful to Lord Cromwell for his good wishes.' Of all people, he was the one she wanted to have on her side; he had made her marriage, and she owed him her goodwill.

Dr Wotton addressed her. 'Lord Cromwell wishes me to tell you that many messages of congratulation are being forwarded to you, as well as rich and princely betrothal gifts from his Majesty, as is customary. And I am to present this to you.'

He handed her a letter bearing the royal seal. It was from the King. She did not open it, but raised it to her lips and kissed it. The men watched with approval as she tucked it into her pocket. She wanted to be alone when she read it.

'I was to give you this also, your Grace,' Olisleger added, handing her a package. 'It was entrusted to me by Lady Lisle, wife of the King's Deputy in Calais, when we passed through there on our way home. Lady Lisle is eager to win your favour.'

Anna opened the packet. It contained some exquisitely embroidered gloves of Spanish leather. 'They are beautiful!' she said.

'Dearest Schwester, you must remember that nothing comes for nothing in this world,' Wilhelm warned. 'You are new to the game of patronage. I assure you that Lady Lisle hopes for some favour in return, when you are in a position to use your influence with the King.'

'That's as may be, but I must thank her for so thoughtful a gift,' Anna insisted. 'Dr Olisleger, will you kindly inform Lady Lisle that I take much pleasure in it, and say how very acceptable it has been to me.'

Wilhelm was shaking his head in mild exasperation. 'Give the woman an inch . . .'

'She has been generous—'

'As will a lot of people appear to be, once the crown is on your head. Vice Chancellor Olisleger and Grand Master Hochsteden will bear that out, will you not, Sirs?'

'Certainly, your Grace. Patronage is a corrupt, but lucrative, business.'

'So exercise it sparingly and wisely,' Wilhelm counselled.

'We *were* made most welcome by Lord and Lady Lisle,' Dr Olisleger recounted. 'The King has commanded Lord Lisle to make all ready in Calais for your Grace's reception there. My lord told me he was having the royal palace renovated; they call it the Exchequer. Indeed, the whole town is to be put in clean order. We saw building works going on at the main gate into the town, and the streets being re-paved.'

'Goodness, so much fuss, just for me!' Anna exclaimed.

'No, Schwester – for the Queen of England!' Wilhelm corrected her. 'You do not quite appreciate how important a person you are now.'

Later, when she and Mutter were sitting by the fire in the ladies' chamber, Anna handed Susanna the King's letter and asked her to translate it. Susanna read it out:

'"To my most dear and entirely beloved wife, the Lady Anna. The bearer of these few lines from your devoted servant will assure you of my loving intentions towards you, since I cannot be there in person to speak to you. I hope to hear from you soon, to be assured that my dearest lady is in good health. I am sending by another bearer a jewel I have commissioned for you, hoping that you will keep it for ever in your sincere love for me. Methinks the time will be long until we meet. Until then, I will be counting the days until your coming. Hoping shortly to receive you into these arms, I end, for the present, your own loving servant and sovereign, Henry R."'

No one, Anna thought, placing the letter in her bosom next to her heart, ever received such a beautiful letter. Suddenly she was glad she had consented to this marriage, glad to be going to England, glad to be the wife of a man who could write so eloquently of love. This was not the letter of a tyrant, a wife-killer or a brute. Rumour had lied, she knew it. Everything was going to be all right.

Mutter was looking over her shoulder. When Anna noticed her, she raised her eyebrows and smiled.

'Most fitting,' she pronounced, 'and quite touching.'

The ambassadors had brought home a copy of the signed treaty. There it was, at the bottom – King Henry's own signature: 'Henry R'.

On the day after their return, Wilhelm sat in state in the great hall at Düsseldorf, where the whole court had gathered to see him ratify the treaty, and to watch Mutter and Anna signifying their approval by the gracious bowing of their heads.

The very next day, word came from the Queen Regent.

'She has granted you a safe-conduct, Anna, with the Emperor's sanction!' Wilhelm announced triumphantly. 'And she is permitting your retinue to accompany you through Flanders, to Calais.'

There was now no obstacle to Anna's journey. The path to her wedding was clear. Her stomach turned over.

The King, they soon heard, was much gratified to hear of the safe-conduct.

'He has urged the Queen Regent to issue orders for your personal comfort, and that of your suite,' Wilhelm told Anna, showing her the royal letter. Again, her insides churned. This was real! There was no going back.

Dr Wotton was a guest at supper that evening. He arrived with a book for Anna, a gift sent by the King. Newly printed, it was by one Richard Taverner, and was a translation of the German reformer Wolfgang Capito's *An Epitome of the Psalms*.

'His Majesty anticipates you would wish to see the dedication to himself,' the doctor said. 'I will read it in German for you. Mr Taverner prays that God will send King Henry that which the wise King Solomon esteemed the sweetest and best portion of man's life, and a treasure inestimable – a prudent and wise lady to be his wife. It is to be hoped, he continues, that she will be a fruitful vine in his Majesty's house, with children like olive branches round about his table. And lo! God has already heard the most ardent petitions of the King's subjects, for a most excellent lady has been sent to him by the Almighty, and is ready to be transported into his realm. Mr Taverner further prays that God might so temper the weather, and so graciously conduct her in her journey, that she might most happily arrive into his Grace's presence, to the fulfilment of his heart's desire, the expectations of his subjects, and the glory of God.'

Listening to this overblown but fervent prose, Anna felt daunted. So many people were expecting so much from her. Would she ever be able to live up to their hopes?

She summoned all her resolve. 'I pray I may bring joy to his Majesty and his subjects,' she said.

'I have no doubt that you will, Madam,' Wotton beamed.

He told her of the great preparations being made in all the places through which she was to pass on her way to London. 'Each town wants to afford your Grace a magnificent entry,' he enthused. 'All the King's subjects wish to express their joy in having a queen who embodies an alliance they think much to their advantage.'

She prayed she would be worthy of it all.

After dinner, Dr Wotton produced a scroll from his leather scrip and handed it to Wilhelm. 'This, your Grace, is a copy of the King's letters patent granting the Lady Anna her dower.'

Wilhelm looked it over, then showed it to Anna. It was a long list of lordships and manors, all with strange English names.

'Madam, on your marriage, all these properties become yours,' Wotton explained. 'They will provide you with an income from rents and dues, to support you as queen – or, God forfend, as queen dowager, in the event of your widowhood. If you wish to travel in England, you may use your own houses as you please; your tenants will be glad to make you welcome.'

Anna was astonished. 'There are so many!'

'Indeed,' Wotton smiled. 'They yield the annual value of the dower agreed in the treaty. You need do nothing. Your officers, councillors, keepers and stewards will manage and administer your properties to your best advantage. This grant is the same as that made to the late Queen Jane, and it is conditional upon your living in England, according to the terms of your marriage treaty.'

'You will be a wealthy woman, Anna,' Wilhelm said, with immense satisfaction.

'I am sensible of my great good fortune,' she replied.

'All that needs to be concluded now is the wedding,' Dr Wotton said.

Everything was going so well that it looked as if Anna might be in England by the end of November.

Early that month, Dr Wotton asked to see her. Wilhelm, of course, was present, and Mutter. The doctor was bursting with news.

'The King is coming to Canterbury to meet your Grace!' he announced. 'He cannot contain himself longer. You will be married there, and he himself will escort you thence to London.'

Anna caught her breath. In a few weeks she would see him, this man who had haunted her waking hours and her dreams for months. 'His Majesty does me great honour,' she said.

'Indeed!' Mutter echoed. 'I must warn Mother Lowe to ensure that you are royally attired when you enter Canterbury.'

'Admirable, admirable!' pronounced Dr Wotton.

'Where is the marriage to take place?' Wilhelm asked. 'Will it be in the cathedral? I hear it is a wonder of the world.'

'I could not say, your Grace. His Majesty's previous weddings were solemnised in private.'

'It matters not to me *where* I am married to the King,' Anna said. 'It is the uniting of ourselves, and our two great countries, that is important.'

Dr Wotton looked at her appreciatively. 'Your Grace has the nub of the matter. You will be pleased to hear that the Lord High Admiral of England and a great company of the lords of the Privy Council are preparing to leave for Calais, even as we speak. They are to receive your Grace there, and escort you across the English Channel.'

'I have arranged for my sister to be conveyed from here by four hundred horsemen,' Wilhelm said, not to be outdone.

Dr Wotton bowed. 'Excellent, Sire.' He turned back to Anna. 'At Dover, the remaining lords of the Council will meet your Grace and conduct you to Canterbury to the King, who will bring you to London to celebrate Christmas. You will enjoy that, Madam, for at court they make merry the whole twelve days of the Yuletide season, with lavish celebrations, which are sure to be greater than ever this year in honour of your marriage. The King has ordained that, on New Year's Day, you are to make your state entry into London; and you shall be crowned at Westminster Abbey on Candlemas Day.'

It all sounded wonderfully splendid, and far beyond Anna's imaginings. Had ever queen received such a welcome?

A courier arrived from London, wearing red livery blazoned with a Tudor rose and spattered with mud from hard riding. The King himself had sent him, from the palace of Hampton Court. His Majesty was eager to know when her Grace would be departing.

'Immediately,' Wilhelm told him.

Part Two
Queen of England

Chapter 6

1539

Wilhelm had gone to Schwanenburg, where Anna's escort was to assemble on 25 November, attired in appropriate clothing and armour. Never let it be said that Kleve did not send its princess in proud estate into England!

He had been planning Anna's retinue for weeks: those who should go with her as far as Calais, those who should go to England, and those who should stay or come home. Many of the highest nobles and officers in the land were to accompany her. Dr Olisleger would head the escort, and Dr Wotton and his party would ride with it.

Back in Düsseldorf, making her final preparations amidst a flurry of packing supervised by Mutter, who – alternately encouraging and haranguing – had performed wonders in the short time allowed her, Anna did not have long to dwell on the final farewells she must soon say. But there was good news from Brussels, brought by a messenger from Wilhelm.

'Anna,' Mutter announced, 'the Queen Regent intends to send a noble person to ensure that you are well treated in the Emperor's dominions till you pass Gravelines, which is where you will enter English territory. It is the most friendly and honourable gesture. Clearly, despite the ill feeling between Wilhelm and the Emperor over Guelders, you will be safe and protected in Flanders.'

'That is a wondrous relief,' Anna smiled. 'Everyone has been so kind.'

'And so they should be!' Mutter said. Her all-seeing gaze travelled around the ladies' chamber, taking in the iron-banded chests piled high, the canvas packs, the bags and boxes, all ready to be laden on the carts and sumpter mules that would follow Anna's procession. She did not know that hidden among Anna's personal possessions was a ring that was all that remained to remind her daughter of how precious love could be.

There was nothing left to do, save help Anna dress on the morrow, when they would depart for Schwanenburg, where she was to bid goodbye to her family.

'I cannot thank you sufficiently for equipping me so well,' Anna said, feeling a lump in her throat. She wanted to reach out and hug her mother, and never let her go, but Mutter had never encouraged overt displays of affection and emotion.

'It was my duty – and my pleasure,' Mutter said. 'Now I am satisfied that you will be going to England accoutred like a queen.'

Anna could not sleep. Her pillow was wet with tears, as it had been on many nights in recent weeks. In the dark hours, one lay vulnerable to gloomy, desperate thoughts. She could *not* go to England and leave all she had ever known behind, probably for ever. How could she have agreed to it? And it was not just Mutter and Emily and Wilhelm whom she could not bear to leave, but also that little boy in Solingen, for whose loss she grieved daily.

She would not go! She would tell them all she had made a terrible mistake. She would write, ever so apologetically, to the King, and explain. He could easily find another bride.

But then her conscience would prick her. What of the alliance, so vital to Kleve's future security? What of the shame her jilting of the English King would bring down on Wilhelm – and on Henry himself? It would be the worst insult. What of Mutter, who had taught her to put duty first, and who had worked so hard to give her a good send-off? What of Dr Olisleger, Dr Wotton and Lord Cromwell, who had been negotiating her marriage for months? What of all the lords and ladies of her escort, waiting for her at Schwanenburg? What would they say if they were ordered to disperse to their homes?

She could not lie there any longer, torn both ways by these tumultuous thoughts. She got up, dried her tears, slipped her feet into her velvet slippers and pulled on her heavy night robe furred with miniver. As she descended the stairs in the tower, a distant clock chimed midnight. And there, coming up the steps towards her, was Mother Lowe, swathed in a black cloak.

'My lady! I was just coming to find you,' she exclaimed in a loud whisper. 'I have brought someone to see you. He is waiting below.'

Anna's heart began to race. No, surely, it could not be . . . Mother Lowe had said it was impossible.

'Is it . . . ?' she began, but her nurse was hastening down the stairs, so Anna followed her broad back to the courtyard below. A man in rich furred robes and a gold chain, a neatly dressed woman and a small boy, wrapped up against the cold, were waiting on the cobbles. At the sight of her, the man made a deep obeisance and the woman bobbed a curtsey, giving the child a nudge. He too bowed.

'Solingen wishes to pay its respects and wish your Grace every felicitation,' Mother Lowe said. 'May I present the Mayor, and Frau Schmidt and her son? These good people would have been here earlier, but they were forced to take shelter in a storm.'

The Mayor stepped forward, and Anna dragged her eyes away from the child.

'Your Grace, I bring the loyal and hearty wishes of all the people of Solingen. We have long had a special devotion to your House, for you and yours are so often at Schloss Burg, and we are sensible of the great good you are doing Kleve by consenting to this marriage. We wish to present you with a gift to mark it, and our gratitude. We decided that it should be presented by one of our youngest citizens. Step forward, boy.'

The child doffed his cap and drew from under his cloak a little casket. Anna could not stop gazing at his face. In the light of the torches in the wall sconces, he was beautiful, with blue eyes, cherry-red lips and fair hair like hers and Otho's; he had her long nose in an otherwise perfect face.

'Your Grace, please accept this humble token,' he said, as he had obviously been schooled to do. Anna bent down and took the casket, savouring the moment when her hand brushed his soft skin. Inside was a beautiful gold pendant in the shape of a heart, enamelled in blue and red, with true-lover's knots.

'Thank you,' she said, and, on impulse, leaned forward and kissed the boy on the cheek. She longed to fold him in her arms, but dared not. One kiss must suffice her hungry heart.

She stood up. 'Herr Mayor,' she said, 'this gift you have given me, and the charming way in which it has been presented, has touched me deeply. It is a beautiful jewel, and I will treasure it always in remembrance of you and the good people of Solingen.' Her voice faltered, and she feared she might break down, for, having briefly seen her child, she must now lose him again, and for good this time.

'Forgive me,' she said, 'I am somewhat overcome with emotion at the thought of leaving Kleve and its people, who are so dear to me. And this gift embodies all that I am leaving behind. I give you my most humble thanks, and shall pray that God will bless you for your kindness.'

So saying, she gazed once more upon the sweet face of her son, then turned back to the tower, so that no one should see her tears.

Mother Lowe caught up with her on the stairs. She held Anna as she cried copiously.

'Oh, thank you, *thank you* for arranging that,' Anna sobbed. 'You cannot know what it means to me.'

'Oh, but I can,' the nurse said, her voice muffled against Anna's shoulder. 'Long ago, before I was widowed, I had a child, a little boy. He died soon after birth. So yes, Anna, I do know what it is to ache for your little one. Any mother would understand it. And it was no trouble. The Mayor is a cousin of mine. When I heard he was thinking of having a child present the gift, a word in his ear was all it took.'

'He is gorgeous, my son. And he speaks so beautifully. The Schmidts have reared him well.'

'They dote on him. You can go to England happy in the knowledge that you have done your best for him.'

'Yes,' Anna conceded reluctantly, dabbing at her eyes.

'Now, let us to bed,' Mother Lowe said. 'We've an early start in the morning.'

* * *

The chariot in which Anna would ride all the way to England stood waiting in the courtyard, an elegant, ornate enclosed carriage in the French style, beautifully carved and gilded, with the arms of Kleve colourfully blazoned, and a well for the driver in front, with the lion of Kleve fashioned in gold going before, like a ship's figurehead. The roof was upholstered in cloth of gold, and blinds of the same material hung over the windows; you could tie them down firmly, for privacy, or to keep out the draughts. The four golden wheels were breast-high, and the interior luxuriously upholstered.

'What a splendid conveyance!' Anna cried, as she stepped out in her new travelling cloak, which had a wide hood and was lined throughout with sables. 'It looks like the one Sybilla rode in to her wedding.'

'It is similar,' Mutter said, 'and it is suspended on chains, so you should have a comfortable ride, weather and roads permitting.'

The courtyard was packed with carts, horses and people. All the luggage was loaded, and before long, chaos had metamorphosed into order and they were ready to depart. Soon, the towers and spires of Düsseldorf were receding into the distance; Anna looked back wistfully as they disappeared from view. Mutter, sitting next to her, quietly laid her hand on hers and squeezed it – a rare gesture that betrayed her own feelings. Mother Lowe, sitting opposite, looked brightly at them both.

'It's less than thirty miles to Duisburg, your Graces,' she said. They were lodging overnight in the castle there.

'And then only three hundred and twenty miles to go,' Anna smiled. 'For me, at any rate.'

'Lucky you,' said Emily, who was sitting next to Mother Lowe. 'I wish I was going to England.'

And you would probably have gone without a qualm, Anna thought. She settled back, cherishing precious memories of the night's encounter, and gazing at her mother and her sister as if she would imprint their faces on her memory for ever.

The next day, they arrived at Schwanenburg, where the Duke was waiting to receive them. The courtyards teemed with the hundreds of men-at-arms who would accompany Anna to Calais. When she entered the Rittersaal, she found it crammed with the more elite members of her escort, who cheered heartily when they saw her. She raised her hand in greeting as the Duke called for hush and steered her to the dais, where she sat down thankfully on the carved chair next to his; it stood beneath the cloth of estate because she was now, effectively, a queen.

As she waited for the presentations to begin, she studied the throng of people gathered before her, recognising many members of the highest noble families of Kleve. There, at the front, was Dr Olisleger, standing with her cousin, the portly Hermann, Count von Neuenahr, his second in command. Anna felt sorry for the Count, for he was leaving behind a sick wife; yet his proficiency in Latin and French was needed.

Mutter, resplendent in figured gold damask, was greeting her half-brother, Uncle Johann, the Bastard of Jülich, who might have been jealous of her inheritance, but was too genial and indolent to resent her. Anna saw her cousins, Anastasia Gunthera Schwarzburg and Franz von Waldeck, sharing a private joke as fourteen-year-olds will. Handsome Franz was the promising son of Anna's aunt, another Anna of Kleve, and Philip, Count of Waldeck; he would serve as one of eight pages, while Anastasia would be one of Anna's five gentlewomen. The others were clustered nearby around Susanna Gilman, who smiled and curtseyed as she caught Anna's eye.

The trumpets sounded suddenly, and the heralds called out the names of those assembled, in order of rank. One by one, the members of Anna's escort came forward, bowed low and bent to kiss her hand. And suddenly, hidden from view until now – no, it could not be . . . Anna wanted to shrink back in her seat, and had to exert the most rigid control, for there, rising from his bow, mature now, and with his handsome face hardened into strong contours, was the man who haunted her memories with reminders of what might have been: Otho von Wylich. With him was a pretty, heavily bejewelled young woman. In that instant, Otho's eyes met hers, and she saw in them a remembered warmth and the memory of the secret that lay between them.

She made herself smile at the couple, trying to ignore her heart pounding in her breast. Always, the past was coming back to taunt her for that one childish sin. Yet Otho was a joy to behold, even as she shrank from him. She held her breath as he came forward, but no one, watching him, would have suspected from his respectful demeanour that he knew her far better than he should. She was high above him now, sitting in state as queen, but all she could feel was terror that he was in her train and bound for England.

How had this happened? Mutter knew what he had done. Why had she not stopped Wilhelm from appointing him?

Dr Olisleger was murmuring in her ear. 'My nephew, your Grace, Florence de Diaceto. My sister married a Florentine, but he was born in Antwerp.'

Anna realised that Otho and his wife had moved on, and that a young man with long wiry hair and a pointed nose was making his obeisance. Despite the pounding of her heart, she made herself smile graciously at the debonair Florence, at Grand Master Hochsteden, and at Vice Chancellor Burchard and Marshal Dultzik; both had been sent by the Elector to show his support for the alliance.

The procession seemed interminable. The herald's voice droned on and on: 'My Lord Johann von Bueren-Drossard . . . My Lord Werner von Pallant, Lord of Bredebent . . .' Anna's eyes were glazing over, and the smile was fixed on her face. 'The Lady Magdalena von Nassau-Dillenborg . . . Lady Keteler . . . the Lady Alexandrine von Tengnagel . . .' The latter was a bent, wizened old lady who must be a hundred years old, and yet, Anna marvelled, she was still coming to Calais. She remembered Wilhelm telling her how the old woman had insisted, saying it was her right. Maybe that was what Otho had said too . . .

As soon as the long ceremony was over, Anna followed Mutter to the ladies' chamber and quickly shut the door behind her before their attendants could catch up.

'Mutter, how did Otho von Wylich come to be in my train?'

Mutter shook her head helplessly. 'He is your cousin. He has the right. What could I have said without arousing Wilhelm's suspicions?'

'You could have said you don't like him.' Anna was beside herself, pacing up and down.

'That would not have been sufficient excuse.'

'But, Mutter, his very presence could put me in danger. If there was any hint that there had been something between us, the King's suspicions might be aroused. He might even think I had brought a lover with me.'

'Anna, you run away with yourself! Otho is married now. He loves his wife, and she him; your aunt told me. He will not imperil a happy marriage, nor his hopes of preferment in England. He too has much to lose. Put your mind at rest, and let us get ready for the feast tonight.'

Mutter was right; she spoke sense. Anna ceased pacing and gradually felt the tension ease. All the same, as soon as she could, she would contrive to have Otho sent home.

The chariot stood waiting by the gatehouse. The courtyard was packed with people and horses. Wilhelm kissed Anna on both cheeks.

'God go with you, Schwester. Write and let us know how you are faring in England.' Being Wilhelm, he could not resist a pompous exhortation. 'Remember, you are there to maintain the honour of Kleve.'

'I will do all in my power to further the interests of my fatherland,' Anna promised. 'Farewell. God keep you in health.' She took his hand and squeezed it. Tempted as she was, one did not hug Wilhelm.

Emily, by contrast, threw her arms around Anna. 'I shall miss you so much,' she wept.

Anna was choked – just when she had determined not to be. 'I shall miss you too, *Liebling*,' she murmured. 'Take great care of yourself. Maybe, next year, it will be you setting off on your wedding journey.' She had a sudden vision of the years flying by, and of them all getting older, but staying the same in memory. 'Come and visit me in England if you can.'

'I will, I will!' Emily cried, face wet, hood askew.

The worst parting had been saved for last. Anna knelt for her mother's blessing, for one final time.

'May God preserve and keep you, my dearest child,' Mutter said, her voice unwavering. 'May He bless you all the days of your life, and keep you safe on your journey, and bring you to a happy and fruitful marriage.'

Anna stood up and embraced her, gazing into that beloved face. For the first time, she realised that Mutter was growing old. She would be fifty soon. Pray God they would meet again in this life. She felt tears welling once more. It was like a dam in her, waiting to burst.

'Farewell, Anna,' Mutter said, tracing Anna's cheek with her finger. It was the tenderest gesture Anna could remember her making. 'Go and be a good queen, for Kleve.'

'I will, dearest Mutter,' Anna promised, her voice unsteady. 'Farewell.'

She climbed into the chariot, settling herself on the crimson velvet cushions. Mother Lowe was seated opposite, with Susanna Gilman. They had placed stone bottles filled with hot water by Anna's seat to keep everyone warm.

Anna pushed back the window blind and forced herself to smile at her family. She did not want their last memory of her to be of a tearful face. There would be letters, she reminded herself, although Mutter had said she would wait until she heard that Anna was safely in England before writing to her. Anna suspected Mutter did not wish to unsettle her, in the early days of their parting, with thoughts of home.

Trumpets sounded some way ahead, and she heard the driver crack his whip, and the clatter of hooves on cobblestones as the great parade moved forward. She waved to Mutter and Wilhelm and Emily, feeling as if her chest would burst with emotion, and then her chariot was lumbering through the gatehouse, at the heart of the great procession that was to accompany her to Calais, and then England.

Before and behind her she could hear the thundering of the 228 horses conveying her retinue of 263 persons, and the marching tramp of the soldiers of her escort. Wilhelm had provided her with a hundred personal servants. They included her cofferer, the broad-set Jasper Brockhausen, with his wife Gertie, both of whom she had liked on sight. She had her own cook, Meister Schoulenburg, under whose fierce tutelage she had spent many an industrious hour in the palace kitchens. And, at Mutter's instance, Wilhelm had allowed her to bring the good

Dr Cepher. She had also her own chaplain, secretary, grooms, pages and footmen. Her brother-in-law the Elector had lent her thirteen trumpeters and two drummers to proclaim her coming at every place she stayed en route. It was they who had sounded her departure.

Most of her German train would return to Kleve after the wedding. She prayed, though, that King Henry would allow her to keep Mother Lowe and some of her maids, and Dr Cepher, at the very least. But not, please God, Otho von Wylich.

Their progress towards Flanders was slow. The first night was spent at Duke Wilhelm's castle of Wijnendale at Ravenstein. They covered only three miles on the second day, and lodged in Batenburg Castle in Guelders, on the banks of the Meuse. Anna retired quickly to her chamber, where she would not have to worry about running into Otho von Wylich.

The next morning, Dr Wotton asked to see her while she was eating breakfast.

'Your Grace, I have received word from England. His Majesty has decided not to have your marriage solemnised at Canterbury. He considers that your Grace should have more time to recover from your journey, and will receive you at his palace at Greenwich, where you will be married.'

'I am content with whatever his Majesty thinks best,' Anna said, secretly glad of the short respite, for trepidation was building in her already at the prospect of meeting her future husband.

They had passed through Tilburg and Hoogstraaten, and were now making for Antwerp. As each mile took Anna further from all that was dear and familiar, homesickness threatened to engulf her. It was all right in the towns, being feted and feasted; but on the long stretches of road, and in the night, she had too much leisure to brood on everything she had left behind.

'This journey is taking a frustratingly long time,' she complained, lifting the blind and peering out at yet another endless expanse of flat frosted fields. 'We will be very late arriving at Calais. It is December already. The King had hoped for us to be married by now.'

'It cannot be helped,' Mother Lowe said.

'But I do not like to keep him waiting,' Anna fretted.

'Men need to be kept waiting,' Susanna observed. 'It increases their ardour. They do not value what they obtain easily. By the time your Grace gets to Greenwich, the King will be in a fever of impatience!'

'Or annoyance!' Anna retorted. 'I will tell Dr Olisleger and Dr Wotton I do not mean to stay at Antwerp more than one day. With luck, we may be in Calais six days afterwards.'

She shivered. The stone bottles, which were refilled with boiled water each morning, had cooled, the blinds were next to useless at keeping out draughts, and they were huddled in cloaks, hoods, blankets and thick gloves. Almost, Anna wished she had gone by sea!

As they neared Antwerp, Dr Wotton rode alongside the chariot. 'Your Grace,' he called, as Susanna pushed back the blind, 'when we are four miles out, the English merchants of the Company of Merchant Adventurers will meet you to escort you to your lodgings.'

'That is most gracious of them,' Anna replied, 'but I hope they will understand if we do not stay long. Time is pressing.'

'Yes, Madam, but we may be at the mercy of the weather. The lack of wind concerns me.'

'Oh, dear.' Anna's spirits plummeted.

'Do not fret, your Grace. His Majesty is a seasoned sailor; he understands these things. And I bring good news too. The Emperor's representatives will conduct you from Antwerp to Gravelines. They will join your train at Antwerp.'

'I have heard that Antwerp is a prosperous and wealthy city,' Anna said.

'It is one of the greatest trading centres in Christendom, with more than a thousand foreign commercial houses, many of them English. My Lord Cromwell and the English merchants have worked together to ensure that you are well received. Look, I see the merchants in the distance!'

Anna too could see a party approaching, and behind them the mighty walls and bastions of Antwerp.

The Saxon trumpeters blew a fanfare when the chariot drew to a halt and its blinds were thrown up. Anna alighted as the fifty Merchant Adventurers in their velvet coats and gold chains bowed low. The governor of their company, Master Vaughan, knelt to kiss her hand.

'Welcome to Antwerp, your Grace!' he beamed.

Although it was still afternoon, the merchants had brought with them a procession of eighty torch-bearers to light her way into the city. At the Red Gate, the Emperor's representatives, the Count of Buren and Ferry de Melen, with a handsome Imperial escort, were waiting to ride into the city on either side of Anna's chariot.

'My lords,' she said, 'I am indebted to his Imperial Majesty for his kindness in sending you both to me.'

The two men bowed. 'It is our pleasure as well as our privilege,' the Count said.

Anna was astonished and moved to see so many crowds thronging the broad streets, cheering and waving heartily to her. Was this a foretaste of what it would be like in England? she wondered, raising her gloved hand in greeting and bowing her head graciously from right to left.

'I never saw so many people gathered in Antwerp at any entry, even the Emperor's,' Count von Buren exclaimed. He pointed out landmarks as they passed slowly through the crowds into the centre of the city. 'The English House, where you will lodge, is along here.'

Moments later, Anna saw before her a grand facade, three storeys high, stretching for what must be a hundred yards. It was surmounted by the stepped gables so popular in Flanders.

Governor Vaughan came forward. 'Welcome to our humble house, Madam.'

'But it is the most handsome lodging,' Anna smiled, as he showed her into her beautifully appointed rooms, 'and I am so grateful to you for all your care for me.'

He bowed, and announced that open household would be kept in the English House for one day, for Anna and her train. In the evening, there would be a great feast in her honour. But of course, she must rest before they threw wide the doors to those who wished to be presented to her.

Anna was too wound up to rest. She bade her maids help her wash and change, then went downstairs and asked to see the garden behind the house, which she had glimpsed from her window. Governor Vaughan and Dr Wotton showed her the way, and walked with her around the covered gallery bordering the garden. It was packed with stalls and booths, where a few vendors were hastily shutting up shop.

'We have over a hundred stalls, Madam,' Vaughan told her. 'Here we sell our good English wool cloth to merchants from all over Europe.'

'Wool is the source of England's wealth,' Dr Wotton added. 'It is much in demand everywhere.'

Anna would have liked to explore the garden, but he asked that she come inside, as people would be waiting to see her. After that, she was swept up in a whirl of receiving, pleasantries and feasting. So many had come to greet her, or just to stare curiously at her; the benches around the laden tables were crammed with her hosts, and with dignitaries and officials, the good and the great of Antwerp, all eager to make her acquaintance. She barely had time to eat. With Susanna translating, she was learning fast how to make small talk with strangers while appearing to delight in their company. It did not come easily.

It was after midnight when she fell into bed. She must be up early tomorrow, for the open house was to last until late afternoon, and they must stay another night before they could be on their way again.

As many people flocked to see Anna on the second day as they had on the first. When she was at last free, dusk was falling, and her head was spinning as she led her attendants upstairs to her chamber. The fire was roaring up the chimney, making her swelter in her black-and-gold finery.

'I must get some air,' she said to Mother Lowe, who was sitting sewing, very red-faced. 'It's stifling in here!' She reached for her cloak.

On her way downstairs, with Susanna just behind her, she encountered Dr Wotton.

'Your Grace!' he greeted her, with his ever-ready smile. 'I was on my way to find you. May we speak?'

'Of course. Come with me to the garden.'

'I've had a letter from Lord Cromwell,' he told her as they walked along the gravelled path, past curiously shaped parterres and ornamental trees in large pots. 'His Majesty is anxious to learn of the German customs your Grace might wish to follow in England, to help ease your transition into your new life. He asks in particular about one called "breadsticks".'

Susanna laughed. 'He means *Brautstückes!*' she told Anna. 'Dr Wotton, it means "bride pieces". In Germany, on the morning after their marriage, a man of rank gives his wife a gift. It might be money, land or jewels. He also gives *Brautstückes* to her gentlewomen, usually rings, brooches or garlands; and to the men who serve her, gowns, doublets or jackets of silk or velvet. This is what the Elector of Saxony did when he married the Lady Sybilla.'

'Mayhap his Majesty will give your Grace *Brautstückes* on your wedding morn!' Dr Wotton smiled.

'That would be most thoughtful of him,' Anna said. 'I very much appreciate his Majesty's care for my happiness. I am as impatient to meet him as he is to see me. We do leave tomorrow, I hope?'

'Yes, Madam, and I trust we shall be at Bruges on Saturday.'

'And from there it is not far to Calais?'

'About seventy miles, Madam. The best part of the journey is behind you.'

'That is a relief!'

Dr Wotton excused himself, and Anna and Susanna continued their walk around the garden. They encountered Anastasia von Schwarzburg walking back towards the house with Gerberge, another of Anna's young gentlewomen, giggling together. They reddened, and hastily curtseyed, when they saw their mistress.

'Hurry in,' Anna urged. 'If Mother Lowe catches you out unsupervised, you'll get a scolding!' The young ladies thanked her and ran to the house.

'You had best go after them, and make it look as if they were with you,' Anna told Susanna. 'I'll wait here for you.'

It was bliss to be alone, if only for a few moments. Anna stood there in the middle of the garden, which was lit only by the glow of the lights blazing from the windows of the house, from which there issued the sounds of supper being prepared. Someone was tuning a lute.

A man stepped out of the shadows. 'Your Grace, forgive me!' Suddenly, Otho von Wylich was on one knee before her.

Anna was so astonished she did not know what to say. 'Forgive you?' she echoed.

'For startling you, my lady, and . . . for my youthful self.' He hung his handsome head; his hair was still long and wild.

'Oh . . . Do rise, please.'

'I wanted your Grace to know that I did not seek this position, or wish to discomfit you in any way. It was my kinsman, the Erbhofmeister von Wylich, who put me forward, and the Duke approved. I would have excused myself to you before, but it has been impossible to get near your Grace, and . . . well, I confess I was reluctant to face you. I owe you the most profound apology for what happened when we were young. Could you ever find it in your heart to forgive me?'

He was so changed, but there was something of the unruly boy he had been in the man he was now. And while his had been the greater sin, for he had known what he was doing while she had not, she had been complicit. And he was happily married now.

'Willingly I forgive you,' she said, and gave him her hand to kiss. She felt a frisson at the touch of his lips, and drew it away. 'It is on one condition: that you vow never to speak of it to anyone.'

'Of course,' he said, his blue eyes full of understanding, and something else – surely she was mistaken in recognising it as more than admiration? 'I solemnly vow never to speak of it. I too have my reasons for wishing to forget what happened.' His smile was self-deprecating. Anna was tempted to tell him that he had a son, but saw Susanna returning and knew that he must never find out. She felt a lump rise in her throat.

'Thank you, Sir,' she said, as Susanna approached. 'I will consider your request, but I should warn you there is no place at present for your wife among my ladies.'

Otho took the hint, and bowed. 'Thank you, Madam.'

'A good-looking young man, that,' Susanna commented as they continued their circuit of the garden.

'Indeed,' Anna agreed. 'He is a cousin of mine.' She was suffused with all kinds of emotions, but the one that was paramount was relief. Otho was no threat to her – and her fear of him had vanished.

Chapter 7

1539

Anna arrived in Bruges a day late, cold, damp and dispirited at the delay, and retired to her chamber, too tired even to think of seeing some of the wonders of the famed city.

She was cheered by the delivery of a crate of wine, a gift from the civic authorities, and gratefully accepted a glass, and then another, and another. The first helped her to relax; the second gave her a glowing feeling, and after the third, she was positively merry. She and her ladies spent a very convivial evening telling each other jests over supper.

From Bruges, Anna journeyed to Oudenburg, Nieuwport and Dunkirk. On Monday, 8 December, her chariot was halted by fast messengers from Calais. The Lord Admiral and his suite had been there some time, they said, and were being entertained while they waited for their new Queen. Dr Wotton, seated on his horse beside her chariot, had a letter from the Admiral. 'Lady Lisle has received many gifts for your Grace, and is preparing a fine table for you,' he recounted. 'I hope you like venison and wild boar!'

Anna smiled. 'I'm sure I will enjoy her hospitality.'

'Her ladyship is a forward woman.'

'I will not mind, if it means I am at last on English soil,' Anna said, as the procession began to move on. 'The delays must have cost my brother a lot more than he anticipated.'

'We shall be in Calais on Thursday,' Wotton assured her, spurring his horse, 'and once your Grace enters the English Pale, you and your whole train will be at the King's charge. With luck, we shall cross the Channel on Saturday.'

The next day, Anna reached Gravelines, where the captain of the town had ordered a shot of guns to salute her. Here, she would rest for two nights and prepare herself for her official reception in Calais. Only sixteen miles further to go . . .

Early on Thursday morning, the Count of Buren and Ferry de Melen said their farewells, having seen Anna safely through the Emperor's dominions. She thanked them heartily, and walked out to the waiting chariot.

It was not quite eight o'clock when, just past Gravelines, they reached a great turnpike. Here, with her trumpeters and drummers going before her, Anna passed into the English Pale. Waiting to receive her was a large company of mounted men, gentlemen-at-arms wearing velvet coats and gold chains, and a guard of archers in the King's own livery.

A tall, middle-aged man with aristocratic features stepped forward and bowed low before her. This must be the King's Deputy, the Governor of Calais. She had been told that Arthur Plantagenet, Viscount Lisle, was uncle to his Majesty, being the bastard son of King Edward IV.

'Your Grace, hearty greetings, and welcome to Calais!' Lord Lisle was courtesy personified. When the pleasantries were done with, the procession reformed, with each of the King's gentlemen-at-arms riding together with one of Anna's escorts.

Within a mile of Calais' gates, in an open space near a church, Anna saw the Lord High Admiral, the Earl of Southampton, waiting at the head of a large deputation to pay his respects. He looked impressive in his coat of purple velvet and cloth of gold, with a bejewelled seaman's whistle hanging on a chain around his neck. The lords with him were wearing similar attire, and in attendance there were hundreds of gentlemen in coats of red damask and blue velvet, the colours of the royal arms of England. It seemed that the full panoply of English pageantry had been mustered in her honour.

As the litter trundled towards the welcoming party, she felt nervous. These were her husband's subjects, and they would be assessing and judging their new Queen. She must conduct herself in such a manner as to win their respect and – hopefully – their love. She sat upright, steeling herself to be smiling and gracious. Mother Lowe squeezed her hand. *Courage!* she seemed to be saying.

The trumpets sounded again and the chariot drew to a halt. As Anna alighted, stepping for the first time on to English soil, every man in the Admiral's suite knelt. He himself stepped forward and bowed low. Imposing and bull-like, with heavy-set features, a prominent nose and shrewd eyes, he looked formidable, a man one would not want to cross, yet as she held out her hand, he smiled warmly.

'Your Grace, these gentlemen are of the King's household,' he told her. Again and again, she extended her hand to be kissed, noticing that Sir Thomas Seymour had a handsome face and a mischievous eye, Sir Francis Bryan a rakish grin under his eyepatch, and that there was an indefinable something about Mr Culpeper that repelled her. Mr Cromwell, a personable young man in well-cut clothes, was surely Lord Cromwell's son.

It was afternoon by the time they came in sight of the harbour at Calais, with its great gate standing sentinel on the quayside. Numerous ships and boats were moored by the watergate, where a round tower guarded the entrance to the harbour.

Anna marvelled at her first ever sight of the sea; she could smell the salt tang of the choppy water, and hear the cries of seagulls wheeling overhead. Very soon, she would be out on that cold, grey expanse, crossing the narrow strait that lay between mainland Europe and England. On the horizon, she could see the English coastline.

'That, Madam, is the Lantern Gate, the main entrance to the town,' the Governor told her, pointing ahead, as Susanna leaned over to translate. 'The city walls extend to the castle of Rysebank. Calais has been an English possession since it fell to King Edward the Third about two hundred years ago. Sadly, it is all that remains of England's lands in France.'

'I am sure the townsfolk are grateful to be English,' Anna said.

The Admiral beamed. 'Indeed they are, Madam. And Calais is of the highest importance to his Majesty, so he spares no expense in maintaining its defences. I have charge of a strong garrison, with five hundred of the best soldiers and a troop of fifty horsemen.'

They were almost at the Lantern Gate now. Suddenly, the royal ships in the harbour let off a salute of what sounded like hundreds of shots of guns, followed by an answering salute from the town, which lasted even longer. The noise was deafening.

'What a marvellous welcome!' Anna shouted to Mother Lowe and Susanna. Leaning out of the chariot's window, she thanked the Governor.

'It was done on the King's own orders, Madam,' he told her, 'and it was my pleasure to obey.'

'Your Grace, do you see that ship yonder?' the Admiral asked. 'It is *The Lyon*, the ship that will carry you to England.' She was bedecked with myriad pennants of silk and gold, while the three vessels anchored beside her were trimmed with streamers, banners and flags, and the sailors were all standing in formation on the rigging or the yardarms. As Anna passed through the Lantern Gate, the ships' guns sounded another deafening salute, and when she emerged the other side, there was such a cloud of smoke that not one of her train could see another. They were all coughing, astonished at what they had witnessed.

'More marvels, my lords!' Anna observed, as soon as she could speak.

Waiting on the other side of the gate was a richly gowned noble-woman dripping with jewels, and many ladies who sank into deep curtseys as Anna's chariot appeared, to much cheering from the waiting crowds.

'May I present my wife, your Grace?' the Governor said, as Anna stepped down from the litter. So this was the ambitious Lady Lisle! She was a proud matron with a dainty figure and a long, aristocratic nose.

'Welcome to Calais, your Grace,' she boomed. Anna extended a gloved hand to be kissed.

With her whole train behind her, and the Admiral walking at her side, she was escorted by Lord and Lady Lisle through narrow streets crammed with people craning their necks for a glimpse of their new Queen. Lined up on both sides, keeping order, were ranked five hundred soldiers in the King's livery.

Anna noticed that some of the spectators were pointing and laughing at her German maids.

'Why do they laugh?' she asked, careful not to betray how discon-certed she felt.

The Admiral looked embarrassed. 'They have no manners,' he said. 'I apologise for them. Madam, you will learn that the English people can be insular and narrow-minded. They regard anything foreign as strange, and seem to find something outlandish in your maids' attire. Pay them no heed.'

Anna glanced back at her maids, who were wearing demure black gowns and *Stickelchen*; their clothes were similar to hers, except that her gown was in black velvet banded with cloth of gold. Of course, the townsfolk would not dare laugh at her! She began fretting that Mutter's sumptuous wardrobe would not be well received in England.

The Governor was pointing out the glories of Calais: the fine church of St Mary, the splendid Hôtel de Ville with its distinctive tower, dominating the marketplace, and the guildhall, which was called the Staple Inn. Drawn up in front were the merchants of the Staple, who presented Anna with a rich purse containing a hundred gold sovereigns. She thanked them heartily, and the procession moved on towards the palace of the Exchequer, where she was to lodge. Here, the Mayor of Calais bowed low and gave her another heavy purse of gold coins, and a jewel in the shape of the letter C.

'It is for Calais, *ja?*' she asked.

'No, Madam,' the interpreter said, 'it stands for Cleves, in honour of your Grace.'

She smiled her gratitude. Now was not the time to point out the correct spelling.

The Exchequer was built around two courtyards, and handsomely appointed. A smell of fresh paint pervaded, and there was new rush matting on the floors. After the lords and the Mayor had brought Anna to the Queen's lodgings, and promised to attend on her daily until she was ready to sail to Dover, she sank down on her bed, exhausted, as her women bustled around her, setting out her possessions.

'There is no need to unpack much,' she told them. 'I hope to leave for England in a day or so.' Dr Wotton had thought they might go today, but it was too late now, and she could not disappoint her generous hosts by departing too soon.

She got up and explored her fine suite of fourteen rooms, which were linked by a gallery overlooking a privy garden. A door, now locked, connected her bedchamber to the empty King's apartments. The initials A.R. were blazoned everywhere, proclaiming to the world her queenly status, but when she looked closely, she discovered that the gilding on one or two was scuffed. These were not new at all. Then it dawned on her. These rooms had been Queen Anne's. Had she ever stayed in them? Anna shivered.

Suddenly, she felt very alone, and homesick. She wished Mutter could be here, and she could have done with Emily's high-spirited chatter to divert her. She even found herself missing Wilhelm's firm guidance. How dreadful it would be if she never saw them again. If it lay within her power, she would, *she would*.

She must not let herself be swamped by self-pity. Her path in life had been set. There was no point in being miserable.

'Let's have some wine!' she said to her ladies. 'Anastasia, will you pour for us, please?'

She took the proffered goblet and walked back into the gallery. It was hung with pictures, which were covered by curtains to preserve them from the sunlight shining through the latticed windows. Today, the skies were grey and overcast.

She opened a pair of curtains to reveal a framed map of Calais, drawn with great skill. Her eyes widened when she uncovered what was hanging beside it – a portrait of a splendidly dressed, handsome man with close-cropped hair, a neatly trimmed beard, merry eyes, and a half-smile playing about his lips. Etched into the golden frame, at the bottom, were the words 'King Henry the Eight'.

She stared, enthralled. In a trice, the prospect of her marriage had become an exciting one. She could love this man, she had no doubt of it. His kindness and care for her comfort – they were all one with his portrait. How she wished she had seen his picture before! She would not have hesitated . . .

She sped back to her bedchamber. Suddenly she could not wait to get to England.

* * *

The Admiral came to see her that evening. She received him in her presence chamber.

'I trust your Grace enjoyed a good supper,' he said.

'The venison was delicious, my lord,' she told him.

'I have written to inform his Majesty of your Grace's arrival,' he said. 'I also took occasion to praise the excellent qualities I have found in your Grace. I pray that your union will be blessed with children, so that, if anything befell my lord Prince, which God forfend, we might have another of the King's blood to reign over us.'

'That is my prayer too,' Anna replied, touched by his words, but troubled too. How would she cope with a pregnancy in a strange country, with a strange husband? Yet it was the lot of princesses to bear such things, and certainly the King would be delighted were she to bear him a child. She would be very pleased herself – and to rediscover that joy she had known with Otho, in doing that which God had intended for procreation. Her flesh warmed as she imagined what love would be like with her handsome King. And there would be another consolation too. Having lost one child, she knew she would find much-needed solace in another.

'His Majesty is not a little desirous to have your Grace arrive in England,' the Admiral was saying.

'I am desirous to meet his Majesty,' she smiled.

'My orders are to escort you there with all speed. I've had a forecast for the tides drawn up for the next week. The afternoon tides will not serve, because it is not easy to make a safe landing by night. So, with your Grace's consent, we will need to be on board, ready to sail, at four o'clock on Tuesday morning.'

'I will be ready,' Anna told him. God send that the weather was kind to them.

On Monday night, the Admiral appeared again, looking worried.

'There is no wind, Madam. We cannot sail tomorrow. I am very sorry.'

'Do you think we will be able to go the next day?' she asked, frustrated at yet another delay.

'I hope so,' he answered. 'In the meantime, I am arranging some entertainments to divert your Grace while you are detained here.'

'That is most kind, my lord,' Anna said.

After dinner, the Admiral took her and her ladies and the lords in her party to see the ships again, and had a banquet served to her on board *The Lyon*, at which marchpane, jellies, biscuits and sugared spices were handed around. Afterwards, jousts were held in her honour. It was enthralling watching the spectacle of the mounted knights, brave in their heraldic colours, charging at each other across the tiltyard, and bracing herself for the clash of lances. The English lords had challenged her German ones, and she could see the colours of Otho von Wylich, and held her breath when he entered the lists, only letting it go when he emerged victorious. Tournaments were rarely seen at the court of Kleve, but Dr Wotton assured her that they were very popular in England, and she would be sure to see another one soon.

'His Majesty himself is one of the greatest champions of the joust,' he informed her. Anna was impressed, for the King was forty-eight, and all the knights she had seen today were young men. It was good to know that her future husband was fit and active.

To her continuing dismay, the weather remained unfavourable on Tuesday, and the Admiral showed himself uneasy at being unable to fulfil his sovereign's orders.

'I have written again to the King's Majesty,' he told Anna on Wednesday morning. 'Of course, he understands that men cannot control the sea, but the delay will be frustrating to him. I have arranged for seven gentlemen to keep watch and give immediate notice of fair conditions. Hopefully, wind and weather serving, we can take passage to England tomorrow.'

'I do hope so,' Anna replied.

'As soon as the weather improves,' he told her, 'I will have the trumpets sounded. Can your Grace hold yourself in readiness to sail as soon as you hear them?'

'I will be ready to leave at an instant's notice,' she promised him. 'I long to go to England!'

They were interrupted by an usher announcing the approach of Lord and Lady Lisle. The Admiral stood up.

'Greetings, your Grace. My lady has two requests to make of you,' the Governor said.

Lady Lisle looked hopefully at Anna. 'Madam, I have two daughters by my first husband, lovely girls, and so willing to serve. The elder, Anne, has been fortunate to be granted a place in your Grace's household, but I have been unable to secure one for the younger, Katherine, and they don't like to be parted—'

'Lady Lisle,' Anna interrupted, 'I understand, but I must refer a matter like this to the King's Grace.'

'Poor Katherine has been so unlucky,' Lady Lisle went on, as if she had not spoken.

'I will do my best,' Anna said firmly. 'You wanted something else, my lady?'

'Oh, yes!' Her ladyship was all smiles again. 'Will your Grace do us the honour of joining us for supper tonight?'

It was the last thing Anna wanted to do. Glancing at the Admiral, she detected a note of sympathy in his eyes. 'That would be most kind, and I thank you both,' she said, not wanting to cause offence by another refusal.

The Admiral and his gentlemen did their utmost to entertain Anna. They played for her, sang to her, and spoke at length about the splendours of the English royal palaces, and the preparations that had been made for her arrival. There was to be a magnificent ceremony of welcome, they told her, to be attended by the entire nobility and all the chief worthies of the realm.

'There has been such a rush for the making of new clothes for your Grace's coming that the tailors cannot keep up with the demand,' Sir Francis Bryan said. He was the sardonic-looking one with the eyepatch. 'My outfit was ready only hours before I left for Dover.'

Again Anna felt humbled by the stirrings her coming had caused. On Dr Wotton's advice, she announced she would keep open household. All were welcome to visit her and pay their respects.

'I wish to become better acquainted with my lord the King's sub-jects,' she said. She wanted to please Henry, to give him cause to love her. Daily, she sat with Susanna, trying to make sense of the English language.

'Why do you spell "bough", "cough" and "rough" the same way, and yet say them all differently?' she asked, utterly bemused.

'Your Grace will just have to remember them,' grinned Susanna.

'I will never master this English!' Anna sighed. Yet how else would she communicate with her husband? They could not always have an interpreter present!

In the meantime, she would learn other ways of keeping the King happy. That afternoon, she approached Dr Olisleger.

'I have heard that his Majesty enjoys playing cards,' she said, 'but I was never taught how to play. I pray you, ask the Admiral to teach me some game the King likes.'

Dr Olisleger looked dubious – cards and gambling were frowned on in Kleve – but the Admiral was happy to comply. Presently, Anna found herself seated at table with him and Lord William Howard, learning to play the game of Sent, with Dr Wotton, Susanna and some English gentlemen standing by. It did not take her long to master the rules.

'Your Grace plays as pleasantly as ever I saw any noblewoman do,' the Admiral complimented her.

She found she was enjoying herself, especially after a fine French wine was brought to the table. Remembering how, in Kleve, she had entertained favoured guests, she resolved that tonight she would invite these good gentlemen, whose company had so enlivened her day.

'My lord,' she said to the Admiral, 'would you do me the pleasure of coming to sup with me this evening, and bringing some noble folks to join us? I would learn more about the manners you English observe at table.'

She had said something wrong. She knew it by the silence that fell on the merry gathering, and the looks on the men's faces as Dr Wotton translated her words. Susanna was sending her warning looks.

'Madam,' the Admiral said at length, 'saving your pardon, I fear it is not thought seemly in England for an unmarried lady, still less a queen, to invite a gentleman to supper. I would not for the world anger his Majesty by accepting your kind invitation, and yet I would not offend you by declining.'

Anna felt embarrassed. She turned to Dr Wotton. 'I think there has been some misunderstanding. Please repeat my invitation, and explain to my lord that it is the custom in Kleve for an unmarried lady to invite gentlemen to table, and that my father and mother encouraged it.'

After Wotton had translated, the Admiral graciously accepted the invitation, and brought with him to supper eight other gentlemen. Anna enjoyed playing hostess. She had never entertained so many guests before, and set herself to charm them. The meal was excellent, and, with Susanna's help, the conversation, like the wine, flowed.

Later, as the Admiral made to depart, Anna detained him. 'My lord, was there in our pleasant supper anything of which his Majesty would have disapproved?' she asked mischievously.

'Madam,' he replied, 'there was nothing. I shall inform his Majesty that your graciousness to us, and your excellent conduct, could not have been more commendable.'

Two days later, they were still stuck in Calais. The wind had returned, but with such force that it was now too dangerous to put to sea.

'There is nothing we can do but hope for its abatement,' the Admiral lamented. 'Some foolhardy masters are setting sail in it, much to their peril. I heard today that a Dutch hulk has been lost near Boulogne.'

'How dreadful.' Anna sighed. 'At this rate, I will not be married before Christmas. I hope the King will not be angry.'

'Not at all,' the Admiral assured her. 'He would be far more angry if we risked your life by putting to sea. Fortunately, the wind is better in the other direction, and a messenger from England has been able to get here, although at some peril. His Majesty has received my letters. Though he desires your Grace's arrival, he takes the delay in good part, and heartily desires me to cheer you and your train.'

It was more evidence of the King's care for her. 'I do thank his

Majesty,' she said, her spirits lifting. 'I am deeply sensible of his kindness.'

The Admiral and the Governor were prompt to obey the King's wishes. In the days leading up to Christmas, there were feasts and jousts, all for Anna's solace and recreation. It was on Christmas night, as spiced wine and wafers were served to her and many guests, that the Admiral arrived unexpectedly, in a jubilant mood.

'Your Grace,' he announced, 'the wind is turning.'

At last, at midday on 27 December, the Admiral conducted Anna on board *The Lyon*, to the sound of trumpets. It was strange, and a little frightening, to be on a ship, feeling it roll beneath her and knowing that underneath was only deep water, but she thrust down her fear. In a few hours, she would be in England, where her King was waiting for her.

The shipmaster greeted her respectfully and, with Susanna in tow as interpreter, she was shown into her well-appointed cabin, which was panelled in polished oak, with a wide latticed window overlooking the sea. The Admiral urged her to remain there for the duration of the voyage.

'Sailors are superstitious about having ladies on board,' he told her, but she waved her hand.

'I am a little nervous of the sea, my lord. I had rather be out on deck, seeing what is happening.'

The Admiral hesitated. 'Very well, Madam. But if it gets rough, the master will expect you to return to your cabin.'

He escorted her and Susanna back on deck, where some of her party were waiting to be shown to their cabins. The rest were sailing on some of the fifty ships accompanying *The Lyon* to England. Anna stood by the port-side bulwark with Susanna, watching the anchor being raised. A woman wrapped in a green cloak stood a few feet away, with one of the soldiers of Anna's escort. Seeing Anna looking at her, she curtseyed.

Anna smiled. 'You were at the Lantern Gate with Lady Lisle when I was received in Calais, yes?'

'I was, your Grace,' the woman said. She was English, about forty, with dark hair and a narrow face and pointed chin.

'You were in her service?'

'No, Madam. My husband here is a soldier in the Calais garrison, but has now obtained a place at court in the King's guard, so we are returning to England.'

'And you are . . . ?'

'Mistress Stafford, Madam.' The woman curtseyed again. Anna noticed that Susanna, who was translating, was staring coldly at her.

'You have been in Calais long?'

'These past five years and more, Madam.'

They were casting off now. The wind billowed out the sails, and gracefully the vessel moved away from the quayside. The Admiral joined them.

'It is very gentle, the movement of the ship,' Anna observed hopefully.

'It usually is in the harbour, Madam.'

It wasn't gentle when they reached the sea. At once, *The Lyon* started rolling and bucking on the waves. Anna felt sick, and frightened. She did not know how she would stand this.

'How long will it take to get to England?' she asked.

'With a good wind like this, Madam, we should be in Dover by evening.' The Admiral did not seem disconcerted at all, from which Anna understood that the motion of the ship was normal. She tried to fight down her rising panic, as she staggered and swayed, gripping the bulwark to stop herself falling over. A princess of Kleve must never lose her composure.

'Forgive me, Madam, I think I will retire to the ladies' cabin,' Mistress Stafford said, and reeled away.

'You will get your sea legs soon,' the Admiral smiled.

Anna found that hard to believe. 'I think I will retire too,' she said, and made her way to her cabin, with Susanna close behind her. No sooner had a grey-faced Mother Lowe shut the door behind them than Susanna said, 'Do you know who that woman is, Madam?'

'No,' Anna replied. 'Should I?'

'That is Mary Boleyn, sister to the late Queen Anne. She has a poor reputation. She left court in disgrace after marrying that soldier, Stafford. Queen Anne did not approve, for he was far beneath Mary, and penniless, and she got the King to banish them. Mary never saw Queen Anne after that.'

'It must be hard for her to live with the memory of what was done to her sister,' Anna said. 'Why does she have a reputation?'

The ship bucked again. Anna hastily sat down on the bed, and Susanna grabbed the door handle to steady herself. 'She was free with her favours,' she sniffed. 'Your Grace ought not to be seen with her.' Mother Lowe was shaking her head, her lips pursed in disapproval.

'No, I suppose not,' Anna said. 'She is not coming to court?'

'No, Madam. There is no place for her there.'

That was as well. Anna looked out of the window, watching the coast of France recede in the distance. Far behind her lay Kleve and all those she loved; but ahead was King Henry.

She lay down, praying the sea would calm a little. It was horrible being tossed back and forth, with no rhythm to it. She willed the hours away, wanting only to be on dry land, and not at the mercy of this pitiless swell. The Admiral had said she would get used to it, but she was still waiting for that to happen. All she could do was lie there and pray to God and His Holy Mother to keep them all safe.

It was dark when the Admiral appeared at the door of her cabin and informed her that they had been driven north of Dover by the wind, but would make land soon near the town of Deal. They were the most welcome words she had ever heard.

She had hoped to be on deck when she saw England for the first time. She peered out of the window, yet could see nothing but a few distant lights in the blackness.

'We had best get your Grace ready for your arrival,' Mother Lowe said, and beckoned Gerberge and Anastasia, both of whom looked green and wan. Gerberge combed Anna's hair and re-plaited it, put on her *Stickelchen*, and brushed down her black velvet gown. Unsteadily, Anastasia fetched water from a barrel, slopping it over the silver bowl, for Anna to wash her face and hands. Mother Lowe brought her jewellery and her sable-lined cloak.

Outside, they could hear the sailors shouting. Gradually, the rolling abated, bringing a blessed respite.

The Admiral came knocking.

'Madam, we have reached England!' He looked at Anna approvingly. 'If I may say so, your Grace looks every inch the Queen. Pray hasten, as the boats are ready.'

Boats? It seemed she had come through one ordeal only to face another, for the master was waiting to assist her into a rowing boat that was poised to be lowered over the side on ropes. She thanked him for bringing her to England safely, summoned all her courage and clambered in. The Admiral followed her, with Susanna and her other gentlewomen. Fortunately, the short journey was calmer than she had anticipated.

'Those hills are the Downs, Madam,' the Admiral explained, 'and they make for a sheltered anchorage. Out yonder in the sea are the treacherous Goodwin Sands, where many ships have been lost. I confess I was a little worried when we were blown north, but the master steered us here without mishap.'

Anna crossed herself, thinking of what might have happened if he had not.

'Where are we?' she asked. The lights on the shore were much closer now.

'That's Deal, Madam.' A distant church bell chimed five times. 'We have made good time,' the Admiral smiled.

The sailors rowed the boat up to the beach and helped Anna out. She was utterly relieved to be on firm ground. As the men sent up flares, a man on horseback hastened towards them, followed by a rider bearing a torch. When he drew up, he almost leapt from the saddle.

'Is it the Queen's Grace?' he asked breathlessly.

'It is, Sir.' Anna had practised her greeting in English. 'I am most happy to be in England.'

He knelt and kissed her hand, then rose. 'Sir Thomas Cheyney, Lord Warden of the Cinque Ports, at your service. Welcome, Madam, in the

King's name! My Lord Admiral.' He bowed again. 'We thought you might put in here, after we did not see you at Dover.'

Behind him a steady stream of riders approached. Soon a great multitude was gathered on the beach to receive Anna.

'It is cold, Madam,' Sir Thomas said. 'Let us not linger. Come, I will escort you to the castle.'

Anna's chariot had now been unloaded from the ship. She climbed into it with Susanna, and was led in procession a short way along the coast to Deal Castle.

Sir Thomas apologised for its being unprepared to receive her. 'It is a fortress, Madam, built by the King's Grace to defend the realm in the event of a French invasion. But at least you may refresh yourself there before we go on to Dover.'

When Anna entered the squat, concentric building, she was struck by how spartan it was, but it was clean, and the kitchen had been busy. An inviting array of comfits and sweetmeats had been laid out for her, and, not having eaten since breakfast, she gratefully tucked in, washing the delicacies down with some spiced wine, which the English called hippocras.

She had barely finished when the Duke of Suffolk was announced. A portly, expensively dressed gentleman with a white spade beard and a prominent nose strode in, bowed and kissed her hand.

'Welcome to England, your Grace,' he said, appraising her with seasoned eyes. 'I trust you had a good crossing. I am come with the Bishop of Chichester and many knights and ladies to escort you to Dover Castle.'

Anna smiled. Cloaked again, she followed him across the drawbridge. Many of her own party, including Dr Olisleger, Dr Wotton, Mother Lowe and Otho von Wylich, had now made land and were waiting for her amidst a throng of English courtiers and men-at-arms, all staring at her.

Again she climbed into her chariot. Would her journey ever end? They rode through the night for about nine miles, until she saw, rising up in front of her, a mighty stronghold on top of a towering cliff, overlooking the sea.

'Dover Castle ahead!' someone called.

Up and up they climbed, through a series of massive gateways, until at last they came to the inmost bailey, which was bright with torchlight. There stood the Great Tower, where the Duke had said she would lodge. Before it, another crowd had gathered. Suffolk presented to Anna more than forty lords and gentlemen, as well as his young wife, a pretty redhead with lively eyes and a retroussé nose, and other richly attired ladies.

It was now eleven o'clock, and Anna was wilting. The Duchess of Suffolk and the English ladies, with Anna's women following, led her up a winding stair to her apartments, which had been made as comfortably luxurious as was possible in such an ancient building. Her great chests had already arrived, and her German maids swooped to unpack them.

'I think her Grace is ready for her bed,' Mother Lowe said firmly, and the English ladies stepped back to allow Anna's gentlewomen to undress her.

'*Gute nacht!*' Mother Lowe said meaningfully. The Duchess took the hint and shooed the ladies out.

Anna swayed on her feet as she was robed in her night-rail. She was utterly grateful to sink into bed. She lay there, her head teeming with impressions of England, and was asleep within minutes.

Chapter 8

1539–1540

Anna awoke greatly refreshed. At Lady Suffolk's suggestion, she climbed up to the roof, gasping at the view. It was a clear, crisp day, and far below the sun glittered on the sea. She could even see the coast of France. England lay around her, green and hilly and densely wooded.

When she was back in her chamber, having breakfast, Dr Olisleger arrived. 'I am glad to see you safely in England,' he said, smiling paternally. 'The Duke of Suffolk, Dr Wotton and I think that you and your train should rest at Dover all this Sunday and Monday.'

Anna was glad of the respite from travelling. Even so, she was eager to press on, and the next morning, she summoned the Duke of Suffolk and asked if they might be on their way.

'Madam, have you looked outside?' he asked. 'The day is foul and windy.'

'My lord,' she said, 'I am very desirous to make haste to the King.'

He gave her his gruff smile. 'Well, Madam, I shall be glad to escort you on your way.'

The baggage was stowed, and the great procession formed again, snaking its way down the hill and westwards through Kent. The weather was truly awful. The wind was back with a vengeance, and it was impossible to keep the chariot's blinds from flapping open. Anna endured the journey with freezing hail and sleet blowing continually in her face, the Duke and the Lord Warden riding on either side of her, their faces pinched with cold.

Ten miles from Canterbury, on Barham Downs, the Archbishop was waiting, his vestments flapping in the gale, with three other bishops and a great number of well-dressed gentlemen of Kent, who escorted

Anna into the city. Archbishop Cranmer was a serious, scholarly man, with a swarthy face and a lugubrious demeanour; apart from his being a little reserved in manner, Anna could not fault him in politeness, and when the fine city of Canterbury came into view, and she leaned out of the window to gaze, awestruck, at the mighty spires of the cathedral, he seemed most gratified.

Dusk was falling as they passed through the gates; torches had been lit all along the streets, and as the Mayor and the chief citizens welcomed Anna, there was a loud crack of guns.

'Your kindness gives me great joy,' she told the Mayor in English, and was touched when Cranmer came forward and presented her with a cup full of gold sovereigns. Crowds had braved the storm to see her as she rode through the city, and she kept a smile on her face as the wind and rain whipped around her. Just beyond the walls on the far side, the Archbishop conducted her through the gatehouse of the ancient monastery of St Augustine, where she was to spend the night.

Of course, it was a monastery no longer. Wilhelm had told her that King Henry had closed down most of the English monasteries and seized their treasure. But apparently he had kept this one for himself, and converted it into a palace.

'It is a most convenient lodging,' the Archbishop explained, 'for it lies on the road between London and Dover. It has been much improved against your Grace's coming. The works have only just been completed.' The new Queen's Side lay at right angles to the King's, and was built of brick and timber with a tiled roof. At the intersection, Cranmer explained, was the former Abbot's Chapel, now the Chapel Royal. 'This was one of the first abbeys in England,' he told her. 'It was founded in the sixth century by the saint himself.' Anna wondered if St Augustine's shrine had survived the King's religious reforms, but did not like to ask.

In the great chamber, a room of vast splendour, she encountered forty or fifty gentlewomen in velvet bonnets waiting to attend her. She greeted them warmly, confident enough now to do so in English. 'I am so glad to see the King's subjects coming so lovingly to see me that I have forgot the bad weather.'

119

She explored her new apartments in wonder. The fireplaces had stone mantels, the walls were plastered in white, and the mullioned windows held stained glass depicting her badges next to those of the King. Her arms had been painted on the walls of her presence chamber and her watching chamber. The rooms smelt of the charcoal burned in them to dry out the plaster and paint.

The Archbishop hosted a feast that night in the King's presence chamber and, as the evening wore on and wine goblets were refilled, he proved unexpectedly witty. Anna enjoyed herself, and began to relax.

'Everyone is singing your Grace's praises,' Cranmer told her. 'I admit, I was a little concerned about the King marrying a lady who could not speak English, but, having seen your Grace and heard for myself how well you have progressed in learning our tongue, my doubts are banished. You have conducted yourself faultlessly.'

'Thank you, my lord,' Anna said. Cranmer was flattering her, she knew, for her English left much to be desired. Yet she felt happy, as a bride should feel.

It could not be long now before she came face to face with the King her husband!

The next day, Anna left Canterbury for the small village of Sittingbourne.

'We will not linger long here,' the Duke of Suffolk said as they passed along a street lined with pretty cottages. 'There is no royal house nearby, so your Grace must be accommodated at an inn. It is an excellent one, though, and many kings and queens have lodged there in the past, on their way to or from Dover.'

Anna thought the Red Lion very pleasant, with its low, beamed ceilings, brick floor and genial innkeeper, who was most anxious to please. He served her a hearty supper of juicy roast beef and apple tart, washed down with two mugs of local ale, which she asked to try and much enjoyed. Heaven knew where all her retinue and the English contingent were staying. They must be billeted in houses for miles around!

After dinner, she invited Dr Wotton to join her in the parlour set aside for her, and offered him some ale, which he gratefully accepted.

'Your Grace will be pleased to hear that the King will greet you formally at your official reception four days hence, at Blackheath,' he told her, as her heart began to thump with anticipation. Soon she would see him, that handsome man in the portrait. She would be counting down the hours . . .

That night, in the cosy bedchamber under the eaves, with its carved tester bed, she examined her reflection in her mirror. Would the King like what he saw? Did he prefer ladies of a more diminutive stature, and like them buxom? She was hardly that – she had lost weight in the past weeks, and feared she was now thin rather than slender. The weeks of travel and the bad weather had done nothing for her. Her nose looked longer, her chin more pointed. Oh, to perdition with it! She was all but married now, and there was no turning back. The King had seen her picture and been enchanted.

On New Year's Eve, Anna left Sittingbourne for Rochester. Two miles outside the city, on Rainham Down, she was greeted by the Duke of Norfolk, a martinet of a man with a face like a wall and a brusque manner. Behind him, bowing low in the icy rain, were two other lords, several ranks of horsemen and a large company of gentlemen in drenched velvet.

'Your Grace, the King bids me greet you and escort you to your lodging,' the Duke barked. 'You will stay here for the next two nights, to give your Grace a chance to rest, and on New Year's Day there will be entertainment laid on for you, and a feast in the evening.' He sounded begrudging.

Riding through the Rochester crowds, who were muffled up against the weather, Anna put up the blinds and waved as she passed, braving the icy chill. At length, she was handed down outside the cathedral priory, which, by some miracle, had not yet been closed down by the King. Here, she was shown to the Bishop's Palace. It was not lived in, Cranmer explained. The last incumbent to stay there had, ahem, committed treason and been justly punished.

In the great chamber, Anna found a lady waiting to greet her. Lady Browne stared hard at Anna as she rose from her curtsey, seeming, like

Norfolk, to emanate distaste. Anna wondered if she had committed some faux pas in dress or courtesy, but Lady Browne's manner, if cool, was perfectly correct as she informed Anna that she had been appointed to help supervise the new maids-of-honour who would join them at Dartford, the last stopping place before Greenwich. Anna thought it strange that the woman would act so disdainfully towards her Queen. Maybe, she thought, in charity, she is unaware of it. Well, Mother Lowe would deal with her. She too would have charge of the maids, and Anna could guess who would soon have the upper hand.

The Bishop's Palace was a fine old house, and well furnished, although it had a forlorn look, as if preserved as a memorial to its late unfortunate occupant. Yet in the bedchamber stood a rich bed with gorgeous hangings, which eclipsed everything else.

'It is one of his Majesty's finest beds,' Lady Browne informed Anna. 'He ordered it to be brought here for you.'

'How very kind of him,' Anna said, touched again by his care for her.

Part of the bedchamber had clearly been a study, with a desk and shelves, all now bare. The late Bishop must have been a man of great learning, for there were two separate studies, and two galleries lined with shelves full of books, some with chains attached, just like a library. Anna's rooms were ranged around a three-sided courtyard, with a garden behind it. The palace had probably been splendid in its day, but that day was evidently long past.

'It's cold here,' Anna said, shivering in her cloak. Yet there was a lively fire crackling in the hearth, and thick curtains covered the windows. Even so, that night, the sheets felt damp. Susanna, lying on a pallet bed at the foot of Anna's, felt it too.

'It's the situation of this place, Madam,' she murmured in the darkness. 'The sea is near and the shore is muddy.'

Anna huddled into a ball under the bedclothes. 'What happened to the Bishop of Rochester?' she asked.

Susanna hesitated. 'Bishop Fisher? He was beheaded, Madam, for refusing to acknowledge the King as head of the Church, and his Grace's marriage to Queen Anne. He was put to death around the same time as Sir Thomas More, five years ago.'

Anna had heard much about More from her father and Wilhelm, for he had been a great friend of Erasmus and a universally respected scholar. She, like all Europe, had been shocked to hear of his dreadful end.

'They would not accept Anne for queen,' she murmured, 'yet within a year, the King had her beheaded too. How the wheel of Fate does turn.' *And pray God it does not turn that way for me too!*

She sighed. 'This does not feel like New Year's Eve. In Kleve, they will be having feasting and music.' Her quiet supper with the two dukes and Cranmer had been a little strained. The three men, one quiet and scholarly, one bluff and blunt, and the other haughty and gruff, had not made for congenial company.

'As we do here, normally, Madam,' Susanna was saying. 'But what with our late arrival and the weather, it would not have been easy to arrange. There will be feasting tomorrow.'

'It's hard to believe it will be 1540,' Anna said. 'Let us hope that the new year will bring us joy.'

In the afternoon of New Year's Day, it was dry for once, and there was a bull-baiting in the courtyard below Anna's window. She watched through the greenish glass, her gentlewomen crowded behind her. The central area of the court had been roped off, and many of her retinue were standing behind the cordon, or at other windows, anticipating the coming fight. She saw money changing hands. They would be taking wagers on the winner.

The bull, decked in coloured ribbons, was paraded around the arena before being chained to an iron ring attached to a stout post in the centre.

'The aim is for the dog to take the bull by the nose and not let go,' Susanna explained. 'The nose is the most tender part. The bull will try to throw off the dog, of course. Many die in the process.'

'This is a popular sport in England?' Anna asked, feeling rather sorry for the bull, and for the dog, a great mastiff that was brought into the courtyard to loud cheers. It looked very fierce, and was slavering at the mouth.

'It certainly is, Madam,' Susanna said.

Just then, a page announced Sir Anthony Browne, Lady Browne's husband. A tall, hook-nosed man with heavy-lidded eyes entered and made his obeisance.

He seemed to hesitate momentarily when he stood up and stared at Anna. What was wrong with her? she wondered, dismayed.

However, he was affable enough, unlike his lady. 'Your Grace, a gentleman of his Majesty's Privy Chamber will be arriving shortly with a New Year's gift from the King.'

'That is most gracious of his Majesty,' Anna said, smiling.

Sir Anthony withdrew, and she turned back to the window. The dog was circling the tethered bull, making ready to leap. As it did so, there was a collective gasp from the spectators at the windows. But the bull butted the dog and tossed it aside. It stood up, bleeding yet undaunted, and made ready to pounce again.

'Madam,' Susanna murmured in her ear. 'There are some gentlemen here to see you.'

Reluctantly, Anna dragged her eyes away from the sport and turned around to find eight gentlemen, all dressed the same, in glossy mottled hooded coats, bowing to her. What pleasantry was this? And why did she sense an air of excitement among them? Why was Susanna looking dumbstruck?

One of the gentlemen, a tall, massively fat man with thinning red hair, ruddy cheeks, a Roman nose and a prim little mouth, was appraising her intently. Without warning, he stepped forward and, to her shock, embraced and kissed her. She was outraged. How dare he treat her so familiarly! The King would hear of this!

Recoiling from the sour, sickly smell of sweat and something worse, she was astonished to see that the other gentlemen had taken nothing amiss, but were beaming broadly. She glared at the fellow who had insulted her, but he had turned away and was taking from one of his fellows a small ivory casket.

'A New Year's gift from the King, Madam,' he said, presenting it to her with a flourish. His voice was strangely high-pitched for such a big man.

She opened the casket. Inside was an ornate gold pendant adorned with two rubies, a sapphire and a pendant pearl. It must have cost a king's ransom.

She closed the box and clasped it to her breast. 'Pray thank his Majesty, Sir,' she said in her halting English. 'Tell him I will treasure this always.'

'I will tell him,' the fat man said. There was a pause, in which his narrowed eyes continued to scrutinise her.

'Have you come all the way from Greenwich, Sirs?' she asked, trying to engage with the other gentlemen.

'We have, Madam,' the fat man replied, as she tried not to breathe in the stench of him. 'We had a good journey by boat, only four hours, and then an hour's brisk ride from Gravesend.'

'Well, Sirs, I wish you a good journey back,' she said, hoping they would know themselves dismissed. But they just stood there, looking at her, so she turned again to the window to reinforce the message. The dog was lying broken on the cobbles, while the bull had a bloody nose and was bellowing out his anger. Behind her, she heard the door close.

'Oh, what a rel—' she began, but Susanna silenced her with a look. Turning round, she saw that the rest of the gentlemen were still standing there, but that the fat man had gone. Well, that was something! Anger still simmered in her.

'Is there anything else you wish of me, Sirs?' she asked.

'Your Grace might ask if there is anything we can do for you,' replied a young man standing at the far side of the group. She had seen him before, in Calais, and disliked him on sight. Now she remembered: this was Mr Culpeper, one of the King's favourite gentlemen.

Before she could answer, the door was thrown open again, and there, to her astonishment, was the fat man, now resplendent in a coat of purple velvet. When the lords and knights knelt, doing him reverence, Anna realised, to her horror and disbelief, that this – this monstrosity of a man – was the King himself.

Astounded, she fell to her knees, feeling her cheeks grow crimson with embarrassment and confusion. This could not be the man in the portrait she had seen at Calais! *He* had been in his prime, attractive and smooth-featured. He bore barely any resemblance to the man standing before her now. Why had no one thought to prepare her for the reality? For the King looked far older than a man not yet fifty; his face was stern, and bore the marks of temper and ill health. And he was huge! His coat had massive puffed shoulders and bulky sleeves, to boot, making him appear almost as wide as he was tall, and there were bulges under the white hose encasing the trunk-like legs below his bases; were they bandages? Was that where the smell was coming from?

And she was to be married to this man, and share his bed, and endure the stink of him! She felt faint at the prospect.

She was quivering with shock as the King raised her and their eyes met. His were steely blue, beneath winged brows that made him look as if he was permanently scowling. He bowed courteously. Mortified that she had not guessed who he was, and at the dismissive way she had behaved towards him, she did her best to put on a loving countenance, which she feared might look more like a grimace. Bowing her head, she sank again to her knees, but he gently raised her up, and once more embraced and kissed her. She tried not to flinch.

'I trust your journey here has not been too arduous, Madam,' he said, 'and that everything has been to your comfort?'

Anna looked helplessly at Susanna, who hurriedly stepped forward and translated the King's words. Anna was grateful for her support.

'It was a long journey, Sir,' she faltered, 'but I thank your Majesty for your care for my comfort. Sir, I am sorry for my rude receiving of you, but I did not know it was your Grace.'

The King gave a short laugh. 'I was ever fond of disguisings, Madam,' he told her, 'and risking the consequences!' As Susanna translated, he held out a hand laden with rings. 'If you will do me the pleasure, shall we go in to supper?'

Anna put her hand in his, signalling to Susanna to follow as interpreter and chaperone, and the King led them into the parlour, where a table for two had been set up in front of the fire. Unobtrusively, Susanna seated herself in the chair he indicated, by the fireside.

'You were expecting a feast, Anne – I may call you Anne?' the King asked.

'It is Anna, your Grace,' she corrected him.

'Ah!' For a moment, his face was pensive. 'I like that.' She wondered if he was thinking of another Anne, of whom he probably did not wish to be reminded.

'Instead of feasting, I thought we could become acquainted in private,' he said.

Anna was in such a turmoil, she did not know if she was equal to becoming better acquainted just now, and at the thought of what that might ultimately mean, she felt faint, but she made herself accept a goblet of Rhenish. Soon, her veins infused with its warmth, she felt herself relax a little. The horror was still there – but it was at a distance.

The food set before them was lavish. Roast swan, served in its plumage, a great Christmas pie full of meat and spiced dried fruits, pickled brawn, white meat called turkey, which was delicious, and a great venison pasty. No wonder the King was fat! Yet, for all the rich, tasty food, she could eat little. She was put off by the smell of him, and too distressed to be hungry.

His table manners were exquisite; despite herself, she found his conversation entertaining. He spoke of pleasant things, telling her how Christmas was observed at his court, and about the magnificent reception being planned for her two days hence, near Greenwich. He told her their marriage would be solemnised on Sunday, the day after the reception. Only three days away, she thought, in something like panic.

'I must apologise, Anna, for surprising you today,' the King said. 'I wanted to meet you in private before I welcome you officially. My ancestor, King Henry the Sixth, did much the same thing at the coming of his bride, nearly a hundred years ago.'

Anna relaxed a little at this sign of a romantic side to him. She liked his respect for history and tradition. It made for a common meeting ground. 'I shall be interested to hear about your ancestors, Sir,' she said.

He beamed, and proceeded to tell her of the rival royal houses of Lancaster and York, from which he had sprung, and of the red rose and the white, their emblems, which had been combined in the Tudor rose badge of his family, a device she had already seen emblazoned everywhere in the royal houses and on the royal livery.

She tried, in vain, to get the measure of him, and his opinion of her, as the conversation wore on. The English, she had heard, were a reserved people, and of course Susanna was present; conversation through an interpreter was always stilted. Yet Henry did not seem to be behaving like a man enchanted with his bride. She imagined that the thirty long years of his rule had toughened him, so that he would not wear his heart on his sleeve and was used to keeping his inmost thoughts and feelings to himself. Maybe he was as disappointed in her as she was in him, but was exerting himself to be good company. She had to concede that he was unfailingly courteous and solicitous. Even so, there was about him the air of a beast waiting to pounce. For all his courtesy, he frightened her, and she could not imagine ever being intimate with him. She tried not to shudder at the thought.

At the end of the evening, he kissed her hand and bade her good night. 'I will be able to dine with you tomorrow,' he told her. 'I have to wait for a favourable tide to carry me back to Greenwich, and that will not be until the afternoon.'

She curtseyed low as he left, and when his footsteps had died away, she took one look at Susanna and threw herself into her arms.

'Oh, God!' she cried. 'Oh, God, help me!'

In the morning, Sir Anthony Browne arrived with more gifts from the King.

'These are for your Grace, with his Majesty's compliments.'

Anna wondered why Henry had not brought them himself, but was distracted by the sumptuous furs that were laid out with a flourish for her to admire – a partlet furred with sables, sable skins to wrap around her neck, a muffler and a fur cap. He could not have chosen anything more welcome in this wintry weather.

She wore the partlet to dinner, over which she thanked him fulsomely. He seemed less affable today, and again she had the impression that he was brooding or angry about something, so the meal was eaten with awkward silences. Finally, the King's cloak was brought. After he had escorted Anna downstairs to the door, and kissed her hand in farewell, she stood in the porch with her ladies, waving him off, relieved to see him go.

If only, *if only*, she could pack up and go back to Kleve and all she held dear! If only he could have been like his picture! Tears blurred her eyes, and she stumbled indoors, unheeding of Susanna calling after her, and desperate to find Mother Lowe and blurt out her misery on that comforting bosom.

Mother Lowe was firm with her. Duty must always come before one's personal feelings, she declared, while repacking a chest with Anna's personal possessions, ready for their departure for Dartford later that afternoon. 'Your lady mother would say the same, Anna. It will be your duty as a wife to study your husband and learn how to please him.'

'I dare not do anything else,' Anna mourned, staring into the fire. 'He scares me. I keep thinking of all the things I have heard about him, which I wanted so much not to believe, and now I fear they were true. It's easy to imagine him being cruel and ruthless.' *As he might be to me if I do not please him.*

'Then you must be careful to obey him, and please him. God has sent you to each other, and you must make the best of it.' Mother Lowe's lips were pursed primly, but her grey eyes were full of compassion. 'Now, no more talk of running back to Kleve.'

'Oh, I dare not.' Anna managed a smile. 'My brother's anger would be more terrible than the King's. I think he would kill me.' *And the King might kill me too, if he found out that I have borne a bastard child.* Icy fingers of fear gripped her spine.

There was a knock at the door. 'May I come in, Madam?' Susanna called.

'Yes, of course,' Anna replied, but at the sight of her dear friend, carrying an armful of clothing and looking at her with sympathetic concern, she felt tears welling anew. 'We are talking about the King.' She knew she shouldn't be discussing him with people of lesser rank, but also that she could trust them both. They knew how unhappy she was.

'What did you think of that charade?' she asked Susanna, as she helped her to fold the gowns.

Susanna paused. 'I thought he played an unkind trick on you.'

'He did apologise. I think he had some romantic notion of himself as a knight errant, come to surprise his princess.'

'There wasn't much that was romantic about it,' Mother Lowe sniffed. 'Anna was very upset afterwards.'

Susanna nodded. 'I know. At dinner, he seemed to be holding back, and, at times, I thought he was angry about something. Maybe there has been a hitch in the wedding preparations, or some matter of state has displeased him.'

'Or maybe it's me,' Anna sighed. 'He came specially to see me, yet he gave no sign that he was pleased with me, nor did he act like an eager bridegroom.'

'Well, if he's not an eager bridegroom, then he's a fool,' the old nurse huffed.

'He *was* very courteous to you,' Susanna said to Anna.

'I was hoping for more than courtesy,' Anna sniffed, twisting her belt between her fingers.

'Child, a king marries for the good of his realm,' Mother Lowe said, locking the chest. 'Love comes later. His courtesy is a good start.'

Susanna, whose own marriage had been made for love, and who was demonstrably happy in it, threw Anna a look of commiseration.

'But there has to be some liking, surely, and I'm not sure the King even likes me,' Anna replied. 'I know I'm not beautiful, but, in all modesty, I think I am seemly.'

'You are lovely,' Susanna said. 'And beauty is a matter of personal perception.'

'Yes, but my nose is too long, and my chin too pointed!' Anna protested.

'And the King is a model of manly beauty?' Susanna challenged.

Anna sighed. 'Of course he is not, although I dare say it would be treason to say so. But what matters, of course, is how *I* look to *him*. You remember my telling you that he was most insistent on seeing my portrait? If he hadn't liked it, I doubt I would be here now. What worries me is that Meister Holbein painted me full-face, from the most flattering angle. You can't see my shortcomings, and the King might be angry because he feels he has been deceived.' He would, without doubt, be angry if he found out about her other shortcoming: that she lacked a maidenhead.

'Anna, it was a good likeness, and there is no proof that the King is displeased with you,' Mother Lowe declared. 'He must have many cares to preoccupy him. He has been most solicitous and generous. Look at that jewel he gave you, and those wondrous furs! He has not hesitated in the past to rid himself of his wives. Be sure that, if he was not pleased with you, he would have no hesitation in sending you back to Kleve!'

Anna was not so certain. 'Then he would risk alienating my brother and the other German princes, and standing alone without allies against France and the Empire. No, he might be angry because he *cannot* send me home.' *But I wish he would!*

'Nonsense! You are building this up into something it is not, and on what grounds? A feeling, an impression! You say the King has shown you no more than courtesy, but he has kissed and embraced you. His conduct has been entirely seemly.'

Anna wanted to be convinced.

'Wait until you are married,' Mother Lowe counselled, 'then he will show you the proper affection of a husband for his wife.'

Heaven forbid! she thought, visions of herself in bed with the King coming unbidden, visions that would become reality in just three days. She did not know how she would bear it. All she could envisage was herself, shrinking in fear on her wedding night . . .

Outside the town of Dartford, the household officers appointed by the King to serve Anna were waiting to receive her. She stood, buffeted by icy winds, as Norfolk presented to her the Earl of Rutland, who was the King's cousin and her new lord chamberlain; Sir Edward Baynton, her vice chamberlain; Sir Thomas Denny, her chancellor; Sir John Dudley, her master of horse, and all who were to serve on the council that would manage her affairs. Then Archbishop Cranmer and the Duke of Suffolk presented to her thirty English ladies and maids-of-honour, who did her due reverence. By the time he had finished, she was frozen stiff.

'These ladies will from now on be in waiting permanently on your Grace,' Norfolk informed her, as they walked through the gatehouse towards her lodging, where, please God, it would be warm. 'For the time being, they will serve alongside your German attendants.' *For the time being.* Anna was distressed to hear that; she had been praying inwardly that her countrywomen would be allowed to stay. Susanna would be, of course, but Anna hated the thought of losing those who had served her faithfully and been her constant companions. Above all, she could not bear to lose Mother Lowe. She would beg the King on her knees for her, if need be. Cast adrift as she was in a land full of strangers, far from her mother, sister or brother, Mother Lowe was her anchor. With dread of her coming marriage now dominating her waking moments, she needed her old nurse more than she had ever needed her before.

She forced herself to listen as Norfolk explained that the house she was staying in was an abandoned priory closed by the King last year.

'His Grace is having it demolished,' he said, his manner gruff as usual. 'He intends to build a fine palace here.' Anna looked about her at the traceried cloister and the big church standing behind. This had been a great nunnery in its day. She felt a pang for the sisters who had been cast out into the world to fend for themselves. And they were by no means alone. Nearly every abbey and priory in England had been closed down in the past four years.

That evening, Anna entered the room serving as her privy chamber to find her new ladies waiting for her. It was unnerving to realise that she would be spending her life with these strangers, for, as queen, she would rarely be left unattended. She must win them over if she wanted a harmonious existence and moral support.

She invited them to rise from their curtseys and be seated. With Susanna acting as interpreter, she managed to speak to each of them. Foremost was the King's niece Lady Margaret Douglas, an auburn-haired beauty whom Anna had liked on sight for her warm welcome.

Next in rank came Norfolk's daughter, my lady the Duchess of Richmond, widow of the King's bastard son; she too was comely, but had a less friendly manner, confirming Anna's suspicion that the Howard family did not like her. And – it came to her – why should they, the foremost Catholic family in the land, when she represented the King's alliance with the Protestant princes of Germany?

The Duchess of Suffolk she knew already, for she had journeyed with Anna from Dover. Katherine Willoughby was a lively, headstrong young woman of decidedly reformist views, who was popular with all. By contrast, the Countess of Rutland, who was cousin-in-law to the King, appeared a little haughty; nor could Anna warm to the heart-faced Lady Rochford, or Lady Edgcumbe, for both had an unappealing superior air, and she had seen them, more than once, whispering and nodding knowingly in her direction.

Of her gentlewomen, she liked Margaret Wyatt, Lady Lee, whose brother was a poet, and the scholarly Anne Parr, Mrs Herbert, who was a humanist. Anna was intrigued to meet Elizabeth Seymour, sister of the late Queen Jane and wife to Lord Cromwell's son. She was a sweet-faced creature with a gentle manner, and most congenial company. If Jane had been like her sister, it was easy to see why the King had mourned her deeply.

Anne Bassett, Lady Lisle's daughter, was blonde, buxom, and full of herself, as Anna had feared. With her comely face, she would attract attention anywhere. Anna decided not to press the King for a place for Anne's sister; one of that family in her household was enough!

Norfolk's diminutive niece, Katheryn Howard, one of the maids-of-honour, dimpled prettily when spoken to, eyeing Anna gauchely. She had a pert manner and a ready laugh. Although she told Anna she was nineteen, she was like a little girl, with her tiny hands and feet, and her evident delight in her new position. Already, Anna felt protective towards her.

The other maids were a lively crowd. Fifteen-year-old Kate Carey looked so like the King that Anna suspected she was his bastard daughter. She was not surprised when Susanna murmured in her ear that Kate was Mary Stafford's daughter. It did not bother her, this evidence of the King's infidelity; it had happened a long time ago. She did not think he would be disposed to such amours now, given his bad legs and his obesity.

'Did your Grace know that the King's aunt the Lady Bridget was a nun here?' Lady Rutland asked. 'She died years ago, before the closure.' Anna thought it sad that Henry had not spared Dartford in his aunt's memory.

'This convent was renowned for its devotion and its learning,' Lady Rochford said. 'It enjoyed royal patronage.'

'Yes,' said Mrs Herbert, 'but his Majesty was right to dissolve it. It was one of the richest nunneries in the land, and a school of popery, no doubt.'

Sensing religious tension between the ladies, Anna encouraged them to make the acquaintance of her German women, who were sitting by themselves to one side of the chamber. But there was really no common meeting ground for, unlike the English ladies, the Germans did not play cards, or sing, dance or make music, and they could not speak the English tongue. She feared they might become isolated, being so outnumbered; it was happening already.

At nine o'clock, aware that she had to be up early for her official reception at Greenwich, Anna retired dispiritedly to the former prioress's house. Here, as at Canterbury, another of the King's rich beds had been set up. She fell asleep reminding herself of all his care for her, which must, surely, betoken some affection in him . . .

Chapter 9

As Anna descended Shooter's Hill at noon the next day, seated with Mother Lowe and Susanna in the gilded chariot, she saw a vast gathering of people on the green expanse of Blackheath below her. Behind her followed twelve of her German ladies, all wearing gowns similar to hers, with heavy gold chains around their necks, and the rest of her great retinue from Kleve; after them, in stately manner, came the dukes of Norfolk and Suffolk, the Archbishop of Canterbury and other bishops, and the lords and ladies who had joined Anna on her journey through Kent.

Susanna pointed out the Mayor and Corporation of London, in their red gowns, and the German merchants of the Steelyard. The broad heath was thronged with hundreds of knights, soldiers and liveried servants, and crowds of ordinary citizens. It seemed the entire nobility of England was here too, and there must have been at least five thousand horses. All eyes were upon Anna's chariot, waiting for a glimpse of her.

'I cannot believe this is all for me,' she said, awed.

'The Duke your brother would be much gratified,' Mother Lowe said. 'The King has gone to much trouble and expense to afford you this princely welcome. It is a measure of his love for you.' There was a meaningful edge to her voice.

At the foot of the hill, the chariot halted outside a gorgeous silken pavilion, which was surrounded by other, smaller tents. Ranked on either side of the entrance, Anna's newly appointed household was waiting for her, having left Dartford at dawn and ridden ahead. Her lord chamberlain, the Earl of Rutland, bowed before her, looking so like his cousin the King, and Lady Margaret Douglas came forward to welcome her, attended by the Duchess of Richmond and the King's other niece, the blunt-faced Marchioness of Dorset, accompanied by a throng of peeresses. As the entire household saluted and greeted her, Anna alighted from the chariot.

'I give you all hearty thanks,' she said in English. Then she turned to her chief ladies and kissed them all in turn.

Her new almoner, Dr Kaye, made a long speech in Latin, of which she did not understand a word, then formally presented to her all those sworn to serve her, which took some considerable time, while each knelt in turn to kiss her hand. Everyone was shivering when the presentation was finished, but they had to endure the cold for a few minutes more to hear Dr Olisleger reply to the address on Anna's behalf. Only then could she and her ladies enter the pavilion, where she was grateful to find braziers containing scented fires, against the January chill. A banquet had been laid out on a long table, and they all descended on it hungrily, relieved to have a little respite from ceremony.

After Anna had eaten, her attendants helped her to change into a gorgeous taffeta gown of cloth of gold, cut in the Dutch fashion, with a round skirt. The English ladies were intrigued that it lacked the train customarily worn by women of rank at court, but some were complimentary.

'It is much easier to wear than these twenty yards trailing at my back,' Lady Margaret said.

Mother Lowe re-plaited Anna's hair and placed a sheer linen caul over it, then, on top of that, a *Stickelchen* studded with Orient pearls and surmounted by a coronet of black velvet. Around Anna's shoulders she set a partlet encrusted with rich gemstones, and high on her breast, a fiery ruby brooch.

With not a hair out of place, Anna stood in the pavilion, waiting for the arrival of the King. She was trembling, unable to forget that it lacked less than a day to her marriage. Word of her arrival had been sent to Greenwich, three miles away, and when the Earl of Rutland came to say that his Majesty would not be long, she swallowed in trepidation, praying she would acquit herself well. And please, God, she breathed, make me like the King a little better.

Moments later, in the distance, trumpets sounded, and her heart began to pound. He was coming.

'Your Grace, it is time,' Rutland told her. 'The King is about half a mile away. You are to meet him as he approaches.'

Outside the pavilion, she saw, to her dismay, a richly caparisoned palfrey waiting for her, its reins held by Sir John Dudley, her master of horse. Ladies were not encouraged to ride back in Kleve – she had been taken everywhere in litters or chariots, and she was nervous of horses. One look at Sir John's hard, swarthy face decided her against confiding her fear. Determinedly she climbed the mounting block and carefully seated herself sideways on the wooden saddle. Fortunately, the palfrey seemed docile and sturdy beneath her. Grasping the reins, she set off with her footmen about her, all wearing livery bearing the black lion of Kleve in goldsmiths' work.

In front of her rode a great company of her German and English gentlemen; after them followed Sir John Dudley, leading her horse of honour, and behind came her ladies, mounted in order of rank, then her yeomen and serving men on foot, bringing up the rear.

The mounted merchants of the Steelyard had positioned themselves on either side of the road that led to Greenwich. Behind stood numerous gentlemen and esquires, and in front the Mayor and his brethren and the leading citizens of London. As Anna rode forward, she could see the royal trumpeters approaching; in their wake, marching towards her in orderly rank, advanced a company of spearmen, wearing dark velvet doublets and gold medallions of office.

'Your Grace, that is the King's elite guard, the Gentlemen Pensioners,' Sir John said, with Susanna translating.

The procession halted to allow the guard to pass. After them came ranks of clerics, lawyers, officers of the royal household, Privy councillors and the gentlemen of the King's Privy Chamber; Sir John pointed them all out.

At last, there, before her, was the King, attended by Norfolk, Suffolk and Cranmer, and encircled by ten footmen, richly apparelled in goldsmiths' work. For all his bulk, Henry looked magnificent, quite unlike how he had appeared at Rochester. He rode a splendid courser trapped in rich cloth of gold embellished with gilded ornaments and pearls. His coat of purple velvet was embroidered with gold damask and heavily criss-crossed with matching laces: the slashed sleeves were lined with cloth of gold, and clasped with great buttons of diamonds, rubies and Orient pearls. Across his breast was slung a collar of rubies and pearls. His sword and girdle glinted with diamonds and emeralds. His bonnet too was edged with precious stones, and on it he wore a cap rich with jewels. He glittered, god-like, in the weak January sunlight, and the crowds gaped in awe as he passed. To left and right he turned a princely countenance, raising his hand in greeting, and Anna felt something stir in her. Never had she seen a ruler treated with such deference, by courtiers and commons alike.

The ranks of gentlemen before her drew back on each side, leaving a clear path between her and the King. Henry spurred his horse a little way beyond the stone cross that stood on Blackheath, and halted there. As Dr Olisleger stepped forward to act as interpreter, the King doffed his cap and, not waiting for Anna to come to him, as was proper, trotted forward to greet her, looking – she observed with relief – pleased to see her.

'My Lady Anna, welcome to England!' he cried, so that all could hear, and he bowed in the saddle.

Anna bowed too. 'Your Majesty, I am both honoured and joyful to be here,' she replied in English, gratified by his warm welcome, and conscious of the hundreds of people watching. Smiling at her most kindly, the King reined in his horse beside hers, leaned over, and embraced her, to loud cheers from the spectators. He smelt fresher today, of herbs and soap.

'See how my subjects welcome you, Madam!' he said.

Anna returned his smile. She had rehearsed her words. 'Sir, I mind to be a good and loving mistress to them, and a humble and loving wife to your Majesty,' she said loudly. 'I thank you, and all the good people here, for this wonderful welcome.'

While they exchanged pleasantries, and Anna dared to think that the King might indeed come to like her, the members of his retinue were taking their places amidst the great concourse of people on Blackheath.

She saw some of the King's guard ride off towards Greenwich, to be ready for his coming there. As she and Henry rode back together towards the pavilion, he accorded her the place of honour on his right hand, and rode so close that their arms kept touching. Everyone was cheering and rejoicing at the sight, and Anna felt that, if they did not love her yet, the people of England certainly seemed to bear her much goodwill.

In the pavilion, the King called for spiced wine to warm them, picked at the replenished banquet, and presented to Anna the Lord Chancellor and Lord Cromwell. Anna was most interested to meet Cromwell, for he had done more than anyone to bring about her marriage.

He bowed over her hand, a portly, eagle-eyed man with heavy features and a polished manner. 'Welcome to England, your Grace. I trust your journey was as comfortable as we could make it.'

We? She had thought the orders for the kindnesses afforded her had come from the King. But, of course, Cromwell would have implemented his orders. Even so, she did not like the presumptuous way the man coupled his name with the King's, as if they were a single entity. Nor did she like Cromwell's appraising look. It seemed rude. But she had been told that he was the son of a blacksmith, so what could one expect?

She was glad when it was time to leave for Greenwich.

Outside the pavilion, there stood an empty litter, hung and upholstered with cloth of gold and crimson velvet.

'It is my gift to you, my lady,' the King said. 'After we are married, you must ride in an English conveyance.'

'I thank your Grace.' Anna curtseyed. It was a handsome litter, yet she felt sad at the prospect of abandoning her magnificent golden chariot adorned with the lion of Kleve. But, for now, the King said, she could use it for the processional journey.

With the trumpets going before, and the King riding beside her, they passed through the assembled ranks of knights and esquires, preceded and followed by their joint entourages. In the chariot behind Anna's sat six of her German gentlewomen, whose fair faces and ornate gowns drew appreciative cheers from some Englishmen watching. Then followed chariots bearing Anna's English ladies, chamberers and laundresses, and behind them was drawn her new litter, in the wake of which rode her serving men.

On they passed through the deer park. As the chariot crested the hill, the red-brick palace of Greenwich appeared, spread out below them on the banks of the Thames. Anna stared in wonder at the painted roofs and soaring turrets. It looked like a palace from a German legend.

'Greenwich!' the King announced. 'Madam, I was born here, and it is the second of my great houses after Whitehall.'

Anna could see the citizens of London in their boats on the Thames, watching the procession.

'All the guilds of London have come out in their barges,' the King said. As they drew nearer, Anna saw that some of the barges had been painted with the royal arms of England or the arms of Kleve; she could hear the melodious sounds of minstrels and men and children singing. The King halted the procession on the wharf near the palace, so they could listen.

'Do you not think it praiseworthy, Madam?' he asked.

'It is very good,' Anna answered, fearing that her limited English could not sufficiently convey how excellent the music was.

On arrival at the palace, they were saluted by guns positioned on top of the massive central tower. It dominated the river frontage, a long range of apartments boasting a costly expanse of glass in a row of splendid bay windows. Passing through the gatehouse at the base of the tower, they arrived in an inner courtyard, where the King dismounted, assisted Anna from her chariot, and lovingly embraced and kissed her in front of their cheering, clapping retinues.

'Welcome to your own, Madam!' he said grandly, and led her arm-in-arm through the magnificent great hall, where the guards were lined up like statues along the walls, and beyond, to her apartments. They were sumptuous, with every surface painted and gilded, and again she was aware of the smells of new wood and paint – and of the distant sounds of sawing and hammering.

'Forgive the noise, Madam, but men are still working on refurbishments to my own apartments,' the King explained. 'They work only in the day, and should be finished soon. They have been ordered not to disturb you any more than is strictly necessary.'

They entered her presence chamber. 'Here,' he said, 'you will hold court.'

Anna gazed in awe at the ceiling decorated with gilded bosses, the expensive Seville tiles lining the hearth, and the alcoves tiled in green and yellow with windows overlooking the river. At the far end of the room, a velvet-upholstered faldstool stood on the dais beneath a rich canopy of estate bearing the combined arms of England and Kleve. This was to be her throne.

They passed through to her privy chamber, the ushers opening the doors and saluting.

'This, Madam, is your private apartment,' the King explained. 'Only the most privileged, those you favour, may enter.'

It was as lavishly fitted out as the presence chamber, but what drew Anna's eye was the wood-burning stove of green-glazed earthenware that stood in a corner. It was just like the stoves in Germany! The King really had gone far beyond what was needful in providing for her.

She swept him a curtsey. 'I thank your Majesty for giving me *gut* rooms, and that *Ofen*,' she said.

'I trust you will be comfortable here, Madam,' he replied. Again, she was aware of the detached, practised courtesy of his manner. 'And now your ladies are waiting to attend you and help you to settle in. I must leave you for a time, to attend to a matter of state. But I will see you this evening, for there is to be a feast in your honour.' He kissed her hand and bowed, at which she made a low curtsey.

'There!' Mother Lowe said, when he had gone. 'I told you there was nothing to worry about!'

'I do hope not,' Anna breathed, sinking into a chair.

'No queen could have had a greater welcome,' Susanna told her. 'There was no such fanfare for Queen Jane. The first we knew of her marriage to the King was when, suddenly, there she was, enthroned in the Queen's presence chamber at Whitehall, with her title being cried out to the court. Of course, there had been talk that his Grace would marry her.'

'But the Lady Anna is royal!' Mother Lowe bristled. 'Queen Jane was but a gentlewoman. She brought no great alliance.'

'She brought the King love, which is just as important,' Anna said.

Mother Lowe opened her mouth to protest, but was silenced by the sounds of the English ladies arriving.

'I do not think I can ever love him,' Anna whispered to Susanna, as Mother Lowe moved hastily to greet the newcomers as if she were their mistress, intent no doubt on establishing her supremacy.

Susanna regarded Anna with sympathy.

'I am dreading tomorrow more than I can say,' Anna confessed. She had tried to suppress all thought of her wedding night, but in vain. In two days, she might be in the Tower!

'There is nothing to fear,' Susanna murmured. 'There might be some pain at first, but it soon passes.'

Anna said nothing; not even to this dear friend could she unburden herself.

'All will be well, I am sure,' Susanna smiled.

Anna's gown was of the plushest velvet, the colour of the fir trees that grew on the hills surrounding Schloss Burg. Over its long, tight sleeves, with their borders of embroidery and goldsmiths' work at the cuffs, she wore the rich sables the King had given her. Her head was crowned with a cap encrusted with pearls and precious stones. She could feel all eyes on her as she arrived in the King's presence chamber, followed by her long train of ladies. This was how it would be from now on. She realised she had been lucky to enjoy so much seclusion at the court of Kleve; she had resented it then, but now – how she longed for it!

The banquet was sumptuous, the King as attentive as ever, yet again she was aware of irritation simmering beneath the surface. She would have liked to ask him if all was well, and thus show him she meant to be a helpmeet as well as a wife, but she did not dare. As always, when in his presence, she found herself overawed and tongue-tied, even with the reassuring presence of Susanna, who was acting as interpreter.

'We will have to choose a motto to be engraved on your wedding ring, and for use by you at other times,' Henry said, as a huge sugar subtlety in the shape of a swan, in tribute to Kleve, was carried in by two confectioners and offered to the high table. Henry nodded graciously, beaming at the applause from the courtiers, and the men set it down at the centre of the table and began to carve it.

'What motto shall I choose, Sir?' Anna asked.

'It is for you to say. What do you think it should be?'

She thought for a moment. 'Something along the lines of asking for God's protection to keep me from harm or trouble.'

Henry nodded approvingly. 'Maybe this will serve – "God send me well to keep".'

'That is perfect, Sir.'

'Good. I will instruct my goldsmith. Now you must choose a badge as your emblem.'

'May I use the swan of Kleve, Sir? Or, if that does not please you, the ducal coronet?'

'You may use both, as you wish,' Henry said benignly.

After the banquet, Anna changed into a taffeta gown and returned to watch the dancing in the presence chamber. She sat on the dais, on a stool at the King's right hand, praying he would not ask her to dance. She did not know how, for it had been frowned upon in Kleve. But he did not; maybe he himself could not dance these days, although she'd heard he had been skilled at it in his youth, as he had excelled at sports and nearly every other accomplishment. He remained enthroned, watching the couples before him weaving in and out of line, touching hands, then whirling away again. From time to time he spoke to Anna, pointing out this lord or that, or explaining some rule of dancing. Something still troubled him – or maybe he was as tired after the long day as she was herself, or sad that youth had flown and he could no longer participate in its pleasures.

She was glad when he stood up and called for spiced wine and wafers to be served, a signal that the festivities were at an end. She gulped down the wine, needing to quell her fears about the morrow. Despite the general air of anticipation among the courtiers, and the wedding talk she had heard in snatches, the King had not mentioned their imminent nuptials, or even told her what time to be ready. This, she knew, was not how things should be.

Her fears were confirmed when, as soon as she had returned to her apartments, Vice Chancellor Olisleger and Grand Master Hochsteden were announced, both looking worried. When they asked if they might speak with her in private, she was convinced they would tell her the King was sending her home.

'Your Grace,' Dr Olisleger said, once they were alone in her closet, 'we are sorry to disturb you so late, but we have only just come from a meeting with Lord Cromwell and the Privy Council. A difficulty has arisen that you should know about. Lord Cromwell summoned us because the King and his councillors are concerned that your betrothal to the Duke of Lorraine's son was not properly dissolved. If that were indeed the case, it would prevent your marriage.'

For a moment, Anna was speechless. It was clear now why the King had been preoccupied. She did not know whether to laugh, cry or slump in relief. 'But it is not the case,' she managed to declare.

'No, Madam,' agreed Hochsteden. 'Last summer, Duke Wilhelm's council assured Dr Wotton that your Grace was not bound by any covenants made between Kleve and Lorraine, and that you were at liberty to marry whom you wished. But Lord Cromwell says that at Windsor, in the autumn, the King repeatedly insisted he would not sign the marriage treaty without proof of a formal annulment. Yet, Madam, his Majesty said no such thing to us. He did not raise the matter at all. Indeed, he was more than happy to sign the marriage treaty. However, at the meeting tonight, Dr Wotton declared that *he* had asked us to bring the proofs, and the Privy councillors said we promised at Windsor to do so, but we have no recollection of that. Indeed, Madam, we believed the Duke's council had given sufficient assurances to satisfy the King, so we brought nothing in writing.'

'But why is his Majesty raising these doubts now, at the very last minute?' Anna asked, incredulous. 'Is this all a pretext to get rid of me?'

'Not at all, Madam!' Dr Olisleger was shocked. 'He was expecting us to bring the proofs he says he asked for. I was told that, having entered into two incestuous unions in the past, with much trouble ensuing, his

Majesty is troubled in his conscience that he might again be marrying a lady who is forbidden to him. He cannot frame his mind or his heart to love you until his doubts have been resolved.'

How could you frame your heart to love someone? Anna herself had tried to do that, and failed. You either loved, or you didn't. No, the King's qualms of conscience were surely born of the fact that, put simply, he did not want to marry her. She had guessed it from the first.

'*Can* those doubts be resolved?' she asked, foreseeing herself returning to Kleve, abandoned and shamed through no fault of her own, yet secretly relieved to be free of this man.

'I am sure they can, and speedily,' Hochsteden assured her. 'There have clearly been misunderstandings, on both sides.'

'Neither your Grace nor the Marquis ever made vows, so there was no need for an ecclesiastical court to dissolve the betrothal,' Olisleger said. 'We said this to Lord Cromwell, who went to the King, then told us his Majesty was not prepared to go through with the marriage. Lord Cromwell urged us to assure him that, as soon as we returned to Kleve, we would send the proofs that will put all out of doubt. Madam, it was most embarrassing. We were made to look like incompetent fools.' Dr Olisleger's normally urbane manner was showing signs of fragmenting.

'So what will happen now?' Anna asked, for it seemed a deadlock had been reached.

'We have said we will confer with you and give them an answer in the morning.'

'But I am to be married in the morning!'

'Madam, the King has deferred the solemnisation until Tuesday to allow time for the matter to be resolved,' Hochsteden informed her. 'Rest assured, all will be well.'

Anna was not so sure of that, and it must have shown in her face.

'Far better to have a happy bridegroom than a reluctant one,' Dr Olisleger observed.

Anna retired to her bedchamber, relieved to find that Mother Lowe had shooed everyone else away and was waiting up for her. Her eye alighted on her wedding finery, all laid out for the morrow. How she longed for the calm serenity of her mother's presence.

'Is everything all right?' Mother Lowe asked.

Anna shook her head, and pulled off her cap. 'No. The wedding is postponed until Tuesday. A problem has arisen.' She explained what it was. 'I think the King is making an occasion to be rid of me, but Dr Olisleger and Grand Master Hochsteden say no. I am not convinced.' She sank into her chair by the fire.

Mother Lowe began unplaiting Anna's hair. 'I am amazed,' she said. 'He's had time enough to satisfy his conscience on that score. If he had doubts, why sign the treaty?'

'Could it be that, when he saw me in person, he did not like me? That's the only explanation I can think of.'

'Or someone has planted these doubts in his mind,' Mother Lowe suggested. 'I have eyes and ears, and I can understand English better than I can speak it. The Catholics do not want this marriage. They abhor the King allying himself with the Protestant princes.'

The Duke of Norfolk's sour face came to mind. Anna could well imagine him working secretly to prevent her marriage.

'Maybe,' she said slowly. 'But what if there *are* no proofs? I shall for ever after be known as the bride sent home by the King of England. I would never live it down. No man would want me—'

'Stop!' Mother Lowe cried. 'The King needs this alliance.'

'He does as he pleases. Luther said that of him.'

Mother Lowe bristled. 'I've never heard of a princess arriving in a foreign country to wed a king, and being sent home. Even this King would not dare. Your brother would not stand for it.'

'What can he do? Kleve is in no position to wage war on England.'

'He could turn the German princes against the King. The Elector of Saxony pushed for this marriage. He will not see you insulted.'

Anna sighed. 'No prince goes to war for the honour of a princess. When the King divorced Queen Katherine, did the Emperor go to her rescue? No. If it comes to it, I will go home willingly. I wish I had never come here!' The tears she had been fighting back burst forth in a flood, and there was her old nurse, holding her as she rocked in misery.

'I would do anything to avoid my wedding night,' she sobbed. 'You, of all people, know why! What if the King discovers I am no virgin? What will he do to me?'

'Hush, hush,' Mother Lowe soothed, stroking Anna's hair. 'No man can tell if a woman is a virgin.'

'But what of those silvery marks on my belly where the skin was stretched? And my breasts are not as firm as they were before I gave birth. Are these not telltale signs?'

'The King is a man,' Mother Lowe said dismissively. 'He will not notice such things.'

'He may expect me to bleed,' Anna fretted.

Mother Lowe thought for a moment. 'Keep a needle handy, under the pillow. Prick your finger, then smear it on the sheet. He won't know the difference. All will be well, you'll see.'

Anna prayed she was right.

The next morning, she waited in suspense. It was near dinner time, and she was about to scream with frustration, when Olisleger and Hochsteden came to her. One look at their faces told her the meeting had not gone as hoped.

'What news?' she asked, without preamble.

Dr Olisleger spoke. 'Madam, we told the lords we were much perplexed. We stressed that the precontract had certainly been renounced, and I offered to remain here as a prisoner until proof of that could be sent from Kleve. They told us they would see the King after dinner, to know his mind on the matter. So we await his answer.'

Anna could eat little of the choice fare served at dinner. Whatever the King decided, there would be a sting in the tail for her.

At four o'clock, just when she was ready to climb the walls in anxiety, Lord Cromwell appeared, his face inscrutable. With him were two clerks in black gowns.

'Your Grace,' he said, nodding to Susanna to interpret, 'I understand you know of the difficulty in regard to the precontract with Lorraine. Be assured his Grace wishes only to remove all room for doubt. He has taken advice from Archbishop Cranmer, who confirmed that, since you were under age when you were betrothed to the Marquis, a formal renunciation by either you or the young gentleman could render that betrothal invalid. The King now asks that you make that renunciation yourself. He feels that such a protestation, in the presence of a person of honour, before notaries, should be a sufficient discharge in law.'

His words astonished Anna. It seemed the King was now doing his best to remove the impediment, not, as she had feared, using it as an excuse to reject her.

Cromwell was still speaking. 'His Grace has appointed me to be that person of honour, and these gentlemen are notaries, who can act as witnesses. Lady Anna, I ask you now, formally, to confirm that you renounce your betrothal and that you are at liberty to wed.'

Anna thought for a moment. There seemed no reason why she should not do as he asked. 'I renounce my betrothal,' she said. 'I am free from all contracts.'

'Thank you, Madam,' Cromwell said. 'I will tell his Grace of your conformability. You have done well.' For a moment he paused, and she thought she detected a hint of vulnerability in his expression. It came to her that she was not the only one suffering anxiety over her coming marriage. Cromwell had been its maker; for him, its success was crucial. His glittering career might be staked upon it. She found it in herself to feel sympathy for him.

She thought he might say more, but he bowed and made to leave.

'My lord,' she said, 'be assured I will do all I can to be a good wife to the King. I am sensible of the honour he has done me, and of all that you yourself have done on my behalf. If you wish it, I am ready to be your friend.'

Those shrewd eyes were staring at her, calculating, cynical. 'I thank your Grace,' Cromwell said. 'Consider me ever yours.'

Anna was still not certain if the wedding would go ahead on Tuesday. On Epiphany Eve, before the Twelfth Night feast, the King accompanied her to Mass. As they processed through the court, smiling to left and right at the press of courtiers, he said nothing of the drama that had just been played out. He was courteous as ever, and just as inscrutable.

After Mass, he escorted her to her presence chamber, and there, summoning Cromwell and his lawyers, he issued letters patent granting Anna her dower. 'Henry, by the Grace of God . . .' she deciphered at the top, when he gave her the document. She could not read it, but she could see the long list of lands and privileges that were now hers. She was thankful she could rely on her council to take care of her estates and collect her dues. What struck her most forcibly was how great a landowner she must now be. It seemed she had properties all over England.

'This dower, Madam, is the same as that held by Queen Jane,' Henry told her. It was the first time he had mentioned his late wife.

'It is a most generous settlement,' she said. 'I thank your Grace, from my heart.'

'It is your due,' he told her. 'My Queen must be seen to live in the comfort and magnificence befitting her rank.' He bowed. 'Make ready, Madam. We will be wed in the morning. I will send my lords to escort you to the Chapel Royal at eight o'clock.'

Chapter 10

1540

The wedding gown was beautiful. Made of cloth of gold in a pattern of large flowers, stitched with large Orient pearls, it had long, hanging sleeves and a round skirt in the Dutch fashion. As became a bride who was supposed to be a virgin, Anna wore her fair hair loose, placing on her head a coronal of gold set with brilliant gems. In her hair, and pinned to her gown, were sprigs of rosemary. 'Rosemary symbolises love, faithfulness and fruitfulness,' Mother Lowe told her. The great ladies of the household brought gold chains and a jewelled crucifix, which Mother Lowe insisted on hanging around Anna's neck herself, and a belt adorned with gold and stones. When she was ready, she shimmered, so glittering was the effect.

Wilhelm had sent Baron Oberstein, a nobleman of Kleve, to England to stand as his proxy at the wedding and give Anna away. He was a rather dashing young man with a good opinion of himself, and punctilious in his duty. He was waiting for her in her presence chamber at seven o'clock with Grand Master Hochsteden. The Earl of Essex, who was also to escort her to the chapel, was late. Shortly before eight o'clock, a very apologetic Lord Cromwell arrived, saying he would take Essex's place, but no sooner had he spoken than the elderly Earl tottered in, reeking of strong drink. He almost fell over while bowing to Anna, and insisted, in no dulcet tone, that he perform his duty. Shaking his head behind the old man's back, Cromwell reluctantly agreed. Hochsteden's face was a study in incredulity. Anna fervently hoped that Essex would behave himself. She threw an anxious glance at Baron Oberstein, but he was standing stiffly to attention, ready to depart.

Preceded by Cromwell, with Oberstein and Hochsteden walking on either side of her, and Essex lumbering behind, Anna passed through the crowds of courtiers who had lined the way to see her. Still not used to so many people doing reverence to her, she kept her eyes downcast and her head bowed.

The many lords waiting for her in the King's presence chamber went before her to the chapel gallery. There she saw the King, dazzlingly dressed in a doublet and bases of cloth of gold embossed with large flowers of silver, and a coat of crimson satin slashed and embroidered, and tied with great diamonds, with a rich collar about his neck. She made three low obeisances as she approached, and he doffed his cap, making an elegant bow. His face gave away nothing, no hint of whether he was pleased to be marrying her. She told herself this was probably his way, to be formal in public. Later, when they were alone, he might reveal his true self and his feelings for her. *When they were alone . . .* She trembled at the thought.

The King held out his hand. She placed hers on it, and together they proceeded into the Chapel Royal, where Archbishop Cranmer was waiting. Baron Oberstein gave Anna away, in the Duke's name, with the utmost correctitude.

Cranmer looked intently at Henry and Anna. 'Have either of you two persons come here to this solemn ceremony with deceitful intentions?'

'No,' said the King, his face impassive.

'No,' Anna answered.

'I must warn you both,' the Archbishop continued, 'in the name of the Father, the Son and the Holy Ghost, that, if either of you know of any just impediment why you should not be wed, you should immediately state it.'

There was the slightest of pauses. 'I know of none,' the King said, and Anna echoed him. Then Cranmer turned to the wedding guests, and asked them to declare if they knew of any legal obstacle to the marriage. They answered, to a man, that they knew of none. The Archbishop looked satisfied, and proceeded to the nuptial ceremony. At his nod, the King placed a ring on Anna's finger. She glimpsed the motto he had chosen for her: 'God send me well to keep'. Never had she had more need of the Almighty's protection and succour.

There was no going back now, no going home to Kleve. They were pronounced man and wife, and Cranmer blessed them and wished them a fruitful union. Anna was queen of England at last.

The watching lords bowed low as the King led her, hand in hand, into his adjacent holyday closet for the nuptial Mass. Cranmer said the *Agnus Dei* and the *Pax Domini*, then gave the kiss of peace to Anna, upon which the King, in turn, kissed and embraced her. After they had received the Eucharist, Henry and Anna offered their tapers at the altar.

When the service ended, they were offered wine and spices, as the trumpets sounded, and a herald strode grandly through the court, proclaiming Anna's title and style. When he returned, amidst a throng of courtiers eager to see – and be seen by – the new Queen, the King rewarded him with a purse of silver shillings.

Laying down his goblet, Henry kissed Anna's hand, and departed for his privy chamber to change, while the dukes of Norfolk and Suffolk escorted Anna to her own chamber, with all her ladies following. She was still in her wedding clothes when, shortly after nine o'clock, she was summoned to attend the Mass of the Trinity, for today was the Feast of Epiphany. She went in procession with her serjeant-of-arms and all her officers before her, as was proper for the Queen of England, and arrived at the holyday closet at the same time as the King, who was now attired in a gown of rich taffeta lined with embroidered crimson velvet. Side by side, they led their trains into the Chapel Royal for a magnificent service, taking part in the great offertory procession as if they were following in the footsteps of the Three Kings.

After Mass, to another fanfare, Henry and Anna entered the King's presence chamber to dine together in full view of the court, with the chief lords and officers of state standing in attendance. Anna sat on a smaller chair beside the King's throne, stiff with anxiety. The meal was served with great formality, and eaten mostly in silence, save for when the King asked her if she was enjoying her meat – she was barely picking at it – or addressed a remark to Norfolk or Suffolk. When dinner was over, she escaped with relief to her apartments, but even there she could not relax, for her ladies were clustering around, congratulating her and saying how well she had acquitted herself.

'You were every inch the Queen, Madam!' Margaret Douglas enthused.

'And you bore yourself so handsomely; every eye was upon you!' Susanna exclaimed. Only the Duchess of Richmond and Lady Rochford held themselves aloof. Maybe she did embody an alliance they deplored, but could they not try to like her for herself?

She rested on her bed in the afternoon, glad to be divested of the heavy golden gown. She tried to sleep, but it was impossible. All she could think of was the night to come.

It was dark when Mother Lowe came to rouse her, handing her a cup of aleberry, the spiced ale so enjoyed at court that it was poured freely for all comers every night at the servery by the kitchens. She drank it gratefully, hoping it would distance her from her fears.

It was time to make ready for the evening's celebrations. Her ladies dressed her in a taffeta gown with voluminous sleeves and the *Stickelchen* she had worn on Saturday for her reception at Blackheath. Her German ladies were in high spirits as they donned similar attire, with an abundance of gold chains. She wished she felt like celebrating, and could be as light-hearted as they. They did not have to face going to bed with a terrifying man who smelt, and who might have cause to be very angry with her.

She joined the terrifying man in chapel for Vespers, and they supped in private afterwards, with just Susanna present. Again, Henry was attentive and solicitous. He spoke of his daughters, Mary and Elizabeth, and of Prince Edward, who sounded a very confident child, and who was looking forward to meeting Anna.

'I would be a mother to him,' Anna said, sipping her wine, trying not to think of another little boy who had lost his mother. 'He must miss Queen Jane.'

'He never knew her. She died twelve days after he was born,' the King said, a shadow passing across his face. 'He has his nurse, Mother Jack, of whom he is fond, and Lady Bryan runs his nursery most capably. She has been lady mistress to all my children.' It seemed there would be no place for Anna in the Prince's life. She tried not to feel disheartened. She was grateful when Henry made a jest and became animated talking about his horses. But still there was that distance.

The remains of the second course were removed, and Anna downed her third glass of wine. They adjourned to the presence chamber, where privileged courtiers had gathered to partake of a banquet of sweet treats. Anna was grateful for the entertainment that followed, since it distracted her a little from her fears. She had never seen anything like *The Masque of Hymen*. What would they say in Kleve if they could see lords and ladies dancing together in the most revealing costumes, or hear jests that were plainly bawdy, judging by the guffaws of the audience? She was glad she could not understand them. But some of the German lords of her escort could; Olisleger and Hochsteden were both red in the face. She felt sorry for their embarrassment. Yet no one else seemed to be bothered; the courtiers were laughing raucously. Many were drunk. She had tried to get a little drunk herself, but tonight, when she most needed it, the wine seemed to have no effect.

The King, sitting beside her, was explaining that Hymen, the god of marriage, was acting as arbiter in a dispute between Juno, the goddess of marriage, and Venus, the goddess of love and desire, who preferred to retain her freedom. Of course, there was no real contest, especially on this occasion: marriage won outright – as anyone could have predicted.

Anna had not expected that, once the victory had been assured, the players, men and women both, would hasten over to the audience and pull everyone to their feet, urging them to dance. A beguiling nymph who looked a lot like Anne Bassett – gracious, it *was* Anne Bassett, the forward minx! – approached the King himself, smiling and reaching out to him. But to Anna's astonishment, he turned to her. 'Forgive me, fair nymph, but tonight I must honour my Queen.'

Anna stared at the podgy hand he was holding out to her. Was he really asking her to join him among the couples whirling around the chamber?

'Will you join me, Madam?' he asked.

She could not dance! What should she do? Dare she risk making a fool of herself in front of the court? Or dare she risk turning him down? Which was worse?

She took a deep breath. 'If it pleases your Majesty,' she said, accepting his hand, 'although I fear I am not skilled in dancing.'

'Then I will teach you,' he said.

The courtiers drew back as Henry and Anna stepped off the dais, and the music ceased. He was still holding her hand, and he swung her round to face him. 'We will dance a pavane – the King's Pavane!' he cried, and the musicians struck up another tune, slower this time, with a compelling tabor beat.

'You take one step to two beats,' Henry said. 'You move sideways, and then forward. It is a very slow and stately dance, and most apt for special occasions.'

Anna quickly got the measure of it, and soon she was moving about the floor with ease. At the end, she curtseyed low as the King bowed, and they returned to the dais amidst loud cheering.

Henry leaned over to her. 'It grows late,' he murmured. 'It is time to take our rest.'

Anna felt faint.

The King signalled to Mother Lowe. 'Have the ladies attend the Queen to bed,' he commanded, and stood up. The dancers halted, and everyone made low obeisances.

'Madam, I will see you presently,' he said, bowing. Followed by his lords and gentlemen, who were smirking and nudging each other, he departed.

Anna was fighting down panic by the time she got back to her apartments. Shaking, she hurried through to her bedchamber, her ladies striving to keep pace.

She was astonished to find that, while she had been revelling downstairs, her bed had been replaced with a fine one of oak with painted decorations. On the headboard, '1539', the date of her betrothal, was chiselled above her initials and the King's. She blushed to see the carvings at either end – a startlingly priapic cherub and a pregnant one. The message could not have been clearer.

She tried to still her juddering heart as she was divested of her finery and Mother Lowe attired her in a chemise of the finest lawn. Anastasia had picked off the rosemary from Anna's wedding dress, and was strewing the sprigs across the counterpane. With her hair combed until it shone, Anna climbed into bed on the side that sported the pregnant cherub, and settled herself against the high pillows, pulling the sheet up over her bosom. Mother Lowe spread her hair out like a glossy golden cape around her shoulders.

They waited in silence for the King to arrive and the ceremonial putting-to-bed of the bride and groom to commence. Whoever had thought up such a humiliating ritual ought to have been boiled in oil, Anna fumed. What passed between two people in bed should be a private matter. But here she was, in her night-rail, waiting to be ravished (there was no other word for it) – and a public spectacle to boot!

She had forgotten to put a bodkin under the pillow! It was too late now. From behind the door leading to the King's lodgings, she heard footsteps approaching, and a voice crying, 'Make way for the King's Grace!' Anna pulled the sheet up further, to her chin. The door opened and there was Henry, clad in a furred nightgown over a long nightshirt, with a night-bonnet on his head. Behind him, his gentlemen crowded into the room, joking and laughing, and peering to get a good view of Anna, to her mortification. The King ignored them – or maybe he too was embarrassed, for he looked like a man forced to endure something unpalatable. She prayed that she herself was not the object of his distaste.

At the last, Archbishop Cranmer entered the bedchamber. Anna understood now why Henry was uncomfortable. He would not wish a man of God to hear unseemly jests. Like her, he probably wanted the whole charade over.

'For England and St George!' cried one of the young men, as the King bowed to Anna and heaved himself into bed beside her. A whiff of corruption rose from his diseased leg. They lay together, not touching, as Cranmer blessed the bed, sprinkled it with holy water and prayed that man and wife be fruitful. Then, at the King's nod, everyone left the chamber. Mother Lowe was the last to depart, after dousing all the candles.

This was one place where Susanna could not act as interpreter, and Anna lay in dread. Wine had been left at the ready on top of the court cupboard on the far wall, and she longed desperately to be fortified for the ordeal that lay ahead.

Henry turned towards her. He had his back to the firelight, so she could not read his expression.

'Would you like some wine, Sir?' she asked carefully.

'I think I've had enough,' he said. 'Maybe we can have some later.'

She felt his arm snaking across her, drawing her to the middle of the bed, so that she lay pressed against him, with the bulk of his stomach against hers. His leg was bandaged and beneath the covers, so the smell was not so offensive. She could bear it. She could bear a lot, she told herself.

'Do not fear me, Anna,' Henry murmured in her ear. 'I know how to please a lady, as a gentleman should.' His beard was rough against her temple. She felt his body stir against her thigh. She squirmed inwardly as he pulled up her night-rail and threw back the sheet and counterpane. She hated being so exposed to him, yet she dared not protest; it was her duty to submit to him in all things, from this day forward. Mutter, blushing, had said so, impressing on Anna the need to be a dutiful and loving wife.

How different this would be with Otho! No, she dared not think of him now.

Henry kissed her lips, his breath smelling of wine, and then she felt his hand travelling over her body. It moved hungrily over her breasts, and then down to her buttocks, before snaking around to her belly. It was there that it paused, and Henry drew back, his eyes raking over her body in the flickering light. She shrank from his scrutiny. Could he see those marks?

After a short silence, he drew his hand away and lay back on the pillow.

'Alas, Madam,' he murmured, 'it seems I have indeed partaken of too much wine, and it has made me sleepy. I will come to you again another night.'

He had not been sleepy a minute before. 'Have I offended your Grace?' Anna whispered, in terror.

'How could you have offended me?' he asked, his eyes glinting in the firelight. She feared his words had more than one meaning.

'All I want to do is please you,' she said.

He got stiffly out of bed and reached for his robe. 'I know that,' he said. 'If you would please me, Anna, then go to sleep. Good night.'

He fastened the robe and crossed to the door. It closed silently behind him.

He had guessed, she was sure of it. Yet he had not said anything. Probably he had been too shocked. No one would expect a princess such as she to be concealing so dark a secret. Was Henry thinking he had been sold a bad bargain, duped and made a fool of? She had sensed he had chosen his words with care. He had not known how to react, or what to say or do. But he would when he had slept on the matter. She did not for a moment think she had got away with it.

In the morning, she woke early. It was as if a pall lay over her. She turned on her back, lying rigid, expecting to hear at any moment the sound of the King's guard coming for her.

Mother Lowe bustled in at seven o'clock. 'Good morning to your Grace,' she said, drawing back the curtains. She smiled at Anna. 'Are you going to tell me? Was all well?'

'No,' Anna whispered, tears streaming down her face. 'He guessed. I know he did! He touched me, and looked . . . Then he stopped and said he was tired. And he left me. Oh, dear God, what is to become of me?'

Mother Lowe sat on the bed and took Anna in her arms. 'Hush, sweeting. This does not come as a surprise to me. His leaving at that point may not betoken what you think.'

'What do you mean?' Anna struggled to sit up.

'Last night, after you had been put to bed, Susanna and I sat up, and

158

a few of the English ladies were disposed to be friendly. We had some wine, and Lady Rochford got rather merry. She told us the King lacks vigour; he can be useless with a woman.'

'She said that? How can she know?'

'Her late husband was brother to Queen Anne.'

Anna made the connection. '*He* was the one executed for incest with her.'

Mother Lowe pursed her lips. 'The Duchess of Richmond told me afterwards, in confidence, that Lady Rochford laid evidence against them.'

'Why would she do that?' Anna was so appalled, she had almost forgotten her own predicament.

'Maybe she was jealous of the love between brother and sister.'

'What love? An incestuous love?'

'Who knows? Most people here won't talk about what happened. All Lady Rochford said was that Queen Anne had told her the King was impotent.'

'But he got a son on Queen Jane.'

'Anna, I was not married long before I lost my husband, but it was long enough for me to understand that men's lust is subject to their health and their moods. It can be unpredictable.'

Anna felt a sense of relief seeping through her veins. How humiliating for a man as powerful as the King to suffer impotence. Perhaps he had been dreading this marriage as much as she! And yet, he had been aroused – she had felt it. Was it the sight of her body that had unmanned him?

'He did desire me, I know,' she said, feeling her face flush. 'But when he had touched me, and looked at me, he stopped, and said he had drunk too much.'

'There you are,' Mother Lowe said, nodding. 'Drink can do that to a man, especially one in his state of health. His leg gives him much pain, it's clear to see. That isn't conducive to lust. Anna, you must be patient. Act as if nothing is amiss. Play the innocent. And be grateful you are not expected to show yourself in the court today. Now dry your eyes, and when you have had time to calm yourself, I will summon your women to help you dress. We cannot have them seeing you like this. Imagine the gossip!'

Anna lay there, trying to still her thumping heart. Maybe the King's behaviour did have nothing to do with her. If he was incapable, so be it; she would be spared his embraces. But she would be barren – and blamed for it, no doubt. There could be grave implications for the succession, and it would be a great grief to her not to bear more children to replace the one lost to her; but it would be better than being publicly shamed.

She forced herself to rise and suffer the ministrations of her attendants, wondering if the King would come to see her. She hoped he would remember the custom of *Brautstückes*; it would be in keeping with his thoughtfulness towards her. But, though she looked for him, or for a messenger bearing gifts, no one came.

She sat in her privy chamber, trying to concentrate on copying the *Kreuzstich* in an embroidery pattern book she had brought from Kleve. She had last used the book in Düsseldorf, and memories of her homeland and everything and everyone she had loved and lost overwhelmed her. A tear dripped on the linen in her lap.

This would not do! She was supposed to be a happy bride. No one must know that anything was wrong. She had to do something to divert herself. She asked Susanna and Margaret Douglas if they would join her for a walk in her privy garden. Cheerfully, they wrapped themselves in their furs, pulled on their gloves and stepped with her into the secluded, frosted little pleasance. They walked past flower beds laid out in neat rectangles, with low railings surrounding them and striped poles supporting heraldic beasts at each corner. They strolled along the paths between, talking of the wedding and yesterday's grand festivities. Anna took care to display appropriate enthusiasm and appreciation.

The King did not come that day, or at night either. At dinner time, his waiter arrived, to wish Anna, on his behalf, an enjoyable repast.

'He will come daily, Madam,' the Duchess of Suffolk explained. 'It is the King's custom to send him.'

Anna did not know whether to be relieved or fearful when Henry did not come to her bed. Grateful to be alone, she summoned Susanna to sleep on the pallet.

'I like the Lady Margaret,' she said. 'I wonder that she is as yet unwed. Surely she is a valuable prize for any man?'

'Madam, she fell in love with Lord Thomas Howard, the Duke of Norfolk's younger brother,' Susanna told her. 'They secretly precontracted themselves, which was foolhardy, for the Lady Margaret is the King's own niece, and her marriage was in his gift. They were sent to the Tower for it – a fine scandal it was – and condemned to death.'

Anna's hand flew to her mouth. Henry had condemned his own niece to death? The pretty, vital, charming Lady Margaret!

'They were spared,' Susanna went on, 'but held in prison for many months. In the end, the Lady Margaret was released, but Lord Thomas became ill and died. She was in great grief, and went to live with the Duchess of Richmond at Norfolk's palace at Kenninghall for a long time after. She only returned to court to serve you. She loved Lord Thomas truly, and I think she still mourns him.'

'What a tragic story,' Anna observed, with feeling. It made her own troubles seem trivial.

When they had doused the candles, she lay wakeful and sad, thinking she would never now know the kind of enduring love Margaret Douglas had experienced, and that, if the King could condemn his own flesh and blood to death, not to mention a wife he had once adored, what might he not do to one who had transgressed as she herself had?

The next day, her period of seclusion at an end, Anna walked in Greenwich Park, taking only Susanna and her English ladies with her. Already, she could sense some resentment at the favour she showed to her German attendants, and towards Mother Lowe in particular. She knew she must not let her household remain divided; if she did, factions would form, which could lead to unpleasantness and rivalry.

At the top of the hill behind the palace, near an old abandoned tower, she encountered four young gentlemen of her retinue, out hawking on horseback. She recognised Florence de Diaceto, Franz von Waldeck, and Hermann, Count von Neuenahr. The fourth was Otho von Wylich, clad in black velvet and looking very gallant on his fine steed. They all bowed in the saddle to her.

Her eyes met Otho's. How beautiful he was, with his blue eyes, high cheekbones and tousled curls. He gave her an engaging smile, and she felt a faint throb of desire. How she envied his wife.

Pleasantries were exchanged. Anna found herself wanting to confide her troubles to Otho. It would be madness, she knew, but she felt he would understand. He was her kinsman, after all. Yet it was unthinkable. She could not – dared not – see him, or any man, alone. So she smiled at all four gentlemen, and walked on.

Henry came to Anna's bed that night, having sent notice by an usher of the time of his arrival. He entered through the connecting door, smiling, although those shrewd eyes were regarding her appraisingly. Thankfully he did not look angry with her.

'Good evening, Anna,' he said, casting off his night robe.

'Good evening, your Grace,' she replied, hoping she looked pleased to see him, and grateful that she had learned a little more English. She had been practising hard; sleeping with him without being able to talk to him made her feel greatly at a disadvantage.

'There is no need for ceremony in our chamber,' he told her. 'You may call me Henry.'

'Thank you, your . . . Henry,' she said, and smiled.

'I'm holding a tournament next week, in honour of our marriage,' he told her, as he divested himself of his nightgown. He sounded more enthusiastic than Anna had ever heard him.

It seemed strange that no other festivities had been planned. She remembered that, when Sybilla wed, the wedding celebrations had gone on for days. Surely they would be even more lavish when a king married a foreign princess? Maybe this King considered her costly welcome in Calais and her reception at Blackheath sufficient to mark their nuptials.

She remembered Mutter telling her that Henry was planning to honeymoon with her at St James's Palace, but there had been no word of them removing there. It was so frustrating, being isolated from what was going on behind the closed doors of the King's apartments and the council chamber! If only she knew what was in Henry's mind.

He blew out the candle by the bed and turned to her. This time, there was no divesting her of her night-rail. 'Come here,' he said, and pulled her to him. Then he heaved himself on top of her, pressing her deep into the mattress. He was so heavy that she could barely breathe. She opened her legs to accommodate him, and waited for him to enter her. But she could feel that nothing was happening. After a few unbearable moments, in which she feared she might suffocate, he rolled off her, panting.

'I cannot, Anna,' he said. 'I am sorry.' He gestured at his leg. 'I am in constant pain, and it is worse tonight. Forgive me.'

She understood what he was trying to tell her. The faint, sickly stench had made it clear. 'Sir – Henry – there is nothing to forgive,' she protested. 'I am sorry for your pain. Can I help?'

'That is kind, but my doctors have tried everything. Maybe tomorrow it will be better. Let us sleep now.' He made himself comfortable in the bed. Evidently he was not going back to his apartments tonight.

'I do hope so,' she said. 'Good night, Henry.'

'Good night, sweetheart,' he said, and dropped a kiss on her forehead. The endearment threw her, it was so utterly unexpected. It was as Mother Lowe had said: things would be different after they were wed, and tonight, the kindness they had shown each other had broken the ice. There had, in the end, been no need for artifice. Henry had revealed himself to her in all his vulnerability, and she had shown herself willing to help. He had clearly liked that.

In the morning, she feared she might have read the situation incorrectly, but no.

'Good morning, Anna,' he said, when he awoke. 'What hour is it?'

She looked at the clock on the mantel. '*Sieben* – seven,' she said.

'Is it? Then I must go. I have ambassadors to see.' He slid from the bed, wincing as he limped across the room, and picked up his robe. Putting it on, he came back to the bed, took Anna's hand and kissed it.

'Farewell, darling,' he said. 'I will see you tonight.'

* * *

The next night, things were no better, nor were they on the night after that. Mother Lowe had been right. The King was impotent.

When he joined Anna on the fifth night, he did not even attempt to enter her. They lay there, making halting conversation, until Henry got up and invited her to play cards with him.

'Sent, *ja?*' she asked.

'Yes, if you wish,' he agreed.

'You play well, Anna,' he said, after beating her at the first game. 'Now I will teach you Primero.'

She found herself enjoying his company, and suspected he liked hers too. He was doing his best to put her at her ease and help her to understand what he said. He had even asked her to teach him a few words in German. It was one o'clock before they fell asleep.

Henry returned the next night, and the one after that, and then again, after a gap of one night. A pattern was being established. He had apparently given up all pretence of trying to consummate the marriage, for he made no move to touch her. Instead they played cards or chess, or slept. Anna's fears were beginning to recede.

She was still aware of her shortcomings. The language barrier did not make for the intimacy and easy conversation that might have awakened deeper feelings between them. She had no idea how to charm a man. She could not entertain Henry with music or dancing because she did not know how. All she could do was offer him a warm welcome and show her pleasure in his company. But was that enough?

Chapter 11

1540

Anna had been married less than a week when Lord Cromwell craved an audience. She was wary of him, aware that he knew the King's mind and might say things she would not want to hear. He had great power, which he might use to her benefit or detriment, and although she had offered him friendship, she did not know if it was reciprocated.

She sat beneath her canopy of estate to receive him. She felt more confident asserting her rank.

'Your Grace,' he said, kissing her hand. When he rose from his bow, his eyes were impassive, giving nothing away. 'I come on a delicate matter.'

Her heart missed a beat. Had the King complained of her lack of virginity? Please God it was not that!

'His Majesty does not wish to offend you, Madam, but he wishes you to cease wearing German dress. You are queen of England, and he would like you to wear English attire.'

And she had feared she was about to be sent to the Tower!

She had with her the English gowns Meister Wilkinson had made for her, most of them unworn because, even at this distance, Mutter's disapproval was a powerful deterrent. She thought of all the rich German clothes Mutter had caused to be made for her – all that labour and expense gone to waste. What rankled most was that Henry hadn't raised the matter himself, but had sent Cromwell. So much for their friendship! She dared not meet the eyes of Susanna, who was translating for them.

'My lord, as ever, I am ready to comply with his Majesty's wishes,' she told Cromwell, 'but my German clothes are worth a princely sum.'

'Madam, you may send for your tailor at any time. The King will defray the cost of altering them to such fashions as will be to his comfort.'

'Please thank his Majesty for me, since he has preferred to broach this matter through your lordship.' Cromwell gave her a sharp look, which she chose to ignore. 'And what of the attire of my German ladies?'

'They would be well advised to adopt English dress too, as I'm sure you will appreciate.'

'Of course,' she said, standing up. 'Was there anything else, my lord?'

Cromwell bowed himself out. Anna looked at her ladies, conscious that she had been wrong-footed in front of them. Cromwell had made her feel she had given offence, when Mutter's intention had been to send her to England as richly attired as was fitting for the honour, not only of Kleve, but also of King Henry.

'Lord Cromwell said as much to us too, Madam, only this morning, when you were walking in the gardens,' Susanna said. 'He told us to use all pleasantness to induce you to wear English fashions.'

'He should have spoken to me first!' Anna fumed. *As should Henry!*

She hastened to her wardrobe. With an outraged Mother Lowe at her elbow, and some maids standing behind, she dragged out one gown after another, in increasing dismay. It did not help that the English ladies were staring at them with disdain.

'It will take a lot of work to alter these,' Anna moaned. 'And they have no trains. I don't know where to begin.'

'Madam,' said Margaret Douglas, 'you have English gowns already. These can be altered at leisure.'

Anna tried not to cry. All the care her mother had taken for her – all set at naught. And yet another link with Kleve broken.

Resolutely, she straightened up. 'Summon the tailor,' she commanded.

She wore one of the English gowns for the tournament, with a halo-like French hood of the kind that was so popular at court that it was now considered an English fashion. Her ladies told her she looked most becoming, but she felt half naked in the low, square-cut bodice, with her hair uncovered. It was gratifying, however, to see the approval in Henry's face as he escorted her to the royal stand, and to bask in the admiring looks of the spectators. Even Cromwell complimented her.

She felt she was settling into queenship with dignity. She was growing more proficient in English. She dutifully observed all the rites of the Church of England. She was discovering that English gowns were more comfortable to wear than German ones, although the trains took some getting used to. She ordered several more in black satin or damask, so that she could show off the jewels Henry gave her to greater effect. He might have forgotten about the *Brautstückes*, but he had arrived to sup one evening with a handsome brooch and matching pendant designed by Holbein himself, and fashioned with the entwined initials H and A.

During a lull in the jousts, she asked Henry if she might spend some of her income on jewellery.

'Yes, of course,' he said. 'You may do as you please.'

He sent his goldsmith to her that afternoon, with a selection of pieces for her inspection.

'Of course, your Grace can commission a jewel, if you wish,' Master Hayes told her. Anna looked at the exquisite selection spread out before her.

'I need look no further,' she said. 'That one is gorgeous.' She pointed to a diamond brooch inset with miniature scenes.

'They tell the story of Samson, Madam,' the goldsmith said.

It was very costly, but she bought it.

Her presence in a court that had not seen a queen for over two years made her the object of great interest, and many nobles and gentlemen were already frequenting her apartments, all seeming to want something from her.

'How will I know who to favour, and who to avoid?' she asked Dr Olisleger, on the afternoon after the tournament. 'I know nothing about any of them.'

'They seek your patronage, Madam,' he told her. 'They hope you will convey their requests to the King, and say a word in their favour. Some lords get rich by charging for their intercession, or calling in favours. It is how courts work.'

'But I have no idea of the King's preferences in these matters. I fear many are going to be very disappointed in me.'

'It is best not to get involved, Madam, until you know this King and his court better.'

Over the next few days, Anna noticed people staring at her with ill-concealed curiosity, one or two even smirking, or talking behind their hands.

It was Susanna who enlightened her. She came back to the privy chamber one evening, her gentle features flushed.

'Oh, Madam,' she said, sinking to her knees before an astonished Anna. 'I hardly know how to tell you what people are saying in the court, but you should know. I only wish I wasn't the one to have to tell you.'

'*What are* they saying?' Anna cried in alarm.

Susanna swallowed. 'They are saying – forgive me, Madam – that the King has said he will never have any more children for the comfort of the realm, for, although he is able to do the act of procreation with others, he cannot do it with you. Some whisper he is impotent, but most of those I overheard think the fault lies with your Grace.'

Fury rose in Anna. 'It lies with him!' she cried, unable to stop herself. 'I had resolved never to speak to anyone of his inability to consummate our marriage, yet now, it appears, he has blazoned it to all, *and* laid the blame at my feet. And he thinks himself a man of honour! How dare he make me the scapegoat for his own inadequacy!'

Susanna was staring at her, speechless. 'Madam, I had no idea—'

But the dam in Anna had burst. 'No wonder people have been staring at me! Are they wondering what horrors are concealed under my royal robes, and what is so awful about me that the King cannot bring himself to make love to me? It is horrible, and utterly humiliating! How will I ever show my face outside my apartments again?'

'Madam, please calm yourself—'

'How can I? Something must be done to stop this scurrilous talk!' Anna paused, dizzy with indignation, and strove to regain control of herself.

There was one man who had the power and the means to stop it.

'Send for Lord Cromwell,' she commanded. 'Say I would see him alone, at once.'

Back came the messenger. His lordship craved her forbearance, but he was busy with matters of state. He would obey her summons as soon as he could.

When Henry came to her bed that night, she could barely bring herself to be civil to him. If it had been any lesser man, she would have raged and let him have a goodly piece of her mind. But, always, she was aware that the King must not be offended. Of course, it did not matter that *she* had been offended!

He dealt out the cards, then paused. 'What is wrong, Anna?'

She did not have sufficient English to go into detail. 'People are talking,' she said at length. 'About us. They know we do not . . .'

He had the grace to look uncomfortable. His fair skin reddened.

'They think I am not good,' she went on. 'That you do not like me. It makes me very unhappy. How do they know these things?' She looked him directly in the eye.

'It is mere gossip,' he said. 'The court is full of it. Just ignore it.'

'It is said you say you can do the act with others, but not me,' she countered. 'But where do they hear it from?' She was determined to pin him down.

'Anna, what is this?' he blustered. 'Do you presume to interrogate me?'

'Tell me you did not say those things!' she cried.

'Of course I did not!' he barked. 'Enough!' He would not look at her. She thought he was lying.

He rose, flinging down his cards. 'I think I will go and find more congenial company,' he muttered. 'I bid you good night, Madam.' And he was gone, stamping out of the door.

* * *

When morning came, Anna woke feeling miserable and anxious. It had been foolhardy to anger the King. Upset with him as she was, she would apologise at the first opportunity.

She hoped Cromwell would come soon, then she could explain how wronged she felt. He would know the truth of it, and how to approach Henry. She waited and waited, but still he did not appear. Anger and frustration mounted in her at the realisation that he might be avoiding her. If she had offended the King, or he considered the catastrophe of their private life her fault, it was only natural that Cromwell would not dare engage in a confrontation with her. He would be falling over backwards to distance himself from her. He would not want to be blamed for the failure of her marriage, or be seen to be supporting her.

She was still in turmoil when her chamberlain presented himself in her privy chamber, looking uncharacteristically awkward.

'Yes, my lord?' she invited.

'Your Grace,' Rutland said, 'my Lord Cromwell has asked me to speak with you on a personal matter. He has your interests at heart and desires to see you and his Majesty happy and contented. He advises you to conduct yourself pleasantly in your behaviour towards the King.'

Anna was speechless. She feared she might explode in fury. Henry had gone running to Cromwell to complain of her, as if this vile business was all her fault. And it followed that the problems in their marriage were her fault too.

The Earl was regarding her with sympathy. 'I think there has been some misunderstanding, Madam, which the King has taken amiss. If I may be so bold, I have observed how you conduct yourself towards him, and I can honestly say that no one could find fault with it.'

At his kindness, tears threatened. He was Henry's cousin, and close to him. He would not criticise him, yet he had opened up a way forward, a means to restore the fragile equilibrium between her and the King. *It had been a misunderstanding.*

'I fear I spoke out of turn to his Majesty last night,' she confessed. 'I was upset after Susanna reported some idle talk to me that she, quite rightly, thought I should hear. My English is poor, and his Grace took my words to mean that I was accusing him of being the source of it. He left before I could explain or apologise.'

'I am sure his Grace will accept your apology,' Rutland reassured her. He paused. 'I am aware of the gossip, Madam. Having had long experience of serving at court, I have learned to ignore idle chatter. I counsel your Grace to do the same.'

'I will do as you advise,' Anna replied, forcing herself to smile. 'Would you kindly ask his Grace if he will visit me this evening?'

'Of course, Madam.' The chamberlain bowed and left.

Henry came. She guessed Rutland had handled things well, for her husband was in a congenial mood and waved away her apologies. Maybe he was feeling guilty about causing her so much upset – if, indeed, he had caused it.

He ordered supper to be served in the Queen's privy chamber with only Susanna in attendance, and told Anna he had appointed a secretary for her. 'William Paget is a good man, sound and dependable, and clever with money too. He's been serving as clerk to the Privy Council.' He groaned. 'And Lady Lisle has been pestering me to place her daughter Katherine in your household. That woman never knows when to stop. She even sent me marmalade, to sweeten me, and got Dr Olisleger to speak for her.'

'It is all my fault,' Anna told him. 'I asked him to, not knowing your pleasure in the matter. Sir, for my part, I would tell her that, however earnestly Dr Olisleger has prayed your Grace that an extra gentlewoman might be taken on, it is not possible. The ladies and gentlewomen of my chamber were appointed before my coming here, and, for now, patience must be had.'

'Indeed!' Henry nodded approvingly.

His pleasant mood evaporated when Lady Rutland approached him after supper. 'Sir, Lady Lisle has asked me to persuade your Grace to appoint her daughter as one of the Queen's maids. You should know she has sent me inducements – barrels of wine and herring.'

'Bribes, Madam!' Henry roared. 'Tell her ladyship the King does not wish more maids to be taken on until some of those now with the Queen are preferred to other posts.'

Lady Rutland bowed her head. 'Of course, Sir.'

'Tell her to apply to Mother Lowe,' Anna said. 'Tell her she can do as much good in this matter as anyone here. That will be the end of it!'

That had Henry chuckling, his good humour restored. 'By God, Anna, you would make Machiavelli blush! We should have you on the Council.'

Two days later, he arrived to supper in a testy humour. 'You had best watch that wench Anne Bassett,' he grumbled. 'She waylaid me this afternoon, when I was about to take my turn at the butts. She asked me to remember her sister.'

'I will speak to her,' Anna said.

'No need,' he sniffed. 'I told her many had spoken to me on her sister's behalf, but I will not grant a place, as I intend to have young ladies who are fair and meet for the honour. That silenced her!'

'Mother Lowe received a large bribe from Lady Lisle today,' Anna revealed. 'She has written back in the firmest terms to say your Grace has decreed there shall be no new maids appointed unless one leaves to get married.'

'Quite so,' Henry said, then his tone changed. 'Anna, I must raise with you the matter of your countrymen. Baron von Oberstein, Dr Olisleger, Grand Master Hochsteden and many others of your escort are to return to Cleves in a few days, as planned.' She had known that, and was dreading it, for it would be the breaking of more ties with home. She would have liked to correct Henry on his pronunciation of Kleve, but did not dare. Most English people called it Cleves, to rhyme with 'sleeves', rather than Kleve, to rhyme with 'waver'. In time, perhaps, she would herself.

'But,' Henry was saying, 'I am retaining the Count of Waldeck and many other of your German gentlemen and damsels, until you are better acquainted with this realm.' Again, there was that kindness in him, which had rarely been in evidence since they married.

'I am most grateful to your Grace,' she told him, deeply touched and relieved. When he behaved like this, she could forgive him a lot.

In the third week of January, the King hosted a feast in his presence chamber for the departing lords and dignitaries, which was attended by Anna and many nobles. Cromwell was there – Cromwell who had been conspicuous by his failure to attend Anna's summons. But never mind that now.

'We have been greatly honoured,' Dr Olisleger said, seated at Anna's right hand, 'and so I will tell the Duke your brother on my return. The King has been most generous. Truly, I think you have been very fortunately bestowed in marriage.'

Anna looked into the wise, weathered face of this loyal counsellor who had done so much to make her a queen, and saw there no irony. Olisleger did not know what was lacking in her marriage. She thought of Wilhelm, and how much store he set by the alliance, and how he needed England's friendship to bolster him against the ambitions of the Emperor. No, she would not burden either of them with the truth. Anyway, despite herself, she was growing to like the King more; daily, she prayed that the problem that lay like an invisible sword between them would be resolved, and that she would be able to bear him children, and so make herself beloved by him and his subjects.

To her joy, Henry said she might keep Mother Lowe, and her favourite German maids, Katharina and Gertrude, and more than twenty other of her compatriots. Her English ladies were still loath to befriend her German ones; she was beginning to learn that the English distrusted all foreigners, or strangers, as they called them. They looked askance at the Germans' clothes and mimicked their guttural accents. Anna suspected that some of her maids, including Anastasia, were homesick and glad to leave, but the strong-willed and vivacious Katharina and the gentle and devout Gertrude were content to remain. Both were devoted to Anna, and to Mother Lowe, who treated them like her own granddaughters.

Anna was pleased that her fourteen-year-old cousin, Franz von Waldeck, was to remain as her page, and that Otho von Wylich, his wife, Hanna, Florence de Diaceto, the Brockhausens, Dr Cepher and her cook, Schoulenburg, had been given leave to stay too. Her household now constituted a great court. No queen, she thought, had ever been so well attended.

She was not so delighted that her stiff-necked receiver general, Wymond Carew, was to replace Dr Olisleger as her official interpreter, although Susanna Gilman would continue to act for her in that capacity in private. She had disliked Carew's manner on sight. This big-set man with his calculating eyes and long, bushy beard was too correct, too aloof, too intimidating – but apparently a brilliant administrator. She must try to get on with him, as was her duty. She smiled with genuine pleasure when he told her that he had been charged by the King to purchase gifts and rewards for all those returning to Germany. She had offered to advise him on what to choose, only to be rebuffed, politely yet firmly. But today, as she stood in her presence chamber waiting to bid farewell to her people, she had to concede that he had done her proud. The lords and ambassadors of Kleve and Saxony were greatly impressed with their rich gifts of money and plate. The cost of such presents must have been immense!

It was time to say goodbye. As she stood on the dais, her eyes lingered on all those who must now depart, looking fondly on Dr Olisleger, Grand Master Hochsteden, Baron von Oberstein and Franz Burchard, good men all, who had served her and hers loyally; and she feared that her grief might burst forth uncontrollably. Yet the King's wife must maintain her composure. The impression they would take back with them to Kleve was of a queen who was serene and happy in her exalted station.

One by one, they came forward to take their leave. As Dr Olisleger bent to kiss her hand, she was almost overcome. 'May God go with you, dear friend,' she said. 'I owe you so much.'

'May He watch over your Grace,' he replied, looking a little emotional himself, 'and bring you the greatest good fortune.'

Watching the procession of her countrymen passing out through the great doors, Anna was seized with the need to ensure that her family would not worry about her. She hoped that no one leaving here today had heard those horrible rumours, but if they had, and repeated them in Kleve, she was determined to give the lie to them.

When Lady Keteler came up to say farewell, Anna detained her. 'My lady,' she said, 'I ask you to say to the Duchess, my mother, and the Duke, my brother, that I thank them most heartily for having preferred me to such a marriage that I could wish for no better. No other would content me so well.'

'I will tell them, Madam,' Lady Keteler promised. Then she too was gone.

Anna was in her bedchamber, writing reassuring letters to her mother and brother, for Dr Wotton to take with him when he returned to Kleve, and Susanna was making up the fire, when the King was announced. They had been married for three weeks now, and still he had not made her his. She supposed that this night would be like all the others. He would come to her bed, lie beside her, trying to make conversation for a while, then fall to snoring or suggest a game of cards. He was always pleasant and courteous, but he made no move to touch her.

Tonight, he was in a good mood. 'I have sent for the Prince, Anna, to come to court to meet his new stepmother.'

'*Ach*, I am so pleased!' Anna exclaimed. 'I have wanted so much to meet your children.'

'You will meet Mary and Elizabeth soon. Mary has been unwell, but is much amended, praised be God. Edward is in excellent health, which is a great comfort to me. He is a most forward child, as you will find.'

Anna laid down her quill. She was already in her night robe. Susanna doused the candles and left, as the King sank heavily into bed. Presently, when she had sealed her letters, Anna joined him. Maybe it was the remembrance that he had only one son, who could be struck down any day by some childish ailment, that made him reach for her. Tonight, she prayed, she might become a wife in truth.

But no. As Henry held and kissed her, it was clear that nothing would happen. Soon, he gave a little sigh and released her. They lay there, silent, in the firelight.

'I like you, Anna,' Henry said at length. 'I like you very much, but it seems God does not intend that I should love you.'

'There are more ways than one of loving,' she whispered.

'Yes, but a king needs heirs, and my mind will not be stirred to do what gets them.'

'Are you ill, Henry?' she ventured.

'My leg gives me much pain,' he admitted.

'Can it be made better?'

'The doctors do their best. I am sorry, Anna.'

'I am sorry for your suffering.' Her hand reached for his. She was still holding it when they fell asleep.

The Prince was very fair, blonde-haired and solemn-faced, with grave blue eyes, chubby cheeks and a pointed chin. Anna's heart turned over, for he reminded her so much of Johann. Not yet two and a half years old, he swept off his feathered bonnet, made a perfect bow before the assembled court, then toddled from his governess and knelt before his father.

'Edward, my son!' Henry cried, lifting him up and kissing him. 'Anna, this is England's greatest jewel. Edward, greet your new step-mother.'

He set the child down, and Edward bowed to Anna, then looked up, regarding her in an almost imperious manner. Anna would have liked to draw him on to her knee, but did not feel she could. This was no ordinary child. This little boy had been worshipped and deferred to from birth, as the precious heir to a great prince, and already, it appeared, he was conscious of it. So she curtseyed to him, wishing that his eyes were not so cold. Maybe, like many young children, he was shy at first with newcomers – but she doubted it. This was a king in the making.

'And here is the redoubtable Lady Bryan,' Henry announced, presenting the Prince's governess to Anna. Lady Bryan was getting on in years, but gave the impression of being capable and dedicated. As Henry questioned her about his son's progress, Anna tried to make headway with the little boy, who stood in his long skirts of red damask, looking impassively at the sumptuous decoration of his father's privy chamber.

Anna held out a ball she had bought for him, a pretty thing, gaily painted, the kind of toy she would dearly have loved to give her own son.

Edward took it as if it were his due. 'Thank you, my lady,' he said formally. She wondered if he knew what to do with it, so she showed him how to bounce it before tossing it gently back to him. He dropped it, of course, for he was too young to catch it with dexterity, but then picked it up and threw it back. Soon, he was laughing, especially when Anna missed the ball. She made a big show of pretending not to see where it had rolled.

'There! There!' he cried, pointing, just like any normal child. Poor little boy. He had never known his mother, and his father, with his great height, and his bulk clad in velvet and furs, must seem an awesome figure in the eyes of a small child. Anna hoped she could play a mother's part to Edward. It would do her as much good as it would him.

The King and his courtiers were watching them. 'Go on, Edward, catch it!' Henry encouraged. The Prince eyed him warily. Henry bent down, taking his turn with the ball, and Edward chuckled with delight.

'Do you ride on the hobby horse I gave you?' his father asked.

'Yes, Sir,' the boy lisped.

'Good, good,' Henry beamed. 'Soon, you will have a real pony to ride. You will like that, won't you?'

Edward looked dubious. Horses, like kings, were clearly daunting to him.

'And then we will teach you swordsmanship!' Henry was running away with himself. The child was two! And yet, Anna thought, gazing at them together, perhaps the King had reason to want his heir to grow up quickly. Anyone with eyes to look could see he was ailing and might not live long enough to watch his son grow to adulthood. Maybe he himself was aware of it.

When Edward tired of the game, the King sat down, with his son on a stool at his feet, and called for music. Music was one of the joys of this court. Already, Anna had engaged some musicians, and they had been summoned to play today, so that Henry could hear for himself how well they performed.

'Bravo!' he cried, as they struck up a *ronde*, which, at his nod, had the courtiers up and dancing. The Prince sat staring at them. Henry leaned across to Anna. 'My Lord Cromwell tells me there are accomplished Jewish musicians in Venice who are hiding from the Inquisition. I am of a mind to offer them asylum in England. They are skilled recorder players. Will you take them into your household, Anna?'

'Willingly, Sir,' she smiled, marvelling again at the kindness in him.

Anna was becoming used to the English way of doing things. Her life was settling into a pattern. She spent much of it sitting in her privy chamber, plying her needle, or gambling with cards or dice with her ladies and gentlemen. The best games were those she played with Otho, for then she could legitimately enjoy his company. Sometimes she summoned entertainers to divert her attendants, like Will Somers, the King's fool, whose droll jests drew much laughter, or the acrobat who had them all gaping at his triple somersaults. Hanna von Wylich, who acted as an occasional lady-in-waiting, gave her a parrot, which drew much attention with its exotic plumage, and amusement when it repeated things it was not supposed to say. There was a heart-stopping moment when the King was visiting, and suddenly, from the gold cage hanging by the window, there came a cackle, 'Harry's a bad boy!'

Anna felt herself go crimson as Henry jerked his head around, then roared with laughter.

'Forgive me, your Grace!' she cried. 'The parrot is called Harry, in your honour. We tell him he's a bad boy when he bites us.'

Henry grinned. 'At least I don't bite!' The ladies all giggled.

Anna still devoted time to mastering English. She could make herself understood, in broken sentences and with gestures, and hold a stilted conversation, but was by no means fluent. It was as well that she was living quietly, for it gave her a chance to become more proficient before she must play a larger public role. Next month, she would be crowned, then spring would come, and with it Easter and the great court festivals of which her ladies had spoken. Her English must be more polished by then!

Henry was patient with her. He took the time to understand her, especially when she searched in her mind for words. Gradually, her vocabulary grew. Growing too was her concern that the time for her coronation was approaching and so far no word had been said about it, or preparations made. She reminded herself that the late Queen had never been crowned.

At the end of January, the King came to sup with her, which he had taken to doing two or three times a week. He was in an ebullient mood.

'The Emperor is falling out with the King of France!' he announced gleefully. 'I always said they would make sorry bedfellows. They have both begun suing for my friendship. Not many months ago, they were uniting to make war on me!'

Anna smiled brightly, but her mind raced, thinking of the possible consequences if Henry made a pact with either ruler.

'The Emperor especially is showing himself interested in renewing our friendship,' Henry went on. 'Charles was so sanctimonious about my being excommunicated, but now, evidently, it doesn't matter, so long as I side with him against that fox François! My dear, this places me in a very strong position indeed!'

Anna was not skilled in politics, but she knew that, if he concluded a new treaty with Charles, Henry would no longer need the alliance with Kleve.

She could not stay silent. 'Sir, you will stay a friend to Kleve, I pray? The Emperor is threatening Guelders.'

Henry raised his eyebrows. 'I did not know you were a politician, Madam! Well, well. Rest assured, I intend to remain a friend to your brother. An alliance with the Emperor is by no means a certainty, and if I decide on it, safeguards will be put in place. I dictate my own terms!'

He leaned back in his chair, downing his wine, well pleased with himself. 'Next week, you are to be officially welcomed to London,' he said.

She was to be crowned after all! Lady Rochford had said that kings and queens always went in procession through London before going to Westminster Abbey for their crowning. 'And there are pageants in the streets, and free wine runs in the conduits,' she'd told Anna.

'We will leave Greenwich by barge on Sunday next,' Henry was saying. 'Anna, wear an English gown.'

'Of course, Sir,' she agreed. 'I have had one made up in cloth of gold, which I will wear for my coronation.'

There was a pause.

'That is deferred until Whitsun,' Henry said, carving more roast beef. 'The weather will be better then.'

She bit back her disappointment, and the suspicion that something was wrong. It had persisted all the while she had known Henry. She had never been sure of him or fathomed what was really going on inside that kingly head. She would fret about it, then it would seem that all was going well until something – like this – gave her pause to wonder.

'Then I will keep the gown until then,' she said, forcing herself to smile.

Chapter 12

1540

Crowds lined the banks of the River Thames, all the way from Greenwich, to see Anna sail past in her barge.

'They are all wearing their best clothes, Madam,' Margaret Douglas observed. She, Mother Lowe, Susanna and the duchesses of Richmond and Suffolk were squeezed in beside the Queen in the luxuriously upholstered cabin – which the English called a state house – towards the back of the vessel. In front of them, eighteen oarsmen rowed in unison, speeding them towards Westminster.

Anna's barge was fourth in the magnificent flotilla of gaily bedecked boats. Immediately ahead was the vessel carrying the King's guard, and in front of that sailed Henry's own barge, with another carrying his household preceding it. She had expected that he and she would be together, side by side, as she made her entry into London, and had been disconcerted to discover that they would be travelling separately. It sparked another attack of the anxiety that had become a part of her life, but she made herself smile at the people and wave to them.

Banners and pennants whipped in the breeze. Behind Anna's barge came others containing her ladies and servants, the Mayor and aldermen, and all the London guilds, their boats richly decorated with shields and cloth of gold. After them, in a fleet of smaller barges, followed the nobility of England and the bishops. It seemed that every ship they passed shot a salute as they sailed by. The air was thick with gunpowder.

The Tower of London loomed ahead, standing sentinel on the edge of the City. Anna suppressed a shudder, remembering that Queen Anne had been imprisoned and beheaded there – and Sir Thomas More. Had

Anne shrunk in terror at the sight, knowing that she might never leave it?

Suddenly, as they neared the great fortress, the air was rent by the crack of guns as the cannon on the wharf shot off a thousand chambers of ordnance in salute. The noise was louder than thunder, and Anna clapped her hands over her ears.

Thankfully, the Tower was soon behind them, and now they were skimming the rapids under London Bridge. To Anna's right was the City of London itself, with great houses and gardens lining the shore, and numerous church spires rising behind. She could hear the bells pealing joyfully, and the cheers of the citizens crowded along the banks.

The boat rounded a bend in the river, and ahead lay Whitehall Palace and the great abbey of Westminster. The barge pulled in by Westminster Stairs, where the King was waiting for Anna. She alighted to rousing applause from the crowds, and curtseyed to her husband, who led her through a great gatehouse and so to the palace itself.

And that was it. No pageants, no procession through the City, no formal welcome by the Mayor. Maybe, Anna thought, as Henry brought her to her lodgings, that too had been deferred until her coronation. But it was not long till Whitsun: May was less than three months away. At least London's welcome had been warm.

She marvelled at the rich decor of Whitehall, the fine galleries, the glorious tapestries, the luxuriously appointed rooms. The palace was so large, and so rambling, that it would be easy to get lost in it. Her rooms overlooked the river and the privy garden below her windows. It felt exciting to be here, on the doorstep of London. She was seized with a sense of elation. Perhaps all would be well, after all, and she would be crowned before she knew it.

They had been at Whitehall for five days when Henry, kissing Anna farewell one morning, informed her that he would not be visiting her that night.

'It is Lent, Anna,' he explained. 'I must abstain from your bed.'

She nodded. 'Of course.' She realised they would not sleep together again until Easter, in six weeks' time. In some ways, she would miss

Henry's massive presence beside her at night. The intimacy of their shared bed had brought them closer in mind, if not in hearts or bodies.

She thought he looked a touch relieved, glad perhaps to be spared the nightly humiliation of lying with her to no effect. He had not tried to make her his since that embarrassing night at Greenwich. If she were honest, she too was feeling some relief, yet she was sad they had not consummated their marriage, and that the joy she had looked for had eluded her. By now, she had hoped to be carrying the King's son. Soon, she feared, people would begin to believe the rumours to be true.

When Henry had gone, she lay listlessly, already feeling lonely. She wondered if all devout couples refrained from loving each other during Lent. She could not imagine Otho von Wylich deserting the bed of his beloved Hanna for so long a time.

Her thoughts kept straying to Otho these days. Although they rarely spoke, and then only to exchange pleasantries, she could feel his eyes on her, encouraging, admiring. She wished he could know about their son. She felt guilty for deceiving him; morally, he had a right to know about his child – but she had to be pragmatic. She had striven to banish Johann to the inmost recesses of her mind. To think of him brought only pain, so she tried not to. Instead, she thought of Otho.

He was the only man she had ever truly desired, the man to whom she had given her virginity. She realised he would always be the one against whom she judged all others; beside him, the King was a sorry husband. Of course, there was more to marriage than physical love, but what would she not give for a night of pleasure such as Otho had given her? She was living on the memory now. It might be all of love she would ever know.

She could not bear to watch the tender way he treated his wife. Despite the kindness Henry often showed, his demeanour towards Anna was in glaring contrast to the way Otho treated Hanna, underpinned as it clearly was by a strong bond of love and intimacy. She tried not to hate Hanna, but it was hard.

She must not lie here and mope. She rose and called for her maids. As she splashed water on her face, she wondered if Dr Wotton had reached Kleve and given her letters to Mutter and Wilhelm. How she longed for news of them. She realised, with some alarm, that she could no longer quite remember Mutter's voice.

Early in March, they left Whitehall for Hampton Court. Anna had seen Greenwich and Whitehall, and thought them splendid, but she gasped at her first sight of the great red-brick palace as the barge carrying her and Henry glided around the bend in the river at Thames Ditton. Nestling on the banks of the Thames amidst vast acres of parkland, Hampton Court was magnificent!

They alighted at the watergate, and walked along a covered gallery with oriel windows, which brought them straight to the King's private apartments.

'I do not wish my subjects always to see what I am doing or where I am going,' Henry said. Anna had become aware that he was almost obsessive in guarding his privacy, and supposed it had everything to do with his fear of treason. From what she had heard, he had had to deal with treacherous plots and betrayals throughout his reign. Susanna had hinted – it was too dangerous to say such things outright – that there were those who considered they had a better claim to the throne.

It was as if he had read her thoughts. 'Never reveal your hand, Anna,' he advised. 'If I thought my cap knew my mind, I would throw it in the fire.' It was one of the most revealing things he had ever said to her.

The doors opened on to the most splendid apartments she had ever seen. They were panelled in oak, with moulded ceilings and rich friezes of *putti* and classical motifs. The walls shimmered with gold and silver, some from the glittering embroideries on hangings of cloth of gold and velvet embroidered with the royal arms. Exquisite heraldic glass sparkled in windows glazed with crystal. Anna walked on sumptuous carpets, thinking that Mutter would have had a fit – carpets were to be laid on tables, to preserve them!

Henry escorted her through his privy chamber, which had an alabaster fountain set into the wall. The door on the opposite wall opened, as if by magic, and they walked into the presence chamber, the guards lining the walls standing to attention.

'We call this the Paradise Chamber,' Henry said proudly. Struck with wonder, Anna could see why. Everything glittered with jewels and precious metals; the effect was dazzling. Persian tapestries hung on the walls, and there was a beautiful painted ceiling and a cloth-of-gold canopy above the throne on the dais.

She had never seen such rich apartments, but even these did not prepare her for the breathtaking magnificence of the Great Hall. Standing on the chequered floor tiled in green and white, she gazed at the impressive oak screen and the minstrels' gallery above, broad stained-glass windows, and vast stretches of wall hung with tapestries depicting, Henry told her, the story of Abraham, and glinting with gold and silver thread. Crowning all was a magnificent hammer-beam roof.

'So you like Hampton Court?' Henry was asking.

'It is wonderful, like a palace out of legend,' Anna breathed. She could not quite believe that all this splendour was hers to enjoy.

'Then you will like your apartments,' Henry said. He took her arm and escorted her back through his lodgings to his bedchamber. There, a door opened on to a privy gallery lined with religious paintings, mirrors and maps.

'The door at the far end leads to the Queen's apartments,' he said. Anna wondered how many of her predecessors had enjoyed them. She stepped into her bedchamber – and looked about her in awe.

'I had these rooms decorated in the antique style by a German craftsman, you will be pleased to hear,' Henry said. 'They were refurbished for you before your coming.' Anna looked up at the mirrors set into the ceilings, and at the intricate grotesque work on the walls. The bed boasted a wooden roundel newly painted with her arms.

The other chambers were just as luxuriously appointed. On one side, they overlooked a spacious courtyard with a cloister; on the other was the privy garden, with the park beyond. What Anna liked most was the wide balcony outside her windows.

'You and your ladies can watch the hunting in the park from there,' the King told her. 'Now, Madam, I will leave you to settle in. I will see you at supper.' He bowed and departed.

Anna's women were busily unpacking, so she beckoned Susanna and descended the private stair to the garden. There was a man working there, an old fellow with ruddy cheeks. He straightened when he saw her and touched his cap.

'This is a beautiful garden,' Anna said.

'Aye, lady. Laid out by her.'

'Her?'

'The Queen. She loved it here. We worked together on it. I be Chapman, head gardener. Dead now she is, but I still see her, with her fair face and her sweet smile.'

Anna and Susanna exchanged glances.

'You oughta see the other gardens, mistresses,' Chapman went on. 'You ain't never seen anything like 'em, and a lot of it's my doing. King Harry, he says to me, "I wants my box hedges crenellated", or "I wants topiary fashioned like a centaur" – and I did it all, much to his pleasure. You go have a look one day soon.'

'We will,' Anna promised, looking around. Flowers were coming into bud in the pale March sunlight, and there was a hint of spring in the air.

'You ladies with the new Queen?' Chapman asked, eyeing them curiously.

Susanna stifled a giggle.

'I am the new Queen,' Anna said, smiling.

The old gardener pulled off his cap and bowed, gawping. 'Beg pardon, your Grace. This be your garden now. You tell Chapman what you wants.'

'It's lovely as it is,' Anna told him. 'I want it to stay like this.'

He peered at her. 'As you command, your Grace. You're as fair as she was, you know – not like they said.'

'He's a little crazed,' Susanna murmured, as they strolled away along the gravelled paths between rectangular railed beds of lawn, bordered with flowers and sporting the ubiquitous green-and-white-striped posts bearing painted statues of the King's heraldic beasts.

'He was clearly devoted to Queen Jane,' Anna said.

'She was much liked,' Susanna told her. 'My brother Lucas painted her several times, all in miniature. Maybe he will paint your Grace one day?'

186

'I must ask him to,' Anna smiled.

'It is for your Grace to command!'

'These were Queen Jane's apartments?' Anna asked, looking up at the windows above her.

'They were meant to be, but she did not live to occupy them. The King wanted them altered after Queen Anne . . . Queen Jane used the old Queen's lodgings in the tower. That's where Prince Edward was born.'

'And where she died,' Anna supplied, glad she was not staying in those apartments.

'Yes. They laid her in state in the chapel. The Lady Mary and all the ladies kept vigil over her for days.'

'What did she die of? Was it a very terrible birth?'

'Her travail was prolonged, but she actually became ill a few days later. It was a terrible tragedy, for England, and for the Prince, of course.'

And a tragedy that there is no hope of the Prince having a brother, Anna thought. 'I mind to be a mother to him, poor little boy,' she declared.

The next morning, the King came to see her. She received him in her privy chamber, her ladies sinking into billowing skirts as they made their obeisances around her. Henry waved them away and eased himself into the chair by the fire.

'I've just received news from Cleves that will cheer you, Anna,' he said. 'Your brother is sending a resident ambassador to England.'

'That *is* good tidings, Sir!' she replied.

'Anna, he wants military aid against the Emperor.'

'Has he invaded Guelders?' she cried in alarm.

'No, although he threatens it. Your brother says you know the new ambassador. His name is Dr Karl Harst.'

'I do know him,' Anna said, pleased. 'He has served my father and brother as a councillor for many years, and been ambassador to the Emperor. He's a very learned man.'

'So Duke Wilhelm tells me. He says the good doctor has degrees from the universities of Heidelberg, Cologne, Orléans and Louvain. He is eminently fitted for the post of ambassador, being a doctor of law and a jurist, and having travelled in Italy. I look forward to talking with him. Does he speak English?'

'No, Sir, but he is fluent in Latin – and he was a personal friend of Erasmus.'

'Ha! Then I am most eager to greet him. You have met Erasmus, Anna?'

'Alas, no, but my father much admired and emulated him. You could say we have an Erasmian court in Kleve!'

'I met Erasmus once, when I was a child,' Henry recalled. 'He came to Eltham Palace.' His eyes filled suddenly with tears.

'Sir? What is wrong?' Anne was amazed to see him so emotional.

'It is nothing,' he muttered. 'I was just remembering how it felt to be young, with the world and the future before you, and all set to be fair. Erasmus brought Thomas More with him. I made More write something for me. He was the best man in my kingdom . . .' He sounded choked.

She did not know what to say.

'Dr Harst will be here soon,' Henry said, recovering himself. 'I mean to give him the kind of welcome I gave the ambassadors of Cleves last autumn. Anna, Dr Wotton has informed me that he presented your letters to the Duchess your mother and the Duke, at which they showed great joy. They were heartily glad to hear of your welfare, and afforded Wotton a most cordial welcome. He reports that they are in good health, and your sister too, you will be pleased to hear.'

'It is the most welcome news I could have received,' Anna told him, feeling near to tears herself at the memory of Mutter and Emily – and the child whose name must never be spoken. 'When does Dr Harst arrive?'

'Any day now. He left only just a little ahead of Wotton's letter.'

Anna began counting the hours. It would be wonderful to have more news of her family, and to keep abreast of what was happening in Kleve.

Two days later, the King came stumping into her chamber in a foul mood.

'Your ambassador is here!' he barked, as Anna and her attendants sank into hasty reverences. 'Out, out, ladies! I would talk with the Queen!' The women scattered.

'Sir, what is wrong?' Anna cried.

'Was I deceived?' Henry roared. 'Is Cleves so poor it cannot afford to equip its ambassador in a manner befitting his master's status? He arrived looking like some varlet, in an old black gown, with barely any servants. He should be presenting himself at my court splendidly dressed and attended by a retinue that reflects the magnificence of a duchy to which I have bound myself in alliance!'

Anna was perplexed, and indignant. 'Sir, Dr Harst is a good man. He cares little for courtly trappings, but his loyalty and wisdom are much respected in Kleve.'

'If he is so wise, Madam, why does he not know how to do honour to his country and to me?' the King growled.

'I am sure he means you no disrespect,' she countered.

'I'll not receive him! He'll get no fine welcome from me!' He turned, the colour high in his face, and, in an angry rustle of damask and silk, stalked out.

Anna stood there nonplussed. What should she do? If Dr Harst's mission was to succeed, he should be told how best to mollify the King. If need be, she herself would give him money for better attire and hiring servants.

'Summon the ambassador of Kleve,' she ordered an usher.

Smiling, Anna held out her hand to Dr Harst. Someone should make him feel welcome!

He looked presentable enough in his furred gown and velvet cap, but his swarthy, jowly face with its heavy brows and fleshy features was creased in concern.

'Your Grace, I did not look for such courtesy, after the King's chamberlain informed me he would not receive me.'

'Dr Harst, the King is angered that you did not come in sufficient state. But I can help with that.'

The ambassador looked uncomfortable. 'Madam, it is not my dress, or my lack of a retinue, that has offended his Majesty. No sooner had I arrived than Lord Cromwell was at my ear, demanding to know if I had brought the proofs.'

'The proofs? What proofs?'

'The documents proving that your Grace's precontract to the Duke of Lorraine's son was formally dissolved.'

Anna caught her breath. 'Were you asked to bring them?'

'No, Madam, I was not. Dr Wotton was sent to Kleve to obtain them, since his Majesty is determined to be satisfied in this matter. When I left, a great search of the archives was in progress.'

She sighed. 'This is all unnecessary!'

'I was assured the King wishes only to satisfy himself that your marriage is lawful and its issue indisputably legitimate. Given his marital history, that is not unreasonable.'

'No, I suppose not.' She was willing to be convinced. 'But I am forgetting my manners.' She poured some wine. 'I trust you have rested after your journey, and that you are comfortably lodged.'

Harst looked distressed. 'Alas, Madam, I have not been assigned any lodging. I am going to seek an inn.'

This was most embarrassing. 'I am very sorry you have been slighted like this. I will speak to the King.'

Dr Harst raised a hand to stay her. 'No matter. When the King is less angry with me, I will try to talk my way into his good graces. Cordial relations must be preserved at all costs. The Duke needs men and arms against the Emperor.'

'The King is aware of that, Dr Harst. I will add my voice to yours on my brother's behalf.'

The ambassador sipped his wine. 'I am gratified to see that your Grace is so well treated, and to hear that you already have some influence with the King.'

'Oh, I would not say that! His Grace does as he pleases, but he has heeded me on one or two matters.'

'You have made an excellent beginning,' Dr Harst said. 'The gentlemen who greeted me on my arrival told me the King's subjects love your Grace and thank God for bringing into their realm such a good queen.'

'I am touched to hear that,' Anna smiled. 'I received a wonderful reception in England, especially at Blackheath, where the King formally welcomed me. I had never seen so many people gathered in one place.'

'Dr Wotton told your brother how well the King likes your Grace, saying he rejoiced greatly that the affection was mutual.'

'The King has been very kind to me,' Anna said, gratified to hear what Wotton – who should know – had said about her marriage. 'He has given me every reason to love him.' She thought of the vile rumours, the barren nights, her inability to fathom Henry's true feelings towards her, and knew herself for a liar. But then she remembered his constant thoughtfulness, the growing liking between them, and the pain that blighted his life, and knew there was some truth in her words.

'We heard from the Elector of Saxony's envoys that your marriage began joyfully, and all in Kleve desire God to bless you, that you may continue in your good fortune.'

It sounded as if Wilhelm, and everyone else abroad, was confident all was well. Anna had wondered if one of her returning servants, or even Dr Wotton himself, might have said something to give him pause for thought. Did it perturb her brother at all that Wotton was pursuing the matter of the precontract?

'Do let me help you with some money for equipping yourself for court,' she said. 'We need to soften the King.'

'Bless you, but no,' Harst replied. 'I have money, although I can think of better things to spend it on. And now, Madam, with your leave, I must go and find some lodgings.'

When Anna next attended Mass, she was astounded by the beauty of the Chapel Royal. Seated beside the King in the royal pew overlooking the nave, where their households had gathered to worship, her eyes were drawn to the glorious fan-vaulted ceiling, painted vivid blue and gold, with pendants, piping *putti*, and the King's motto, '*Dieu et mon Droit*', blazoned everywhere on the ribs. The chapel was resplendent with vibrant stained-glass windows, carved choir stalls, paintings, tapestries and a chequered marble floor.

Here, Queen Jane had lain in state; here, the Prince had been christened. Here, God willing, Anna's own child might be baptised one day, although it was a faint hope.

After Mass, she asked Henry if she might linger to look at the carvings, and he bade the chaplain leave her be, with just Susanna in attendance. She was absorbed in the delicate rendering of pious scenes in the glass when she was interrupted by a footfall.

'They told me I might find your Grace here,' said Dr Harst, looking resplendent in a furred damask gown, and doffing a feathered cap with a jewel. 'I hope I am not disturbing you.'

'Not at all,' Anna said, inviting him to sit with her in the front pew. 'Is all well now between you and the King?'

Harst gave her a rueful smile. 'I am grovelling and he is slowly unbending, so yes, things are improving!'

'I am glad to hear it. I am learning that the King can be all bluster and pride, and that he is very short-tempered. I think he will soon be more friendly, especially if you talk to him about Erasmus! Now, how can I help you today?'

'It is more a matter of what you should know, Madam. The King is pressing the Duke to add a new article to the marriage treaty. His Majesty wants a guarantee of advance warning if the Duke plans to make war on the Emperor. The Duke fears he wants to avoid England being drawn into the conflict.'

'But he is pledged to help Kleve!' Anna was shocked.

'Indeed, Madam. Possibly he just wants time to prepare and arm. But the Duke is loath to agree; he fears to provoke the Emperor and the King of France. However, he is willing to consent privately to the King's request.'

'Is the King content with that?'

'No, Madam.' Harst's expression told her Henry had been difficult. 'But I shall do my best to persuade him. I do have some good news. A notarial certificate has been issued by your brother, confirming that the precontract with Lorraine was repudiated. The Duke is certain this certificate will satisfy the King.' He paused. 'Of more concern, I think, is my impression that the reformers, both at this court and abroad, are rejoicing at the prospect of your championing the Protestant cause.'

'What?' Anna was alarmed. 'Have they not seen that I have never failed to observe the rites of my faith?'

'They think you but conform to what is expected, Madam, and that you will work on the King to bring him around to their opinions, like the late Queen Anne did.'

'I have no desire to emulate Queen Anne in any way, still less champion the Lutheran faith,' she declared.

'Nevertheless, this new friendship of the King with Kleve and the Schmalkaldic League has led many to entertain great hopes of you. Already, people are saying there has been no persecution since you became queen.'

'That is mere coincidence, Dr Harst. I have only been married for two months. I fear the reformists will be disappointed, for I can never espouse their cause.'

'I knew that would be your answer,' the ambassador said. 'It would be prudent not to involve yourself in the religious conflicts that divide this court, and indeed, all Europe.'

'That is wise advice, my good friend,' Anna answered. 'I will remember it.'

When she left the chapel, she saw Lord Cromwell just along the gallery, in conversation with two clerks. He was watching her. Again, she realised that Dr Harst's advice was sound.

Chapter 13

1540

Standing at the table in her privy chamber, Anna opened the package. Inside the delicate tissue lay a miniature crimson bonnet and cap adorned with gold buttons and a jaunty feather.

'This will be perfect for Prince Edward,' she said to the tailor. 'Thank you for your trouble.'

She could not wait to give the bonnet to Henry, who was going to Richmond two days hence to visit his children, but would be back in time to spend Easter with her at Hampton Court. Lent would have ended by then, and he could return to her bed. She found, to her surprise, that she was looking forward to it. How things did change, she reflected, remembering how appalled she had been when Henry had revealed himself at Rochester. But she had learned that affection had nothing to do with outward appearances; it was the character within that won hearts. Not for a moment did she think this was love, but her husband's courtesy to her, and his kindness, had wrought a sea change in her feelings towards him.

When he arrived for supper that evening, she showed him the little bonnet.

'What a kind thought, Anna!' he exclaimed, admiring it. 'This will suit Edward perfectly, and I believe it will be a good fit.'

He greeted Susanna and sat down in a high humour. 'I look forward to seeing my children again. It is not often that they are all lodged together in one place.' He had told Anna that he tried to keep Edward and Elizabeth away from the court as much as possible, in the healthier air of the country houses he had appointed their nursery palaces.

'That is a pity, Sir, for I would be a mother to them,' she said, trying not to betray her neediness.

'I will bring them to court soon,' he promised.

'I especially look forward to meeting the Lady Mary,' she told him. 'We are almost of an age.' Poor Mary; from what Anna had gathered, she had had a difficult time after her parents' marriage had foundered. Suitor after suitor had been considered, and rejected. Having been bastardised and excluded from the succession, like her half-sister, Elizabeth, she was no longer so desirable a bride. Anna had heard that Mary was a martyr to one minor complaint after another; it was easy to see why. She hoped to do her stepdaughter some good. There was no reason, now that Henry had a son and heir, why he should not restore her to the succession. That would improve her chances of finding a husband immeasurably.

'We will invite her to court soon,' Henry promised. 'I know she is eager to meet you.'

Anna hoped Mary had not heard what the reformists were saying. She was staunch in the old faith, like her mother, Queen Katherine. She might not think kindly of a stepmother whom she believed to have Lutheran sympathies.

'I have heard her Grace has many virtues,' she said, spearing a slice of chicken on her knife. 'Henry, do you worry they are being wasted?'

He frowned. 'Wasted?'

'Married to a great prince, she could be an asset to you,' Anna ventured. 'Given her excellent qualities, she could do much to further your interests abroad, especially with her blood connections, and being cousin to the Emperor. It seems a shame that no suitable husband has been found.'

'It is not for the want of looking,' Henry said, his eyes taking on that steely look. 'Having just the one precious son, I have to consider what would ensue if, God forfend, anything happened to him. An ambitious husband might seek to enforce Mary's claim to the throne.'

'But she is your Grace's next heir.'

His eyes narrowed. 'You misunderstand, Anna. My union with her mother was no true marriage. A bastard cannot inherit the throne.'

'But failing the Prince, surely she is the next best choice, being of your Grace's blood?'

Henry banged his fist on the table, making her jump. 'Enough, Madam! Do not meddle in matters you do not understand! Mary is my daughter, and I shall do with her as stands with my pleasure.'

'I am very sorry, Sir.' Anna wrung her hands. She had gone too far, she knew it. 'I but wished to help.'

'It's meddling, Madam! I have dealt with queens who meddled too much in politics.' He stood up, wiping his mouth with his napkin. 'I will leave you to consider the proper conduct of a wife.'

When he had gone, Anna burst into tears.

The Earl of Rutland came to her chamber. Seeing his heavy expression, she knew what it was about.

'The King has complained of me again,' she said flatly. 'I know I have offended him, although I never intended to.'

'It *is* that, I fear, Madam,' the chamberlain sighed, 'and I know your Grace would never willingly anger his Majesty. But Lord Cromwell told me this morning that the King has complained to him that you showed yourself stubborn and wilful.'

'I suggested that the Lady Mary be restored to the succession,' Anna admitted.

The normally urbane Rutland could not hide his dismay. 'Madam, it is treason to suggest that the Lady Mary is legitimate.'

'I meant no treason!' Anna cried, alarmed. 'The King expressed concern about having only one son, and I was trying to help him find a way to secure the succession to his own blood.'

'It was well meant,' Rutland answered, 'and no doubt the King will come to understand that, and forgive you your ignorance. Madam, *you* did not live through those difficult years of the Great Matter, when the King was trying to divorce Queen Katherine, or the Princess Dowager, as I should call her. It is still a sensitive issue with him. My advice is to avoid the subject, and that of the succession, at all costs.'

'Have no fear, I shall take it!' Anna said fervently, wondering if she would ever be back in the King's favour.

To her surprise, Henry came to her privy chamber that night. She was so pleased to see him that she threw herself to her knees at his feet. 'Oh, your Grace, I am sorry if I said the wrong thing. I wanted only to be helpful!'

She felt his hands on her forearms, raising her up; then he bent forward and kissed her on the lips.

'You are forgiven,' he said. 'I have been told you spoke only out of concern for my security.' Rutland, that kind, brave man, had spoken up for her again. She would thank him as soon as she got the chance.

'I am so grateful to your Grace,' she said. 'In future, I will leave all great matters to your wisdom.'

He sat down by the fire, and she asked Susanna to bring him some of the rich sack he loved, which he had sent specially from Spain.

'I need to ask you something, Anna,' he said, savouring the wine. 'It concerns your precontract with the Duke of Lorraine's son. What do you know about it?'

Anna did not hesitate. 'It is true I was espoused to him in childhood, but, later on, my father told me the precontract had been dissolved.'

'You made no promises yourself?'

'No. I was too young, and when I *was* old enough, it was not required of me.'

'Hmm.' Henry was pensive for the rest of supper, after which he departed, leaving her deep in thought. Why, if he was so worried about the precontract, had he gone ahead and married her, *and* declared he knew of no impediment? It made no sense. She prayed that the certificate Dr Harst had mentioned would set the King's mind at rest.

On a fair day in March, Anna ventured into her garden with just Susanna for company. Their conversation led to reminiscences about their younger days, and she was pleased to hear that Susanna had had as happy a childhood as she had, although in very different circumstances. Certainly, she had enjoyed more liberty, and she had even been allowed to encourage the attentions of young men, which Anna thought a little scandalous. Truth to tell, she envied Susanna for having known such freedom.

And then Susanna asked, quite innocently, if Anna had ever loved anyone before the King?

Anna stared at her. 'Of course not. How could I? I had no opportunity. And it would not have been allowed.'

'Of course,' Susanna said. 'But did you ever admire a young man from afar? I have seen some handsome German gentlemen in your train. There is a chestnut-haired one who is particularly charming.'

'I was taught custody of the eyes, like a nun,' Anna replied tersely, fearing that Susanna was referring to Otho, and not wanting to continue this discussion. Such questions touched a tender spot, and came too close to home. But how could Susanna know anything of what had passed between Anna and Otho?

Thereafter, Anna was a little wary of Susanna. Although she liked her as a friend, she was aware of the necessity for steering clear of certain subjects, and for not encouraging too great a familiarity. It was safer, in the circumstances.

Henry and Anna celebrated Easter together at Hampton Court, and the conjugal visits resumed. But nothing had changed. He made no move to touch her, and seemed troubled. Sometimes, as she lay there wakeful beside him, she would hear him gasp and moan in his sleep. She wished he would unburden himself to her. Maybe she could help him. But all she could do was try to please him and avoid giving offence.

Spring was flowering, and she took delight in the awakening gardens at Hampton Court. Her favourite seat was in the little banqueting house near the fishponds. There were several such bowers in the palace grounds, and one evening, as Anna strolled about, enjoying the sunset, she heard music and voices coming from the one on a high mound in the Mount Garden. Henry must be entertaining. Feeling excluded, she stared at the candlelit windows, and listened to musicians playing and men laughing.

'It will be for the gentlemen only, Madam,' Lady Suffolk told her, making a face.

A little cheered, Anna entered an orchard, admiring the hundreds of rose bushes Henry had had planted in it, and then returned by way of the herb garden, breathing in its heady fragrances. There were gardeners working there, and, spontaneously, she drew some gold coins from her pocket and pressed the men to take them.

'Your work gives me much pleasure,' she told them, as they stammered their gratitude.

She saw Dr Harst walking towards her.

'They told me I might find your Grace in the gardens,' he said, bowing. 'Might we speak in private?'

'Of course.' She led him into her privy garden.

'I had an audience with the King today,' Harst told her. 'When he received me, I knew something had displeased him. He offered no courtesies, but complained of the Duke's unwillingness to agree to adding that article to the treaty. He was ranting, Madam!' Anna could well imagine it. 'He is still angry about my lack of trappings. He said the Duke had done you and me a great disservice in failing to furnish me with the attire and household suitable to my standing; he had demonstrated that my embassy was of little significance to him, which was insulting to himself and to your Grace.'

'Oh dear.' Anna shook her head. 'I am so sorry.'

The doctor sighed. 'In faith, Madam, I am asking myself if I can be of service to the Duke at this court. I feel I am despised here, or taken for a nonentity. Neither the Imperial ambassador nor the French one holds me of any account; in fact, they do not deign to acknowledge me.'

'The Emperor's ambassador will have his reasons, of course,' Anna said. 'His master is becoming more hostile towards Kleve, and he must guess you are here to seek support from the King.'

'There is small chance of that at present,' Harst muttered. 'I fear I am failing everyone.'

'Dr Harst,' Anna said firmly, 'my brother could not have sent a better, or more qualified, emissary. You are loyal to me and mine, and I feel happier having you here. I know I can count on you to come to my assistance if I ever need it.'

'Your Grace is kind to say so,' he sighed, 'but I fear I have no influence.'

'I wish I could do more for you, but recently I spoke out of turn, and the King has warned me not to meddle in politics. I would plead for the aid my brother craves, but I dare not anger his Majesty again.'

Harst's lugubrious eyes were full of concern. 'There has been no falling-out?'

'Not at all. I am forgiven. His Majesty is being kind and polite, and good company. We are friends again.'

'I am glad to hear it, and so will the Duke be.'

'Take heart,' Anna counselled. 'The King will not be angry for ever, as I know from experience.'

Everyone was talking about the coming coronation, and the jousts and pastimes that would mark it. But it was now April, and Anna was worried.

'No preparations are being made,' she told Dr Harst, having summoned him to wait on her in her privy chamber. 'Whitsun is only six weeks away. Surely arrangements should have been set in train by now?'

'I have been concerned too,' Harst admitted. 'I think I should inform the Duke. I doubt the King will listen to any complaints from me.'

'I have a better idea,' Anna told him. 'You tell Lord Cromwell and the Earl of Southampton you have heard talk that I am to be crowned, and ask them what the King intends.'

Harst looked dubious. 'That may not be politic, Madam. It might irritate his Majesty, when Kleve needs his friendship. I have just heard from Dr Olisleger. The Emperor has demanded that Duke Wilhelm surrender Guelders.'

Anna's hand flew to her mouth. 'No! How dare he? This will mean war, I know it. I must beg the King for aid!' She rose, and would have sped away, but Harst grabbed her hand.

'No, Madam! Your brother wants to avoid war. But there is tension between the Emperor and the King of France, and both are tentatively looking to England for friendship. From what I've been able to glean from the councillors I've spoken to, the King is leaning towards the Emperor. He might not want to provoke him by taking Kleve's part in this conflict.'

Anna heard him out in mounting dismay. 'Then the alliance was all for nothing.'

'Not at all, Madam!' Harst was adamant. 'The King has gained a wife of whom he may be proud. He has not denied Kleve his support. He has not sued for the Emperor's friendship. We must trust in his good faith, and not anger him.'

As in the bedchamber, so in the council chamber, Anna thought: Henry would never declare his intentions, or reveal his mind.

'I will pray that all will turn out to Kleve's advantage,' she said. 'In the grand scale of things, my coronation is of little importance.'

Anna walked into her privy chamber to hear her ladies talking about the closure of the last of the great abbeys. Canterbury, Christchurch, Waltham, and Rochester, where she had stayed, had all surrendered themselves to the King's commissioners.

'I never thought to see this day,' Margaret Douglas mourned, viciously jabbing her embroidery tambour with her needle. 'At the outset, the King intended only to dissolve the smaller religious houses.'

'Good riddance, I say,' chimed in Lady Suffolk. 'Hotbeds of popery, all of them.' Most of the ladies were nodding their agreement. Margaret, a devout Catholic, seemed poised to retort, but kept silent. It was tantamount to treason to criticise the King, and she had known what it was to be sentenced to death and languish in the Tower.

Only last night, Henry had come to sup with Anna wearing on his thumb the great ruby that had adorned the shrine of St Thomas Becket at Canterbury.

'Becket was a traitor to his King,' he'd told her. 'Last year, I had his bones exhumed and thrown on a dung heap, which is all the shrine he deserved.' She had shrunk from the violence in his tone.

For all that he upheld the old faith and its rituals, and was effectively pope in his own realm, it worried Anna that he had appropriated the Church's riches for his own coffers, and was now selling off monastic land to loyal noblemen. It was a clever ploy, for he was binding his lords to the Crown by ties of gratitude and obligation. They were hardly likely to oppose religious reforms that had so lavishly benefited them.

Dr Harst shared her concerns. When they were next alone, taking the air together in her privy garden, he opened his mind.

'Forgive me, Madam, I do not wish to speak ill of the King, but I have learned that, in England now, the sick and the poor go destitute, since they can no longer receive succour from the monasteries.'

'Not to mention the monks and nuns who have been turned out,' Anna murmured. 'The King says they have all been given pensions, but it is not much – and it cannot compensate those who had vocations. Yet who will dare speak up for them?'

'Two abbots who refused to surrender their houses were hanged. That probably silenced dissent.'

'It is almost as if the King is encouraging Lutheranism,' Anna reflected, sitting down on a stone bench. 'The Protestants applaud the dissolution. What worries me is that people here, both Catholics and reformists, see me as a champion of reform, and some even think I hold Lutheran views.'

'I know, Madam,' Harst said, sitting down beside her. 'I had to correct a clerk who asserted that your Grace refused to come to England while there was still one abbey standing.'

'I can believe it,' she said bitterly. 'I am sure they are blaming me for the closure of these last monasteries.'

'Your Grace must give the lie to them by assiduously observing the rites of the Church.'

'I do, Dr Harst, I do! I would not be a Protestant in England for the world. The penalty for heresy is terrible.' She shuddered, imagining what it must mean to go to the stake. 'Yet the reformists flourish. Even Lord Cromwell is one.'

'They are not heretics. They want the Church reformed from within. As for Lord Cromwell, there is talk in the court.' Harst lowered his voice. 'He is tottering. You are acquainted with Bishop Gardiner of Winchester? He is a staunch Catholic and hates all reformers, and Cromwell in particular. Cromwell had him dismissed from the Council, but now he is back, and in favour with the King, a sure sign that Cromwell's influence is not what it was.'

'It was Cromwell who made my marriage.' Anna looked fearfully at Harst. 'Gardiner, I hear, is hand-in-glove with the Duke of Norfolk. The Howards resent me. They might persuade the King to divorce me, and there would be good grounds—' She clamped her mouth shut as she realised what she had said.

'You mean the precontract, Madam?' Harst looked puzzled. 'That is no impediment, and the matter is being dealt with. Your marriage is valid, and there are no good grounds for dissolving it, whatever Norfolk and Gardiner may say.'

Anna bit her tongue. 'If the King decides to get rid of me, a way will be found. Look what happened to his first two queens!'

'Madam,' Harst said firmly, 'you are seeing trouble where there is none. Has the King given any hint that he wants to be rid of you?'

She thought back. 'There were rumours he found me unappealing, but, apart from that, no.'

'Then your Grace has nothing to fear. And if anything perturbs you, I am here to serve you and protect your interests – and I would make myself heard!'

She allowed herself to be reassured. But underneath there remained an insidious, worming doubt. The repeated resurrection of the tiresome matter of the precontract, her unconsummated marriage, her deferred coronation, not to mention the forces that might be working against her at court, and her inability to read the King's mind, were making her feel very vulnerable. If only Henry could, or would, make her his wife in every sense! If only she could bear him a son! Then she would be invincible.

How often, she wondered, had her predecessors had that very same thought?

In the second week of April, the court moved back to Whitehall, so that the King could be present when Parliament opened. Anna was sad to be leaving Hampton Court and hoped they would return soon.

It seemed the rumours about Cromwell were baseless as, soon

afterwards, Henry created him earl of Essex and appointed him Lord Great Chamberlain of England. Anna watched Cromwell kneeling before the King in the presence chamber to be invested with his coronet and mantle and given his patent of nobility. Harst had been wrong. It was the Catholic party who would be tottering now, in the face of Cromwell's elevation. She felt a little safer.

After the ceremony, Henry supped with Anna in her privy chamber.

'Did you see Norfolk's face?' he asked gleefully, breaking his manchet bread in half. 'He hates Cromwell because Cromwell wasn't born in a castle with a pedigree stretching back to Adam. He told me to my face I shouldn't be giving the earldom of the noble Bourchiers to a black-smith's son. I told him that blacksmith's boy had been of far more use to me than the Bourchiers ever were.'

'I have heard that Norfolk resents Cromwell because he is for reform,' Anna ventured.

'Norfolk is jealous of Cromwell's power,' Henry said. 'He hates everything he stands for. I'm well aware of the political tilting that goes on, Anna. Let me help you to some of this brawn – it's excellent.' He placed slices on her plate. 'The French King's sister, the Queen of Navarre, has asked for miniature pictures of us.' He turned to Susanna, who was interpreting as usual. 'Mistress Gilman, would you ask Master Horenbout to attend me. He can paint them.'

Susanna curtseyed and left. Henry turned to Anna. 'I want you to be the first to know that I am making your brother a Knight of the Garter, alongside Prince Edward, when I hold a chapter of the Order later this month.'

That *was* good news! So great an honour bestowed on Wilhelm, and thereby on Kleve too, surely augured well for Kleve receiving English aid.

'The Duke will be overjoyed, as I am,' she said, from her heart. 'Sir, I cannot sufficiently express my appreciation.'

Looking pleased with himself, Henry patted her hand.

Anna sat with the King in the oriel window of the gatehouse at Whitehall, awaiting the start of the triumphal jousts that were being staged to celebrate May Day, a festival – she had learned – that was traditionally observed with great entertainments by the English court. It was a glorious day, with the sun shining down and a gentle breeze blowing, and everyone had donned new attire in honour of the occasion. Anna wore a pale grey gown of gossamer silk with a gold and pearl biliment at the neckline; it rippled about her as she moved, and the French hood of grey damask became her well, she thought.

It was hard to believe it was five months since she had left Kleve. She missed her family still, of course – their letters always unsettled her – but she felt she was beginning to adapt to her adoptive land and was making the best of the hand Fate had dealt her.

Beside her, Henry was applauding the arrival of the contestants in the wide thoroughfare below, which was being used as a tiltyard. The lords and ladies surrounding him and Anna were leaning forward for a better view. The jousts had been proclaimed in France, Flanders, Scotland and Spain, inviting the flower of European chivalry to respond to the English challengers, and knights from far and wide had come for a tournament that would last five days. Forty-six defenders, led by the gallant and accomplished Earl of Surrey, were parading around the arena, followed by the richly apparelled challengers, all wearing white doublets and hose in the Burgundian fashion, and riding horses trapped in white velvet. At their head rode Sir John Dudley, Anna's own master of horse, and among them she recognised the debonair Sir Thomas Seymour and the faintly repellent Thomas Culpeper.

The jousts began with a fanfare, then the great destriers were thundering towards each other; there was a clash of lances, and shouts erupted. Anna was on the edge of her seat, expecting to see someone killed at any moment. But Henry was in his element, jerking in his chair whenever the contestants engaged, and living each move as if he were taking part himself – which doubtless he wished he was. Anna almost screamed when Culpeper was unhorsed and crashed to the ground, but to her immense relief he got up and walked away. When victory was declared for the defenders, Henry roared his approval. Anna added her congratulations, as he presented the winners with handsome prizes of money and the deeds to fine houses.

At the end of the afternoon, he led Anna in procession along Whitehall to the great chequered gatehouse at the far end, and through it to the Strand. Crowds had gathered to see them, and Henry raised his hand in greeting as he and Anna passed through their ranks.

'What is that?' she asked, indicating a beautifully sculpted stone monument adorned with statues of a queen, which stood to their right.

'It's the cross that Edward the First built in memory of his beloved Queen Eleanor,' Henry replied, almost shouting against the hubbub.

How wonderful to be remembered in such a way, Anna thought. What great love there must have been between them.

The challengers had ridden ahead to Durham Place, an imposing mansion on the Strand. Here, they were keeping open house, to feast the King and Queen, her ladies, the courtiers and the visiting knights. The stately chambers had been hung with sumptuous tapestries and furnished with massive cupboards of plate. Sitting at the high table in the hall, Henry and Anna were served choice dishes to the pleasant sound of minstrelsy. It was a fitting finale to a lovely day.

Anna attended all the tournaments held that week, during which open house was maintained at Durham Place, where she and Henry – and the whole court, it seemed – resorted in the evenings for suppers and banquets. The weather was balmy and on the last night they gathered in the gardens by the Thames, eating sweetmeats offered by servitors carrying large gold salvers, and sipping wine from jewelled goblets. Henry was in an expansive mood, going over every move in the jousts with the crowd of young combatants encircling him. Anna and the ladies listened in admiration, while the knights made eyes at her maids-of-honour. Anna was keeping a watchful gaze on the latter. As their mistress, she was *in loco parentis*, and responsible for their good conduct.

It was then that she noticed the King smiling familiarly at Katheryn Howard. Little auburn-haired Katheryn was full of beauty and sweetness, a frivolous girl who seemed to care only for clothes and lap dogs. She had always served Anna well and willingly, and never given her any trouble – until now.

Anna could not help herself. She stared, shocked, as Katheryn smiled pertly back and Henry's eyes narrowed lasciviously in a way they had never done for her. She remembered where she was and realised she had not the faintest idea of what the young knight on her left had been saying. He was looking at her curiously, as was Susanna, so she made herself smile at him, and hastened to excuse herself. 'My apologies, Sir. I felt faint for a moment, but I am better now.'

Escaping his solicitude, she made her way back indoors, evading the few courtiers who made to speak to her. She found an empty chamber, and closed the door behind her, finding herself in a study furnished with a desk and bookshelves. The latticed window overlooked the garden. She peered through it. Katheryn Howard had moved nearer to Henry now. Her girlish laughter rang out.

Surely it was nothing! The King, everyone knew, had always had an eye for the ladies. Why should he not find Katheryn appealing? Smiling at her did not mean he was pursuing her. But what was it someone had said, in Anna's hearing? *When he takes a fancy for a person or a thing, he goes the whole way.* Now she really was running away with her imagination. Stop it! she admonished herself. It was a passing flirtation.

Or was it?

She could never confront him, of course. It was beneath her dignity to do so, and anyway, he was the King, and accountable to no one. If he took a mistress, the best course was to ignore it. So long as he did not humiliate her in public, she would try not to mind. She did not love him, so it should not matter to her.

But it did.

Smoothing her skirts, she returned to the banquet, waving away the trays of food offered her. She rejoined the King, smiling and nodding as they conversed with the guests. She was pleased to see that Katheryn Howard had drifted away.

That night, she asked Mother Lowe and Susanna to help her prepare for bed. She didn't want her English ladies present. It would cause resentment, she knew, but she had more pressing things to worry about.

'What do you know of Katheryn Howard?' she asked.

Susanna's face tautened. Don't tell me it's all around the court, Anna prayed.

'She is a niece of the Duke of Norfolk,' Susanna said. 'That makes her first cousin to Queen Anne. This is her first post at court, secured by her uncle, no doubt.'

And for what purpose? No one would be more pleased than Norfolk if Henry pursued another of his nieces. It must have galled him to see Anne toppled from the consort's throne; how he would welcome another aspiring to the same dignity. Anna would not have put it past the wily old fox to have pushed Katheryn in Henry's path. A good, dutiful little Catholic queen, untainted by any connection to the reformers – that would suit Norfolk well! She hoped she was straying into the land of fancy.

'She's poor as a peasant,' Mother Lowe said. 'She told me her father died last year, and that she has no fortune. Her mother passed away when she was a child, and she was brought up in the household of her grandmother, the Dowager Duchess of Norfolk. She didn't seem to want to talk about that, only about how pleased she was to be at court.'

'I find her too forward,' Susanna said, unplaiting Anna's hair. 'She's a Howard, through and through.'

'Why are you asking about her, Anna?' Mother Lowe wanted to know.

Anna sat down so that they could remove her shoes and stockings. She decided it was best not to utter her fears. 'It occurred to me that I have never paid her very much attention, and that I ought to know more about her. I am surprised the Howards have not found her a husband.'

But maybe they have, an unwelcome inner voice taunted her.

She would have liked to ask Susanna outright if she had heard gossip connecting the King to Katheryn, but was too afraid of the answer. It was probably better to remain in ignorance.

Or was it? Over the days that followed, she found herself torn by doubt, watching Henry when he came to visit her, to see if his eyes strayed in Katheryn's direction, and watching Katheryn too; but neither gave her further cause to wonder. After a week, she concluded that she must have been mistaken in the first place. And when she received a gift of a jewel from the Dowager Duchess of Norfolk, she exhaled in relief, because it seemed inconceivable that the Duchess would court the Queen's favour with presents if she knew the Queen's husband was pursuing her granddaughter.

After the jousts, the King seemed sad and pensive. Anna feared that the contrast between his ageing self and the young combatants had depressed him, reminding him of pleasures in which he could no longer partake. He had good cause to feel sorry for himself anyway, for he was not well. The malady in his legs was slowing him down, and some days he could hardly walk, let alone ride. Worse still, he had an abscess that oozed pus and had to be dressed daily, not a pleasant task as the wound stank. Anna could smell it as she sat at table with him. Sorry for him as she was, it quite put her off her food. She felt humiliated for him. He was in great pain, and once or twice she saw him close his eyes and take rapid breaths, as if he were at the limit of his endurance.

One night, at supper, he sighed and laid down his knife. 'I am weary of my life,' he said.

'Can the doctors not do something to ease you?' Anna asked, feeling helpless.

He shook his head. 'Not unless I face the knife. I am summoning up my courage.'

He did not come to her bed that night, or the next, and on the third day, he sent her a message to say he had been forced to submit to the attentions of the barber surgeons and have the abscess lanced.

When she saw him again, he looked much better, and the pain had eased, although the leg was still bandaged.

'I have ordered a new suit of tiltyard armour,' he told her. She could have wept for him, for it was plain to see that he would never wear it, never again be the athletic hero of his glory days.

Two days later, Anna's new consort of musicians, the Bassanos of Venice, to whom Henry had succeeded in granting asylum, performed in her chamber. The King was present, seated with her in the midst of her ladies, when the music was interrupted by a loud sob. All eyes turned, and Anna saw Anne Bassett weeping on Mrs Cromwell's shoulder.

'Take her out,' she bade Mother Lowe, who hastened to do her bidding.

Henry signalled to the musicians to play on.

'I wonder what upset Mrs Bassett,' she said to him when they had finished and the ladies were setting the table for supper.

'This morning, I had her stepfather, Lord Lisle, arrested for treason,' Henry said, his mouth pursed primly. 'I was shown proof that he plotted to sell Calais to the French. He is now in the Tower. I expect Mistress Bassett had just been informed.'

'How dreadful for her – and for your Grace!' Anna exclaimed, thinking how devastating this must be for Anne's ambitious mother. 'Should I dismiss her?'

'No, Anna. She has committed no treason, and I like the little minx. You may tell her that my displeasure does not extend to her.'

'Will her father be executed?' Anna dared to ask.

'He is my cousin. I will not shed his blood. He can rue his folly in the Tower for a space.' She had not expected him to be so merciful.

Weeks before, all the talk had been of Anna's coronation. Everyone had been looking forward to it. But still no arrangements had been made, and Whitsun came and went without any mention of a crowning.

When Anna complained to Dr Harst, his response was firm. 'I have raised the matter with the King. It is your right to be crowned.'

'Thank you. I have dreaded broaching the subject, lest it provoke his anger. His temper has been volatile these past weeks.'

'I am well aware of that, Madam,' Harst smiled wryly, 'and I am sure that Lord Cromwell, or my lord of Essex, as I should now call him, is too, for I heard that the King boxed his ears the other day and threw him out of his chamber. He emerged battered, but smiling, and I dare say all was soon forgotten. If you say to the King that Duke Wilhelm is asking when you are to be crowned, I think he will be reasonable.'

'Then I will gather my courage,' Anna promised.

'Sir,' she said, strolling on Henry's arm in her garden after supper, 'my brother the Duke is asking when I am to be crowned.'

'Has that fool of an ambassador been talking to you?' Henry snapped, his benign mood evaporating. 'He keeps asking me the same question. You will be crowned when I will it.'

'But, Henry, I was to have been crowned last week, and before that at Candlemas. There was much talk of it. I feel shamed because it did not happen, and no explanation was given. I fear people will be wondering if I have displeased you in some way.'

He glared at her. Clearly she had displeased him by bringing up the subject. Then he sighed, and the dangerous moment passed. 'The truth is, Anna, there are too many other calls on my treasury. If your brother wants me to join him in a war against the Emperor, I will need funds for that. So do not press me on the matter of your coronation. My late Queen did not trouble herself about it, and hers was deferred again and again because of plague and rebellion. In the end, she never had one.' There was great sadness in his eyes.

'And she, of all your queens, most deserved it, because she gave you a son,' Anna said softly.

He stared at her. Gone was the steely gaze. 'You have a rare understanding, Anna.'

'Against such a fine example, I feel very much lacking,' she confessed, thinking they had never spoken so candidly. 'I try to emulate what I know of her in all I do.'

Henry grasped her hand. 'You have a good heart, Anna,' he said.

211

Chapter 14

1540

When the Earl of Rutland and Anna's council asked for a formal audience, she knew there was trouble afoot.

'Your Grace,' Rutland said, 'my lord of Essex has required us to counsel you to use all pleasantries to the King.'

He might have slapped her, for his words had the same effect.

'My lord,' she faltered, 'everything is pleasant between myself and the King, so I do not understand your meaning.'

Rutland hesitated.

'Is my lord Essex implying I have done something amiss?' Anna cried, anger overriding dismay. 'My lords, I take great pains to study and please his Majesty. I am an obedient wife, always conformable to his pleasure. Maybe my lord of Essex would like to give me specific advice, for I do not know what more I can do! And maybe you can all go back and ask him for it.'

Rutland paled. Anna stepped off the dais and faced him. It was like confronting Henry, for the Earl looked so like him. 'I remember your giving me similar counsel back in January, and I have borne it in mind ever since. Is my lord of Essex implying that you failed sufficiently to impress upon me his advice the first time? I am not sure I approve of his unwarranted interference in my affairs. Be assured, I shall speak to the King about this.'

Rutland looked stricken.

'You may go, my lords,' Anna said. She signalled to her ladies to follow her, and swept out of the presence chamber.

While she was still impelled by indignation, she sent an usher to enquire where the King was. Informed that he was in his library, she hurried there, and was admitted to find Henry alone, reading. Seeing her, he stood up and bowed. He did not seem angry at being interrupted.

'This is a pleasant surprise, Anna,' he said. 'Pray be seated. What can I do for you?'

She took the chair opposite his at the table. 'Speak to my lord of Essex, your Grace!' she cried.

Henry's eyes narrowed. 'What has he done?'

'For the second time this year, he has instructed my chamberlain to urge me to be pleasant to you! Sir, am I not pleasant? Have I offended you in some way?'

An angry flush had suffused Henry's face. He held up his hand. 'Cease, Anna! You must not concern yourself with this. Cromwell is tilting at phantoms. The Catholics are out for his blood; they did not want me to ally myself with the German princes, but he persisted. He is desperate to safeguard his own position by ensuring that our marriage is a success. He is not reacting to anything you have done – and be sure you have done nothing to offend me – but pre-empting any chance of its failure. You may leave this with me. I will speak to him.'

Only later did she begin to wonder what part Henry was playing in this feud between Cromwell and the Catholic party. Was he supporting his chief minister? Or was he distancing himself from the alliance that Cromwell had brokered?

When Anna returned to her apartments, the Duchess of Richmond brought her embroidery basket.

'Your Grace, I heard what Lord Rutland said. It was outrageous of Cromwell to lay such a task on him.' She did not give Cromwell his proper title, the title Norfolk had complained about. 'I told my father the Duke about it. He was most indignant on your Grace's behalf.'

Anna did not for a moment believe the Howards were concerned for her; she was convinced they had resented her from the start. 'I thank him for his concern,' she said, suspecting that Norfolk might use her to make mischief for Cromwell, 'but I have already spoken to the King, and he is dealing with the matter.'

The Duchess stiffened. 'I am glad of it, Madam,' she said, and went back to sit with Margaret Douglas and Lady Rutland.

'Cromwell has apologised,' Henry said, when he came to Anna's bedchamber that night. 'He says he was misinformed. I don't believe a word of it.'

Anna next saw Cromwell on a hot June afternoon, when she went to watch the King shooting at the butts. He doffed his bonnet to her and bowed, but his eyes were wary. He had thought her his instrument, passive and malleable. It must have felt as if a lamb had turned and bitten him.

Two days later, when she and her ladies were seated in her garden, listening to the Bassanos playing, Margaret Douglas came running along the path.

'Madam, have you heard? Cromwell is arrested.' The music ceased and everyone gaped, as Margaret caught her breath. 'Sir Anthony Browne just told me he was taken as he entered the council chamber, ready for the day's business. The Captain of the Guard suddenly appeared and apprehended him for treason and heresy.'

'Heresy?' Anna echoed in disbelief.

'He was ever a friend to the reformers,' Margaret reminded her. 'My lord of Norfolk and the Lord Admiral stripped him of his Garter insignia. Cromwell was shouting that he was no traitor, but he was literally dragged off to the Tower. Many are rejoicing at it.'

'And some must be lamenting,' the Duchess of Suffolk said bitterly. 'This is a sad day for reform.'

'What chills me is that one who rose so high could be brought down so suddenly,' Anna said. The world knew how heavily Henry had relied on Cromwell, how far Cromwell's power had reached. His enemies must have been busy! And they were not far to seek. The smug smile on the Duchess of Richmond's face said it all.

When Henry came to Anna's bedchamber that night, he slumped down in a chair, looking exhausted.

'You will have heard about Cromwell,' he said.

'Yes, Sir, I did. My ladies have spoken of little else all day.'

Henry sighed. 'I want you to know the facts, Anna. It is my intention, using all possible means, to lead religion in my realm back to the way of truth. I relied on Cromwell to assist me in that. But he had become too attached to the German Lutherans, and dangerously influenced by them. I had my suspicions, and then, I thank God, I was warned by some of my principal lords that he was working against my will and pleasure, and that of Parliament.'

Anna feared that those same principal lords had been plain envious of Cromwell's meteoric career and his intimacy with the King. They had despised his birth, and become jealous. They had ulterior motives for bringing him down, which had little to do with religion. But she must not be seen to question the King's justice.

'I have nourished a snake in my bosom!' Henry snarled, working himself up into a rage. 'I will abolish all memory of him. He is the greatest wretch ever born in England!'

And what of me? Anna thought fearfully. What of the Queen Cromwell had set up on the throne? If people believed she was a Protestant or reformist, would she not share in the infamy that must now attach itself to Cromwell's name?

'What will happen to him?' she ventured, knowing that, with Henry in this mood, the answer was obvious.

'Tomorrow, a Bill of Attainder against him will be drawn up and laid before Parliament.'

'A Bill of Attainder? What is that?'

'It is an Act passed by Parliament condemning a traitor to the loss of his life and goods.'

'So Cromwell will be tried by Parliament?'

'No, Anna, there will be no trial. Parliament considers the evidence in the Bill of Attainder, and acts accordingly.'

It did not seem fair that Cromwell would be deprived of the chance to plead his case. But who was she, a foreigner, to criticise English justice?

On the day the House of Lords approved the Bill, Anna looked out of her window and saw a group of ladies and gentlemen strolling in the gardens down by the river. As they drew nearer, she recognised the King – his massive figure was unmistakable – and the tiny woman beside him. It was Katheryn Howard, leaning on his arm and laughing.

It really upset her – and frightened her. Norfolk and his party had brought down Cromwell. Katheryn Howard was Norfolk's niece. Was he using her to bring down the Queen too?

She turned away from the window and beckoned Susanna to follow her into the closet she used for private prayer.

'My good friend, tell me truly,' she said, as soon as the door was closed. 'Do you know if the King has cast his fancy on Katheryn Howard?'

She could tell from the distress in Susanna's face that it was true.

'There was gossip back in April,' Susanna said. 'We did not want to upset you, as you had enough to contend with.'

'Who knew?' Anna asked, hurt turning to anger that anyone should have kept this from her.

Susanna faltered. 'Nearly all your ladies, Madam.' She could not meet Anna's eye. 'We were hoping it was just a passing fancy.'

'From what I've seen, and the time it has being going on, that is unlikely.' Anna did not know whether she was more grieved by the affair, or by the failure of her own ladies to warn her – especially Susanna, her special friend, on whom she had relied to be her ears at court. She felt like a fool.

She steeled herself not to cry. She did not love Henry, but she was his wife and Queen, and she felt slighted, humiliated and stupid.

'Tell me what you know,' she insisted.

Susanna looked uncomfortable. 'Kate Carey overheard Katheryn telling the Duchess of Richmond that the King had made her a grant of land. This was some weeks ago, when first we came to Whitehall. He has given her jewels too; she told Lady Rochford, and Lady Rochford – well, you know how she enjoys stirring things up – said she'd perceived his Grace was marvellously set on her, more than he had been on any woman in his life.'

It was easy to see why. Katheryn was young, graceful and pretty;

having her as his mistress would flatter Henry's vanity. He would be rejuvenated by her youth and vivacity. It made Anna feel old and drab and useless.

'Are they lovers?' she whispered. Could Henry do with Katheryn what he had failed to do with her?

Susanna swallowed. 'She hinted to Lady Rochford that he was laying siege to her virtue, as Lady Rochford took great pleasure in telling us, but she said she would not stain her family's honour by granting him favours. Madam, it is the same game Anne Boleyn played, and look where it got *her*.'

'It got her beheaded,' Anna snapped, pacing up and down in turmoil. 'These Howards, they are behind this. I know it.'

Susanna spread her hands helplessly. 'I fear you are right. The ladies think Katheryn is alienating the King's affections from you.'

Strangely, Anna felt little anger against Katheryn herself. When the King had beckoned, Katheryn would have had no choice, nor the strength of character to say no to him and the puppet masters who were probably priming her for queenship. As an ageing man, Henry had little to offer a giddy young girl, but the prospect of a crown would compensate for that.

She was furious with Henry, with Norfolk and his faction – and with those who had kept this from her and left her to her false illusions. She was scared too, because if Henry wanted to marry Katheryn – it would not be the first, or even the second, time he had resolved to advance a maid-of-honour to the consort's throne – then what might he not do to rid himself of her?

'Who else knows about this affair?' She was terse towards Susanna, deeply wounded by her concealing a matter that touched herself so closely.

'I think it is common knowledge, Madam,' Susanna whispered.

Of course. It made sense now that there had been a decrease in the numbers resorting to her court. Her star was falling. Naturally, the courtiers would be fawning over Katheryn Howard now.

'I will not have gossip about it in my household,' she said. 'Will you make that clear to everyone?'

'Yes, Madam,' Susanna said, curtseying as if they were on the most formal of terms.

'You may go,' Anna said.

Left alone, she wept. Susanna had been a cherished friend, but Anna could not see past her betrayal. What sort of friend kept something so vital to herself? She did not think she could ever trust Susanna again, or forgive her. And what of those who had colluded in the deception? Was there anyone who was loyal to her?

She did not tax Henry with what she knew. She tried to continue as if all were well, although she was alert for the slightest indication that it was not. But he gave nothing away, as usual.

She behaved as normal to Katheryn, making sure she gave the girl no cause to complain about her. Katheryn was probably as much a victim of circumstances as she herself was, and there was no malice in her; you could not help liking her.

That night, as Henry snored beside her, oblivious to the turmoil raging in her heart, she lay wakeful and restless, obsessing over the fates of her predecessors. Both Katherine and Anne had been supplanted by their maids-of-honour. Might Henry use similar means to rid himself of her? Yet surely he could not so easily set aside a princess of Kleve?

Indeed he could, for he had put away a princess of mighty Spain!

The next day, Anna summoned Dr Harst, and received him with only Mother Lowe present. Mother Lowe, she was relieved to find, had known nothing about Henry's pursuit of Katheryn Howard, and had been shocked when Anna confided in her.

'Dr Harst,' she said, 'it has come to my notice that the King is enamoured of one of my maids-of-honour.' She saw from his expression that he knew. 'You are aware of it,' she said, feeling again that sense of betrayal, and making it sound like an accusation. Did the whole court know? Were people laughing behind their hands at her? Was she considered so weak in character that even her friends had conspired to keep silent about what was going on?

'I have become aware of it lately, Madam,' he replied. She wondered if he was telling the truth.

'It seems his Majesty has been pursuing Mistress Katheryn Howard for some time,' she said. 'It is a great grievance to me that no one saw fit to inform me. Forewarned is forearmed, as they say.'

'Madam, I believe, from what I have heard, that it is mere dalliance. Such things should be beneath your Grace's notice, of course, and I have been debating with myself whether it was better to spare you pain, or to cause it through telling you about a circumstance that is probably of no account.'

Anna was not sure if she believed him. 'I have my interests to protect,' she retorted, 'and it is in my interests to know what is going on, however trivial the affair might be. It is my duty to preserve the alliance I represent.'

'I am sure it *is* trivial, Madam, so do not be too concerned. I hear this King is often given to amours of no consequence.'

'And were they of no consequence when his eye lighted on Anne Boleyn, and Jane Seymour? Dr Harst, it has happened before, and it may happen again, if the King's fancy turns to another lady. What of my position then? Do I merely acquiesce, and retire gracefully? Or do I oppose him, as Queen Katherine did, and face the consequences?'

'Madam, with respect, you are inflating this matter out of all proportion. I'm sure the King will soon be inviting you to join him on his annual summer progress, and this young lady will be forgotten.'

'He has given her land and jewels. I saw them together. He did not look as if he would soon be forgetting her. Believe me, Dr Harst, that girl is a threat – to me, and to Kleve!' Anna was nearly beside herself with anxiety.

'It is a pity your Grace is not yet with child,' Dr Harst blurted out, then reddened. 'Forgive me, that was unpardonable.'

'But most apposite,' Anna replied. 'I pray for it daily.'

He looked as if he would have said more, but had thought better of it. Maybe he was wondering if those rumours had been true. She would not enlighten him.

'We shall see,' she said. 'The summer progress is only two months hence. I shall look forward to accompanying the King.'

She could not bring herself to forgive Susanna. She kept looking covertly at her ladies in turn, as they sat sewing, and thinking: Did you know?

And then, miracle of miracles, Katheryn was curtseying before her, asking for permission to leave court and go to the house of her grandmother at Lambeth, on the Surrey shore of the Thames. Anna's first thought was that Henry was becoming too persistent, and that Katheryn was running away from his unwelcome advances.

'And how long do you wish to stay there?' she asked.

Katheryn's blue eyes filled with tears; she could even cry prettily. 'I wish to leave court, Madam,' she whispered.

'Why? Has someone been unkind to you?' Anna persisted, wondering if the girl was fleeing from her uncle's bullying. Norfolk was not a man for niceties, she would wager. He would take little account of his niece's feelings.

'No, Madam,' Katheryn sobbed.

'But I thought you were happy here?'

'Madam, I was.'

'Is it a young man?'

Katheryn dabbed at her eyes. 'No, Madam. My grandmother needs me.'

Anna thought it astonishing that a daughter of the Howards would leave court just because she was needed at home. From what she had heard, their mission was to secure advancement for every member of their grasping family. Maybe the grandmother was arranging a match for Katheryn, and Katheryn did not favour it. And who was she, Anna, to disrupt the Howards' schemes? Besides, it would be much to her advantage if the girl went home.

When next they took what had become a regular walk in the gardens, Anna told Dr Harst about Katheryn's departure.

'I am relieved to hear it, Madam,' he said. 'I trust your Grace is happier now.'

'I am indeed. The King is being very kind to me.' Henry had supped with her every evening lately and brought her two gifts, a brooch and a book. He had not behaved like a man desperately missing his lady love. 'I think Mistress Howard's absence is to be permanent. Possibly a husband is in the offing.'

'Ah.' Harst looked pleased.

But Anna's good mood soon dissipated. Later that day, as she was sitting in her privy garden, embroidering with her ladies and enjoying the June sunshine, Lady Rochford looked up from her tambour and smiled. Anna had never liked that smile – it made the woman look like a vixen.

'It is hard to believe your Grace has been married nearly seven months,' she said.

'The time has gone quickly,' Anna replied. She noticed the ladies exchanging glances.

'We all wish that your Grace could be with child,' Lady Rutland said.

'Indeed we do,' Lady Rochford echoed.

'I know I am not with child,' Anna declared, resenting them raising so delicate a matter.

'How is it possible for your Grace to know that?' asked Lady Edgcumbe.

'I know it well, I am not,' she retorted, in a tone she hoped would silence them.

'It would be such a great benefit to the realm, to have a duke of York join his brother in the nursery,' Lady Rutland persisted. 'It must be his Majesty's chief desire.'

Anna felt herself flushing. She knew how catty the English ladies could be. Were they implying it was her fault that she was not pregnant?

Lady Edgcumbe laughed. 'I think your Grace is a maid still!'

Anna's cheeks grew hotter.

'By Our Lady, Madam, I think your Grace *is* a maid still,' Lady Rochford chimed in.

This was intolerable. 'How can I be a maid and sleep every night with the King?' Anna snapped.

'Sleep? There must be more than that,' chuckled Lady Rochford, 'or else the King might as well lie in his own chamber.'

'Well of course there is more than that!' Anna snapped again. Her words oozed sarcasm. 'When the King comes to bed, he kisses me, and takes me by the hand, and bids me, "Good night, sweetheart"; and in the morning, he kisses me and bids me, "Farewell, darling." Is this not enough?'

There was a silence.

Lady Rutland swallowed. 'Madam, there must be more than this, or it will be long before we have a duke of York, which all this realm most desires.'

Anna shrugged. 'I am contented with what I have, for I know no more.' Let them think her ignorant!

Lady Rutland pressed her. 'Did your Grace not tell this to Mother Lowe?'

Anna had had enough of being interrogated. 'For shame!' she exclaimed. 'I receive quite as much of his Majesty's attention as I wish!'

Afterwards, she regretted having admitted that her marriage was a sham. The ladies would probably gossip, and gossip spread fast in this court. She prayed it would not come to the King's ears.

On the evening of Midsummer Day, Anna was in her bedchamber, trying to mend the clasp on a necklace. Susanna and Gertrude were tidying away her day clothes, and from outside the open window she could hear the shouts of boatmen on the Thames.

Henry was coming to supper. Next door, her ladies were setting the table. Anna could hear them chatting. Suddenly, she was alert, having heard the name Katheryn Howard.

'It seems the King is still much taken with her,' came Lady Edgcumbe's voice. 'I hear he frequently passes over the river in a little boat to visit her, in full view of the citizens of London.'

'And sometimes he goes at midnight,' said the Duchess of Richmond.

Anna froze.

Susanna, who had been trying hard to win back her favour, looked at her in sympathy. 'Pay no heed, Madam,' she said. 'It is just malicious talk. You do not need to hear it.'

'Yes, I do!' Anna flared. 'You kept too much from me before.'

Susanna fell silent.

'My lord Bishop of Winchester seems to be playing pimp!' Anna heard Lady Rochford say. 'He entertains them in his palace.'

'We know what mark he shoots at!' someone giggled.

'My lord says the gossip is rife in the City.' That was the Duchess of Suffolk. 'It's rife at court too. People are saying these signs betoken that the King intends to divorce the Queen.'

'All they betoken is adultery!' Lady Rochford tutted.

Anna felt sick. Just then, the King's arrival was announced. She would have liked to slap her ladies, and him, for good measure, or at least send him away, so that she could curl up somewhere and weep, but she did not dare. No, whatever it cost her, she must exert herself to be a gracious supper companion, and do all she could to preserve her marriage and the alliance.

She joined Henry, sinking into a deep obeisance. He was in a good mood, and over the repast they talked of his plans for the progress, the building works at Hampton Court, and the excellence of the beef. He did not stay the night, but bade her a very cheerful farewell.

The next day, she was perturbed when a deputation of Privy councillors requested an audience. She received them in her presence chamber, with her ladies present, wondering, in some trepidation, why they had come.

The Duke of Suffolk acted as spokesman. 'Your Grace,' he said, his expression unreadable, 'the King desires you to remove from court to Richmond Palace two days hence, for your health and pleasure.'

Alarums began sounding in Anna's head. Why send a deputation to tell her that? It came to her that Queen Katherine had been banished from court prior to being divorced. Was she too to be repudiated? In a flash, she understood how vulnerable she was – a foreigner, isolated in England, far from her friends. Unlike Katherine, she had no court faction, no powerful Emperor to support her. What was she to do?

The only course, it seemed, was to do the King's bidding and hope for the best.

'My lords,' she said, making herself smile at them, 'I am content to depart at his Majesty's pleasure. I will be ready as soon as I can.'

'Thank you, Madam,' the Duke said, looking more cheerful. 'Every arrangement will be made for your comfort.'

After the Privy councillors had left, Anna gave Mother Lowe orders for the packing of her household gear and belongings. Trying not to read too much into the King's order, she went to her closet to pray for guidance. But the remembrance of Henry last night, at supper, kept intruding. He had said nothing of sending her to Richmond, so why the sudden concern for her health?

She lay awake for much of the night. In the dark hours, it seemed certain that this move was a preamble to his divorcing her. Even in the morning, she was still convinced it boded no good.

Unable to bear the uncertainty any longer, she summoned Dr Harst.

'Madam, what is wrong?' he asked. 'I am dismayed to see you looking so sorrowful.'

'The King is sending me away,' she said, fighting back tears, and recounted what had happened.

Harst hastened to reassure her. 'Madam, I was told that he is sending you to Richmond to protect you from plague in the City.'

'I had not heard there was plague in London. My ladies say the King is mortally terrified of plague, and removes to a safe distance upon any hint of it. Is he departing too, then?'

'I cannot say, Madam.'

'Dr Harst, I fear this is just an excuse to get me out of the way.'

'Madam, I think not!' Harst protested. 'I sensed the motive was concern for your well-being. It did not occur to me that you would be upset by this. And Richmond is not so very far from the court; less than two hours along the river, they say.'

Anna was far from convinced. 'Dr Harst, there are rumours at court, and in the City, that the King means to repudiate me for Katheryn Howard, just as he repudiated Queen Katherine for Queen Anne, and Queen Anne for Queen Jane.'

'Madam, this is mere gossip. I have heard nothing to substantiate it, I assure you. Please, do not worry any more. I will come to visit you at Richmond, and if I hear anything that perturbs me in the meantime, I will tell you.'

His words were reassuring, but the concern in his eyes led Anna to believe otherwise.

With a heavy heart, she prepared to leave Whitehall. On the morning of her departure, Rutland came to say that her barge awaited her outside. 'His Majesty has asked me to inform you that he will visit you at Richmond in two days' time.'

The relief was overwhelming. Henry's concern had been genuine. 'I am surprised he does not come now, to escape the plague,' she said.

'Plague?' Rutland looked bewildered. 'Madam, there is no plague.'

'That is strange,' she observed, her heart sinking. 'Dr Harst was informed I was being sent away to avoid the plague.'

Rutland seemed at a loss for words.

'If there is no plague, why am I being sent to the country to escape it?' she persisted.

'Madam, I cannot answer that. Perchance Dr Harst was mistaken. You are being sent there for your health, because the air is clean. That's what I have been told.'

He knew more than he would say, she was sure. She was certain now that Dr Harst had been lied to.

'His Majesty will see you in two days,' Rutland said brightly.

'I shall look forward to it,' Anna replied.

But, as the barge pulled away from the jetty, she was full of forebodings.

Despite her anxieties, she found Richmond a little paradise on earth. As her barge made its tranquil way westwards along the Thames, the beautiful palace rose up ahead of her, distinguished by vast expanses of bay windows, fairy-tale pinnacles, and turrets surmounted by bell-shaped domes and gilded weathervanes. Encircling it was a mighty brick wall, with a tower at each corner, and beyond that lay a large deer park.

Soon she had to admit that it was wonderful to have this little Eden to herself, with the freedom to wander undisturbed through the courtyards, sit by the splashing fountains and take the air in the pleasant knot gardens. When it rained the next day, she walked in the galleried cloisters around the gardens, and explored the great tower, which contained the royal lodgings built by Henry's father. Hers were on the second floor, Henry's on the first. She heard Mass in the richly appointed chapel, and leafed through precious illuminated manuscripts in the library.

'It's sad that the King rarely stays here now,' Lady Edgcumbe said; she was in attendance with Lady Rutland, the two of them accompanying Anna as she walked along a path bordered by lime trees.

'I marvel at that, seeing it is so beautiful,' Anna said.

'He came here often in the early years of his reign,' Lady Rutland recalled.

'Why doesn't he come now?' Anna asked.

'He prefers his more modern palaces, like Hampton Court and Whitehall, where the royal lodgings are all on the first floor, in the French fashion. This tower seems so old-fashioned now.'

'That does not worry *me*,' Anna smiled. 'I grew up in ancient castles – and I think Richmond is lovely.'

Chapter 15

1540

Anna tried to see things in perspective and persuade herself there was nothing sinister about her being sent to this beautiful place. She reminded herself that Henry would be here tomorrow, and she would know then whether something was amiss, although one could never tell with Henry.

The next day, she waited, counting down the hours, trying to estimate the time of his arrival. When dusk fell, she had to accept the fact that she, like Richmond itself, had been forgotten, abandoned . . .

Yet someone did come – two people she very much wanted to meet. The following afternoon, as Anna was racked with fevered speculation over Henry's failure to visit her, the Lady Mary and the Lady Elizabeth were announced. A small, slight young woman, overladen with finery and jewels, entered the room, holding by the hand a slender child with red hair, an unusually old face for one so young, and a bearing way ahead of her six years. Both curtseyed gracefully.

'My Lady Mary, my Lady Elizabeth, you are most welcome!' Anna declared, wondering if Mary had come as the King's emissary. 'I am overjoyed to meet you both at last.'

'Your Grace, we are on our way to Whitehall, and I thought we should seize the opportunity of making your acquaintance.' Mary spoke in a deep, gruff voice, and had a disconcerting way of peering at you as she did so. There was no mistaking whose daughter she was, with her red hair and blue eyes, although her features were blunter than Henry's. Clearly, though, she had not come from the King, which sent Anna's spirits plummeting, yet she provided a welcome distraction. While the Duchess of Richmond took Elizabeth off to the stool room, Mary greeted Anna's ladies warmly, especially her cousin Margaret Douglas.

'The Lady Margaret was my lady-of-honour at one time,' she told Anna.

'Until I was made to serve Anne Boleyn.' Margaret made a face.

Mary stiffened. 'That woman gave my mother and me much grief,' she said vehemently.

'I have heard that Queen Katherine was a most gracious and devout lady,' Anna said soothingly.

'Oh, she was!' Mary breathed. 'She was a wonderful mother, and true to her principles to the last. She was ready to face a terrible death, rather than compromise them. Anne Boleyn was utterly cruel to her, and to me. It was thanks to her that my father broke with Rome. I pray constantly that he will one day be reconciled to the Holy Father.'

Anna judged it safer to nod rather than reply, fearing that Henry would not approve of his daughter's sentiments. She sensed in Mary a banked-up tide of bitterness at the blows life – and Anne Boleyn – had dealt her.

'But I hear Queen Jane was kind to you and helped you to be reconciled to the King,' she ventured.

'She was a good woman and a kindly soul, God rest her.' Mary crossed herself. 'And now, I must call your Grace "Mother".'

'Nothing would give me greater pleasure,' Anna said, taking Mary's hands in hers. 'Although I can hardly be that in truth, because we are almost of an age, yet I mean to show you a mother's kindness, and be your friend. Pray, sit with me, and I will send for refreshments. Then we can talk.'

She sent for wine, poured some for Mary and Margaret and gratefully downed a goblet herself. It left her feeling distanced from her fears. She poured another.

'Before Elizabeth returns, I should warn your Grace that we do not mention Anne Boleyn in her presence,' Mary said. 'She is a winning child, and I do the best I can for her, but there is a wayward, capricious side to her, and she needs firm moral guidance to prevent her from turning out like her mother.'

228

Obviously Mary knew Elizabeth better, but Anna was captivated by the six-year-old's charm and precocious wit. As they talked, she became aware of how bright and perceptive Elizabeth was. There was about her an air of brilliance that Mary lacked. Maybe it had surrounded Mary once, and the troubles she had suffered had extinguished it.

When Elizabeth impulsively took Anna's hand and squeezed it, then gently touched her face, as if she was hardly able to believe that this new stepmother was real, Anna felt choked. The child clearly needed a mother's love and stability in her life. Mary, with her enduring hatred of Elizabeth's mother, was perhaps not the best mentor, although it was plain she loved her half-sister.

As Mary relaxed, her kindness and innate sincerity became evident, and Anna began to enjoy her company, warming to her more and more, but it was Elizabeth who captured her heart.

They spent the afternoon discussing Elizabeth's education, her dogs, her dolls, court entertainments and their different upbringings; they swapped anecdotes about mutual acquaintances and agreeing on the merits of Richmond. Anna noticed how relieved Mary showed herself when told she had been brought up a Catholic.

'I must confess, I thought you were one of those dreadful German Protestants!' she said.

'So do many people,' Anna replied. 'I wish they didn't. I go to Mass often enough.'

Mary beamed approvingly. 'I rejoice to hear it. And I'm impressed to find that you speak English well.'

'I have worked hard at it,' Anna admitted, pleased.

After that, Mary seemed even more disposed to be friendly. By the time the princesses left, to take their barge to Whitehall, Anna felt she had found a new friend – and an adoptive daughter.

It was now the end of June. Waiting at Richmond for a husband who never came, Anna wondered if the King's barge was still being rowed across the Thames to the house of the Duchess of Norfolk, so that he could pass his evenings with Katheryn Howard.

Most of her attendants were in touch with friends or relations at court, so news and gossip did reach Richmond, although Anna suspected that some was censored before it got to her. The most sensational, if not unexpected, news was that Cromwell had been attainted by Parliament, and adjudged a traitor.

'That means he will die, and his family will be left destitute,' Anna said to Mother Lowe as they sunned themselves by the riverbank. She could not stop thinking of Elizabeth Seymour and Cromwell's son, Gregory, and what a dreadful blow this must be for them; but the worst blow would be that which would fall on Cromwell. She shivered. 'How terrible, on such a beautiful day, to be shut away in the Tower, knowing you will soon be led out to execution.' In England, her ladies had told her, they cut off traitors' heads with an axe. In Germany, at least, decapitation was by the sword, which was kinder. Queen Anne had been accorded the dubious privilege of being beheaded by a swordsman, and it had been mercifully quick. Pray God Cromwell's end would be as speedy when his time came.

Deep down, Anna wondered if, when it came to it, Henry would destroy the man who had been his chief minister and mainstay. Had arranging her marriage really been what had brought Cromwell down? Or had it merely been a pretext for the Catholic party to remove him?

Helping herself to an apple from the basket of food Mother Lowe had brought with her, Anna had an alarming thought. What if Henry himself was punishing Cromwell for arranging a marriage he no longer wanted? The Emperor and the French King were now vying for England's friendship. What if the alliance with Kleve was no longer needed? Suddenly, it seemed she was standing on the brink of an abyss.

'It's clear that Norfolk was instrumental in his fall,' she said. 'Lord Rutland says the King was so appalled by the evidence that he did not question it. But who can his Grace trust hereafter, if he could not trust Cromwell?'

Mother Lowe did not answer. She had drifted off to sleep, leaving Anna alone with her teeming thoughts.

* * *

Just when she had given up hope of ever seeing him at Richmond, Henry arrived.

'A thousand apologies, Anna!' he said. 'State and parliamentary affairs have detained me – and this miserable business with Cromwell.'

'It is no matter,' she said. 'You are here now.' She wished she had worn her jewels, and a headdress, but maybe she looked becoming enough in her simple rose-coloured gown, with her fair hair unbound. She called for wine, and when they had drunk each other's health, Henry led her to the bowling alley, where he taught her how to play. His leg was not troubling him today.

'You beat me!' he cried, incredulous, when, by a very lucky chance, she won. Certainly she had not intended to.

'Again!' he cried, and this time he emerged victorious.

They had supper early, so that he could catch the tide. She was tempted to ask him why she was being kept here at Richmond, but it had been a most pleasant afternoon, and she did not want to risk spoiling it.

'I do hope your Grace will come again another day,' she said, as Henry kissed her hand in farewell.

'I will come again tomorrow,' he told her.

He left her happier than she had felt in weeks. She poured herself a glass of wine to celebrate.

The next day, she took more care in choosing what to wear, determined to entice Henry to her bed. She selected a low-necked gown of red and black embellished with heavy goldsmiths' work, with full sleeves slashed and puffed with bows and bands. With it, she wore an ornate necklace from which hung a great crucifix with pendant pearls. She left her hair loose, like a bride.

When Henry arrived, she noticed his eyes on her bosom. But he was in a different mood today, nowhere near as talkative, and seemed barely to be listening to what she was saying. Supper was a rushed affair, as he was anxious to get back to Whitehall.

Maybe, she thought later, as she tossed and turned in bed, it was beginning to dawn on him that it would be a mistake to execute Cromwell. Or maybe – God forbid – he had been offended by the immodest gown. Her cheeks burned to think he might have guessed at her ploy to seduce him, and that she had humiliated herself. Next time, she would wear something discreet.

But when would next time be?

'Madam, wake up!' Mother Lowe was shaking her. Reluctantly, Anna dragged herself away from a dream in which she was back in Kleve, safe in the knowledge that she would never have to leave it again. She awoke and saw it was still dark outside.

'What's happening?' she mumbled, rubbing sleep from her eyes. She could see the clock on the mantel in the flickering light of Mother Lowe's candle. It was a little after two o'clock.

'Madam, Mr Berde of the King's Privy Chamber is here to see you. You must rise and make haste to receive him.' From the urgency in her nurse's voice, and the unearthliness of the hour, Anna deduced that someone must have died. Not the King, Heaven forbid?

She was shaking as Mother Lowe put on her velvet night robe, linking its clasps right up to her neck. Having slipped on her shoes and had her hair brushed and her face washed, she stepped into her privy chamber, where her women, who had heard the commotion, were gathering in consternation, some wearing wraps or cloaks, others still in their night-rails.

'Make yourselves decent and attend me in the presence chamber,' Anna instructed. 'I have a visitor from the King.'

Even at this hour, Mr Berde was immaculately dressed, clean-shaven and brisk in manner. As Anna took her seat on the dais, he gave a brief bow and proceeded quickly to his business.

'Your Grace, I bring a message from the King,' he said.

'At this hour?' she asked.

'Alas, Madam, the matter will not wait, and it must be submitted before Parliament in the morning.'

Anna steeled herself for bad news.

'His Majesty wishes to inform you that he has grave doubts about the validity of your marriage.'

In the deepest core of her heart she had expected this. It prompted fear and perplexity rather than shock. *What will happen to me? How should I respond?* She felt faint and dizzy.

'His Majesty,' Berde continued in his officious manner, 'has unburdened himself of his doubts to Parliament, which, aware that there is but one male heir of his body to ensure the succession, and of the likelihood of civil war should that line fail, has petitioned him to commit the examination of validity of your marriage to the bishops and clergy.'

Anna heard his words through a buzzing in her temples. Was Henry such a moral coward that he could not face discussing his doubts with her? Did he have to arm himself with a body of official opinion before sending a messenger?

'Madam, for the validity of the marriage to be examined by an ecclesiastical court, your Grace's consent is essential, which is why I am here,' Berde was saying.

Now it became clear. Berde's visit had been timed to intimidate her into complying. At night, human defences are down, and even little issues seem like big ones. She was trembling now, understanding the reality of the situation, and the enormity of the decision she had to make. Queen Katherine had faced this dilemma, and chosen what she believed to be the right path – and she had suffered for it, hounded to an early death. Since then, the King had had a wife beheaded. If Anna proved obdurate, would he have any scruples in sending her to the scaffold too?

She could not speak. Her mind was teeming with fear and anger. She had done no wrong, and should not be in this position. The alliance must be protected – but at the cost of her suffering, her very life, even? If the King rejected her now and sent her home disgraced, no other man would consider her. Worse still, her brother, impoverished though he was, might feel obliged to retaliate by declaring war on England – when he had the Emperor baying at his gates. Wilhelm might even blame her for the failure of the alliance, and for not trying hard enough to please the King. He would see her conduct as detrimental to Kleve, treason even . . .

Any moment now, she thought, she would fall in a faint.

Berde was waiting for her answer. If she denied him what he had come for, she could be on her way to the Tower within the hour. Her every instinct was telling her to say, 'Yes, yes, do what you will!' – but duty to her brother, and to Kleve, prevented her.

With a huge effort of will, she stood up. 'Mr Berde, I will give this weighty matter the most thorough consideration. You shall have my answer presently. Please wait here.'

She could see from his face that he was not best pleased, but he made no complaint and bowed as she led her ladies out.

She had thought to sleep on the matter, but when she returned to her bedchamber, she knew that getting back to sleep would be impossible. What she needed now was wise counsel. She summoned an usher, who came stumbling in, half awake and hastily dressed.

'Send for Dr Harst,' she commanded. 'Apologise for disturbing his rest, but ask him to come at once. It is a matter of vital importance.'

The usher lumbered off. Anna prayed he would catch a convenient tide for Westminster, where Harst was lodging. She called for wine, to steady herself. She waited – and waited, her women sitting around her, stifling yawns. They had all heard Berde's words, or been told of the purpose of his visit. No one spoke. It was as if everything was in suspension until Harst came with what Anna prayed would be a magical solution to her dilemma.

When three o'clock chimed, she ordered that wine and little cakes be served to Mr Berde in the presence chamber, and had a second drink herself. Another hour passed. She tried not to feel guilty about keeping him waiting; after all, he had not scrupled to disturb her slumber.

At last, at four o'clock, Dr Harst was brought in, through the door of the privy stair that led up from the deserted King's apartments. Anna had sent a groom to conduct him that way, so he should not meet Berde.

'Oh, my good friend, I was never more glad to see anyone!' she cried, holding out her hands to the ambassador. She had now downed three goblets of wine, and was feeling emotional.

'What has happened, Madam?' Harst asked, his brow furrowed with concern.

'The King has grave doubts about the validity of our marriage. He has consulted Parliament and wants an ecclesiastical inquiry, for which my consent is essential. He sent one of his gentlemen, Mr Berde, here tonight, at two o'clock, to obtain it.'

'I trust you have not given him an answer,' Harst said, in alarm. 'This needs the weightiest consideration.'

'Which is why I have sent for you. I said I will give my answer presently. Mr Berde is waiting without. Dr Harst, what shall I do?' A tear rolled down her cheek.

Harst took her hand and squeezed it. She recognised the uncharacteristic gesture as a measure of his sympathy. 'I think we should take advice from your chamberlain,' he said. 'He is the King's cousin, and knows him well, and he is also your friend. My guess is that he has heard something of this matter already. Let us confer with him, and agree on the best course to take.'

Anna dismissed her ladies and sent for Rutland, who brought Wymond Carew as his interpreter. Anna would have preferred not to discuss the matter before the stiff-necked Carew, but she had no choice, since she did not want Susanna Gilman gossiping about it. She was still sore with Susanna, still smarting from her betrayal.

'My lord,' Dr Harst said to the Earl, 'the King's Highness has sent the Queen a certain message, to which he requires an answer.'

Anna could see, from the look of comprehension on Rutland's drawn face, that he already knew what that message contained.

'I know of this matter,' he admitted. He turned to Anna. 'My instructions were not to mention it until the King had informed your Grace.'

'It seems I am always the last to know what is going on,' she observed drily, noticing Carew regarding her with something like sympathy, which made her warm to him a little. 'My lord, I have summoned you and Dr Harst because I do not know what answer I should make to the King. Mr Berde is waiting for it. I cannot keep him waiting much longer.'

Rutland considered for a moment. 'My advice, Madam, would be to send whatever answer you think fit, either in writing or by mouth.'

'I will not write anything down,' she declared. 'Could you take my answer to the King, Dr Harst?'

'By no means, Madam! He will not welcome my involvement, and might try to prevent me from helping you in future.'

'Very well, I will send Mr Berde. But what shall I say?'

'Do not immediately give consent,' Harst urged. 'Promise the King his request will receive serious consideration. Tell him his messenger took you unawares. Play for time.'

'But that only defers the decision,' Anna said, disappointed that neither Harst nor Rutland would advise her what course to take. 'If I consent, I fear his Grace will find a way to divorce me. That means returning to Kleve in disgrace, which could imperil the friendship between my brother and the King. It might even mean war – and punishment for me. But, if I refuse his Majesty's request, it may go hard for me . . .' She began weeping uncontrollably.

'Madam, be of good comfort,' Rutland said gently. 'The King's Highness wishes only to abide by the law of God and discharge his conscience and yours. All will be done for the best, so your Grace has cause to rejoice, not to be sorry.'

Anna dabbed her eyes and nodded, feeling drained. Maybe Henry really was just making sure that all was sound and lawful.

She looked at Dr Harst for guidance, but he merely smiled sympathetically. She turned back to Rutland. 'Pray tell Mr Berde I am considering the King's request,' she said.

When Rutland had gone, Harst's smile vanished. 'Madam, I cannot express the outrage I feel on your behalf. Matters must not be allowed to progress until Duke Wilhelm has been consulted. You are right to be concerned. If you resist an annulment, as Queen Katherine did, you risk repercussions, and your brother may well feel bound to go to war on your behalf. That is why I would not take any message to the King. I do not want my actions, or yours, misinterpreted.'

'What should I do?' Anna asked desperately. 'Shouldn't I just consent? If the King is grateful and well disposed towards me, then he will remain well disposed towards Kleve as well, and the alliance will not be at risk.'

'Alas, Madam, I fear the King no longer needs that alliance. The Emperor and the King of France are now falling over each other to gain his friendship.'

'So Wilhelm will not blame me if the alliance fails?'

'Why should he? Madam, if the King divorces you, he will surely wish to placate the Duke by any means he can. He does not want war.'

'But if he forges a friendship with the Emperor, Charles may require his support in the matter of Guelders.'

'I think his Majesty is in a position to dictate terms, Madam. We must do all we can to ensure he remains friendly towards Kleve. If he does not, it will be a rift of his own making, not yours.'

'You do not know my brother!' Anna wrung her hands. 'He has very firm views on how wives should conduct themselves. He will blame *me*! If I am sent back to Kleve in disgrace, he may kill me!'

'Madam, calm yourself, please!' Harst urged. 'Leave this with me. I will go to Whitehall as soon as it is light, and try to sound out some of the Privy councillors, to see if the King really does just need to be reassured that your union is lawful. Given the previous troubles that have befallen his marriages, that is entirely possible.'

Anna doubted it, but she let Harst go and went back to bed, evading the questions of her ladies. 'I am tired, I must sleep,' she told them. Sleep was impossible, of course, but she must get some rest. She poured another glass of wine.

In the morning, she felt drained, nervy and sick. Harst had left soon after dawn, and Anna could not settle to anything, not even her embroidery. When the Duchess of Suffolk asked the musicians to play, Anna had to ask them to stop, for a headache was threatening. She sat there, unable to engage in conversation, turning around in her mind the events of the night, wondering what Harst was doing, and when he would return. At dinner, she could not eat.

Shortly before one o'clock, she heard footsteps approaching and jumped up eagerly. But it was not Dr Harst. Instead, Lord Chancellor Audley, Bishop Gardiner, the Duke of Suffolk and other Privy councillors were announced.

She knocked over her chair in her haste to get to the presence chamber.

'I must not keep these lords waiting,' she told her ladies. 'They come from the King.' She would give Henry no cause for criticism.

Suffolk was his usual bluff, hearty self, a King's man through and through. The Lord Chancellor was impassive, with a bland manner, the Bishop dark-browed, sardonic and uncompromising. Apart from Mr Carew, who had been brought as interpreter, Anna did not know who the other men were, but at least they all made a respectful reverence as she entered.

'Madam,' said Audley, 'may I present Bishop Gardiner, Sir Thomas Cheyney, Sir Richard Rich, all of the Privy Council, and Sir William Kingston, Comptroller of the King's Household and Constable of the Tower.'

The Tower! Anna felt her blood run cold as she struggled for words to greet a wizened old man who looked near death, but offered a courtly greeting. Were there soldiers outside, waiting to arrest her? Or was Sir William's presence here meant purely to intimidate her?

'Madam,' Suffolk said, 'we are here to reiterate the King's request that you consent to an ecclesiastical inquiry into the validity of your marriage, and to hear your answer.'

She made herself smile graciously. 'My lord, I am giving the matter the most serious consideration. You will have my answer very soon.'

Suffolk grunted his annoyance. 'Very well, Madam, but it would be convenient if you did not delay too long. The matter is pressing.'

She inclined her head, saying nothing.

Audley's voice filled the silence. 'We have received certain documents relating to your Grace's precontract. To your knowledge, were there any formal proceedings to annul it?'

Anna strove to stay calm. 'My lords, as I have told the King already, I was a child when that betrothal was made. I was only told of it after everything had been agreed. Some years later, I was informed that it had been broken. I'm afraid that is all I know.'

'So, when your marriage to his Majesty was mooted, you believed that you were free to wed?'

'I did, my lords.'

'You were not aware that your betrothal had not been formally dissolved?'

'I believed it had been.'

Audley sighed. 'Madam, your brother has sent the King, as proof, a notary's certificate written and signed in the presence of Grand Master Hochsteden and Vice Chancellor Olisleger. It states that the precontract was repudiated on the fifteenth of February 1535.'

'Then you have the proof you need,' Anna said, relieved.

'No, Madam, we do not,' Gardiner snapped. 'This certificate has an odour of trickery about it. It was sealed with the emblem of a beer pot! How could anyone give such a document any credence?'

'Moreover,' Audley added, 'it does not contain the proof that was promised by the Duke's councillors.'

'It appears, therefore, that no one in Cleves can produce any proofs, because such proofs do not exist,' Gardiner barked. 'There should be a record in the appropriate church archive, and in the ducal archives of Cleves too, yet it appears neither can be found.'

Anna realised that the case for an annulment could be strong. Yet she would say nothing until she had conferred with Dr Harst.

'It sounds as if you are blaming me for the apparent lack of proofs, my lords,' she said.

Audley cleared his throat. 'Not at all, Madam. We merely wish to make your Grace aware of the difficulties we have faced in trying to establish that your marriage is valid.'

'But I have formally renounced the precontract, at his Majesty's request.'

'I fear that does not satisfy the King,' Gardiner said. 'He cannot risk a disputed succession, should your Grace bear him children. All must be incontrovertibly lawful. The other question we must ask is . . .' He paused and studied her in his hawk-like fashion. '*Is* your Grace like to bear the King children?'

She felt the heat rising in her face. *They knew the answer to that.* But she would not confirm it. Non-consummation of a marriage was grounds for an annulment. Admit that, and they wouldn't be bothering with legal niceties about precontracts!

'I pray daily for that blessing,' she said.

'And you know of no impediment to it being vouchsafed?' Gardiner persisted, his black eyes boring into hers.

'I know of none, my lord.' Let them think her an innocent!

'We would like to speak to your ladies,' Lord Audley said.

Anna's mind went winging back to the odd conversation she had had with Lady Rutland, Lady Rochford and Lady Edgcumbe not two weeks earlier. It had seemed almost like an interrogation, and now she suspected that they had been ordered to quiz her about what happened with Henry in the marital bed.

'I will send for them,' she said. She knew what they would say.

Audley and Gardiner spent the next hour or so taking depositions from her ladies, questioning them each in turn. One by one, the women emerged, embarrassed, upset or tight-lipped.

'We cannot say anything, Madam,' was their constant refrain, when Anna pressed them to tell her what had transpired. But she could well imagine what they had been asked.

Mother Lowe was defiant. 'I told them I spoke no English. In the end, they gave up, and with Katharina and Gertrude too. They'll not get me conniving at any annulment!'

Anna hugged her. 'Thank you, dear friend. What were they asking?'

'If you were a maid still.' Mother Lowe gave her a look.

Anna confided her suspicions that Lady Rochford, Lady Edgcumbe and Lady Rutland had been instructed to get the truth out of her. 'No doubt they are all gleefully recounting it now.'

Within an hour, the last of the maids-of-honour had returned from the presence chamber. Minutes later, Anna was summoned back.

'I am still queen!' she told the usher. 'No one summons me! Tell the lords I will grant them an audience in a quarter of an hour.'

She had made her point, but at some cost to herself, for it was the longest fifteen minutes she had ever spent. And when she did enter the presence chamber, her ladies in train, she found Audley and Gardiner in no very good mood. They wasted little time in getting to the nub of the matter.

'Madam, we have heard testimony that your marriage to the King remains unconsummated.'

She had not expected them to be so direct.

'That is a matter for the King to answer,' she said. 'He has always been the most attentive husband.'

'His Majesty has already revealed that he has never had relations with your Grace,' Gardiner said. 'He said his mind could not consent to it, for he knew in his heart that you are another man's wife and forbidden to him.'

'We would like your Grace to make a deposition confirming his Majesty's testimony,' Audley invited.

'My lords, I should like to take counsel of the ambassador of Kleve before I write or sign anything,' Anna insisted. 'I am expecting him this afternoon. I pray you, grant me grace to speak with him. I must have consideration for what my brother the Duke would expect of me.'

She could see they were displeased by her response.

'Very well, Madam,' Audley sighed. 'We will return to Whitehall and await your pleasure.'

Anna was now in no doubt that Henry was determined upon a divorce, and that the outcome of any inquiry was already decided. But what about what *she* wanted? What of the alliance it was her duty to preserve?

While she waited for Dr Harst, she took a brisk walk in the fresh air, under louring storm clouds that reflected her mood, and asked herself what she *did* want. She didn't love Henry, but she had grown fond of him, thinking the good in him outweighed the bad. She could have sworn he was becoming fond of her too. He had given a very good impression of it, for all he had apparently been nursing these doubts. Maybe rumour had spoken truth, and he had not liked her at the first. Yet he had made an effort to be kind to her, and she was certain a friendship had been building between them. There might have come a time when Henry liked her enough to forget about the precontract. But then his eye had been captivated by Katheryn Howard. Had his doubts been revived by his lust for her?

Did she really want him now? Anna asked herself. She could live without the constant worry, the fear of not being good enough, yet the prospect of losing Henry's friendship and company saddened her, even though she was angry with him. She liked being queen, with all the deference and privileges it brought, and she liked to feel she was making a difference to Kleve, and to England. She had begun to accept that the price she must pay was never again to know sexual love or the joy of children.

Henry had much to answer for! As Anna strode on, anger got the upper hand. This fuss about the precontract was nonsense. Wilhelm was a cautious man: he would not have let her wed if she was not free to do so. She was the King's true wife, and always would be, until death parted them. It was outrageous of his ministers to humiliate her like this. She was a princess of Kleve, and could not just be packed off home as unwanted goods. Her father would be turning in his grave if he knew how she was being treated. The Elector of Saxony and his Protestant allies would be shocked. A declaration of war was no less than the King deserved . . .

'Your Grace!' Kate Carey was calling her. 'Dr Harst is here.'

She flew indoors.

Harst was waiting in her presence chamber.

'Thank God, thank God!' she cried, motioning him to rise. 'The Lord Chancellor and Bishop Gardiner have been here. I have never felt so humiliated . . .' She recounted the events of the morning. 'They have gone back to court and are waiting on my answer.'

Harst was furious. 'They questioned you in my absence? No doubt they waited until I was at a safe distance! Well, Madam, I shall return to court in the morning, to complain about these unjust interrogations – *and* these highly dubious proceedings. I shall ask if it is the custom in England for a queen such as your Grace to be married, and then got rid of on a whim. I cannot credit that the King has sanctioned such treatment, and I shall demand that the Council inform him what they have done.'

'May God bless you,' Anna breathed. Truly, this good man was her champion. Yet she was not so sure that the King's proceedings were dubious at all, or that he was unaware of the tactics his councillors were deploying.

'Tell me, what happened at court?' she asked.

The doctor sighed. 'I asked for a meeting with the Privy Council. I was kept waiting until after dinner, when I was summoned before the Duke of Norfolk, Archbishop Cranmer, Sir Anthony Browne and the Bishop of Durham. They had the grace to apologise for not having invited me to dine with them; they said it was an oversight. When I asked what the King's message to your Grace portended, the Bishop told me the common people are circulating rumours about the legitimacy of your marriage. Therefore, for reassurance, and to avoid civil war in the future, his Majesty had ordered that the matter be tried. In the meantime, they assured me you would be treated as befitted your queenly rank.'

'The King wants an annulment, not reassurance,' Anna said. 'They are cozening you with fair words.'

'The Bishop of Durham assured me that the King is friendly towards your Grace, and will probably keep you as his wife, whatever the outcome. But I too am not convinced. I left with the impression that the King and his Council are working against your interests, and after what you have told me of their proceedings today, I agree, they are determined on an annulment. But I will still make a protest, on your behalf, in the strongest possible terms.'

Anna's heart was sinking. 'I am so grateful to you, Dr Harst. Did they say more?'

'They asked me if I would write to Duke Wilhelm explaining the matter, but I refused. They can explain themselves to him! After the meeting, I tried to persuade the Bishop to delay the inquiry until the dukes of Kleve and Saxony could send envoys to England, but he would not hear of it. So, Madam, I must be your sole advocate.'

'I could not have a better one,' Anna told him.

They were interrupted by shouts from the gatehouse below. She hastened to the window. 'A party of gentlemen have arrived,' she said. 'Oh, no. It is the Lord Chancellor and Bishop Gardiner again, with Suffolk and the rest. The Constable of the Tower is there too. Why have they returned? They said they would await my pleasure.' She was trembling, fearing they had come to arrest her; that the King was displeased by her failure to cooperate, and was punishing her for her defiance.

She felt dizzy, and wished she had eaten something. Had Anne Boleyn felt like this on the day they came for her?

'I imagine the King has insisted they obtain your consent to an inquiry,' Dr Harst said.

'I hope that is their only purpose.' Anna sounded far braver than she felt. 'Maybe I *should* give my consent. I'd hate to be seen to be clinging on to a husband who does not want me. I shall be reasonable.' *If it's not too late.*

'It is your decision to make, Madam,' Harst said. 'Whatever you decide, I will support it.'

Seating herself again in her chair of estate, she smoothed her skirts and checked that her hood was straight. She would receive them like the Queen she was. She would not be intimidated. Harst stood at her right hand, Wymond Carew on her left, as interpreter. Her heart was pounding in fear. This, she was convinced, was the beginning of the end.

As the councillors entered, she felt the world spin away, and everything went black.

When she opened her eyes, Mother Lowe was pressing her head forward, down to her knees.

'You fainted, Madam,' she said. 'Are you back with us now?' Anna sat up slowly, feeling dazed. Her women had clustered around her, and Dr Harst and the lords were staring at her, all looking concerned.

'I am perfectly well,' she told her ladies. 'Leave us now.'

'Is your Grace quite recovered?' Suffolk asked. 'We can wait if you need time to rest.'

All Anna's anxieties flooded back.

'I think her Grace would appreciate—' Harst began.

'I am better, thank you, my lords,' she said. 'Please proceed.'

Suffolk smiled gratefully. 'Madam, you are aware that Parliament wants the legality of your marriage investigated by a convocation of the clergy. Does your Grace understand what that means?'

'Yes, I do,' she answered. 'The bishops will determine if my precontract was properly dissolved.'

'That is so, Madam,' said Audley. 'And if they find there was no formal revocation, they may declare the marriage invalid. We are here to assure you that his Majesty is ready to do everything in his power to ensure that you do not suffer any ill consequences.'

'I appreciate his Majesty's consideration,' Anna said, overwhelmed with relief that they had not come on a more sinister errand.

'Of course, the bishops may find your matrimony good,' Audley smiled. She was not deceived for a moment.

'Has his Majesty granted the petition?' she asked.

'He has, Madam. He said today he had no other object in view but the glory of God, the welfare of the realm and the triumph of truth. All that remains is for your Grace to say you agree to the matter being committed to the clergy as competent judges.'

Anna made her decision. She faced the councillors, trying not to betray her fear. 'I am content always with his Majesty's determinations,' she said.

'Then, Madam,' Gardiner said, his manner much warmer, 'in our opinion, everything will proceed well, and the King's virtuous desire to have the truth established will be accomplished.'

'Doubtless his Majesty will be delighted to hear I am being so reasonable,' Anna observed to Harst, after the councillors had departed with smiles of approval and many good wishes. Some must be, at heart, decent men who did not like intimidating a blameless woman. 'He cannot have forgotten how stoutly Queen Katherine opposed him. Lady Rochford was telling me she held out for more than eight years, even after he divorced her and married Queen Anne. But I am not made of such strong clay, and I have no child to protect.' *But I have, of course, and for his sake I have made the right decision.* 'All that concerns me now is that my brother will not be too angry about my consenting to this inquiry.'

'He is more likely to be angry with the King,' Harst predicted. 'Although it pains me to say it, I am in no doubt now that his Majesty wants a divorce. Mr Rich told me, almost as a parting shot, that if you and the King are married in name only, the Church has the power to annul your union anyway.'

'They have me on all counts, with everything covered,' Anna said miserably.

Harst's voice was tight with indignation. 'The King must be sure indeed of the Emperor's goodwill to risk angering the Duke. The best we can hope for is that he will make generous financial provision for you, to placate your brother.'

Anna was hoping for that too. In justness, Henry should compensate her for the loss of the crown she had never yet worn.

She wrote to him that evening. She assured him she was amenable to Convocation examining the validity of their marriage, although she had no doubt that it was lawful. Yet, should the bishops decide otherwise, she hoped his Grace would look kindly on her. She sent it to court by the last tide.

The next morning, there arrived a letter from the Council: she must cease sending messages to the King.

It reduced her to tears. When Harst arrived from Whitehall, she cut him off before he could speak. 'Read this.' She swallowed, trying to compose herself. 'There is more.'

Harst read aloud: '"The envoys of Cleves have not kept their promise to produce proof of the annulment of the betrothal between the Lady Anna and the Duke of Lorraine's son. On the contrary, they have sent such documentation as puts the matter in much more doubt, and thus it appears plainly that the King's marriage cannot be in any way validated." Madam, this is appalling! They are muzzling you when you have most cause to speak out in your defence.'

'There are those in Kleve who are to blame as well.' Anna would not mention names, for if fault there was, surely it was her father's, or his advisers'. 'Had my betrothal been properly broken, with written authority, I would not now be in this peril.'

'You are not in peril, Madam,' Harst reassured her.

'I might have angered the King; is that not peril enough? What can I do from now on but show myself conformable? I shall write to the

Council, assure them of my good intentions and say I mean never to deviate from my resolve to please his Majesty.'

'Do nothing yet, Madam, I beg you,' Harst remonstrated. 'I think it will all be resolved soon. Yesterday, the bishops convened in Westminster Abbey, with Archbishop Cranmer presiding. I heard they were taking depositions from witnesses, on oath.'

'Ah. No doubt my ladies have been busy!' Anna gave a mirthless laugh. 'I shall take your advice, my good friend.'

She left Harst to finish his ale before he returned to Whitehall, and wandered into her privy chamber, where her maids were playing cards. She poured herself a large goblet of wine – never had she so needed the courage it gave her – and sipped it gratefully. She sat down and picked up her embroidery tambour, trying not to think about what those witnesses might be saying. Would they claim the King had never wanted her? Would it all be written down for posterity to read?

Her cheeks burned when it occurred to her that Henry himself might reveal what had – or had not – passed in bed between them, and that she was still as good a maid as he had found her. What she feared most was that he would say he had found her no maid at all. She quailed at the shame of it. If she came home a rejected bride, Wilhelm might, if she was lucky, be merciful – but if he found out she had gone sullied to her bridegroom, he would kill her, there was no doubt of it, and no one would blame him. She could not bear this suspense of waiting to find out what was happening. The bishops would be reassembling today. They would be looking at the depositions and discussing them, and that which should have remained private would be laid bare. She had had her suspicions since their wedding night that Henry had guessed her secret. Would he spare her the disgrace of exposure, and all its terrible consequences?

Part Three
The King's Sister

Chapter 16

1540

Late that afternoon, Mr Berde arrived at Richmond, asking to see Anna at once.

'He called your Grace "the Lady Anna"!' the Duchess of Suffolk exclaimed. 'How impertinent of him!'

Anna said nothing. She knew what that imported. What am I now? she wondered.

Mr Berde did at least do her the courtesy of bowing to her. 'Madam,' he said, his voice grave. 'This afternoon, at three o'clock, the bishops agreed that his Majesty and your Grace are in no wise bound by the marriage solemnised between you, and have pronounced it null and void.'

She had been expecting this, but still it came as a shock. She thought she might faint, as she had yesterday, but no, she was still standing, still breathing. Her head teemed with questions, but she could not speak.

Berde stared at her, no doubt bracing himself for the storm. 'His Majesty has been informed, as have both houses of Parliament, and Convocation has been prorogued until eight o'clock on Friday morning, when the bishops' ruling will be formalised and take effect.'

So she was still queen – but only for four more days. At least Berde had given no hint that her terrible secret had been laid bare. More than shock and indignation, she felt relief.

She found her voice. 'On what grounds am I to be divorced, Mr Berde?'

'On three counts, Madam. Firstly, by reason of the precontract between your Grace and the present Marquis of Lorraine; secondly, that the King's Majesty, suspecting this impediment, entered into the marriage against his will, and never gave his inward consent to it; and thirdly, that this whole nation has a great interest in the King's having more issue, which it is clear he can never have by your Grace, since the marriage remains unconsummated on account of his Majesty knowing in his heart that you were forbidden to him. Both his Majesty and your Grace will be at liberty to marry elsewhere.'

And Henry can now have his Katheryn! Anna did not begrudge him that happiness. She did not regret the loss of him as a husband, only as a friend – and lately he had certainly not been much of that to her.

And then something odd occurred to her. Had no one noticed the contradiction in the bishops' pronouncement? Her marriage had been dissolved on the grounds that she was still precontracted to Francis of Lorraine, so she could not be free to wed again – and yet their lordships had stated that she was. It made little difference, for there was no denying that the marriage had not been consummated, which was sufficient grounds in itself for an annulment.

What would happen now? Henry had effectively condemned her to a life of celibacy and sterility. The disgrace she had so feared would have to be faced. What would Harst say? She wished he was here. What would the world say, come to that? More to the point, what would Wilhelm say?

Mr Berde was watching her warily as she gathered her thoughts.

'Madam,' he said, 'it is the King's command that you should assent to the clergy's determination.'

'Forgive me, Mr Berde,' she replied, 'but this news has upset me, as you may imagine.' *If you had any heart.* 'Allow me time to compose myself. I will give you my answer anon.' And with that she nodded, signalling that the audience was at an end. Berde backed away, looking vexed.

She told no one. All that evening, she sat among her ladies and gentle-men, sipping wine, listening to the musicians playing and trying to master her teeming thoughts. In less than two days, the whole edifice of her life – the great household, the fine palaces, the deference, the jewels and other accoutrements of her rank – would crumble, and she had no idea what would happen to her afterwards.

Soon she would have to give Mr Berde an answer. He was waiting in the grooms' room, where she had ordered supper to be served to him.

She noticed Otho von Wylich looking at her. She was aware of the sympathy in his blue eyes. He was sitting alone, a little apart from the other gentlemen.

'Where is your wife tonight, Otho?' she asked.

There was a slight hesitation. 'She is indisposed, Madam.' Another pause. 'I trust your Grace is well?'

'I am perfectly well, thank you,' she answered, wondering if something was amiss with him. Maybe they were both lying. She wished she could confide in him, and that he could give her the comfort she craved. But she had no right to that kind of comfort, and she had enough to cope with just now without other complications in her life.

She knew she would not sleep, so when a distant church bell chimed eleven, she dismissed her attendants, picked up the ewer and retired to her bedchamber, where she sat drinking more wine and fretting about what to do.

What would become of her? If she returned to Kleve, it could only be in humiliation – galling, after the grand send-off she had had, to fulfil a magnificent destiny that was now no longer hers. Putting the problem in the most basic terms, she would be devalued in the royal marriage market, and unlikely to find another husband. She would be returning to her mother's tutelage and vigilance, and the dull daily round of prayers and embroidery. Wilhelm would surely appropriate any settlement Henry made on her, as compensation for the cost of her marriage. He would be angry with her. Men did commonly blame the wife if anything went wrong, and in this case, an alliance was at stake.

But here, in England, she was a long way from Wilhelm's jurisdiction. Here, especially at Richmond, she could enjoy certain freedoms. If she kept the King's goodwill, he might continue to be kind to her. Perhaps she could retain control over her own money, and keep at least some of her own people about her; he would surely agree to that – he owed her, after all. She had come to like England and its pleasant landscapes; she was growing used to the ways of its people.

She was torn; it was only natural, for she loved Mutter and Emily – yet the truth was, she had grown used to being without them, and enjoying a degree of independence. Maybe, when all this trouble had died down, she could visit them one day. There were other things in Kleve she missed too, but certainly it would be better to stay in England. Here, she could be her own woman. Her resolve hardened. But that did not solve her immediate problem.

When midnight struck, she sent a messenger to Whitehall to summon Dr Harst back to Richmond. She longed to confide in someone, and was badly in need of his counsel. He would know what to do. All her instincts told her to assent to what Henry wanted.

Harst made good speed and arrived at three in the morning, by which time Anna was feeling drained and dizzy from the effects of wine and lack of sleep. Without preamble, she related to him what Berde had said.

'Madam.' His hand was on her arm, a breach of etiquette, but one intended to comfort her. Besides, what did it matter now? Tomorrow, she would be queen no longer. Yet she would still be royal, and a princess of Kleve.

Harst had no doubt as to what she should do. 'Madam, I strongly recommend that you accept Convocation's sentence, and have patience.'

Suddenly, the awfulness of what was happening struck her like a stinging blow. This was real, and there was nothing she, or Dr Harst, or Wilhelm could do about it. She could bear it no longer: the shame of having everyone know she had been found wanting; that she was unlovable, rejected, abandoned . . . Her shoulders heaved, and she was seized with great gasping sobs. What had she done to deserve it all? Was she being punished for the sin of her youth?

She could not control herself. The tears came like a flood. Had she been building castles in the air, imagining a happy future for herself here? She was alone in this land, with only the good Dr Harst to protect her, which was hardly reassuring. Effectively, Henry could do what he liked with her. He might even find some pretext to have her beheaded, like Anne Boleyn. Panic gripped her, as she saw in her mind's eye the sinister bulk of the Tower of London looming ahead as she was carried there, a prisoner; she saw herself kneeling in the straw, blindfolded, imagining the agony, the blood . . .

Suddenly, she was screaming in terror. Doors banged, and there were voices outside, and urgent knocks, but she could not heed them. She was too far immersed in mortal fear. If only God would let her die here, of her misery, and spare her what was to come. Whatever it was, it would not be good, she was sure of it.

Strong arms were holding her, drawing her down on a bench. Her head was cradled against her old nurse's motherly bosom. 'There, there, *mein Liebling*,' Mother Lowe murmured, gentling her. 'Hush now.'

'Thank God you came,' Anna heard Harst say. 'It broke my heart to hear her Grace lament thus. This has all been too much for her, poor lady.' He knelt and took Anna's hand. 'If it was anything I said that upset your Grace, I am deeply sorry for it,' he murmured.

The hysteria had subsided. Anna struggled to regain her composure. 'I am sorry, forgive me,' she gasped.

'There is no need to apologise, Madam,' said another voice, and Anna looked up to see Lord Rutland in his night robe and cap, with several anxious faces peering from behind him. She sat up, releasing Mother Lowe's hand.

'Thank you, thank you,' she said, her eyes embracing them all.

'Madam, you have nothing to fear from the King,' Rutland said. 'If his Majesty could see you now, I know his heart would be moved. He would be touched that you are so saddened at the prospect of losing him.' Anna did not correct him.

'What happened?' Rutland asked Harst, and the doctor told him.

'You gave her Grace good advice,' the chamberlain observed. 'Madam, as I said before, you should respond to his Majesty as you think right.'

Calmer now, Anna rose, smoothing her skirts. She knew what she must say. If she did not, it would fester inside her like a wound for the rest of her life. 'Please send for Mr Berde. Mother Lowe, if you could kindly bring me some water and a cloth.'

She dabbed at her face and let the nurse comb her hair. A glance in the mirror told her she looked dreadful, but no matter. It would not hurt Henry to hear that she appeared devastated.

Mr Berde looked shocked when he saw her. And so he ought!

She took a deep breath and summoned her courage. Henry should know she had never taken their matrimony as lightly as he had. 'Pray convey my answer to the King,' she said. 'Tell him that I gladly accepted him as my husband and master. I gave myself to him, and in my heart I will remain his wife until the bitter death.' Even as she said it, she was wishing the words unsaid, fearing that a bitter death might well be her reward. What had she done? Had she gone mad?

Berde visibly flinched. Harst and Rutland were staring at her as if she were crazed. 'The King will not be pleased with such an answer,' Berde said at length.

'I do not wish to anger or offend his Majesty,' Anna replied. 'I will not oppose him on this matter, but I must speak as my conscience dictates – as he does.'

She could sense the exasperation of the men around her.

'Very well, I will tell his Majesty that,' Berde replied grimly. He gave a perfunctory bow, and left.

Unable to bear the dismay in the faces of those who remained, Anna wished them good night and retreated to her chamber. She was too exhausted for explanations tonight.

In the morning, Harst came, but not – thank Heaven – to castigate her. 'I am for the court, Madam,' he said. 'I am deeply unhappy about the speed with which this annulment has been obtained, and the way the King has treated you, and I intend to go before the Council and say so! You are a princess of Kleve, and should not be kept in suspense as to what the future holds or what kind of settlement is being made on your divorce. I hope to rectify that today.'

'I think you are hoping also to repair any damage I may have done,' she said. She had not slept at all, and suspected, from the look of him, that Harst had not either. 'Tell me, was I wrong to state my view?'

'Brave, Madam,' he replied. 'I would not say wise, especially as we are looking to the King to be generous.'

'I am regretting it today,' she confessed. 'I fear I spoke rashly, impulsively. I was not thinking straight. Any moment now, I am expecting soldiers to come and arrest me.'

'The King is not a man to be gainsaid, but even he would not dare go that far,' Harst assured her.

'I do hope not! Good Dr Harst, make speed to the court, I pray you, and say it was never my intention to imply any criticism of the King or his bishops. Say, I beg you, that I was crazed at the prospect of losing his love.'

'That is very wise.' Harst smiled. 'Your Grace should have been a diplomat.'

He was back after dinner, and Anna invited him to walk with her in the privy garden.

'Madam, I think the King fears you as much as you fear him,' he smiled.

'Why?' she asked, astonished.

'Clearly, he fears you might incite your brother to war, for the first thing the Council did today was assure me his Majesty would not abandon the alliance with Kleve, and that he intends to treat your Grace as his sister. Madam, I urge you now to accept the ruling of Convocation. If you do, all will go well for you, for the councillors still bear you much goodwill, which they would not do if you had incurred the King's displeasure. But if you refuse to accept it, then I fear undue pressure will be brought to bear on you, with disastrous consequences.'

Anna could well imagine what 'undue pressure' might mean. 'I will accept it,' she declared. 'Shall I send for Mr Berde?'

'No, Madam. The councillors will come to you, very soon. Convocation is due to publish its sentence in the morning.'

Anna felt her stomach clench. In a few hours, she would no longer be a queen.

* * *

The deputation from the Privy Council waited upon her in her privy chamber, as the sun sparkled on the window panes and a light summer breeze played at the open casement. She was anxious to show herself cooperative and amenable. Behind the Duke of Suffolk she saw Southampton, now Lord Privy Seal in place of Cromwell, who still languished in the Tower. Beside him stood Sir Richard Rich and Mr Berde. She had insisted on receiving them with Dr Harst and Wymond Carew present, and her ladies in a semicircle around her. She saw Lady Rutland, Lady Rochford and Lady Edgcumbe exchanging glances. She knew they had helped to bring her to this day.

Suffolk cleared his throat. 'Madam, you are aware of the late proceedings at Westminster, and that your marriage has been annulled. Convocation has determined that both you and the King may lawfully marry again. Furthermore, Parliament has enacted that you be acknowledged no more as queen, but called the Lady Anna of Cleves.'

She could not prevent a tear trickling down her cheek. It was so final, so starkly put. Queen no more. She had been so proud, for herself, but more for her country.

'Madam, do not distress yourself,' Suffolk said gently.

'It is on account of the great love and affection I bear to the King,' she sobbed. 'And I have no idea what is to become of me, bereft of his protection.'

'Madam, let me assure you that, if you accept Convocation's sentence, you will be very well treated.' He could not have put it more clearly. What sounded like words of comfort was a veiled threat.

She made an effort and mastered herself. She would show them she was a true daughter of Kleve, sensible and pragmatic.

'I do here and now declare my consent to the bishops' ruling,' she said. 'I am amenable to it, content always with what his Majesty wishes and determines. I do indeed confirm that my marriage was never consummated.' She was not going to admit to the precontract nonsense. 'In the face of all, even my mother, my brother and any who would move me to the contrary, I commit myself wholly to the King, wishing to remain here in England as his servant and subject.' She took a deep breath. If she had judged aright, her carefully prepared speech would save her life, and her brother and Kleve from a war that would have crippled the duchy.

Dr Harst stepped forward. 'Madam, I must warn you not to grant anything to the prejudice of your own rights or your brother's position.'

Anna stayed him with a discreet gesture. 'I will obey the King my lord. I have not forgotten the great kindness he has extended towards me. My firm intention is to endure all he thinks fit, and to remain always in this country.'

Harst stared at her, but Suffolk was beaming. 'His Majesty will be most gratified to hear that, Madam.' Of course. It would suit Henry very well: he would not want her going back to Kleve and trumpeting it around Europe that she had been unlawfully divorced.

'He intends to make a very generous settlement,' the Duke continued, 'and, for the honour of your house, and his respect for you, he means to treat you as a sister. You will have precedence over all the ladies in England, after any future queen the King might marry, and his Majesty's daughters.'

Anna could not have hoped for more. She would have her own income, her freedom, and be honoured by the King as his sister! Her fears began to recede. 'His Majesty is, as ever, very good to me,' she said, and smiled at Harst to show him she really was content with how matters were turning out.

'Madam, will you freely write a letter to the King, formally consenting to the dissolution of your marriage?' Suffolk asked. 'You will understand that your written consent is essential.'

'Of course, my lord,' Anna said, and called for Mr Paget, her secretary. 'Will you dictate what I should say, my lord?' she asked Suffolk.

He beamed at her again, doubtless surprised and gratified at being able to deal with a discarded queen who *was* conformable. 'My lady, you might say you have been informed by the lords of his Grace's council of the doubts that have moved him to question the validity of your matrimony, and that you knew Parliament had petitioned his Highness to have the matter determined by the holy clergy of this realm, which was duly done.' Anna nodded, and Suffolk paused to give Paget time to get it all down.

'Next,' the Duke went on, 'you need to assure the King that you freely consent to Convocation's ruling.'

'I know what I would like to say,' Anna said, seized with sudden inspiration. 'Mr Carew, with my lord of Suffolk's approval, please ask Mr Paget to write: "May it please your Majesty to know that, although this ruling is most hard and sorrowful to me, for the great love I bear to your most noble person, yet I must have more regard to God and His truth than to any worldly affection. I testify to your Highness, by this letter, that I promise, on my word, that I do accept and approve the sentence, wholly and entirely putting myself at your Highness's goodness and pleasure."'

She hoped her words conveyed a fitting sense of loss that would flatter Henry and make him feel even more well disposed to her.

The lords were nodding approvingly.

'Excellent, Madam, excellent,' Suffolk commented.

'Thank you, my lord,' Anna said. 'I would like to say further: "I most humbly beseech your Majesty to understand that, since the matrimony between us is void, I will never again call myself your Grace's wife. I shall be very grateful if it will please you to take me for one of your humble servants, and that I may sometimes have the pleasure of your most noble presence, which I shall esteem a great benefit. My lords of your Majesty's council, now being with me, have comforted me with assurances of your Highness's good intentions towards me, and said you will take me for your sister, for the which I most humbly thank you." Mr Paget, pray end the letter: "Thus, most gracious Prince, I beseech our Lord God to send your Majesty long life and good health, to God's glory, your own honour, and the wealth of this noble realm. Your Majesty's most humble sister and servant."'

'You have done very well, Madam,' Suffolk said. 'His Majesty will be most pleased.'

Paget passed her the letter. The ink was still wet, so she took care when she signed it: 'Anna, the daughter of Kleve'. Using her former style was a tacit acknowledgement that she was no longer queen.

To her surprise, she felt a burgeoning sense of well-being. For the first time since meeting Henry, she knew where she stood. The worst that could happen had not happened. From a humiliating bondage, she had suddenly been liberated to a life of luxurious freedom; she was, for the first time, her own mistress. She had not lost the King's goodwill: he was still her friend – and brother! What did it matter that she now lacked the title of queen, when she could stay in England, take precedence over all but the foremost ladies in the land, and always be assured of a welcome at court?

When the lords had gone, Dr Harst spread his hands in admiration.

'Madam, you were magnificent. You struck just the right note. I am in no doubt now that his Majesty will be well disposed to be generous.'

'We shall see,' Anna said. 'In the meantime, I will continue as I am, until I am commanded otherwise.'

Parliament had confirmed the sentence of the bishops and formally annulled her marriage. Dr Harst brought the news late the next day, arriving just as her supper was being served. She invited him to join her at table.

'You look troubled, my friend,' she said.

'Not at all, Madam,' he assured her. 'You will be pleased to hear that your letter to the King was read out to both houses of Parliament, where it was well received.'

'Was the King there?'

'No, Madam. He had written a statement that the Lord Chancellor read to the Lords.'

Anna felt a creeping unease. Harst's manner had changed since yesterday. It was unusually stiff. She was sure he was holding something back. 'Something is amiss,' she said. 'Please tell me.'

'It is probably nothing, Madam. But the statement prompted some speculation.'

'Speculation about what?' She was alarmed now.

Harst was focusing busily on his food, not looking at her. 'Aside from enumerating the three grounds given for the annulment, his Majesty stated the bishops had also considered other great causes *not to be published.*'

No! Oh, dear God! Was it possible Henry meant her to know that, should she fail in her compliance, he might yet expose her shameful secret?

'Have you any idea what those causes might be, my lady?' Harst asked.

'I have no idea,' she said, praying he would not detect the lie. Lying was her only armour.

'I heard Sir Richard Rich saying secret causes could have been used to prove the invalidity of the marriage, but that the King refused to disclose them because they touched your honour.'

This was terrible. Letting it be known that something had touched her honour was as good as saying she had behaved immorally. Her anger mounted.

'That is unwarranted speculation!' she cried. 'How impertinent of him! I never did take to Sir Richard.'

Harst was looking at her searchingly. 'Forgive me, Madam, but would he have dared say such a thing, which touches the King's honour and yours so nearly, if he had not heard it from a reputable source? Could it be that it came from the King himself?'

'I cannot believe the King would be so unchivalrous as to spread false calumnies about me – and I would not give credence to anything Sir Richard says. This is the man, I am told, who lied when giving evidence at Sir Thomas More's trial. My ladies say he also helped to bring down Cromwell. Such a man would not hesitate to slander me.'

Harst hesitated. 'Madam, something else fuelled the speculation. It was the wording of the Act of Parliament, which stated you had openly confessed that you never carnally knew the King's body.'

'And so I did,' Anna said, anger and fear making her sound sharp. 'What is wrong with that?'

'Some were wondering if you had carnally known *another's* body.'

Anna froze. 'This is outrageous!' she said, rising, obliging the ambassador to rise too. 'And it does not behove you, Dr Harst, to give credence to malicious talk, or to interrogate me like this. My brother shall hear of it. I thought you were my friend!'

'Madam, I am your friend, which is why I have, reluctantly, broached this matter,' Harst protested. 'Naturally I defended you against their talk, strongly and vehemently, but you should be aware of what is being said.'

'As you once counselled me, Dr Harst, it is best not to pay heed to gossip.'

'This is gossip at the highest level, Madam. It must be stopped. With your consent, I will complain on your behalf to the King.'

'No!' Anna gasped, and their eyes met. There was an awful silence.

'*Was* there some other cause?' he asked, searching her face.

Dare she confide in him? He was her brother's man, and his first loyalty might well be to Wilhelm. The fewer people who knew her secret, the better.

'No, there was not,' she declared. 'And I do not want to prejudice my settlement by making complaints to the King.'

She feared she had not convinced him, that there had been some irreparable breach in the trust that had built up between them.

'Then I shall say nothing, Madam,' he said, swallowing.

Wanting to make things right, she indicated his seat. 'Let us finish our supper,' she invited, sitting down. 'Is there any more of note to report?'

'Only that Parliament has decreed that anyone calling you the King's wife, or denying the judgement, will be guilty of high treason. My lady, you will be pleased to hear that many like you. I heard several lords praising your courage and common sense.' It was an olive branch, and she was grateful to Harst for extending it, hating herself for having lied to him. 'One said it might please the King to mislike you, but he himself always thought you a brave lady.'

'That is heartening to know,' Anna said, still fretting about how near she had come to exposure.

'One gentleman even stated it was a shame the King had married another man's wife,' Harst went on, 'and that you were an admirable queen.'

'I wish I had known people thought so well of me when I *was* queen,' Anna said wistfully. 'But I knew little of what was going on outside my apartments. Maybe the King wanted to isolate me. Maybe he was planning this for a long time.'

'I am not so sure,' Harst said. 'In my view, and from what you have told me, he grew fonder of you after your marriage, but then took a fancy to Mistress Howard, and it was only when that fancy deepened that he decided to pursue an annulment.'

Anna shook her head. 'I doubt we will ever know the truth. I too thought we were growing closer, but then suddenly I was banished to Richmond. And now we know why.'

There was a knock, and Lady Rutland entered. 'Excuse me, Madam, but the lords of the Council are here again, wishing to speak with you.'

'I will come,' Anna said, wiping her mouth with her napkin and downing the last of her wine. 'Dr Harst, will you attend me, please?'

Suffolk, Southampton and Sir Thomas Wriothesley were waiting in the presence chamber. Anna was unsure if it was appropriate now for her to sit in the consort's throne, so she received them standing in front of the dais, with the duchesses of Suffolk and Richmond standing on either side.

Suffolk was his customary hearty self. 'My Lady Anna, the King is most grateful for your good conformity, and wishes us to convey his thanks, and to impart to you the arrangements that have been made for the maintenance of your estate here in England.'

At his signal, Southampton stepped forward. 'Madam, we bring you a letter from his Majesty.' He presented it to her, bowing. 'It is full of friendly intentions, and we are instructed to deliver it, with this token, to his dearest sister by adoption.'

Suffolk handed Anna a velvet purse. 'It contains five hundred marks in gold.'

Anna fell to her knees, wondering if she had jumped too hastily to the conclusion that Henry had subtly threatened her. 'His Majesty is most gracious. Please offer him my humble thanks. My lords, could someone read the letter to me?'

'We will leave you to read it with your own interpreter,' Suffolk said, indicating Dr Harst. 'We will wait in the antechamber.'

'What does it say?' Anna asked Harst, when they were alone.

He read it aloud:

'"Right dear and right entirely beloved sister, from the report of our Council, and your letter, we perceive the continuance of your conformity. We take your wise and honourable proceedings in most thankful part, for you have done everything in respect of God and His truth. Continuing in your conformity, you shall find in us a perfect friend, content to call you our dearest sister."'

Harst's face lit up. 'Here it is, Madam, what we have been hoping for! The King goes on:

'"We shall, within five or six days, when our Parliament ends, determine your estate so honourably that you will have good cause to be content, for we mind to endow you with four thousand pounds in yearly revenue. We have appointed you two houses, Richmond and Bletchingley, not far from London, so that you may be near us and, whenever you desire, can come to our court to see us, as we shall come to you. When Parliament ends, we shall see and speak with you, and you shall see what a friend you have in us. We require you to be quiet and merry. Your loving brother and friend, H.R."'

'It is a very kind letter,' Anna said, after digesting its import. 'The King is being very generous. The settlement is not much less than my dower as queen. It sounds as if I shall want for nothing. What pleases me most is that I shall have Richmond, for I have come to love it here.'

'It is no less than you deserve, Madam,' Harst said. 'This generosity has been prompted not only by the King's gratitude to you for making things so easy for him, but by his desire to retain your brother's friendship.'

'He is making it easy for Wilhelm to accept the annulment,' Anna replied. 'How could Wilhelm not, in the circumstances?'

'I would be surprised if the Duke did not make some protest,' Harst said. 'But it will be circumspect, I am sure. Shall I ask the councillors to come in?'

'Yes, please do.'

When the lords returned, she smiled at them. 'Please inform his Majesty that I send him most hearty thanks for his generous settlement. I have only one question. Where is Bletchingley? I have never heard of it.'

'Bletchingley, Madam, is south of London, in the country of Surrey, less than twenty miles from here,' Sir Thomas Wriothesley told her. 'It is a splendid house with a fine hunting park. His Majesty also grants you Hever Castle in Kent. That too is not far from here.'

Anna was sure she had heard Hever Castle mentioned somewhere. Was it Lady Rochford who had referred to it?

'You will, in addition, be given The More, which lies to the north of London.'

Four residences. She might no longer be a queen, but she would still be a great lady.

'Now, my lady,' Suffolk said, 'we have been instructed to declare to you the arrangements that will be made in respect of your estate and household.'

'I am content to have those his Majesty shall appoint to serve me,' Anna said.

'Be assured that you will be allocated a suitable household headed by noble officers and composed mainly of your German servants. His Majesty intends to give you regular grants of money to fund it. It will take some time to sort out the financial settlement, but in the meantime, you are to retain the lands of your jointure. I must advise you that the settlement is conditional upon your remaining in England.'

'That is my desire and intention,' she said.

'You must surrender those jewels that are the hereditary property of the queens of England, but you may keep all your other jewels, including those the King gave you, and your pearls, plate, clothes and hangings. Madam, the King trusts these arrangements are satisfactory to you.'

'More than satisfactory, Sir Thomas. I thank his Majesty for so generously providing for me. Please assure him that I will maintain the truth in regard to the annulment, especially touching the integrity of my body, which I here declare the King left in a state of virginity.' She could sense Harst's eyes on her. He would understand why she was making this statement, and God would surely forgive the lie. He would know that she had to safeguard her reputation in order to protect everything she held dear.

'Lady Suffolk,' she asked, 'would you fetch the casket containing the queen's jewels? My lords, please take this ring to the King, as a token of my pledge.' She drew it from her finger; it had a fair diamond that caught the sunlight.

When the Duchess returned, Anna bade her hand the casket to her husband, the Duke. 'My lord, please convey these to the King.'

'Thank you, my lady,' Suffolk said, and smiled at his wife. Anna had long wondered what passed between them, this ageing man in his mid fifties and his young Duchess, who must be little more than twenty. Yet they seemed to get on well. Suffolk clearly adored his Katherine, and Katherine seemed happy enough with him.

'There is one other request I must make of you, Madam,' the Duke said to Anna. 'Naturally, the King is anxious to prevent any unpleasantness between England and Kleve. For the avoidance of this, he asks that you write to Duke Wilhelm in your own language, explaining that you are content to be divorced.'

Anna baulked at this request. It put her in a very difficult position. She had no idea how Wilhelm would react when he heard the news. Her decision to stay in England might seem cowardly or even treacherous to him. She did not want to contact him until she knew his response. Surely it was up to Henry to inform him of the annulment? It was nothing of her doing.

'It is not fitting that I write to my brother before he writes to me,' she said. 'But when he does send to me, the King's Grace shall see the letter; and, according to what my brother writes, I will answer him with the best will and pleasure. And I trust that, however he or the Duke of Saxony take this matter, his Grace will be good to me.'

The lords nodded understandingly. 'No matter, Madam,' Suffolk said.

'I will not vary from my agreement to the annulment,' Anna declared. 'To be honest with you, I fear that my brother will blame me for what has happened. If I return to Germany, he might slay me. That is why I wish to stay in England.'

They were regarding her with some sympathy and concern, these hardened, experienced men. She suspected that candour and honesty were not qualities they encountered very often at court.

'I can hardly believe the Duke would treat his sister so,' Suffolk said. 'Not such a gracious lady. You are blameless in this matter, Madam.'

'I trust my brother will see it that way,' she answered.

'His Majesty will make sure of it, I have no doubt. He is sending Dr Wotton back to Kleve to inform the Duke of the late proceedings.'

Anna did not envy Wotton, but felt reassured that the urbane cleric, with all his experience and diplomatic skills, would be breaking the news to Wilhelm.

'Now, we will take our leave,' Suffolk said. 'We bid you farewell, Madam.' He bowed most courteously.

Anna stayed them. 'Before you go, my lords, may I request, as a great favour, that I might be permitted to see the Lady Elizabeth sometimes. She is the most delightful child.' If it was not possible for her to remarry and have children of her own, Elizabeth could help to fill that empty space in her life. She could not be a mother to the child, but she could be a friend. She hoped, of course, that the Lady Mary would visit her too.

'Madam, we will convey your request to the King,' Suffolk promised. 'In the light of your praiseworthy and exemplary conduct, I do not see how he could refuse.'

Chapter 17

1540

Anna kept wondering if Henry *would* marry Katheryn Howard. There was no doubt that he must marry again, and soon. At his age, and in his state of health, he could not afford to waste time.

Well, it was no business of hers any more. She got on with her quiet daily tasks and pleasures, taking care to be circumspect in all her doings, and saying to those who would have commiserated with her over her divorce that she wished for nothing but what pleased the King her lord. In her heart, she was resolved to accept what could not be remedied.

Two days after they had departed, the councillors returned to see her. This time, they seemed a little warier than before.

Suffolk cleared his throat. 'Madam, the King still wishes you to write to your brother to make it clear to him that you have freely consented to the sentence of the bishops, and are satisfied with the provision that is being made for you.'

It came to her that Henry was worried she might change her mind, especially if Wilhelm protested about her being divorced.

'His Grace would prefer that you do not put off writing until your brother writes to you,' Wriothesley added. 'He feels that, considering how you have so honourably and virtuously behaved in this matter, and, indeed, earned yourself much love and favour, it would be for the best if you informed your brother of all the proceedings, so that he may not heed tales and rumours.'

'My lords,' Anna protested, 'I wish to do nothing but what pleases the King, yet I have made clear to you my reason for not wanting to write to my brother at this time. After I have heard from him, and know where he stands in this matter, I will do so, I give you my word.'

Suffolk was almost dancing in perplexity. 'Madam, I do not wish to offend you, but his Majesty is aware that the nature of ladies is to be changeable. Mindful of the treaty with Cleves and the surety of his realm, he fears that, unless you do write and assure your brother that you are content, everything hangs upon a woman's promise.'

Anna felt indignation rising in her. 'I am a princess of Kleve, my lord, and when I give my word, I keep it. I fear my brother, as you know, so I dare not write at this time.'

'Madam, for your comfort, the King has commanded us to tell you that, however your brother may conduct himself, so long as you continue in your conformity, you shall never fare the worse.'

'I thank his Majesty. But pray give me grace to wait upon my brother's response.'

The councillors exchanged glances.

'Very well, Madam.' Suffolk sighed.

Anna fretted for three days, worrying she might lose Henry's favour and goodwill by refusing to write to Wilhelm. She did not want him to think her lacking in gratitude. Probably he was stunned that she had been so cooperative. After his long battle with Queen Katherine, he must be finding it hard to believe that she, Anna, had capitulated without a fight. He might be wondering if she meant to complain to Wilhelm, which would really jeopardise England's relations with Kleve.

She could not let Henry think her capable of such duplicity, and to show her good intentions, she decided to write to him.

Seated at her desk, she sent for Mr Paget and Mr Carew. 'I wish to dictate a letter,' she told them. 'Address it to "the King's Most Royal Majesty" and write: "Most excellent and noble Prince, my good brother. I do most humbly thank you for your great goodness, favour, and liberality, which it has pleased you to determine towards me. I can say no more, but that I shall ever remain your Majesty's most humble sister and servant, as I have informed your Grace through your councillors, which is what I have intended from the first. I have neither varied from that, nor will hereafter; and, if any man has said anything to the contrary, I assure your Grace that he has done it without my consent. Thus I beseech our Lord to send your Majesty long life with good health, and perpetual felicity. Your Majesty's humble sister and servant.'"

She signed the letter and sent Paget with it to Whitehall, hoping it would set Henry's mind at rest.

The sensational news of her divorce must be all over England by now, and soon it would reach the courts of Europe. Anna thought the Emperor would be pleased. Courteous as he had shown himself to her on her journey to England, her marriage to Henry had been an obstacle to their friendship.

The reformist party at court must be disgruntled to hear of the annulment. Already, Lady Suffolk had told her, their power had been weakened by the fall of Cromwell. The Catholic Howards now held sway. But here at Richmond, that all seemed a world away.

On the day after Anna wrote to the King, the lords of the Council came to Richmond to discharge some of those who had attended on her when she was queen, and swear in those who were to stay and serve her as the King's sister.

She was dismayed to discover that her household was to be severely reduced. Instead of having more than a hundred and thirty officers and servants, she would now have only thirty-six. But she was gracious to the lords when they told her. At least she was to be allowed to retain her Germans. Mother Lowe would now come into her own, with no rivals to challenge her authority.

At Suffolk's instance, Anna formally dismissed those who must leave her service, and put on a smiling face when she said farewell to them, as they bowed and curtseyed in turn before her. For the most part, she was not sorry to see the back of her English ladies and maids. Some she had liked – especially Margaret Douglas and the Duchess of Suffolk – but the rest she had not. Their presence in her chamber had felt intrusive, even though they had had every right to be there. Some had been catty, and most had made little effort to bond with her German ladies and maids, which had made for a divided household with all its awkwardnesses.

She was aware of Susanna Gilman searching her face for any sign of affection or regret when her turn came, but she merely inclined her head and let Susanna move on. It would be a relief not to be constantly reminded of the woman's betrayal.

She was sad, though, to be losing the Earl of Rutland, who had been a kind and efficient chamberlain. No longer, either, would she have her own chancellor, master of horse, surveyor or auditors. Her councillors had all been dismissed.

When the presence chamber had emptied, she received the new servants selected for her by the Privy Council. They had been waiting downstairs in the great hall and, one by one, were summoned to be presented to her and sworn in. She received them kindly, and welcomed them to her service.

Sir William Goring was her new chamberlain. He was a Sussex man, a courtier through and through, clearly loyal to the King, and jovial in spirit. Anna liked him instantly.

Jasper Horsey, whose equine looks did not belie his name, was to be her steward.

'Mr Horsey is well qualified for the office,' Sir Thomas Wriothesley told her. 'He was comptroller to the late Marquess of Exeter, whose treason he helped to uncover. In reward, he was made a gentleman usher of the King's Privy Chamber and granted the lands of the manor of Bletchingley that are now in your ladyship's hands. Mr Horsey has been given another estate in compensation.' Anna hoped Jasper Horsey did not begrudge her the exchange, but his manner towards her was deferential, even friendly.

Wymond Carew was to stay in post as her receiver general.

'He will also act as envoy between yourself and the King,' Suffolk told her. 'His Majesty wishes you to show to him any letters you receive from your brother.' Anna nodded. It was not an unreasonable request to make.

On, on they came. The majority now were Germans who had accompanied her to England, and who were required to be sworn again. She was ridiculously pleased to see Otho von Wylich walking towards her, and hoped it was not too obvious. He was followed by Franz von Waldeck, Florence de Diaceto, Dr Cepher, and her cook, Schoulenburg. Katharina and Gertrude had now been promoted to gentlewomen of her chamber, and would serve alongside the five other gentlewomen appointed by the Council. Katherine Bassett had secured a place at last, which would doubtless please her mother, especially with Lord Lisle still in the Tower, and no one any the wiser as to what was to happen to him.

Frances Lilgrave, a plump, dark-haired woman in her forties, told Anna she was an embroiderer, and that her husband had been embroiderer to the late Queen Anne. Then came the amiable Dorothy Wingfield, pale-faced Jane Ratsey and an older woman called Mistress Simpson. Next to last, rustling over in her good black gown and over-large *Stickelchen*, was the redoubtable Mother Lowe. Elya Turpen, the laundress, brought up the rear. It seemed all too small a household after the great establishment that had been Anna's for the past seven months.

When everyone was assembled, Anna addressed them. 'Again, a hearty welcome to you all. I need not remind you, and my lords here present, how bound I am to the King, who has been pleased to appoint you to my service.' Let no one think her in any way resentful of the man who had spurned her. 'In serving me well, you will be serving him.'

She turned to the councillors. 'I know myself to be under great obligations to the King's Majesty, and I am determined to submit myself wholly to his goodness. I will never vary or change in that regard, and all the letters and messages I receive from my brother, my kin and my friends I will send to the King's Majesty, and be guided by his determination.'

'You have done well, my lady,' Suffolk murmured. He turned to the waiting servants. 'Now, all of you, to your duties!'

Hastily, Anna's new household began to disperse. Mother Lowe was already in charge, in her element, issuing orders. Anna saw Sir William Goring staring at the nurse in dismay, probably wondering if this old woman was intent on subverting his authority. She hid a smile.

The lords came back four days later, at the King's behest, to see that Anna's new household was settling in efficiently, and surprised her elbow-deep in flour in the kitchen, making a pie. Having quickly washed her hands, she hastened to the hall and exclaimed in delight when they showed her the jewels, tapestries and plate they had brought, all gifts from Henry. They also gave her a letter from Wilhelm. It was addressed not to her, but to the King.

She was stunned when she read it. Wilhelm's response was milder than she could ever have expected. He was sorry for what had happened; he would have wished it otherwise, yet he would never depart from his friendship for his Majesty for such a matter. Both he and Dr Olisleger were concerned about his sister being ill treated, but trusted the King would never allow that. He could have wished for her to return to Germany, but if she preferred to remain, he was confident the King would act uprightly towards her, and he himself would not press for her to come home.

Anna could have danced with relief. It did not sound as if Wilhelm was angry with her at all. She handed back the letter. 'Please convey my most humble thanks to the King's Majesty for letting me have sight of this,' she said. 'Now I can write to my brother without fear. I want to reassure him and Dr Olisleger that all is well with me. My lords, if you would kindly wait, I will write to him now.'

When Paget had finished, she had Wymond Carew read the letter back to her in English and then translated into German. Her heart lightened with every word, and she nodded in approval, confident she had conveyed everything she needed Wilhelm – and Mutter – to know.

'Will that do, Madam?'

'Thank you, Mr Carew, and Mr Paget,' Anna said. 'It will do very well. Pray ask the lords to return.'

They came, and read the letter in turn, nodding their approval. 'This will be conveyed to the Duke by Dr Olisleger's nephew, Mr Diaceto,' Suffolk said. 'He has agreed to carry it for you. He departs for Dover after dinner.'

'Then, with your leave, Sirs, I will send for him. I wish to give him a personal message for my brother.'

Florence de Diaceto was summoned, and when the swarthy young man appeared before her, already dressed and booted for travel, she spoke to him, the councillors looking on. 'Florence, when you get to

Kleve, I desire you to convey my hearty commendations to the Duke, and to tell him I am merry, and honourably treated, and that I have written my whole mind to him in my letter.' She smiled at him and held out her hand. 'God speed you.' He would be able to tell Wilhelm that she was not looking miserable or discontented.

When he had left, Anna invited the lords of the Council to dine with her. Now that they had her letter, they were relaxed and less on their guard. She had choice wines served to them, and good English roast lamb, which she much enjoyed herself. It was a very convivial dinner, and the conversation flowed, touching greatly on her new properties, about which the councillors were able to tell her a great deal. Afterwards, when she stood, they leapt to their feet.

'My lords,' she said, feeling rosy from the wine, 'I want you to return this to the King. It is the ring he gave me at our pretended marriage. Take it, I pray, with my most humble commendations. I desire that it be broken in pieces as a thing of no force or value.' As she held it out in her palm, she caught sight of the inscription engraved on the inner side of the band: 'God send me well to keep'. God had done that most effectively, she reflected. Without doubt, He had been keeping her safe these past days.

Dr Harst found her walking in the cloister. She was pleased to see him, eager to tell him about Wilhelm's letter.

'I have heard from the Duke too,' he told her. 'As you may imagine, he did not entirely open his mind to the King. He was much dismayed to hear of the annulment of your marriage. He thinks his Majesty's conduct deplorable, and fears you might be persecuted in England, or that some dreadful fate might befall you. Naturally, I have sent a fast messenger to assure him his fears are completely unfounded.'

'I have reassured him too,' Anna said, realising how hard this business must have hit her family, and the anguish it would be causing them. How well Wilhelm had dissembled in his letter to the King – she had been so relieved to read it that she had never guessed how concerned for her he had been. She had completely misjudged him.

They passed into Anna's privy garden, where fat bees buzzed drowsily among the blooms. 'You may have heard,' Harst said, 'that the King has instructed all vicars and curates to announce to their parishes that you are no longer to be prayed for in church.'

'That's rather sad. It was a comfort to have so many people praying for me.'

'Then it will comfort you to know, Madam, that when I went to the church near my lodgings last Sunday, people were expressing regret at your divorce, saying it was a great pity that so good a lady should so soon have lost her greatest joy.'

Anna smiled wryly. 'I would not have put it quite like that.'

'No, but they were saying they loved and esteemed you as the sweetest, most gracious and kindest queen they ever had, and that they greatly wished you could continue as their queen. It seems that word of your estimable conduct in a difficult situation has seeped out.'

'I do not deserve such esteem. I am overwhelmed by it.'

Harst sighed. 'You do, believe me. But, Madam, there is more talk, especially at court, and I'd rather you heard it from me than anyone else.'

'What is it?' Anna asked, immediately concerned. 'I thought you were not going to heed mere gossip.'

'I fear there is some truth in it, Madam. It is said that the King is going to marry Katheryn Howard. Some even report that their marriage has already taken place in secret.'

It was a blow, but not a hard one. 'It is no more than I expected. If the King remarries, I shall take it in good part. He needs heirs – and someone he can love.'

'You are more generous than he deserves,' Harst said severely. 'He risked bringing great shame on you.'

Anna looked at him sharply. Was he still drawing his own conclusions? 'I will not hear any criticism of him, dear friend,' she said, sitting down on a stone bench and indicating that he should join her.

'Your patience in affliction is superhuman!' he observed. 'Some are even saying that Mistress Howard is already *enceinte*, though I cannot confirm the truth of it.'

Anna tried not to mind. But, if Henry *had* sired a child on Katheryn, it must have been revulsion for her own person that had prevented him from paying her the same compliment. She sighed. There was no accounting for individual fancy.

'Tell me,' Dr Harst asked, 'how long are you going to be immured here at Richmond?'

'I am not a prisoner here,' she corrected him. 'I can leave if I wish, but I have judged it wise not to appear in public until things have quietened down. Maybe it would be politic to retire to the country soon. After all, I have all these houses to live in!'

'And you are a lady of means.'

'Indeed! I mean to enjoy my freedom. Now that the friendship between my brother and the King is assured, I will be happy to distance myself from politics. I will have the privileges of royalty, but not the cares. I might no longer be queen, but I mean to maintain a privy chamber, and there seems to be no objection to my styling myself in the royal plural.'

'Madam, the King has won the main argument; he will not concern himself with what, compared to that, are trifles.'

'I am in good cheer. You may report that,' she smiled.

Another letter arrived from Wilhelm, written in his own hand. Faithful to her promise, Anna sent it to the King, who speedily returned it. She replied to her brother: 'I am very content, and I wish you and my mother to know this.'

That day, her steward, Jasper Horsey, came to her closet to inform her that an officer of the Royal Wardrobe had come riding over from Hampton Court, by the King's command, to inform him that beds and furnishings from the Crown's store were being transported to her new residences. 'The officer said he and his clerk had been kept busy for four days sorting out what was needed from the Earl of Essex's house at the Austin Friars in London, and the royal wardrobes at the Tower of London and Westminster Abbey.'

Anna was grateful to Henry for his ongoing generosity, yet dismayed that some of her new furnishings were the confiscated possessions of Cromwell, who still lay in the Tower under sentence of death.

She could so easily have shared his fate, had she chosen to defy the King.

She wondered why Cromwell had not been executed ere now. Could it be that Henry had decided to commute his sentence to imprisonment? She very much hoped so. She loathed the thought of that clever, brilliant man suffering a traitor's death. Margaret Douglas had not long ago spelled out for Anna the dreadful details, and they did not bear thinking about. Besides, Anna still felt she had some affiliation with Cromwell because of her marriage. She did not want his furniture; it seemed wrong that she should profit by his misfortune. The things would be tainted, for ever associated with his downfall. She vowed to store them in a lumber room.

On Dr Harst's next visit, he reported that, after dissolving Parliament for the summer recess, the King had left Whitehall and moved with a small household to the palace of Oatlands.

'It is less than ten miles from here,' he told Anna, as they strolled along the gravelled path that ran parallel with the River Thames.

'Do you think he might visit me?' she asked.

'I do not know, Madam.' He paused. 'I bring grave news too. Cromwell was beheaded this morning on Tower Hill. I was there to see it.'

Her hand flew to her mouth. 'No! I had thought the King would spare him. Oh, he will regret this, I am sure, for few princes ever had a more able or dedicated minister.'

'Or one who made him so rich!'

'Did he suffer greatly?'

Harst hesitated momentarily. 'The King had graciously commuted the sentence to decapitation, but the executioner was a ragged and butcherly youth, who didn't know what he was doing. Yes, I'm afraid he did suffer a little.'

Anna shuddered. 'I fear it was my marriage that did for Cromwell. I feel somehow responsible for his death. Dr Harst, I did not know how to make my husband love me! I lack the arts other women practise. I tried, I did try, to be dutiful and loving, and I think there was a time

278

when the King began really to like me – but then it was too late. If Katheryn Howard had not caught his eye, Cromwell might still be here among us.'

'Who can tell where attraction lies, Madam. This King wants a wife he can love. That came across strongly during the marriage negotiations, when he was most concerned to see your portrait. As you yourself pointed out, it overrode all other considerations. Thus it was a dangerous matter for Cromwell to arrange this match. He believed all Germany would ever afterwards assist this country for your sake. Instead, the marriage ruined him.'

'It did, poor wretch. It so nearly ruined me too.' They paused, watching the boats sail by on the Thames. Anna lifted her eyes to the fields that stretched beyond into the distance.

'The Catholics at court are rejoicing, of course,' Harst said. 'Cromwell's fall represents a victory for them. This will drive the reformers underground. Mark me, you will see the King uphold religious orthodoxy more vigorously than ever. Mr Barnes, who helped negotiate your marriage and is a notorious Protestant, is to be burned as a heretic at Smithfield two days hence. It is a grim pointer as to the way the wind is blowing.'

Anna had never spoken with Mr Barnes, but she remembered seeing him at Düsseldorf, and being struck by the intensity of his gaze. She could well believe he had a fanatical zeal for the Lutheran faith. He must have, to maintain it in the face of such a terrible death.

Harst was speaking. 'Never again, I think, will the King rely on one minister, as he did on Cromwell, and on Cardinal Wolsey before him. There is no statesman here of equal merit.'

'But Norfolk's influence is prevailing; and if the King marries his niece, it will grow stronger.'

'Norfolk is no Cromwell. He's a soldier, essentially, and ambitious for his family. The King knows that. No, we will not see any man rise so high as those that are gone, only factions fighting for precedence, mark my words.'

Anna walked ahead, reflecting that it was probably true. Well, she was glad not to have any part in it.

Dr Harst caught up with her. 'Changing the subject, Madam, I learned today that Hans Holbein has fallen out of favour. He was with me at Tower Hill this morning, for Cromwell was his patron, and his friend too, I suspect. He was complaining that his royal commissions had dried up.'

'That is because he painted the portrait of me that led the King to believe I was beautiful,' Anna said sadly. 'Dr Wotton thought it a good likeness.'

'I haven't seen it, Madam, but I do not need to. I speak as a friend when I say you are a lovely lady; there can be no denying it. Beauty comes from within; it illuminates the features. Others, I know, have seen this in you. The King may come belatedly to see it too; I think he has glimpsed it already, but has been blinded by infatuation for another.'

Never had the scholarly Dr Harst spoken so familiarly to her. 'You are very kind, but you are embarrassing me,' she told him, feeling herself blush.

'It is my job to speak the truth!' he retorted amiably. She could have hugged him or squeezed his hand, but she was still the Princess of Kleve and he was still her brother's ambassador. They walked on in companionable silence.

Chapter 18

1540

It was so hot. Anna was sewing with her new gentlewomen, and they had the windows wide open, yet still they sweltered. They had thrown off their gowns and were sitting in their kirtles, with the sleeves of their undersmocks rolled up.

'Look at us! We are so indecorous!' Anna laughed, when Mother Lowe came in and stared at them.

'What would your lady mother say?' the nurse asked, shaking her head and chuckling. She laid down two bolts of silk that had just been delivered by the mercer's apprentice.

Anna was enjoying the days spent with her new attendants. Frances Lilgrave was brilliant with a needle, and had helped Anna improve her stitches and design some elegant embroidery patterns. She loved a gossip too, and it was hard not to relish her scandalous tales of who was having secret trysts, and who was no better than she should be.

Katherine Bassett was a paler version of her sister, Anne, and not, thank Heaven, as forward. She had become friends with Jane Ratsey, whom Anna found to be empty-headed, yet willing and kind. Mrs Wingfield and Mrs Simpson were pleasant company, and, of course, the lively Katharina and the gentle Gertrude were as amiable and loyal as ever. Fortunately, Katharina now had enough English to act as a reasonable interpreter, while Anna's knowledge of the language had improved vastly.

Today, the talk was all of her proposed visits to her new houses.

'I think I will go to Hever first, and then Bletchingley,' she said. 'You will all come with me, and we shall make a merry party.'

'I marvel that your Highness wants to stay at Hever Castle,' Frances

Lilgrave said, her beady black eyes alight with the hint of another juicy tale to tell.

'Why should I not?' Anna asked.

'It was *her* family seat. Anne Boleyn's, I mean. It came to the King when her father died last year.'

Of course. It *had* been Lady Rochford, Anne's sister-in-law, who had spoken of Hever. She'd lived there, and hated it. Small wonder, for she made no secret of the fact that she had loathed the Boleyns.

'Do you think it's haunted?' Jane Ratsey asked fearfully.

'I should hope not!' Anna said, hoping to discourage such talk. Even so, she found herself not looking forward to visiting Hever as much as she had been.

'If *she* had cause to walk, it would surely be at the Tower, wouldn't it?' Katherine Bassett put in.

'We shouldn't speak of her,' Mrs Simpson reproved. 'It's frowned on at court, I hear.'

'I think we should talk about something more pleasant,' Anna intervened. 'Like how many new gowns we need to order for the trip!' There was a chorus of assent.

Just then, Hanna von Wylich came in, accompanied by Jasper Horsey's wife, Joanna. They had been keeping watch in the antechamber and gatehouse lest anyone approach while their mistress and her gentlewomen were in a state of *déshabillé*.

Joanna was amiable enough, when she wasn't ruling her husband – and thus Anna's lower servants – with a staff of iron (although she did it so capably that Anna had no wish to complain); but Anna had never forged any kind of friendship with Hanna von Wylich, whom she thought brittle, sly and secretive. Something was going on between her and Otho; it was clear to all that no longer were they a happy couple. He wore his misery like a cloak. His wife, by contrast, didn't seem to care.

But today, she was animated. 'A barge is mooring below, my lady. It bears men in the King's livery!'

'Make haste, Madam,' Joanna urged. 'They will surely be here to see you.'

At mention of the King, Anna had leapt to her feet, and Mother Lowe began pulling on her gown, fumbling with the laces.

'Someone bring a comb!' she cried. 'You girls, make yourselves decent.'

By a miracle, they were all looking presentable when two men in red livery bearing the Tudor rose emblem were shown in by John Bekinsale, Anna's punctilious gentleman usher.

They bowed to her. 'My Lady Anna, the King asks if he may visit you tomorrow, and dine with you,' the taller man said.

She was astonished. Henry had said he would come to see her, but she had thought it just fair words. 'His Majesty will be most welcome,' she said. 'At what time will he arrive?'

'At eleven o'clock, my lady. He is coming by barge from Hampton Court.'

'And will there be any other guests?'

'No, my lady. His Majesty will bring just his master of horse, three lords in attendance, two grooms and a small escort. If your kitchens could provide them with an adequate repast, that would be much appreciated.'

'Of course,' she said, thinking she could have a table set up for them in the watching chamber. 'Pray tell the King I am sensible of the honour he is paying me, and will be glad to see him.'

When they had gone, she wondered if her last words might be misconstrued as meaning she had been pining for Henry. Well, he would soon – she hoped – see that she wasn't.

'We have much to make ready,' she said, turning to her women. A buzz of excitement broke out, especially among the younger ones, who must have been longing for some diversion from their humdrum days. She summoned Jasper Horsey and informed him of the King's visit, then sped down to the kitchens and spent an hour with Meister Schoulenburg and Henry, her butler, discussing what was to be served at dinner. She inspected the many kitchen offices that would be spurred to action, checking that all was clean, after which she went through the napery chests, selecting the finest linen for the table. Richmond had become a hive of activity, with the assembling of provisions, the polishing of glasses and gold plate and the rattle of pans.

Escaping the hubbub she had set in train, Anna raced upstairs to search in her wardrobe. She must look her best for the King; there must be no hint that without him she had let herself go. He would see a happy, confident woman, contented with her lot. She would never again wear in his presence anything like that low-necked gown of red and black she had naively donned to arouse his ardour. *That* could be cut up and made into cushion covers. There were other gowns too that held uncomfortable memories; it was a shame, after all Mutter's care, and so much money, had gone into providing them. But there was one Henry had never seen, one of the English ones Anna had had made, in a dark green damask. It fitted tight to the waist, with a pointed stomacher, standing collar and long hanging sleeves, and it suited her well, she thought. There was a matching French hood edged with pearls, and she could wear the pendant Henry had given her.

The next morning, thus attired, she waited at the waterside, her household behind her, for the royal barge to make its serene way to the jetty. And there he was, the King, broader than ever in a sumptuous suit of cloth of silver, lumbering heavily along the gangway towards her. She sank to her knees, bowing her head, then felt the shadow of Henry's bulk loom over her, and his hands grasping hers and raising her up.

'Anna, my dearest sister!' he greeted her, kissing her on the mouth in the English manner.

'Your Majesty – Brother – this is a great honour,' she told him, searching his face for any sign of embarrassment. There was none. She had expected their meeting to be awkward, underpinned with wariness, even guilt, but Henry was in an ebullient mood, and looking a lot happier than when she had last seen him. She should have known he would feel no unease with her; he had such a deep-rooted belief in his own righteousness that it would never occur to him that he might have wrecked her life.

'You are looking very well, Anna,' he said, taking her hand and leading her through the gatehouse.

'I was going to say the same about your Grace,' she laughed.

'I have not felt so well in ages,' he replied. 'That's a most becoming gown. It suits you.'

This was a very different Henry from the one to whom she had been married. For the first time, she understood why people called him more of a good fellow than a king. If only he had exerted such charm when they were man and wife, she might have gained the confidence to be a little seductive and win him. But no matter. It was strange how, now she was free of him, she seemed to have that confidence.

'I have had dinner laid in my privy chamber,' she said, as they ascended the stair to the Queen's lodgings. She had taken care with the seating arrangements, to demonstrate her obedience to his will. His chair had been placed at the centre of the table beneath the cloth of estate bearing the arms of England, which the harbingers had thoughtfully brought for her use. A separate, smaller table for her had been placed at right angles, at the corner of the high table, to denote that she no longer merited the distinction of dining at the King's side.

Henry made no comment, but she saw his eyes take in her arrangement. Once seated, he looked about him in admiration at the bowls of flowers she had caused to be set around the room, the brightly embroidered fire screen she had made, the sparkling Venetian glasses and the snowy napery.

'By God, Anna, you know how to make a house comfortable!' he said.

'I would not go to such trouble for just any guest,' she smiled. At her nod, a servitor stepped forward and laid napkins over the King's shoulder and then hers, while another placed the finest white manchet bread beside their chargers, which were of heavy gold plate. She signalled to her butler to pour the wine.

'Mmm,' murmured Henry. 'Rhenish? It's very good.'

'In Germany, Sir, we have been making good wines for hundreds of years,' she said, tasting hers. 'Yes, this is excellent.' She smiled at the butler.

The first course was brought in: six dishes of the choicest fish to choose from, garnished with spices and herbs. Henry tucked in zestfully, complimenting Anna on her table. 'Mmm, this is delicious,' he said, polishing off the last of the carp in verjuice.

He had made no mention of the annulment, or the momentous

events of the past weeks, and Anna certainly wasn't going to. He had made it clear that this was to be the beginning of a new relationship between them, and she was rather enjoying it. Freed from the ties that had bound them, it was obvious that they were both realising how much they really liked each other.

When the main course arrived, and Henry had exclaimed over the great venison pasty that Anna had commanded to be presented to him, knowing it to be his favourite dish, and he had served them both the choicest cuts from all the other meats on offer, he waved the servants away, reached over and took her hand.

'I am glad you are contented with the ruling of the bishops, Anna. Thanks to your conformity and reasonableness, the matter was dealt with speedily, and to our mutual benefit.'

Anna chose her words with care. 'It was a heavy matter to me,' she confessed, 'but I saw the necessity for the inquiry, and I do believe the sentence was the right one. It was very wise of your Grace to entertain those doubts. In my ignorance, I had not the faintest idea that something might be amiss.'

Henry was watching her intently. Now he nodded. 'I knew, from the first, that you were not my lawful wife. I knew it when Kleve could not produce the promised proofs. I told my Council my conscience would not permit me to consummate the marriage, as I felt sure I was not entitled to do so since you were another man's wife.'

'I understand, Sir,' Anna said, aware that he was explaining away his impotence. 'And there I was thinking that my person was displeasing to you.' She could not resist teasing him a little, and was gratified to see his fair skin flush. Now he *was* embarrassed!

'It was nothing personal, I assure you, Anna,' he said. 'It was just that I knew I had no right to love you.'

He did not know she had heard the gossip. It came to her that he really believed in the myth he had created.

'I like you, Anna,' he continued, regarding her with those piercing blue eyes. 'I like you very well, and I am indebted to you too. I know, from bitter experience, that divorce can be a messy and fraught business that can drag on for years, so I did not pursue an annulment lightly.

I will tell you, my Council shrank from the prospect. But you were so amenable, so understanding of my concerns. I thought you would play the woman and prove capricious and obstructive, but you surprised me, and I began to realise what a gem I was losing. Notwithstanding, we could not remain in a marriage that was no marriage. I am heartily grateful to you for easing its ending.'

'Your Grace was ever good to me,' she said, 'and you have been most generous in the settlement you made on me.' She waved her hand to indicate the ornate room and the palace beyond the window. 'And I like being in England – and being your sister.'

'Martin Luther was not so charitable!' Henry grimaced. 'Do you know what he said when they told him of the annulment? "Squire Harry wishes to be God, and do as he wills!" As if he can talk! He is severely discountenanced, for he thinks his followers have been deprived of an ally in England.'

'I was never that,' Anna said sharply.

'I know.' Henry raised his glass to her. 'I know you for a devout Catholic, and no Pope-lover. But I fear your name is inextricably linked to the reformers in Germany.'

'As long as your Grace knows the truth of it,' she replied. 'I would not want my name tainted by heresy.'

'Rest assured, Anna, I could never believe that. Some more of this excellent beef?'

As he served her, carving the meat with skill, as a gentleman should, Anna noticed that the door was open a chink and that, just behind it, there was, unmistakably, a damask skirt. Frances Lilgrave was eavesdropping. She could not risk exposing the woman to Henry's wrath, so she excused herself, got up and closed the door.

'A slight draught,' she explained.

'I am glad we are private together,' Henry said gently, making her wonder for a mad moment if he was about to make an advance to her. 'I have some news I wanted to tell you myself. I have a new queen. When I was at Oatlands, on the twenty-eighth of July, I married Katheryn Howard.' It was so at odds with what Anna had expected that she was momentarily speechless.

'I think you knew I would wed her,' he said, his cheeks again flushed. 'I was attracted to her maidenly behaviour, and it came to me that I should honour her with my hand, thinking that, in my old days – after the many troubles of mind that have plagued me in my marriages – I must obtain such a perfect jewel of womanhood. Anna, her love for me is not only to my quietness and peace of mind, but also leads me to hope she will bring forth the desired fruits of marriage.'

Anna did not want to hear all this. It made her feel even more unwanted, and not a little jealous of her former maid-of-honour, to whom – she realised – she must from now on bend the knee. Now she had an inkling of how Queen Katherine and Queen Anne had felt when they, in their turn, were supplanted. She could have shaken Henry for his insensitivity. Yet she would not let it matter; she *must* not let it matter. So she kept a cheerful countenance – and found her voice. 'I am so happy for your Grace, and I will be the first to congratulate Queen Katheryn on her great good fortune.'

'Thank you, Anna,' Henry beamed. 'I knew you would understand. I need sons, and at my age I cannot afford to wait. Besides, it was not as if I had been widowed and must wait a decent interval. Katheryn is young, and I look for a child soon.' He was telling her he had done with Katheryn what he had failed to do with her.

'I wish your Grace many strong, strapping sons,' Anna said. 'I always liked Katheryn. She was kind and thoughtful.' And so young, to be tied fast to an ageing, ailing man.

'She is, she is!' Henry agreed enthusiastically. 'She has great qualities, and aptness for a crown.'

As he waxed on lyrically about Katheryn's charms and loving ways, Anna realised he was truly, genuinely in love, and it was this that had illuminated him and made him genial and expansive. She did not blame him, or begrudge him his happiness, even though it made her feel distinctly lacking. He could not help the way he felt. If he had had more love like this in his life, he – and his reign – might have turned out very differently. Maybe everything *had* happened for the best, and God's hand *was* evident in Henry's affairs.

Something was nagging at her, though. Henry had said he was married on 28 July. The date had rung bells. Now she remembered. It was the day Cromwell had gone to his execution. Had Henry chosen it deliberately, to mark the beginning of a new chapter in his life and the end of another?

When the bowls of fruit and the remaining custard tarts had been removed, the King rose. 'Before I depart, Anna, I should be grateful if you would sign the deed of separation.'

'Of course,' she agreed, and was surprised when he summoned the three lords who had accompanied him to Richmond; they were all Privy councillors. So *this* was the real reason he had come to see her. And yet he had enjoyed himself, she knew; he had liked her company. They had got on well, become firmer friends.

When they laid the document before her, she signed it willingly.

After seeing the King and his lords off, standing waving from the jetty, Anna led her ladies back to her privy chamber, where the servants were removing the tables. As soon as the door closed behind them, the ladies broke out in excited chatter.

'Madam, we were thrilled to see the King on the best possible terms with you,' Gertrude cried.

'Maybe he has changed his mind about the divorce,' Katherine Bassett speculated.

'He is realising he loves you after all,' Frances added.

'Frances, you were listening at the door! I saw you,' Anna reproved. 'What if the King had noticed you?'

Frances flushed. 'I'm sorry, Madam, but I could not resist. We were all bursting to know how you were faring with his Grace. And it was wonderful to see you dining so pleasantly together. I'll wager we will see you restored to your place.'

'Nonsense!' Anna snapped, her good mood dissipating. What if the King heard that her ladies, the people closest to her, and in the best position to influence her, were conjecturing that he would take her back? Might he wonder if she was encouraging such speculation?

'It would reflect too much on the King's honour to put me away on a plea of conscience and take me back so easily,' she said coldly. 'It would argue too great an inconsistency. There were lawful impediments to the marriage, so the annulment must stand, however well the King and I accord together. Besides, as Frances has no doubt told you all, he has taken another wife.'

Frances clearly had not told them, for she – and the others – looked utterly dumbfounded.

'Yes, it is true,' Anna went on. 'He has married Katheryn Howard, and I enjoin you all to honour her as your Queen.'

Mother Lowe made a face. There were murmurs of disbelief and incredulity. 'That girl . . . Far too young for him . . . Little slut . . .'

'Enough!' Anna cried. 'I will not have her maligned in my presence – or anywhere else, for that matter. You will speak of her with respect, and think well of her, as I do.'

'You are a saint, Madam,' Gertrude said.

'I am the King's dutiful sister!' Anna reminded her.

Florence had returned from Kleve. Anna summoned him at once.

'You delivered my letter to the Duke?' she asked.

'I did, my lady.'

'And how did he respond?'

'He retired immediately to consider its contents in private. Then he sent my uncle to inform me that, although he was sorry about what had happened, he would not depart from his amity with the King.'

'I am relieved to hear it,' Anna said, with feeling.

Florence's handsome features were a picture of concern. 'My lady, do not think the Duke was indifferent to your situation. He was troubled at your remaining here, and asked whether the King could be induced to suffer you to return home. But we told him it truly was your choice to remain, which you had made clear from the first.'

'Did he comment on the causes of the annulment?'

'He said that, as far as he knew, there never was any binding contract between yourself and the Marquis of Lorraine; he was sorry it was otherwise found, but he trusted the King to order the matter to his honour. However, he would not give any formal assent to the annulment.' And that, Anna realised, was as far as Wilhelm was prepared to go. He would not risk overturning the alliance with England.

'But we spoke privately later,' Florence went on, 'and he said he was glad you had fared no worse, for he had not the means to oppose King Henry. He will rejoice to hear you are to be restored to your place.'

'What?' Anna was confused. 'What place?'

'As queen,' he replied, looking at her in puzzlement.

She was aghast. 'Where did you hear that?'

'It is all over the court, and even in the taverns. People are speaking of it as something to be greatly wondered at.'

This could not be happening. 'Florence, they know not what they are talking about. The King has remarried, although it is a secret for now.'

The young man looked confused.

'I am sorry,' Anna said. 'I did not mean to speak so sharply. Go and get some refreshments at the servery – and keep all this to yourself!'

When he had gone, she paced the floor, deeply troubled. This bruit might have arisen from her ladies gossiping, especially Frances. If it was traced back to her household, she would be implicated, and the bright carapace that had convinced Henry she was not pining for him would be shattered. If the court was buzzing with rumours, surely he would hear them. He had once said he never heeded them, but this matter touched him too nearly.

She determined to show the world she was happy and contented in her single state. For the next week, she took care to appear in public with a joyous face, and donned a new gown every day, each more sumptuous than the last. She rode her palfrey to the edges of Richmond Park, where she could be seen by large numbers of the King's subjects; she took pleasure jaunts with her ladies along the Thames, and hosted a dinner for local worthies, serving the choicest food and wines. For that she wore a glorious gown of black velvet edged with fur from Pamplona. Let none say she was languishing!

Afterwards, she was to wonder if this vile gossip had prompted Henry to announce his marriage. Two days after his visit, Dr Harst described to her how Katheryn Howard had appeared as queen at

Hampton Court, and dined publicly under a cloth of estate. She had comported herself with dignity and grace, and been well received by the courtiers, he reported, though many had shown surprise at her elevation, thinking her no more than just another royal mistress.

Dr Harst was somewhat agitated. After much blustering, he blurted out, 'Madam, I hear you are showing yourself unduly gay and frolicsome. There is talk about you in the court. People are arguing whether such behaviour displays prudent dissimulation or stupid forgetfulness of what should so closely touch your heart.'

'It's neither!' Anna cried, goaded to fury. 'I just don't want people thinking I wish the King to take me back. There were rumours to that effect. I feared they emanated from my ladies, and that people would think I was encouraging them.'

'I doubt your ladies are informants of the French ambassador,' Harst observed. 'He has taken the greatest pleasure in fuelling the gossip.'

'That's as may be, but I *am* happy, and I see no reason why you, Dr Harst, or anyone else, should look askance at my simple pleasures. Does everyone expect me to sit here mourning my lost husband? Am I not entitled to build a new life for myself? Or should I be rending my clothes and beating my bosom to show the man who put me away that I miss him? Dr Harst, I have my pride!'

Harst had the grace to look chastened. 'Forgive me, Madam. I'm sure the gossip will abate, as it always does.'

'I trust it will, and that you and everyone else will stop judging me and finding me wanting. Whatever I do, I cannot win!' She was still seething. But later, after Harst had gone, and she had calmed down, she could not help feeling she had alienated a friend.

When Anna next went to Sunday Mass, a new bidding prayer enjoined her and the whole congregation to pray for the King, Queen Katheryn and Prince Edward. It would be the same in every church in the land. She prayed fervently, as she was bid, trying not to mind. She had been doing that a lot lately.

She spent the long summer days enjoying sports and recreations, which were a great antidote to regret. At Richmond, there was plenty of scope for such pursuits. At the lower end of the gardens there were pleasant galleries and houses of pleasure where you could play chess, backgammon, dice, cards or even billiards, with the warm breeze whispering through the latticed walls. There were bowling alleys, butts for archery, and tennis courts. Anna went often to the courts, to sit in the gallery and watch her household playing.

She found herself taking special pleasure in seeing Otho bounding around the court and dealing fast serves to Franz von Waldeck, his tall, muscular body lithe and agile. She could not stop remembering how intimately she had once known that body, or imagining that the mature man would be a far more accomplished lover than the callow youth he had been. Once, she was sure he saw her staring at him, and blushed to think he might guess that she was indulging in such fantasies. Another time, his wife was waiting for him when he left the play, and there were hard words between them. Anna could not hear what was said, but the tone was acrimonious on his wife's part, and defeated on his. For the hundredth time, she wondered what had happened to turn such a loving couple against each other.

She was aware, from the reactions of her guests, that her table was becoming renowned. Now that the King had set the precedent and dined with her, and come again three weeks later, others followed suit. Courtiers called upon her, among them Sir Anthony Browne and Sir Thomas Seymour, all angling to be feasted, and she discovered an aptitude for playing hostess.

She found herself increasingly enjoying the food of her adoptive land. 'There is no place like England for feeding well!' she declared, serving a generous portion of quails to the Duchess of Suffolk, who visited on a beautiful summer's day.

'But surely you had good fare in Germany?' the Duchess replied, savouring the rich sauce in which the meat was steeped.

'Yes, I did,' Anna agreed, filling their goblets. 'I come from near Cologne, where the food is very rich and varied because it is a great trading place. Next time you come, I will have for you some *Sauerbraten*, cherries in wine, and pretzels.'

Seeing her guest looking dubious, she laughed. 'You will enjoy them all, I promise you!'

In this glorious, golden summer, Anna's thoughts kept turning to Otho. Twice lately, her eyes had met his and, beyond the unhappiness in his gaze, she could sense a flicker of something else. Another time, his hand – she knew it – had deliberately brushed against hers and lingered a second longer than was seemly. It made her feel, momentarily, something of the pleasure he had once awakened in her. How sad, at just twenty-four, to have experienced physical love only once, and that once furtive and clandestine – and to know she might never experience it again. And there was no one to whom she could unburden herself. Mother Lowe, to whom she confided most things, would be shocked. In her book, honest young ladies did not think about such things, let alone yearn for them. If only Emily were here. Emily would understand, would even giggle about it. But Emily was lost to Anna, far away in Kleve.

She knew there was little prospect of her being able to remarry, even though she was purportedly free to do so. The smallest suggestion that the King might want her back would deter any would-be suitor. If she did marry, the whole distressing business of the precontract might be raked up again.

But did she want to be married? Her only experience of it had ended in humiliation. Free to live her life much as she pleased, she did not relish the prospect of being under subjugation to another overbearing husband. Countless wives accepted their lot without question, but they had not had a glorious taste of what it was to be your own mistress. No, she wanted love rather than wedlock; shocking as it sounded, she wanted a lover! The realisation astonished her a little, but she was surprised to find she felt no shame at the prospect of an illicit affair. That heady sense of liberation had clearly had its effect on her. She must be the true granddaughter of 'the Childmaker'!

Early in August, Anna left with her household on the little progress to her new properties. The scandal of her divorce had subsided, to the point where she judged it permissible to go abroad. Besides, most people would think she was just another great lady perambulating her domains. So she left behind her chariot and took the handsome litter Henry had given her, riding with Mother Lowe while her ladies, gentlemen and servants followed behind on horseback or in covered wagons.

She took with her Henry's permission to make the trip, and for his daughter Elizabeth to join her. When he had last visited, she had asked if the child might come to stay with her, and he had readily agreed. Mrs Astley, Elizabeth's governess, was to accompany her to Hever Castle and, surprisingly, Henry had betrayed no reservations about Elizabeth visiting her mother's family home.

As Anna and her train wended their way south-east down the pretty, leafy lanes of Kent, she found herself approaching Hever with a sense of trepidation, fearing it might be tainted with the tragedies that had befallen its former owners. Five years ago, they had been riding high at court, puffed up with power. Now they were all dead, annihilated by violence and grief, save for the self-effacing Mistress Stafford, whose daughter Kate had served her when she was queen. How those two must regret the loss of their family seat – unless, of course, for them too it was a bitter reminder of the ruin of all they held dear.

Such thoughts filled Anna's head as she was conveyed through the beautiful undulating countryside and into the hunting park that surrounded the castle. And there it was, nestling in a sheltered valley, a small, mellow-stoned fortified residence surrounded by a moat and lovely gardens.

Anna had been told that Hever had been stripped of the Boleyns' possessions, and refurnished – with more of the rich pickings from Cromwell's houses, no doubt. Her sense of foreboding increased. How could Hever be a lucky or happy house, with its bloody connections? In owning it, she feared she was profiting from others' misfortunes; and that it might be unlucky for her too.

Nevertheless, she had to admire the costly furnishings that had been provided for her. It was better not to speculate on where they had come from. But as she wandered through the rooms and ascended spiral staircases, exploring her new domain, she saw that some traces of the

Boleyns still remained. In her bedchamber was a tester bed bearing the initials T.B. and carvings of bulls; doubtless it had been too big to remove. And, in the attic, she found, turned against a wall, a portrait of an elegantly dressed brunette that bore the Latin inscription '*Anna Bolina uxor Henry Octa*'. Certainly the King would not have wanted such a vivid reminder of the wife he had sent to her death, which was probably why the picture had been left here. Anna wondered if it was a true likeness. If so, Anne had been no beauty. With her long, thin face, dark, watchful eyes and prim mouth, she bore a strong resemblance to her daughter, although Elizabeth had Henry's colouring and Roman nose. Yet she had an indefinable something about her, at which the artist had hinted; and Anna liked the portrait. She would have it rehung in the gallery; it seemed a just reparation, for it was only on account of Anne's tragedy that she herself owned Hever. The picture could always be put away if the King visited.

Anna could imagine the Boleyn family entertaining him in the great hall, with its vast fireplace and screens passage. Maybe Henry had wooed Anne in the family's private parlour, or walked with her in the long gallery. In the cavernous kitchen, with its well sunk in the floor, feasts had been prepared, and the bustle of everyday life had pre-dominated. All gone now, faded to a distant memory. How quickly – and devastatingly – the wheel of fortune could turn.

Well, she would do her best to bring Hever to new life, honour its past and banish its ghosts. It really was a most beautiful place.

Anna watched from a window as the little cavalcade crested the hill, and saw the nearly-seven-year-old Elizabeth spur on her palfrey. Wearing her green gown, Anna sped downstairs and opened the main door, calling for her household to assemble with her. There she waited until, with two men-at-arms riding behind, and three waiting women in attendance, Elizabeth and her governess clattered over the drawbridge and into the courtyard. At Elizabeth's approach, Anna swept a deep curtsey, and the child returned the courtesy as soon as she had dismounted. Her sallow skin had a rosy tinge from being out in the fresh air, and her long red hair streamed loose over her shoulders.

'Welcome, my Lady Elizabeth!' Anna smiled. 'It is most kind of his Majesty to allow you to visit me.' She was proud of her growing command of English.

Elizabeth inclined her head regally, as if bestowing the favour of her presence on her hostess, and allowed Anna to lead her into the castle. Here, on trestles in the hall, were laid out cold meats, raised pies and custard tarts, and a selection of candied fruits that made the little girl's eyes shine. Anna had ordered them specially, for Henry had warned her his daughter had a sweet tooth.

'We have also a dish from Kleve!' she announced proudly, as they seated themselves at the high table, with Elizabeth in the place of honour. At Anna's nod, two servants came forward. One poured wine, watered for their young guest; the other carried a platter piled high with what must look to the child like a greenish-white mess.

'What is that, my lady?' Elizabeth was curious.

'It is sauerkraut,' Anna said. 'Cabbage with salt, wine and juniper.' Another nod, and the servant spooned a generous amount on to Elizabeth's plate. Elizabeth tasted it.

'Very good!' she pronounced, and began eating voraciously.

Delighted that the visit had got off to a promising start, Anna smiled at Mrs Astley, the governess, a well-spoken, cultivated lady who clearly adored her charge and was only too willing to sing her praises.

After they had eaten their fill, Elizabeth wanted to be shown around the castle. She had not mentioned her mother, but Anna suspected she was curious to see the house where Anne had grown up. It was half her heritage, after all.

In the long gallery, Elizabeth spotted the portrait. Anna could have kicked herself. She had meant to have it removed for the Princess's visit, but in the bustle of preparations she had forgotten to give the order.

'It's my mother!' the little girl cried impulsively, then clapped her hand over her mouth, plainly realising what she had said. Poor thing, she already knew that Queen Anne was never to be mentioned publicly.

Anna saw Mrs Astley staring at the portrait with misty eyes.

'I should have remembered,' Anna murmured. 'I meant to have it replaced. I have been so busy making ready . . .'

The governess came to her rescue. 'No matter, your Highness. The Lady Elizabeth has seen pictures of her mother. I made sure of it. I think it is important that she knows something of her.'

'Oh, yes,' Anna said, with feeling. 'The poor child. And that poor woman.' She shuddered. 'That is why I wish to do something for the Lady Elizabeth. I would be a friend to her.'

'Your Highness's kindness is deeply appreciated,' said Mrs Astley. The two women exchanged sympathetic looks.

Elizabeth was gazing at the picture.

'She looks so beautiful,' she said.

'It's a fair likeness,' said the governess.

'I was pleased to find it here,' Anna told them. 'No one would talk about her at court.'

'They are too afraid of the King,' Mrs Astley said quietly. 'It would not do to express an opinion.' From the tone of her voice, Anna comprehended exactly what her opinion was.

She took Elizabeth's hand.

'Come. I have something else to show you,' she smiled, and led the child along the gallery to her bedchamber. 'This bed was owned by someone in your mother's family,' she said.

Elizabeth's eyes widened.

'Why is it kept here?' she asked.

'This was her home,' revealed the governess, and Anna realised that Elizabeth had not known of Hever's connection with her mother. 'She spent her childhood here, and the King your father came here to pay court to her. Not that she would have him then: she kept turning him down!'

'But he was the King!' Elizabeth looked shocked.

'Yes, and in asking your mother to be his chosen lady, he was placing her above him, to be worshipped like a goddess, so to speak. It was ever so, in the courtly game of love.' Mrs Astley smiled.

'Not in Kleve!' Anna put in tartly. 'There, young ladies have always been made to marry the men their fathers choose for them.'

'And here too that is the custom,' said Mrs Astley. 'It is why lovers sigh for the unattainable.'

Anna smiled. 'In my case, it was all signed and sealed before ever I met his Majesty. That is what happens to princesses.'

Elizabeth stared hard at her. 'No one will make me marry a man I have not seen, and I will not trust portrait painters!'

Her words gave Anna a jolt. Had the child heard that Henry, having been much taken with Anna's portrait, had not liked the real thing? Was that why she kept looking at Anna appraisingly?

'You will have to marry the man the King your father chooses, my little lady,' Mrs Astley said firmly. 'When he met your mother, he was already married. He could not ask her to be his wife, so he asked her to be his mistress.'

'His mistress?' Elizabeth asked, running her fingers over the carvings on the bedposts.

'The one who ruled his heart,' Mrs Astley said, telling only half the truth. 'As your lady mistress rules you!'

'And she refused? She was a brave woman!' Anna declared.

'Did my father love her very much?' Elizabeth asked.

Mrs Astley hesitated. 'He did. He thought of no one else. He broke with the Pope and made himself head of the Church of England so that he could marry her, and in the end he won her.'

After that, of course, things had gone badly wrong, so Anna resolved to divert Elizabeth from further questions.

'Let's find your bedchamber, shall we?' she said. 'Come this way.'

'Can't I sleep here?' Elizabeth asked.

'This is the Lady Anna's room,' Mrs Astley told her. 'And that bed was probably your grandfather's; I'll wager those initials stand for Thomas Boleyn.'

'I did wonder,' Anna said. 'Of course you may sleep here, my Lady Elizabeth. I will order it.' She beamed down at the little girl, who looked at her gratefully. 'Now, I want to show you the beautiful gardens!'

Anna was aware that wherever Elizabeth went at Hever, there would be reminders of her mother. Anne's memory was there in every room, every garden walk, every shady arbour. Lying wakeful that night in the bedchamber that was to have been Elizabeth's, she wondered if the

299

child was sleeping well in her grandfather's bed. The unfamiliar room, the strange house, the revelations of the day – any or all of it could have unsettled her. Yet she was a self-contained child, more inquisitive than emotional, and did not appear to be affected by the loss of a mother she could hardly have known; but who knew what went on in that little red head?

Anna herself did not like being in the dark at Hever. A shadow cast by a piece of furniture, or the hoot of an owl, could make the hairs on the nape of her neck stand up. Always, at night, she kept a candle burning, and had one of her maids sleep on the pallet at the foot of her bed for company. She had never seen or heard anything untoward, but for a child with a vivid imagination, night might bring terrors. Thank goodness the estimable Mrs Astley was sleeping nearby.

The next morning, Elizabeth said she had slept well, but Mrs Astley looked tired. After breakfast, she drew Anna aside.

'Madam,' she said, 'was it you I heard sobbing in the night?'

'No,' Anna answered, surprised. 'It wasn't the Lady Elizabeth, I hope?'

'It wasn't. I checked on her. But someone sounded very distressed.'

Anna asked her ladies, and anyone else who had slept within earshot of Mrs Astley, but no one admitted to having been crying, and Anna believed they were telling the truth. It was a mystery, and she was beginning to entertain the suspicion that the castle was indeed haunted. Could it have been Anne, weeping because she was not there to give her daughter a mother's love?

The days flew by. The weeping was heard no more, and all too soon, Elizabeth was curtseying farewell.

'Your Grace must come again,' Anna told her. 'Your visit has given me great pleasure. I hope you will think of me as your friend.'

'I do, my lady,' declared Elizabeth fervently, extending her hand. But Anna ignored it. Bending, she drew the child into a warm embrace, and kissed her.

'Come back soon!' she said.

* * *

That very day, after Elizabeth had gone, Anna was sitting in her favourite spot in the gardens, enjoying the sunshine and some rare solitude, when, from behind the box hedge to her rear, she heard an angry exchange of voices. It was Otho and his wife.

'I *loved* you!' she heard him say. 'I loved you with my whole heart, yet you have treated me as if I am nothing, like the dirt beneath your feet. Are you surprised that I no longer want to be anywhere near you?'

'I was merely your trophy,' Hanna snapped, 'someone you could parade to the world. Werner loves me for myself.'

Werner? Werner von Gymnich, Anna's cupbearer? He was a handsome fellow in his way, but by no means as handsome as Otho.

'I loved you truly,' Otho repeated, as if through gritted teeth, 'but you chose to betray me, and now you are trying to justify what you did by shifting the blame onto me. Well, Hanna, I am not listening any more. You are not worthy of my love.'

'Who's shifting the blame now?' Hanna screeched. 'It's *her* you want, isn't it? I've known for some time that your heart is hers now, as it was before. Well, she's welcome to you!'

Anna knew she should not be listening to this conversation, but her curiosity had rooted her to the spot. She dared not move now, fearing they might hear her and realise she had been there for some time.

'Would that I could have her!' Otho flared. 'She's worth a hundred of you. I have never seen a woman so brave and dignified in adversity.' Anna drew in her breath.

'Oh, we feel sorry for her, do we? Has she been playing the damsel in distress for your benefit?'

'No, her behaviour towards me has always been irreproachable, and you know it! Hanna, let's end this. We no longer want each other, and living with these constant recriminations is Hell on earth. Go back to Kleve; tell the Lady Anna your family needs you, or whatever you want to say. But, for God's sake, leave me in peace.'

'But Werner is here,' Hanna protested. 'Why should I leave you free to pursue the Lady Anna, and deprive myself of the man I love?'

Anna's hand flew to her throat as her heart began thumping. He

301

loved her. Otho loved her. A miracle, sent by God to reassure her that a man could desire her. It was enough just to know it, because she could never, in all conscience, have him. He was married, and she must leave him to make things right with his wife. Inwardly, though, her soul was singing.

She had to go. Stealthily, she crept back along the path by the hedge, then looked to check that she had not been seen. The pair of them were standing at the other end of the path, staring at her. She nodded her head and walked on, praying they had not guessed that she had overheard them.

Chapter 19

1540

In the middle of August, Anna moved her household to Bletchingley in Surrey, a dozen miles' ride westwards from Hever. The splendid red-brick manor house stood within a mile of the village. Waiting there to greet Anna was its newly appointed keeper, Thomas Cawarden, a magnificent-looking man in his mid twenties who carried about him an air of barely constrained energy and virility. He had a cherubic face, heavy-lidded eyes and a devastating smile, and held himself as if he owned the manor and was welcoming an honoured guest. His chestnut hair was cropped neatly short, and he was finely dressed in a doublet and short gown of showy damask. When he rose from his bow, Anna found herself unsettled by his gaze.

He lost no time in telling her how well he had been looking after the manor and, as her master of the deer hunt, the two hunting parks that surrounded it and extended for seven miles. He was not so much giving an account of himself to his mistress as boasting.

'I live at Hextalls Farm, which is close by,' he told her.

'You live alone, Mr Cawarden?'

'Yes, just me and the servants.' So he was unmarried, then. She was surprised.

He led her through the arch of the large gatehouse into an outer courtyard. Anna looked around with interest, uncomfortably aware of the vitality and allure of Thomas Cawarden. He could never compare to Otho, of course; she could never love Otho any the less, just because some good-looking fellow had crossed her path and laid about her with his charm. Looking back at her household, who were following, she glimpsed Otho walking stony-faced beside Hanna, and felt again the new-found rush of love and desire that had been her intermittent companion these past few days.

'Your private apartments are here,' Cawarden said, pointing to the range ahead of them. He led her through an arched door and into a great hall with brightly decorated floor tiles, then through to the chapel. Beyond, there were myriad chambers, parlours, closets and oratories, all panelled with wainscot – ceilings, floors and walls.

'There are sixty-three rooms here,' he said proudly.

'It is a fine house,' Anna observed.

They ascended a spiral stair to a first-floor gallery, from which the private rooms led off. They were apartments of vast size and great splendour, and furnished sumptuously, perhaps in anticipation of a visit from the King. In the enormous state bedchamber, the huge bed, chairs and tables were made, Cawarden told her, of walnut, very rare.

'The King has a bed of walnut at Whitehall,' Anna said, wanting to impress upon him that she had lived in palaces and was used to surroundings of such magnificence.

The bed hangings and cushions were of gold and silver, embroidered in coloured silks, the chairs and benches strewn with satin cushions in red, yellow, green and blue. Anna reckoned there were about forty yards of costly tapestry hanging on the walls.

Two other bedchambers were almost as large and luxurious. In a fit of guilt, Anna assigned one to the von Wylichs. She had no right to love Otho, and must afford him and his wife the chance to make all well between them. Offering such fine accommodation must go some way towards assuring Hanna that her mistress was no threat to her. But, from the look on Hanna's face, the prospect of sharing this beautiful room with Otho was not appealing. Anna realised belatedly that others in her household were more entitled to the grander bedchambers. Hastily, she invited her chamberlain, Sir William Goring, to take the remaining one.

At the head of the stairs, Anna inspected the great chamber and, beyond it, the rooms her other staff would occupy. Then, leaving them to unpack, she followed Thomas Cawarden down to the ground floor to take a closer look at the hall and the two parlours.

'Your Highness can use these as reception and dining rooms,' he said, as if he had already made the choice for her. It irritated her, his presumption, and his manner of lordly proprietorship. She noticed that, in the dining parlour, the trestles had been set in place for dinner; two young girls in aprons and lawn caps were laying out plates and napkins for six people.

'I thought your Highness might appreciate having supper with me, and inviting your chamberlain and steward, and two of your ladies, as there is much with which to acquaint you concerning the manor,' Cawarden said.

Again, the presumption of the man! It was for Anna, as mistress of the house, to decide where, and with whom, she would dine. Yet what he was suggesting was quite reasonable, and changing the arrangements now would make her seem petulant, so she nodded graciously.

'Thank you. I will be down at six o'clock,' she said.

In the other parlour, she was pleased to find gaming tables, musical instruments, and cupboards well stocked with playing cards, board games, dice and music books.

'We shall not lack for diversion,' she said, smiling at her ladies.

'Your Highness enjoys cards?' Cawarden asked, those intense eyes raking her face.

'I do,' Anna answered.

'Splendid! We can have a game after supper,' he said.

Did he not know that it was those of higher rank who extended such invitations? Again, she bristled.

'I may be tired after my journey, Mr Cawarden. Now I would see the kitchens, if you would be so good.'

He shrugged, and showed her beyond the hall to the offices. She made a close inspection of the buttery, cellar, spicery, starching house, milking house, bakehouse, brewhouse and mill house, and was almost annoyed to find no cause for complaint. Everything was spotlessly clean and in excellent order. In the kitchen, Meister Schoulenburg was already establishing his authority, while laying out the pans, pots and ingredients he would need for the evening repast. Anna smiled at him. 'Is everything to your satisfaction, my friend?'

'It will be when I can get these damned scullions to do their job properly,' he growled in German, with no respect for niceties, as usual.

Anna laughed. 'I'm sure you will have them jumping at your command in no time.' She turned to Cawarden, who was waiting with ill-concealed impatience. 'I will rest a little now, Mr Cawarden. I will see you at dinner.'

At six o'clock promptly, a bell in the gatehouse tower rang out. Anna was ready, dressed in a gown of black velvet with a crimson kirtle beneath, and a French hood edged with pearls. On her way to the stairs, she met Sir William Goring coming out of his chamber. He bowed to her.

'Your Highness, I am glad to have the chance to speak with you,' he said. 'I think that you, as well as I, were a little overwhelmed by Mr Cawarden. I was watching your face as he made presumption after presumption. He acts as if he owns this house.'

'That was indeed my impression,' Anna told him. 'He has a high opinion of himself.'

'I think he is a man to be reckoned with, Madam, and not one to be crossed. He is one of the "new men" who have risen by ability rather than on account of who their father is. His, I am informed, was a cloth fuller. Cawarden was lucky enough to secure the patronage of Lord Cromwell, and that's how he rose to become a gentleman of the King's Privy Chamber. He is close to his Majesty, and therefore to be treated with caution.'

'Thank you for the warning, Sir William. However, I hardly think the King would approve of his audacity. If it continues, I will mention it to his Grace.'

She descended to the dining chamber, Katharina and Gertrude in her wake. Cawarden bowed respectfully enough as she entered, and set himself to charm her. As the meal progressed, and wine was imbibed, she found that despite herself, she was drawn in by his vitality, his wit and his beauty.

'This house was once owned by the dukes of Buckingham,' he told her, waving a hand to encompass the splendour of their surroundings. 'One was sent to the block for leading a rebellion against King Richard, after which all his possessions were confiscated. His son, the last Duke, got everything back, and he tore down the old house and built this one. He had good taste, wouldn't you agree?' Before Anna could answer, he rattled on, 'It seems, however, that he learned nothing from his father's example, because he too was beheaded for treason. That's how Bletchingley came to the Crown.'

Anna was dismayed that two of her houses were hers because their owners or occupants had died bloodily. And The More, which she had not yet seen, had belonged to Cardinal Wolsey, who, had he lived long enough after his disgrace, might well have shared the same fate.

'I would rather not be the beneficiary of tragedy,' she said, laying down her knife.

'Oh, you're not the first owner since Buckingham died,' Cawarden blithely assured her. 'The King granted it to Sir Nicholas Carew. It was only after his execution last year that it again reverted to the Crown.'

'So that makes its history less tragic?' Anna asked drily. Truly, this beautiful house was unlucky.

'They were traitors; what did they expect?' Cawarden was dismissive. 'No point in getting sentimental about them.'

Anna felt anger rising at his flippancy. She changed the subject. 'You mentioned that there are two large parks here?'

'Well-stocked hunting parks to the north and south,' he answered proudly. 'The Little Park and the Great Park. And, over to the west of them, are the ruins of Bletchingley Castle.'

'I must ride out and see it,' Anna said.

'I will myself be your escort,' Cawarden stated. Anna saw Sir William Goring and Jasper Horsey exchange glances. Again, she felt irritated. It was perfectly reasonable that Cawarden should show her around her lands; he was more familiar with them than anyone else. And yet once more she felt she was being manoeuvred.

'You live at this place called Hextalls?' she asked, without giving him an answer.

'Yes, Madam. It's nearby, at Little Pickle.'

Anna had to smile. She was learning to like these strange English place names.

'It is part of the Bletchingley domain,' Cawarden was saying. 'The house is old, but it's been kept up, and it offers reasonable accommodation.'

'I heard that it has two courtyards, a great hall and a large deer pound,' Goring interjected. 'It sounds very reasonable to me.' *Especially for a fuller's son.* The words were unsaid, but Anna caught Goring's meaning, and saw Cawarden flush.

The talk turned to the King's progress, the new Queen and the rising price of virtually everything. It was a combative conversation, as if Cawarden and Goring were trying to score points off each other. Eventually, Anna grew weary of their sparring, and rose. 'Sirs, I am tired, and must go to bed. I bid you good night.' She would not thank Cawarden for the fine food. Effectively, she had been his hostess.

As the days passed, and she grew familiar with Bletchingley, although never entirely at ease there, Anna came to realise that the overbearing Thomas Cawarden was not her only problem. She was sure now that Wymond Carew was intercepting her correspondence, through the covert offices of his wife, Martha.

It had gradually dawned on her that letters she had sent were taking longer than usual to arrive, judging by the delay before she received responses; she was sure her seal had been moved at least twice; and then Mrs Carew let slip something she could only have read in one of Anna's letters. Anna had written to Mutter of her abhorrence of the English custom of greeting people with a kiss on the lips, something she would never have confided to anyone in England, lest her words be repeated and give offence. But Mrs Carew, having received Otho von Wylich's kiss when he joined them at bowls one day, had said, 'Don't kiss my Lady Anna on the lips; she hates it!' It was that which alerted Anna to the possibility that the Carews were spying on her.

It was not the surveillance itself that troubled her, for she knew she had nothing to fear. The King himself could read all her correspondence and find no fault with it. Dutifully, at Sir William Goring's suggestion, she handed him any letters she received, to forward to the court, and within a day or so they would be returned. But now, it seemed, her outgoing correspondence was being scrutinised too.

She sent for Carew and challenged him. 'You and your wife have no right to intercept the letters I write myself,' she reproved, her voice sharp. 'If it continues, I will report you to the King.'

He smirked superciliously at that, and she lost her temper.

'So you find this funny, *ja*? Mr Carew, I will not have members of my household spying on me. You may go.'

She resolved to keep her distance from both him and his meddling wife. Where Mrs Carew had assisted her, she took to calling upon Joanna Horsey. It was the deceit that galled her, so much so that, when a letter arrived from Wilhelm, giving her news of Mutter and Emily and affairs in Kleve, she decided to thwart those watching her and keep it, rather than send it immediately to the King. After all, it was a personal letter, and dealt only with domestic matters.

Three days later, she was surprised to receive an evening visit from Dr Harst. She had not seen him since she had upbraided him for accusing her of frivolity, and had feared he was no longer her champion, or her friend.

His manner was pained and distant. 'Madam, I have today received a letter from Mr Carew, complaining of you. He has asked his brother-in-law, Mr Denny, who is head of the Privy Chamber, to obtain the King's permission for him to leave your service. Mr Carew says you are bent on doing him displeasure.'

'I do *him* displeasure?' Anna cried. 'He has been spying on me! Whose displeasure is the greater? He should ask himself where his loyalty lies.'

'It lies with the King, Madam, first and foremost. Plainly there are still concerns that there might be reprisals from the divorce, or that Duke Wilhelm might be allying with other princes against England. You did promise to show all the letters you receive to his Majesty. Mr Carew was also commanded by the Duke of Suffolk to show to the King's Council any letters you sent.'

'I did not know the Duke told him to do it!' Anna snapped. 'I should have been told.'

'Mr Carew believes you did know. He complains that you do your best to ignore him, and that you esteem his wife far less than you do Mrs Horsey.'

'Oh, that is pathetic!' Anna seethed. 'Does he expect me to esteem her after she spied on me?'

'That is not the main thrust of his complaint, Madam,' Harst frowned. 'Mr Carew states you had a letter three days past from your brother, and do not seem minded to send it to the King, as is your duty. I made excuses for you, Madam. I said it was a letter of congratulation from your brother on being divorced.' His tone was droll.

Anna gaped at him. 'That is not a matter for sarcasm.'

'Madam, I was trying to make them look ridiculous. I am sure his Majesty will not be interested in reading about which book the Duke has enjoyed, or that the Lady Amalia has learned how to cook *Bratwurst*. Such matters hardly offer incitement to war. Nevertheless, Mr Carew was quite firm. He said I should advise you to send the letter to the King.'

'Very well,' Anna agreed.

She sent for Carew, and received him in Harst's presence. 'I have had a letter from Duke Wilhelm,' she said. 'Pray give it to Sir William to send to the Privy Council. They will find it treats of high matters of state.' She could not resist the dig.

'Thank you, Madam,' Carew said, his manner stiff. But he made no move to leave.

'Is something wrong?' Anna asked him.

He glanced at the ambassador. 'My lady, I must speak. I have learned from your cofferer that Mr Horsey receives substantially more in salary than I do.'

Ah, so this was why he had complained of her favouring Joanna Horsey over his wife. She'd wager that Mrs Carew was behind this!

'Madam, I pray that I and my wife shall have the same allowance as Mr Horsey and his wife, for I think myself no meaner than he.'

Biting back a tart retort, Anna paused. She could not have jealousies in her household. They could escalate and lead to strife and ill feeling. And yet, granting Carew an increase in salary now would seem like rewarding him for his perfidy, and might embolden him to further disloyalty.

'I'm sorry, but I cannot,' she said. 'I have no authority to increase the salaries of my household. That would be a matter for the King, and I would wish him to bestow increases only on those who have rendered me loyal service.'

She inclined her head to show Carew that he was dismissed, and he went out glowering.

'You have made an enemy there,' Dr Harst observed.

'He was already my enemy,' she told him.

There was a distinct chill in the household for days afterwards. Carew continued to act as go-between for Anna and the King, but with ill grace. His wife would not speak to her.

When Sir William Goring took their part, Anna rounded on him.

'I think you know why I am displeased with them. You should have told me what was going on. Am I to have no privacy? Is not my word good enough, that I would do nothing to injure the King?'

'The orders came from above, Madam.' Sir William looked perplexed. 'To obey your Highness would have been to contravene them. In faith, Madam, none of us can do our duty to you as you desire. I ask you to understand our position.'

Anna did understand, but it galled her to have to concede that the Carews had done no wrong. Even Mr Horsey stood up for Carew, asking if he might assist with costing the household provisioning when they returned to Richmond.

'He is good at his office, Madam, and sound with figures. Believe me, I have little liking for him, and I know he resents me, but he is as grieved in this matter as you are. It is affecting all of us.'

'As it is affecting me!' she blurted out. Horsey just stood there, not meeting her eyes. How would he feel if *his* privacy had been violated?

'Was there anything else?' she asked, her tone cold.

'Madam, I need to know where you will sojourn over the winter, so that we might make provision.'

'I don't know,' she said, feeling distressed. Right now, the only place she wanted to be was a long way from here, away from them all. 'I will give it some thought, but I can't do it now.' She heard her voice break, and knew that Horsey must have heard it too.

At the end of August, Dr Harst came again, disturbing her peace as she sat apart from her ladies by an open window, trying to read. But he was relentless.

'Your Highness, are you aware that your chamberlain has asked the Council for licence to go home with his wife; and that he, Mr Horsey and Mr Carew have been driven to asking their lordships where you will winter, because you will not tell them?'

She stared at him. She had known nothing of this. 'Is Sir William leaving my service then?'

'The councillors are reluctant to permit it. Until your divorce settlement is finalised, the King is effectively running households for two queens, and good men like Goring are thin on the ground. Madam, this situation is escalating, and your behaviour is only making it worse. Accept that Carew did what he had to. Show yourself above such squabbles.'

She roused herself, weighing his words. She resented being harangued yet again, but in her heart she knew Harst was right. It pained her that she had been so enveloped in her sense of betrayal that she had lost sight of how she should conduct herself as mistress of the household. Guilt washed over her. She should have let it go and moved on. 'You are right, my good friend. I will summon them all now.' For the first time in weeks, Dr Harst smiled at her.

Her officers filed in, and stood looking warily at her.

'Sirs,' she said, and made herself sound pleasant and cheerful, 'we will be removing to Richmond next Monday. I am sorry I did not inform you of this before, but I have not been feeling myself lately.' It sounded like the transparent excuse it was, yet she hoped they would take it as the olive branch it was meant to be. 'I wish to thank you all for your patience with me at this time, and for your good service. If I can be of any assistance in matters relating to our move, you know where to find me. And, Mr Carew, I will be writing to my brother this night. The letter will be ready for you to take to the Council in the morning.'

Carew looked gratified, and relieved, as well he might. There was relief too in Horsey's face, and in Goring's.

'When I next see the King,' Anna informed them, 'I will ask if he will graciously consider raising your salaries equitably. Thank you.'

They left looking happier, and she heard a burst of conversation as the door closed behind them. Harst was regarding her with approval.

'Well said, Madam. I knew you would do the right thing. I doubt they will give you more trouble.'

No sooner had Anna arrived back at Richmond than the Lady Mary paid her a visit.

'This is an unexpected pleasure,' Anna told her, beckoning for wine to be served.

'None for me,' Mary said, waving it away.

'You won't mind if I do.' Anna accepted a glass, aware of Mary's gaze on her. 'I trust your Grace is well.'

'Tolerably,' Mary replied, 'though it is getting to that season when I suffer all kinds of ailments. The autumn is never good for my health. But you are in fine fettle, I see.'

'I ride out daily now,' Anna said proudly. 'I am become a reasonable horsewoman, and I go for long walks, taking the air. Tell me, is there news of the court?'

Mary sighed. 'Yes, but not what you might want to hear. Queen Katheryn daily discovers some new caprice, and my father leaps to indulge her. She is become greedy, greedy for new gowns, jewels and endless diversions. Anna, she will wear him out. He is besotted.'

'You do not like her?'

'It's not that; but she is so immature, so giddy, and so oblivious to the fact that he is no longer young.'

Anna rather doubted that, remembering how she herself had been shocked to find the King looking old and grossly obese – and the nightly reminders of it in the marriage bed. 'She comes of a good Catholic family,' she pointed out, knowing that must find favour with Mary. 'She will be able to influence the King in the way of truth.'

Mary snorted. 'I doubt she has the brains for it.' Her voice was bitter. Anna wondered if she was jealous of this stepmother who was younger than herself, and married to a man who adored her.

'You know there is still talk that the King will take you back,' Mary said, making Anna start.

'Not again!' she cried.

'Many of us wish he would,' Mary murmured.

'I appreciate the sentiment, but I am contented as I am,' Anna assured her.

'It will not happen. That girl is entrenched. He's taken her on progress so that he can show her off. It's embarrassing, the way he constantly caresses her and makes a great show of his affection.'

Anna felt a pang. He had never shown her that kind of affection. Yet who could account for what attracted one human to another? She was glad Henry had found someone he could love.

They spent a while talking, and Anna insisted Mary stay to dinner before she left for Essex and her palace of New Hall. Mary much enjoyed the game pie Anna had ordered, and the custard flavoured with nutmeg, and left full of thanks for the hospitality.

Shortly afterwards, a messenger from Dr Harst arrived with a letter for Anna from her older sister Sybilla. Anna settled down in her chamber to read it, but stood up in consternation on learning that Sybilla was furious with the King for setting her aside, insisting she would never acknowledge the annulment and would continue to refer to Anna as queen. Her husband, the Elector, was outraged too, and the Schmalkaldic League, of which he was head, had wasted no time in severing diplomatic relations with England. Anna winced, but there was worse to follow. Never mind that these princes had united against the might of the Emperor and needed Henry's support, Sybilla wrote; they would never renew the alliance.

She had not known that her sister had become such a firebrand.

Mother Lowe appeared, and Anna showed her the letter. 'That's what comes of fraternising with Luther,' Mother Lowe muttered. 'She always was an opinionated young lady. Still, she does have your interests at heart.'

'That may be so, but I dare not show this to the King,' Anna fretted. 'What shall I do?'

The nurse squeezed her hand. 'Burn it.'

'Someone may have seen the messenger arrive, and ask what he brought.'

Mother Lowe fumbled in her pocket and handed over a folded piece of paper. 'You can show them this. It came from Solingen.'

Their eyes met. It was Anna's great grief that she had word of her son all too rarely.

'It's from Frau Schmidt,' the old nurse said. 'You can say the messenger brought it for me.'

Anna took the creased letter and devoured it avidly. The boy was well. He was now serving his apprenticeship under his father and showing promise.

'How good it is to know that,' she whispered, near to tears, suddenly consumed with the longing she had so resolutely repressed. 'His father is proud of him, it says. *His father is here!* He does not even know he has a son.'

'And it's imperative it stays that way,' Mother Lowe said severely.

Anna was about to protest, but subsided.

As she lay wakeful that night, aching for her child, she began to feel angry. Johann had the ducal blood of Kleve in him, yet he was hidden away as a shameful secret, and being trained as a swordsmith. He had no idea who his real parents were, or even that he was adopted. And Otho – he had a right to know he had a son, surely, and now that she was her own mistress, and a private person, the danger of exposure was not so great. She was sorely tempted to tell him.

She was still agonising over what to do two days later, when the King came to dine at Richmond. He was again the hearty self she had seen since their divorce, and still full of the joys of his new marriage.

They sat up late together, alone in her dining chamber, talking and playing cards until the candles were dying, and she found herself enjoying it immensely. Replete with good Riesling, she even found herself flirting a little. She did not want Henry back, but she was very glad to have him as a friend. It was extraordinary how two people who had made such a bad beginning had now come together in genuine affection.

When he got up to leave, he embraced her warmly. 'God bless you, my dear Anna. I will come again soon. And maybe you would like to come to court at Christmas.'

'I would like that very much, Brother,' she said, with a twinkle in her eye. 'God go with you.'

After waving him off by torchlight, she turned back towards the palace, and there was Otho, sprawled on a stone bench in the shadows, looking dejected.

'Go ahead; I'll be with you directly,' she ordered Katharina and Gertrude, and walked over to him.

'What is wrong?' she asked, as he sprang to his feet. 'No, sit down, please.' She sat beside him. 'I know that all is not well between you and Hanna.'

'It is no secret,' he muttered. 'She is playing me false with your cupbearer, and cares not how she humiliates me. I've tried, God knows, to win her back. It was losing the child that did for us. It changed her.'

'She lost a child? I did not know.' Anna laid her hand on his. 'I am so sorry.'

'I loved her,' Otho declared, his voice taut, 'but she is no longer interested in me. We both desired that child so much.'

Anna did not hesitate. She was the one person who could offer him comfort and consolation; and she had been longing to tell him her secret, the secret that should be his too. 'Otho, you have a son,' she said.

His head jerked up. 'I have a son?' He seemed bewildered.

'*We* have a son,' she amended.

There was a long silence.

316

'Oh, my God,' he blurted out, sounding choked. 'My God. Why did you not tell me?'

'How could I? I was commanded to keep it a secret. The only other people who know are my mother and my nurse. They arranged for me to go to Schloss Burg to have the child. I called him Johann, after my father. He was taken away from me and placed with a swordsmith in Solingen.' She was weeping now. 'I have seen him only once since. He is a darling child, and happy, I believe, but I want more for him. And I miss him, I yearn for him . . .'

Otho reached for her, and suddenly they were holding each other tightly, both sobbing helplessly, and then they were kissing, hungrily, desperately, tasting salt tears on each other's lips.

'God forgive me, I had no idea,' Otho said in her ear. 'I was young and foolish, and unthinkingly took my pleasure. It grieves me that I caused you such shame and sorrow.'

'But you brought me joy too,' she murmured, surrendering her lips to his once more. 'And now this . . .'

'I have dreamed of it,' he whispered, as she clung to him tightly.

'I have wanted to tell you for years,' Anna said a little later, 'but they would not let me. There was too much to lose.'

'There would have been for me too! I had Hanna to consider. But not any more.' He drew back and grasped her hands. 'Anna, I am overjoyed and proud to know I have a son, especially since he is your son too. I am a bastard myself, but my father has always treated me as if I were trueborn, and my stepmother has been kind. I want that for Johann.'

His words made Anna weep again. This was beyond all her hopes.

'I will go to Solingen,' he declared. 'I am not known there. I will make some pretext to buy a sword, and try to befriend the family and see the boy, to ascertain that he is happy and well cared for. Then . . . I do not know what I will do, but if money can help, I am not poor. My father is generous to me.'

'If he is happy, that is what matters,' Anna said, pulling her hands away to find her handkerchief. 'I want what is best for Johann. And yet, I cannot help thinking that there must be a better future for him. But how to ensure it, and whether he would be happier, I cannot say.'

Otho was thoughtful. Anna shivered. 'Let us go in. I think we both need a drink. There might be some wine left in the dining chamber.'

There was. The servants had left a cloth over the ewer after clearing the table. Anna poured two large goblets, and they drank deeply. And then Otho was pulling her into his embrace once more, and this time there was no gaucheness, no ignorance, just two troubled souls seeking comfort in each other.

When Anna came to her senses, she was lying on the Turkey rug before the empty hearth, with Otho's arm flung across her breasts. He was pressed against the full length of her body, facing her, gazing into her eyes.

She remembered telling her maids she would be with them shortly. Heavens, what time was it?

Reluctantly, she lifted Otho's arm and sat up.

'Anna?' he asked.

'I must go to my chamber. My maids will be wondering where I am.'

'I don't want you to go.'

'I have to.'

He sat up beside her and kissed her tenderly. 'Thank you for that. I had long hoped that, one day, when our lives were less complicated, we might come together again. Yet I never expected this. Anna, you mean a great deal to me.'

'As you do to me, Otho. And I am grateful to you for ensuring . . .' Her voice tailed away as she felt her cheeks grow warm. He had foregone his full pleasure to keep her safe, yet he'd brought her to that joy she had longed for all these years. And it had been even better, infinitely better, than she had remembered.

'There are more ways than one of loving,' he smiled, kissing her again.

She rose, straightening her skirts and retrieving her hood from the table. 'I still have your ring,' she told him.

'You kept it all these years?' He seemed stunned.

'I could not forget the father of my child – and the man who taught me how to love,' she whispered.

'Will you wear it now?'

'Yes, Otho, I will.' She smiled at him.

'Shall I see you again?' he asked. 'Shall we . . . ?'

'Yes,' she said, and he drew her to him for a last embrace.

'We *will* do what's best for our son,' he assured her. 'I will leave for Solingen on Saturday.'

Chapter 20

1540–1541

Anna stared at Dr Harst. 'I assure you, I am *not* with child! Where *did* these rumours come from?'

'In faith, Madam, I do not know, but the court is agog with them. And people are saying the King is the father.'

'What? This is outrageous.'

'They impute much to his visit here in August. Some claim you were alone with him.'

'And so I was, at his Majesty's instance. Who was I to gainsay him? We talked and played cards. He told me how much he loves the Queen. What more can I say?'

'Madam, it is said he is troubled because the Queen is not yet with child; and – forgive me – it is being alleged that you have been suffering the sickness common to women in that condition.' Harst's tone was so strained that Anna wondered if he actually believed the rumours.

'I *have* been sick, but it was something I ate, and I am better now. How dare people draw such baseless conclusions! And how do they know I was ill?'

'There are those in your household who regularly visit the court. People will talk.'

Anna wondered who had talked. It was ironic that she was being accused of a sin she had not committed, when all the while she had been agonising lest the sin of which she *was* guilty should be exposed.

'I hope that his Majesty is also being taxed with these rumours,' she said tartly. 'It's unfair that they rebound on me. Let him refute the gossip!'

'He will not condescend so far.'

'He might, if it touches his honour – and mine! And I pray he will. In the meantime, Dr Harst, my brother the Duke will be counting on you to defend my reputation at every opportunity.'

'It is not just your reputation that is at stake, Madam. There is also talk that the King will now leave Queen Katheryn and take you back.'

'That is nonsense,' Anna cried, 'and if anyone raises the subject, you must say so. The King makes such singular demonstrations of affection to the Queen that it cannot be.' She got up from her seat by the fireside and went over to the window, staring out at the autumnal colours of the garden below. 'I think I will remove to Bletchingley or Hever, or even Rickmansworth. I don't want my servants going in and out of the court as easily as they do from here. I want these evil bruits stopped.'

'To remove now, Madam, might be to fuel the rumours. If you were to seclude yourself at a distance from the court, people may jump to the wrong conclusions.'

'Well, I will think on it,' Anna said, exasperated. 'Tell me, Dr Harst, you do believe me blameless in this?'

'Yes, Madam, I do.' His expression was sincere, she was gratified to see. 'Forgive me if I seemed to doubt you. Believe me, I will do all in my power to refute the rumours.'

Anna was overjoyed when, on a grey and windy December day, Otho presented himself in her chamber, where he found her surrounded by her ladies. He had been gone for weeks, without word, and she was in a fever of anticipation, wondering what he had to tell her.

'Otho, dear cousin, this is a pleasure,' she said as he bowed before her. 'I do hope you have had a good journey. How is my brother, the Duke?'

As Otho's blue eyes sought hers, she saw in them the memory of what had passed between them, and her heart leapt. 'The tide was with us, Madam, so we made excellent speed from the Zuyder Zee. And I have much in the way of news for you. Some is for your ears alone.'

She caught his drift. 'Ladies, please leave us. My cousin and I would speak in private. Frances, please pour us some wine before you go.'

They waited until the last footsteps had echoed away. Anna held out her hand, but Otho bent to embrace her and kiss her long and lovingly on the lips. She had missed him dreadfully, and ached to continue, but her need to hear about Johann was paramount, greater even than her desire for his father.

'Did you see him?' she asked eagerly.

'I did,' he smiled, 'and I have talked with him on several occasions and become his friend, as he assures me. He is a fine boy, and shows great promise. Anna, I can see both of us in him, but not so plainly that people would guess. The Schmidts are good people, the house is clean and the father's trade thriving.'

'But is he happy?'

'Yes, happy in the sense that he knows no other life. I think he could benefit from a sounder education, for he is intelligent, and forward for his age.'

Anna was twisting her rings. 'Does he love the Schmidts?'

'Yes, I believe so. They are kind to him, and indulge him a little, but the father is strict when teaching him his trade. Johann is treated no differently from the other apprentices. Anna, he *is* happy, for now. I asked him, by way of a jest, if he would like to come and live in England with me, in a great palace, and serve the Princess of Kleve, and he laughed and said he would like that very much. So I said that, one day, we will consider it, but in the meantime he must serve his apprenticeship, and serve it well.'

She was conscious of a searing sense of disappointment. Almost, she had wanted Otho to find the boy keen to leave his foster home, so that he would have had to bring him to England. A place could readily be found for him at Hever or one of her other houses, where no one would guess who he was.

'I wanted him with me,' she said, near to tears.

Otho took her hands. 'Anna, you must be patient.' Reluctantly, she realised he was right.

'How long? Can an apprenticeship be broken?'

'In theory, Johann is bound by his indenture for seven years; in practice, palms can be smoothed.'

'Seven years?' she cried.

'Anna, calm yourself.' His arms enfolded her again. 'I promise you, as soon as the time is right, I will fetch him.'

She clutched at him, kissing him fervently, overcome by the moment. 'Thank you, my dear heart!' Their kisses grew violent, and then they were coming together in a tangle of laces and heavy skirts, both consumed with desire, and aware of the need for haste.

Having spent the last Christmas miserably immured in Calais, Anna was determined that this one should be celebrated in true German style, and that her whole household should enjoy it. Early December found her in the kitchens, standing beside Meister Schoulenburg at the long table, making spice cakes and gingerbread, and humming as she did so, for she was happy in the knowledge that, at last, she was loved for herself. Otho made her feel cherished and protected. If only they could see each other openly, and not have to snatch time together at opportune moments, how wonderful life would be. But they had to be so careful, and that meant a considerable degree of self-denial. Yesterday, however, they had ridden out hunting in the park and managed to lose Anna's attendants, and, for a brief, breathless moment, they had made love in an old hut screened from view by trees. It had left her sleek and contented, like the cat stretched out by the kitchen fire.

On Christmas Eve, *Heilige Abend*, Anna's household watched curiously as she set up a little fir tree in the hall, and decorated it with apples, nuts and some paper flowers she had made.

'Martin Luther may be a heretic,' she told them, fixing candles to the branches, 'but he started a delightful custom that we in Kleve like to observe. One night, he was walking through a forest when he looked up and saw thousands of stars twinkling through the branches of the trees. It inspired him to set up a fir tree in his house, lit with candles, to remind his children of the starry heavens whence our Saviour came.'

Some looked dubious, clearly wondering whether any deed of the arch-heretic Luther could be accounted good; but others were smiling.

'Pray light the candles, Sir William,' Anna said, and the chamberlain came forward with a glowing taper. The tree did look pretty, and even the dubious admired it.

'And now I will give you all your presents, like the *Christkind*, the bringer of gifts,' Anna smiled. This too, she knew, was not their custom, for they exchanged gifts at New Year, but it would be an extra treat for them. It would be compensation for her absence after New Year – for she was going to court, having accepted the King's invitation.

She had chosen her gifts with care, commissioning silver-gilt cups and goblets from a goldsmith in nearby Kingston, and was thrilled to see faces light up as she presented them. Gertrude and Katharina exclaimed in delight. Even Wymond Carew thanked her effusively. It had been worth the expense.

Then it was time for supper, and sausages, as was traditional. Anna presided at the high table in the hall, the Advent wreath with its four candles sitting proud on a platter before her. After supper, flushed with wine, they all sang carols, some of which, she was surprised to find, had both German and English words. As she looked around the hall, at the laughing faces of her servants and the handsome features of her lover, she felt truly contented.

A week later, New Year's gifts for Anna arrived from the King: jewels, bolts of rich fabrics, several fine pieces of gold plate, and money too. He had been lavish! She saw her ladies staring at the exquisite presents, and her heart sank. Heaven forbid that the gossips got to hear of it, for they might raise another bruit that Henry would take her back. She now wished she had not sent him those two great horses in their velvet trappings. No doubt that would be misconstrued too!

As she sat in her chariot, wrapped in furs, on the third day of January, making the short journey to Hampton Court, she felt a certain trepidation. Would she find the palace a hotbed of gossip about her? Would people be pointing the finger and laughing behind their hands? God, let it not be so. She was praying too that the meeting with Queen Katheryn would not be an occasion for any awkwardness, now their positions had been reversed. Certainly there would be no resentment on her part; she was approaching it with a willing heart.

As she rode with her small entourage through Kingston, she saw a horseman approaching, and recognised Lord William Howard, the Queen's uncle, who hailed her jovially.

'My Lady Anna, well met! How fortunate that I was passing this way. Let me escort you to the court.'

Anna thanked him, and he turned his horse and rode ahead, alongside Otho and Sir William Goring. At Hampton Court, he led her to the Inner Court, where she was received by the Duchess of Suffolk, the Countess of Hertford and other ladies, who conducted her to her lodgings. She was gratified to find that she had been allocated a spacious apartment with luxurious furnishings.

It was good to see the Duchess of Suffolk again, and although Anna would dearly have liked to complain about the Duchess's husband getting Wymond Carew to spy on her, now was not the occasion. They chatted for a while, catching up on their news, while Anna's maids fussed about her, making sure that not a hair was out of place. Lady Hertford, whom Anna barely knew, stood silently appraising her, making her feel uncomfortable. Heaven forbid she was looking for signs of a pregnancy!

'We should make haste,' Lady Hertford said at last. 'The Queen awaits your Highness.'

The ladies escorted Anna to the Queen's apartments. It seemed strange being here again; the last time she had occupied these rooms, she had been in constant perplexity about her marriage to the King and her future. It seemed a long while ago now.

When she was announced in the presence chamber and walked to the dais, she saw that the gorgeously attired little Queen looked as plump and pretty as ever, and had acquired a consciously regal manner. Anna knelt at her feet with as much reverence as if she herself was now the maid-of-honour.

'Oh, please, my Lady Anna, do not kneel to me!' Katheryn cried, bending forward to raise her. 'I am so happy to see you! I have dearly hoped that we can be friends. You were always a kind mistress to me, and now I long to do you favour in return.' She embraced Anna and kissed her. You could not help liking the girl. Her charm was irresistible;

she was like an eager puppy. Anna could see how she had cast an enchantment over Henry.

'Make way for his Majesty the King!' an usher intoned, and there was Henry, stumping into the room and beaming broadly.

'Welcome, Anna, my dear sister!' he said, opening his arms to her and pressing his lips to hers. 'I see you two ladies are pleasantly according together. The horses are splendid – I cannot thank you sufficiently. My love . . .' He broke away and folded his arms around Katheryn. His lust for her was palpable. Anna had never seen him like this. The courtiers were exchanging knowing grins.

Henry led them into supper, with Katheryn on his right hand and Anna on his left. His presence chamber was festooned with evergreens, and filled with a seasonal aroma from candles set amidst festive arrangements of pine cones, spiced dried oranges and juniper berries. Anna was delighted to find the Lady Mary present, and they exchanged warm greetings. Then she was shown to a seat near the bottom of the high table. It was no less than she had expected, and she was still close enough to talk to the King and Queen. She relaxed and began to enjoy herself, and had to suppress a smile when she noticed Messire Chapuys, the Imperial ambassador, and other courtiers observing her carefully. What had they expected, a cat fight between her and Katheryn?

During, and after, supper, the conversation was lively, with much merriment, and Anna found herself getting on very well with Katheryn. Even Mary seemed to have forgotten her reservations about her young stepmother, and joined in the laughter.

Anna was aware that Henry had aged a little since she last saw him. She caught him wincing once or twice, and guessed his bad leg was paining him. But Katheryn seemed oblivious. She was prattling on about the coming Twelfth Night celebrations, her latest gowns, the wonderful poems written by her cousin, the Earl of Surrey, and the gifts the King had showered on her at New Year.

'Are we going to dance?' she asked. 'Oh, Henry, please say we can dance. I love it when you lead me out before the court!'

He smiled at her indulgently. Anna would never have dared call him Henry in public, but he did not seem to mind.

'I think I am rather tired and would prefer to go to bed,' he said. 'But you ladies can dance together.' He signalled to the musicians in the gallery, and they struck up a lively tune.

'Oh, thank you, Henry!' Katheryn cried.

'Don't be too late,' he said, caressing her cheek as he rose to leave. Everyone stood, but he waved them down. 'Be seated, my friends! Enjoy the rest of the evening.'

When he had gone, Katheryn held out her hand. 'My Lady Anna, please dance with me!'

Anna had practised steps with her ladies at Richmond, anticipating that there would be dancing during the court festivities, but she had not anticipated being singled out like this. She glanced pleadingly at Mary, but Mary merely smiled encouragement.

Anna steeled herself. 'It will be my pleasure,' she said, taking the Queen's hand, and they stepped down to the floor, all eyes upon them.

'The pavane!' Katheryn cried, and the music began, slow and stately, to Anna's relief, for she knew the paces. By the time the measure had ended, she was feeling more confident, and when the Queen called for a lively *branle*, she entered into it with enthusiasm. Katheryn danced prettily, as she did everything else, and Anna could not hope to match her, but what did it matter?

The courtiers were flushed with wine and clapping heartily. Soon, at the Queen's invitation, many couples took to the floor, and Anna found herself brushing shoulders with Otho. He was partnering one of the maids-of-honour, which caused her a pang, for the girl was looking up at him adoringly; but when they next passed, he sent Anna such a longing look as to set all her senses singing, and she gave him a secret smile.

At that moment, she spied Chapuys watching her again. Had he noticed? She prayed not, else that brief exchange would soon be all over Christendom. She *must* be more circumspect, she chided herself, and warn Otho that he must try harder not to betray their love in public.

But, oh, she wanted him. She wanted him badly, and she knew he wanted her too. They had had too little of each other.

When the dancing had ended, the wine was all drunk, Katheryn had finally, reluctantly, gone to bed, and the great palace had settled down to sleep, Anna looked out of her window, and there was Otho, standing in the courtyard below. Flinging on her cloak, pulling the hood down to hide her face, she tiptoed through her lodging, praying she would not wake her women, then down the stair and out into the night air. She saw Otho put a finger to his lips and nod in the direction of the guards standing at the entrance to the royal apartments. She drew back into the stairwell, and he followed, closing the door and taking her there and then, without warning. It was glorious, all the more so for being illicit. She was sure no one saw or heard them.

The next day, Anna dined with the King and Queen, again amidst much conversation and laughter. In the afternoon, when she and Katheryn were playing backgammon in the Queen's privy chamber, an usher arrived holding the leashes of two sweet little lap dogs. He bowed to Katheryn.

'Your Grace, the King has sent you these gifts.' He passed her the leads and handed her a velvet pouch, from which she pulled a ruby ring, exclaiming in delight. The puppies were sniffing at the rush matting.

'Oh, they're adorable!' she cried, sweeping them up on her lap, where they crouched, quivering, their silky ears pressed back. 'Oh, you silly things, you mustn't be afraid of little Kafwyn,' she murmured, nuzzling their smooth heads. She looked up. 'Anna, don't you just love them?'

Anna reached over to pet the little creatures. 'I do. They are so pretty.'

'They are yours!' Katheryn announced impulsively, plonking them on Anna's lap.

'Oh, but I couldn't . . .'

'I want you to have them.' She was like an eager child. 'And the ring!'

Anna was astonished, and thrilled. The ring was exquisite, and she could not imagine two more delightful pets than the little dogs. 'Thank you!' She leaned forward and kissed Katheryn. 'I'm so grateful, and really touched.'

Katheryn turned to the messenger. 'Pray thank his Majesty for his goodness to me, and say I will thank him properly when I see him later.' She smiled archly.

The usher bowed. 'I will, Madam.' He turned to Anna. 'The King sent this for your Highness.' He handed her a scroll bearing the royal seal. It was a grant of an annual rent of five hundred pounds. She could have bought over a hundred horses with that sum! 'I cannot sufficiently express my gratitude to his Grace,' she declared – and she said the same, later on, to Henry himself, when he came to bid her farewell and himself escorted her to Base Court, where her party's horses were saddled and waiting.

'Prices are rising,' he said. 'You may find that the settlement I made on you will not be sufficient. But do not worry. I will supplement it as necessary. You have only to ask.'

She kissed him, moved by his thoughtfulness, resolving to make some gesture in return. When she got back to Richmond, she searched out an exquisite French Book of Hours Mutter had given her. It would be the ideal gift. Inside, she wrote: 'I beseech your Grace humbly, when you look on this, to remember me. Your Grace's assured friend, Anna, the daughter of Kleve.' Then she wrapped it in silk and arranged for a messenger to take it to Hampton Court.

'You were a great success at court,' Mother Lowe observed as they watched him depart. 'Do you know what people were saying? That the King likes you so much that he will have two wives!'

Anna laughed. 'The very idea! He seems a changed man. He really is like a brother to me. I am glad the Queen makes him happy.'

Mother Lowe gave her a shrewd look. 'And there is one who makes you happy too, if I am not mistaken.'

Anna felt her cheeks burning.

'I've known you all your life,' Mother Lowe said. 'You're glowing with it, child. Anyone can see the looks you give each other. Be careful, Anna. He is married – and he brought you down once before.'

'We were children then! Not now, though. And we are being careful.'

Mother Lowe harrumphed. 'If *I* can see what's going on, others can too. I agree, his wife is a shrew, and does not trouble to hide her infidelity. But they are fast married, and there's nothing to be done about that. Take care, Anna, I beg you. Things are good now, *ja*? Let them stay that way.'

Anna nodded, chastened. Her nurse's concern was sincere, and born of love. And she was right. Life was good for them all. She must not put that at risk. But she could never end things with Otho. How could she return to her barren existence, yet still see him every day? She could not do it. She would rather die. She must therefore ensure that they were even more discreet in future.

A few days later, a royal messenger arrived from Hampton Court with a missive for Anna from the King. He had issued letters patent making her an English subject, on condition that she did not leave England without licence. The lands she had held as queen had at last been reassigned to Katheryn, and Anna held in her hand a long list of the manors, boroughs, rectories, parks, farms, mills, tithes and annuities that were now hers in their place, again on condition of her remaining in England, and in consideration of her submission to the laws of the realm and the authority of Parliament, which had declared her marriage invalid. Heavens, she even had the right to a tithe of beans at some place in Sussex!

As she looked down the list, which she must pass over to Wymond Carew as soon as possible, for he would have all to do sorting out her rents, she saw that many of the properties had been confiscated from Cromwell. A good number had clearly been monastic lands of which he had availed himself. Again, she was profiting from the misfortunes of others. She wished it could have been otherwise, but the decision had not been hers to make.

Most of the place names meant little to her, but there were quite a few in Sussex, not far from Richmond. She promised herself another progress soon, to see some of them.

She summoned Carew, and he looked over the document. 'A handsome settlement,' he pronounced. 'Barely less in value than you had when you were queen. You are assured of a good income.'

'His Majesty has been most bountiful,' she said. 'I am indebted to him. And I mean always to abide by the terms of my settlement.' Let Carew report that back to Suffolk!

Anna could barely concentrate on the preparations for her journey into Sussex that spring. She was too worried, too preoccupied with a problem that had at first seemed a trifle, but had rapidly assumed monumental proportions. She was longing for an opportunity to speak in private with Otho. Their secret trysts had continued, but far less often than she would have liked. Always, discretion had to come first. But she needed him more than ever now.

Mother Lowe bustled in, weighed down by a pile of towels, which she dumped on the bed. 'There's been a delivery of wine. The King sent it. The carter told me the Queen is expecting at last. He said it was the talk of the court.'

Anna swallowed. 'Since his Grace has been good enough to send us the wine, we should make an occasion to celebrate,' she said, although she had no appetite for celebrations just now, and the thought of wine made her queasy. 'This news will be a very great joy to the King.'

She walked through to her closet, looking for books and games to take with her on progress. She felt bowed down by her own fears, and with worry about Master Mandeville, a groom of her stable who had been arrested for heresy while performing errands in London, and was being held in the Marshalsea prison for questioning. She barely knew him, and had no idea what heresy he was supposed to have committed – Henry had not gone into detail in his letter informing her of the arrest – but she feared for him, being well aware of the penalty.

Mother Lowe followed her into the bedchamber. 'Something is troubling you, child,' she said. 'Do you want to talk about it?'

'I can't stop thinking about poor Mandeville,' Anna told her. 'I hope no one here betrayed him, and that no one else in my household is tainted with heresy, because, if they are, we all risk being thought guilty by association. I have written to the King, telling him I am shocked to hear the news of Mandeville, and that I had no suspicions of him at any time, which is the truth. I don't think I ever spoke to him, beyond saying thank you.'

'Hopefully he will clear himself,' Mother Lowe said, but she did not sound convinced. Anna wondered if those accused of heresy in England ever escaped the stake.

At dinner, she asked Sir William Goring if he knew.

'You are thinking of Mandeville, Madam?'

'Yes, Sir William.'

'My understanding is that a heretic may recant and escape punishment, but if they then lapse, it is the stake for them. I have not heard that Mandeville ever recanted before. I was not even aware he entertained heretical views.'

'He didn't receive the Sacrament at Easter,' Mr Horsey recalled. 'I thought that a bit strange.'

'He denied the miracle of transubstantiation,' Wymond Carew said. They all stared at him.

'I heard it in the court,' he told them. Yes, Anna thought, no doubt your good friend, the Duke of Suffolk, told you. She hoped it was not Carew who had laid evidence against Mandeville. Yet, even if it had been, and she taxed him with it, he would doubtless say he had acted in her interests – and he would be right.

She did not know what to do. She dared not ask Henry to show mercy in such a serious case, yet she could not stop thinking of her wretched groom languishing in prison with no one to help him.

Spring was in the air. All around Anna the gardens were bursting into new life, and there was a mild breeze and the smell of newly scythed grass. Yet the beauty of her surroundings failed to move her; it seemed cruel that the season was fulfilling its promise while she fretted in fear, unable to take any joy in it, and made one of the hardest decisions of her life.

Her preparations for the journey completed, she went walking alone in the orchard, seeking some peace in which to ease her despairing soul. It was there that Otho found her. At the sight of him, tears welled in her eyes.

'Is something wrong?' His blue eyes searched hers.

'Something is very wrong,' she replied. 'I am with child.'

He looked stunned. 'No, you cannot be. I was careful . . .'

'I am. I know the signs.' She fought back the tears. 'I have been here before, and I cannot believe it has happened again.'

'Oh, Anna. I am so sorry.' He pulled her to him and stroked her hair. 'What shall we do?'

She was glad he had said 'we'.

'I have thought of a plan,' she said, breaking away. 'It might just work. During the progress, I hope to find one of my houses lying in a remote spot. As soon as my condition starts to show, I will lodge there on some pretext, then pretend to be ill and stay until the child is born. Mother Lowe will have to be told. She helped me before and, though I know she will be angry, and disappointed in me, I'm sure she will help again.'

'There will be talk if you have just one lady attending you,' Otho pointed out, his beloved face creased in concern.

'I will take others, but they will not be allowed to enter the sickroom, lest I am contagious. You see, I have thought of everything.' She forced a smile.

'And what can *I* do?' he asked.

This was going to be the hard part. She had been dreading this moment. 'Nothing,' she said. 'No one must guess there has been anything between us. If my brother found out, he would demand that we be sent back to Kleve for punishment, if King Henry does not punish us first. Otho, my dearest love, this must end. We dare not risk exposure. It will be hard enough as it is to keep my condition a secret.' Her voice broke; she could hold back the flood of tears no longer.

'No! Anna, don't do this!' Otho tried again to embrace her, but she stood back.

'Don't touch me,' she begged, 'or I will forget all my good intentions. I am so sorry . . .'

'This is my fault.' He punched his forehead. 'May God forgive me!'

'We did it together,' she reminded him. 'I do not blame you. But now, it must be farewell. It will be hard, but we have to be strong.'

'Anna,' he pleaded, 'Anna, please . . .' But she was walking away, forcing herself not to look back.

'The Queen is not with child,' Katherine Bassett said. 'My sister wrote to me.'

'Did she miscarry?' Anna asked, as the chariot conveyed them along the sun-baked track towards the town of Lewes, the next stop on their progress.

'No, I think it was wishful thinking. The King is very disappointed.'

Poor Katheryn, Anna thought. It must be dreadful, being under such pressure to give Henry a son. 'I feel for them both,' she said.

They had travelled south from Richmond and Anna had already inspected her properties at Maresfield and Alfriston. She could not see all those in Sussex, for there were too many; she would visit more another time. She wanted to gain an idea of what she owned, and see more of her adoptive land. It was taking her mind off the dreadful decision she had just made, but not numbing the pain. She did not think she could sink lower in misery than this.

Ahead, she could see Lewes on its high hill. Tonight, she would stay in her house at Southover, at the foot of the hill, and tomorrow she would visit the nearby manors of Le Hyde and Kingston before riding on to Ditchling.

The house at Southover was delightful, a fine timbered building with a stream running through the gardens and an orchard. Just along the road was an abandoned priory. Her tenant, Master Freeman, and his wife, were at pains to ensure that Anna enjoyed every comfort, and after enduring the jolting of the chariot on ill-kept roads, she gratefully seated herself on a settle in the beamed hall and accepted a goblet of wine.

Ten minutes later, a messenger wearing her own livery caught up with her. Mandeville and two others had been found guilty of heresy and burned at the stake in Southwark. The news made her feel so sick that she feared she might lose the child. As her officers and ladies expressed their shock, she saw Otho, seated at an adjacent table, looking at her with the most profound sympathy and yearning, and had to summon all her resources to keep control of her emotions. How she longed to be comforted in his arms.

She made a hasty excuse and retired to the great chamber that had been prepared for her, where she vomited and gave herself up to the ministrations of her maids. She could not stop imagining the terrible torments Mandeville must have endured, against which her own suffering seemed unimportant. It was too awful even for tears. The only consolation was that he was at peace now.

'Bring me more wine,' she directed, desperate to calm herself, and gulped it down quickly. But, this time, it did not bring comfort. She lay wakeful for what seemed like hours, and when she eventually fell asleep, she dreamed of devils dancing in the flames.

The manor house of Nyetimber was perfect for her purpose. Tucked away in its grounds, in the heart of a sleepy village, the magnificent half-timbered mansion would afford complete privacy when she most needed it – and it was much further from London than the other houses she had visited. Sitting at table in the hall, listening to the lute player thoughtfully engaged by her hosts strumming in the minstrels' gallery, she felt some sense of peace here – and, Heaven knew, she needed it.

Her decision made, she asked Mother Lowe to attend her in her bedchamber that night.

'I need your help,' she said as soon as they were alone. 'You will think me beyond redemption, I fear, and it grieves me to risk losing your good opinion of me, for I cannot plead the folly of youth this time – but, dear Mother Lowe, I am with child!' Again, the ready tears spilled.

'I know, Anna,' Mother Lowe said gently. 'I am not blind. You've not had your courses for some time. Elya Turpen told me.'

And she had thought she'd been discreet. Even the laundress knew her secret.

'She will not talk?' she asked fearfully. 'No one must know. Tell me no one else suspects!' Her knees felt weak, and she sank down on the bed, pulling off her hood.

Mother Lowe bent and took her hand. 'No one else has said anything, and I warned Elya not to. I think, if anyone had guessed, there would be talk. You know how fast gossip spreads – and there are those in this household who would take the greatest pleasure in repeating it at court.'

'I know,' Anna wept. 'We tried hard to be discreet, and careful. Do not think ill of me!'

'How could I, Anna?' The nurse stroked her hair. 'There is no likelihood for the present of your being able to remarry, despite what was said at the time of your divorce. No one could blame you for seeking consolation, and you have been extremely unlucky. I wish Otho was not married; but, even if he were, it would not be easy for you to wed. How you make your peace with God is your business, not mine. I'm only concerned about what is to be done.'

Anna sagged with relief. How fortunate she was that her nurse loved her unconditionally. She threw her arms around her, surprising the old woman.

'Thank you! Thank you!' she said.

Mother Lowe disentangled herself, pink with emotion. 'We must think what to do!' she said.

'I have it all planned,' Anna told her. She outlined what she had decided, and Mother Lowe nodded approvingly.

'It could work,' she pronounced. 'No – we will make it work.'

By June, Anna knew that, soon, she would be unable to hide her condition any longer. She reckoned she was now five months gone with child, counting from when she had last made love with Otho.

She announced she would be making another visit to Sussex, but only a short one this time – nothing on the scale of last month's progress. Mother Lowe would be accompanying her, with Katharina and Gertrude, Florence de Diaceto, John Bekinsale and two grooms. She dared not risk taking her English ladies, for she did not know if she could trust any of them absolutely.

Mother Lowe packed English gowns that could be unlaced to accommodate Anna's increasing girth, and a good store of night-rails, with books and games against the coming months when she would be confined to her chamber.

They were nearly ready to leave when two letters arrived. Recognising

Wilhelm's seal, Anna opened his first, and was delighted to read that he was married. He had secured a great prize, no less a personage than Jeanne d'Albret, the heiress of Navarre, who would be a queen in her own right one day. She was the niece of the French King, and marriage to her would bind Wilhelm closer to France and bolster him against the territorial ambitions of the Emperor. It was the most splendid match, and Anna was overjoyed for him.

Her eyes widened in disbelief as she read on. Wilhelm's bride, for all that she was only twelve years old, had at first refused to consent to the marriage. 'She was whipped for it, and did in the end agree,' he had written, 'yet even then she signed a statement that it was against her will. Her father made her obey him, but still she protested, and had to be taken by the collar and carried forcibly to the altar by the Constable of France. It was not an edifying sight, and occasioned me much embarrassment. She has gone back to her mother now, for it has been agreed that the marriage will not be consummated until she is older. It is my hope that, before then, she will learn to be obedient and dutiful.'

Anna wondered why the young Jeanne had so taken against Wilhelm. Many girls married husbands who were a dozen years or more older, and this was a good match for both parties. In time, Wilhelm would be king of Navarre, one of the greatest princes in Europe. And he was handsome. Surely the Princess had been taught that she must marry the man chosen for her, as Anna had done? Yet Anna could also remember her own fears and anxieties about marriage. She had some sympathy for the girl, who was, after all, very young.

Shaking her head, she opened the other letter. It was from Dr Harst, informing her that her erstwhile betrothed, Francis of Lorraine, was to marry the Duchess of Milan. 'The King has protested,' he wrote, 'and declared that he holds your Highness as the real and legitimate wife of the Marquis.'

Well, Henry would say that, Anna thought. He must pre-empt Francis's marriage casting doubt on the legitimacy of their divorce and his marriage to Queen Katheryn. It was best not to comment. It all seemed so unimportant beside the challenges that lay ahead of her.

At dinner that last night before Anna's departure, Katherine Bassett revealed that there was tension between Henry and Katheryn. Anne Bassett sent regular letters about life in the Queen's household, with which Katherine always regaled Anna and the rest, and mostly they were filled with gossip of little consequence. But Anne had now reported that the Queen had been sad and thoughtful for some days, prompting the King to ask what ailed her.

'She heard the Queen say she was upset on account of some rumour that his Grace was about to take back your Highness as his wife,' Katherine said.

Anna shook her head in despair. 'Not again, please God! What did the King say?'

'He said she was wrong to attach faith to rumours, and if he had to marry again, he would never take your Highness, for you were precontracted to another. Yet Anne says many think he might be reconciled to you for fear of the King of France making war on him at the solicitation of the Duke of Cleves.'

'That won't happen either,' Anna said flatly. 'My brother has only the friendliest of intentions towards the King.'

She sighed. When would they end, these silly rumours?

They set out on a brilliant June morning. Waving to those staying behind from the window of her litter, Anna caught a last glimpse of Otho, his hand raised, his expression unbearably poignant. It would be a hard separation for them both.

The little party took the same road south as before, which led them to Anna's manor of Chailey, where they lodged overnight. The next night they were at Offham, then they travelled on to the manor of Falmer, where she was much taken with the ancient parish church in its picturesque location by a tranquil duck pond.

Their next stop was at Ovingdean, near the sea, after which they swung westwards to visit Anna's properties in and around the fishing village of Brighthelmstone. From there, they rode further west, lodging at her rectory at Cuckfield, and at an inn north of Arundel, before finally arriving at Nyetimber, where they received a joyous welcome from Anna's tenant, Thomas Bowyer, and his wife. Bowyer was a gentleman in every sense of the word, a respected local worthy and a Member of Parliament.

After two days, Anna complained of feeling sick and feverish. Mrs Bowyer, a nervous woman, became flustered, but Mother Lowe calmed her.

'Her Highness just needs to rest in her chamber until she is better.'

'I am sorry for the inconvenience,' Anna murmured, pressing her hand to her temple, as if to dull a throbbing pain. 'There is no need to go to any trouble.'

Mother Lowe helped her upstairs, as her concerned tenants looked on.

'Take it slowly, my lady,' she said. 'You'll feel better soon.'

But of course Anna did not. Mother Lowe told the Bowyers she had aches in her joints, and felt very weak. It must be a rheumatic ague, she declared, caught as a result of staying in that inn near Arundel. The sheets, she could have sworn, had been damp . . .

Fortunately, the travail was quick, otherwise Anna would not have been able to keep from crying out for much longer. It had been hard enough as it was to stifle her moans. But soon after five o'clock, on a late September afternoon, when she was supposed to be resting and convalescing after her long illness, Anna delivered her silent child into the waiting hands of Mother Lowe, who wrapped it in a towel.

Lying there exhausted, she saw the nurse shake her head, hurriedly cover the infant's face and lay it on a chair.

'I am so sorry,' Mother Lowe whispered, her face crumpling in distress.

All for nothing, Anna thought. Probably it was for the best. Maybe God, seeing her plight, had shown His hand and taken her child to Himself, knowing it had no place on earth.

'What is it?' she asked weakly, wondering why she felt so numb.

'A girl,' Mother Lowe told her, as she busied herself with the afterbirth. 'Perfect to look at, but tiny. Poor little lamb.'

At that, Anna did cry. 'It seems I am never to know the joy of motherhood!' And there was no comfort for her.

She sobbed herself to sleep, and after she had slept a long time, she woke feeling stronger and asked for some food. But before Mother Lowe could hasten away to the kitchen, she grasped her hand.

'I want to see her,' she said. 'Where is she?'

'Are you sure?' the nurse asked. 'The memory will be with you all your life.'

'It will be my only memory of her,' Anna replied. 'The only thing I can cherish.'

Mother Lowe reached into Anna's iron-bound travelling chest and brought out the locked coffer in which her money and valuables were kept. 'I've put everything into a bag,' she said, and placed the coffer on the bed next to Anna.

Anna pulled herself into a sitting position, grateful that she had suffered no damage during the birth. She looked at the coffer for a few heartbeats, then turned the key, lifted the lid and drew aside the fine Holland cloth that covered her baby, gazing down on the little white face and the tiny delicate hands. Her daughter was her very image, even down to the pointed chin; there was nothing of Otho in her.

A great lump formed in her throat, and she feared she would cry out her grief. Tenderly she touched the infant's cold cheek, then bent to kiss it. She was too chilled in the presence of death to pick up the child and hold it to her bosom. Maybe she was not worthy to be a mother after all. But there was something she could do for her daughter.

'I want her to be decently buried,' she told Mother Lowe, looking for the last time on the still little face and resolutely closing the coffer. 'That lovely church at Falmer . . .'

'But it's miles away,' the nurse protested.

'The weather is turning,' Anna pointed out. 'It's not so warm. If we keep her in the coffer, inside the chest, she will be all right.'

'But Anna, you're in childbed! You have to lie in for a time. You're supposed to be recovering from an illness.'

'Am I? No one but you knows I have given birth. I am not injured, and I feel strong. Tomorrow I will go downstairs and tell them that I have presumed on their kindness for too long, and am well enough to leave. I'll say we are taking the journey in easy stages.'

Mother Lowe was shaking her head. 'And have you thought of what will happen when we get to Falmer? How do we explain why we've brought with us a child that needs burial?'

Anna thought for a moment. 'We can say we found her abandoned and near death by the roadside, and that she died soon after we spoke the words of baptism over her. I'm sure that's allowed when no priest is nearby. We daren't say she was unbaptised, or the priest will bury her in unconsecrated ground. I *am* lady of the manor – he is hardly likely to gainsay me. He seemed a mild man.'

Mother Lowe was still looking uncertain, but Anna could tell she was coming around to the idea.

'It could work,' she urged. 'Luck has been with us so far. We just need a little more of it. Heaven knows, I've probably committed most sins known to man recently, and in doing this I will doubtless commit more, but my child deserves a decent Christian burial, and she will have it, as God is my witness.'

'She will go to her grave unnamed,' Mother Lowe mourned.

'God will know who she is,' Anna replied.

It was a pretty spot, in the shelter of an ancient elm near the lychgate. They stood there, the two women, heads bowed, as the old priest read the burial rite over the little coffer and nodded to the sexton to commit it to the grave. Anna felt as if her heart were being buried with her child, along with all her earthly happiness. But she dared not show too much emotion, and it took all her self-control to stem the torrent of weeping welling within her. When it was over, and the final Amen had been intoned, she thanked the priest for helping her to do her Christian duty; then, summoning all her inner reserves of strength, she turned away and walked back to her chariot.

Chapter 21

1541

'The Queen has been arrested! Queen Katheryn has been arrested!'
Katherine Bassett came running up the stairs, calling out the news
and waving a letter, and Anna, who had been sitting sewing with her
women, listening to Otho playing his lute, felt her heart begin to
pound.

'No!' she cried out. Not Katheryn, kind-hearted, childlike Katheryn,
whom the King adored! 'Why? What crime can she possibly have
committed?'

'My sister is in great anxiety,' Katherine told them. 'The Queen
has been confined to her rooms at Hampton Court, and no one
knows what's going on. She confessed to one of her ladies that she had
indulged in naughty behaviour before her marriage, but surely that's
not a crime?'

'Of course it's not,' Anna replied, trembling inwardly at the thought
of her own 'naughty behaviour'. Her eyes met Otho's; he looked as
troubled as she.

Poor Katheryn. The girl was foolish enough to have let herself be led
astray – she must have been very young at the time – and who could
blame her for not telling the King? Anna could well imagine Henry
being devastated at discovering that his beloved Queen was not as pure
as he had thought – but to have her arrested for it? 'There must be
something else,' she said. 'Let's pray that she is found to be innocent. Is
your sister all right?'

'She is confined with the Queen – a few of the maids are – but she is
allowed out to take the air. That's how she got this letter to me.'

Anna's household was soon buzzing with speculation, waiting

impatiently for news. A letter from Dr Harst was seized on eagerly, almost before Anna had read it. The King had come to Whitehall, he wrote, and left the Queen under guard at Hampton Court. He had been sitting in Council for hours, from which Dr Harst deduced that a matter of great importance was under discussion. He'd seen some councillors emerge with troubled faces, especially Norfolk. The court was seething with rumours, and it was bruited that the King would change queens yet again.

'It is not a vain fancy,' the doctor wrote. 'The King of France has allied himself with the German princes and wants the King to join forces with him against the Emperor. The time is ripe for reinforcing the alliance between England and Kleve. Monsieur de Marillac, the French ambassador, is hoping for a reconciliation between his Majesty and your Highness, for he believes the King will soon be a free man.'

Anna was greatly disturbed to read this. Harst had clearly taken the French ambassador seriously.

'Monsieur de Marillac said he had heard that the Queen was accused of being entertained by a gentleman while she was in the house of the old Duchess of Norfolk. He told me the process against her is the same taken against Queen Anne, who was beheaded. She is allowed no kind of pastime, but must keep to her chamber, whereas, before, she did nothing but dance and rejoice; and now, when the musicians come, they are told that it is no more the time to dance.'

Anna passed the letter to her ladies. This was truly dreadful; she could barely imagine what that poor girl at Hampton Court was suffering.

She could not but ask herself: if Katheryn were set aside – she dared not think of what that might mean – would she want to go back to Henry? And would she have a choice? If he and Wilhelm agreed on it, there would be no room for objections. Had she not fallen so deeply in love with Otho, it might not have been so unwelcome a prospect, especially if Henry continued to show the same kindness and affection towards her. She had to admit that the prospect of being queen still held some appeal, although she could not bear to relinquish her cherished freedom. Nor, conscious of all she must keep secret – which, in the wake of Katheryn's arrest, was all the more imperative now – did she want to lay herself open to the deadly intrigues of the court.

At Richmond, they were collectively holding their breath. Several of Anna's household had already assumed that if the King put away Katheryn Howard, their mistress would be queen again, and all she could do was keep saying, 'We must not leap to any conclusions.'

Another letter arrived from Dr Harst, who had been extracting information from anyone who would talk to him. 'Monsieur Chapuys suspects that the lords in Parliament will revoke the annulment of your Highness's marriage. Monsieur de Marillac thinks there is a strong likelihood of this, because Bishop Gardiner has lately returned from Germany, where it is thought he may have obtained new information about the causes for which you were divorced.' Harst thought a reconciliation between Anna and Henry would promote many advantageous alliances. Yet Anna could not credit that the King really would consider taking her back, for it would not profit him dynastically – unless, of course, having grown fonder of her as a friend, he could be moved to do that which he had been unable to do when they were married.

More shocking news from the court arrived in another letter from Anne Bassett. Sir Thomas Wriothesley had assembled Queen Katheryn's household together and informed them that she had been charged with treason for lewd and adulterous behaviour.

'Adultery?' Anna exclaimed, as they all looked at each other in amazement. 'With whom?' Surely Katheryn had not been so stupid, especially with the example of her own cousin before her?

Katherine read on: '"We were informed that she had traitorously committed adultery with Thomas Culpeper, a gentleman of the Privy Chamber, who was greatly favoured by the King."'

Culpeper! Anna had always sensed something unsavoury about him. He was clearly an opportunist and an unprincipled rat!

'She is no longer to be called queen,' Katherine was saying, 'and has been sent to Syon Abbey, under house arrest. Her household has been dismissed. I know not what our mother will say when she hears.' She looked up from the letter, plainly distressed. 'She will be distraught, especially with my father still in prison in the Tower. She laboured so hard to get that place for Anne. Madam, I beg you, if you see the King, will you speak for Anne and ask him to be a good lord to her?'

'I will, if I see him, Katherine.' Anna looked at the stunned faces of her women, and thought of how silly Katheryn had been, the grief she had inflicted on herself, the people who would be hurt by her unthinking acts – and Henry. This would break him, she feared.

'She is young,' Jane Ratsey said.

'Old enough to know right from wrong,' Mother Lowe declared.

'And the danger she risked,' Anna said. 'What if she had become pregnant with another man's child?'

Bearing a bastard child had not, in Anna's case, hurt anyone but herself, but Katheryn had betrayed a loving husband, and risked impugning the royal succession. At least Anna had known when to say *no more*, condemning herself to living daily in close proximity to the lover she had rejected, with both of them suffering for it, as was plain in the misery in Otho's face, which people naturally imputed to his wife's notorious infidelity. Katheryn had apparently exercised no such restraint.

'I cannot bear to think what they will do to her,' Frances Lilgrave said mournfully.

'Surely the King will not sign her death warrant?'

'She has done a very wicked thing,' Mother Lowe sniffed. 'How can he forgive her?'

'I shall beseech God to move him to mercy,' Anna vowed. Inwardly, she was not confident. The reformers at court would be jumping at this chance to overthrow Norfolk and the Catholic party, and they would be out for Katheryn's blood like a pack of baying hounds.

Tongues were clacking furiously. Speculation that Henry might take Anna back was becoming rampant, at court and in her household, as it became clear that the reformists were pressing the King to rid himself of Queen Katheryn and the entire Howard faction. And who would they set up in her place? One who, despite her Catholic faith, was unavoidably aligned to the cause of reform because she represented an alliance with the German princes.

Anna was not surprised to receive a letter from Dr Harst, in which he insisted on her being ready for the summons he was certain would come. She was to hold herself in readiness at Richmond, or at a place nearer the King, if possible. Above all, she was to show herself joyous at the prospect of being restored to the throne. Her brother, and all Kleve, would wish it.

She stared at the letter. Her restoration would depend on Katheryn's ruin. She could not stop thinking about the terrible fate that had over-taken the vivacious young woman who had been so friendly and generous to her the previous winter. She might deplore Katheryn's stupidity and its far-spreading consequences, but she still felt sympathy for her, all alone at Syon, where she must be wondering what they would do to her.

'You must show yourself glad that such wicked treason has been discovered,' Harst exhorted. It was wise advice, yet how could Anna be glad about something that was causing such pain to others?

She tried to reconcile herself to what Fate probably had in store for her. She was tense with anticipation. Henry might soon be a free man, and she would have no choice but to do as Wilhelm wished.

She took Harst's advice. 'I cannot but rejoice at the uncovering of this heinous treason,' she told her officers and ladies, as they were discussing the scandal over dinner. 'I shudder when I think how closely it touches the King.'

'The Queen will pay dearly for it, poor soul,' Frances said.

'His Grace has been suffering too,' Anna reminded her. 'He is no longer young or in good health. I fear for him, what with the shock of finding she was not the rose without a thorn he had thought her, and the grief of his loss.'

'But think of what *she* is going through.' Jane Ratsey spoke up. 'Is that not worse suffering? To live daily in fear of death?'

'We should all live daily in fear of death,' Anna said gently. 'We never know when our souls will be gathered. I do feel sorry for her. But, whatever my personal feelings, I cannot condone her treason, and neither should any of you. Who are we to question the King's justice? If I am restored as queen, as my brother wants, you will all benefit.'

'So your Highness really thinks it will happen?' Gertrude asked.

'I have been advised to hold myself in readiness and wait for a summons to court.'

They all stared at her, awestruck.

She waited for news. The short November days ran into each other, and the skies were louring and grey, reflecting the heaviness that lay upon the kingdom. The only messenger who came was a Privy councillor with orders to retrieve the ring Katheryn had given Anna. Anna handed him the pretty thing, remembering how impulsively Katheryn had made a gift of it – and the little dogs, who were full-grown now. It had been such a happy occasion.

Harst wrote again. He had heard from Dr Olisleger, who had written to the Earl of Southampton and Archbishop Cranmer begging them to urge Anna's reinstatement. 'The Archbishop is a great reformer,' Anna read, 'and has been instrumental in the proceedings against her who was lately queen. He and the Earl might be counted on to press for an alliance with the German princes. The general opinion here at court is that his Majesty will remarry you. Nearly everyone thinks it. I urge your Highness to exert prudence and patience.'

'You may count on me to do that,' she wrote back, aware that her letter would probably be intercepted and read. 'I will never utter a word by which anyone might suppose I am discontented; have I not always said I wish for nothing but what pleases the King my lord?'

All her life, she had been enjoined to patience. Dissembling her passions had become second nature to her. Mutter had always said that patience could only come of a singular grace from God, and a heart resolved to accept what could not be remedied. She would be proud to read how Dr Harst admired Anna's circumspection. 'Your Highness has conducted yourself, with your household, very wisely,' he wrote. 'Those who have visited you have marvelled to me at such great virtue, and are loud in your praise. I rejoice to hear that you are well. People even say you are looking more beautiful than when you were queen. In truth, you are more regretted and commiserated over than the late Queen Katherine.'

His letter had her reaching for her mirror. Was she more beautiful these days? There was no doubt that French hoods did more for her than the *Stickelchen* ever had. Whatever the truth of the matter, it bolstered her confidence. How ironic it would be if Henry came to desire her after all, when she did not want him.

Harst arrived at Richmond, grave-faced, in early December. Receiving him in her parlour, where a fire had been lit, Anna's first thought was that the Queen had been sentenced to death.

'Madam,' he said, unable to conceal his distress, 'I must speak to you about a delicate matter, which, if not dealt with properly, could mean the end of all our plans.'

Anna immediately thought of Otho, and the little grave in the shadow of the elm tree. If she had not been sitting in her chair, she feared she would have collapsed.

Harst took the chair on the opposite side of the fireplace, looking as if he would rather be anywhere else. 'Monsieur Chapuys came to see me. The King had gone hunting, and many thought he would come here to visit you, my lady. But Monsieur Chapuys took pleasure in informing me that he took another road, *and* reminded me that there has been no sign, as yet, of his Majesty taking you back. I said that could hardly be expected, given that he is still wedded to Queen Katheryn.' Harst hesitated. 'Then he said there was something I should know, and he thought, in friendship and charity, that he ought to tell me.'

'In friendship?' Anna interjected, nearly mad with apprehension. 'How can there be friendship between the Empire and Kleve, when the Emperor threatens our borders?'

'It was not friendly at all,' Harst replied. 'It was a ploy to undermine your chances of being restored, and I'm sure, Madam, you will tell me that what he said was groundless.'

Anna was praying that too. Her future, her very life, seemed suspended on the brink of disaster. 'What *did* he say?'

'He said he had spoken with the Clerk of the Council, Mr Paget, who was your Highness's secretary, and that Paget had said something strange – that, if his Majesty separated from this Queen on account of her having had connection with another man before she married him, he would have been justified in doing the same with the lady of Kleve for the same cause, if the rumour current in the Low countries is true.'

Anna felt herself grow hot. 'What rumour? What was he talking about?'

'I have no idea, Madam. And, as you clearly have none either, we must dismiss it as mere calumny. But – forgive me for repeating this, Madam – Monsieur Chapuys said it was not difficult to believe at your age, considering that you are fond of wine and indulge in other excesses.'

The room began spinning, and there was a rushing in her ears. She felt she was standing on the edge of a precipice. Chapuys had skirted too close to the truth.

She leapt hotly to her defence. 'I condescend? I may enjoy a glass of wine from time to time, but all I indulge in is innocent good cheer with my household. Is that very wrong? And what does he mean, *at my age?*'

'Madam,' Harst replied, his face pained, 'his drift was clear. He meant you are of an age to enjoy certain pleasures, and, I think, that you condescend to grant favours.'

'This is outrageous!' she seethed.

'It's even more outrageous that Mr Paget did not deny it. As one who worked for you, he should be in a position to know the truth of it.'

'I wish I had been there and made them explain themselves,' Anna fumed. 'Did you not defend my honour to Monsieur Chapuys?'

Harst bristled. 'Of course! I said I knew you for a virtuous lady, and that Mr Paget should have better things to do than spread malicious gossip.'

'Thank you, my friend.' Anna relaxed a little. 'I cannot bear to have people thinking or saying such things about me. Do you think it is the Catholics at court, trying to dissuade the King from taking me back?'

'Very likely,' Harst agreed, looking relieved himself. Anna thought she had been rather deft in diverting his attention to an alternative, and very plausible, explanation, and decided to move the conversation along further.

'I imagine Monsieur Chapuys believes there will be no reconciliation.'

'He said Mr Paget did not believe the King would take you back or marry again unless Parliament forced him. Bishop Gardiner himself told me that the King will never restore you as his wife. However, that might be wishful thinking. He helped the Howards push the Queen in the King's path, and has his own future to think of. I imagine he would oppose your remarriage with all his might.'

'But his teeth have been drawn.' Anna forced a smile.

Her heart was still pounding after the doctor had left. Who? she kept asking herself. Who had begun spreading the gossip about her, gossip that was rooted in truth? How had they known her secrets? Only Mutter, Mother Lowe and Otho knew of Johann's existence, and she trusted them all implicitly. How could anyone here know what had happened within the stout walls of a secluded castle in Germany? But that, of course, was not all there was to know.

Was the gossip just about her 'condescending' to men in general? It worried her that Paget had mentioned it being rife in the Low countries. Who knew her secrets? Again, only Mother Lowe, Elya Turpen and Otho had been privy to her second pregnancy. Had the Bowyers guessed? It was unlikely they would have risked losing their comfortable tenancy by spreading gossip.

There were too many questions spinning in her head. In the end, as she lay wakeful that night, it came to her that there were only two people, Mother Lowe and Otho, who knew the truth of what had happened on both occasions. Anna knew, as surely as she knew God was in Heaven and the Devil in Hell, that wild horses would have torn Mother Lowe apart before she said anything. And she would never believe that Otho had deliberately betrayed her, but what if he had inadvertently done so? She remembered Mr Horsey complaining how he had found Otho lying drunk on the stairs one night, soon after she had ended their trysts. Had Otho said something while in his cups?

She slept late the next morning, having not drifted off until four o'clock, and when she was dressed, she decided that she must steel herself and send for Otho. She made sure her ladies were present, and wondered why Jane and Katherine weren't with them.

'My lady,' Otho said, bowing low. When he straightened up, she could see the pain of loss and longing in his eyes. 'You have heard the news?'

'What news?'

'Mrs Ratsey and Mrs Bassett were summoned before the Council this morning.'

'No!' Anna's heart began thudding alarmingly. 'Why?'

'I cannot say. None of us know.'

'Ladies, please leave us,' Anna managed to say. The women departed, looking at her in bafflement.

'They will come for me next!' she cried. Otho hastened to her and took her hand, which she promptly withdrew. He listened, his frown deepening, as she poured out her fears.

'Did you say anything at all?' she asked him.

'To be honest, I don't remember,' he admitted, shamefaced. 'I was drunk, and out cold more than once. If I did, I am truly, truly sorry.'

'It's too late. I think we are undone already.' Anna was convinced of it, and would not be comforted. When Otho tried to put his arms about her, and apologised for the tenth time, she sent him away.

Had hours ever passed so slowly? Was this what it was like to be waiting for the summons to execution? Anna dared not let herself think about that, but tried to divert herself with books she could not read and embroidery stitches she kept dropping.

At last, at last, she heard the splash of oars below her window, and looked out to see Jane and Katherine stepping up to the jetty. Picking up her skirts, she raced down the stairs and through the gatehouse, and ran towards them.

'I have been so worried about you,' she cried. 'What happened? Why were you called before the Council?'

'For gossiping.' Katherine snorted in disgust. 'Really, you'd think they'd have better things to do.'

'Gossip may be of great significance in this matter of the Queen,' Anna said, suffused with such overwhelming relief that she felt quite light-headed. 'What have you been saying?'

'Madam, I had only speculated what would happen if God worked to make you queen again,' Jane said.

'And Mr Carew overheard us, and saw fit to report us,' Katherine sniffed. 'I'd merely said it was impossible that so sweet a queen as yourself could be put away.'

'Oh dear,' Anna fretted. 'Didn't you remember, you silly girls, that it is treason to criticise my divorce?'

'I think the councillors were more annoyed at me saying, "What a man the King is!" And because I wondered aloud how many wives he would have. I told them it was just idle talk, and that I had never spoken at any other time of your Highness, and I thought the King's divorce from you a good thing. I said I was sorry about it at the time, but I knew not so much then as I know now.'

'And that was all?' Anna asked, as they mounted the stairs.

'Yes. They warned us never to gossip about the King again, and let us go.'

Reprieved! Her fears had been unfounded. She could have hugged the girls, and kissed them. Instead, she said, 'How about some wine to calm us all down?'

The next morning, Anna roused herself to start baking gingerbread for Christmas. She was feeling relieved that yesterday's interrogation had turned out to be a trifle, but anxious all the same lest someone else reveal her secrets. She seemed always to be anxious these days, and when a frantic Mother Lowe came bustling into the kitchen to say that Sir Anthony Browne and Sir Richard Rich of the Privy Council had arrived with four guards and were asking to see her, she thought she might die from shock. They had come for her, as she had feared. She was shaking so much she could barely utter the words of greeting.

'We are sorry to trouble you, my Lady Anna,' Browne said, not looking or sounding as if he were about to arrest her, 'but we are directed to apprehend your servant Frances Lilgrave. She is to be taken to the Tower for questioning.'

Anna felt faint. Light became dark and her vision was scrambled by flashes like lightning. The sensation was momentary, but it frightened her. She must catch a grip on herself. They had not come for her, but for Frances, who loved nothing more than to gossip. Not for the first time, Anna wondered if *she* had been responsible for the rumours. But what did Frances actually know? And could Anna trust her not to betray her?

'What has she done?' she asked.

'She has slandered you, Madam, and the King also,' Sir Richard told her.

Anna felt again that she might faint.

'Do you know Mr Taverner, Clerk of the Signet?' Sir Anthony asked.

'Is that the same Richard Taverner who dedicated *An Epitome of the Psalms* to the King?' Anna asked, remembering that flowery dedication welcoming her coming to England. 'Why?'

'It is indeed him, and he is involved in this.'

'In what, precisely?' Her heart was thudding so loudly she feared they might hear it. 'If my honour is being slandered, I have a right to know what is being said about me.'

Sir Richard looked at Sir Anthony and indicated he should speak.

'A few days ago, Madam, we had word of an abominable slander: that your Highness had been delivered of a fair boy, and that it was the King's Majesty's, begotten back in January when you were at Hampton Court.'

Anna was genuinely stunned. It was perilously near the truth, but the details were all wrong and could honestly be denied. Whoever had spread this slander had not known her secret. 'It's a foul lie,' she said, 'and I'd like to know who is responsible, and why.'

'That is what his Majesty would like to know too,' Rich said. There was an edge to his voice, and she trembled to think that Henry himself might be wondering if there was some truth in the gossip. 'Taverner learned of this from his mother-in-law, Mrs Lambert, who said she'd heard it from Mrs Lilgrave, and from old Lady Carew. They discussed it among themselves and with others, but Taverner thought he ought to divulge what he had heard to Dr Cox, who advises the King on religious matters. Dr Cox immediately disclosed it to the Lord Privy Seal, which was how the matter came to the Council's attention.' His face softened. 'Madam, please don't worry. We know there is no truth in it, but it is treason to slander the King. We need to find out where this malicious slander originated, and deal with the culprit accordingly. Fear not, we will root them out. The King will not have his honour, or yours, impugned.'

The last thing Anna wanted was for them to do any rooting-out. Who knew what they might dig up?

When summoned, Frances Lilgrave became hysterical, pleading with Anna not to let them take her, but the guards marched her away, leaving Anna shocked and fearful.

Would she be next?

Tossing sleepless in bed later, she racked her brains trying to make sense of what she had heard.

It worried her that the King, who had told her to ignore gossip, was taking this matter so seriously. He knew there was no basis to the story that he had fathered a child on her, so he must be concerned either to discover where it had originated, or whether Anna had indeed given birth. At the very least, the uncovering of such misconduct on her part would provide him with an excuse to free himself of his financial obligations to her. Even if he did not punish her more severely, now that she was his subject, she would be left destitute, and could not possibly go home to Kleve disgraced and beggared, for Wilhelm would surely exact a severe penalty.

Hopefully, Henry was merely being touchy about his honour, and wanted to bring the offenders to justice. But who were these people who had slandered him – and her? She knew that, as fine embroiderers, Frances and her husband had close links to the court, but who was

Taverner to Frances? And who was old Lady Carew? Anna could not place her. She had met so many people at court, it was hard to recall them all. Wymond Carew was not of knightly rank, so it couldn't be his wife, who was plain Mistress Carew, and she had heard him say his mother was dead.

Could it be that the Catholics were doing their best to discredit Anna so that the King would not take her back?

As Anna waited to hear word of Frances, more news about Katheryn Howard's crimes filtered its way through to Richmond. It was said that she had fornicated before her marriage with one Francis Dereham, and after it with Thomas Culpeper. Both men had been sentenced to death. The King had shown mercy and commuted Culpeper's sentence to beheading, but Dereham was to suffer the full penalty for treason. Anna was horrified. What had he done to deserve such savagery, save seduce a young girl? But maybe there was more to it than she knew. She had heard that Dereham had inveigled his way into the Queen's household, which looked suspicious in itself, given their previous relationship.

No one now doubted that Katheryn would die. The sentences handed down to her lovers presaged that. Anna could not bear to think of her suffering such a fate at such a tender age.

It was cried in London that the men's executions would take place on 9 December, at Tyburn. Some of Anna's household were planning to take a barge and be present, but, that morning, a butcher delivering sides of beef told them the word was that the traitors were to die on the morrow instead. He had no idea why there had been a postponement.

The next day, Anna again gave permission for her servants to go to Tyburn. They returned subdued, sickened by what they had witnessed, and she did not press them to talk about it. She could all too easily imagine how horrible Dereham's suffering had been.

A pall lay over Richmond. There had been no word of Frances Lilgrave. Surely, if she or Taverner had said anything incriminating, the councillors would have been here with their guards before you could say a Hail Mary.

Anna got a nasty jolt when Browne and Rich did arrive that evening, until she saw they had no armed company. She invited them to be seated and called for wine, of which she herself had need.

'Thank you, my lady,' Sir Anthony said. Of the two, he was by far the more pleasant. Sir Richard reminded her of a snake. She did not like his abrupt manner or the way he stared at her as if weighing up the veracity of what she was saying, although maybe it was her guilty conscience making her think that.

But Sir Anthony was genial; she had always liked him.

'We came to tell you, Madam, that his Majesty thinks it requisite to have this abominable slander thoroughly examined. I regret I must ask you a delicate question, since he has instructed me to inquire whether your Highness has indeed had any child.'

She had not expected this. She felt her cheeks grow hot. 'I am astonished his Majesty should even ask. It's bad enough that one of my servants has been spreading this rumour, without it being taken for the truth. Of course I have not had a child.' There, the lie was out, but she had had no choice. After the dread sentence passed on Francis Dereham for misconduct outside marriage, she would defend herself even unto perjury.

There was a pause. Panic welled in her. What did they know?

Sir Richard broke the silence. 'Taverner is in trouble because, in conversation with his wife and Lilgrave, he said the Queen's treason seemed like a judgement of God, since you, my lady, were still the King's wife, and you had gone away from London in the family way, and been confined last summer. I should tell you, Madam, that this rumour has been widely circulated.'

She was a whisper away from disaster. Someone had known her secret; someone had told Frances Lilgrave. Yet surely the Council could have no proof that the story was true?

'Again, it is a wicked calumny,' she declared, looking her visitors directly in the eye. 'You, Sirs, like everyone else, saw how greatly the King loved Katheryn Howard. To suggest he had relations with me in that time is implausible in the extreme. It must be plain to you how baseless these slanders are.'

'We are more concerned with where they originated, Madam,' Sir Richard said, 'but, before we proceed to charging Lilgrave and Taverner with treasonously slandering his Majesty, we have to establish that there is no truth in what was said.'

'Of course,' Anna said, her fears receding a little. 'I understand that. But I am shocked to hear that such vile things have been said about me, and about his Grace.'

'Taverner has been committed to the Tower, with Lilgrave and his mother-in-law, who is a devil, for she took pleasure in spreading the slander, but Lilgrave appears to have been the first author of the bruit.'

That was too close to home for comfort. If the slander had originated from someone close to Anna, and in a position to know the truth, it would be the more readily believed.

'What of Lady Carew?' she asked. 'Her name means nothing to me.'

Sir Anthony Browne answered. 'She is the widow of the traitor Sir Nicholas Carew, and I assure you, Madam, your name means much to her. Through no fault of your own, you now possess her former house at Bletchingley. Thus she had a motive for desiring to slander you. When her husband was attainted, his property forfeit to the Crown, she sought refuge with her children and her mother-in-law in one of his lesser houses at Wallington, which the King, in his mercy, permitted her to keep. Mrs Lambert's people live nearby, and the families know each other. But it was Lilgrave who broke open the slander to Lady Carew. She, however, refuses to reveal her source. Taverner is charged only with concealing it.'

Taverner was lucky not to have been accused of treason for speaking out in favour of her marriage. Yet he had not concealed the slander for long. If they were being this harsh with him for such a small offence, what might they not do to Anna if the truth came out? And why would Frances refuse to reveal her source? Was she protecting someone? If so, who?

'We will be summoning your officers for questioning, Madam, and we would like Mrs Ratsey to accompany us back to court now,'

Sir Richard said. Anna wondered what, if anything, Jane and the other members of her household knew. Had *she* talked to Frances Lilgrave?

'This is ridiculous!' she snapped, thrusting down her fear. 'It's just idle gossip.'

'His Majesty thinks otherwise,' Sir Richard said stiffly, 'and if you, Madam, are not concerned about your honour being sullied, he is!'

Stung by the insult, Anna glared at him and summoned Jane Ratsey, who looked terrified, and burst into tears when told that she must go with the councillors. Sobbing, she was escorted from the presence chamber, leaving Anna to her tumultuous thoughts.

Naturally, the visits of the councillors and the absence of Jane Ratsey gave rise to much talk in Anna's household. Two royal scandals in the space of a few weeks – everyone was agog, and some fearful lest they themselves be taken away for questioning.

The very next day, Sir William Goring came to tell Anna that he had received a formal letter commanding himself, Mr Horsey and the amiable, inoffensive Dorothy Wingfield, a gentlewoman of her chamber, to repair to the Privy Council. Anna knew Dorothy to have been an acolyte of the garrulous Frances, and wondered if Jane had mentioned her under questioning. It pained her to see Dorothy's fright when informed she was to be interrogated.

Anna could settle to nothing. How could she prepare for Christmas with this dread matter hanging over her? Yet, if she was to maintain an innocent stance, she must not be seen to let it touch her. Summoning all her resolve, she began drawing up lists of the gifts she needed to buy and food for the Christmas table. There would be no going to court this year, and certainly the King would not be making merry.

Daily, she waited for news, barely able to suppress her trepidation. Her household were still excitedly anticipating that the King would take her back, but she was more concerned about the continuing absence of Frances and Jane. The others had returned, having – they told her – been unable to assist the lords. The councillors had given little away, apart from telling Sir William that Jane had admitted she knew of the gossip, but had refused to say more.

'I told them that was more than *I* knew,' said the chamberlain. 'Nevertheless, the Lord Chancellor is keeping her in custody, for clearly they think she knows more than she admits to.'

But how could she have known? Anna wondered.

When Dr Harst arrived a day later, Anna thought he had come to discuss the slander, but it soon became clear that he knew nothing about it. In fact, he was unusually ebullient and full of purpose.

'Madam, I have this morning received letters of credence from the Duke your brother, and also a letter from Dr Olisleger to my lord of Canterbury. I now have the authority to seek a reconciliation between your Highness and the King. I have already seen my lord of Southampton and asked if I may declare my charge to the Council and wait upon the King; but I wanted to tell your Highness the good news before proceeding further.'

Now that the moment had come, Anna shrank from the prospect of being reconciled to the King. Besides it seeming like a betrayal of her love for Otho, she could see herself facing the same fate as Katheryn Howard. Yet, she reassured herself, it was unlikely Henry would consider a reconciliation with this slander under examination. She calmed down a little.

'What did the Earl of Southampton say?' she asked.

'He undertook to show my letter of credence to the King. This afternoon, I am for Lambeth, to see the Archbishop. Being of the reformist persuasion, I have no doubt he will support a reconciliation.'

'You will let me know what he says?'

Harst looked pained. 'Madam, if I may say so, you could look a little more pleased about the remarkable change of fortune that might come to you.'

'Would that I could feel pleasure in it, Dr Harst, but something is troubling me deeply. The King has ordered the Council to investigate a slander that I have borne him a child. Two of my women are in prison. One is the person who first spread the bruit, but she will not name her source. What with that, and this dreadful business of the Queen, I feel quite upset. The worst of it is that, at one point, the Council, and perhaps even the King, seemed to believe there was some truth in the slander.'

Harst's eyes had widened in dismay.

'You have, of course, told them there isn't.'

'Of course I have. I think they are more concerned to discover the author of the slander.'

'I'm sure they are. But do not let the malicious actions of envious rogues trouble you, Madam, I pray you. Think on this advantageous chance that has come your way.'

'I will, Dr Harst,' she promised, forcing herself to smile. 'I will.'

The next day he wrote to her as he had promised, but the news was not what he had hoped. Archbishop Cranmer had spoken to the King, but his Majesty had asked him to state most firmly to Dr Harst that there could never be any question of a reconciliation. 'He thought it not a little strange that Dr Olisleger should urge for a reconciliation in regard to a marriage that had justly been dissolved,' Harst had written. Anna could imagine how dejected he was feeling. She felt offended that Henry had rejected her so categorically, and wondered anxiously if it was because he entertained suspicions about her morals.

Harst had tried to see the King, but had been told his Majesty was too grief-stricken over the treason of the Queen to receive him. He had then approached Monsieur de Marillac, hoping the French would back Anna's reinstatement. Marillac had been eager to help, but had advised him to defer the matter until it was known what would happen to the Queen. So Harst had gone before the Council, declared Duke Wilhelm's gratitude for the King's liberality to his sister, and prayed the lords to find some means to effect a reconciliation and restore Anna to the estate of queen.

'I am sorry to report that they answered, on the King's behalf, that his Majesty had seen you graciously provided for, and had asked them to remind me that the annulment had been made for such compelling causes that he prayed the Duke never again to make such a request.'

It was painfully clear to Anna that Dr Harst had little influence at court, and that Henry would never take her back. Part of her was saddened to realise he still did not like her enough; the other part could feel only relief. Harst, though, sounded defeated. 'I can do no more here, Madam. I am not welcome, and no one pays any attention to what I say. If you or the Duke need me, I will be at my new lodging in the Bell Savage Inn on Ludgate Hill. There is no point in my being at court.'

Anna felt sorry for him. He had done his best for her, and championed her interests. It was not his fault that Henry had been prejudiced against him from the first and the councillors deemed him of little account. Now, she supposed, she must fight her own battles.

Chapter 22

1542

They had done their best to make merry at Christmas, but for Anna, the season was overshadowed by anxiety as to what the new year of 1542 would bring. She had sent Henry a gift of some lengths of fine crimson cloth, and was relieved to receive presents from him. She exclaimed in delight over the exquisite glass bowls and flagons he had chosen, having half expected to receive nothing.

A few days after Twelfth Night, Sir William Goring surprised her as she was kneeling on the floor, playing with her dogs.

'Madam, I have heard from the Privy Council.' He sounded unusually excited. 'You will be glad to hear that Mrs Lilgrave has finally admitted to having slandered you and touched the King's person. She maintains she heard the report from others whom she refuses to name, but I think she is lying. Since she has admitted her offence, the Council has refuted the rumours publicly, stating that the King did not behave to you like a husband, and it was not true that you went to the country and bore him a son.'

The relief was overwhelming, yet Anna was angry that Frances had taken so long to make that admission, and caused her weeks of worry. Personally she doubted that Frances *had* lied, and feared someone else had talked. It was disconcerting to realise she might never know who it had been. She could never ask Frances, lest Frances guess the truth. Always she would be looking at those close to her and asking herself: Was it you?

'What is to happen to her?' she asked Sir William.

'She is to remain in the Tower, and Taverner also, for concealing the slander. I imagine they will be detained for as long as it takes to teach them a salutary lesson.'

'I will not have Frances back in my employ,' Anna said, 'or Jane Ratsey. They have done me a great disservice and caused me and the King much grief.'

'That is quite understandable, Madam,' Sir William agreed. 'I will have their service formally terminated.'

Proof that Anna was still in the King's favour arrived later that month, in the form of a royal grant bestowing on her estates in Berkshire and Yorkshire. She wondered if this was compensation for his having given credence to the slander. How lucky she had been, she reflected, still unable to believe that the horrible business was behind her and that she had escaped unscathed. She prayed that Fortune would be as bountiful to poor Katheryn Howard, of whom there had been no word for weeks.

Her household were elated when they were told of the King's gift and, predictably, saw it as a sign that he might take Anna back. She merely smiled to herself. They would soon realise that it would never happen.

It was the second week of February, and Wymond Carew had, as usual, been about his business at the court. He was still wearing his cloak when he returned, slightly out of breath, and intercepted Anna as she was going to supper.

'The Queen was executed this morning,' he told her, his face grave, 'and Lady Rochford too, for abetting her adultery.'

Anna crossed herself. Even though she had half expected this news, she was still shocked. That poor girl. Yes, she had been foolish, and unfaithful, yet she had paid a terrible penalty – as had Lady Rochford. Anna had not known that she was involved. She had not liked the woman, but would never have wished this on her.

'God rest their souls,' she whispered. 'Do you know how the King is taking it?'

'The word is that he is looking very old and grey, and will not yet hear of taking another queen, although his ministers beg and urge him to marry again. They say he is now very stout and daily growing heavier, yet many believe he will not be long without a wife, on account of the great desire he has to have more children.'

'No doubt some will be speculating that I will be restored to my former place,' Anna sighed.

'They are, but there is, as yet, no sign of it.'

A page appeared. 'Madam, a letter has arrived from Dr Harst.' He handed it to her with a bow.

'Thank you for bringing me the news, Mr Carew, unwelcome as it was to me,' Anna said, hoping he would take the hint and depart, leaving her to open her letter.

Carew looked pointedly at it. 'I trust I will be seeing that later, Madam,' he said. If Anna hadn't been so shocked by the news of Katheryn Howard, she would have given him a tart answer, but she let it go.

Seating herself at the table, she broke the seal. She had not been expecting to hear from Harst, so clearly his missive contained something of import. She raised her eyebrows as she read that he was still hopeful of her being reconciled to the King. He had received many letters from German princes, saying they were urging Henry to reinstate her, and he was waiting only for Monsieur de Marillac to inform him of King François' support before he handed them over to the King. He added, somewhat gleefully, that Monsieur Chapuys was in torment at the prospect of England allying itself in a joint pact with France and Kleve.

The good doctor was building castles in the air. To be honest, she wished that everyone would leave her be. She did not want to be restored as queen, especially after what had happened to Katheryn Howard, or be wife to a prematurely aged man who was not in the best of health, fond of Henry as she was. What price a crown!

In the middle of March, Anna fell ill. It began with a simple ague, but soon she had to take to her bed, suffering rigours, vomiting, headaches, bitter bile and painful waves of heat and thirst. The odd thing was that, the next day, she would feel well enough to get up, but the symptoms would recur two days later.

'It is a tertian fever, my lady,' Dr Cepher pronounced, holding up his glass and examining her urine. 'So called because it comes in three-day cycles. I'm told it's common in these southern parts of England.'

'It's a misery,' Anna groaned, so exhausted she barely had the strength to get up to the privy.

'Just rest and keep warm, Madam. It will pass in a few days.'

'That's not soon enough.' She managed a weak smile.

Dr Cepher turned to Mother Lowe. 'Heap the bedclothes over her Highness to make her sweat, and give her plenty of posset ale through a goose quill, if you have one.'

'We do,' Mother Lowe nodded. 'What is posset ale?'

'Hot milk mixed in equal parts with ale. A sovereign remedy for fevers.'

'Very good, Doctor,' Mother Lowe said, bustling over to the window to fetch more blankets from the chest.

Anna was alarmed when the nurse came into the sickroom the next morning to say that Sir Anthony Browne and Sir Anthony Denny, the head of the Privy Chamber, were below, but relieved and touched when told they had been sent by the King to enquire after her health. 'They say his Grace has offered you the services of his own physicians.'

How good it was of Henry to remember her when he was, by all accounts, in very low spirits. 'That's very kind, but Dr Cepher is highly competent, and might resent other doctors being called in. But please say I am deeply grateful for his Majesty's thoughtfulness, and will certainly call on his physicians if I have need.'

Her recovery was slow. Easter came and went, and April blossom bloomed like snow on the trees, but still Anna was suffering rigours, although not so badly as to make her stay in bed. The Duchess of Suffolk visited, bringing spring flowers and sweetmeats. At her suggestion, Anna sent a letter to Dr Butts, the royal physician, enquiring after the King's health, and asking if his Grace would send some of the cramp rings he himself had blessed on Good Friday, which were believed to be efficacious against cramps, convulsions and fits. The rings duly arrived, but with no word or letter from Henry, which was disappointing – and disconcerting.

Anna summoned Wymond Carew and instructed him to write on her behalf to someone in the Privy Chamber.

'I do not know who best to approach,' she told him, 'but I expect you will. Please say I have been very sad since I last wrote to his Grace, for he did not respond to my gentle enquiry after his health. It troubles me that he ignored it, for I fear he is unwell.'

'The King is in a low mood these days,' Carew told her. 'Do not take his silence amiss. I will write, though. Sir John Gates is the man; he gets things done. And I will ask my brother-in-law, Sir Anthony Denny, to declare your concern for the King to him.'

'That is most kind,' Anna said, realising that, of late, she had seen more kindness in Carew than of old. Maybe it was because she was unwell.

'Charity binds me to comfort the comfortless,' he said softly, 'and especially you, my lady.'

He left her astonished at this glimpse of the humanity she had not known him to possess.

A few days later, Anna began to feel better, and decided she fancied a change of scene. Soon, she and her household were on their way to Hever Castle, where she could convalesce in the tranquil Kent country-side. Slowly, her strength was returning, and she took care to walk daily in the gardens and rest in the afternoons.

One morning at the end of April, John Bekinsale came hurrying into the parlour to say they had visitors. 'A party of horsemen is coming down the hill, Madam.'

Anna hoped this was not another visitation from the lords of the Council. Just then, Franz von Waldeck dashed in, without ceremony.

'Madam, it's the King! The King is here!'

'Oh, Heaven save us!' Mother Lowe cried. But Anna was overjoyed. He had come; he had not spurned her kindness. She hastened out to the courtyard, and there he was, dressed in his hunting clothes, dismounting awkwardly from his horse.

'My dear sister Anna!' he cried, as she sank into her curtsey. He raised her up and kissed her on the lips, and she was saddened by how changed he was. The recent tragedy had made an old man of him.

'It is a pleasure to see your Majesty,' she told him. 'I trust you are in good health.'

'I get by,' he said, pulling off his gloves. 'I am pleased to see that you have recovered from your illness.'

'I am much improved, Sir,' she assured him, standing back to allow him to precede her into the castle. He was looking around the courtyard, a place that would once have been very familiar. This house must hold many memories for him.

'I've just ridden down from my lord of Suffolk's house at Beckenham,' he told her, as they entered the hall. 'He entertained me most royally there.'

'Alas, Sir, I fear I am unprepared, and cannot offer any royal entertainment. But, if you will give me leave to speak to my steward, I will ensure that you are served with a hearty meal.'

'Anna, I did not come to put you to any trouble. Some wine or good English ale would be sufficient.'

Anna sent for some, and they sat together in the parlour.

'Dr Butts has prescribed a plaster for you,' Henry said, drawing a small package from his doublet. 'He says it will comfort and ease the rigours, if you still have them. It's also good for aches and rheums that come from being in the cold or in draughts. It's made up of linseed, chamomile and hyssop.' Henry was fascinated by medicines, and even made up his own remedies. Anna had been impressed to find how knowledgeable he was. 'Linseed is good for inflammation,' he told her.

As she took the packet from him, he squeezed her hand. Their eyes met for a moment before he let it go. 'I have been worried about you, Anna,' he said. 'I did get your message, but I have been in no fit state of mind to see people of late. This late mishap with the Queen has caused me great grief. You know how much I loved her.' There were tears in his eyes. 'It was enough for me to hear that you were not in any danger. I could not have faced your sympathy.'

This time, it was Anna who reached over and took his hand. 'I do not know how she could have betrayed you so, knowing how greatly you loved her.'

'I have been asking myself that,' Henry sighed. 'The truth is, I am old and overweight, and I have a bad leg. I could not offer her what a young man could. Even so, she had made her vow to me, and owed me love and duty, not only as her husband, but as her King. Treason can never be right, or condoned. She had her just punishment. But, Anna, I miss her . . .'

'Of course you do,' she said. 'It is but natural. And it will ease with time.'

'The hardest thing is existing until it does,' he observed.

'I know,' she sympathised.

Henry cleared his throat and looked about him. 'Anna, I am noticing how pleasant you have made this house. The bright embroideries, the bowls of dried flowers, that painted fire screen – you've made your mark on it.'

'I embroidered the cushions myself,' she told him proudly. 'Would your Grace like to be shown around?'

'I would like nothing better,' Henry replied, and heaved himself to his feet.

Too late, she remembered that Anne Boleyn's portrait was still hanging in the long gallery. As they ascended the stairs, she tried desperately to think of something to say to justify its being there.

So far, Henry had not made any reference to having been at Hever in the past, or to the Boleyns, those silent presences no one was mentioning. At the end of the gallery, he paused to get his breath, bathing in the sun streaming in through the armorial glass window. Anna waited as he peered at a portrait of Wilhelm she had hung there – a drawing by the French artist Clouet, in which her brother looked far more handsome and cheerful than he did in the flesh.

'I am glad the amity between the Duke and me has not diminished,' Henry said. 'He has more sense than the Elector and his friends!'

They passed on, looking at portraits of Mutter, kneeling gravely before the Virgin, and Erasmus, wittily smiling in a little picture once owned by Vater.

'My father embraced Erasmus's teachings wholly,' Anna said.

'Your father and I had much in common. I admired Erasmus too. Alas, all those high ideals we shared got swept up in the religious quarrels. People now think that to be a humanist is to be a heretic.'

They were nearing the other end of the gallery, where the portrait hung. Anna was aware of Henry halting beside her. 'I thought they would have removed that,' he said tersely.

He had given her the perfect opening. 'So did I, Sir. I did not know what to do with it, for it is Crown property, so I left it here. I was going to ask what your pleasure is in the matter.'

'Take it down and put it away somewhere,' he said. 'You don't want that witch staring at you.'

'I will give the order,' Anna said. 'Shall we go downstairs? I can smell something good cooking. I think your Grace will like it.'

His Grace did. He stayed to dinner after all, his good humour restored, and it was not until late in the afternoon that he departed, bound for nearby Penshurst Place, where he was to stay the night.

'Penshurst is a fine house, Anna,' he said, as he kissed her goodbye. 'You must visit me there and I will show it to you. And now, farewell!' With a final squeeze of her hand, he mounted his horse, not without difficulty, and wheeled it around, his hand raised in a salute.

Chapter 23

1543

Anna was in her closet at Richmond, writing letters, when Wymond Carew knocked and popped his head around the door. 'Forgive me, Madam, but there is a royal messenger below, come to say that the King will be at Hampton Court shortly, and would like to have your company there.'

Anna rose. She had not seen Henry for some months, so she was delighted to receive this invitation. She dismissed her ladies' speculation that there might be a subtext to it.

'More than a year has passed since the death of the Queen,' Gertrude reminded her. 'His Grace might be looking for a new wife.'

'Nonsense!' Anna replied. Privately, she thought that Henry's infirmity might be a barrier to his marrying again.

They ignored her, being too busy looking out her most becoming gowns.

She had forgotten how big, how noisy and how teeming with people the court was. Her lodgings in Clock Court were spacious and comfortable, but they were on the ground floor and people were always walking past. She found herself longing for the peace of Richmond or Hever, yet she was looking forward to seeing Henry, and could not leave, of course, until after he had sent for her.

There were no women at court because there was no queen to be served. Anna had brought with her Mother Lowe and Katherine Bassett, who had pleaded to be taken. Anna and Katherine drew some masculine interest as they walked in the gardens or watched games of tennis or bowls – at least until the men realised who Anna was, and hastily averted their eyes. She wondered if they believed she was still untouchable – or that she might soon be their Queen again.

It was the French ambassador, Monsieur de Marillac, who enlightened her. Standing beside her as she was enjoying an archery contest, and laying on the courtesy, he assured her his master was her friend, especially in these present troubles of her brother with the Emperor. She did not know whether to trust his smooth Gallic charm, and could not decide whether his swarthy features were interesting or repellent, but she warmed to him.

'The Lady Mary was at court two months past,' he told her. 'Almost all the gentlemen of the court went out to welcome her, and the King met her as she entered the park and received her most lovingly.' Anna felt a pang that Henry had not afforded her the same courtesy.

Marillac was observing her closely, and she noticed his rival Chapuys in the group of spectators opposite. He was watching her too, but in a less friendly manner.

'Many are of the opinion that the King is thinking of marrying again,' Marillac said. 'Your Highness may not be aware that, during the past month, your brother's ambassador has been three or four times at court – where he has not been seen for many moons – and the last time, he came upon the King's summons.' He waited for her to digest that.

She had not seen or heard from Dr Harst for well over a year. She had thought all this business about her remarrying the King had been forgotten, and was alarmed to find that someone as well informed as Marillac thought it a real possibility.

'It may be that my brother has been asking England for aid against the Emperor.'

'It may indeed, Madam. Yet many think this embassy concerns yourself.'

'Well, Monsieur, this is the first I have heard of it.'

'The strange thing is, Madam, that when I asked some councillors what your brother's ambassador was doing at court, they told me he was not an ambassador, but a representative of yourself, there to assist you in your private affairs.'

Anna wondered what game was being played out behind the closed doors of the council chamber. 'That is news to me,' she said. 'I would far rather they were talking about aiding Kleve. Since last October, as you know, my brother has been in desperate need of King Henry's help.' She had endured months of anxiety since learning that the Emperor had defeated Wilhelm in battle and captured Guelders at last. Wilhelm's ally, King François, had not been able to come to his aid because he was fighting the Imperial forces in Italy. She feared for her family – and for her child. What if the Emperor was not content with Guelders?

'Let us hope King Henry can send aid, my lady. It is noble of you to put your brother's interests before your own.'

'My brother's interests are mine,' she said. 'They are more important to me than any other consideration.'

On the third day of her visit, Henry sent for her, and received her in his privy gallery. The day being rainy, they walked up and down for a space, Anna leaning on his arm.

'I am sorry I could not see you earlier,' he said. 'I have been plagued with business and petitioners. They never go away.' He smiled ruefully. 'And I had one of my headaches.'

'I trust you are better now,' Anna said.

'Greatly,' he told her. 'It's the close reading of all those official papers that does it. It keeps me up at night, and I can't see to read as well in candlelight as I used to.'

'Maybe your Grace needs new spectacles,' she suggested. 'That might alleviate the headaches.'

'I will think about that,' he said.

'I trust I find your Grace feeling happier than when I last saw you.'

Henry grinned. 'Much happier. And I'll tell you a secret I know I can trust you to keep. There is a lady . . .'

He was looking at her expectantly.

'I am *so* pleased for your Grace,' she said, meaning it. 'May I ask who the lady is?'

'Lady Latimer. I don't think you know her, for she is rarely at court.'

Anna tried not to betray her dismay. She knew of Lady Latimer, who was the sister of Mrs Herbert, one of her former ladies-in-waiting. Indignation mounted in her. She had not realised till now how much she had liked the idea of Henry taking her back as his queen, as opposed to the reality. It had been gratifying to know that people still hoped for her restoration. Now, learning he had set his sights on a commoner, whose sister had been her servant, she felt slighted and disparaged. At least Katheryn Howard had come from an ancient noble house!

'Her brother is captain of my Gentlemen Pensioners,' Henry was saying. 'She visits him from time to time, and is an occasional lady-in-waiting to the Lady Mary. She came with her to court in January, which was when I saw that in her which I knew I could love. But her husband has only just died, so I must be discreet for now.'

'And she returns your Grace's affection?' Anna chose the word with care. For all she knew, this widow might be Henry's mistress, although, given the size and the increasing infirmity of him, which had struck her today after so long an absence, she doubted he would have any use for a mistress.

'I like to think so,' he said. 'She was fond of her husband, although he was ill for a long time, so she was more nurse than wife. I am allowing her time to mourn.'

'I do hope your Grace will find true happiness,' Anna made herself say.

'Anna, you will be discreet? I know not if my suit will find favour.' He sounded like an eager young swain.

'Of course, Sir. I will speak of this to no one.' How could he not think his suit would find favour? He was the King!

'How *is* the Lady Mary?' Anna asked, not wishing to speak of Lady Latimer any more. She felt humiliated, disparaged . . .

'In good health, and much in demand as a godmother, she tells me.'

Anna thought it sad that Mary, who was now twenty-seven, was not yet a mother herself. Sometimes she could not fathom Henry's reasoning. Bastard though she might be, Mary was still his daughter. Yet here she was, unmarried still, and lavishing her thwarted maternal instincts on other people's children.

'I should love to see her,' she said.

'You may see her whenever you wish, Anna, with my blessing.'

'Then I will invite her to Richmond,' she told him. 'Thank you, Sir. It will be a great pleasure to me to have her company.'

Anna had been back at Richmond for a fortnight when Otho suddenly appeared in her privy chamber, jubilantly waving a letter.

'My lady, I have great news from my father in Kleve! Your brother has defeated the Emperor's troops at Sittard!'

'Oh, joy!' Anna leapt up, thrilled. 'That is the best news you could have brought me.'

Their eyes met. She could see in Otho's all the love and desire he felt for her, and it was tempting, in this surge of elation, to give him some sign that it was reciprocated. Perhaps it was plain to him anyway. It took all her resolve not to give him any encouragement.

But the news was wonderful, and cause for rejoicing. As her German servants hugged and congratulated each other, she called for wine, so that they could all toast Wilhelm's victory. God grant that the Emperor would now retreat and leave Kleve alone.

As summer bloomed, Anna took herself and her entourage down to Bletchingley, where she again had to suffer Thomas Cawarden's insufferable arrogance. This time, he took pleasure in informing her she was to be guest of honour at a feast he was hosting at Hextalls. And, of course, she could not refuse, after he had bragged of the trouble he and his wife had gone to on her behalf.

He had not thought to inform her that he had got married. He was not obliged to, but it would have been a courtesy. His bride, Elizabeth, was his complete antithesis, a pretty, self-effacing woman of good breeding who seemed content to defer to his every word and stay in his shadow. She was very pleasant to Anna, but rarely joined in the conversation at table, and it was her husband who barked orders to the servants.

Anna was disconcerted to find, on the high table, where Cawarden had seated himself in the place of honour at her right hand, some distinctive German pottery she had brought with her from Kleve. The last time she had seen these pieces, they had been in the court cupboard in her house nearby.

Sir Thomas saw her looking at them.

'These are mine, aren't they?' she asked.

He did not turn a hair. 'Yes, my lady. I thought they would be more fitting for your service than those I have.'

'Well, I don't mind, of course,' she said pointedly, but the gentle barb fell on deaf ears.

'I knew you wouldn't,' he smiled. Oh, he was exasperating!

Nevertheless, the food was good, and again Cawarden proved to be an attentive host. Anna was admiring the lavish displays of fruit set out for dessert when a gentleman in a tawny gown – one of the local worthies Sir Thomas had invited, no doubt wishing to impress them – asked if there was any news of the gentlemen at Windsor.

'Which gentlemen?' Anna asked, to be greeted by a bewildering silence.

'The gentlemen who were arrested for heresy in March,' Cawarden said at length. 'You had not heard? Or that I myself was arrested soon after? It was that bastard Gardiner – saving your pardon, my lady – who was behind it. Having rooted out what he was pleased to call a nest of heretics in the Chapel Royal at Windsor, he thought he might find more lurking in the court, and I, my dear wife here and ten others were arrested.'

Anna recoiled. She wanted nothing to do with heretics. It was all too easy for people to believe she herself was one, because of her connection to the German Lutherans, and showing favour to a tenant who had already attracted the attention of Bishop Gardiner might serve only to confirm people's suspicions.

'But I'd been fore-armed, thanks to Lady Latimer sending advance warning,' Cawarden was saying.

Was this the same Lady Latimer the King had spoken of? Nearly all the guests, except Anna's own people, seemed to know who Cawarden was talking about. Heavens, there *was* a nest of heretics here, and she was sitting in the midst of them! He was taking a huge risk in presuming that none of his visitors would report him.

'This Lady Latimer is a friend of yours?' she asked. 'And she is a Lutheran?'

'Indeed she is, Madam, one who is zealous for the Gospel.'

The sheer bravado of the man! Surely he knew he could be burned for this – and all his friends, for that matter. He must have seen the images and ornaments in Anna's chapel at Bletchingley, and realised she could not possibly be the Lutheran she was reputed to be. But evidently he chose to believe what he wanted to believe. She was beginning to think he was stupid.

'Despite the warning, several were imprisoned, including Elizabeth and me. None of us talked. Gardiner was fuming that the Devil himself could not make one of us betray the other, but we knew it was the hand of God, because, when the King found out, he promptly pardoned us all. Yet the poor wretches at Windsor are still under guard, and I fear Gardiner will have his way and make martyrs of them.'

'Aye,' several people agreed, looking distressed.

'Gardiner is the pawn of the Devil!' Cawarden sneered.

Anna said nothing. She was wondering how soon she could make her excuses and leave. Sir Thomas had placed her in an impossible position, for her first loyalty was to God, and then to the King. Yet Henry had pardoned Cawarden and the others. Evidently he did not believe them to be heretics – but he did not know the half of it!

'Was Lady Latimer arrested too?' Otho asked, looking as uncomfortable as Anna felt.

'No. Their inquiries did not lead them to her. And anyway, they could not have touched her. You all know why. We are hoping to see changes when she marries the King.'

Anna's jaw nearly dropped. Was the King really going to wed this heretic? It must have been she who influenced him to free Cawarden and his friends. Had he not smelled a rat?

'I had not heard the King was to marry again,' she said.

They all looked at her as if she was to be pitied, which had her bristling with annoyance. Cawarden even patted her hand, which she quickly drew away.

'I am happy for his Majesty,' she lied. 'He did tell me there was a special lady. And now, if you will excuse me, I have a headache and must say good night.'

Striding home in the dark, her attendants trailing behind her, Anna found herself fretting about the dangerous Lady Latimer. It sounded as if the King knew nothing of her heretical sympathies.

He loathed heresy; he saw it as a canker to be ruthlessly excised. Dare she warn him about the viper he was nurturing in his bosom?

She was still wrestling with her dilemma when they entered the hall and found a messenger wearing the stained livery of the Duke of Kleve waiting there.

'Lady Anna!' he cried in German, his face working in distress. 'I bring dread news. The Duke has suffered a terrible defeat at the hands of the Emperor, at Heinsberg, and has been forced to retreat. I am just come from the court, where I informed the King's Council of it.'

Defeat. Retreat. Such shameful words. And yet Wilhelm's courage had never been in doubt. As Anna knelt in her chapel, beseeching and bargaining with God to grant a reversal of his fortunes, she wished she could be with them all, Wilhelm and Mutter and Emily. It seemed wrong that she was living in safety and comfort here while they were in peril.

Later in June, Anna welcomed the Lady Mary to Richmond. Mary was good company, and generous in rewarding Anna's household for the services they performed for her. She even tipped the porters at the gate. She also insisted on giving Anna money towards the extra expenses of her kitchen, buttery and cellar.

'I would not hear of taking it!' Anna protested.

'My father instructed me to offer it,' Mary told her, and Anna subsided. It was another of Henry's generous gestures, the latest of several in recent months. Prices were rising higher and higher, and her allowance did not stretch as far as it had just three years before. Henry kept making up the deficit, ensuring she did not lack for comforts. She hoped he would continue to do so after he married – *if* he married, for there had, as yet, been no announcement.

'I've kept the Spanish silk your Grace sent me last year,' Anna said. 'I would appreciate your advice on what style I should follow, as I was planning to make it up into a gown while you are here.'

'I'd be delighted to help,' Mary replied. 'The stand-up collar is very popular now, so you'll need some buckram. Do you have any pearls with which you can edge it?'

Having cut out the pattern, they took their sewing baskets into the privy garden and settled down on a stone bench.

'Has your Grace heard of Lady Latimer?' Anna asked, unable to restrain herself.

'Yes.' Mary hesitated. 'I assume you're aware that my father has grown close to her.'

'I heard talk of it, and that she serves you.'

'She does, and I like her. She is a very intelligent woman, warm and attractive. She will probably be good for my father.' Obviously, Mary knew nothing of the lady's religious views.

'So they are to marry?'

'So people say, although he has not said anything to me. Why, are you disappointed, Anna? I heard speculation that you would be queen again.'

Anna made herself smile. 'Not at all. I love the King from my heart, but I've known for a long while that he will never take me back. Our marriage was dissolved for just causes, and nothing has changed. I ask only to remain his friend. He has been very good to me, you know.'

'I do know, and I know that he values your friendship too. He calls you his beloved sister.' Mary cast off and began re-threading her needle. 'I think we need not worry that Lady Latimer will be another Katheryn Howard.'

'And yet I sense that your Grace has some reservation about the King marrying her?' Anna ventured.

'I heard gossip among my ladies that she loves Sir Thomas Seymour, Queen Jane's brother. He's a handsome catch.' Mary sounded wistful.

'Over-bold too, I've heard,' Anna said. Seymour was a rogue, by all accounts. 'If the gossip be true, then Lady Latimer is in a difficult situation. For, if the King proposes marriage, she dare not refuse him.'

'I think she is very unhappy about it, but she is too loyal and discreet to say so. She gives nothing away, and she never mentions my father.'

'So you are worried that Sir Thomas Seymour might make trouble for her?'

'I am.' Mary looked distressed. 'He could compromise her. He's outspoken enough to do it – a liability, really.'

Anna could have mentioned something more deadly that could make trouble for Lady Latimer. 'Well, let us hope that she puts him off kindly, and firmly – if things progress,' she said.

'*If,*' Mary added.

Henry's eyes filled with tears as he kissed his bride, and everyone crowded into the Queen's holyday closet in the July heat applauded, including Archbishop Cranmer, who had performed the ceremony.

Anna followed with Margaret Douglas, the bride's chief attendant, as Henry led the new Queen Katharine through the ranks of wedding guests and out to the gallery beyond, where the avid courtiers thronged. He had himself bidden Anna attend his wedding. It was a signal honour, given how few could squeeze into the closet, yet she suspected that, for the avoidance of any doubt, he wanted her to be there to signify her approval of the marriage, and to show the world she still had no doubts about their divorce.

Her heart was heavy with the morning's bad news from Kleve, but she was making an effort to appear delighted for the couple. Let none think she was sour at being passed over. She *did* approve of Henry marrying again; she did not have to feign that. He needed more children, for the good of his realm. It was his smiling, auburn-haired bride, with her unremarkable features and her determined chin, of whom Anna could not approve. What had Henry seen in her? Katheryn Howard had been very pretty, so she had expected a woman with looks, but this one was nothing special – *and* she was a secret Lutheran. The reformers must have pushed her in the King's path. Anna was troubled. Should she have warned him? Well, it was too late now. It worried her to see him smiling so jubilantly. Pray God the new Queen never gave him cause to regret this day.

Returning Henry's smile, she realised that she herself could now think of marrying again – although, with Otho still bound to Hanna, there was little likelihood of it happening. Hopefully, she would be under less scrutiny after today, and could at least indulge in the occasional flirtation with him. And she needed some comfort now, especially after being informed, in a letter from Emily, that Mutter was gravely ill.

Had it been in her power, Anna would have rushed off to Kleve immediately, but Sir William Goring had told her it would take time to obtain a safe-conduct, even if one were to be forthcoming, for the Emperor's forces were occupying Guelders. It was doubtful, too, that the King would permit her to undertake such a perilous journey, for the war could break out again at any time. So she had put on a brave countenance and come here today to celebrate, trying not to think of her poor mother lying sick, with only Emily to comfort her.

As the guests gathered in the presence chamber to toast the royal pair, Anna turned to Margaret Douglas.

'I am glad to see you, my lady,' she said. It had been a long time since they had met.

'The pleasure is mine. You are looking so well, and most elegant in your English gown. Well, here we are again!' Margaret made a face. 'My uncle has grown so large that three men could fit into his doublet!'

'A fine burden the lady has taken on,' Anna observed, more tartly than she had intended, and then noticed Chapuys standing behind her. Pray God he had not heard her speaking so disrespectfully about the King, or it would be all over Europe within a week.

Margaret giggled. 'They might have to find other ways of doing it!'

Anna nudged her. Margaret saw who was nearby, and subsided. 'Oops,' she muttered. 'My uncle will have me in the Tower again!'

Anna peered round surreptitiously. Chapuys was deep in conversation with Sir Anthony Denny. He had not heard them, she decided.

She turned back to Margaret. 'Forgive me if I am poor company,' she murmured. 'I am in great grief, for I heard today that my mother is very ill.' Tears welled in her eyes.

'I am so sorry to hear that,' Margaret said, looking genuinely concerned. 'Let's slip down to the privy garden for a moment. I will tell my uncle you are feeling a little faint and need some air.' She swept over to Henry, who nodded, then looked across at Anna, frowning.

When they got down the stair, Anna leaned against the brick wall and let the tears fall.

'Sit down,' Margaret said, leading her to a seat beneath a hornbeam tree. 'You must be desperately worried.'

Anna nodded. 'At this moment, I would give up everything I have to be with my mother in Germany. I wish I could go now.'

'Oh, my dear Anna.'

'And I can't help it, but I feel humiliated by the King spurning me to marry this lady who can offer him so little. She is not as handsome as I am, she can bring him no great alliance, and there is no hope of her having children, seeing she had none by her two other husbands.'

Margaret was startled. 'You really thought he would take you back?'

'First I did not, and then I did. It was as if the wheel of fortune were spinning, and I never knew where it would stop. I did not want it, really. It was the idea of it, the being wanted as queen. And now . . . I could have been contented if he had married a French princess, say, but . . . Forgive me, I should not have spoken. I've probably committed all kinds of treason.'

Margaret patted Anna's shoulder. 'Don't worry. It helps to unburden yourself, I have found, and I'm the one person who can understand. I know what it's like to be accused of treason – and condemned.' She shuddered.

Anna wondered if she dared confide to Margaret what she knew about Queen Katharine. Her secret knowledge was a burden she did not relish bearing alone, and if ever it came out that she had concealed that information, she might be deemed guilty of abetting heresy. And it *could* come out, for Thomas Cawarden and his friends were rashly indiscreet about their dangerous activities, and had already come under suspicion. They might say she had known, and even approved. Oh, what should she do?

'Try not to brood on it,' Margaret said, misreading the cause of her silence. 'Queen Katharine is gentle and kind. I am to be her chief lady-of-honour, and she has been most gracious to me.'

Anna deemed it best to stay silent and pray that Cawarden and his associates never fell foul of the law. She could not be responsible for setting in motion a chain of events that might bring him and others to the stake.

'We should return,' she said, rising. 'Thank you for listening.'

When they got back upstairs, there was the King, tall, massive and expansive, coming to embrace his dear niece and his dear sister, and to ask if Anna was feeling better. He beamed as he received their good wishes and presented to them his new Queen.

'Kate,' he said, 'this is the Lady Anna.'

Katharine smiled charmingly as Anna curtseyed, and extended her hand to be kissed. Already, Anna thought resentfully, she had the poise of a queen. 'It is a pleasure to meet you, my Lady Anna,' she said.

'The pleasure is mine,' Anna answered, in what she hoped was a friendly tone. 'Please accept my warmest congratulations. I am overjoyed for you both.'

A week later, Henry came alone to Richmond, to dine with Anna.

'I am glad you like Katharine,' he said, tucking eagerly into a meat pie flavoured with honey and mustard. 'Mmm, is this another of your German dishes, Anna? It's delicious. I swear, no one keeps as good a table as you do.'

'I thought your Grace would enjoy it,' Anna said, pleased. She was delighted that he had come, having feared that such visits might cease now he had remarried.

After dinner, he played his lute for her, and they strolled down to the river and stood there for a while watching the boats pass. A party of merrymakers, playing loud music in their barge, waved to them, then realised who it was they were saluting. Henry roared with laughter when he saw their faces. 'A very good evening to you all!' he called.

All too soon, it was time for him to leave. As he kissed Anna on the jetty, he took her hands. 'You are still my dearest sister. That will never change. I will see you again soon. And, if you lack for anything, let my Council know.'

* * *

In early August, Anna was deeply perturbed to hear that the Windsor heretics had been burned at the stake. She imagined how the news would affect Cawarden and his colleagues, and Queen Katharine, of course, who must never betray her dismay to the King.

She was busying herself making fruit tarts with Meister Schoulenburg when, to her astonishment, a page appeared and announced that Dr Harst had come to see her. Hastily she took off her voluminous apron, and hurried to her presence chamber.

'This is an unexpected pleasure,' she said, extending her hand. Then she saw his face.

'Madam, you must prepare yourself for the worst news. Kleve has been overrun by the armies of the Emperor.'

Anna felt faint. It was almost worse than the news she had long dreaded to hear, that her mother had died. She had known of Charles's determination to have Guelders, but had never dreamed he would take Kleve itself.

'This is terrible,' she breathed. 'What of my brother, and my mother? She is ill, and this will nearly kill her.' *And what of my little boy?* That was a question she dared not ask.

'She is at Schloss Düren, and appears to be safe for the moment,' Harst replied. 'I have not heard that the town has been taken, but the news comes piecemeal, of necessity.'

'How could this happen?' Anna was beside herself with horror and anxiety.

'The Emperor surprised Duke Wilhelm by suddenly appearing in Flanders with a great army. There was nothing the Duke could do. Now the Emperor has demanded that King Henry break off diplomatic ties with Kleve and send me home, but the King has refused. He summoned me this morning and told me he would not do it, and that I must stay.'

Bless him! Anna thought. Henry would come to Wilhelm's aid, she was sure of it.

'It is my mother I am most worried about,' she said, wringing her hands. 'I want to go home and be with her.' *And I need desperately to know that Johann is safe.*

'I too wish to leave, Madam, however well meant the King's intentions. Yet, as he warned me, the situation in Kleve is too perilous to permit my return. We dare not attempt it. Imagine if you were taken hostage.'

Anna realised Harst was speaking the truth. She felt like bursting with frustration.

'We must rely on the Duke's diplomacy to save the day,' he told her. 'I understand he is appealing to King François for aid.'

'I pray he will get it,' Anna said, 'and that God will move the French King to compassion for the plight of our country.' She was not optimistic. François had been too preoccupied with his own problems to aid Kleve last time.

Waiting for news was dreadful; not hearing anything was worse. But worst of all were the tidings that came late in August. The Emperor had taken and sacked Düren, the chief town of Jülich.

'Six hundred houses have been fired,' Harst mourned. 'There was great panic and bloodshed. Madam, they burned Schloss Düren too.'

'My mother was there!' Anna shrieked. 'What news of her?'

'Alas, there is, as yet, no word.' Harst looked near to tears himself. 'I wish I could offer your Highness more comfort.'

Horrific images filled Anna's head, of her mother trapped, or overcome by smoke and flames . . . As she broke down in tearing sobs, gasping out her grief, she felt strong arms around her, and there was Dr Harst, forgetting all the rules of etiquette and holding her gently, weeping himself, and Mother Lowe, embracing them both, tears flooding her cheeks.

'What is amiss? Is someone hurt?' Otho had come bursting through the door. Harst left Anna and Mother Lowe to support each other, and she heard him relate in lowered tones what had happened.

Otho was visibly moved. 'Would you like me to go to Kleve now to discover what has happened to your lady mother?' he offered, his voice hoarse with emotion. 'I can go through France, and approach from the south. King François is our ally; he will not prevent me.'

'That is so brave and kind of you,' Anna sobbed. 'I have not the words to thank you.'

'It might be best to wait for news,' Dr Harst said. 'It might well arrive sooner than you can get word to us.'

'Yes, wait,' Anna said, seeing the wisdom in his advice. 'But for only a day or so, for I do not know how I can bear the not knowing. Do you know if any of our other castles have been sacked?' She was thinking of Schloss Burg, hard by Solingen, and trembling in fear lest Johann had been caught up in the Imperial onslaught. Düren was not that far from Solingen.

'Not that I have heard,' Harst said. 'But I have been assured that the Duke and your sister are safe.'

No news was good news, Anna told herself, praying as she had never prayed before that Mutter and Johann were still alive.

The waiting was cruel and hard, especially when they got word that the Imperial forces were now marching through Jülich unopposed, and so terrifying the people that every town was surrendering its keys to the Emperor. But there was no word of the Duchess's whereabouts, and Anna was beginning to give up hope that she had survived the fire. Even if she had, the occupation of her own duchy of Jülich would be the end of her.

Early in September, Dr Harst sought out Anna, his countenance so heavy that she shrank from hearing what he had to say and gripped Mother Lowe's hand for support.

'Madam, I have received word of your lady mother. God be thanked, she did not die in the fire.'

'Oh, that is the most blessed relief!' Anna cried. 'But was she hurt?'

'Not in the fire, but I am deeply sorry to tell your Highness that she died four days afterwards. Please accept my profound condolences.'

Anna closed her eyes, trying to ward off the pain and grief that were overwhelming her. She was remembering Mutter's gentleness, her devotion, her care for her children and her abiding love for Vater. She was united with him now, in Heaven, for surely a soul as pious as hers would not have suffered long in Purgatory.

'How did it happen?' she asked, too numb for tears.

'Dr Olisleger writes that she fled the castle in some terror,' Dr Harst told her. 'Her attendants reported that she was almost out of her wits with anger over the loss of her country. In her state of health, the ordeal proved too much for her. Mercifully, she did not live to see all Jülich subdued.'

'What of Kleve?' Mother Lowe asked anxiously, wrapping her arm protectively around Anna, who was desperately trying to come to terms with her loss.

'I fear that few towns in Kleve could resist such an army as the Emperor has under his command. The taking of Düren has made them all afraid. Dr Olisleger predicts there will be no resistance, and that the Imperial forces will cut a swathe through to Nijmegen, by which time the town of Kleve and all the country on that side of the Rhine will be at the Emperor's commandment.'

The world as Anna had known it was falling to pieces. Her grief for Kleve was almost as intense as that for her mother. Suddenly she was howling at the awfulness, the unjustness of it all.

The white linen cap and long veil seemed an appropriate choice; it felt fitting, and oddly comforting, to be mourning Mutter in a German headdress. It made a simple contrast to the heavy black velvet gown with its wide partlet, stand-up collar and tight sleeves. No jewellery, apart from the rosary hanging from a chain around her waist. Her face stared back at her from the mirror, pale and etched with grief. It had been a fortnight now, and still the pain of loss was raw. And now she must rouse herself and receive Dr Harst, whose arrival had just been announced.

She thought she had reached the nadir of despair, and that she could not feel worse, but she was wrong. Harst's gloomy face struck fear into her heart. His news was shocking. Wilhelm had conceded defeat and formally submitted to the Emperor.

'He had no choice, my lady,' Harst said, as she reeled from the blow. 'The King of France appears to have abandoned him, and he is ravaged by grief for your lady mother. He met with the Emperor at Venlo, and came dressed in deepest mourning. He was made to kneel before his Imperial Majesty in submission and sign a treaty ceding Guelders and Zutphen. In return, he was allowed to keep his duchies of Kleve and Jülich, although there will be some diminishing of the autonomy he has hitherto enjoyed. Furthermore, he has agreed to divorce Jeanne d'Albret so that he can marry a niece of the Emperor.'

Anna listened to it all with mounting shame. She could not bear to think how humiliating it must have been for Wilhelm, that proud man, to suffer such public abasement and dishonour. If *she* felt she could not face the world on account of her country's degradation, how must he be feeling? And this while they were mourning their mother. The only consolation was that, now the war was over, Johann was safe. To Anna's inestimable relief, Mother Lowe had heard from the Schmidts that Solingen had not been touched by the invaders.

'I will go to King Henry myself and beg his aid,' Anna said. 'He will help, I am sure.'

'I would advise against it, Madam,' Harst replied gloomily. 'There is no sign at court of compassion for Kleve. The councillors made it very clear to me that the King will not risk a war with the Emperor.'

Another blow. Anna had thought Henry would welcome a chance to prove his friendship with Kleve; she had thought he would intervene for her, as well. Her disappointment was profound.

'There is nothing to be done, my lady,' Dr Harst said sadly. 'At least your brother has retained his duchy, and rules there still. I doubt the Emperor will interfere in the daily business of government.'

'Yes, but we enjoyed such independence in Kleve! My father would be horrified if he knew what had happened.'

'Your father would have made the same choice. Who dares withstand the might of the Holy Roman Empire?'

Late that autumn, after she had put off her mourning, Henry invited Anna to court. Still smarting over Wilhelm's humiliation, she arrived resolved to ask the King if there was anything he could do, but soon realised, from his commiserations over Kleve, that he too was tied, and there was no point. So she made small talk with Queen Katharine, joined her and Henry to feast and watch the courtiers dancing, and tried not to think of how much the King had aged since she had last seen him in July. It grieved her to see him declining so fast. If only he could lose some weight, he would feel better, and his leg might improve, affording him better mobility. But there he sat, with rich food piled high before him, and a goblet that was continually being refilled. And no one dared give him any wise advice.

She was glad to get back to Richmond, glad too to be told by Wymond Carew that he had been offered the prestigious post of treasurer to the Queen, and would be leaving her service.

'It is a great honour, and I am very pleased for you, Mr Carew,' she told him. 'I am pleased also to hear that your surveillance is to be withdrawn. I trust I am no longer under suspicion of intriguing against the King my brother, whom I would never hurt.'

Carew had the grace to look uncomfortable. 'I was but obeying orders, Madam. I have never doubted your loyalty.'

She let it go. The man was leaving; soon she would be free of him. 'Who is to replace you as my receiver general?' she asked.

'On my recommendation, my kinsman Thomas Carew.' Thomas was a kindly, cultivated man who had been serving Anna as a gentleman of her chamber. She could not imagine him ever agreeing to spy on her.

'The choice pleases me very well,' she said, 'although I trust his duties will be limited to those of his office!'

'I have not heard otherwise, Madam,' Carew said stiffly.

She smiled at him. 'I wish you well in your new position,' she said.

It came to her that night, as she snuffed out the candle and curled up for sleep, that, since she was no longer to be spied on, certain possibilities might open out to her. The image of Otho's beloved face came to mind – and that of little Johann, in faraway Solingen, although he would not be so little now: he was twelve, and no doubt she would not recognise him. He was three years into his apprenticeship, and excelling at his craft, Mother Lowe had told her. Dare she now – if it could be arranged – bring him over from Kleve and install him in her household, through the good offices of Otho? Surely there could be little risk. No one would know who he was, least of all Johann himself. And they could be together, a family of sorts, her, Otho and their son.

The more she thought about it, the more it seemed feasible. Yet was it fair to uproot the boy from all he knew? Was she being selfish?

She broached the matter with Otho, having invited him and some of her other gentlemen out riding so that she could put the white osprey Duke Albert of Prussia had sent her through its paces. It had come to England, fully trained, with a gift of a dozen falcons for King Henry, and the King had sent it on to her. It was a fine hawk, and she was pleased that Duke Albert, one of the Protestant princes of Germany, had thought of her.

Riding ahead of the rest through Richmond Park, with Otho keeping abreast, she confided to him her idea.

'There is now no chance of my remarrying the King, so I have no political importance here. I am no longer being spied upon. I can, at last, lead the life of a private person. Why should I not employ someone from Kleve in my household – as an old favour to a friend, say?'

Otho appeared torn. 'I want to be with our son as much as you do, Anna, but I still think it would be wrong to bring him here now. Let us wait until he is a young man and has finished his apprenticeship, then I will make some pretext to visit Solingen and renew my offer to find him a position in England. By then, people will have largely forgotten about your marriage to the King, and the risk of scandal will be far less.'

Johann would not finish his apprenticeship for four years. It seemed an eternity. Anna knew that Otho spoke sense – and that he would keep his word. But how, now that the idea was born, would she ever find the patience to wait so long?

Chapter 24

Anna stood with the ladies Mary and Elizabeth and the duchesses of Richmond and Suffolk, watching the King and Queen receive the Admiral of France, the new French ambassador. The presence chamber at Greenwich was packed with the lords and ladies summoned to do him honour. Anna felt honoured too, to be accorded a place beside the King's daughters, whom Henry had restored to the royal succession two years since, in order of seniority after Prince Edward.

The Lady Mary stood stiff and unsmiling, for she was her Spanish mother's daughter through and through, and could never love the French. No doubt she was regretting the retirement of Messire Chapuys, who had left England last year. But he had never been a friend to Anna, unlike the faithful Dr Harst, who had also gone home, many months ago, having no need to remain. Anna missed him, and the news he had brought of the court and the wider world at large. Now she had to rely on her household for it, or her occasional guests. She did not entertain so much these days, for she could not afford to, even with the King supplementing her income.

The Lady Elizabeth was smiling graciously at all, basking in this rare chance to be a focus of attention. She had her mother's dark eyes, and even now, at the tender age of twelve, she knew how to use them to effect. She was accomplished and learned – and very vain.

It was the King who drew Anna's eye most. When he had raised and embraced her on her arrival, she had seen that he was in much pain, and that he could not stand for long. He had collapsed on his chair of estate immediately afterwards and signed to a page to bring his footstool. Anna saw that it was stained with pus, which was seeping through the bandages under his hose.

That evening, during a lull in the festivities to mark the ambassador's coming, the Lady Mary sought out Anna.

'I am worried about my father,' she muttered, hardly audible against the chatter going on around them. 'He is ill. Anyone can see it. The Queen says he spends most of his time in his secret lodgings, and seldom stirs out of his chamber, unless it is to walk in his privy garden – when he is able. I think she is having a difficult time, for his temper is worse than ever. His legs give him so much pain that he becomes exceedingly perverse, and is inclined to lash out on the slightest provocation.'

Anna took Mary's hand and squeezed it. 'I am aware his health is failing. It is plain how badly his legs trouble him.'

'He tries to hide it, but you can see by his face that it is worse than he pretends.' Mary looked distressed. 'He cannot go up and down stairs now; he has to be hauled up and down by a pulley device, and he has had two chairs made with extended arms, so he can be carried to and fro in his galleries and chambers.' She glanced around at the company, then bent close to Anna's ear. 'Let us walk in the gallery, where we can be private. We might be overheard here.'

The gallery, by good fortune, was deserted. They sat down on a window seat.

'In faith, Anna, I do not see how my father can last much longer,' Mary said. 'And then we shall have my brother, and I fear for us, and for England, because he is being tutored by Cambridge gospellers – heretics all, I do not doubt! And she, the Queen, encouraged it.'

Anna awoke to the bleak prospect of an England ruled by reformers. No wonder Mary was so worried.

'You heard what happened last month? Bishop Gardiner tried to have her arrested for heresy, but she managed to convince the King of her innocence.'

Anna wondered if she should tell Mary what she knew of Katharine Parr's activities before her marriage to the King, but shrank at the prospect of what the consequences might be, should Mary think fit to tell Henry. So she kept silent. She had spent these last years living contentedly away from court, far from the intrigues and jealousies that pervaded it, and she was looking forward to going home, to Otho, who was now dearer to her than he had ever been, and the people she now regarded as her family. And Johann was fifteen now. Only a few more months to wait . . .

'I trust she has profited from the experience,' she said. 'It may have jolted her into an appreciation of her error.'

'I don't think she would call it that,' Mary said, tart. 'No, Anna, the future is very uncertain for those of us who are of the true faith. We must pray that my father lives longer, but already the wolves are chafing at the muzzle for a new order. And there is nothing to be done about it!' Her voice was bitter. 'Do they not fear for their immortal souls?' She sighed deeply, fingering her rosary. 'We should rejoin the company, lest we are missed.'

Again and again, over the days that followed, Anna was struck anew by the luxury and lavishness of the court, which seemed greater than ever. She dined every day, with the princesses, at the King's table; in the afternoons, she enjoyed the chase and, in the evenings, she sat next to Queen Katharine as they watched the extravagant masques staged every night in honour of the French Admiral. Afterwards, she was among the privileged guests invited to gather privately with the King and Queen in the new banqueting house that had been erected in the gardens, an exquisite small pavilion hung with tapestry and furnished with cupboards laden with gold plate set with rich stones and pearls, and salvers of sweetmeats. Henry, Anna saw, was acting as if he still had many years ahead of him, doing his best to ignore the pain in his legs and determinedly driving himself to lead as normal a life as possible.

From Greenwich, the court moved to Hampton Court for yet more triumphs and celebrations, and Anna was commanded by the Council to accompany it. It seemed as if Henry, recalling the glorious days of his youth, was bent on one last great festival before the darkness closed in on him. She was aware of an air of expectancy, of suppressed speculation – suppressed, of course, because it was treason to predict or even imagine the King's death.

One evening, she was on her way to sup with the King when she encountered Susanna Gilman in a gallery. Susanna looked at her warily, yet Anna found she no longer felt any rancour towards her erstwhile friend. What had happened six years ago no longer mattered now. So she smiled and asked after Susanna's health, and walked on, feeling pleased that there remained no ill feeling between them.

She left Hampton Court on a blazing-hot August day, weeping in her litter because some intuitive instinct told her she would not see Henry again. He had sent for her to bid her farewell. She had found him in a reflective mood, and suspected he too had an inkling that his time was short, for he had held her tight in their last embrace, and there had been tears in his eyes as he looked into her face.

'You have ever been a good friend to me, Anna, more than I deserve. You have such excellent qualities and virtues, gifts of which I recognise myself both bare and barren. But for such small qualities as God has endowed me with, I render to His goodness my most humble thanks, and I thank him, most heartily, that I have enjoyed the friendship of a good woman such as you.' He had let her go and kissed her hand in the most courtly fashion. 'Love, dread and serve God,' he'd exhorted her. 'Be in charity with all.' It was as if earthly concerns no longer mattered to him, only his immortal soul.

'I have loved your Grace as a sister,' Anna had told him, 'and I am ever grateful for your goodness to me.' She had been remembering all the money he had sent her, the properties he had transferred to her on the Duke of Suffolk's death, to augment her income, and the sum he had outlaid to Dr Cepher last autumn, when she had suffered a recurrence of tertian fever. 'May God keep your Grace in health, and bless you.'

'Farewell, dear Anna.' Henry had bent and kissed her on the lips. She had curtseyed, and was conscious of his eyes lingering on her as she left his presence.

She returned to Richmond feeling emotional, and informed her household that they would be removing to Bletchingley. She hoped a change of scene would lift the pall of sadness that lay over her.

When they rode out to Bletchingley, Otho was beside her, as he always was these days. For the last year they had secretly been lovers again, not in the fullest sense – Anna was resolved not to risk any more illicit pregnancies – but in every other way, and her household, who must have noticed, had turned a blind eye. Anna knew, from the way her servants treated her, that she was much beloved, and she was grateful that they were so protective towards her. She sensed they thought she deserved some happiness, after all the troubles she had suffered; and things became easier that August, when Hanna left Otho in England and went back to her family in Kleve. There was much disapproval, and sympathy for the abandoned husband; no one begrudged him the love he had found. Yet Anna and Otho were discreet, and took care never to make demonstrations of their affection in public. For Anna, it was enough just to be with him, especially on this beautiful summer day, riding through the pleasant leafy lanes of Surrey.

Word of their coming had been sent ahead the day before, and Thomas Cawarden, now knighted by the King, was waiting to receive them. Anna was still wary of him, still worrying that he was involved in some nefarious activity or other. He seemed to have a finger in every pie, and to have cultivated everyone of standing round about, and in the court. He was good at putting pressure on people.

She had to concede that Sir Thomas was a diligent steward at Bletchingley. He cared for the place as if it were his own, and no doubt he was hoping that one day it would be. It was his proprietorial attitude that irked, and sometimes infuriated, her.

He had done well for himself, as he never ceased reminding her, and was now doing so again over the supper he had prepared in her honour. Two years ago, when the King had enjoyed a brief period of respite from his ailments and led an army into France and taken Boulogne, Sir Thomas had been appointed Master of Revels and Tents, with the responsibility of providing tents for the troops. He had also led a company of horsemen and foot soldiers, and it was for these services that he had been knighted.

'These days,' he informed the company, 'his Majesty licenses me to keep forty liveried retainers. I shall need a larger house to keep them in!' Anna was aware of him casting his eye over the splendours of her dining chamber. Her eyes met Otho's, and she knew he was having the same thoughts.

Sir Thomas leaned towards her. 'Madam, you will be pleased to hear that the King has granted me the reversion of Hextalls, as well as other lands in Surrey, Kent and Sussex.'

The arrogance of the man! Hextalls was hers too, so why would she be pleased to hear that it would come to him on her death? She might yet marry and bear children; she was, after all, only thirty. Yet this insufferable fellow had deprived her posterity of part of its inheritance.

'You'll be looking for the reversion of Bletchingley next, Sir Thomas!' She said it as a jest, but meant it as a warning.

There was a pause, then he laughed. 'There would certainly be enough room here for all my retainers!'

Sir William Goring came to Anna's rescue. 'Sir Thomas, you may not have heard that the Duke of Cleves has married the Emperor's niece, the Princess Maria of Austria.'

'We are all very pleased for him,' Anna said. She omitted to add that Emily had written to say that the new Duchess Maria was very nice, but positively ugly, for she had the notoriously long Habsburg jaw and a face like a horse. Anna had smiled when she read that, glad to see that her sister was still her old irrepressible self. Emily had never married, but that might be remedied now that Wilhelm was allied to the Emperor, who seemed to have an endless store of relatives.

'My brother is delighted with his bride,' Anna confirmed. 'Certainly she is more amenable than the first one!'

'How long will you be staying at Bletchingley, my lady?' Sir Thomas asked.

'Oh, I think for quite some time,' she replied, and saw the fleeting dismay in his eyes. Of course, while she was elsewhere, he could treat the place as his own. She would not have put it past him to move into the great house in her absence. 'I do so love it here,' she went on, feeling mischievous. 'I have decided I prefer it above my other houses, and mean to make it my chief residence.' She was enjoying herself now, seeing his discomfiture. 'I intend to undertake some improvements.'

'May I ask what they will be, Madam?'

'I will tell you when I have decided, Sir Thomas.'

The next day, she looked around the house, with Otho, Sir William and Mr Chomley, her cofferer, in attendance, and drew up a list of every improvement she wanted to make. She meant to establish her presence here, and transform the house to reflect her own tastes.

She summoned a wood carver and asked him to make a magnificent chimney piece in the antique style for her great chamber, instructing him to include the figure of the King. She ordered carved wooden panels bearing her initials and emblems.

She set in train the building of new dwellings on the estate for her poorer tenants, a communal brewhouse for their convenience, and a tavern for their recreation. She wanted her people to look upon her as a kind benefactor.

Soon, Bletchingley was filled with the smells of sawdust and fresh paint. Anna spent hours with her ladies making hangings, curtains, drapes for beds, and even rugs. It was good to have a project on which to focus, and to make the house her own.

By the time winter drew in, Bletchingley was looking brighter and more colourful, and everything smelt so fresh. Looking around her, admiring it, Anna felt even more possessive towards the house.

They were preparing for Christmas now, but in an atmosphere of sorrow, for the cold weather had taken its toll. Early in Advent, poor Dr Cepher had caught a chill and died of it, and the chaplain had followed him to the grave within days. Anna had ordered that they be buried in the parish church, and attended the committal service herself, thinking how sad it was to be summoned from this world as the festive season approached.

On the day after the funerals, Sir Thomas came to look at the improvements Anna had made, and pointed out that the roof needed attention and some of the window frames were leaking.

'Your Highness needs to address these things, or the problems will get worse,' he warned.

'But I have spent all my money,' she pointed out, keeping him standing. 'I must wait until the next quarter.'

He lost patience. 'Madam, it is a question of priorities. It is foolhardy to lavish a fortune on a chimney piece when the roof has holes in it and the rain can get in.'

'*I* will decide on the priorities here,' Anna snapped, outraged that he felt he could speak to her like that. 'I marvel you did not tell me that repairs were needed before I outlaid money on refurbishment. It's your job as steward to know these things.'

'I had not then undertaken an inspection of the roof,' he snarled. 'It's not easy to access.'

'Well, we shall just have to wait until March,' she said.

'There is another matter I wish to raise,' he hissed, clearly furious. 'Since you first came here, I have given you all the wood you could need for your fires. Yet your servants are felling good trees in the parks for charcoal, wasting the timber. Quite blatantly, they told me it was theirs to do as they pleased with, and I could not deny them. They were about to take forty loads away! I have impounded it all. They do not need that wood for fuel, so I suspect they are secretly planning to sell it to the iron foundries in Sussex and make a profit!'

Anna made to answer, but Cawarden held up his hand. 'That is not all, Madam. After I delivered the timber you requested for the improvements to the house, your servants, without my consent, felled a great many more trees, and built four new houses of timber. This cannot be justified by the law. They even took my wood-axe to help build a brewhouse and a tavern, and—'

'Will you let me speak?' Anna interrupted, stopping him in full flight. 'First, Sir Thomas, shall we get one thing clear? The trees are all on *my* lands, and are therefore mine. My servants cut down the trees on my authority, and they were to sell the charcoal on my authority too. You must be aware that, nowadays, money does not go as far as it did, and that I am no longer a wealthy woman. I do not have to explain myself to you, but, as a courtesy, I will tell you that I need the profits from the sales to the foundries, so you will let them have that wood. No, Sir Thomas, I will finish what I have to say! As for the law preventing me from building houses, I know nothing of that, but I am sure that, if I asked the King's Majesty, he would give me permission. I have never heard of a lord or lady being prevented from providing houses for their tenants!'

Sir Thomas was almost purple with rage. 'Madam, you and your servants are running down the estate!'

'That is my concern, Sir – unless, of course, you are looking to the future and anticipating that it might be yours?'

He glared at her. 'Madam, woodland needs managing. It is my duty to see to that.'

'And this is my property. I will not allow you to criticise me for acting for my own benefit and that of others.'

He stood there fuming, then turned on his heel and stalked out without a word.

'There's a man to be wary of,' Mother Lowe observed. 'He has ambitions, that one.'

'Don't I know it!' Anna muttered.

One afternoon, as Anna was making a Christmas wreath for the table, Sir William Goring asked for a word.

'Madam, Sir Thomas Cawarden has complained that your servants are wasting good timber and cutting down trees without his permission.'

'They had my permission!' she said firmly. 'I have had the matter out with him. Really, Sir William, I am sick of the man's presumption.'

'Yes, Madam, he does rather exceed his remit. Fear not, I have persuaded him to let you have the forty loads of timber he has been keeping back. However, he wants you to acknowledge that they are a gift to you from him.'

'What?' Anna was seething with rage. 'How can he make me a gift of my own property? The impertinence of it!'

'I did point that out, my lady. He also asks you to make a present of an apron to the park-keeper's wife, as recompense for the trouble the tree-felling caused her.'

'The answer is no,' Anna declared. 'On both counts.'

Cawarden would not take no for an answer. Grudgingly he surrendered the wood, but he became ever-more vehement when she permitted her servants to cut down more trees. The quarrel dragged on, with considerable bad feeling, especially on the part of Anna's servants, who resented being shouted at for merely doing what their mistress had ordered.

Anna considered appealing to the King to have Cawarden removed from his post as steward of Bletchingley. But she had heard that Henry was unwell, and did not like to disturb him. Sir Thomas had no such scruples, however. One day, near Christmas, he disappeared. When he returned later, he was triumphantly brandishing a document bearing the royal seal.

'You see, Madam,' he said nastily, 'his Majesty understands the need for careful management of an estate, especially one in the gift of the Crown.' He thrust the paper under her nose.

As she read it, she felt her anger rising. Henry had granted his faithful Sir Thomas Cawarden the reversion of Bletchingley with its parks and all the lands attached to it. It would be his upon her death.

Fury got the better of her. 'You may now be the next owner here, Sir Thomas,' she seethed, 'but, while I live, Bletchingley is mine, and you will run it as I order. Now go. You are dismissed.' As he went out, smirking, she resolved to ask the King to dismiss him. She was sure that, when Henry learned of his insolence, he would withdraw the grant.

Her resolve hardened when Sir William Goring came to give his resignation. 'My lady, I have been offered a place in the King's Privy Chamber. I did think twice about it, as it has been a privilege to serve you, but of late there have been too many trials. You know who I mean . . .'

Anna understood, although her heart was sinking. She had a great liking for her chamberlain. 'Of course you must accept the post, Sir William. It is a great honour. Do you know who will replace you?'

'I have recommended Sir John Guildford, Madam. You will recall that the King awarded him a pension earlier this year, in acknowledgement of his good service to you.' Sir John, a lawyer who had sat in Parliament and held various offices under the Crown before he joined her household, was a good administrator and reliable, affable and witty too.

'I am sure he will prove most efficient,' Anna said, 'yet I am sorry to be losing you.'

As Sir William bowed himself out, she prayed that Sir John Guildford would be as staunch in taking her part against Sir Thomas Cawarden. His presence blighted all her pleasure in Bletchingley, and it was utterly galling to know that he would get this beautiful house on her death. She resolved to go to court herself and ask the King to have him removed. She would tell Henry the truth!

Part Four

Repudiated Wife

Chapter 25

1547–1549

January came in on a tide of hail. It was freezing cold, and the wind whistled through the vast chambers, obliging Anna to have the leaking windows sealed up, much to Cawarden's unconcealed amusement. It snowed, and the roads became impassable, then waterlogged with the thaw. She could not go to court, so nothing could be done about Sir Thomas.

Early in February, the weather improved, and Anna decided she would travel to Whitehall on the morrow.

A fire was crackling merrily in the hearth, and there was the pleasant scent of burning applewood in her chamber. She began looking through her gowns, wondering what to wear to court. As she was rubbing at a grease spot on her tawny velvet, Mother Lowe knocked and said a royal messenger was asking to see her. Already, she could hear him thumping up the stairs. He had not even waited for her to go down to receive him.

He knelt before her. 'My lady, I bring heavy news. The King is dead.'

She cast off her bright attire and put on the mourning clothes she had worn for her mother. She ordered her whole household, down to the scullions, to wear black. She re-read the letters the King had sent her, and cried over them. She got out the jewels he had given her, and pressed her lips to their cold surfaces. She could not believe he had gone from her – and from England. What would become of her adopted land now that a boy king ruled over it? Would it turn Protestant, as the Lady Mary had feared? And would young Edward be as good a friend to her as Henry had been? It was a lot to expect from a nine-year-old child who barely knew her, she thought dismally.

Needing a change of scene, and having no stomach for repeatedly running into Sir Thomas Cawarden, she sought refuge for herself and her household at Hever Castle, where she could grieve in peace. She wanted something to mark the King's passing, so she commissioned a local artist to paint her in her mourning weeds, seated on her great chair. She hung the portrait in her bedchamber, alongside one of Henry.

Every day, as she walked through the castle, the memories of his visit were vivid. She imagined she heard the clatter of his horse's hooves as he rode into the courtyard. Almost it was as if he walked beside her in the long gallery. He had been such a solid, reassuring presence in her life, and in the life of the kingdom, that it was hard to believe he was gone. She had loved him more than she had realised.

It was as the Lady Mary had feared. It had been proclaimed that, under the leadership of Queen Jane's brother, Edward Seymour – who had promptly created himself duke of Somerset, and been named Lord Protector – the Council was to rule England in the name of the young King Edward VI. One of its first decrees was that the Protestant faith was to be the official religion of England; Catholicism and the Mass were outlawed.

Through Sir John Guildford, Anna learned what was happening at court. It was amazing how many people had kept their Lutheran leanings secret under King Henry and were now hastening to express their zeal for the new religion. Queen Katharine was among them. Sir Thomas Cawarden had quickly made his strong Protestant convictions clear, and was high in the graces of the Council and the young King, who had given him lands near the royal palace of Nonsuch in Surrey.

'Not only does he have the use of a fine house at Blackfriars, as Master of the Revels, but he also boasts he now has estates in seven counties,' Sir John told Anne over supper the night after he returned from one of his regular visits to Whitehall.

'Hopefully, he will not be satisfied to remain as my steward at Bletchingley,' Anna said.

'Alas, Madam, it suits him very nicely. He is well entrenched in those parts, where he has much influence.'

'Then I shall stay here at Hever. I was thinking of going to court to congratulate King Edward, and remind him and the Council that I exist, but with all these religious changes, it might be wiser to stay away. Without a queen in residence, there would be no place for me at court anyway.' And, she thought, possibly no welcome. She had found out that King Henry had been dead for four days before anyone thought to tell her. She had a feeling that, for those now in power, she had ceased to be of any importance.

She had decided that, if she was asked to conform to the new religion, she would pay lip service to it, to stay safe. God would know what was in her heart. In the meantime, she had bidden Sir Otto Rumpello, her new German chaplain, to continue to celebrate Mass. Surely no one would object if it was in the privacy of her own home?

No one did. Probably no one cared enough.

She was more worried about money. Mr Chomley having retired, her trusty countryman, Jasper Brockhausen, had replaced him as cofferer, and yesterday he had come to her with his account books.

'Madam,' he said as he laid them before her, 'we have a problem. While the late King lived, your annual allowance of four thousand pounds was paid regularly, and he often supplemented it with grants. But, since his passing, the payments have fallen into arrears. There is a deficit of a hundred and twenty-six pounds in the annual accounts.'

'Oh dear,' Anna groaned. 'Our finances are tight enough as it is.'

'They are.' Jasper's sandy eyes were full of concern. 'Sir John says prices have doubled in a decade. He blames the old King, for debasing the currency.'

'Well, there's nothing I can do about that, and I suppose, if I am feeling the pinch, the Council is too. But I have no choice. I must appeal to them for help.'

She sent Sir John Guildford and her other household officers to present her petition. They returned the same day, and her spirits soared to see them looking more buoyant than they had when they set out.

'Their lordships were sympathetic,' Sir John told her. 'They have confirmed all the grants made to your Highness, and are granting you an extra one hundred and eighty pounds yearly. These arrangements will remain in place until the King reaches his majority at the age of eighteen.'

'Oh, that is such a relief!' Anna cried. The normally reserved Jasper smiled at her.

But Sir John had not finished. 'The Council suggested that the grant of another estate might make up any shortfall.' He appeared to be choosing his words with care. 'Madam, they have decided that you should rent out Bletchingley to increase your income, and take Penshurst Place and park in Kent in its stead. It is a fine house . . .'

Anna was not listening. Rent out Bletchingley, after she had done so much to it? Of course, it made sense practically. Yet she would have preferred to have rented out Hever. She could not rely on a tenant to keep in check the pretensions of Sir Thomas Cawarden; the man was too intimidating. Besides, she loved Bletchingley.

'Madam?'

'Yes, Sir John?' She tried to focus on what he was saying about the glories of Penshurst.

'Madam, I had no choice but to agree to the exchange on your behalf. I have here a letter from Lord Protector Somerset for you.'

She read it quickly. The Lord Protector and his fellows considered that Penshurst would be perfect for her, for it was near to Hever. Her eyes widened in outrage as she read that Somerset had thought it good to 'plant' Sir Thomas Cawarden in Bletchingley. Worse still, he required Anne to surrender to him all her interest in the house and its lands, in return for a yearly rent of £34. In Sir Thomas, she was assured, she would have an honest tenant who would see her revenue assured, and the arrangement would be in keeping with the late King Henry's wishes, which the Lord Protector doubted not that she would wish to respect.

She was shaking by the time she got to the end of the letter. He had won. He had wrested Bletchingley from her; now it was as good as his, and he could live there in great style at a very reasonable rent.

She was not going down without a fight.

'I will consent to this on two conditions,' she declared. 'First, that Sir Thomas agrees I can stay at Bletchingley whenever I wish, and that when I do, he will take himself off elsewhere; and second, that he will give me each year twelve haunches of venison from the deer park. The venison is very good there, as you know.'

'I do not foresee any difficulty with those conditions,' Sir John said.

'When is Sir Thomas to be *planted* in Bletchingley?' she asked bitterly.

'Two days hence, Madam.'

'Really? He *has* been busy!'

She was still smarting over being displaced by the scheming Cawarden when, a week later, an emissary from her brother arrived at Hever. It was the learned Konrad Heresbach, Wilhelm's former tutor, now his councillor, a man she had once known quite well.

She led him to her parlour, where a fire was burning on the hearth.

'It is so good to see you, Herr Doktor. How are the Duke and my sister?'

'In good health, Madam. I have letters from them for you, and also one from the Duchess Maria.' He opened his scrip and handed them over. 'The Duke has sent me to console you in your bereavement, to look to your welfare and ensure that you are managing financially. In Germany, we hear there is great inflation in England.'

Anna told him about the accommodation she had reached with the Council. She did not say how unhappy she was about it, for, on the face of it, it seemed a sensible arrangement.

'King Edward did tell me you are now well provided for. I had an audience with him in London before riding down here.'

'What did you make of him?'

'He is a remarkable child, very learned and self-assured; sharp-witted too, and zealous for the Protestant faith. But there is a coldness there, a lack of feeling.'

'Unlike his father,' Anna observed.

'Now there, by all accounts, was a terrifying man!' Heresbach said. 'I have heard him called the English Nero.'

'He was always a friend to me,' Anna said. 'I think he had many frustrations in his life, which made him what he was in his later years. I miss him greatly.' She could feel the ever-ready tears threatening.

'But I am cheered to see you. Please stay for a few days, and consider my house your own.'

Three days later, after Dr Heresbach had departed, satisfied that Anna was well provided for, she decided to move her household to Penshurst, a grand house of mellow sandstone, with four corner towers and a magnificent beamed hall. The gardens were glorious, arranged like a series of open-air rooms bordered by box hedges, and they were just coming into bloom as she and Otho wandered from one to the other, exploring, and snatching an occasional kiss.

'It is not such a bad place after all,' he said, pausing by an ornamental fountain. She sensed a suppressed excitement in him, as if he were about to tell her some good news.

'True,' she agreed. 'It's not Penshurst that annoys me; it's that man getting his hands on Bletchingley.'

'Forget him,' Otho urged, drawing her into his arms. 'It's idyllic here.' He kissed her tenderly. Always he aroused her, yet still she resisted her desire for him. Being caught out in any misconduct might give the Council an excuse to withdraw her settlement.

'You are preoccupied,' he said, as they strolled on.

'Yes. The steward told me that this house, like Bletchingley, once belonged to the Duke of Buckingham, who was beheaded for treason. It seems I am fated to acquire houses with a sad history.' She looked around her, listening. There was nothing but birdsong and the coo of a pigeon, but she lowered her voice. 'There is something else. My brother writes that the Emperor has destroyed the Schmalkaldic League. He is determined to crush the Protestant religion. My brother-in-law, the Elector of Saxony, is now a prisoner. He and my sister Sybilla are very close, and I am concerned for them.'

'Understandably,' Otho said, and put a protective arm around her.

'There is nothing I can do, and I imagine Wilhelm is powerless in the face of the Emperor. Thank goodness Kleve never joined the Schmalkaldic League.'

'I have news too,' Otho said. 'Hanna is dead of a fever, God rest her. I wish I could mourn her more than I do.' He turned to face her, taking her hands and gazing at her with longing. 'Anna, you realise what this means? We are both free. Will you marry me?'

No wonder she had sensed his excitement. A surge of happiness, the first she had felt in months, rose in her. She wanted to laugh out loud, dance, cry and sing, all at once.

'Say yes!' Otho urged, his eyes shining.

'I so want to,' Anna breathed. 'I would say yes now, but there are so many considerations . . .'

'Such as?' He was still smiling at her.

'I might lose my allowance, my houses and the means to support my household.'

'You were assured that you could marry again. It was one of the terms of your divorce settlement.'

'Yes, but this new government might seize on any excuse to rescind that.'

'You could send Sir John to ask permission to remarry.'

'I could.' She wondered what was holding her back. She needed time to collect her thoughts.

'Think on it, Anna! We could be a family. Johann is sixteen now; he will have completed his apprenticeship and can come here. I will myself go and fetch him.'

'That would be wonderful!' she cried, ecstatic with joy.

'Say yes!' Otho pressed her. 'I know I could make you happy. Think on it.'

She did think. She thought about little else in the days that followed, as Otho prepared for his journey to Kleve. He had the perfect pretext, that he was going to attend his wife's funeral. Most of the household, having seen how it had been between them, thought it a noble gesture.

'The court is in an uproar!' Sir John Guildford announced, as he joined the household at table in the solar, having just returned from London. 'It's emerged that the Lord High Admiral, Sir Thomas Seymour that was, secretly married Queen Katharine not long after King Henry's death.'

'He took a risk!' Thomas Carew observed, passing the salt. He had proved a most reliable servant, and had taken on several of the steward's duties after Mr Horsey had died last year.

'Aye. The Protector is furious that his own brother should have presumed so far, especially since, if the Queen proved to be with child, there might be a chance it was the late King's – and that would have implications for the succession.'

'What will happen to them?' Anna asked, jolted into a new awareness of how perilous it was for redundant queens to attempt matrimony.

'It'll to be the Tower for them, mark my words,' said Mother Lowe, ladling some pottage into her bowl.

'It could be construed as treason,' Sir John said. 'Impugning the succession is a capital crime.'

Anna made up her mind. When Otho returned from Kleve, she would tell him marriage was out of the question – at least for now. In its present mood, the Council might not look kindly on it, and she dared not risk being forbidden to marry Otho – a bastard whom some might deem no match for a princess – or wedding him without permission. She might lose her settlement and so many depended on her.

She had been counting down the days until his return, desperate to see her son, but now she was half dreading it. She must do her utmost to convince him they were better off as they were. It was enough to know he wanted her as his wife.

As the tall youth bowed before her, Anna's heart felt as if it would burst. Her eyes met Otho's, and she could read in them the answering emotion he was feeling, and the triumph.

'Welcome, Johann,' she said, yearning to embrace her son, but knowing she must not. He looked up, in awe of her, and she could see both herself and his father in him, yet not so plainly that people would notice. She was filled to the brim with love for him. That feeling had not lessened since she had seen him as a young child; indeed, it was fiercer. She could not believe he was here.

'I hear you are a journeyman swordsmith,' she said.

'I have just completed my apprenticeship, my lady,' he said in German, in the deep tones of incipient manhood. 'My father wanted me to practise my craft and gain customers, but I wanted to see more of the world, as I told Herr von Wylich. I am very grateful to him for bringing me to England to serve your Highness.' Anna marvelled that he spoke so well and courteously.

'And your parents, they are happy about this?'

'Yes, my lady. My father says I must appease my wanderlust before I settle down to my craft, but I am not so sure now that I want to be a swordsmith. The world is full of opportunities!' He smiled, and Anna melted.

'We have not the wherewithal for you to make swords here anyway,' she said, 'but you may serve in my chamber as a groom. If you give good service, you can look for preferment.' She could not give him any higher position for fear of arousing suspicion. Already Jasper had expressed surprise that she was taking on a new servant.

'It is as a favour to Otho,' she had told him. 'He is anxious to find a place for a young kinsman.' Which was true.

When, reluctantly, she had sent Johann off with Mr Carew to settle in, and she and Otho escaped to the gardens to sing their son's praises and catch up on news, she knew she had to tell him of her decision. She could put it off no longer.

'Dear heart, we cannot marry just now.' As she explained why, he looked as if she had dealt him a mortal blow. 'It's not that I don't love you,' she said, when he opened his mouth to protest. 'I do! But for the present, I want us to go on as we are. I could not bear to lose you. If things were otherwise, I would marry you at once – need you doubt it?'

His face was filled with such pain that she felt it physically.

'My Anna!' he said brokenly. 'All the time I was away, I was cherishing the thought that, when I returned, you would be my wife, and mine entirely. Will you not reconsider? Queen Katharine took a foolhardy risk in marrying so soon after King Henry's death. We would not be taking such a risk. Who cares what the likes of us do? You are thirty-one, I am thirty-three; we are no longer young, and we don't have time to waste. Go to the Council! Ask them. It can do no harm. It's not as if we've taken matters into our own hands.'

He was right.

'I will,' she said. 'For you, I will ask.'

'For us,' he corrected her, and drew her to him.

She told her household she was going on a hunting expedition, and then, with Otho and just two grooms accompanying her, rode north-wards towards Greenwich, where the court was in residence. It took them three days, and they had to stay overnight at wayside inns. To Anna's dismay, when she got to the palace, she found long queues of petitioners waiting to go before the Council. Fortunately, an usher recognised her and arranged for her to be seen next.

Seated at a long table was the Lord Protector himself, with Sir William Paget on one side and Sir Thomas Wriothesley, now Earl of Southampton, on the other. The previous Earl – the Admiral who had brought her to England – had been dead these five years.

'My lady of Cleves,' said the Protector, giving her what passed for a smile. 'How can we help you?'

'My lord, I have come to ask if the King's Majesty will graciously consent to my marrying a German gentleman of my household.'

'Indeed!' The lords exchanged looks. 'And who might the gentleman be?'

'Otho von Wylich. He is the son of the Lord of Gennep in Limburg.'

The Duke paused, before murmuring something in Paget's ear. She saw Paget nod. Then Somerset conferred with Wriothesley, who also seemed in agreement. The Duke turned back to Anna. His eyes were cold.

'We are sure his Majesty will make no objection to your Highness remarrying. However, your divorce settlement was made on the under-standing that you remain in England, and it follows that, to retain that settlement, you must marry an English subject. Has Mr Wylich been granted letters of naturalisation?'

'No, my lord,' Anna had to admit.

'Then I am sorry, but I do not see that his Majesty can approve your marriage to an alien *and* allow you to keep your settlement. You may, of course, wish to consider returning to Germany.'

She had known they would put an obstruction in her way. They just wanted to be rid of their financial obligations to her.

There was no point in making a scene. 'My lords, you have made yourselves very clear,' she said. 'As you force me to choose, I will stay in England. I have not the means to support myself in Kleve, and Herr von Wylich has no inheritance or expectations.' She could not resist a little dig. 'I had, my lords, hoped to find a little happiness after all my troubles.'

They said nothing, but just sat there, waiting for her to leave.

'Good day to you,' she said.

She was nearly in tears when she found Otho at the end of the gallery, where the press of people was not so great.

'They said no,' he muttered, searching her face.

'They said yes, but I forfeit my settlement if I marry an alien. I'm not even sure it's legal.'

He took her arm and steered her towards the door. 'No matter. We have each other, and Johann, and that is what is important.'

He was right, and yes, they did now have Johann. It was a constant joy to see him daily, to drink in every detail of him – her beloved boy. It was hard not to favour him above everyone else, and thus betray, by any word or gesture, that he meant so much to her.

Johann, however, soon proved worthy of reward, so it was possible for Anna to allocate to him privileged tasks that would keep him near her. He must serve her at table, or drive her chariot, or wait on her when she received guests. If anyone thought he was enjoying too much favour too soon, let them. The lad had earned it.

Standing in the December sunlight, amidst her household, wrapped in her fur cloak, Anna watched with some emotion as the young couple made their vows in the porch of the parish church of Hever. Katherine Bassett was marrying Henry Ashley, the local Member of Parliament, and looked radiantly happy.

Anna glanced across at Otho. She knew that, like her, he was wishing they too could know this peaceful happiness; that life could be as simple as this, and they could go to church and be married in the eyes of God. Tears welled as she took her place in her pew. Assisting in the preparations for the wedding had been difficult for her, and she had been tempted to break her resolve and damn the consequences. She had resisted the temptation. Now she made herself keep smiling, genuinely pleased for Katherine, who was kneeling before the altar with her bridegroom.

What could not be mended must be endured! Sad thoughts should not mar this happy day.

The letter arrived in May, when Anna was in the still room, helping Mother Lowe to distil some physick. It bore the King's seal.

She read it in mounting dismay. 'The Crown has repossessed Richmond Palace!'

Mother Lowe's jaw dropped. 'Why?'

'The King likes it, and wants it for himself,' Anna replied. 'Isn't it bad enough that they forced me to rent out Bletchingley? Hasn't the King got enough palaces?'

They were both bristling with outrage.

'I love Richmond!' Anna declared. 'I'm not giving in without a fight.' It was time for another visit to court.

Again she found herself before the Lord Protector, this time with Sir Anthony Browne and her former master of horse, the bull-faced John Dudley, who had risen high since leaving her service and lately been made earl of Warwick. Of them all, she sensed that Sir Anthony alone was sympathetic to her.

'My lords, I am deeply unhappy about losing Richmond,' she said, 'especially after it was granted to me for life by his late Majesty.'

Somerset shrugged and spread his hands helplessly. 'Alas, Madam, it was the King's will, and we may not deny it.'

'But I have been given nothing in compensation!'

Dudley spoke, or rather growled. 'I am surprised you expect it, Madam. You did nothing to maintain the palace in the eight years of your tenure, and it is now in a state of dilapidation.' It was true. There had not been the money for repairs. 'We have had to allocate the surveyor of the King's works two thousand pounds to cover what needs to be done.'

'I could not afford to repair the house, my lords. The extra allowance granted me last year is now barely sufficient to cover my outgoings.'

'My lady has a point,' Sir Anthony said. Bless him.

'Which is why his Majesty is giving your ladyship his house and manor of Dartford in exchange,' the Protector said, as Dudley sat there scowling. Anna remembered staying at Dartford soon after her arrival in England.

'King Henry had the priory pulled down,' Sir Anthony told her, 'and built in its place the King's Manor. It is large and luxurious, most suitable for your Highness. And with it are houses, gardens and orchards, a great park and even an inn at the gate.'

'It is newer than Richmond, and more convenient in many ways,' Somerset said.

Anna capitulated, knowing herself bested. 'Please thank his Majesty for his goodness to me.' The words nearly stuck in her throat.

If only Henry were here. He would never have taken away her beloved Richmond. How she missed him still.

The autumn of 1549 was as cold as winter, and the trees were bare, apart from the odd brave golden leaf. It was time, Anna thought, to make another visit to Bletchingley. She had been meaning to do so for a while, but had repeatedly shrunk from it, not relishing the prospect of seeing Sir Thomas Cawarden lording it over her house, or of crossing swords with him. She had visited on five occasions now. Twice he had been mercifully absent; the other times he had flouted his agreement with Anna, and been at Bletchingley when she arrived, only very reluctantly withdrawing to Hextalls, which – he made no secret of it – was not grand enough for him these days. Anna hoped he would not be in evidence this time.

She rode out from Hever with Otho at her side, her four grooms riding ahead. Among them was Johann, quite the man now. Anna never tired of looking at him, marvelling that he seemed genuinely to like her, and to be happy in England. He was learning the language far more quickly than she had, and making friends. She fancied there was a special, unacknowledged rapport between them. When she'd mentioned this to Otho, he had laughed.

'All your people love you, Anna. Why should Johann be any exception?'

'I think there is an instinctive bond between mother and child. He feels it too, I am sure.'

Passing through the gatehouse of Hever, Anna was reminded of Elizabeth, cantering through it on her palfrey. Her heart grieved for the girl, now sixteen and enduring the aftermath of a great scandal in which her reputation had been torn to shreds.

'It's hard to believe it is six months since the Admiral was beheaded,' she said. She had found it shocking that he had tried to seduce Elizabeth, without a care for the honour of the Queen his wife; and that, barely a widower, he had plotted to marry her. The man must have been crazed. Well, he had paid with his head for it.

'Thank God the Queen did not live to see it,' Otho said.

Anna almost crossed herself at the mention of Katharine Parr, who had died in childbed last year, but such Popish gestures were forbidden these days. She was silent for a moment, thinking hard. 'Sir Thomas Cawarden had dealings with the Admiral. I thought they were friends.'

'If they were, Sir Thomas quickly abandoned him. Sir John told me he helped to sequester the Admiral's confiscated estates.'

'Sir Thomas is one who will always bend with the wind,' Anna said tartly.

It still galled her to see the great gatehouse Sir Thomas had built in front of the house at Bletchingley. There had been other changes too. She had not forgotten the complaints made to her last year by the villagers, who were appalled by his determination to rid their parish church of all trace of its Catholic past. She had seen for herself the rood loft he had torn down lying in the nave, the crucified Christ crushed and broken beneath it. The building had been stripped of statues and vestments, the walls whitewashed, covering the old paintings of scenes from Scripture, and the altar horribly defaced.

'All the gold and silver plate and the furniture and carvings have been carted off to his house in London,' the innkeeper had grumbled. 'He called them the symbols of idolatry.'

'If y'ask me,' an old man said, 'he just wants 'em for hisself.'

Anna had been powerless to do anything beyond sending four of her servants to help clear up the mess. If she had tried to have the church restored, Cawarden would only have desecrated it again – and might have lodged a complaint against her with the Council.

Mercifully, he was not in occupation when she arrived. Everything, she had to concede, was in immaculate order. Surfaces gleamed, glass sparkled, plate shimmered, and the larder was bountifully stocked. Sir Thomas lived like a king.

As Anna and Otho inspected the gardens and grounds – which were also in perfect order – she noticed that a large barn had recently been refurbished. Pushing open the door, she gasped, for it was crammed with armour, guns and weapons of all kinds.

'Otho, why is Sir Thomas keeping an armoury?' she asked, perturbed.

He stared around the barn. 'He does represent Surrey in Parliament, and he is also High Sheriff. Maybe he needs a store of weapons for keeping the peace.'

Anna was not convinced, for she could never believe that Sir Thomas was the upright public servant he aspired – or pretended – to be. She suspected his influence hereabouts was malign, rather than benign. And he had amassed a *very* large arsenal of weapons.

She tried not to think about it, and enjoyed her stay; and she did not hesitate when her servants asked if they could fell timber in the park. It was hers, after all.

'Why should I not make a profit from it?' she asked Mr Carew. 'We need it more than ever now. My allowance is once more in arrears, and I am so low in funds I have been obliged to ask my brother for aid.'

That evening, Sir Thomas Cawarden returned to Bletchingley. There was about him less of his usual swagger, and more of a sense of elation.

'My Lady Anna, lords and ladies all!' he said, sweeping off his bonnet and bowing, as if he had every right to be at Bletchingley while Anna was there. 'I have news. The Duke of Somerset has been forced to step down as Lord Protector.'

'Why?' Anna asked, as those around her gaped in astonishment. 'What has he done?'

'What has he *not* done, you might ask! I could mention his overweening ambition, his vainglory, his entering into rash wars, enriching himself with the King's treasure, and doing all by his own authority. The lords were sick of it, and decided he had to go. And good riddance, I say.'

'So who will replace him?' Sir John asked. 'Who is to govern England?'

'I think you can look to see my lord of Warwick advanced to that honour,' Sir Thomas said, drawing up a stool and sitting down uninvited at the end of the high table. 'Is there any wine here?' Unsmiling, Jasper passed the ewer.

Anna had not liked Warwick when he had been her master of horse, and he had known it. But Sir John Guildford looked pleased. 'My lord of Warwick is married to my cousin. I hope he will remember me.'

Sir Thomas smiled at Anna. 'I too am hoping Warwick is promoted. I am also a kinsman by marriage, and I look for great things at his hands.'

Oh, no, Anna thought. You are not having Bletchingley. Only over my dead body.

Sir Thomas rode out in the morning, and Anna had hoped that would be the last they would see of him. But he was back late in the afternoon, in a glowering temper.

'Have your people been cutting down my trees again?' he snarled at her, without any courtesy or proper greeting.

'*My* trees, I think,' she corrected him.

'I pay you rent for them!' he countered.

'And *I* own them. And yes, I did sanction the felling of some of them.'

'I shall complain to the Council!' he flared.

'What about? People chop down trees all the time, for firewood, building and all sorts of things. The lords will laugh at you! But pray go ahead, make a fool of yourself.'

She could hear her officers stifling their mirth.

'You'll have nothing to grin about when I'm done with you!' shouted Sir Thomas, stamping out and banging the door behind him.

Anna sighed. He would never concede defeat. If only he would leave her alone!

In the midst of December, Anna was overjoyed to hear from Sir John Guildford that her brother had sent envoys to the English court.

'They sought me out at court, Madam, and told me to inform you that they are here to obtain payment of the arrears of the pension owed you by the Crown. They said also that the Emperor's ambassador is supporting them in this, at his personal instance.' Maybe, Anna thought wryly, there were advantages to having Kleve under the heel of his Imperial Majesty. 'They are to have an audience with the King tomorrow.'

'This *is* good news,' Anna said. 'Who is their spokesman?'

'Dr Herman Cruser, Madam.'

'I know him. He is a doctor of law and a councillor to my brother – a very learned man, and a good one, I assure you.'

Yet the good man's efforts were apparently of little avail, for she heard nothing more, and had to start making further economies. The sale of the timber helped – at least it afforded them some cheer at Christmas – but, as the new year loomed, Anna began to panic about the future.

It would be the year of our Lord 1550. A new decade was about to dawn. Ten years ago, she had been in Calais, waiting for a fair wind to take her to England. How hopeful she had been, anticipating a glorious future as queen. Now she was thirty-four and nearly middle-aged – loved, it was true, by all the good people who depended on her, but with not enough money to support them.

Chapter 26

Sir Thomas's prediction had been correct. The Earl of Warwick was now Lord President of the Council, ruling England in Somerset's place. When she'd heard the news, Anna's spirits had sunk even lower, for she knew she could expect nothing from him.

Sir Thomas, by contrast, was riding high. When Anna visited Bletchingley that spring, the estate was agog with talk of the signal proofs of Warwick's confidence in him. He had been given the house at Blackfriars, which he had long held as Master of the Revels. He was away just now, arranging for the reinforcement of the Tower garrison, so that prisoners of state could be held more securely. Probably the government had anticipated some protests at Somerset's downfall – or maybe it was just nervous after the great uprising against land enclosures last year. When she took a surreptitious look, Anna noticed that the store of arms in the great barn was a little depleted; yet there was still enough here to equip a small force.

Cawarden had also been made keeper of Nonsuch Palace, which had been built by King Henry in what Anna had heard was the most fantastical style – hence its name, None-such, or the Pearl of the Realm. She had never seen it, so when Sir Thomas, in his usual high-handed way, sent a messenger bidding her and her officers join him at a banquet he was hosting there, since he had missed having the pleasure of her company at Bletchingley – the impudence of the man! – her curiosity got the better of her.

To her surprise, the banquet was not held in the palace, which was smaller than she had expected, and much like any other great house, with its turrets and battlements – at least from the back view. She would see it later, when she went there to sleep. For now, she and Otho were escorted some way across the park to a banqueting house set high on a stone platform on rising ground. It was a small, octagonal, timber-framed building that looked like a fort, and was surrounded by a low brick wall. Lifting up her silver skirts, Anna ascended one of the three staircases up to the entrance, and was surprised to find the interior brilliantly lit with candles and sumptuously hung with tapestries that she suspected had been brought over from the palace. A table was laid with all kinds of delicacies, and wine spouted from a little stone fountain set in the wall. Such luxury was an uncomfortable reminder that she could no longer afford to entertain lavishly, as she was deeply in debt. She brushed the unpleasant thought aside, smiled at Otho and joined the throng. She would forget her troubles for this one evening.

Soon, all the guests were chattering away, and growing merrier by the moment. Anna stood by the fireplace, talking to Katherine Ashley, who had come up from her home near Hever for the occasion. They were reminiscing about Katherine's wedding, when Anna became aware of her host standing next to her, waiting for her to notice him. Reluctantly she excused herself and extended her hand.

'Sir Thomas, I must thank you for your excellent hospitality,' she said.

'I am glad your Highness has honoured me with your presence,' he said, in a voice all could hear. He never missed an opportunity to show the world how high he had risen.

But then, to her surprise, he bent to her ear. 'Your coming is pleasing to me in a more personal way,' he murmured. 'My lady, let us forget our differences. There has long been friendship between us, and I would there was more than that.'

She stared at him. *Friendship?* Presumption on his part, rather, and irritation and indignation on hers! Now he really had gone too far.

'Sir Thomas, I think you have perhaps had a little too much to drink,' she said gently. 'I will forget we had this conversation – and so should you.' Without another word, she moved away and sought out Otho, her heart racing. She felt sullied. How could that man think she would ever condescend to be his mistress? For that was what he was proposing, since his wife was alive and well. For Heaven's sake!

She spent the rest of the evening avoiding him. Towards midnight she felt a headache coming on, from the wine and the loud chatter, and Otho led her outside to stand in the cool night air.

'Let's make our excuses and leave,' she said. 'I don't want to stay at the palace. I'll tell you why later.'

'We can find an inn somewhere,' Otho said with a grin.

Something long suppressed flowered within her. 'Will you go and say goodbye and thank Sir Thomas for me?' she asked. 'I don't want to go near him.'

His eyes narrowed. 'Has he been pressing his attentions on you? Because if he has, I'll run him through.' He was only half joking.

'He was just being his usual arrogant self,' she said. 'No need for a duel.' She would tell Otho the truth later, when they were at a safe distance.

'I'll go now,' he said, leaving her to savour the peace of the moonlit park.

'I couldn't see him anywhere,' he reported when he returned. 'I asked his wife to say our farewells. Let's find your chariot.' It was waiting for them, with Johann yawning in the front seat, a few yards further on, in the place where all the horses were tethered.

'I trust you had a good evening, my lady,' Johann said, springing to attention.

Anna resisted the urge to hug him. 'I did, thank you, Johann.'

They climbed in, and Otho pulled the velvet counterpane over her lap.

'I noticed an inn in Banstead,' he called to Johann.

'*Ja*, I saw it. I will take you there.'

As they rode past the banqueting house, Anna saw Sir Thomas standing outside, staring into the distance with a forlorn expression. Maybe he did, in his way, have feelings for her.

She turned to Otho, and he folded his arms around her. In a whisper, she told him what had happened, and felt him tauten with anger, which she soothed with kisses and caresses.

That night, in a bed under the eaves of the old inn, she let him love her again, as far as she dared.

By the following spring, Anna felt she could not go on. Her financial situation was now so desperate she was seriously contemplating returning to Kleve. It would mean living under Wilhelm's watchful eye, and losing her independence, but it would afford some respite from her stressful situation. Wilhelm might even permit her and Otho to marry. She could take Johann with her, and her other German servants.

She had written to her brother telling him how bad things were, and was heartened when he immediately sent Dr Cruser back to England with orders to insist that the Council rescue her from her difficulties.

Needing to make stringent economies in the meantime, she instructed her stewards to shut up Hever and Dartford, and travelled north of London to the property she had not yet seen. The More was a smaller house and would be cheaper to run. It was about a century old, and bore poignant traces of the grandeur it had enjoyed when Cardinal Wolsey owned it, but it was not in good condition. No one had stayed here in more than a decade. The gardens, Anna was dismayed to see, were utterly destroyed by years of neglect.

She mustered her servants and allocated the tasks that needed to be done to make the place comfortable. She worked alongside them, sweeping floors, polishing windows and hanging the bright curtains she had brought from Hever. Johann made a passable job of painting window frames, and Jasper Brockhausen and his wife revealed a flair for gardening, assembling a team of volunteers to retrieve what they could.

The More looked far more welcoming by the time Anna heard from Dr Cruser. He was in England and had already met with the Council twice, and pleaded with them to help her. God willing, he might do her some good.

She waited – and waited. Not until the first week in June did she receive a letter from him, telling her the King had written to her brother, promising to settle her bills. Cruser believed Archbishop Cranmer had interceded for her.

The sense of relief was tremendous. She went into the chapel, now free of layers of dust, and knelt to give thanks. Then she wrote to King

Edward, expressing her gratitude for his goodness to her; another letter went to her brother, thanking him for sending her such an excellent champion as Dr Cruser, and informing him she had decided to stay in England.

It occurred to her that the good doctor might be able to assist in another matter.

The long-running dispute over tree-felling at Bletchingley had become utterly wearisome, and she begged him to help her resolve it.

She was gratified to learn that he had obtained from the Privy Council permission for her to enjoy full access to the house and use of the woods there, provided she allowed no waste or despoiling of them. Making and selling charcoal was perfectly permissible.

She was rejoicing over her victory, imagining Sir Thomas's fury when he heard how she had outwitted him, when Sir John Guildford knocked and told her there was a report of plague in London.

'Best not to worry too much, my lady,' he said. 'There is often plague in the summer. You're safe enough here; we're nearly thirty miles north of the City.'

A day later, he ventured as far as he deemed prudent into London, and was back very soon, looking worried. 'It's the sweating sickness,' he said, as the household crowded round. There were gasps of dismay.

'The sweating sickness?' Anna echoed, puzzled.

'It is a dread illness, Madam, that seems only to strike in England, every few years. The last outbreak was in the 1520s. I have heard that it's caused by an atmospheric putrescence. It causes a most profuse sweat, which seizes people without warning. Remedies have no effect.'

Anna shuddered. She imagined Johann stricken with it, Otho dying . . .

'Aye,' said Dr Symonds, who had replaced Dr Cepher as Anna's physician. 'A man can be well at breakfast and dead by dinner time.' His normally urbane and reassuring manner had been replaced by an expression of grave concern. 'Madam, we must ensure that no one from London is admitted to this house. When the sweat struck before, it traversed the whole kingdom, and the death toll was huge.'

Sir John spoke. 'In Edgware, where I was warned about the sweat, I heard that some persons at court had died of it, and that King Edward had been rushed away to Hampton Court.'

'Be honest with me. Are we safe here?' Anna asked Dr Symonds. 'I have properties further away where we could seek refuge.'

'As long as we do not come into contact with any outsiders, we will be safe.'

'We have plenty of food,' Meister Schoulenburg put in.

It was like being under siege. Only afterwards did they learn that nearly a thousand souls had perished in London, amidst widespread panic. All business was suspended, the shops were closed, and the citizens had locked their doors and prayed to be spared. At The More, Anna and her household held their collective breath for twenty tense days, constantly watching themselves and each other for any sign of the contagion, and eating sparingly, as there was only so much meat and fish in the wet larder, and the weather was warm.

At last, in July, as Jasper was working in the garden, a man shouted over the wall that the sweat had abated, and that there had been no cases hereabouts.

Gradually, life returned to normal. In September, Anna was delighted to receive an invitation from the Lady Elizabeth to visit her at Ashridge.

At eighteen, Elizabeth had matured into a slender, poised young woman with an incisive wit and a formidable intellect. With her sandy hair, sallow skin and hooked nose, she was not beautiful, yet she had undeniable charm, and Anna did not doubt that men found her attractive.

They congratulated each other on avoiding the sweat, and walked in the gardens, enjoying the sunshine and catching up on each other's news. Anna gathered that Elizabeth preferred to stay away from the court these days.

'There used to be warmth between my brother and me. He called me his sweet sister Temperance. Yet he is distant towards me now, and the formality at court is daunting. He is like a god to be worshipped. He's not yet fourteen, but he knows everything. I cannot get close to him any more. And when I do see him, he does nothing but complain about our sister Mary's insistence on having her Mass.'

'Her faith is more than life itself to her,' Anna observed.

'Yes, but Mass is illegal now. She should stop provoking the King and be more pragmatic, like you. You were a Catholic, yet you have converted like the rest of us.'

The conversation was taking a dangerous turn.

'I am a private person,' Anna said. 'My conformity is not important to the King. The Lady Mary is his heir. I'm not surprised he wants her to abandon the Mass, although I am certain she will never do that.'

'Then let us pray God preserves my brother for long years to come!' And Elizabeth went tripping ahead along the gravelled path, humming as she went, her long hair flying loose behind her.

January 1552 found Anna at Bletchingley again, digesting the startling news that the former Lord Protector had been beheaded.

'He plotted to overthrow the Duke of Northumberland,' Sir John reported. This was the title Warwick had recently bestowed on himself to underline his greatness. Only twelve years ago, he had been Anna's master of horse – now he was supreme in England!

'There was a great outcry among the people,' Sir John reported. 'They think of Somerset as "the Good Duke". I think even he believed there might be a last-minute reprieve. He died bravely.'

'He was never a friend to me,' Anna said, 'yet I am sorry for him.'

She went back to the accounts Jasper had given her to initial. The deficit was greater than it had been last week. She might have to leave England after all.

She set the ledger to one side and began a letter to Wilhelm, informing him of Somerset's execution. 'God knows what will happen next,' she wrote, 'and everything is so costly here in this country that I do not know how I can run my house. If I do decide to return to Kleve, I will be no trouble to you. England does not feel like my home any more.'

She was still wondering what to do when a letter arrived from the Privy Council, informing her that the King had granted Penshurst to Sir William Sidney. There was no apology, and no mention of her being given another house in exchange. She wrote back, complaining in the strongest terms, but did not receive even the courtesy of a reply.

'It may be for the best,' Otho said, as she lay in his arms that night. 'You have three houses to keep up already.'

'Personally, I would rather only have one,' Anna told him, 'but, as a princess of Kleve, I must live in a style befitting my status. If I had my way, you and I would have a pretty manor house in the country, and I would be playing *Hausfrau*!'

'And what would I be?' he laughed, tickling her and making her squeal.

'Don't do that! People will hear us,' she reproved him. Since that night at the inn, they had been sharing a bed at every opportunity, and it was blissful, yet they had had to be discreet. Anna knew that most of her household sympathised with their situation, but they might not approve of Otho treating her as if she were his wife. Only, of course, he wasn't, because the ultimate joy was denied to them. It was as frustrating for her as it was for him, and often, as she lay beside him, making free with his body, the longing was overpowering – but it was not as great as her fear of the consequences. It was as if she were conditioned always to expect the worst. That was what her life in England had done to her.

'The problem is more in your head than in reality,' he had said to her.

'But the Council made its views clear,' she countered.

'That was Somerset. Now he is gone.'

'And you think Northumberland will be more sympathetic?'

'Let's just get married, Anna, and damn the consequences!'

And always she had said no, denying herself, denying the man she loved.

In March, there was some joyful news from Kleve. Two years ago, the Duchess Maria had borne her first child, Marie Eleonore. Now she had a new daughter, whom Wilhelm had named Anna in honour of his dearest sister. Anna wished she could attend the christening, but she could not afford the journey. Instead, she sent her niece a silver rattle with tinkling bells, and her blessing.

427

It was a little burst of happiness in an otherwise miserable spring. The Council persisted in its relentless policy of reducing Anna's settlement. In April, the King commanded her to exchange her manor of Bisham for another of equal value, but had his officers seize it before a suitable exchange could be made. And it would not be made, Anna knew, for all her protests. Then the Council put pressure on her to exchange her lands in Kent, but she was wise to the game of exchanges by now, and flatly refused, much to their chagrin.

As if this were not enough, Jasper came to her with a long face and warned her that her finances were again in a perilous state.

'Madam, we *must* pare back your expenditure and make economies.'

'Very well,' she agreed, too weary even to ask what he was planning. But what was there to pare back? Jasper had it all worked out. Fewer dishes at meals. Fires to be extinguished at nine o'clock, whatever the weather. Following the old custom in Kleve, no food or wine to be served after that time. Candles were to burn down before they were replaced. This caused the most resentment, for the servants were used to appropriating them as perquisites after only one evening of usage. And then the daily ration of ale was reduced.

Anna was aware of the rising tide of anger in the household. Her cousin, Franz von Waldeck, now twenty-seven and a gentleman of her chamber, was the most vociferous, and took Jasper to task at supper one evening.

'What do you call this?' he challenged, pointing with distaste at his small portion of fish. 'No sauce, and no alternative dish. We might as well be living in a monastery.'

'They eat better there, I'll wager,' Thomas Carew said.

'My Lady Anna,' Franz continued, 'your table used to be famous. Now no one comes, and the food gets worse daily.'

'It is not the fault of Meister Schoulenburg,' Anna said. 'We have to live within our means.'

'No, it's *his* fault,' Franz declared, jabbing a finger at Jasper.

'Forgive me, but since when did you become acquainted with her Highness's accounts?' Jasper retorted. 'She has no money, and is in debt. We *have* to make economies.'

'It is your mismanagement of her finances that has led to this!' Franz snapped.

'You can't talk!' Jasper flared. 'You, with your eight servants, whom she is obliged to support!'

'Gentlemen, desist!' Anna cried. 'Franz, you *are* in no position to criticise.'

'I looked at the books. They're in a hopeless mess.'

'That's a lie!' Jasper roared.

'How dare you!' Gertie spluttered.

'On my family's honour, Herr Brockhausen, I am not a liar, and you will take that back!' Franz had gone red in the face.

Anna banged her fist on the table. 'I will not have this unseemly squabbling. Franz, I check the accounts every week. They are not in a mess; you exaggerate.'

He glared at her. 'Madam, it grieves me to see you so ill served. It is not compatible with your honour or your status to have this penny-pinching inflicted on your household.'

'Nor is it compatible with my honour to have my people starving! None have been let go, or gone unpaid, so if you want to retain your eight servants, you had best stop complaining.'

She turned to the seething Jasper. 'Maybe we could economise in other ways.'

'Don't you think he's tried?' Gertie interrupted.

'I know he has.' Anna smiled placatingly. She could not afford to upset these good, loyal friends. 'But let us put our heads together and see if we can't find a better means of saving money. Now, shall we all change the subject? I hear there is to be a new Book of Common Prayer in English.'

For all her efforts, the quarrel was not done with. Enmity simmered, and she suspected there was more to it than appeared on the surface.

Anna raised some money by selling some of her jewels. Sitting in her garden at Hever one June morning, staring into her depleted casket and wondering if she could bring herself to sell a brooch King Henry had given her, she suddenly became aware that Franz von Waldeck was standing at her elbow, waiting to speak to her.

'Franz, what can I do for you?'

'I'd like to talk to you, Madam,' he said.

'Sit down,' she invited, closing the casket.

Franz hesitated for a moment. 'As your close kinsman, my lady, I have been wondering if you have made a will.'

'A will?'

'It is wise to be provident. You would want your possessions to go to the heir of your choice, surely. But if you die intestate, that might not happen.'

'Franz, I'm thirty-six, and in good health!'

'It's never too soon. None of us knows when God will summon us.'

This was a gloomy conversation to be having on a lovely summer day.

'We are cousins, my lady,' Franz persisted. 'If you will make me your heir, I will do all I can to protect your interests, for they will be my own.'

Ah, Anna thought, now it becomes clear why you are so eager to delve into my finances.

Aloud, she said, 'Franz, I am very fond of you, but there will be no advantage to you in being my heir, for I am poor. These great houses will revert to the Crown on my death, when my income will cease. All I have are my jewels and personal possessions.'

'It is not gain I look for,' he said. 'More a recognition of our kinship and my dozen years of service. As your acknowledged heir, I would enjoy more authority in your household, and could manage things better.'

There was the nub of the matter. 'You mean you want to take over the accounts?'

'That, and other responsibilities. I too am finding things hard financially. I was hoping that, of your goodness, you might release to me some of your personal effects, so I can raise some money.'

You had to admire his effrontery!

'Franz,' she said gently, 'if I die intestate, the heir to my poor fortune is my brother, and then my sister. They are my closest relatives, so it is only right that they should benefit. And, when the time comes, I shall want to reward those who have done me good service. Let's leave the matter there.'

A sulky look clouded Franz's handsome face.

'Was there anything else?' she asked, with more asperity.

'No, my lady,' he muttered, and walked off.

Within moments, Jasper appeared. 'I couldn't believe what I was hearing just then,' he told her.

'You were eavesdropping?' Anna asked.

'Not intentionally. I was coming to tell your Highness that those overdue rents from Norfolk have come in, when I heard Franz speaking to you. Naturally, I waited until he had finished. Frankly, Madam, his presumption is appalling!'

Anna thought so too, but did not want to inflame the enmity between the two men. 'About those rents, Jasper,' she said. 'Will they make us solvent?'

When they were alone that night, she asked Otho what he thought about Franz's astonishing request.

'He's a young hothead,' he said. 'I'm glad you put him in his place.'

'But I did it kindly,' Anna said, running her fingers through the golden hairs on his chest, and marvelling that, at thirty-eight, he was still lean, strong and muscular.

'As a younger son, he has no inheritance. I suppose you can't blame him for trying to better himself. But it was wrong-headed. I don't know what's got into him lately.'

'I think he thought he had a comfortable future assured, and resents having to make economies.'

Otho stroked her hand. 'I don't like the way he carps at Jasper. The man is doing his best to make ends meet.'

'Jasper was very angry today.'

'He showed me the accounts. He was upset that Franz said they were in a mess. They looked pretty orderly to me.'

Anna's lips sought his. 'I hate all this bad feeling. It's casting a cloud over everyone.'

'I will speak to them both,' Otho promised, and gathered her into his arms.

Otho's tactful advice fell on deaf ears. Jasper would not speak to Franz; and Franz did not let an opportunity pass to criticise Jasper. People were taking sides.

Anna was at her wits' end when, out of the blue, a letter arrived from Dr Olisleger, revealing that Jasper had written, urging him to warn Duke Wilhelm that Franz was trying to persuade Anna to recognise him as her heir and advance him some of her property. On the Duke's orders, Dr Olisleger was recalling Franz to Kleve to explain himself, and asked Anna to ensure he departed without delay.

She was deeply relieved to see an outraged Franz go, and asked Otho and Sir John personally to oversee his departure and make sure he did not seek out Jasper and pick a fight. The atmosphere in the household lightened, and she began to hope that Wilhelm would not allow Franz to return.

Her spirits rose further in July, when the Council informed her that the Emperor had finally freed the Elector of Saxony from captivity. She had more than once petitioned King Edward to urge his release, and Sybilla had written that she herself had never ceased pressing for it. To Anna's grateful surprise, the Privy Council had asked the English ambassador to beg the Emperor to show clemency. She took the greatest of pleasure in imagining Sybilla's joy as she was reunited with her beloved husband.

In August, encouraged by the Council's support in this matter, Anna wrote to the King explaining most apologetically that her expenses now exceeded her income by nearly a thousand pounds a year, and begging him, of his goodness, for financial aid.

She was crestfallen to receive only a short reply. His Highness was on progress and resolved not to be troubled with payments until his return; her request could not be satisfied until his coming to London.

Part Five

My Lady of Cleves

Chapter 27

1553–1554

The King was dead.

There had been rumours that he was ill, but Sir John said he had appeared at a window at Greenwich Palace to reassure the crowds below that he was well, so the news came as a shock. To die at fifteen – it was desperately tragic. Anna could not get that poor, isolated, deified boy out of her mind.

And now – what would happen?

'The next heir is the Lady Mary,' Sir John said, as they sat subdued over supper at Bletchingley that evening.

'That will mean we all turn Catholic again,' Mr Carew said.

'The first one she'll overthrow will be Northumberland,' Sir John predicted. 'She has no cause to love him; he was vigorously opposed to her having her Mass, and has done much to strengthen the Protestant faith in England.'

'I can't see him giving up his power without a struggle,' Otho said.

His words were prescient. Three days later, they learned, to their astonishment, that the Lady Jane Grey had been proclaimed queen in London. Anna struggled to place her.

'Who is she?'

'King Henry's great-niece, the granddaughter of the French Queen,' Mr Carew supplied. 'She is but a girl.'

'She was married to Northumberland's son only a few weeks ago,' Sir John related. 'I think the Duke planned this all along. The word is that King Edward changed the succession on his deathbed, disinheriting his sisters.'

435

'I wonder what the Lady Mary will do,' Anna pondered, deeply worried for both Mary and Elizabeth.

'What can she do?' shrugged Mr Carew. 'She is but a woman, with no resources at her command.'

'But she has right on her side,' Sir John insisted. 'As a lawyer, I can tell you with certainty that a deathbed wish, even one made in writing, cannot overturn an Act of Parliament. Thus the Lady Mary is our rightful Queen.'

No sooner had he spoken than they heard the front door bang open and a commotion in the hall. Sir Thomas Cawarden appeared, booted and wearing his riding clothes. 'My lady.' He bowed to Anna, nodded at the rest, then eyed the remains of the joint of beef on the table.

Anna wondered where he had been – and why he kept coming to Bletchingley when she was here. Yet, over the years, she had grown more used to his ways. At least he had never propositioned her again. 'Do join us, Sir Thomas,' she said, obliged by common courtesy to invite him.

'There is a letter waiting for you in the hall,' Mr Carew told him. Sir Thomas fetched it, and came back scanning the page.

'It's from the Council,' he said, 'to all the deputy lieutenants, sheriffs and justices of Surrey.' He did not reveal any more. He had not been at court, then, or the Council would not have had to write to him here. Had he been out and about, drumming up support for Queen Jane?

Conversation turned again to the day's momentous tidings, but Sir Thomas did not appear interested in joining in. Anna had expected him to be elated at the prospect of England having another Protestant monarch, yet he seemed almost indifferent.

A week passed, with no more news. Then Sir Thomas received another letter, one bearing the royal seal. Anna saw him hurrying to the stables as she was picking flowers for the parlour.

'I have to go to London,' he called back over his shoulder. 'They need tents for the garrison at the Tower, where the Queen is.'

He had been gone two days when a carter came by the gate and told the porter that the Lady Mary had been proclaimed queen and Lady

Jane had been overthrown. The porter raced to the house, dragging the man with him.

'I heard it proclaimed in the marketplace at Reigate, lady,' the carter told Anna, clutching his hat, as everyone gathered around her in the hall. 'The herald told us that Queen Mary had raised her standard in Norfolk, and everyone in those parts rallied to her, and the rest of the kingdom did likewise. The traitor Northumberland is taken.'

'And what of the Lady Jane?' Anna asked, thrilled to hear of Mary's triumph.

'She's in the Tower.'

Anna sent the carter to the kitchens for some refreshment, and turned to her household. 'We must all pray for Queen Mary,' she said. 'God grant her long to reign!' It seemed strange to have a queen governing over them, but she was confident that Mary would prove equal to the task. Clearly, she had come to the throne on a vast tide of popular approval.

She went to her closet to write a letter of congratulation to the new Queen. Next door, she could hear Mother Lowe declaring how pleased she was that they could all practise their religion openly again now. Anna sat quietly for a space, savouring the moment – until she remembered Sir Thomas Cawarden. He would have been riding into danger. Had he been caught delivering the tents to the Tower, or had he heard the news before he got to Blackfriars, and escaped capture? Would that save him from the anger of Queen Mary, who would surely find out about his close association with Northumberland?

To her horror, Anna realised that her own connection with Sir Thomas might lead to suspicions that she too had supported the usurper Jane. Yet surely Mary would not believe that of her: Mary, who was her friend.

It had been an anxious few weeks – until the summons arrived at Hever bidding Anna come to London to take part in the Queen's coronation.

'This is such a relief – and most gratifying!' she told Otho, showing him the letter. 'I am deeply touched that her Majesty regards me as worthy of this honour. She is aware, of course, that I share her faith; she must know that I too rejoice that true religion can once again be practised in England.'

'So you think she really will return the realm to obedience to the Pope?'

'I have no doubt of it. Oh, Otho, things are going to be much better from now on!'

Anna had already ordered that Mass be celebrated openly in her household, and asked all her people to attend. As the weeks passed, news of the great changes that were afoot reached Hever. It was said that God was taking pity on His people and His Church in England, through the instrument of a virgin called Mary. Anna wondered if there would be protests from the Queen's Protestant subjects, but so far there had been no demonstrations against the restoration of the old faith. Doubtless it was because the Queen had published an edict promising not to compel her subjects to follow the Catholic religion.

Anna could imagine Mary's joy in having the freedom to worship as she wished. Sir John Guildford had told her that Mass was now celebrated six or seven times a day at court.

'And what of my Lady Elizabeth?' she had asked. 'She is hot for the Protestant faith.'

'She has not been at court yet, but I'm sure she will do as the Queen pleases. She will not risk being disinherited again.'

The barge was crowded with ladies, all looking like rare birds in their fine attire and chattering excitedly about the coronation and the celebrations to come. Feeling like a queen again in her purple velvet gown, Anna sat in the cabin, waving to the crowds lining the riverbanks. They would know who she was when they saw the pennant bearing her coat of arms fluttering in the breeze. Ahead of her she could see the royal barge leading the great procession of boats making their stately way to the Tower of London.

As the Queen's barge turned in towards the Court Gate, the guns on the wharf sounded a mighty salute. Anna's mind turned to the poor souls she had known who had been imprisoned, or met their end, here – Cromwell, Katheryn Howard, the Seymour brothers, and now

Lady Jane Grey, who was still immured somewhere behind the stout walls of the fortress. As Anna alighted from the barge and was escorted along the outer ward to her lodgings in the royal palace, she wondered how Jane felt, hearing all the commotion and the cheers greeting the Queen's arrival. But she would not think of that now. Today was a day for rejoicing, and here was the Lady Elizabeth coming to embrace her.

Two days later, early on a mild late-September morning, Anna climbed into the chariot she was to share with Elizabeth. It was a great privilege, especially as they were to ride immediately behind the Queen's open litter. Elizabeth was already seated, facing the horses and wearing a crimson velvet gown identical to Anna's. Lifting her heavy skirts, Anna sat down opposite. The litter was upholstered in the same crimson velvet, with a canopy of white cloth of silver to protect them from inclement weather.

'Are you looking forward to it, my Lady Anna?' Elizabeth asked, keenly taking in all that was going on around them in the inner ward of the Tower.

'It is most exciting, and a great honour to be sharing it with your Grace,' Anna smiled.

Not by one word or expression had Elizabeth given any hint that she was unhappy about her sister's religious policy. Yet she had been noticeably absent when Anna attended Mass in the Chapel of St John, high in the keep. Anna had watched the Queen, kneeling devoutly, her face rapt, then seen her suddenly glance sideways and look pained at the sight of Elizabeth's empty chair. Mary might have said she would not compel her subjects to follow her religion, but Elizabeth was her heir. You would have thought she would make some compromise with her conscience to please the Queen.

The great ladies of the court were disposing themselves in the chariot behind them, and the many gentlewomen who were to ride after them were mounting horses trapped in red velvet, which matched their gowns. At last, the great procession moved slowly forward, out of the Tower and into the City of London, which the Queen entered in state, to be welcomed by the Lord Mayor and the leading citizens. Anna could see the small crown on Mary's head bobbing up and down as she nodded her head in acknowledgement of the cheering crowds and the pageants put on for her delight along the route. She gazed in wonder at streets hung with tapestry, triumphal arches, colourful pageants and happy, waving people. Her ears were assailed by the roar of the crowds, trumpets sounding fanfares, and the heavenly choirs of children. And so they came to Westminster.

The next day, Anna stood in the cool of Westminster Abbey watching Bishop Gardiner place the crown on Mary's head. She wondered what had become of that radical Protestant, Archbishop Cranmer, who should have been officiating, but did not like to ask.

Afterwards, in the glowing light of a thousand candles, she and Elizabeth were seated together at the end of the Queen's table at the coronation banquet in Westminster Hall. It was wonderful to have the Queen smiling down the table at her and to enjoy such gracious favour. It meant she could look forward with confidence to a happy, assured future.

The celebrations over, Anna returned to Bletchingley, eager to tell Sir Thomas Cawarden all about the coronation – to which he had not been invited – and to make it plain to him which one of them was riding high now. But he was not at home, which left her feeling a little deflated. Always, he seemed to have some mysterious business in hand. Again she thought he had been lucky to escape censure after Queen Mary's accession.

She hoped Mary's favour would extend to her finances. The previous year, she had exchanged her manor house at Bisham for Westhorpe in Suffolk, a beautiful palace of which she had high hopes. But it was proving costly to maintain and her debt was again growing.

She was surprised and glad to see Dr Cruser, come from her brother.

'He has sent me, Madam, to ensure that your settlement is confirmed by the new Queen, to whom I have already paid my respects. I took with me letters from the Duke and Duchess, congratulating her Majesty on her accession, and expressing the hope that the friendship between England and Kleve will be warmly maintained.'

'I do hope so,' Anna said, leading him into the large parlour she used in the mornings, and bidding him take the chair opposite hers on the other side of the hearth. She poured him some wine, and sat down.

'I am confident the Queen will ensure that I will not be left in want,' she said. 'Already, I have received several marks of her favour.' She told him about the coronation and the prominent part she had played.

Dr Cruser nodded approvingly, but his expression became serious. 'My lady, even with the Queen's favour, you cannot rely on her supplementing your income on a regular basis. Duke Wilhelm is well aware that your allowance is now seriously insufficient to meet your expenditure – and this kingdom is all but bankrupt.'

'I'm sure the Queen will help me,' Anna protested.

'Has she said she will?'

Anna had to admit that she had not.

'In that case, Madam, I have a strategy you could follow. Parliament met this week, and the first Act it passed was one declaring the marriage of the Queen's parents lawful.'

Mary must be rejoicing at that, Anna thought.

'Given that, and the favour you have been shown, your Highness might take steps to have your marriage to the late King Henry also declared lawful, so that you can enjoy the lands and prerogatives of a queen dowager. There is no queen dowager now to claim them, nor likely to be for many years.'

Anna stared at him. 'But Parliament and Convocation declared my marriage invalid.'

'That hardly matters now. As things stand, the income from your settlement would be forfeited if ever you left England; but your marriage treaty provided that you could keep your lands if you returned to Kleve a widow. Thus, if you could prove your marriage lawful, you would be a wealthy woman, with the respected status of a queen dowager.'

It was a daring and contentious plan – but, given the Queen's favour, it might just work.

'Would you help me draft a letter to the Council, Dr Cruser?' Anna asked.

* * *

She waited – and waited – for a reply. When it came, she broke the seal eagerly. The Council had received her request, she read, but the matter must be adjourned till later, when more urgent and important affairs had been settled and decided.

At least they had not said no.

According to Sir John, the more urgent matters included the Queen's marriage. Several prospective bridegrooms had been mooted, including Prince Philip of Spain, the Emperor's son and heir, who was said to be Mary's preferred choice. Wilhelm now wrote to Anna proposing another suitor, his brother-in-law Ferdinand of Habsburg, Archduke of Austria, a son of the Emperor's nephew, Ferdinand, King of the Romans, Bohemia and Hungary, heir to the Holy Roman Empire. King Ferdinand was eager for the match, Wilhelm declared, and Anna could see at once that the marriage would bolster her position in England.

Dr Cruser had returned to Kleve, so, at Wilhelm's behest, she donned her stateliest gown, one of scarlet cloth of gold, and took herself to Greenwich, where she was readily granted an audience with the Queen.

'My dearest Anna,' Mary said, extending her hand to be kissed, then embracing Anna warmly. She was gorgeously attired and bejewelled, to the point of ostentation, her rich gown swamping her spare frame.

'I trust I find your Majesty in good health and prospering,' Anna said.

'Yes, I am. My cousin the Emperor has sent me a new ambassador, Monsieur Renard, and he is proving an invaluable support.'

Anna wondered if it was appropriate for the Queen of England to rely on a foreign ambassador. Aloud, she said, 'I am pleased for your Majesty.'

'I needed someone who has my true interests at heart,' Mary confided. 'I cannot rely on my Council. They all supported the usurper Jane. What was I to do? I couldn't execute them all for treason. So they are sworn to me, and I am watching them, hoping they stay loyal. But what can I do for you, Anna?'

'It is more a case of what I can do for your Majesty,' Anna smiled, encouraged by Mary's candour. 'My brother has proposed the Archduke

Ferdinand as an excellent husband for you, and I understand the Archduke himself is greatly desirous of winning your Majesty's hand.'

To her consternation, Mary looked dismayed.

'I hope you do not think I am interfering,' Anna said hastily.

'No, not at all, dear friend,' Mary said. 'The Archduke is eminently suitable, but my heart is set on the Prince of Spain.'

So rumour spoke truth. Mary *was* keen to marry Philip.

'I have seen his portrait,' the Queen breathed, her eyes lighting up. 'He is most . . . comely.' She reddened. 'I feel there can be no other for me. Soon, all will be decided.'

Anna wanted to beg her not to fall in love with a portrait. She herself knew how disastrous that could be. 'I pray the Prince lives up to his picture,' she said, knowing she sounded sceptical.

'I am assured it is a wonderful likeness,' Mary said. 'Pray tell your brother I appreciate his care for my happiness, and that I would have considered the Archduke, but for the fact that my heart is given elsewhere.'

'I will do that, Madam,' Anna promised, trying not to betray her concern.

'And now,' Mary said, 'walk with me awhile in the gallery. I would hear all your news.'

The new year of 1554 came in, and still Anna had heard nothing from the Council. Small wonder really, for the lords had far more pressing matters to occupy them. The Queen's resolve to marry the Prince of Spain had provoked outrage in England and cost her much of the public acclaim that had greeted her accession. Her subjects did not want a foreign king, still less one who persecuted Protestants; it was held against Philip that he was a champion of the Spanish Inquisition. The mood of the country was angry.

Anna could sense an answering anger in Sir Thomas Cawarden, who had come to Bletchingley for Christmas and stayed on at Hextalls. His resentment was palpable when, as soon as the festive greenery had been taken down, Mary's officers appeared and demanded, in the Queen's name, that he surrender his arms and armour for use in the defence of London.

Anna heard the shouting outside, and opened the window to see what was going on. There was Sir Thomas, his breath clouding the freezing air, protesting loudly that he needed his arms, lest the house be attacked. Anna thought of the store of weapons in the barn; there were surely far more than would be needed here!

She worried about the Queen needing arms for the defence of London. Was public feeling against the Spanish marriage so strong that she feared an uprising?

Perhaps Sir Thomas Cawarden, that stout Protestant, was suspected of plotting unrest. She watched as, furious, he stalked off, calling for his men to help deliver the arms the Queen demanded, and disappeared behind the house to the barn.

When she saw the cart loaded, she knew he had handed over only a small part of his arsenal. What game was he playing? Was he planning an insurrection? Or was he determined to retain the rest of the arms for his own defence in the future?

She fretted over the matter, not daring to confide in anyone, not even Otho or Mother Lowe. Mother Lowe was growing old and Anna did not want to trouble her. She thought Otho would press her to warn the Queen of her suspicions. But what if there was an innocent explanation? Relations between her and Sir Thomas were difficult at the best of times; reporting him for stockpiling arms would sour them for ever – and she did not want to feel a pariah in her own house. So she held her peace, and tried not to think of what lay in the barn.

In the last week of January, Anna was appalled when Lord William Howard appeared in her hall with a detachment of guards in his wake, and demanded to know where Sir Thomas was.

Flustered, she sent Johann to find him, and a good quarter-hour later, during which Lord William paced impatiently up and down and refused her timid offer of refreshment, Sir Thomas appeared in the doorway.

'Lord William, what do you want?' he barked. 'Here I am, enjoying my house in perfect quietness and good order, and in obedience to the Queen – and you come and disturb my peace!'

'Nevertheless, Sir Thomas, you must accompany me,' Lord William insisted. 'You are to go before the Star Chamber at Westminster. The Lord Chancellor wishes to ask you certain questions.'

Since Gardiner was now Lord Chancellor, Anne imagined that Sir Thomas would have a hard time. She watched as he was taken away, wondering how his poor wife would take this, and whether she should have said anything about the store of arms that remained in the barn. But it was unwise to get involved in these great affairs – and there was no evidence that Sir Thomas intended to use those arms for some nefarious purpose.

He was soon back, and at liberty. 'Well, I managed to convince the Council of my loyalty,' he growled, sitting down heavily by the fireside without a by-your-leave, leaving Anna still standing. 'They have ordered me to arm my people here and hold myself in readiness to march at an hour's notice. There is a rebellion in Kent, led by Sir Thomas Wyatt, against the Spanish marriage. The Council is mustering forces to suppress it.'

'A rebellion?' Anna echoed, almost forgetting that Cawarden had referred to *his* people at Bletchingley, when most were in fact her people. 'Kent is not far from here!'

'Don't look so worried, my lady. It'll be quickly put down. Even so, the Queen should think twice about pursuing the marriage. This rising is testimony to the strength of feeling against it.'

At least Anna did not have to worry any more about Sir Thomas concealing his arsenal. The Council clearly knew he still had weapons, otherwise they would not have asked him to arm his men. She had been right not to report him.

She wasn't so sure about that the next day, however, when Lord William Howard appeared again, with Sir Thomas Saunders, the Sheriff of Surrey, in tow, demanding the surrender of all unrequired weapons and armour stored at Bletchingley. She stood by in the hall as Sir Thomas argued with them.

'My lord, my patent as Master of the Revels and Tents permits me to keep forty armed servants here.'

'Yes, Sir Thomas, but you also maintain an armoury, as you yourself told us, and we have received information that you have been accumulating weapons to help the rebels.'

'Oh, please!' Cawarden drawled. 'Saunders, you know me of old. Would I do such a thing?'

Sir Thomas Saunders stared at him coldly. 'The last I heard, Cawarden, was that you were the greatest hot gospeller in Surrey. You are under house arrest, and will remain here at Bletchingley, under my supervision.'

Anna bristled. 'Sir Thomas, this is my house, and I do not care to have one who is suspected of colluding with the rebels under my roof.'

Cawarden glared at her, but Saunders bowed. 'Madam, forgive me. I will take Sir Thomas to my constituency house in Reigate until he is summoned to London for questioning. Cawarden, make ready! We must not incommode the Lady Anna any longer.'

Sir Thomas was marched out, protesting.

Again, Anna found herself and her household waiting apprehensively for news, which reached them piecemeal from the few carters, pedlars and merchants who ventured abroad with their wares. Florence of Diaceto returned from a mission he had undertaken for the late King Edward in Denmark, and was able to tell them what he had heard on the way down through Kent.

'The government is obviously frightened,' he said. 'Some letters I brought back, and a gold chain the King of Denmark gave me, were impounded by the port officials at Dover.'

The rebel army's ranks were swelling daily, he reported. It was marching on London. Some said Sir Thomas Wyatt was loyal to the Queen and wanted only to force her to abandon the Spanish marriage. Others were convinced he meant to depose her and set up the Lady Elizabeth in her place, which was treason by anyone's reasoning. Anna realised, with some dismay, that she did not know Elizabeth well enough to predict whether she would consent to such villainy. When she heard of other risings in different parts of the country, she wondered if they were safe at Bletchingley, but Dartford was in Kent, which ruled it out, and The More too far away; any travel would surely be hazardous.

Cawarden's valet wrote to say his master had been taken to London for more questioning by the Lord Chancellor. But the rebels had now converged on the capital.

They learned what had happened afterwards, from a letter written by one of Sir John's friends at Whitehall. The Queen, God bless her, had gone to the Guildhall and rallied the people with a rousing speech. Then London had locked its gates to the rebels. Within days, the revolt had collapsed. Wyatt had been captured, and Sir Thomas Cawarden had been ordered by the Council to remain in his own house at Blackfriars.

Anna had been praying daily for the Queen's deliverance, and now she gave thanks to God for it.

With the roads safe again, Sir John deemed it time to ride to court himself. On his return, he joined Anna, Otho, Jasper and Mother Lowe for supper. They all pressed him for news.

'The Lady Elizabeth is widely believed to have been involved in the rebellion,' Sir John told them. 'I hear she is to be questioned. But the Lady Jane is in greater peril. Her father rose with the rebels in the Midland shires, and proclaimed her the rightful queen. His stupidity is beyond belief. She is already under sentence of death, which the Queen had suspended. But now the Council are urging her to have the Lady Jane executed, for, while she lives, she will always be a figurehead for Protestant malcontents. It is said the Queen is reluctant, for the Lady Jane is but seventeen and had no hand in this latest treason.'

Anna shuddered. Jane had been foolish to accept the crown in the first place, though probably she had had little choice. But to die violently, at such a tender age, was terrible. Her eyes met Otho's, and she could see he thought the same.

'What did the rebels gain?' Mother Lowe asked. 'Nothing but death and misery.'

'Aye,' Sir John said. 'There are gallows at every street corner in the City, it seems. You can't get away from the stench of rotting flesh.'

Anna winced, sickened.

'I think the French were behind it,' Jasper said.

'It's possible,' agreed Sir John. 'King Henri is strongly opposed to the Queen marrying the Prince of Spain. He doesn't want Philip poised to leap across the Channel from England.'

'Which is precisely why Wyatt rebelled,' Jasper said. 'He could see England being dragged into Spain's wars.'

'I don't condone rebellion,' Otho put in, 'but maybe he had a point.'

'He will lose his head for it,' Sir John muttered, 'as will Lady Jane and her father.'

He was right, as he discovered when he was next at court.

'The Lady Jane suffered this morning,' he said gravely, when Anna greeted him on his return.

She crossed herself, imagining how it must have been for that young girl to whom she could not put a face. The news cast a pall over her day, and she sensed a subdued atmosphere in her household.

That evening, she heard the clatter of hooves, and went to the window to see who was approaching. She gasped when she recognised Lord Chancellor Gardiner and her former secretary, now Lord Paget, at the head of a small party of horsemen. What could they want here? Did they not know that Sir Thomas Cawarden was in London? Or maybe he had been released and they thought they might find him at Bletchingley.

She made herself walk slowly into the hall to receive the councillors. This was like the dark days when her marriage was being annulled and she had never known what the next visit from the Privy Council would bring.

'My lords, welcome,' she said, extending her hand, and the lords bowed over it. 'To what do I owe this pleasure?'

Gardiner fixed his eagle eyes on her. 'We would like to ask your Highness some questions relating to the late rebellion.'

They wanted information on Cawarden. She swallowed. She must never say she had known about the arms stashed away in the barn.

'I shall be glad to assist in any way I can,' she told them. 'Do come into my parlour, and I will have my servants bring some refreshments.'

They followed her, and she indicated that they should all sit at the table, where wine and little cakes were served within moments. When the door had closed, she waited.

Gardiner broke the silence. 'Madam, the Queen has received information that you were privy to the plotting of the rebels, and intrigued with your brother, the Duke of Cleves, and the King of France, to help the Lady Elizabeth gain the throne.'

Anna could not speak. She could see herself being arrested, languishing in the Tower, kneeling before the block . . . Had she survived her divorce to come to this? The shame, the pain . . . when she had done nothing!

'You do not say anything in your defence?' Paget asked.

She found her voice. 'No, my lord. I am too shocked. I have no need of a defence. That her Majesty should think me capable of this treason is beyond belief. Who is saying these things about me? It is all lies.'

Gardiner was watching her severely. 'We shall see,' he said. 'In fact, her Majesty is of the opinion that God has miraculously permitted these treasons to come to light, and furnished her with means to put a stop to them by punishing the guilty. Otherwise heresy would have found its way back to the kingdom, while she would have been robbed of her estate and England subjected to the will of the French. So she is absolutely determined to have strict justice done and make herself strong against further eventualities.'

'What treasons?' Anna demanded. 'I am guilty of nothing.'

'You are close to the Lady Elizabeth, are you not?'

'I would not say close, not at all. I rarely see her.'

'Yet you *are* close to Sir Thomas Cawarden.'

She had known from the first that that man was trouble. 'He rents one of my houses. He is not supposed to be there when I am in residence, but somehow he contrives to be.'

'And you have never put a stop to that?'

'My lord, you must know him. He is intimidating, and I do not like to cross swords with him too often. It is my house, and I like it to be a peaceful one.'

'You know that he is close to the Lady Elizabeth, and that she thinks well of him?' Gardiner's eyes were like steel.

'I did not know that. He is most secretive about his affairs.'

Paget leaned forward. He had been making notes while they had been speaking. 'Your servant, Florence of Diaceto, returned from overseas just as the rebellion was breaking out. He had on him letters and a token from the King of Denmark, who is a Lutheran and suspected of trying to aid the rebels. Madam, do you deny that you sent your servant to him for that very purpose?'

'I do indeed! This is nonsense. The late King Edward sent him. I do not know what his mission was.'

'So he was not acting on your behalf?'

'No.' She held Paget's gaze, reminding herself to warn Florence of what was being said about him.

Gardiner returned to the attack. 'We have reason to believe the King of France may make war on England because he desires to prevent the Queen's marriage to the Prince of Spain. Madam, can you tell me any other reason why King Henri would wish to make war on England?'

Anna was bewildered. 'I have no idea why you are asking me this, my lord.'

'Could it be because the Lady Elizabeth asked him to obtain revenge on behalf of the Duke of Cleves for King Henry's repudiation of your Highness?'

Anna gaped. 'That's ludicrous! Why would she do that? I was divorced fourteen years ago, and I have never borne any grudge about it. Always, I have tried to preserve the amity between England and Kleve.'

'We believe the Lady Elizabeth hoped to incite the Protestant German princes to turn their forces against England and so abet the rebels, which would aid her in seizing the throne.'

'And you think I asked her to do it? My lords, this is ridiculous!'

'The Council does not think so, nor the Spanish ambassador. The Lady Elizabeth's plea to the Duke of Cleves, on your behalf, suggests that you were complicit, and probably active, in the plot.'

Anna fought off despair. 'I have no knowledge of these affairs!' she protested. 'I have had no contact with the Lady Elizabeth since the coronation.'

Gardiner and Paget looked unperturbed. Paget reached into his scrip and handed her a letter. 'Read this, Madam. It is from the Emperor himself, stating that you were the author of this conspiracy and incited the Lady Elizabeth to act as intermediary. It was at your request that the King of France promised the Duke of Cleves to avenge the perceived wrongs done to you and him.'

Anna read the letter, fury mounting. 'What wrongs?' she demanded. 'The late King Henry was good to me. Our marriage was dissolved for sound reasons; I never contested them.'

'And yet you recently petitioned the Council to have it declared valid, for your personal gain. Madam, your duplicity is clear.'

'I acted on the advice of my brother's ambassador. He told me it would secure my dower rights and solve my financial problems, and that whether or not the marriage was valid was no longer important.' Gardiner made to speak, but Anna raised her hand to silence him. 'My lords, I am telling the truth. Aside from worrying over money, I have been contented in England. I bear no grudge for the dissolution of my marriage, nor ever have done. I have no desire to involve myself in public matters. Why would I jeopardise the favour Queen Mary shows to me?'

'You might if the Lady Elizabeth promised to be even more generous,' Paget said softly.

'I would have said no, most firmly.'

Gardiner sighed. 'So you deny it all?'

'Of course. I am the Queen's loyal subject, and will ever remain so.'

They stood up. 'Very well, Madam. We will report your answers to the Queen.'

'Pray give her Majesty my love and duty,' Anna said, rising to show them out, and hoping her legs would carry her.

When they had gone, she leaned back against the door, trembling, and waiting for her beating heart to still. Would the Queen believe her? Dear God, she prayed so.

Chapter 28

1554–1556

There followed days of anxiety. Anna could barely focus on anything, so great was her fear. It was as if all normal life had been suspended until she could be assured that she had a future.

'They can prove nothing against me, for there is nothing to prove,' she murmured against Otho's chest as he held her close one night.

'You are so tense,' he said, kneading her shoulder muscles.

'Is it any wonder? I just wish I could have some word from the Queen, to show she believes me. I would not lose her favour for anything.'

'I think, if she believed that you had plotted against her, you would have heard by now.' He kissed the top of her head. 'She must realise it was all nonsense.'

'You're probably right. At the very least, she would have stopped my allowance. But she has just sent money to supplement my servants' wages, as King Henry did. I doubt she would have done that if I was still under suspicion. I just wish she would invite me to court, so I can see for myself that all is well between us.'

But wish as she might, no invitation arrived. Nor was there any response to Anna's plea to have her marriage declared valid. Still she was listless, finding it hard to take an interest in anything. She was aware that her servants were taking advantage of her detachment from daily affairs, and subverting Jasper's efforts to make them economise, but she could not rouse herself to reprove them, or to heed his protests. She could not rid herself of the dread and fear that dominated her waking hours and stalked her dreams.

* * *

In the second week of March, Sir John entered the still room and told Anna that Sir Thomas Cawarden had not only been released from house arrest, but was back at court, and in favour too.

'He has resumed his official duties,' he related. 'He is ever the opportunist. He is diverting the Queen from her troubles by staging plays for her disport and recreation.'

'Are we to assume he has now turned Catholic?' Anna asked drily, pounding herbs in a mortar.

'He will always be a diehard Protestant, Madam, but I suspect he means to live to plot another day. My advice is to steer clear of him.'

'That is what I intend to do,' she declared. 'In fact, I am about to give the order to remove to Dartford. I was going to go to Westhorpe, but Sir Thomas Cornwallis has offered me a goodly sum for it, which will make me solvent for at least the foreseeable future. Jasper says I should keep the house and rent it out, but I have three other houses already.'

'Either way, you would raise money, Madam.'

'Well, I will think on it. Is there any news of the Lady Elizabeth?'

'Yes, Madam. She is in the Tower, being questioned about her part in the rising.'

Anna froze. 'Why?' She heard her voice quaver. 'What is she supposed to have done?'

'Incited Wyatt to rebel, I hear. But apparently there is no proof. One of the councillors, who is secretly her friend, told me they dare not deal with her too harshly, being aware that she might one day be queen.'

Anna was trembling. 'Surely the Queen will not execute her own sister?'

'I doubt it will come to that. There is talk of her being kept under house arrest.'

In trepidation, Anna wrote to Wilhelm, confiding to him how she had come under suspicion, and her fears that she might yet be implicated in whatever crimes Elizabeth was thought to have committed. A week later, she was filled with inexpressible relief to see Dr Cruser at her door, although it was hard to tell from his expression whether he brought good news or bad.

She took him into the garden, for they were enjoying a spell of warm spring weather, and she did not want their conversation to be overheard.

'Is there any word from the Duke?' she asked.

'My lady,' Dr Cruser said, 'there is nothing to fear. The Duke understands your situation, and will protect you. I have just delivered the most tactful letter from him to the Queen herself, in which he thanks her Majesty for the great kindness she has shown you, and congratulates her, on behalf of you both, on suppressing the recent rebellion. From which, Madam, she cannot but deduce that the Duke holds you for her true and loyal subject – and that, were that to be doubted, he would not be a bystander.'

Anna exhaled, much eased in her mind. This was comfort indeed. 'I cannot tell you how much my brother's support means to me. To have my loyalty doubted, without cause, has been a great trial to me. I have lived in fear these past weeks.'

'You need fear no more, Madam,' Dr Cruser said, his eyes kindly. 'The Queen spoke most pleasantly of you. I gained absolutely no impression that she doubts your friendship, or bears you any rancour.'

'Oh, that is good to hear!' Anna cried. She could have wept with relief. 'Tell me, how is my brother?'

'He is in health, Madam, but he is grieving. Alas, it is my melancholy duty to tell you that your sister, the Electress, and her husband, the Elector of Saxony, have both died. They succumbed to the same illness within ten days of each other.'

'Oh, my poor sister,' Anna faltered, stunned. She had not seen Sybilla in seventeen years, but the bonds of blood were strong, and she had always rejoiced that Sybilla had found love in her marriage. That love was legendary, so it was not surprising that the one could not live without the other. It was tragic that their reunion after the Elector's long imprisonment had been so brief.

She rose and led the way back to the house, dabbing her eyes. 'You must sup with us, and stay overnight,' she told Dr Cruser. As they passed through the downstairs rooms to the stairs, she saw him taking in his surroundings, and realised that the place was looking untidy and none too clean. She really must impose better order on her servants.

At supper, not wishing Dr Cruser to think she was letting things go, she wore a black velvet gown furred with ermine, like a queen's. But he was plain with her.

'Madam, it is clear to me that you need someone with authority to govern your servants. Mr Carew is ineffectual as a steward, as he has too many other duties. Herr Brockhausen tells me you do not listen to his advice, and that you are too lenient with your household.'

'I have been somewhat preoccupied by my troubles,' she admitted, 'but I will make amends.'

'Get a good man to run your house,' Dr Cruser advised, 'and don't sell Westhorpe. Herr Brockhausen's counsel is wise, and you would do well to heed it.'

'I shall, my friend,' Anna promised.

The next day, she asked Sir John if he knew of anyone who would make a suitable governor for her household, and he recommended that she approach the Council. In May, they appointed George Throckmorton, a kinsman of the late Queen Katharine, who had been at court serving Queen Mary as a gentleman pensioner. Anna liked him, and he was tactful yet firm with her servants. Having shaken off her melancholy, she took care to keep a watchful eye on how her house was being run, and was glad to see it looking cleaner and in better order.

After Dr Cruser left for Kleve, Anna retreated to Hever. She had resolved to spend her time in the country, and attend solely to domestic affairs. She would make sure that no one could ever again suspect her of treason.

Yet even in this peaceful place, the world intruded. In July, the Queen married the Prince of Spain in a lavish ceremony in Winchester Cathedral. Anna was not invited, which made her wonder if Mary still entertained doubts about her loyalty.

She could not bear to think it. She wrote to Queen Mary, congratulating her on her marriage and sending her humble commendations.

She prayed the Queen would continue to show favour to her, as she desperately needed assistance in paying her servants' wages, and assured her that she desired to wait on her at her pleasure. Having wished the royal couple much joy and the blessing of children, she waited tensely for some sign that Mary still loved her.

Anna clutched the package bearing the royal seal to her breast. The Queen had sent her five thousand pounds, proof, if she had needed it, that she was restored to favour. Her heart was ready to burst with relief.

It was now December, and four months since she had heard from the Queen. Unwillingly, she was coming to the conclusion that, while Mary had done her duty by her financially, she was not ready to fully extend the hand of friendship. Life, Anna reflected, could be deeply unfair, for she had done nothing to deserve this.

She sighed, and dragged her mind back to the present. Mr Carew had just complained that Sir Thomas Cawarden had defaulted on paying this quarter's rent for Bletchingley. Irritated, Anna picked up her quill and dashed off a stern letter, reminding Sir Thomas that his rent was nearly three months overdue, and she expected it to be paid before she departed for Penshurst for Christmas.

The money arrived tardily, on the very day she had planned to depart. The man was impossible! And yet she could not rid herself of him. He was a powder keg waiting to explode, and seemed not to care about the dangers he courted. Queen Mary might have begun her reign in a spirit of religious tolerance, but, in the wake of Wyatt's rebellion, she had taken a harder line. The Protestant faith had been outlawed. Only last month, England had formally been reconciled to Rome, and Parliament had reinstated the old law against heresy. Mary, it was clear, meant to eradicate all trace of religious dissent from her realm. From now on, relapsed heretics were to be burned at the stake.

Shuddering at the thought, Anna fervently hoped that Sir Thomas would keep his religious views to himself in future, for his own sake and the sake of those connected with him.

* * *

Dartford was splendid. When Anna finally made the move there in April, she wished she had done so long before. The place had been transformed since she had last seen it fifteen years ago. The manor house King Henry had built stood on the site of the old priory, and was surrounded by gardens and orchards and the white stone wall that had encircled the monastic buildings. There were two courtyards and a splendid range of royal apartments around the old cloisters. The nuns' church was now an office for the grooms of her chamber. As Anna walked up the processional staircase from the inner court, past pillars supporting the English lion and the Welsh dragon, she felt like the queen she should have been.

Upstairs, the royal chambers led off the staircase on either side. Wandering through the house, with her household trailing excitedly behind, she lost count of the number of rooms it contained. There were more than a hundred, she was sure!

The chapel was beautiful. Looking in awe at the jewelled crucifix, she wondered if the Lord Jesus approved of the burnings that were being carried out in His name. They had begun in February.

Anna feared Sir Thomas Cawarden would be lucky to escape a similar fate. He was in prison right now, because someone had informed on him. Sir John had been unable to find out the charge, for it was too dangerous to enquire closely into such matters, but Anna suspected it was heresy.

There had still been no word of Cawarden when, in May, Dr Cruser returned to England with news that the Duchess Maria had borne Wilhelm a son and heir named Karl, after the Emperor, who had graciously agreed to be the baby's godfather.

'A toast, in celebration of the news!' Anna cried, overjoyed, and her whole household gathered around to drink the infant's health. She looked fondly upon them all, especially Johann and Otho. They had become her family, and it was fitting they should share in her joy at welcoming its newest member.

Later, when the goblets had been cleared away, and everyone had returned to their duties, Anna bade Dr Cruser be seated, so that she could hear his other news.

'I have lately been at court,' he told her, 'where I heard that your tenant, Sir Thomas Cawarden, had been in prison.'

'Yes, but I don't know why,' Anna said, troubled.

'I was told he had defaced the parish church next to his house in London. The local people were so outraged they complained to the Privy Council. He refused to rebuild the church, which is why he was arrested. But he eventually undertook to provide a room for worship, so he was not prosecuted, and is now free.'

'He seems to court trouble.'

'Unfortunately, your Highness seems unwittingly to attract trouble-makers. Did you know that your cofferer, Herr Brockhausen, had written to the Duke complaining that you were low in funds?'

'Yes, I did. What with the upkeep of my houses and my household, we are spending money like water, and I cannot find it in my heart to approach the Queen for more.' She refrained from telling Dr Cruser that she was no longer sure she had the Queen's favour. 'But Jasper Brockhausen is no troublemaker. He nags me, it is true, but only because I'm not good with money, and he is. He's quite firm with me sometimes.'

'Your Highness should know that his letter prompted Franz von Waldeck to complain of him to the Duke.'

'Franz is no friend to him. *He* is the troublemaker, which was why he was summoned home in disgrace.'

'Yes, but he has portrayed himself as the injured party, and has gained the Duke's sympathy. He has accused Herr Brockhausen of various offences, and now your brother wants him removed from your household.'

Anna was bursting with indignation. 'How dare Franz interfere in my affairs? I don't want to lose Jasper. He has been a rock of support to me.'

'Franz has made some serious accusations against him.'

'Then he should hear them, and have the right to answer for himself.'

Anna summoned Jasper, and made Dr Cruser state what Franz was saying about him.

'What?' Jasper was appalled. 'I have *never* stolen from her Highness, or falsified her accounts; nor was I ever overfamiliar with her. How can he say that? And if I have remonstrated with her, it was for her own benefit.'

'That is true. It's all true.' Anna smiled at him to show that she believed and supported him.

'Madam, this is slander of the worst kind,' Jasper protested. 'I feel I must go to Kleve to defend myself against these accusations, if you will permit it.'

'Of course,' Anna said, wondering how she was going to manage while he was away.

'That is the wisest course,' Dr Cruser pronounced. 'But first, Herr Brockhausen, I will myself ask the Duke to guarantee that you will be allowed to return to England to resume your duties.'

'You must not leave until you are assured of that,' Anna told Jasper, and he reluctantly agreed.

After a frustrating delay, during which Wilhelm was persuaded to provide the requested guarantee, Jasper departed for Kleve, leaving behind a furious Gertie, who was ready to do all kinds of violence to Franz von Waldeck, should she get her hands on him.

Anna was already feeling overwhelmed by all this when a letter arrived from the Council, demanding that she dismiss Florence de Diaceto, who was suspected of intriguing with the French, and had been ordered to leave the realm within thirty days, on pain of imprisonment.

'Florence, you must read this!' she cried, when she had raced through the house and found him playing bowls with Otho in the grounds.

He read the letter, raising his eyebrows. 'I've served you loyally for fifteen years, Madam. I can only think that the Council have been suspicious of me since they impounded my letters in Dover last year.'

'I will go to court myself and speak for you,' Anna declared.

'No!' he said, so sharply she wondered if he did have something to hide. 'They might think you guilty by association. Madam, it is not fair that you be drawn into this. It is my problem.' Her suspicion deepened.

'I will seek help from my uncle,' he went on. 'He has friends in Paris, and I will go there.' Why go to Paris and not Kleve? she wondered.

Otho, standing behind Florence, nodded at Anna to agree.

'Very well,' she said, 'but I shall be deeply sorry to lose you, after all the good service you have given me. How will you live? They will stop your pension.'

'I have money saved,' he told her. 'I shall shift as best I can.'

'Are you sure there is nothing I can do?' Anna begged.

'Nothing, Madam,' Florence said.

'He's hiding something,' Otho muttered when Florence had gone. 'He never did tell us what was in those letters he brought from Denmark. And why did he stay all those months there – and come back by Dover, when it would have been easier to make land much further north? I have wondered if he went to France on the way. And these friends in Paris – are they really Dr Olisleger's?'

'But his family have always been loyal,' Anna protested, 'and he receives a pension from the Queen. Sir John is my only other servant so honoured. I think Florence got his for services to King Edward. I cannot believe . . .'

'It's not inconceivable that he was working for the French.'

Anna's thoughts went winging back to the previous year, when she herself had been suspected of doing just that. Had Florence, out of a sense of misplaced loyalty, tried to persuade the French King to make war on England on her behalf? It seemed far-fetched. Yet what other motive could he have had?

As they walked back to the King's Manor, she made up her mind to have it out with him. But when she sent a groom to summon him to her parlour, the young man returned alone. 'He has gone, my lady,' he said helplessly. Anna looked at Otho, whom she had asked to be present at the interview.

'God damn him!' he swore.

Anna sent for Dr Cruser, and related what had happened. 'He said he was going to Paris,' she said. 'I must beg a favour, my friend. Could you go home that way, and see if there is any news of him there?'

'I will do my best,' Cruser promised.

He had been gone for a week when Jasper returned from Kleve in a foul mood. When he came to see Anna, he had a simmering Gertie clinging to his arm.

'The Duke would not listen to me, Madam,' he growled. 'Franz has poisoned his mind against me, and he said that, while he would honour his promise to let me return to England, he will urge your Highness to dismiss me.'

'Rest assured, I will never do that,' Anna declared, 'and, if my brother complains of you to me, I shall tell him the truth.'

The Brockhausens looked relieved.

'Thank you, Madam,' Jasper said. 'With your leave, I will rest a while after my journey, then see to your accounts.'

Anna returned to her closet to find a letter waiting for her. She recognised Dr Cruser's handwriting. He had reached Paris without incident and, by great good chance, had encountered Dr Wotton, who was now serving as England's ambassador there. He had confided to Dr Wotton the purpose of his detour, and the doctor had revealed that he had been charged by the Council to keep an eye on Florence. Furthermore, Dr Cruser had learned that Florence had had many meetings with no less a personage than the Grand Constable of France, *and* with the entire French council. Dr Wotton thought that showed no good intent.

Anna dropped the letter. Maybe Florence *had* been responsible for her coming under suspicion, and all the unpleasant consequences she had suffered. If so, he had a great deal to answer for. The worst of it was, she had trusted him, as she had trusted his uncle – and now she felt she could not rely on her own judgement any more.

Dartford was a big house, and Anna lacked the means to furnish it properly. On a recent visit to Bletchingley, she had mentioned to Sir Thomas Cawarden that she was trying to find funds to buy what she needed for the King's Manor.

Two days after she returned to Dartford, three cartloads of furnishings turned up.

'They were sent by Sir Thomas Cawarden,' Mr Carew informed her.

She did not want to be obliged to Cawarden, yet she did not wish to appear churlish. 'Mr Carew, please write and tell him I am most grateful for his kindness, and will pay him back when I know the cost.'

Back came the prompt reply. The furnishings were a gift. In return, would she do Sir Thomas the great honour of visiting him at his house at the Blackfriars?

After he had been so generous, she could hardly refuse. She only hoped this was not a prelude to his making another unwelcome proposition to her.

Anna stared into her mirror. She was forty now, and had been fretting that it showed, but the reflection that looked out at her seemed little changed, the skin still smooth, the hair still yellow.

Mother Lowe tapped her on the shoulder. 'Mr Carew is here, Madam.'

Anna laid down her glass. 'Good day, Mr Carew,' she said, smiling.

'It is about your Highness's coming visit to London,' he replied, taking the stool she indicated. 'It is customary in this country for visiting royalty to send harbingers ahead with a list of their requirements.' Did she detect a note of mischief in his tone? She knew he did not like Sir Thomas. None of her servants did. That business with the tree-felling still rankled.

'It might be helpful to summon Meister Schoulenburg,' he advised. 'Sir Thomas would wish to be apprised of the foods your Highness enjoys.'

Meister Schoulenburg appeared to have been prepared for the summons. He insisted on Anna asking for lavish amounts of beer and wine, and presented a long list of the foods Sir Thomas might like to order – mutton, capons, rabbits, the best-quality wheat flour, raisins, prunes and costly spices. To this, Mr Carew added wood for the fires – which must not be stinted in this cold season – and torches to light the house.

'We must not forget fish,' he reminded her. Meister Schoulenburg suggested carp, pike, tench and other fresh fish. 'And maybe your

Highness should ask for a kitchen to be set aside, so that you can prepare dishes yourself, as you do here. Also, it might be best to ensure that Sir Thomas's kitchens are well equipped for the service of so many guests. Instruct him to obtain in advance . . . let me think: sixteen dozen earthenware pots, pewter pots for the buttery, pans, kettles, skillets, ladles, peelers, dressing knives, spits, racks, flesh hooks, tubs, baskets, trays and flasks.' The list seemed endless, and had obviously been well rehearsed.

Anna knew what they were doing. They were having their revenge on Sir Thomas.

'Is that everything?' she asked, unhappy at asking for so much. Cawarden might conclude that she meant to stay regularly at Blackfriars in the future, and she did not want him thinking that. 'Are you sure you need it all?'

'In my experience,' Mr Carew said, 'visiting households can face challenges when they find their hosts are not sufficiently prepared to receive them.' Herr Schoulenburg nodded vigorously. Anna gave in and signed the order.

Sir Thomas seemed to mind not one jot that she had made so many demands. His welcome was warm, if not overpowering, and he proudly showed Anna around his domain. His house was not large, having just twelve rooms, but it was in a most desirable part of London. It stood in a precinct, in which she could see the ruins of what appeared to have been a monastery.

'This was the house of the Black Friars, where King Henry's nullity suit against Queen Katherine was heard back in 1529,' Sir Thomas said. Now, there were houses on the site, and business premises. Anna saw a bookbinder's and a printer's.

'I lease the houses,' he said. 'Lord Cobham has one.'

They returned to his parlour, where supper was about to be served.

'Everything your Highness asked for has been provided,' he beamed. 'I outlaid forty-one pounds of my own money on those items and more.' That was substantially above the annual rent he paid for Bletchingley.

It was bad manners to tell a guest how much you had spent on entertaining them, and Anna felt uncomfortable.

The supper was good, the mutton tender and tasty, the fish delicate in flavour, steeped in a rich cheese sauce. Sir Thomas exerted himself to be witty, and Anna began to relax. She caught Otho's eye across the table. It held the promise of private pleasures to come. But they would have to take great care to be discreet.

As ever, their lovemaking left them unsatisfied. Now, more than ever, Anna feared risking a pregnancy. Queen Mary would be utterly shocked.

As they lay entwined, talking about the evening just past. Otho's hand strayed to Anna's breast – and stopped. 'What's that?' he asked, and guided her fingers. There was a hard lump, the size of a pea, beneath her skin.

'It's probably a mole or a spot,' she said. 'It doesn't hurt.'

'I've not felt it before,' he murmured. Anna realised she hadn't either.

She forgot about it the next morning, when she donned an apron and made for the laundry, which was serving as her personal kitchen, to dress the fish that would be served to the top table at dinner. She walked into a scene of devastation. There, scattered about the kitchen floor and table, lay most of the new kitchen equipment, broken and spoiled.

'What has happened?' she cried.

Her servants looked as bewildered as she was.

'I do not know,' Herr Schoulenburg said. 'Someone, it seems, has been a little clumsy.'

'Aye,' some others agreed. Anna frowned. Was this more revenge being exacted for Cawarden's complaints about the tree-felling?

'Clear it up, please,' she said. 'I will tell Sir Thomas.'

He came down himself, frowning, to inspect the damage. 'You have all been wantonly careless!' he shouted. 'You should have more respect for other people's property. This stuff was provided against your mistress's coming, and now it is unusable. How am I to provide her with good service now?'

'It's all right, Sir Thomas,' Anna said hastily, glad of an excuse to leave. 'We will not impose on you any more. I can come another time.'

He rounded on her. 'What about the money I have outlaid, Madam, and the losses I have incurred through your servants' *carelessness?*' His emphasis on the word was deliberate, she knew.

She could not repay him; as usual, she was short of money.

'I am very sorry for it,' she said, feeling humiliated.

'Very well,' he replied, after a pause. 'I shall petition the Privy Council for compensation.'

'I do hope they will help,' Anna said, and fled to her room to pack.

Chapter 29

1556

Cawarden had been arrested again. The household was agog, crowding into the hall as Sir John, standing in his riding clothes, related to Anna what he had learned at court.

'Lord Paget told me the Council uncovered details of a Protestant plot to rob the Exchequer and set the Lady Elizabeth on the throne. Sir Thomas was plainly implicated; he and other gentlemen were to intercept any treasure sent abroad by the Queen to King Philip in Spain. One confessed that some of the conspirators were Members of Parliament who despised the Queen and her faith, and had declared themselves true Protestants.' Anna could easily imagine Sir Thomas doing that. How reckless he was. Did he not know that even Archbishop Cranmer had not been exempt from the heresy laws? He had suffered only this month; Anna had heard he had held his right hand in the flames, saying it should be punished first, as it had signed the recantation he had afterwards abjured.

She was glad to be at Dartford. She felt relatively safe here. Should the Council suspect her of too close an association with Cawarden and his heretical friends, it was well placed for an easy escape from England by sea.

The next she heard, Sir Thomas had been released, after binding himself for four thousand pounds to reappear before the Council by November. So he was still under suspicion.

Anna hoped he would clear himself. She worried that her fate was linked to his, and she did not want to flee England. She had grown fond of the country and its people, and, for all the squabbles, the life she lived in her beautiful houses with those she loved most around her.

Johann was twenty-five now, a tall, blonde giant with a gentle nature and a willing heart. She adored him, and often wondered if he suspected that he meant more to her than any servant could. She wished, more than anything else on earth, that she could tell him she was his mother, and lavish openly on him all the love she had had to keep hidden.

There was little for her now in Kleve, where Wilhelm had strangely prospered under the Emperor's direction, and was building and beautifying fortresses and palaces and earning himself the nickname 'Wilhelm the Rich'. He was preoccupied with his wife and his growing family. Emily was living out a spinster's existence, and seemed to have lost her youthful vivacity, if her letters were anything to go by. From them, Anna learned that her sister spent an inordinate amount of time quarrelling with Wilhelm. She did not want to get caught up in that. All she wanted was peace in which to lead the life she had built for herself.

The late spring brought with it Franz von Waldeck, on a ship from Germany.

Anna received him coldly. 'I did not look to see you here again,' she said.

His blue eyes narrowed. 'The Duke sent me, Madam, as his emissary. He desires you to dismiss the Brockhausens and . . .' his eyes strayed to Otho, who was standing by Anna's chair, 'and Herr von Wylich.'

Anna was so horrified she felt she would faint. It would be bad enough to have to get rid of Jasper and Gertie, but to lose Otho? That would be beyond dreadful . . . She would never, ever allow it to happen.

She could sense indignation emanating from Otho himself.

'Might I remind you, Franz,' she seethed, her voice taut with anger and fear, 'that these good people have given me years of loyal service. Jasper deserves only praise for his efforts to save me money and conserve my funds. And yet, having caused discord in my house in the past, and having presumed too far on our blood tie – for which, I might remind you, you were recalled to Kleve – you come here today and demand that I dismiss them. Well, I declare to you here and now, I will not! Now go.'

Franz glowered at her. He gave a curt bow, and stalked out.

'I will write to my brother,' Anna told Otho. 'I will make him aware of the perfidy of this rogue. Do not worry, my love. I will never let you go.' She reached for his hand and squeezed it, caring not who saw.

After Franz had left, and her letter to Wilhelm had been sent by fast courier, Anna hoped that would be the end of the matter. She was surprised when Dr Harst arrived at Dartford a fortnight later, looking plumper and greyer, and none too pleased to be there.

Wilhelm would have sent him, she did not doubt it. As she attended to the courtesies that must be extended to a visitor, even an unwelcome one, she determined to resist any pressure that might be brought to bear on her. Never would she allow the removal of Otho or the Brockhausens.

'Well, Dr Harst,' she said, when, at last, they were alone in her privy chamber. 'What brings you to England?'

'A delicate matter, Madam. Your brother thought that, as I have known you a long time, I might be best placed to broach it.'

She guessed what was coming.

Harst handed her a letter. It was from Wilhelm, warning her not to persist in retaining those three servants who were causing so much dissension. He had heard from Franz von Waldeck that they were exerting an unhealthy influence over her, even to the extent of un-balancing her mind.

Her eyes narrowed in anger. What on earth did Wilhelm mean? What lies had Franz fed him?

'This is wicked calumny,' she flared. 'It makes no sense to me, unless it is the malice of a troublemaker at work.'

'Madam,' Dr Harst said, 'the Duke believes Herr Brockhausen and his wife are driving you to despair by trying constantly to poison your mind against Herr von Waldeck.'

'They are doing no such thing,' Anna corrected him. 'I have lived here in harmony with them since he left. If anyone is driving me to despair, it is him.'

'Madam, I fear you are labouring under a delusion, and cannot see what is happening under your very nose.'

'Oh, come, Dr Harst, you know me better than that!'

'Madam, Herr von Waldeck is concerned that Frau Brockhausen has bewitched you.'

Anna gaped at him. 'Clearly, it is *he* whose mind has been affected! Really, I marvel that you and my brother pay heed to his poisonous accusations. They are sheer invention. I think, Dr Harst, you had better leave.'

'Madam, please!' He looked distressed. 'I must talk to you, for there is another concern, about the pernicious hold Herr von Wylich appears to have on you. There has been talk in your household about a more familiar association than is seemly.'

Anna was overcome with anger and fear. The world tilted, but she determinedly gathered her thoughts, resolved to fight for the man who meant more to her than any other. 'That too is a calumny,' she declared. 'I resent such an allegation. He is my kinsman, and very dear to me. There is nothing unseemly between us.' Yes, it was a lie, but, if Franz could play a dirty game, so could she.

Dr Harst rose. 'I am relieved to hear it,' he said, not sounding entirely convinced. 'I will return to Kleve and inform the Duke of your response to his letter. In the meantime, for the avoidance of further unpleasantness, I advise your Highness to dismiss those three servants.'

'It is out of the question,' Anna told him.

Wilhelm couldn't make her get rid of them, she told herself. He was in Kleve, many miles away. He had no authority here. Always she had been obedient to his wishes, in great matters as well as small ones – but this was not his concern. It was a domestic matter, just a nasty squabble.

She would defy him if he insisted. The Brockhausens did not deserve to be laid off for no good reason. As for Otho, he was the breath of life to her, and she needed him more than ever now – especially since noticing that the lump in her breast had got bigger. She had mentioned it to Mother Lowe, who had advised her to consult Dr Symonds. But Anna would not. She could not face the embarrassment, and she was too scared of what the doctor might say. But she could talk to Otho, and confide her fears to him. She was putting the moment off, though, because once she had told him why she was worried, there could be no more carrying on as if everything was normal.

She blurted it out that night, unable to tolerate the anxiety on her own any longer.

'You look at it,' she begged. 'I can't bear to touch it, or see it.'

Otho gently probed the place. 'It is bigger. You must see Dr Symonds.' He looked so concerned it frightened her.

'I can't face it,' she wept.

'Anna, it may be nothing. And, if it is, there will be more chance of a cure than if you seek help too late. I'm not trying to frighten you, sweetheart. I just want you to be reassured. Promise me you will see the doctor.'

Anna took a deep breath. 'Very well,' she sniffed.

'You may lace your bodice now, my lady,' Dr Symonds said, his voice calm and professional, giving away nothing.

Holding her breath, Anna made herself decent.

The doctor sat down. 'It is a cancer, my lady, which is not a common ailment. What you have is a hard tumour. It sticks fast to certain parts of the body, as does the crab from which cancer gets its name. It is caused by a dry, melancholic humour in the veins encircling it, and sometimes by evil diet.'

'You can cure it?' she asked anxiously.

'Hopefully, Madam. I shall first try purging the offending humour by bleeding you. If you would bare your arm, please.'

Hoping and praying that this would work, but unsure if the doctor was telling her everything, Anna unfastened her sleeve, and Dr Symonds applied leeches.

'Try to avoid pressing the part, take moderate exercise, especially before meals, get seven or eight hours' sleep every night, and eat a good diet. Abstain from fasting, and things that heat the blood, like salt flesh, hare, venison, spices, cheese and mustard. Eat nourishing meats such as mutton, veal, capons and other sorts of fowl. Whey, a little ale and white wine are good.'

It all sounded very comforting and reassuring. Surely Dr Symonds would not be prescribing such a simple cure, rather than more radical measures, if the disease was serious?

She rose. 'Thank you, Dr Symonds. Do I need to consult you again?'

'Only if you are worried,' he said.

The messenger wore the Queen's livery; the letter he brought carried the royal seal. Anna broke it open. Was this, at last, the summons to court she had longed for?

The first thing she saw was Mary's ornate signature. Then she read the rest.

At the behest of the Duke of Cleves, the Council had been instructed to order the deportation of three alien offenders, viz. Herr Brockhausen and his wife, and Herr von Wylich. My lady of Cleves was ordered to dismiss them from her service forthwith, that they might make their way back to Germany.

'No!' she wailed, and fell to her knees, keening helplessly, bringing her servants running to find out what was the matter, and Otho, inexpressibly dear Otho, who took her in his arms in front of them all and gentled her. With trembling hands, she showed him the Queen's letter.

By the time he had read it, he was shaking too, and passed it to Jasper and Gertie.

'I will fight this!' he said. 'I will go to court and expose that bastard Waldeck for what he is. I will demand to see the Queen!'

Anna laid her hand on his arm. 'I will go, Otho.' She knew she would deal more tactfully with Mary than he would. Righteous fury might get the better of him. It was more advisable to go as a sorrowful plaintiff than as an angry one.

She rode to Greenwich Palace, taking Johann for moral support. Yet, sitting in her litter, she could barely look at him, for, each time she did, she was reminded that he was at risk of losing the father he had never known as his. And she – sweet Jesus, her loss did not bear thinking about! So she would not think about it. She must be strong, and gird her loins for the task that lay ahead.

She found the court overwhelming, after so long an absence: the press of people, the noise, the never-ending scramble for advancement. An usher disappeared with her request for an audience with the Queen, and it was two hours before he returned.

'Her Majesty begs your forgiveness, my lady, but she was giving audience to the Spanish ambassador. Follow me, please.'

Mary's presence chamber was stuffy in the August heat, and she herself looked ill and diminished, despite the gorgeous gown of cloth of gold and the sparkling jewels. As she stretched out her hand to be kissed, she gave Anna a guarded smile. 'It is good to see your Highness. How can I help you?'

'Madam, I have come to plead for my servants,' Anna said. 'Your Majesty is the only person I can turn to for help.'

'You mean the three Clevelanders who are to be deported?'

'Yes, Madam. False accusations about them were made to my brother by one who bears them malice, and whom I have expelled from my household. They are all three good and devoted servants on whom I rely heavily.'

Mary's tired face looked vexed. 'This places a different perspective on the matter,' she said, 'but I am in a difficult position. I was informed that not a stone had been left unturned to have these people removed from your service, but that it had been in vain, which was why the Duke had sent a lawyer to ask me to exercise my authority to expel them from England. He informed me that Mistress Brockhausen especially was a troublemaker, and that, by spells and enchantments, she had driven your Highness to madness.'

'That is nonsense, Madam,' Anna interjected. 'As you can see, I am as sane as any. Gertie Brockhausen is no enchantress, rather a down-to-earth, honest woman who has my interests at heart. Your Majesty, it is all calumny, believe me.' She recounted what had passed between Franz von Waldeck and the others during the past few years, and told her about Franz's attempt to be named her heir. 'Herr Brockhausen reported his presumption, and my brother recalled Herr von Waldeck, who then poisoned his mind against these loyal servants. Your Majesty, I beg of you, do not deprive me of three persons I love and rely upon!'

She was relieved to see Mary looking at her sympathetically.

'In view of what you have told me, I will ask King Philip what he thinks,' the Queen said. There was a touch of wistfulness in her voice as she continued, 'I am expecting him to return to England soon, but he is in Ghent now, so I will send a messenger in order that this business may be settled speedily. I will ask him if, given this new information, it is compatible with my honour and his for us to do as the Duke requires. I trust that in a few days we will hear back and make an end of the matter.'

Anna could not understand why Mary was unable to make the decision herself.

'Does your Majesty need the King's approval in this matter?' she asked, and immediately regretted it, for Mary's smile instantly disappeared.

'You may have forgotten, my Lady Anna, that Kleve is under the protection of his Majesty's father, the Emperor, who takes a keen interest in its affairs.'

'Of course,' Anna said. 'I meant no criticism, Madam.'

'Go home now,' Mary said. 'I will have the Council write to you when I have heard from his Majesty.'

Reluctantly Anna curtseyed and dragged herself away, fearing she had upset Mary and that her mission had been in vain. She went home feeling dejected, and could not shake off a sense that the worst was about to happen – and that it might be her own fault for being tactless.

A week later, the Council summoned Otho and the Brockhausens to come before them, with two other servants as witnesses to the proceedings. Filled with trepidation, Anna delegated two grooms to perform that office, and herself travelled to Greenwich with them all, unable to face waiting at home for news.

She stayed behind with Johann in a crowded gallery after the others had gone into the council chamber. Having been unable to eat breakfast, she was swaying with anxiety, and a worried usher had to fetch a stool for her.

When the council chamber door opened, she sprang up, every nerve taut with apprehension. Otho's heavy expression warned her that the news was not good. Gertie was weeping.

People were staring, so, not allowing herself to think, Anna beckoned the three of them to follow her, and led them down the stairs to the gardens, where Otho took her in his arms and held her tight. He was crying.

'It is bad news, Anna,' he said, trying to master himself. 'The King insisted that the Duke of Kleve's wishes be complied with as soon as possible. We are all to leave England before All Saints' Day.' His voice broke.

She could not speak. Frantically calculating, she realised she had just seven short weeks left with him. She could feel her heart breaking, and wanted to scream, but she saw Johann's face working in distress and put her arms around him, not caring who saw.

'We are ordered to depart from your Highness's house and family, and never after to enter any of your houses,' Jasper muttered. 'I am commanded never more to meddle or busy myself in the administration of your household or other affairs.'

'And none of us can ever return to your service, except at our utmost peril,' Gertie sobbed.

Anna had half a mind to go straight back into the palace and demand that the Council rescind the orders of banishment, but she felt so faint and ill that she could barely stand. And what good would it do? She had already appealed to the Queen and laid her case before her. The King had now spoken, and it was unthinkable that Mary would gainsay him.

They rode back to Dartford in a sombre, dejected mood. Johann wept all the way. Anna gazed out of the window, clutching Otho's hand. It was too late now for discretion. She did not care if the whole world knew of their love. All she could think of was that he would be going from her. She could not, *would* not, let it happen. She would think of a plan.

That night, she clung to him as never before. 'Take me properly,' she begged. 'For you, my beloved, I would risk anything. All I want is to be close to you. Nothing else matters now.'

It felt wonderful to be totally possessed, after the years of abstinence and frustration, and yet it was a bittersweet joy shot through with terrible sorrow. But they *must* have a future together; there had to be a way to contrive it.

'I will come with you,' she said, as they lay in each other's arms afterwards.

'Anna, I could not ask it, although I too have thought of it. By myself, I have nothing to offer you. I am a bastard, and have no fortune of my own. I must go to my cousin and presume on his charity. I dare not ask him to receive you as well. Your brother would be furious; it would go ill for my cousin.'

'Then marry me now. Let us present Wilhelm with a fait accompli.'

'Darling, have you considered the consequences? I would marry you tomorrow, but I am the man whose deportation he demanded. King Philip has ordered it, and your brother will not risk offending the Emperor. I am hardly a desirable bridegroom. If we married and went back to Kleve as man and wife, he might kill us both.'

'Then let us marry and go elsewhere!'

'Where? Anna, be realistic. Don't you think I haven't thought this through already? If you leave England, you will forfeit all your settlement. How could I subject you to that? You have spent your life in comfort. You do not know what true penury is. And there is Johann to think of too. He is happy here, in your service. Would you uproot him from that?'

'He has his craft to fall back on.'

'Yes, but a journeyman needs premises in which to ply his craft, and money to establish them.'

Anna sat up. 'I have the perfect idea. I'm sure that his foster parents would take us in, if we apprised them of the situation.'

'Anna, think what you would be asking of them. They would feel obliged to keep you in a manner befitting your estate. Even if they could afford it, they would live in fear of the Duke's vengeance, should he discover where you were. For, be assured, all Europe would be looking for you. Princesses don't just disappear as it pleases them. No, what I have in mind is better.' He pulled her to him, and cradled her head on his shoulder. 'I will go back to Kleve, do my utmost to show the Duke that Franz was wrong, and prevail on him to request my reinstatement in your household, along with Jasper and Gertie.'

'It might mean a long separation,' she wept.

'It is the best way. I will come back to you, I promise.' His voice faltered, and then his tears were mingling with hers.

Chapter 30

1556–1557

The dreaded day had come. Anna and Otho had said their passionate, desperate farewells in private, and now she was standing in the outer court, with her household lined up behind her, to say goodbye to him, and to Jasper and Gertie. They were all calm and tight-lipped, having steeled themselves for the inevitable.

Otho had never looked so handsome and desirable as when he bowed to her and took her hand, his lips lingering on it for as long as was decently possible. She gazed into his warm blue eyes, praying it was not for the last time.

'Until we meet again,' she said, putting on a brave smile.

'Adieu, dear lady,' he replied, and swung himself up onto his horse.

Anna kissed Jasper and Gertie goodbye, barely taking her eyes off Otho, and then they were spurring their mounts and riding away, through the gatehouse and out of her life.

She had never felt so desolate. That very morning, she had probed the lump in her breast for the first time in weeks, and found it had grown bigger. She had not told Otho. She had not wanted him to go away worrying about her. But her heart was heavy with fear. If, or when, he prevailed upon Wilhelm to let him return to England, would it be too late for her?

It was more than five months now since Otho had gone from Anna – five long, dragging, miserable months, and still Wilhelm would not receive him. She was desperate, wild with her need, and so, so lonely. Time, she knew, was running out for her.

There was now a sore on her breast, loathsome to look at, sordid and stinking. Its appearance had driven her to consult Dr Symonds again, and he had peered at it, wrinkled his nose and frowned.

'There are various remedies I could try,' he said. 'I once treated a nun who had a cancer in her breast, with a sore such as this one. I soaked a cloth in the urine of a young boy and applied it to the wound, and by this remedy, I preserved her life for ten years. I also knew a doctor who swore by the application of goat's dung mixed with honey, which he said could kill a cancer. Shall we try the urine, Madam?'

Anna nodded her head reluctantly. She waited while the doctor summoned his young son to make water, and held her breath as he slapped the wetted cloth, still warm, on her breast.

'We will try this daily until the sore improves,' Dr Symonds said. 'There's plenty more where that came from!'

Anna refrained from checking herself every day to see if the sore was better. Instead, she tried to focus on her financial affairs. She had engaged Sir Richard Freston in Jasper's place, on Mr Carew's recommendation, but he was nowhere near as efficient as Jasper had been, and lacked the authority to impose economies. Once again, she was low in funds.

Late the previous year, when she had asked the Council for help, they had merely taken back The More, saying it would save her money to have one house fewer to keep up. They'd also suggested she exchange Westhorpe for another property, but she had resisted. Now, Sir Richard Freston and Mr Throckmorton were urging her to part with it, and she was seriously considering going ahead. What need did she have of a great palace like Westhorpe, when she had Dartford and Penshurst and the use of Bletchingley?

She did not like to look into her mirror these days. The last time, she had been shocked to see herself looking so pale and thin. Her clothes were now hanging on her, even when laced to the fullest extent. Her strength was failing, she knew it. She had noticed her household fussing around her more than usual, alert to every little need.

Word had reached the Queen that she was unwell. She was informed, by Lord Paget in person, that Mary was sorry to hear it.

'Her Majesty has granted you the use of the palace of Chelsea,' he said, and there was in his eyes a rare gentleness. 'It is in a healthy, rural location by the Thames, and has beautiful gardens, which should be looking their best at this time of year.'

'I am deeply touched by her Majesty's kindness,' Anna told him. 'Chelsea might be just the tonic I need.'

'The Queen thought it would be an excellent place in which to rest and recover,' Paget said. 'For my part, I wish your Highness a speedy return to health. May God have you in His keeping.'

A change, she reckoned, might do her the power of good. In May, as soon as the keys to Chelsea were in her hands, she ordered her household to make ready for the move.

If only Otho could be here with her, she thought, as she beheld the exquisite little palace, its mullioned windows glinting in the sunshine. The longing for him was a constant piercing ache, worse than the pain in her breast. How he would love this place! It was a peaceful haven, and she began to hope that, living in this healthful air, she would at last be cured.

'I will walk a while before exploring the house,' she said. 'The gardens are in glorious bloom.'

Alighting from her litter, she took Johann's arm and strolled slowly along the path to her privy garden, savouring the heady scent emanating from the banks of rosemary, the borders of lavender, the damask roses and the privet hedges. There were cherry trees, filbert and damson trees, even peach trees.

'Didn't Queen Katharine live here with Admiral Seymour?' she asked Sir John Guildford, who was following behind with her other officers and her ladies. Mother Lowe was waddling along, leaning on her stick and admiring the flowers.

'Yes, Madam, and then it was leased to the Duke of Northumberland's widow. I believe it has been in the Crown's hands since her death last year.'

The palace was built of brick. It had three halls, three parlours, three kitchens and fine chambers on the ground floor. Upstairs, Anna found three withdrawing rooms and seventeen bedchambers. The apartment she chose for herself was a summer bedchamber overlooking the Great Garden.

By the time she had finished the tour, she was exhausted, and lay down on her bed to sleep, with a breeze from the open window playing on her face. 'Otho, my beloved,' she murmured. 'Please come soon!'

She awoke to pain. The sore on her breast was throbbing as never before. She caught her breath, wincing.

Mother Lowe was sitting by the bed, peering at her anxiously. She was old now, and weak, so Anna had not confided in her how bad her malady was. But those faded eyes missed little.

'I'm not blind, you know,' Mother Lowe said. 'I can see you are suffering. You've not been well for some time, have you?'

'No,' Anna admitted. 'I did not want you to fret about me, as I knew you would do. But I have felt so poorly lately, and I don't seem to be getting any better. In fact, I feel worse as each day goes by – and I'm frightened!' She gripped Mother Lowe's hand.

'Hush now,' the nurse soothed, stroking Anna's hair. 'Tell me what's the matter.'

'It's this.' Anna unlaced her bodice and pulled down her chemise. She watched Mother Lowe recoil, saw the horrified look on her face, quickly masked by a reassuring smile.

'Well, we'd better get Dr Symonds to have another look at that,' she said, her voice hoarse.

The doctor came quickly and examined the sore, tight-lipped. Anna summoned the courage to peer at it, and wished she hadn't, for it was livid and blackened, with a rough surface.

'The urine cure didn't work,' she whispered.

There was a pause. 'No, my lady, but there are others we can try. I recommend a poultice of oil of roses, burnt lead and camphor, and will have it mixed in a mortar. Applied to the sore, it will corrode the acrimony of the evil humour.'

She prayed he was right. Mother Lowe stood by as the pungent-smelling ointment was applied, and Anna offered up fervent prayers for its efficacy.

That month, Anna learned that Sir Thomas Cawarden had been incarcerated in the Fleet prison. Sir John did not know why, but feared it was to do with some heresy. Anna prayed for Cawarden's deliverance. He was his own worst enemy, for certain, reckless and indiscreet. She would wager he had been involved in every plot against the Queen.

But gradually, as the summer days lengthened, Sir Thomas, the world and its superficial affairs seemed increasingly far away. By June, Anna's universe had narrowed down to her summer bedroom, for she no longer had the strength to leave her bed. The ointment had been of no use, yet still Dr Symonds laboured indefatigably to cure her, or at least alleviate some of the pain she was suffering. It was eating into her now. Her surgeon, Mr Blundey, bled her as often as he dared, to balance her body's humours and rid it of the poison that had invaded it.

Mother Lowe was in constant attendance, insisting on doing even the most menial nursing chores herself, and Anna's ladies and maids were ever at the ready to perform the smallest task for her. Meister Schoulenburg served up the choicest fare, in small portions, for she could eat little, and all her officers and servants took great pains to see to her comfort. She felt surrounded by love. But the love she needed most was denied her.

By the middle of July, she knew she was dying. She could barely endure the pain, which no medicine could relieve, and could only pray that the end would come soon. There had been no good news from Kleve, and she knew now that, short of a miracle, she would never see her beloved Otho again in this world. All she had left of him was their son, whom she rarely saw now, since his duties did not often bring him into the sickroom. How she missed the constant sight of him!

In her dreams, she was whole again, and she and Otho were lovers, untrammelled by convention or the cruel decrees of others. They were such vivid dreams that when she awoke, she thought they had been real. It was a misery to her to be dragged back into her woeful existence.

* * *

It could not be long now, she knew it. She sent for a lawyer, and dictated to him her will. It took four days, since the effort tired her so much.

'I bequeath my soul to the Holy Trinity. My body is to be buried where it shall please God,' she instructed. 'I pray that the Queen's most excellent Majesty will ensure that my debts are paid; and I ask that my executors be good masters to my poor servants, to all of whom, as well as to my faithful officers, I give and bequeath one whole year's wages, and as much black cloth as will make every one of them a mourning gown with a hood and coat. Ooh . . .'

The pain was so bad that she could not go on.

The next day, she felt a little better, and directed the lawyer to draw up a list of bequests to be given to Mother Lowe and the gentlewomen of her privy chamber for the great pains they had taken in serving and, latterly, nursing her. She rested after that, and partook of a little pottage. In the afternoon, she enumerated the bequests to her gentlemen, her yeomen and her grooms, insisting that one pound each be left to all the children of her servants.

On the third day, feeling herself growing weaker, she directed that Wilhelm be given her gold ring with the diamond shaped like a heart. To Wilhelm's wife, she left a ruby ring, and to Emily another diamond ring. She thought too to remember the Duchess of Suffolk, who had been a friend to her in the past; she was to have a gold ring with a table diamond. She left a ring to Lord Paget too, because he had shown kindness to her when they last met.

That was enough for now, she told the lawyer. The pain was gnawing, so badly she could barely speak. She looked down at her wasted body; it was so slight under the light counterpane. She was fading away.

That evening, she felt able to resume. She directed that her plate, jewels and robes be sold with her other goods to pay her debts, legacies and funeral expenses.

She remembered Dr Symonds and Mr Blundey. They must be well rewarded for their pains. Nor did she forget her chaplains, whom she asked to pray for her, or her old laundress. She left money for the education of the alms children she had succoured out of charity, and for the poor people of Richmond, Bletchingley, Hever and Dartford.

It grieved her that she could not openly acknowledge Johann, or give him more than his fellow servants; she had to content herself with leaving him the same sum they would receive. To Otho she left twenty pounds, all she could afford. It was a small price to pay for his devotion over the years, and all that he was to her, but he would understand, and it would help him to start a new life in Kleve.

On the fourth day, Anna remembered everyone else she wanted to benefit from her will. Mindful that her German servants might wish to go home to Kleve, she left money to assist their passage.

'And lastly,' she murmured, 'I earnestly desire our most dear and entirely beloved sovereign lady, Queen Mary, to be the overseer of my will, and to see it carried out as shall seem best for the health of my soul. In token of the special trust and affection I have in her Grace, I wish her to have my best jewel. And because her Majesty's late father of most famous memory, King Henry the Eighth, said to me that, if I died, he would account my servants his own, I beseech her to accept them in this time of their extreme need. And I would like the Lady Elizabeth to have my second-best jewel.'

A few more bequests to her executors, and it was done. The lawyer gave her the document and shakily she wrote, 'Anna, the daughter of Kleve'.

He looked at her, his eyes full of compassion. 'My lady, I have drawn up many wills in my time, but I have never seen one that contains such kindness and compassion for others. May God bless you, and ease your pain.'

Her chaplains stayed with her all that night, kneeling by her bed and praying. She felt death drawing near, yet there was one more thing she must do before she left this world. Lying there feeling her strength ebb away, she had thought long and hard on the matter, and now her mind was made up.

'Send for Johann,' she bade Sir Otto Rumpello, interrupting his prayers. 'This will not wait.'

He gave her a searching look, but rose from his knees and hastened away.

When Johann came, looking plainly shocked to see her so ill, she sent the chaplain away and reached for his hand.

'I am dying,' she said gently, 'and I wanted to see you one more time.'

'No!' he protested, his eyes wet with sorrow. 'No, you cannot be dying.'

She squeezed his hand to still his distress. 'It is God's will,' she said, 'and we must bow to His pleasure. I have left you a bequest. It is not enough, and I want you to know why. You see, my dear Johann, even now I have to keep it a secret . . .' She was so weak with emotion she could barely continue, and lay for a few moments just gazing at his beloved face. Then she made a great effort to speak. 'My darling boy, you are my son, and Otho von Wylich is your father.'

He stared at her, his eyes brimming with tears. 'Am I dreaming?' he asked. 'In faith, I am speechless.'

'Do not be angry with me for failing to tell you,' she pleaded. 'When I am gone, go to your father in Kleve, and he will explain all. I want you to know that I have loved you with all my heart, all your life, and that it has been a tragedy to me that I could never recognise you as my own. But I have loved you, and watched over you, and longed for you, and you will take that love with you wherever you go. It is my true bequest to you.'

To her joy, Johann bent forward, tears streaming down his cheeks, and gathered her gently in his arms. 'My mother,' he said wonderingly. 'In some way I must have known it, for truly I have loved you too.'

'Say you forgive me!' Anna begged, using the last of her strength to embrace him as tightly as she could.

'I would forgive you anything, my lady mother, you know that,' he wept. 'I am sure you had your reasons. And I am proud, proud to be your son!'

The pain struck then, like a knife in Anna's bosom. She cried out, clutching herself, and Johann shouted for help. They came running, the chaplain and the doctor and the women, even Mother Lowe on her creaking legs. Soon the whole household had crowded into the bedchamber.

Sir Otto gave Anna the last rites of the Church, as everyone knelt around the bed. Anna was barely aware of making her peace with God, the pain was so vicious. When she had received the final blessing, and been anointed with holy oil for her final journey, she lay there trying to rise above the agony, with Mother Lowe and Johann holding her hands, one on each side of the bed. She could hear her people weeping. But they should be glad for her. Her ordeal would soon be over.

And then, suddenly, the pain was gone, and he was there, coming through the door, her handsome, shining Otho, and he was standing beside Johann, and they were a family at last, as they had never been before, and her heart was soaring with joy. He had come back for her, as he had promised.

Author's Note

Anna of Kleve was the only one of Henry VIII's queens to be accorded the honour of burial in Westminster Abbey. On 3 August 1557, she was interred, by Queen Mary's order, in the south transept, with great ceremony. The Queen invited Anna's countryman, the stonemason Theodore Haveus, to come over from Kleve and fashion a monument, which bears the earliest examples of a skull and crossbones to appear in England. It remained unfinished a century after Anna's death. Today, it consists only of a freestone base of three bays divided by panelled pedestals, elaborately carved with Renaissance ornament, Anna's initials and the crowned arms of Kleve. The tomb is obscured by two others from the late seventeenth century.

Mary I did not long survive Anna. She died on 17 November 1558, and was succeeded by her sister, Queen Elizabeth I. Mary was buried not far from Anna, in a tomb in one of the side chapels of the Henry VII Chapel in Westminster Abbey, where Elizabeth's body would also be laid to rest when the Tudor dynasty became extinct in 1603.

Anne of Cleves, as she is commonly known, signed herself 'Anna', which is why I have used that form here. Although English sources usually call her Anne, Henry VIII came to refer to her as Anna. Correctly, she should be called Anna von Kleve. Kleve is the German name of the town and duchy, Cleves the anglicised form.

It is difficult to pinpoint exactly what it was about Anna that aroused such distaste in Henry VIII. He was realistic enough to accept that a monarch had to marry for the good of his realm, yet towards Anna he professed to feel such an abhorrence that he was ready to put his own needs before the benefit of his kingdom – and risk alienating her brother and the German princes whose friendship he needed.

It is often said that he found her unattractive, and that she was not like her portrait. In painting her full-faced, Holbein undoubtedly chose the most flattering angle. Wotton thought it a good likeness, and there is no record of Henry VIII complaining that Holbein had deceived him. However, portraits in which Anna is shown three-quarter-faced are less kind to her. One, in St John's College, Oxford, portrays her as having a more angular face with a prominent pointed chin, heavy-lidded eyes and a long pointed nose. Recent X-rays of this portrait reveal an even longer nose. Another portrait, in Trinity College, Cambridge, shows a coarser-featured Anna. She was probably no great beauty – the French ambassador Marillac's reports bear that out. Yet Henry VIII himself was to concede that she was 'well and seemly' in person. Others even described her as beautiful or handsome.

Henry was a fastidious man, and after his wedding night, he complained that his bride had 'very evil smells about her', which probably accounted for his distaste. He may also have been disappointed by her lack of education, wit and musical ability, accomplishments he greatly esteemed in women. But no contemporary source supports Bishop Burnet's assertion, made in the late seventeenth century and repeated by Tobias Smollett in the eighteenth, that the King likened Anna to 'a great Flanders mare'.

It was something Henry VIII said – and kept on saying – that made me wonder if Anna did come to her marriage bed a virgin, and gave me the storyline that runs through this book – a storyline I suspect will provoke some controversy.

On the morning after his wedding night, the King told Thomas Cromwell: 'I liked her before not well, but now I like her much worse, for I have felt her belly and her breasts, and thereby, as I can judge, she should be no maid, which so strake me to the heart when I felt them that I had neither will nor courage to proceed any further in other matters.'

For weeks afterwards, he made similar complaints to others, saying he 'plainly mistrusted her to be no maid by reason of the looseness of her belly and breasts and other tokens', and stating, 'I have left her as good a maid as I found her.'

I puzzled for months over what Henry meant by these remarks. Discovering that your bride was no virgin did not constitute grounds for an annulment, although failing to consummate the marriage did, and blaming that on Anna spared the King any loss of face; there had been talk that he was impotent. But there was no need to blame anyone; he needed only to state that he felt there was an impediment to his marriage that prevented him from consummating it. And there were other grounds for dissolving the marriage, because the Duke of Kleve could not produce proof that Anna's previous betrothal had been properly dissolved.

Even so, Henry *had* gone ahead with the marriage, and initiated sexual activity to the extent of exploring Anna's body, which suggests that he might originally have intended to proceed to intercourse. It may have been the evidence suggesting she was no virgin that put him off going any further.

What if he had been telling Cromwell and others what he believed to be the truth?

Henry had had vast experience of women. He had been married three times before he wed Anna, and his previous wives had had a total of at least eleven pregnancies between them. He must have known the difference between a female body that had borne children and one that had not. Were Anna's loose breasts and belly and the 'other tokens' Henry mentioned indicative of her having been pregnant at some stage?

It is hard to imagine she would have had the opportunity, having been brought up strictly near her mother's elbow, as we read. Yet her innocence could have made her vulnerable to the attentions of some amorous male, possibly one of her many cousins (who might have been regarded as safe company), who seized his opportunity and took advantage of her. She may have been a willing partner: she was, after all, the granddaughter of the libidinous and prolific *Kindermacher*, and there would later be talk of her being fond of wine and indulging in other excesses, and gossip about secret pregnancies. I did fear that speculating along these lines might be doing a great injustice to Anna, but as I re-researched her story further, I found evidence that could be seen as corroborative. It may be significant that, when it came to providing grounds for an annulment, Henry placed far more reliance on the precontract than he did on non-consummation. There was talk of Anna's body being inspected to prove her virginity, which came to nothing. Was Henry concerned that an examination would show her to be no virgin? How would he prove that someone else had deflowered her? Accusing her of fornication could have led to a diplomatic meltdown with Kleve.

During the annulment proceedings, Henry made contradictory statements about whether Anna had been a virgin on their wedding night. In one, he stated, 'I never for love to the woman consented to marry, nor yet, *if she brought maidenhead with her* [author's italics], took any from her by true carnal copulation.' Yet he also affirmed that Anna had come to him a virgin. That spared her any examination, and so avoided exposing her lack – if lack there was – of a maidenhead, which in turn could have compromised the King's case.

Anna herself stated that she had given herself to one man, and would remain his wife until the bitter death. She agreed to the annulment, 'confessing the integrity of her body, the state of [which] remaining entire for any act of carnal knowledge'. She was hardly likely to admit, especially in the circumstances, that she had not come to Henry a virgin. The Act of Parliament confirming the annulment stated: 'The Lady Anna has openly confessed that she remains not carnally known of the King's body.' Was this a qualified statement? Soon afterwards, Anna told the councillors that she would 'maintain the truth, both touching the integrity and cleanness [purity] of her body'. She told her brother that her body was 'preserved with the integrity which I brought into this realm'. Again, in both cases, she may have been telling the strict truth.

But, in the sarcastic opinion of the reformists, 'As to the reply of the Archbishop of Canterbury and the other bishops to the King's letter directing them to judge the case, that they found Anne of Cleves was still a maid, that is a likely thing indeed!' They found it hard to believe that Henry had not deflowered her – and perhaps that she had been a maid anyway.

Henry VIII's seventeenth-century biographer, Lord Herbert, refers mysteriously to 'secret causes' that could have been used to prove the invalidity of the marriage but were never put forward, and adds that 'the King, without great necessity, would not have disclosed [them] because they touched the honour of the lady'. Could those secret causes have been connected with Henry's oft-voiced doubts about Anna's virginity? There can be little doubt that, if she had contested the nullity suit, he would have used them against her.

Within sixteen months of her divorce, Anna had gained something of a reputation. In December 1541, Chapuys reported his conversation with Sir William Paget about Anna's behaviour and the rumours swirling about her. It seems it was widely known – in London and the Low counties – that she enjoyed wine and other excesses. Maybe her new-found freedom, like the wine, had gone to her head.

A strange episode that occurred in December 1541 is the basis for another storyline in the novel. This was when the King's councillors informed him that they had 'examined a new matter, viz., that the Lady Anne of Cleves should be delivered of a fair boy, and whose should it be but the King's Majesty's, and gotten [back in January] when she was at Hampton Court, which is a most abominable slander'. The baby had allegedly been born late in September. Chapuys says the rumour had been widely circulated.

What happened is much as described in the novel. The King *was* most concerned to discover whether there was any basis to the report. It is hard to credit that, at the height of his infatuation with Katheryn Howard, he had slept with Anna. More likely he wanted to know if Anna had committed the kind of misconduct that could have freed him from his financial obligations to her. The great lengths to which the Privy Council went to investigate the matter show how seriously it was regarded. It was treason to slander the King, and treason to speak of his marriage to Anna as valid, which may have accounted for the councillors meeting with an apparent conspiracy of silence.

Clearly the rumour had come from two sources, and Frances Lilgrave's refusal to name hers argues either that she had made it up, or that she was protecting someone. Given that Jane Ratsey had also refused to divulge what she knew, it may have been the latter – or the sources they could have named would have led the investigation directly to Anna.

Although nearly all modern historians insist that Anna had not borne a child, the possibility remains that she had, although it was surely not the King's. Her movements after the early spring are not documented, and she seems to have spent the year living quietly in the country. With the assistance of her women, she could have concealed a pregnancy and a birth from the rest of her household.

One could, of course, interpret these sources in different ways, and conclude that Anna was purely the victim of gossip or malice. But the rumours originated from a source close to her, which may be significant.

Was Anna as innocent as the conversation with Lady Rutland, Lady Rochford and Lady Edgcumbe (which is repeated almost verbatim in the novel) suggests? It was a strange conversation, especially since, the following month, Anna's chamberlain, Lord Rutland, could not understand her because she had not yet learned sufficient English. Yet, in the reported exchange with her ladies, her English is lucid and flawless. Possibly she had managed to make herself understood through an interpreter – or the ladies put words into her mouth. Obviously they were aware that her marriage had not been consummated; and they had probably been given official instructions to get Anna to admit it, to provide grounds for an annulment, for this conversation appears in a deposition in support of the dissolution of the marriage.

But was Anna as innocent as she made out? Her actual words, if she said them at all, may have been ironic. It seems inconceivable that she had reached the age of twenty-four without finding out about sex. She had grown up in a court populated by her grandfather's bastards. Even if she had never speculated about that, or asked awkward questions, and her mother had so far forgotten her duty to inform her daughter what happened in the marriage bed, the carvings Anna must have seen on the nuptial headboard were pretty explicit. Henry's pawing of her body on her wedding night, his attempts to consummate their marriage, and the crucial, oft-voiced expectation that she would bear him children cannot but have alerted her to the fact that there was more to bed sport than kissing.

I found Otho von Wylich in the splendid genealogy that appears on the website http://vanosnabrugge.org. It shows Anna's family connections and those who accompanied her to England. I discovered it when I was looking for a cousin of similar age to Anna, to portray as her seducer. The story of their love affair is fiction, of course, as are the narratives of her pregnancies and her son, Johann – stories that developed organically as my imagination took wings. But Otho von Wylich did come to England in Anna's train, and did serve for seventeen years in her household. His dismissal was as described in the novel.

'John of Jülich' is also listed (in Anna's will) as being in her household towards the end of her life. It's uncertain who he was, and unlikely that he was Anna's bastard Uncle Johann, because the latter was known as the Bastard of Jülich. Although the Bastard had been a member of the escort that brought her to England, he is not listed as being in her household in July 1540, while the John of Jülich to whom she left a small bequest in 1557 seems to have been of lower rank.

Apart from the storylines above, the novel is based very closely on the historical record, although I have modernised the language in the sources in places. In the passages covering the negotiations and preparations for Anna's marriage, I have telescoped events slightly, to avoid repetition. Events that took place over a month or so are portrayed, roughly timeously, in fewer scenes.

Those negotiations for Anna's marriage, her journey to England, her months as queen, her houses and household, and the later tensions in the latter are much as described, as is the career of Sir Thomas Cawarden, who probably was involved in every conspiracy against Mary I. Anna did come under suspicion during Wyatt's rebellion (although there is no record of her being questioned, as shown here), and Queen Mary never showed warm friendship until Anna was dying.

I composed Henry VIII's first letter to Anna, basing it on his love letters to Anne Boleyn and Jane Seymour.

We don't know for certain if Florence of Diaceto was intriguing with the French. The impounding of his papers suggests that he was thought to have been acting on Anna's behalf, and that she was involved in the political manoeuvrings of her brother and Henri II of France against England. In 1555, Dr Wotton, now ambassador to France, wrote to Queen Mary's Secretary of State that Florence, having been in trouble, had left England, and had been seen in Paris. Wotton had him watched, and was informed that he had met many times with the Constable of France and the whole Council, which led Wotton to believe that he was 'here for no good intent'. But we hear no more of the matter.

One of the carved wooden panels Anna ordered is now at Hever Castle. The fireplace (now at Reigate Priory) was once at Bletchingley, and may actually have been made for Henry VIII's Nonsuch Palace. Given that we know Anna installed carved wood panels in a later house of hers, it could have been she who commissioned the chimney breast. Anna's glimpse of Cawarden as she leaves Nonsuch was inspired by stories that ghostly sounds of a banquet have been heard there, and people have reported seeing a tall man with a thin face standing by the eastern gate, watching the park or the palace; he wears a dark cloak and hat and has a forlorn or fixed expression.

The nature of Anna's final illness is unknown. By the spring of 1557, when her health began seriously to decline, she had probably been ailing for some time. Some have speculated that she was suffering from cancer, which is possible. It is clear from her will that her physician, Mother Lowe (who had perhaps become a mother figure to her), her ladies, kitchen staff, household officers and servants had all looked after her in her final illness, 'taking great pains' to tempt her with food and see to her comfort, which suggests she was bedridden and needed careful nursing. She was also attended by her surgeon, Alard Blundey. Barber-surgeons like Blundey, who was rewarded in Anna's will, performed not only operations, but also dentistry and blood-letting, believed to balance the body's 'humours' for the maintenance of good health. Blundey may have operated on Anna, although I have not shown that in the novel –

the final passages are harrowing enough. Surgery without anaesthesia was sheer agony, but a modern examination of the surgeon's chest found aboard the *Mary Rose* showed that Tudor practitioners were far more skilled and advanced in their craft than was hitherto suspected. If Anna did undergo an operation, it was to no avail.

I owe a debt of gratitude to the historian Elizabeth Norton, who afforded me new insights on Anna and drew my attention to the dispatches of Karl Harst, the ambassador of Kleve, which offer a somewhat different narrative of her divorce to the official English sources. Ms Norton's excellent biography of Anna was especially helpful.

For the sources I consulted, the reader is referred to the extensive bibliographies in my Tudor non-fiction books, notably *The Six Wives of Henry VIII* and *Henry VIII: King and Court*. Among the many works I read while updating my research, the following were very useful: *Anne of Cleves* by Mary Saaler (London, 1995); *In the Footsteps of the Six Wives of Henry VIII* by Sarah Morris and Natalie Grueninger (Stroud, 2016) and *The Marrying of Anne of Cleves* by Retha Warnicke (Cambridge, 2000). The Internet Sacred Text Archive was the basis of my research into German legends. The passages relating to the treatment of cancer draw heavily on *A Discourse of the Whole Art of Chyrurgerie* (1612) by Peter Lowe.

I am hugely grateful to my editors, Mari Evans at Headline in the UK, and Susanna Porter at Ballantine in the USA, for commissioning this book and giving me the chance to bring Anna to life – and for their terrific support. I owe a large debt of gratitude to Flora Rees for her sympathetic, creative approach to editing, which has helped me to craft a far better book. Special thanks also to Caitlin Raynor, Jo Liddiard, Sara Adams, Frances Edwards, Jennifer Harlow, Phil Norman and all the fabulous team at Headline in London; and to Emily Hartley, Melanie DeNardo, Kim Hovey and the amazing team at Ballantine in New York.

I am indebted, as ever, to my agent, Julian Alexander, who goes above and beyond to support me, and has now put up with me for over thirty years!

Lastly, a loving thank-you to Rankin, my husband, without whom I could not function. You will never know how much I appreciate all you do for me.

Dramatis Personae

In order of appearance or first mention. Names in italics are fictional, used where the actual name is unknown.

Anna, daughter of Johann III the Peaceful, Duke of Kleve, and Maria of Jülich-Berg.

Johann III, Duke of Kleve, Anna's father.

Otho von Wylich, Lord of Gennep, Anna's maternal uncle.

Elisabeth of Kleve, his wife, Anna's aunt.

Johann I, Duke of Kleve, Anna's great-grandfather.

Otho von Wylich, bastard son of Otho von Wylich, Anna's cousin.

Johann II the Childmaker, Duke of Kleve, Anna's grandfather.

Wilhelm, later Wilhelm V, Duke of Kleve, Anna's brother.

Amalia (nicknamed Emily) of Kleve, Anna's younger sister.

Maria of Jülich-Berg, Duchess of Kleve, Anna's mother.

Charles V, Holy Roman Emperor, kinsman of the dukes of Kleve.

Francis, Marquis of Pont-à-Mousson, Anna's betrothed.

Antoine, Duke of Lorraine, Francis's father.

Dr Heinrich Olisleger, Vice Chancellor of Kleve, Anna's cousin.

Desiderius Erasmus, celebrated Dutch humanist scholar.

Martin Luther, founder of the Protestant religion.

Johann Friedrich, Elector of Saxony, leader of the Protestant German Schmalkaldic League, Anna's brother-in-law.

Sybilla of Kleve, Electress of Saxony, Anna's sister.

Adolf I, Duke of Kleve, Anna's great-great-grandfather.

Mother Lowe, Anna's nurse.

Charles II, Duke of Guelders, great-uncle of Francis, Marquis of Pont-à-Mousson, Anna's betrothed.

Henry VIII, King of England.

Katherine of Aragon, first queen of Henry VIII and aunt of the Emperor Charles V.

Konrad Heresbach, councillor of Kleve and tutor to Wilhelm of Kleve, Anna's brother.

Johann Gerecht of Landsberg, Prior of the Charterhouse at Cantave, Jülich, confessor to Anna's mother.

Dr Schultz, physician to the Duke of Kleve.

Gerda, Anna's maid at Schloss Burg.

Meister Schmidt, swordsmith of Solingen, and his wife.

Johann, Anna's bastard son.

Dr Cepher, physician to the dukes of Kleve, and later to Anna.

Franz Burchard, Vice Chancellor of Saxony.

Thomas, Lord Cromwell, later Earl of Essex; Principal Secretary to Henry VIII, Chancellor of the Exchequer, Lord Privy Seal.

Anne Boleyn, second queen of Henry VIII.

Jane Seymour, third queen of Henry VIII.

Pope Paul III.

Christina of Denmark, Duchess of Milan, niece of the Emperor Charles V.

François I, King of France.

Lucas Cranach, painter to Johann Friedrich, Elector of Saxony.

Dr Nicholas Wotton, English ambassador to Kleve.

Edward Carne, English envoy to Kleve.

Richard Berde, gentleman of Henry VIII's Privy Chamber, envoy to Kleve.

Robert Barnes, Henry VIII's chief emissary to the Protestant princes.

Herr Hograve, Chancellor of Kleve.

Hans Wertinger, German painter.

Hans Holbein, King's Painter to Henry VIII.

Werner von Hochsteden, Grand Master of the court of Kleve.

Mary of Habsburg, Queen of Hungary, Regent of the Netherlands, sister of the Emperor Charles V.

William Fitzwilliam, Earl of Southampton, Lord High Admiral of England.

Susanna Gilman, née Horenbout, painter to Henry VIII, gentlewoman of Anna's privy chamber.

Gerard Horenbout, Flemish painter to Henry VIII, Susanna's father.

John Gilman, vintner, Susanna's husband.

George Boleyn, Viscount Rochford, brother of Queen Anne Boleyn and husband of Jane Parker, Lady Rochford.

Prince Edward, later Edward VI, son of Henry VIII and Jane Seymour.

Lady Bryan, lady mistress to Prince Edward.

The Lady Mary, later Mary I, daughter of Henry VIII and Katherine of Aragon.

The Lady Elizabeth, daughter of Henry VIII and Anna Boleyn.

William Wilkinson, tailor.

Honor Grenville, Viscountess Lisle, wife of Arthur Plantagenet, Viscount Lisle.

Arthur Plantagenet, Viscount Lisle, Deputy Governor of Calais, bastard son of Edward IV and cousin of Henry VIII.

Richard Taverner, Clerk of the Signet, reformist scholar.

Wolfgang Capito, German reformer.

The Mayor of Solingen.

Hermann, Count von Neuenahr, humanist scholar and politician.

Johann, the Bastard of Jülich, Anna's maternal uncle.

Anastasia Gunthera Schwarzburg, Anna's cousin and maid-of-honour.

Franz von Waldeck, Anna's cousin and page.

Anna of Kleve, Countess of Waldeck, Franz's mother and Anna's aunt.

Philip, Count of Waldeck, her husband, and Franz's father.

Hanna von Wylich, Otho von Wylich's wife.

Florence de Diaceto, Dr Olisleger's nephew and a gentleman of Anna's household.

Marshal Dultzik, envoy of the Elector of Saxony.

Johann, Lord of Bueren-Drossard, member of Anna's escort to England.

Werner von Pallant, Lord of Bredebent, member of Anna's escort.

Lady Magdalena von Nassau-Dillenborg, member of Anna's escort.

Lady Keteler, member of Anna's escort.

Lady Alexandrine von Tengnagel, member of Anna's escort.

Jasper Brockhausen, Anna's cofferer.

Gertie Brockhausen, his wife.

Meister Schoulenburg, Anna's cook.

Steven Vaughan, governor of the Merchant Adventurers' Company.

Floris of Egmond, Count of Buren, and Ferry de Melen, Master of the

Emperor's Ordnance, Imperial commissioners conducting Anna from Antwerp to Gravelines.

Gerberge von Ossenbruch, one of Anna's gentlewomen.

Diederik II von Wylich, Erbhofmeister (hereditary chamberlain) of Kleve, kinsman of Otho von Wylich.

Sir Thomas Seymour, brother of Queen Jane Seymour, later Lord High Admiral.

Sir Francis Bryan, English courtier.

Thomas Culpeper, gentleman of Henry VIII's Privy Chamber.

Gregory Cromwell, son of Thomas Cromwell.

Anne Bassett, maid-of-honour to Anna.

Katherine Bassett, Anne's sister, later maid-of-honour to Anna.

Lord William Howard, English courtier, half-brother to the Duke of Norfolk.

Mary Boleyn, Mistress Stafford, former mistress of Henry VIII, sister of Queen Anne Boleyn.

William Stafford, her husband, soldier in the Calais garrison, later Gentleman Pensioner to Henry VIII.

Sir Thomas Cheyney, Lord Warden of the Cinque Ports.

Charles Brandon, Duke of Suffolk, brother-in-law of Henry VIII, former husband of the late Mary Tudor, 'the French Queen'.

Richard Sampson, Bishop of Chichester.

Katherine Willoughby, Duchess of Suffolk, second wife of Charles Brandon, Duke of Suffolk, and lady-of-honour to Anna.

Thomas Cranmer, Archbishop of Canterbury.

Thomas Howard, Duke of Norfolk, England's premier Catholic peer.

Alice Gage, Lady Browne, wife of Sir Anthony Browne.

John Fisher, Bishop of Rochester.

Sir Thomas More, former Lord Chancellor of England.

Sir Anthony Browne, master of the horse to Henry VIII.

Thomas Manners, Earl of Rutland, cousin of Henry VIII, and Anna's chamberlain.

Sir Edward Baynton, Anna's vice chamberlain.

Sir Thomas Denny, Anna's chancellor.

Sir John Dudley, Anna's master of horse, later Duke of Northumberland and Lord President of the Council under Edward VI.

Lady Margaret Douglas, niece of Henry VIII and Anna's chief lady-of-honour.

Mary Howard, Duchess of Richmond, widow of Henry VIII's bastard son, Henry Fitzroy, Duke of Richmond, and lady-of-honour to Anna.

Eleanor Paston, Countess of Rutland, lady of Anna's privy chamber.

Jane Parker, Lady Rochford, lady of Anna's privy chamber.

Catherine St John, Lady Edgcumbe, lady of Anna's privy chamber.

Margaret Wyatt, Lady Lee, sister of the poet Sir Thomas Wyatt, and gentlewoman of Anna's privy chamber.

Anne Parr, Mrs Herbert, gentlewoman of Anna's privy chamber.

Elizabeth Seymour, Mrs Cromwell, sister of Queen Jane Seymour and gentlewoman of Anna's privy chamber.

Katheryn Howard, niece of the Duke of Norfolk and maid-of-honour to Anna.

Katherine (Kate) Carey, daughter of Mary Boleyn and (probably) Henry VIII, and maid-of-honour to Anna.

Bridget of York, daughter of Edward IV, aunt of Henry VIII, and nun at Dartford.

Frances Brandon, Marchioness of Dorset, daughter of Charles Brandon, Duke of Suffolk, and Mary Tudor, sister of Henry VIII.

Dr Kaye, Anna's almoner.

Baron Oberstein, a nobleman of Kleve.

Henry Bourchier, Earl of Essex.

Mother Jack, nurse to Prince Edward.

Lord Thomas Howard, younger brother of the Duke of Norfolk.

Master Cornelius Hayes, goldsmith to Henry VIII.

William Paget, later Sir William, then Lord Paget, and a Privy councillor; Anna's secretary.

Katharina, maid-of-honour to Anna.

Gertrude, maid-of-honour to Anna.

Wymond Carew, Anna's receiver general.

Will Somers, Henry VIII's fool.

Chapman, Anna's gardener, formerly gardener to Queen Jane Seymour.

Lucas Horenbout, son of Gerard Horenbout, brother of Susanna Gilman, and painter to Henry VIII.

Master Cornelius Hayes, goldsmith to Henry VIII.

Dr Karl Harst, Kleve's ambassador to the court of Henry VIII.

Eustache Chapuys, Imperial ambassador to the court of Henry VIII.

Charles de Marillac, French ambassador to the court of Henry VIII.

Stephen Gardiner, Bishop of Winchester, later Lord Chancellor.

Marguerite of Valois, Queen of Navarre, sister of François I, King of France.

Henry Howard, Earl of Surrey, son and heir of Thomas Howard, Duke of Norfolk.

The Bassano family of Venice, Anna's musicians.

Agnes Tilney, Dowager Duchess of Norfolk, step-grandmother of Katheryn Howard.

Thomas, Lord Audley, Lord Chancellor.

Sir Richard Rich, Solicitor General.

Sir William Kingston, Comptroller of the King's Household, Constable of the Tower.

Cuthbert Tunstall, Bishop of Durham.

Sir Thomas Wriothesley, later Earl of Southampton, Principal Secretary to Henry VIII.

Sir William Goring, Anna's chamberlain after her divorce.

Jasper Horsey, Anna's steward.

Henry Courtenay, Marquess of Exeter, cousin of Henry VIII.

Frances Lilgrave, embroiderer, gentlewoman of Anna's privy chamber.

Dorothy Wingfield, gentlewoman of Anna's privy chamber.

Jane Ratsey, gentlewoman of Anna's privy chamber.

Mistress Simpson, gentlewoman of Anna's privy chamber.

Elya Turpen, Anna's laundress.

Thomas, Cardinal Wolsey, Henry VIII's former chief minister.

Joanna, wife of Jasper Horsey.

John Bekinsale, Anna's gentleman usher.

Henry, Anna's butler.

Katherine Astley, governess to the Lady Elizabeth.

Thomas Boleyn, Earl of Wiltshire, father of Queen Anne Boleyn.

Werner von Gymnich, Anna's cupbearer.

Thomas Cawarden, later Sir Thomas, Anna's steward at Bletchingley, and later Master of Revels and Tents to Henry VIII and Edward VI.

Edward Stafford, Duke of Buckingham.

Sir Nicholas Carew, master of horse.

Martha Carew, wife of Wymond Carew.

Sir Anthony Denny, head of Henry VIII's privy chamber.

Anne Stanhope, Countess of Hertford, wife of Edward Seymour, Earl of Hertford, brother of Queen Jane Seymour.

Master Mandeville, groom of Anna's stable.

Master Freeman, and his wife, Anna's tenants at Southover.

Jeanne d'Albret, Duchess of Kleve, later Queen of Navarre, first wife of Anna's brother, Wilhelm V.

Thomas Bowyer, MP, and his wife, Anna's tenants at Nyetimber.

Mrs Lambert, mother-in-law of Richard Taverner, Clerk of the Signet.

Elizabeth Bryan, Lady Carew.

Dr Richard Cox, later tutor to Prince Edward.

Francis Dereham, secretary to Queen Katheryn Howard.

Dr William Butts, physician to Henry VIII.

Sir John Gates, gentleman of Henry VIII's Privy Chamber.

Jean Clouet, French portrait painter.

Katharine Parr, Lady Latimer, a widow.

Elizabeth, wife of Sir Thomas Cawarden.

Thomas Carew, Anna's receiver general, succeeding his kinsman Wymond Carew.

Claude d'Annebault, Admiral of France, French ambassador to the court of Henry VIII.

Maria of Austria, Duchess of Kleve, second wife of Anna's brother, Wilhelm V.

Mr Chomley, Anna's cofferer.

Sir John Guildford, Anna's chamberlain, succeeding Sir William Goring.

Edward Seymour, Duke of Somerset, Lord Protector of England under Edward VI, and brother of Queen Jane Seymour.

Sir Otto Rumpello, Anna's chaplain.

Henry Ashley, MP for Hever, husband of Katherine Bassett.

Dr Herman Cruser, envoy from Kleve.

Dr John Symonds, Anna's physician.

Sir William Sidney, courtier.

Marie Eleonore of Kleve, Anna's niece, eldest child of Wilhelm V and Maria of Austria.

Anna of Kleve, Anna's niece, daughter of Wilhelm V and Maria of Austria.

Lady Jane Grey, great-niece of Henry VIII, nine-days Queen of England.

Philip of Spain, son and heir of the Emperor Charles V, husband of Mary I, and thereby King of England.

Ferdinand of Habsburg, Archduke of Austria, brother-in-law of Wilhelm V and suitor to Mary I.

Ferdinand, King of the Romans, Bohemia and Hungary, heir to the Holy Roman Empire, father of Ferdinand of Habsburg, Archduke of Austria.

Simon Renard, Imperial ambassador to England.

Sir Thomas Wyatt, son of the poet Sir Thomas Wyatt, and leader of a rebellion against Mary I.

Sir Thomas Saunders, the Sheriff of Surrey.

Henry Grey, Duke of Suffolk, father of Lady Jane Grey.

Henri II, King of France.

Christian III, King of Denmark.

Sir Thomas Cornwallis, Steward of the Household to Edward VI.

George Throckmorton, Gentleman Pensioner to Mary I.

Karl, ducal Prince of Kleve, son and heir of Wilhelm V, and Anna's nephew.

Anne de Montmorency, Grand Constable of France.

Lord Cobham, tenant of Sir Thomas Cawarden.

Sir Richard Freston, Anna's steward, succeeding Jasper Brockhausen.

Jane Guildford, Dowager Duchess of Northumberland.

Alard Blundey, Anna's surgeon.

Timeline

1491

– Birth of Henry VIII

1509

– Accession of Henry VIII
– Marriage and coronation of Henry VIII and Katherine of Aragon

1510

– Marriage of Johann (b.1490), heir of Johann II, Duke of Kleve, to Maria (b.1491), heiress of the duchies of Jülich and Berg

1512

– Birth of Sybilla of Kleve (17 January)

1515

– Birth of Anna of Kleve (22 September)

1516

– Birth of the Princess Mary, daughter of Henry VIII and Katherine of Aragon
– Birth of Wilhelm, Duke of Ravenstein, son and heir of Johann of Kleve (28 July)

1517

– Birth of Amalia (Emily) of Kleve (October)

1521

– Johann III succeeds his father, Johann II, as duke of Kleve

1526

– Marriage of Sybilla of Kleve to Johann Friedrich, Elector of Saxony

1527

– Betrothal of Anna of Kleve to Francis, Marquis of Pont-à-Mousson (5 June)
– Anna of Kleve first suggested as a bride for Henry VIII (November)

1533

- Marriage of Henry VIII and Anne Boleyn (January)
- Parliament passes the Act in Restraint of Appeals (to the Pope), the legal cornerstone of the English Reformation
- Archbishop Cranmer pronounces the marriage of Henry VIII and Katherine of Aragon incestuous and unlawful, and confirms the validity of Henry's marriage to Anne Boleyn
- Birth of the Princess Elizabeth, daughter of Henry VIII and Anne Boleyn

1534

- Parliament passes the Act of Supremacy, making Henry VIII Supreme Head of the Church of England, and the Act of Succession, naming the children of Queen Anne the King's lawful heirs

1535

- Revocation of the precontract between Anna of Kleve and Francis, Marquis of Pont-à-Mousson

1536

- Death of Katherine of Aragon
- Execution of Anne Boleyn
- Marriage of Henry VIII and Jane Seymour
- Parliament passes a new Act of Succession settling the succession on Jane's children by the King

1537

- Birth of Prince Edward, son of Henry VIII and Jane Seymour
- Death of Jane Seymour (24 October)
- Henry VIII begins searching for a fourth wife (November)

1538

- Treaty of Nice between the Emperor and the King of France leaves Henry VIII in political isolation (June)
- Henry VIII excommunicated by the Pope (December)

1539

- Treaty of Toledo between the Emperor and the King of France further isolates Henry VIII and puts an end to negotiations for a marriage between Henry and Christina of Denmark (January)
- Henry VIII opens negotiations for a marriage with Anna of Kleve (January)

- Death of Johann III, Duke of Kleve; accession of Wilhelm V, Duke of Kleve (6 February)
- Hans Holbein sent to Kleve to paint portraits of the princesses Anna and Amalia (August)
- Wilhelm V, Duke of Kleve, signs Anna's marriage treaty (4 September)
- Henry VIII signs the marriage treaty (4 October)
- Anna leaves Düsseldorf for England (26 November)
- Anna arrives at Antwerp (2 December)
- Anna received at Calais (11 December)
- Anna sails to England (27 December)

1540

- Meeting of Henry VIII and Anna of Kleve at Rochester (1 January)
- Official reception of Anna of Kleve at Blackheath (3 January)
- Marriage of Henry VIII and Anna of Kleve (6 January)
- Official reception of Anna of Kleve at Westminster (5 February)
- Henry VIII begins courting Katheryn Howard (April)
- The Privy Council begins looking for grounds for an annulment (May)
- Thomas Cromwell arrested (10 June)
- Anna sent to Richmond (27 June)
- Cromwell attainted in Parliament (29 June)
- Parliament begins debating the validity of Anna's marriage (6 July)
- Henry VIII commissions the English clergy to examine the marriage (6 July)
- Convocation declares the marriage invalid (8 July)
- Anna accepts Convocation's ruling (11 July)
- Anna's marriage formally annulled by Act of Parliament (12 July)
- Anna's household dissolved (17 July)
- Execution of Cromwell (28 July)
- Marriage of Henry VIII and Katheryn Howard (28 July)
- Rumours that the King would take back Anna first emerge (September)

1541

- Anna visits court after New Year
- Henry VIII issues letters of denization to Anna, and grants her divorce settlement (January)
- Anna goes on progress

- Fall of Katheryn Howard, followed by rumours of Anna's restoration (November)
- Anna rumoured to have borne a child in September (December)

1542

- Execution of Katheryn Howard (February)

1543

- Marriage of Henry VIII and Katharine Parr (July)
- Kleve overrun by the armies of the Emperor Charles V (August)
- Death of Maria, Dowager Duchess of Kleve, Anna's mother (29 August)
- Wilhelm V, Duke of Kleve, submits to the Emperor (7 September)

1546

- Anna at court for the reception of the Admiral of France (summer)

1547

- Death of Henry VIII (28 January) and accession of Edward VI

1549

- Anna asks Duke Wilhelm for financial aid

1551

- Anna contemplating returning to Kleve

1553

- Death of Edward VI (6 July); Lady Jane Grey proclaimed queen, deposed after nine days; accession of Mary I
- Anna prominent in Mary I's coronation procession

1554

- Anna suspected of complicity in Sir Thomas Wyatt's rebellion (February)

1557

- Death of Anna of Kleve (16 July)
- Burial of Anna of Kleve in Westminster Abbey (3 August)

Reading Group Questions

- Anna is brought up in a court that appears serene but where religious values silently clash. Kleve is modelled on Erasmus's theological ideals by her father, yet Anna and her sister are ruled by their mother's conservative religious morals. The innocence instilled by Mutter proves Anna's undoing in one way; yet, at the same time we see her thirst for new experiences. How does this mix of naivety and a sense of adventure serve Anna as she is forced into a different world, and is it overall a benefit or a drawback during her life?

- One of the novel's pervasive themes is of thwarted hope and expectation. Which characters do you feel are most affected by this, and why? Anna spins ideas of her future, and, like Henry, pins her hopes on a portrait that shows a different version of reality. Both are deeply disappointed in the other. How did you respond to Alison Weir's telling of Henry and Anna's first meeting? Given the negative picture of Anna that has persisted over the centuries, have you ever considered this moment from her point of view before, and did Alison's version change your perception? Does Anna's life ever live up to her early expectations?

- '*I am a princess of Kleve, my lord, and when I give my word, I keep it.*' Anna has grown up certain of her royal position, something that Henry's last two queens lacked. But she is thrown into a very different world on her arrival in England, and has to draw on reserves of courage and dignity to navigate this new environment. How successful is she in creating a persona of 'queen', for the brief time she has, and how does this sharp learning curve create resilience for the future ahead of her?

- 'No one would expect a princess such as she to be concealing so dark a secret.' This novel is filled with secrets and silent deceptions, from the innocuous to the deeply shocking. In addition to keeping her own secrets, how does Anna manage to navigate so much of her life and key decisions while afraid of what others might secretly know? She is willing to lie to protect herself and those she loves, and to choose the path of least resistance and greatest benefit. Do you feel this makes her weak and cowardly, or strong and pragmatic? Which do you think was the hardest secret she had to keep?

- There is a significant clash of cultures between Anna and her retinue and their English counterparts, in addition to the language barrier they face. Did you find that, through Anna's perception of England both from a distance and once she arrives, you were able to view Henry's court from an entirely new perspective? What were your impressions of the Tudor world created by Alison Weir, and how does it change as Anna herself becomes settled in England?

- 'She would have liked to correct Henry on his pronunciation of Kleve, but did not dare.' Anna of Kleve is perhaps one of the least known of Henry's queens – even her name has been wrongly recorded over the centuries. How does Alison Weir create Anna as a rich and believable character, and how does she grow and develop over the decades depicted in *Queen of Secrets*? Does this portrayal of Anna meet your expectations? What did you learn, and what did you find surprising?

- In order to bring Anna's story to life some historical gaps have to be filled. Otho von Wylich and 'John of Jülich' were both members of Anna's household, and Alison worked from Henry VIII's own recorded testimony and real rumours that circulated about Anna bearing a child, but had to let her imagination run with the potential storylines these facts suggested. What was your response to Alison's choice of new narratives for Anna, and the way they are woven into the story?

- *'I was just remembering how it felt to be young, with the world and the future before you.'* As Anna and Henry's friendship matures, the King's infirmity grows along with a sense of regret for what he's lost. How does the Henry of *Queen of Secrets* compare to the Henry that Alison Weir created in the first three Six Tudor Queens novels, and how has his character developed over the series? Do you agree with Anna that Katheryn Howard's betrayal breaks him?

- Anna lives through the reigns of three Tudor monarchs, allowing us insight into the impact of each on society and religious freedoms. Do you agree that Mary plays a pivotal role in Anna's story, particularly in denying Anna a final opportunity at happiness? How does Alison manage to create a vivid picture of Mary, and of her half-sister, Elizabeth, through Anna's brief scenes with each? And how do they compare to Lady Margaret Douglas, also a Tudor royal and with as difficult a background in many ways, yet still vivacious and kind?

- Who do you feel has the most influence on Anna at different stages of her life? Despite being rarely alone, did you find she often seems lonely, and reaches out quickly to those who offer kindness? Her friendship with Susanna Gilman, and its abrupt ending, is an interesting example, and her complicated relationship with Henry is particularly fascinating as she moves from fear and dislike to something close to love over the years. How does her reliance on others, even as she revels in her independence, cause problems throughout her life?

- As with each novel in the Six Tudor Queens series, the whole story is told purely from Anna's point of view. This allows Alison to show the English court and people from Anna's personal perspective, and create elliptical moments in her comprehension of the world she is experiencing. How does this narrative style affect the overall shape of the novel? Does it work for you, and how does Anna's voice compare to those of Henry's first three queens as portrayed by Alison Weir?